TONI MORRISON

BELOVED

Toni Morrison is the author of eleven novels, from *The Bluest Eye* (1970) to *God Help the Child* (2015). She received the National Book Critics Circle Award, the Pulitzer Prize, and in 1993 she was awarded the Nobel Prize in Literature. She died in 2019.

VINTAGE INTERNATIONAL

ACCLAIM FOR TONI MORRISON'S

BELOVED

"Brilliant. . . . Resonates from past to present."
—*San Francisco Chronicle*

"A brutally powerful, mesmerizing story. . . . Read it and tremble."
—*People*

"Toni Morrison is not just an important contemporary novelist but a major figure in our national literature."
—*The New York Review of Books*

"A work of genuine force. . . . Beautifully written."
—*The Washington Post*

"There is something great in *Beloved*: a play of human voices, consciously exalted, perversely stressed, yet holding true. It gets you."
—*The New Yorker*

"A magnificent heroine . . . a glorious book."
—*The Baltimore Sun*

"Superb. . . . A profound and shattering story that carries the weight of history. . . . Exquisitely told."
—*Cosmopolitan*

"Magical . . . rich, provocative, extremely satisfying."
—*Milwaukee Journal*

"Beautifully written. . . . Powerful. . . . Toni Morrison has become one of America's finest novelists."

—*The Plain Dealer*

"Stunning. . . . A lasting achievement."

—*The Christian Science Monitor*

"Written with a force rarely seen in contemporary fiction. . . . One feels deep admiration." —*USA Today*

"Compelling. . . . Morrison shakes that brilliant kaleidoscope of hers again, and the story of pain, endurance, poetry and power she is born to tell comes right out."

—*The Village Voice*

"A book worth many rereadings." —*Glamour*

"In her most probing novel, Toni Morrison has demonstrated once again the stunning powers that place her in the first ranks of our living novelists."

—*St. Louis Post-Dispatch*

"Heart-wrenching . . . mesmerizing."

—*The Atlanta Journal-Constitution*

"Shattering emotional power and impact."

—*New York Daily News*

"A rich, mythical novel . . . a triumph."

—*St. Petersburg Times*

"Powerful . . . voluptuous." —*New York*

ALSO BY TONI MORRISON

FICTION

God Help the Child

Home

A Mercy

Love

Paradise

Jazz

Tar Baby

Song of Solomon

Sula

The Bluest Eye

NONFICTION

The Source of Self-Regard

The Dancing Mind

Playing in the Dark:
Whiteness and the Literary Imagination

The Origin of Others

BELOVED

BELOVED

A NOVEL BY

Toni Morrison

VINTAGE INTERNATIONAL

Vintage Books

A Division of Penguin Random House LLC

New York

FIRST VINTAGE INTERNATIONAL EDITION, JUNE 2004

The Library of Congress has cataloged the Knopf edition as follows:
Morrison, Toni.
Beloved.
I. Title.
PS3563.08749B4 1987
813'.54
86-46157

Vintage International Trade Paperback ISBN: 978-1-4000-3341-6
eBook ISBN: 978-0-307-38862-9

Book design by Dorothy Schmiderer Baker

www.vintagebooks.com

Printed in the United States of America
60 59 58 57 56 55 54 53 52

Sixty Million
and more

I will call them my people,
which were not my people;
and her beloved,
which was not beloved.

ROMANS 9:25

FOREWORD

In 1983 I lost my job—or left it. One, the other, or both. In any case, I had been part-time for a while, coming into the publishing house one day a week to do the correspondence-telephoning-meetings that were part of the job; editing manuscripts at home.

Leaving was a good idea for two reasons. One, I had written four novels and it seemed clear to everyone that writing was my central work. The question of priorities—how can you edit and write at the same time—seemed to me both queer and predictable; it sounded like "How can you both teach and create?" "How can a painter or a sculptor or an actor do her work and guide others?" But to many this edit–write combination was conflicting.

The second reason was less ambiguous. The books I had edited were not earning scads of money, even when "scads" didn't mean what it means now. My list was to me spectacular: writers with outrageous talent (Toni Cade Bambara, June Jordan, Gayle Jones, Lucille Clifton, Henry Dumas, Leon Forrest); scholars with original ideas and hands-on research (William Hinton's *Shen Fan*, Ivan Van Sertima's *They Came Before Columbus*, Karen DeCrow's *Sexist Justice*, Chinweizu's *The West and the Rest of Us*); public figures eager to set the record straight (Angela Davis, Muhammad Ali, Huey Newton). And when there was a book that I thought needed doing, I found an author to write it. My enthusiasm, shared by some, was muted by others, reflecting the indifferent sales figures. I may be wrong about this, but even in the late seventies, acquiring authors who were certain sellers outranked editing manuscripts or supporting emerging or aging authors through their careers. Suffice it to say, I convinced myself that it was time for me to live like a grown-up writer: off royalties and writing only. I don't know what comic book that notion came from, but I grabbed it.

A few days after my last day at work, sitting in front of my house on the pier jutting out into the Hudson River, I began to feel an edginess instead of the calm I had expected. I ran through my index of problem areas and found nothing new or pressing. I couldn't fathom what was so unexpectedly troubling on a day that perfect, watching a river that serene. I had no agenda and couldn't hear the telephone if it rang. I heard my heart, though, stomping away in my chest like a colt. I went back to the house to examine this apprehension, even panic. I knew what fear felt like; this was different. Then it slapped me: I was happy, free in a way I had never been, ever. It was the oddest sensation. Not ecstasy, not satisfaction, not a surfeit of pleasure or accomplishment. It was a purer delight, a rogue anticipation with certainty. Enter *Beloved.*

I think now it was the shock of liberation that drew my thoughts to what "free" could possibly mean to women. In the eighties, the debate was still roiling: equal pay, equal treatment, access to professions, schools . . . and choice without stigma. To marry or not. To have children or not. Inevitably these thoughts led me to the different history of black women in this country—a history in which marriage was discouraged, impossible, or illegal; in which birthing children was required, but "having" them, being responsible for them—being, in other words, their parent—was as out of the question as freedom. Assertions of parenthood under conditions peculiar to the logic of institutional enslavement were criminal.

The idea was riveting, but the canvas overwhelmed me. Summoning characters who could manifest the intellect and the ferocity such logic would provoke proved beyond my imagination until I remembered one of the books I had published back when I had a job. A newspaper clipping in *The Black Book* summarized the story of Margaret Garner, a young mother who, having escaped slavery, was arrested for killing one of her children (and trying to kill the others) rather than let them be returned to the owner's plantation. She became a cause célèbre in the fight against the Fugitive Slave laws, which mandated the return of escapees to their owners. Her sanity and lack of repentance caught the attention of Abolitionists as well as newspapers. She was certainly single-minded and, judging by her comments, she had the intellect, the ferocity, and the willingness to risk everything for what was to her the necessity of freedom.

The historical Margaret Garner is fascinating, but, to a novelist, confining. Too little imaginative space there for my purposes. So I would invent her thoughts, plumb them for a subtext that was historically true in essence, but not strictly factual in order to relate her history to contemporary issues about freedom, responsibility, and women's "place." The heroine would represent the unapologetic acceptance of shame and terror; assume the consequences of choosing infanticide; claim her own freedom. The terrain, slavery, was formidable and pathless. To invite readers (and myself) into the repellant landscape (hidden, but not completely; deliberately buried, but not forgotten) was to pitch a tent in a cemetery inhabited by highly vocal ghosts.

I sat on the porch, rocking in a swing, looking at giant stones piled up to take the river's occasional fist. Above the stones is a path through the lawn, but interrupted by an ironwood gazebo situated under a cluster of trees and in deep shade.

She walked out of the water, climbed the rocks, and leaned against the gazebo. Nice hat.

So she was there from the beginning, and except for me, everybody (the characters) knew it—a sentence that later became "The women in the house knew it." The figure most central to the story would have to be her, the murdered, not the murderer, the one who lost everything and had no say in any of it. She could not linger outside; she would have to enter the house. A real house, not a cabin. One with an address, one where former slaves lived on their own. There would be no lobby into this house, and there would be no "introduction" into it or into the novel. I wanted the reader to be kidnapped, thrown ruthlessly into an alien environment as the first step into a shared experience with the book's population—just as the characters were snatched from one place to another, from any place to any other, without preparation or defense.

It was important to name this house, but not the way "Sweet Home" or other plantations were named. There would be no adjectives suggesting coziness or grandeur or the laying claim to an instant, aristocratic past. Only numbers here to identify the house while simultaneously separating it from a street or city—marking its difference from the houses of other blacks in the neighborhood; allowing it a hint of the superiority, the pride, former slaves would take in having an address of their own. Yet a house that has, literally, a personality—which we call "haunted" when that personality is blatant.

In trying to make the slave experience intimate, I hoped

the sense of things being both under control and out of control would be persuasive throughout; that the order and quietude of everyday life would be violently disrupted by the chaos of the needy dead; that the herculean effort to forget would be threatened by memory desperate to stay alive. To render enslavement as a personal experience, language must get out of the way.

I husband that moment on the pier, the deceptive river, the instant awareness of possibility, the loud heart kicking, the solitude, the danger. And the girl with the nice hat. Then the focus.

I

124 WAS SPITEFUL. Full of a baby's venom. The women in the house knew it and so did the children. For years each put up with the spite in his own way, but by 1873 Sethe and her daughter Denver were its only victims. The grandmother, Baby Suggs, was dead, and the sons, Howard and Buglar, had run away by the time they were thirteen years old—as soon as merely looking in a mirror shattered it (that was the signal for Buglar); as soon as two tiny hand prints appeared in the cake (that was it for Howard). Neither boy waited to see more; another kettleful of chickpeas smoking in a heap on the floor; soda crackers crumbled and strewn in a line next to the doorsill. Nor did they wait for one of the relief periods: the weeks, months even, when nothing was disturbed. No. Each one fled at once—the moment the house committed what was for him the one insult not to be borne or witnessed a second time. Within two months, in the dead of winter, leaving their grandmother, Baby Suggs; Sethe, their mother; and their little sister, Denver, all by themselves in the gray and white house on Bluestone Road. It didn't have a number then, because Cincinnati didn't stretch that far. In fact, Ohio had been calling itself a state only seventy years when first one brother and then the next stuffed quilt packing into his hat, snatched up his shoes, and crept away from the lively spite the house felt for them.

Baby Suggs didn't even raise her head. From her sickbed she heard them go but that wasn't the reason she lay still. It was a wonder to her that her grandsons had taken so long to realize that every house wasn't like the one on Bluestone Road. Suspended between the nastiness of life and the meanness of the dead, she couldn't get interested in leaving life or living it, let alone the fright of two creeping-off boys. Her past had been like her present—intolerable—and since she knew death was anything but forgetfulness, she used the little energy left her for pondering color.

"Bring a little lavender in, if you got any. Pink, if you don't."

And Sethe would oblige her with anything from fabric to her own tongue. Winter in Ohio was especially rough if you had an appetite for color. Sky provided the only drama, and counting on a Cincinnati horizon for life's principal joy was reckless indeed. So Sethe and the girl Denver did what they could, and what the house permitted, for her. Together they waged a perfunctory battle against the outrageous behavior of that place; against turned-over slop jars, smacks on the behind, and gusts of sour air. For they understood the source of the outrage as well as they knew the source of light.

Baby Suggs died shortly after the brothers left, with no interest whatsoever in their leave-taking or hers, and right afterward Sethe and Denver decided to end the persecution by calling forth the ghost that tried them so. Perhaps a conversation, they thought, an exchange of views or something would help. So they held hands and said, "Come on. Come on. You may as well just come on."

The sideboard took a step forward but nothing else did.

"Grandma Baby must be stopping it," said Denver. She was ten and still mad at Baby Suggs for dying.

Sethe opened her eyes. "I doubt that," she said.

"Then why don't it come?"

"You forgetting how little it is," said her mother. "She wasn't even two years old when she died. Too little to understand. Too little to talk much even."

"Maybe she don't want to understand," said Denver.

"Maybe. But if she'd only come, I could make it clear to her." Sethe released her daughter's hand and together they pushed the sideboard back against the wall. Outside a driver whipped his horse into the gallop local people felt necessary when they passed 124.

"For a baby she throws a powerful spell," said Denver.

"No more powerful than the way I loved her," Sethe answered and there it was again. The welcoming cool of unchiseled headstones; the one she selected to lean against on tiptoe, her knees wide open as any grave. Pink as a fingernail it was, and sprinkled with glittering chips. Ten minutes, he said. You got ten minutes I'll do it for free.

Ten minutes for seven letters. With another ten could she have gotten "Dearly" too? She had not thought to ask him and it bothered her still that it might have been possible—that for twenty minutes, a half hour, say, she could have had the whole thing, every word she heard the preacher say at the funeral (and all there was to say, surely) engraved on her baby's headstone: Dearly Beloved. But what she got, settled for, was the one word that mattered. She thought it would be enough, rutting among the headstones with the engraver, his young son looking on, the anger in his face so old; the appetite in it quite new. That should certainly be enough. Enough to answer one more preacher, one more abolitionist and a town full of disgust.

Counting on the stillness of her own soul, she had forgotten the other one: the soul of her baby girl. Who would have thought that a little old baby could harbor so much rage? Rutting among the stones under the eyes of the engraver's son was not enough. Not only did she have to live out her years in a house palsied by the baby's fury at having its throat cut, but those ten minutes she spent pressed up against dawn-colored stone studded with star chips, her knees wide open as the grave, were longer than life, more alive, more pulsating than the baby blood that soaked her fingers like oil.

"We could move," she suggested once to her mother-in-law.

"What'd be the point?" asked Baby Suggs. "Not a house in the country ain't packed to its rafters with some dead Negro's grief. We lucky this ghost is a baby. My husband's spirit was to come back in here? or yours? Don't talk to me. You lucky. You got three left. Three pulling at your skirts and just one raising hell from the other side. Be thankful, why don't you? I had eight. Every one of them gone away from me. Four taken, four chased, and all, I expect, worrying somebody's house into evil." Baby Suggs rubbed her eyebrows. "My first-born. All I can remember of her is how she loved the burned bottom of bread. Can you beat that? Eight children and that's all I remember."

"That's all you let yourself remember," Sethe had told her, but she was down to one herself—one alive, that is—the boys chased off by the dead one, and her memory of Buglar was fading fast. Howard at least had a head shape nobody could forget. As for the rest, she worked hard to remember as close to nothing as was safe. Unfortunately her brain was devious. She might be hurrying across a field, running practically, to get to the pump quickly and rinse the chamomile sap from her legs. Nothing else would be in her mind. The picture of the men coming to nurse her was as lifeless as the nerves in her back where the skin buckled like a washboard. Nor was there the faintest scent of ink or the cherry gum and oak bark from which it was made. Nothing. Just the breeze cooling her face as she rushed toward water. And then sopping the chamomile away with pump water and rags, her mind fixed on getting every last bit of sap off—on her carelessness in taking a shortcut across the field just to save a half mile, and not noticing how high the weeds had grown until the itching was all the way to her knees. Then something. The plash of water, the sight of her shoes and stockings awry on the path where she had flung them; or Here Boy lapping in the puddle near her feet, and suddenly there was Sweet Home rolling, rolling, rolling out before her eyes, and although there was not a leaf on that farm that did not make her want to scream, it rolled itself out before her in shameless beauty. It never looked as terrible as it was and it made her wonder if hell was a pretty place too. Fire and brimstone all right, but hidden in lacy groves. Boys hanging from the most beautiful sycamores in the world. It shamed her—remembering the wonderful soughing trees rather than the boys. Try as she might to make it otherwise, the sycamores beat out the children every time and she could not forgive her memory for that.

When the last of the chamomile was gone, she went around to the front of the house, collecting her shoes and stockings on the way. As if to punish her further for her terrible memory, sitting on the porch not forty feet away was Paul D, the last of the Sweet Home men. And although she could never mistake his face for another's, she said, "Is that you?"

"What's left." He stood up and smiled. "How you been, girl, besides barefoot?"

When she laughed it came out loose and young. "Messed up my legs back yonder. Chamomile."

He made a face as though tasting a teaspoon of something bitter. "I don't want to even hear 'bout it. Always did hate that stuff."

Sethe balled up her stockings and jammed them into her pocket. "Come on in."

"Porch is fine, Sethe. Cool out here." He sat back down and looked at the meadow on the other side of the road, knowing the eagerness he felt would be in his eyes.

"Eighteen years," she said softly.

"Eighteen," he repeated. "And I swear I been walking every one of em. Mind if I join you?" He nodded toward her feet and began unlacing his shoes.

"You want to soak them? Let me get you a basin of water." She moved closer to him to enter the house.

"No, uh uh. Can't baby feet. A whole lot more tramping they got to do yet."

"You can't leave right away, Paul D. You got to stay awhile."

"Well, long enough to see Baby Suggs, anyway. Where is she?"

"Dead."

"Aw no. When?"

"Eight years now. Almost nine."

"Was it hard? I hope she didn't die hard."

Sethe shook her head. "Soft as cream. Being alive was the hard part. Sorry you missed her though. Is that what you came by for?"

"That's some of what I came for. The rest is you. But if all the truth be known, I go anywhere these days. Anywhere they let me sit down."

"You looking good."

"Devil's confusion. He lets me look good long as I feel bad." He looked at her and the word "bad" took on another meaning.

Sethe smiled. This is the way they were—had been. All of the Sweet Home men, before and after Halle, treated her to a mild brotherly flirtation, so subtle you had to scratch for it.

Except for a heap more hair and some waiting in his eyes, he looked the way he had in Kentucky. Peachstone skin;

straight-backed. For a man with an immobile face it was amazing how ready it was to smile, or blaze or be sorry with you. As though all you had to do was get his attention and right away he produced the feeling you were feeling. With less than a blink, his face seemed to change—underneath it lay the activity.

"I wouldn't have to ask about him, would I? You'd tell me if there was anything to tell, wouldn't you?" Sethe looked down at her feet and saw again the sycamores.

"I'd tell you. Sure I'd tell you. I don't know any more now than I did then." Except for the churn, he thought, and you don't need to know that. "You must think he's still alive."

"No. I think he's dead. It's not being sure that keeps him alive."

"What did Baby Suggs think?"

"Same, but to listen to her, all her children is dead. Claimed she felt each one go the very day and hour."

"When she say Halle went?"

"Eighteen fifty-five. The day my baby was born."

"You had that baby, did you? Never thought you'd make it." He chuckled. "Running off pregnant."

"Had to. Couldn't be no waiting." She lowered her head and thought, as he did, how unlikely it was that she had made it. And if it hadn't been for that girl looking for velvet, she never would have.

"All by yourself too." He was proud of her and annoyed by her. Proud she had done it; annoyed that she had not needed Halle or him in the doing.

"Almost by myself. Not all by myself. A whitegirl helped me."

"Then she helped herself too, God bless her."

"You could stay the night, Paul D."

"You don't sound too steady in the offer."

Sethe glanced beyond his shoulder toward the closed door.

"Oh it's truly meant. I just hope you'll pardon my house. Come on in. Talk to Denver while I cook you something."

Paul D tied his shoes together, hung them over his shoulder and followed her through the door straight into a pool of red and undulating light that locked him where he stood.

"You got company?" he whispered, frowning.

"Off and on," said Sethe.

"Good God." He backed out the door onto the porch. "What kind of evil you got in here?"

"It's not evil, just sad. Come on. Just step through."

He looked at her then, closely. Closer than he had when she first rounded the house on wet and shining legs, holding her shoes and stockings up in one hand, her skirts in the other. Halle's girl—the one with iron eyes and backbone to match. He had never seen her hair in Kentucky. And though her face was eighteen years older than when last he saw her, it was softer now. Because of the hair. A face too still for comfort; irises the same color as her skin, which, in that still face, used to make him think of a mask with mercifully punched-out eyes. Halle's woman. Pregnant every year including the year she sat by the fire telling him she was going to run. Her three children she had already packed into a wagonload of others in a caravan of Negroes crossing the river. They were to be left with Halle's mother near Cincinnati. Even in that tiny shack, leaning so close to the fire you could smell the heat in her dress, her eyes did not pick up a flicker of light. They were like two wells into which he had trouble gazing. Even punched out they needed to be covered, lidded, marked with some sign to warn folks of what that emptiness held. So he looked instead at the fire while she told him, because her husband was not there for the telling. Mr. Garner was dead and his wife had a lump in her neck the size of a sweet potato and unable to speak to anyone. She leaned as close to the fire as her pregnant belly allowed and told him, Paul D, the last of the Sweet Home men.

There had been six of them who belonged to the farm, Sethe the only female. Mrs. Garner, crying like a baby, had sold his brother to pay off the debts that surfaced the minute she was widowed. Then schoolteacher arrived to put things in order. But what he did broke three more Sweet Home men and punched the glittering iron out of Sethe's eyes, leaving two open wells that did not reflect firelight.

Now the iron was back but the face, softened by hair, made him trust her enough to step inside her door smack into a pool of pulsing red light.

She was right. It was sad. Walking through it, a wave of grief soaked him so thoroughly he wanted to cry. It seemed a long way to the normal light surrounding the table, but he made it—dry-eyed and lucky.

"You said she died soft. Soft as cream," he reminded her.

"That's not Baby Suggs," she said.

"Who then?"

"My daughter. The one I sent ahead with the boys."

"She didn't live?"

"No. The one I was carrying when I run away is all I got left. Boys gone too. Both of em walked off just before Baby Suggs died."

Paul D looked at the spot where the grief had soaked him. The red was gone but a kind of weeping clung to the air where it had been.

Probably best, he thought. If a Negro got legs he ought to use them. Sit down too long, somebody will figure out a way to tie them up. Still . . . if her boys were gone . . .

"No man? You here by yourself?"

"Me and Denver," she said.

"That all right by you?"

"That's all right by me."

She saw his skepticism and went on. "I cook at a restaurant in town. And I sew a little on the sly."

Paul D smiled then, remembering the bedding dress. Sethe was thirteen when she came to Sweet Home and already iron-eyed. She was a timely present for Mrs. Garner who had lost Baby Suggs to her husband's high principles. The five Sweet Home men looked at the new girl and decided to let her be. They were young and so sick with the absence of women they had taken to calves. Yet they let the iron-eyed girl be, so she could choose in spite of the fact that each one would have beaten the others to mush to have her. It took her a year to choose—a long, tough year of thrashing on pallets eaten up with dreams of her. A year of yearning, when rape seemed the solitary gift of life. The restraint they had exercised possible only because they were Sweet Home men—the ones Mr. Garner bragged about while other farmers shook their heads in warning at the phrase.

"Y'all got boys," he told them. "Young boys, old boys, picky boys, stroppin boys. Now at Sweet Home, my niggers is men every one of em. Bought em thataway, raised em thataway. Men every one."

"Beg to differ, Garner. Ain't no nigger men."

"Not if you scared, they ain't." Garner's smile was wide. "But if you a man yourself, you'll want your niggers to be men too."

"I wouldn't have no nigger men round my wife."

It was the reaction Garner loved and waited for. "Neither would I," he said. "Neither would I," and there was always a pause before the neighbor, or stranger, or peddler, or brother-in-law or whoever it was got the meaning. Then a fierce argument, sometimes a fight, and Garner came home bruised and pleased, having demonstrated one more time what a real Kentuckian was: one tough enough and smart enough to make and call his own niggers men.

And so they were: Paul D Garner, Paul F Garner, Paul A Garner, Halle Suggs and Sixo, the wild man. All in their twenties, minus women, fucking cows, dreaming of rape, thrashing on pallets, rubbing their thighs and waiting for the new girl—the one who took Baby Suggs' place after Halle bought her with five years of Sundays. Maybe that was why she chose him. A twenty-year-old man so in love with his mother he gave up five years of Sabbaths just to see her sit down for a change was a serious recommendation.

She waited a year. And the Sweet Home men abused cows while they waited with her. She chose Halle and for their first bedding she sewed herself a dress on the sly.

"Won't you stay on awhile? Can't nobody catch up on eighteen years in a day."

Out of the dimness of the room in which they sat, a white staircase climbed toward the blue-and-white wallpaper of the second floor. Paul D could see just the beginning of the paper; discreet flecks of yellow sprinkled among a blizzard of snowdrops all backed by blue. The luminous white of the railing and steps kept him glancing toward it. Every sense he had told him the air above the stairwell was charmed and very thin. But the girl who walked down out of that air was round and brown with the face of an alert doll.

Paul D looked at the girl and then at Sethe who smiled saying, "Here she is my Denver. This is Paul D, honey, from Sweet Home."

"Good morning, Mr. D."

"Garner, baby. Paul D Garner."

"Yes sir."

"Glad to get a look at you. Last time I saw your mama, you were pushing out the front of her dress."

"Still is," Sethe smiled, "provided she can get in it."

Denver stood on the bottom step and was suddenly hot and shy. It had been a long time since anybody (good-willed whitewoman, preacher, speaker or newspaperman) sat at their table, their sympathetic voices called liar by the revulsion in their eyes. For twelve years, long before Grandma Baby died, there had been no visitors of any sort and certainly no friends. No coloredpeople. Certainly no hazelnut man with too long hair and no notebook, no charcoal, no oranges, no questions. Someone her mother wanted to talk to and would even consider talking to while barefoot. Looking, in fact acting, like a girl instead of the quiet, queenly woman Denver had known all her life. The one who never looked away, who when a man got stomped to death by a mare right in front of Sawyer's restaurant did not look away; and when a sow began eating her own litter did not look away then either. And when the baby's spirit picked up Here Boy and slammed him into the wall hard enough to break two of his legs and dislocate his eye, so hard he went into convulsions and chewed up his tongue, still her mother had not looked away. She had taken a hammer, knocked the dog unconscious, wiped away the blood and saliva, pushed his eye back in his head and set his leg bones. He recovered, mute and off-balance, more because of his untrustworthy eye than his bent legs, and winter, summer, drizzle or dry, nothing could persuade him to enter the house again.

Now here was this woman with the presence of mind to repair a dog gone savage with pain rocking her crossed ankles and looking away from her own daughter's body. As though the size of it was more than vision could bear. And neither she nor he had on shoes. Hot, shy, now Denver was lonely. All that leaving: first her brothers, then her grandmother—serious losses since there were no children willing to circle her in a game or hang by their knees from her porch railing. None of that had mattered as long as her mother did not look away as she was doing now, making Denver long, downright *long*, for a sign of spite from the baby ghost.

"She's a fine-looking young lady," said Paul D. "Fine-looking. Got her daddy's sweet face."

"You know my father?"

"Knew him. Knew him well."

"Did he, Ma'am?" Denver fought an urge to realign her affection.

"Of course he knew your daddy. I told you, he's from Sweet Home."

Denver sat down on the bottom step. There was nowhere else gracefully to go. They were a twosome, saying "Your daddy" and "Sweet Home" in a way that made it clear both belonged to them and not to her. That her own father's absence was not hers. Once the absence had belonged to Grandma Baby—a son, deeply mourned because he was the one who had bought her out of there. Then it was her mother's absent husband. Now it was this hazelnut stranger's absent friend. Only those who knew him ("knew him well") could claim his absence for themselves. Just as only those who lived in Sweet Home could remember it, whisper it and glance sideways at one another while they did. Again she wished for the baby ghost—its anger thrilling her now where it used to wear her out. Wear her out.

"We have a ghost in here," she said, and it worked. They were not a twosome anymore. Her mother left off swinging her feet and being girlish. Memory of Sweet Home dropped away from the eyes of the man she was being girlish for. He looked quickly up the lightning-white stairs behind her.

"So I hear," he said. "But sad, your mama said. Not evil."

"No sir," said Denver, "not evil. But not sad either."

"What then?"

"Rebuked. Lonely and rebuked."

"Is that right?" Paul D turned to Sethe.

"I don't know about lonely," said Denver's mother. "Mad, maybe, but I don't see how it could be lonely spending every minute with us like it does."

"Must be something you got it wants."

Sethe shrugged. "It's just a baby."

"My sister," said Denver. "She died in this house."

Paul D scratched the hair under his jaw. "Reminds me of that headless bride back behind Sweet Home. Remember that, Sethe? Used to roam them woods regular."

"How could I forget? Worrisome . . ."

"How come everybody run off from Sweet Home can't stop talking about it? Look like if it was so sweet you would have stayed."

"Girl, who you talking to?"

Paul D laughed. "True, true. She's right, Sethe. It wasn't sweet and it sure wasn't home." He shook his head.

"But it's where we were," said Sethe. "All together. Comes back whether we want it to or not." She shivered a little. A light ripple of skin on her arm, which she caressed back into sleep. "Denver," she said, "start up that stove. Can't have a friend stop by and don't feed him."

"Don't go to any trouble on my account," Paul D said.

"Bread ain't trouble. The rest I brought back from where I work. Least I can do, cooking from dawn to noon, is bring dinner home. You got any objections to pike?"

"If he don't object to me I don't object to him."

At it again, thought Denver. Her back to them, she jostled the kindlin and almost lost the fire. "Why don't you spend the night, Mr. Garner? You and Ma'am can talk about Sweet Home all night long."

Sethe took two swift steps to the stove, but before she could yank Denver's collar, the girl leaned forward and began to cry.

"What is the matter with you? I never knew you to behave this way."

"Leave her be," said Paul D. "I'm a stranger to her."

"That's just it. She got no cause to act up with a stranger. Oh baby, what is it? Did something happen?"

But Denver was shaking now and sobbing so she could not speak. The tears she had not shed for nine years wetting her far too womanly breasts.

"I can't no more. I can't no more."

"Can't what? What can't you?"

"I can't live here. I don't know where to go or what to do, but I can't live here. Nobody speaks to us. Nobody comes by. Boys don't like me. Girls don't either."

"Honey, honey."

"What's she talking 'bout nobody speaks to you?" asked Paul D.

"It's the house. People don't—"

"It's not! It's not the house. It's us! And it's you!"

"Denver!"

"Leave off, Sethe. It's hard for a young girl living in a haunted house. That can't be easy."

"It's easier than some other things."

"Think, Sethe. I'm a grown man with nothing new left to see or do and I'm telling you it ain't easy. Maybe you all ought to move. Who owns this house?"

Over Denver's shoulder Sethe shot Paul D a look of snow. "What you care?"

"They won't let you leave?"

"No."

"Sethe."

"No moving. No leaving. It's all right the way it is."

"You going to tell me it's all right with this child half out of her mind?"

Something in the house braced, and in the listening quiet that followed Sethe spoke.

"I got a tree on my back and a haint in my house, and nothing in between but the daughter I am holding in my arms. No more running—from nothing. I will never run from another thing on this earth. I took one journey and I paid for the ticket, but let me tell you something, Paul D Garner: it cost too much! Do you hear me? It cost too much. Now sit down and eat with us or leave us be."

Paul D fished in his vest for a little pouch of tobacco—concentrating on its contents and the knot of its string while Sethe led Denver into the keeping room that opened off the large room he was sitting in. He had no smoking papers, so he fiddled with the pouch and listened through the open door to Sethe quieting her daughter. When she came back she avoided his look and went straight to a small table next to the stove. Her back was to him and he could see all the hair he wanted without the distraction of her face.

"What tree on your back?"

"Huh." Sethe put a bowl on the table and reached under it for flour.

"What tree on your back? Is something growing on your back? I don't see nothing growing on your back."

"It's there all the same."

"Who told you that?"

"Whitegirl. That's what she called it. I've never seen it and never will. But that's what she said it looked like. A chokecherry tree. Trunk, branches, and even leaves. Tiny little chokecherry leaves. But that was eighteen years ago. Could have cherries too now for all I know."

Sethe took a little spit from the tip of her tongue with her forefinger. Quickly, lightly she touched the stove. Then she trailed her fingers through the flour, parting, separating small hills and ridges of it, looking for mites. Finding none, she poured soda and salt into the crease of her folded hand and tossed both into the flour. Then she reached into a can and scooped half a handful of lard. Deftly she squeezed the flour through it, then with her left hand sprinkling water, she formed the dough.

"I had milk," she said. "I was pregnant with Denver but I had milk for my baby girl. I hadn't stopped nursing her when I sent her on ahead with Howard and Buglar."

Now she rolled the dough out with a wooden pin. "Anybody could smell me long before he saw me. And when he saw me he'd see the drops of it on the front of my dress. Nothing I could do about that. All I knew was I had to get my milk to my baby girl. Nobody was going to nurse her like me. Nobody was going to get it to her fast enough, or take it away when she had enough and didn't know it. Nobody knew that she couldn't pass her air if you held her up on your shoulder, only if she was lying on my knees. Nobody knew that but me and nobody had her milk but me. I told that to the women in the wagon. Told them to put sugar water in cloth to suck from so when I got there in a few days she wouldn't have forgot me. The milk would be there and I would be there with it."

"Men don't know nothing much," said Paul D, tucking his pouch back into his vest pocket, "but they do know a suckling can't be away from its mother for long."

"Then they know what it's like to send your children off when your breasts are full."

"We was talking 'bout a tree, Sethe."

"After I left you, those boys came in there and took my milk. That's what they came in there for. Held me down and took it. I told Mrs. Garner on em. She had that lump and couldn't speak but her eyes rolled out tears. Them boys found out I told on em. Schoolteacher made one open up my back, and when it closed it made a tree. It grows there still."

"They used cowhide on you?"

"And they took my milk."

"They beat you and you was pregnant?"

"And they took my milk!"

The fat white circles of dough lined the pan in rows. Once more Sethe touched a wet forefinger to the stove. She opened the oven door and slid the pan of biscuits in. As she raised up from the heat she felt Paul D behind her and his hands under her breasts. She straightened up and knew, but could not feel, that his cheek was pressing into the branches of her chokecherry tree.

Not even trying, he had become the kind of man who could walk into a house and make the women cry. Because with him, in his presence, they could. There was something blessed in his manner. Women saw him and wanted to weep—to tell him that their chest hurt and their knees did too. Strong women and wise saw him and told him things they only told each other: that way past the Change of Life, desire in them had suddenly become enormous, greedy, more savage than when they were fifteen, and that it embarrassed them and made them sad; that secretly they longed to die—to be quit of it—that sleep was more precious to them than any waking day. Young girls sidled up to him to confess or describe how well-dressed the visitations were that had followed them straight from their dreams. Therefore, although he did not understand why this was so, he was not surprised when Denver dripped tears into the stovefire. Nor, fifteen minutes later, after telling him about her stolen milk, her mother wept as well. Behind her, bending down, his body an arc of kindness, he held her breasts in the palms of his hands. He rubbed his cheek on her back and learned that way her sorrow, the roots of it; its wide trunk and intricate branches. Raising his fingers to the hooks of her dress, he knew without seeing them or hearing any sigh that the tears were coming fast. And when the top of her dress was around her hips and he saw the sculpture her back had become, like the decorative work of an ironsmith too passionate for display, he could think but not say, "Aw, Lord, girl." And he would tolerate no peace until he had touched every ridge and leaf of it with his mouth, none of which Sethe could feel because her back skin had been dead for years. What she knew was that the responsibility for her breasts, at last, was in somebody else's hands.

Would there be a little space, she wondered, a little time, some way to hold off eventfulness, to push busyness into the corners of the room and just stand there a minute or two, naked from shoulder blade to waist, relieved of the weight of her breasts, smelling the stolen milk again and the pleasure of baking bread? Maybe this one time she could stop dead still in the middle of a cooking meal—not even leave the stove—and feel the hurt her back ought to. Trust things and remember things because the last of the Sweet Home men was there to catch her if she sank?

The stove didn't shudder as it adjusted to its heat. Denver wasn't stirring in the next room. The pulse of red light hadn't come back and Paul D had not trembled since 1856 and then for eighty-three days in a row. Locked up and chained down, his hands shook so bad he couldn't smoke or even scratch properly. Now he was trembling again but in the legs this time. It took him a while to realize that his legs were not shaking because of worry, but because the floorboards were and the grinding, shoving floor was only part of it. The house itself was pitching. Sethe slid to the floor and struggled to get back into her dress. While down on all fours, as though she were holding her house down on the ground, Denver burst from the keeping room, terror in her eyes, a vague smile on her lips.

"God damn it! Hush up!" Paul D was shouting, falling, reaching for anchor. "Leave the place alone! Get the hell out!" A table rushed toward him and he grabbed its leg. Somehow he managed to stand at an angle and, holding the table by two legs, he bashed it about, wrecking everything, screaming back at the screaming house. "You want to fight, come on! God damn it! She got enough without you. She got enough!"

The quaking slowed to an occasional lurch, but Paul D did not stop whipping the table around until everything was rock quiet. Sweating and breathing hard, he leaned against the wall in the space the sideboard left. Sethe was still crouched next to the stove, clutching her salvaged shoes to her chest. The three of them, Sethe, Denver, and Paul D, breathed to the same beat, like one tired person. Another breathing was just as tired.

It was gone. Denver wandered through the silence to the stove. She ashed over the fire and pulled the pan of biscuits from the oven. The jelly cupboard was on its back, its contents lying in a heap in the corner of the bottom shelf. She took out a jar, and, looking around for a plate, found half of one by the door. These things she carried out to the porch steps, where she sat down.

The two of them had gone up there. Stepping lightly, easy-footed, they had climbed the white stairs, leaving her down below. She pried the wire from the top of the jar and then the lid. Under it was cloth and under that a thin cake of wax. She removed it all and coaxed the jelly onto one half of the half a plate. She took a biscuit and pulled off its black top. Smoke curled from the soft white insides.

She missed her brothers. Buglar and Howard would be twenty-two and twenty-three now. Although they had been polite to her during the quiet time and gave her the whole top of the bed, she remembered how it was before: the pleasure they had sitting clustered on the white stairs—she between the knees of Howard or Buglar—while they made up die-witch! stories with proven ways of killing her dead. And Baby Suggs telling her things in the keeping room. She smelled like bark in the day and leaves at night, for Denver would not sleep in her old room after her brothers ran away.

Now her mother was upstairs with the man who had gotten rid of the only other company she had. Denver dipped a bit of bread into the jelly. Slowly, methodically, miserably she ate it.

NOT QUITE in a hurry, but losing no time, Sethe and Paul D climbed the white stairs. Overwhelmed as much by the downright luck of finding her house and her in it as by the certainty of giving her his sex, Paul D dropped twenty-five years from his recent memory. A stair step before him was Baby Suggs' replacement, the new girl they dreamed of at night and fucked cows for at dawn while waiting for her to choose. Merely kissing the wrought iron on her back had shook the house, had made it necessary for him to beat it to pieces. Now he would do more.

She led him to the top of the stairs, where light came straight from the sky because the second-story windows of that house had been placed in the pitched ceiling and not the walls. There were two rooms and she took him into one of them, hoping he wouldn't mind the fact that she was not prepared; that though she could remember desire, she had forgotten how it worked; the clutch and helplessness that resided in the hands; how blindness was altered so that what leapt to the eye were places to lie down, and all else—doorknobs, straps, hooks, the sadness that crouched in corners, and the passing of time—was interference.

It was over before they could get their clothes off. Half-dressed and short of breath, they lay side by side resentful of one another and the skylight above them. His dreaming of her had been too long and too long ago. Her deprivation had been not having any dreams of her own at all. Now they were sorry and too shy to make talk.

Sethe lay on her back, her head turned from him. Out of the corner of his eye, Paul D saw the float of her breasts and disliked it, the spread-away, flat roundness of them that he could definitely live without, never mind that downstairs he had held them as though they were the most expensive part of himself. And the wrought-iron maze he had explored in the kitchen like a gold miner pawing through pay dirt was in fact a revolting clump of scars. Not a tree, as she said. Maybe shaped like one, but nothing like any tree he knew because trees were inviting; things you could trust and be near; talk to if you wanted to as he frequently did since way back when he took the midday meal in the fields of Sweet Home. Always in the same place if he could, and choosing the place had been hard because Sweet Home had more pretty trees than any farm around. His choice he called Brother, and sat under it, alone sometimes, sometimes with Halle or the other Pauls, but more often with Sixo, who was gentle then and still speaking English. Indigo with a flame-red tongue, Sixo experimented with night-cooked potatoes, trying to pin down exactly when to put smoking-hot rocks in a hole, potatoes on top, and cover the whole thing with twigs so that by the time they broke for the meal, hitched the animals, left the field and got to Brother, the potatoes would be at the peak of perfection. He might get up in the middle of the night, go all the way out there, start the earth-over by starlight; or he would make the stones less hot and put the next day's potatoes on them right after the meal. He never got it right, but they ate those undercooked, overcooked, dried-out or raw potatoes anyway, laughing, spitting and giving him advice.

Time never worked the way Sixo thought, so of course he never got it right. Once he plotted down to the minute a thirty-mile trip to see a woman. He left on a Saturday when the moon was in the place he wanted it to be, arrived at her cabin before church on Sunday and had just enough time to say good morning before he had to start back again so he'd make the field call on time Monday morning. He had walked for seventeen hours, sat down for one, turned around and walked seventeen more. Halle and the Pauls spent the whole day covering Sixo's fatigue from Mr. Garner. They ate no potatoes that day, sweet or white. Sprawled near Brother, his flame-red tongue hidden from them, his indigo face closed, Sixo slept through dinner like a corpse. Now *there* was a man, and *that* was a tree. Himself lying in the bed and the "tree" lying next to him didn't compare.

Paul D looked through the window above his feet and folded his hands behind his head. An elbow grazed Sethe's shoulder. The touch of cloth on her skin startled her. She had forgotten he had not taken off his shirt. Dog, she thought, and then remembered that she had not allowed him the time for taking it off. Nor herself time to take off her petticoat, and considering she had begun undressing before she saw him on the porch, that her shoes and stockings were already in her hand and she had never put them back on; that he had looked at her wet bare feet and asked to join her; that when she rose to cook he had undressed her further; considering how quickly they had started getting naked, you'd think by now they would be. But maybe a man was nothing but a man, which is what Baby Suggs always said. They encouraged you to put some of your weight in their hands and soon as you felt how light and lovely that was, they studied your scars and tribulations, after which they did what he had done: ran her children out and tore up the house.

She needed to get up from there, go downstairs and piece it all back together. This house he told her to leave as though a house was a little thing—a shirtwaist or a sewing basket you could walk off from or give away any old time. She who had never had one but this one; she who left a dirt floor to come to this one; she who had to bring a fistful of salsify into Mrs. Garner's kitchen every day just to be able to work in it, feel like some part of it was hers, because she wanted to love the work she did, to take the ugly out of it, and the only way she could feel at home on Sweet Home was if she picked some pretty growing thing and took it with her. The day she forgot was the day butter wouldn't come or the brine in the barrel blistered her arms.

At least it seemed so. A few yellow flowers on the table, some myrtle tied around the handle of the flatiron holding the door open for a breeze calmed her, and when Mrs. Garner and she sat down to sort bristle, or make ink, she felt fine. Fine. Not scared of the men beyond. The five who slept in quarters near her, but never came in the night. Just touched their raggedy hats when they saw her and stared. And if she brought food to them in the fields, bacon and bread wrapped in a piece of clean sheeting, they never took it from her hands. They stood back and waited for her to put it on the ground (at the foot of a tree) and leave. Either they did not want to take anything from her, or did not want her to see them eat. Twice or three times she lingered. Hidden behind honeysuckle she watched them. How different they were without her, how they laughed and played and urinated and sang. All but Sixo, who laughed once—at the very end. Halle, of course, was the nicest. Baby Suggs' eighth and last child, who rented himself out all over the county to buy her away from there. But he too, as it turned out, was nothing but a man.

"A man ain't nothing but a man," said Baby Suggs. "But a son? Well now, that's *somebody*."

It made sense for a lot of reasons because in all of Baby's life, as well as Sethe's own, men and women were moved around like checkers. Anybody Baby Suggs knew, let alone loved, who hadn't run off or been hanged, got rented out, loaned out, bought up, brought back, stored up, mortgaged, won, stolen or seized. So Baby's eight children had six fathers. What she called the nastiness of life was the shock she received upon learning that nobody stopped playing checkers just because the pieces included her children. Halle she was able to keep the longest. Twenty years. A lifetime. Given to her, no doubt, to make up for *hearing* that her two girls, neither of whom had their adult teeth, were sold and gone and she had not been able to wave goodbye. To make up for coupling with a straw boss for four months in exchange for keeping her third child, a boy, with her—only to have him traded for lumber in the spring of the next year and to find herself pregnant by the man who promised not to and did. That child she could not love and the rest she would not. "God take what He would," she said. And He did, and He did, and He did and then gave her Halle who gave her freedom when it didn't mean a thing.

Sethe had the amazing luck of six whole years of marriage to that "somebody" son who had fathered every one of her children. A blessing she was reckless enough to take for granted, lean on, as though Sweet Home really was one. As though a handful of myrtle stuck in the handle of a pressing iron propped against the door in a whitewoman's kitchen could make it hers. As though mint sprig in the mouth changed the breath as well as its odor. A bigger fool never lived.

Sethe started to turn over on her stomach but changed her mind. She did not want to call Paul D's attention back to her, so she settled for crossing her ankles.

But Paul D noticed the movement as well as the change in her breathing. He felt obliged to try again, slower this time, but the appetite was gone. Actually it was a good feeling—not wanting her. Twenty-five years and blip! The kind of thing

Sixo would do—like the time he arranged a meeting with Patsy the Thirty-Mile Woman. It took three months and two thirty-four-mile round trips to do it. To persuade her to walk one-third of the way toward him, to a place he knew. A deserted stone structure that Redmen used way back when they thought the land was theirs. Sixo discovered it on one of his night creeps, and asked its permission to enter. Inside, having felt what it felt like, he asked the Redmen's Presence if he could bring his woman there. It said yes and Sixo painstakingly instructed her how to get there, exactly when to start out, how his welcoming or warning whistles would sound. Since neither could go anywhere on business of their own, and since the Thirty-Mile Woman was already fourteen and scheduled for somebody's arms, the danger was real. When he arrived, she had not. He whistled and got no answer. He went into the Redmen's deserted lodge. She was not there. He returned to the meeting spot. She was not there. He waited longer. She still did not come. He grew frightened for her and walked down the road in the direction she should be coming from. Three or four miles, and he stopped. It was hopeless to go on that way, so he stood in the wind and asked for help. Listening close for some sign, he heard a whimper. He turned toward it, waited and heard it again. Uncautious now, he hollered her name. She answered in a voice that sounded like life to him—not death. "Not move!" he shouted. "Breathe hard I can find you." He did. She believed she was already at the meeting place and was crying because she thought he had not kept his promise. Now it was too late for the rendezvous to happen at the Redmen's house, so they dropped where they were. Later he punctured her calf to simulate snakebite so she could use it in some way as an excuse for not being on time to shake worms from tobacco leaves. He gave her detailed directions about following the stream as a shortcut back, and saw her off. When he got to the road it was very light and he had his clothes in his hands. Suddenly from around a bend a wagon trundled toward him. Its driver, wide-eyed, raised a whip while the woman seated beside him covered her face. But Sixo had already melted into the woods before the lash could unfurl itself on his indigo behind.

He told the story to Paul F, Halle, Paul A and Paul D in the peculiar way that made them cry-laugh. Sixo went among trees at night. For dancing, he said, to keep his bloodlines open, he said. Privately, alone, he did it. None of the rest of them had seen him at it, but they could imagine it, and the picture they pictured made them eager to laugh at him—in daylight, that is, when it was safe.

But that was before he stopped speaking English because there was no future in it. Because of the Thirty-Mile Woman Sixo was the only one not paralyzed by yearning for Sethe. Nothing could be as good as the sex with her Paul D had been imagining off and on for twenty-five years. His foolishness made him smile and think fondly of himself as he turned over on his side, facing her. Sethe's eyes were closed, her hair a mess. Looked at this way, minus the polished eyes, her face was not so attractive. So it must have been her eyes that kept him both guarded and stirred up. Without them her face was manageable—a face he could handle. Maybe if she would keep them closed like that . . . But no, there was her mouth. Nice. Halle never knew what he had.

Although her eyes were closed, Sethe knew his gaze was on her face, and a paper picture of just how bad she must look raised itself up before her mind's eye. Still, there was no mockery coming from his gaze. Soft. It felt soft in a waiting kind of way. He was not judging her—or rather he was judging but not comparing her. Not since Halle had a man looked at her that way: not loving or passionate, but interested, as though he were examining an ear of corn for quality. Halle was more like a brother than a husband. His care suggested a family relationship rather than a man's laying claim. For years they saw each other in full daylight only on Sundays. The rest of the time they spoke or touched or ate in darkness. Predawn darkness and the afterlight of sunset. So looking at each other intently was a Sunday-morning pleasure and Halle examined her as though storing up what he saw in sunlight for the shadow he saw the rest of the week. And he had so little time. After his Sweet Home work and on Sunday afternoons was the debt work he owed for his mother. When he asked her to be his wife, Sethe happily agreed and then was stuck not knowing the next step. There should be a ceremony, shouldn't there? A preacher, some dancing, a party, a something. She and Mrs. Garner were the only women there, so she decided to ask her.

"Halle and me want to be married, Mrs. Garner."

"So I heard." She smiled. "He talked to Mr. Garner about it. Are you already expecting?"

"No, ma'am."

"Well, you will be. You know that, don't you?"

"Yes, ma'am."

"Halle's nice, Sethe. He'll be good to you."

"But I mean we want to get married."

"You just said so. And I said all right."

"Is there a wedding?"

Mrs. Garner put down her cooking spoon. Laughing a little, she touched Sethe on the head, saying, "You are one sweet child." And then no more.

Sethe made a dress on the sly and Halle hung his hitching rope from a nail on the wall of her cabin. And there on top of a mattress on top of the dirt floor of the cabin they coupled for the third time, the first two having been in the tiny cornfield Mr. Garner kept because it was a crop animals could use as well as humans. Both Halle and Sethe were under the impression that they were hidden. Scrunched down among the stalks they couldn't see anything, including the corn tops waving over their heads and visible to everyone else.

Sethe smiled at her and Halle's stupidity. Even the crows knew and came to look. Uncrossing her ankles, she managed not to laugh aloud.

The jump, thought Paul D, from a calf to a girl wasn't all that mighty. Not the leap Halle believed it would be. And taking her in the corn rather than her quarters, a yard away from the cabins of the others who had lost out, was a gesture of tenderness. Halle wanted privacy for her and got public display. Who could miss a ripple in a cornfield on a quiet cloudless day? He, Sixo and both of the Pauls sat under Brother pouring water from a gourd over their heads, and through eyes streaming with well water, they watched the confusion of tassels in the field below. It had been hard, hard, hard sitting there erect as dogs, watching corn stalks dance at noon. The water running over their heads made it worse.

Paul D sighed and turned over. Sethe took the opportunity afforded by his movement to shift as well. Looking at Paul D's back, she remembered that some of the corn stalks broke, folded down over Halle's back, and among the things her fingers clutched were husk and cornsilk hair.

How loose the silk. How jailed down the juice.

The jealous admiration of the watching men melted with the feast of new corn they allowed themselves that night. Plucked from the broken stalks that Mr. Garner could not doubt was the fault of the raccoon. Paul F wanted his roasted; Paul A wanted his boiled and now Paul D couldn't remember how finally they'd cooked those ears too young to eat. What he did remember was parting the hair to get to the tip, the edge of his fingernail just under, so as not to graze a single kernel.

The pulling down of the tight sheath, the ripping sound always convinced her it hurt.

33

As soon as one strip of husk was down, the rest obeyed and the ear yielded up to him its shy rows, exposed at last. How loose the silk. How quick the jailed-up flavor ran free.

No matter what all your teeth and wet fingers anticipated, there was no accounting for the way that simple joy could shake you.

How loose the silk. How fine and loose and free.

DENVER'S SECRETS were sweet. Accompanied every time by wild veronica until she discovered cologne. The first bottle was a gift, the next she stole from her mother and hid among boxwood until it froze and cracked. That was the year winter came in a hurry at suppertime and stayed eight months. One of the War years when Miss Bodwin, the whitewoman, brought Christmas cologne for her mother and herself, oranges for the boys and another good wool shawl for Baby Suggs. Talking of a war full of dead people, she looked happy—flush-faced, and although her voice was heavy as a man's, she smelled like a roomful of flowers—excitement that Denver could have all for herself in the boxwood. Back beyond 124 was a narrow field that stopped itself at a wood. On the yonder side of these woods, a stream. In these woods, between the field and the stream, hidden by post oaks, five boxwood bushes, planted in a ring, had started stretching toward each other four feet off the ground to form a round, empty room seven feet high, its walls fifty inches of murmuring leaves.

Bent low, Denver could crawl into this room, and once there she could stand all the way up in emerald light.

It began as a little girl's houseplay, but as her desires changed, so did the play. Quiet, private and completely secret except for the noisome cologne signal that thrilled the rabbits before it confused them. First a playroom (where the silence was softer), then a refuge (from her brothers' fright), soon the place became the point. In that bower, closed off from the hurt of the hurt world, Denver's imagination produced its own hunger and its own food, which she badly needed because loneliness wore her out. *Wore her out.* Veiled and protected by the live green walls, she felt ripe and clear, and salvation was as easy as a wish.

Once when she was in the boxwood, an autumn long before Paul D moved into the house with her mother, she was made suddenly cold by a combination of wind and the perfume on her skin. She dressed herself, bent down to leave and stood up in snowfall: a thin and whipping snow very like the picture her mother had painted as she described the circumstances of Denver's birth in a canoe straddled by a whitegirl for whom she was named.

Shivering, Denver approached the house, regarding it, as she always did, as a person rather than a structure. A person that wept, sighed, trembled and fell into fits. Her steps and her gaze were the cautious ones of a child approaching a nervous, idle relative (someone dependent but proud). A breastplate of darkness hid all the windows except one. Its dim glow came from Baby Suggs' room. When Denver looked in, she saw her mother on her knees in prayer, which was not unusual. What was unusual (even for a girl who had lived all her life in a house peopled by the living activity of the dead) was that a white dress knelt down next to her mother and had its sleeve around her mother's waist. And it was the tender embrace of the dress sleeve that made Denver remember the details of her birth—that and the thin, whipping snow she was standing in, like the fruit of common flowers. The dress and her mother together looked like two friendly grown-up women—one (the dress) helping out the other. And the magic of her birth, its miracle in fact, testified to that friendliness as did her own name.

Easily she stepped into the told story that lay before her eyes on the path she followed away from the window. There was only one door to the house and to get to it from the back you had to walk all the way around to the front of 124, past the storeroom, past the cold house, the privy, the shed, on around to the porch. And to get to the part of the story she liked best, she had to start way back: hear the birds in the thick woods, the crunch of leaves underfoot; see her mother making her way up into the hills where no houses were likely to be. How Sethe was walking on two feet meant for standing still. How they were so swollen she could not see her arch or feel her ankles. Her leg shaft ended in a loaf of flesh scalloped by five toenails. But she could not, would not, stop, for when she did the little antelope rammed her with horns and pawed the ground of her womb with impatient hooves. While she was walking, it seemed to graze, quietly—so she walked, on two feet meant, in this sixth month of pregnancy, for standing still. Still, near a kettle; still, at the churn; still, at the tub and ironing board. Milk, sticky and sour on her dress, attracted every small flying thing from gnats to grasshoppers. By the time she reached the hill skirt she had long ago stopped waving them off. The clanging in her head, begun as a churchbell heard from a distance, was by then a tight cap of pealing bells around her ears. She sank and had to look down to see whether she was in a hole or kneeling. Nothing was alive but her nipples and the little antelope. Finally, she was horizontal—or must have been because blades of wild onion were scratching her temple and her cheek. Concerned as she was for the life of her children's mother, Sethe told Denver, she remembered thinking: Well, at least I don't have to take another step. A dying thought if ever there was one, and she waited for the little antelope to protest, and why she thought of an antelope Sethe could not imagine since she had never seen one. She guessed it must have been an invention held on to from before Sweet Home, when she was very young. Of that place where she was born (Carolina maybe? or was it Louisiana?) she remembered only song and dance. Not even her own mother, who was pointed out to her by the eight-year-old child who watched over the young ones—pointed out as the one among many backs turned away from her, stooping in a watery field. Patiently Sethe waited for this particular back to gain the row's end and stand. What she saw was a cloth hat as opposed to a straw one, singularity enough in that world of cooing women each of whom was called Ma'am.

"Seth—thuh."

"Ma'am."

"Hold on to the baby."

"Yes, Ma'am."

"Seth—thuh."

"Ma'am."

"Get some kindlin in here."

"Yes, Ma'am."

Oh but when they sang. And oh but when they danced and sometimes they danced the antelope. The men as well as the ma'ams, one of whom was certainly her own. They shifted shapes and became something other. Some unchained, demanding other whose feet knew her pulse better than she did. Just like this one in her stomach.

"I believe this baby's ma'am is gonna die in wild onions on the bloody side of the Ohio River." That's what was on her mind and what she told Denver. Her exact words. And it didn't seem such a bad idea, all in all, in view of the step she would not have to take, but the thought of herself stretched out dead while the little antelope lived on—an hour? a day? a day and a night?—in her lifeless body grieved her so she made the groan that made the person walking on a path not ten yards away halt and stand right still. Sethe had not heard the walking, but suddenly she heard the standing still and then she smelled the hair. The voice, saying, "Who's in there?" was all she needed to know that she was about to be discovered by a whiteboy. That he too had mossy teeth, an appetite. That on a ridge of pine near the Ohio River, trying to get to her three children, one of whom was starving for the food she carried; that after her husband had disappeared; that after her milk had been stolen, her back pulped, her children orphaned, she was not to have an easeful death. No.

She told Denver that a *something* came up out of the earth into her—like a freezing, but moving too, like jaws inside. "Look like I was just cold jaws grinding," she said. Suddenly she was eager for his eyes, to bite into them; to gnaw his cheek.

"I was hungry," she told Denver, "just as hungry as I could be for his eyes. I couldn't wait."

So she raised up on her elbow and dragged herself, one pull, two, three, four, toward the young white voice talking about "Who that back in there?"

" 'Come see,' I was thinking. 'Be the last thing you behold,' and sure enough here come the feet so I thought well that's where I'll have to start God do what He would, I'm gonna eat his feet off. I'm laughing now, but it's true. I wasn't just set to do it. I was hungry to do it. Like a snake. All jaws and hungry.

"It wasn't no whiteboy at all. Was a girl. The raggediest-looking trash you ever saw saying, 'Look there. A nigger. If that don't beat all.' "

And now the part Denver loved the best:

Her name was Amy and she needed beef and pot liquor

like nobody in this world. Arms like cane stalks and enough hair for four or five heads. Slow-moving eyes. She didn't look at anything quick. Talked so much it wasn't clear how she could breathe at the same time. And those cane-stalk arms, as it turned out, were as strong as iron.

"You 'bout the scariest-looking something I ever seen. What you doing back up in here?"

Down in the grass, like the snake she believed she was, Sethe opened her mouth, and instead of fangs and a split tongue, out shot the truth.

"Running," Sethe told her. It was the first word she had spoken all day and it came out thick because of her tender tongue.

"Them the feet you running on? My Jesus my." She squatted down and stared at Sethe's feet. "You got anything on you, gal, pass for food?"

"No." Sethe tried to shift to a sitting position but couldn't.

"I like to die I'm so hungry." The girl moved her eyes slowly, examining the greenery around her. "Thought there'd be huckleberries. Look like it. That's why I come up in here. Didn't expect to find no nigger woman. If they was any, birds ate em. You like huckleberries?"

"I'm having a baby, miss."

Amy looked at her. "That mean you don't have no appetite? Well I got to eat me something."

Combing her hair with her fingers, she carefully surveyed the landscape once more. Satisfied nothing edible was around, she stood up to go and Sethe's heart stood up too at the thought of being left alone in the grass without a fang in her head.

"Where you on your way to, miss?"

She turned and looked at Sethe with freshly lit eyes.

"Boston. Get me some velvet. It's a store there called Wilson. I seen the pictures of it and they have the prettiest velvet. They don't believe I'm a get it, but I am."

Sethe nodded and shifted her elbow. "Your ma'am know you on the lookout for velvet?"

The girl shook her hair out of her face. "My mama worked for these here people to pay for her passage. But then she had me and since she died right after, well, they said I had to work for em to pay it off. I did, but now I want me some velvet."

They did not look directly at each other, not straight into the eyes anyway. Yet they slipped effortlessly into yard chat about nothing in particular—except one lay on the ground.

"Boston," said Sethe. "Is that far?"

"Ooooh, yeah. A hundred miles. Maybe more."

"Must be velvet closer by."

"Not like in Boston. Boston got the best. Be so pretty on me. You ever touch it?"

"No, miss. I never touched no velvet." Sethe didn't know if it was the voice, or Boston or velvet, but while the whitegirl talked, the baby slept. Not one butt or kick, so she guessed her luck had turned.

"Ever see any?" she asked Sethe. "I bet you never even seen any."

"If I did I didn't know it. What's it like, velvet?"

Amy dragged her eyes over Sethe's face as though she would never give out so confidential a piece of information as that to a perfect stranger.

"What they call you?" she asked.

However far she was from Sweet Home, there was no point in giving out her real name to the first person she saw. "Lu," said Sethe. "They call me Lu."

"Well, Lu, velvet is like the world was just born. Clean

and new and so smooth. The velvet I seen was brown, but in Boston they got all colors. Carmine. That means red but when you talk about velvet you got to say 'carmine.' " She raised her eyes to the sky and then, as though she had wasted enough time away from Boston, she moved off saying, "I gotta go."

Picking her way through the brush she hollered back to Sethe, "What you gonna do, just lay there and foal?"

"I can't get up from here," said Sethe.

"What?" She stopped and turned to hear.

"I said I can't get up."

Amy drew her arm across her nose and came slowly back to where Sethe lay. "It's a house back yonder," she said.

"A house?"

"Mmmmm. I passed it. Ain't no regular house with people in it though. A lean-to, kinda."

"How far?"

"Make a difference, does it? You stay the night here snake get you."

"Well he may as well come on. I can't stand up let alone walk and God help me, miss, I can't crawl."

"Sure you can, Lu. Come on," said Amy and, with a toss of hair enough for five heads, she moved toward the path.

So she crawled and Amy walked alongside her, and when Sethe needed to rest, Amy stopped too and talked some more about Boston and velvet and good things to eat. The sound of that voice, like a sixteen-year-old boy's, going on and on and on, kept the little antelope quiet and grazing. During the whole hateful crawl to the lean-to, it never bucked once.

Nothing of Sethe's was intact by the time they reached it except the cloth that covered her hair. Below her bloody knees, there was no feeling at all; her chest was two cushions of pins. It was the voice full of velvet and Boston and good things to eat that urged her along and made her think that maybe she wasn't, after all, just a crawling graveyard for a six-month baby's last hours.

The lean-to was full of leaves, which Amy pushed into a pile for Sethe to lie on. Then she gathered rocks, covered them with more leaves and made Sethe put her feet on them, saying: "I know a woman had her feet cut off they was so swole." And she made sawing gestures with the blade of her hand across Sethe's ankles. "Zzz Zzz Zzz Zzz."

"I used to be a good size. Nice arms and everything. Wouldn't think it, would you? That was before they put me in the root cellar. I was fishing off the Beaver once. Catfish in Beaver River sweet as chicken. Well I was just fishing there and a nigger floated right by me. I don't like drowned people, you? Your feet remind me of him. All swole like."

Then she did the magic: lifted Sethe's feet and legs and massaged them until she cried salt tears.

"It's gonna hurt, now," said Amy. "Anything dead coming back to life hurts."

A truth for all times, thought Denver. Maybe the white dress holding its arm around her mother's waist was in pain. If so, it could mean the baby ghost had plans. When she opened the door, Sethe was just leaving the keeping room.

"I saw a white dress holding on to you," Denver said.

"White? Maybe it was my bedding dress. Describe it to me."

"Had a high neck. Whole mess of buttons coming down the back."

"Buttons. Well, that lets out my bedding dress. I never had a button on nothing."

"Did Grandma Baby?"

Sethe shook her head. "She couldn't handle them. Even on her shoes. What else?"

"A bunch at the back. On the sit-down part."

"A bustle? It had a bustle?"

"I don't know what it's called."

"Sort of gathered-like? Below the waist in the back?"

"Um hm."

"A rich lady's dress. Silk?"

"Cotton, look like."

"Lisle probably. White cotton lisle. You say it was holding on to me. How?"

"Like you. It looked just like you. Kneeling next to you while you were praying. Had its arm around your waist."

"Well, I'll be."

"What were you praying for, Ma'am?"

"Not *for* anything. I don't pray anymore. I just talk."

"What were you talking about?"

"You won't understand, baby."

"Yes, I will."

"I was talking about time. It's so hard for me to believe in it. Some things go. Pass on. Some things just stay. I used to think it was my rememory. You know. Some things you forget. Other things you never do. But it's not. Places, places are still there. If a house burns down, it's gone, but the place—the picture of it—stays, and not just in my rememory, but out there, in the world. What I remember is a picture floating around out there outside my head. I mean, even if I don't think it, even if I die, the picture of what I did, or knew, or saw is still out there. Right in the place where it happened."

"Can other people see it?" asked Denver.

"Oh, yes. Oh, yes, yes, yes. Someday you be walking down the road and you hear something or see something going on. So clear. And you think it's you thinking it up. A thought picture. But no. It's when you bump into a rememory that belongs to somebody else. Where I was before I came here, that place is real. It's never going away. Even if the whole farm—every tree and grass blade of it dies. The picture is still there and what's more, if you go there—you who never was there—if you go there and stand in the place where it was, it will happen again; it will be there for you, waiting for you. So, Denver, you can't never go there. Never. Because even though it's all over—over and done with—it's going to always be there waiting for you. That's how come I had to get all my children out. No matter what."

Denver picked at her fingernails. "If it's still there, waiting, that must mean that nothing ever dies."

Sethe looked right in Denver's face. "Nothing ever does," she said.

"You never told me all what happened. Just that they whipped you and you run off, pregnant. With me."

"Nothing to tell except schoolteacher. He was a little man. Short. Always wore a collar, even in the fields. A schoolteacher, she said. That made her feel good that her husband's sister's husband had book learning and was willing to come farm Sweet Home after Mr. Garner passed. The men could have done it, even with Paul F sold. But it was like Halle said. She didn't want to be the only white person on the farm and a woman too. So she was satisfied when the schoolteacher agreed to come. He brought two boys with him. Sons or nephews. I don't know. They called him Onka and had pretty manners, all of em. Talked soft and spit in handkerchiefs. Gentle in a lot of ways. You know, the kind who know Jesus by His first name, but out of politeness never use it even to His face. A pretty good farmer, Halle said. Not strong as Mr. Garner but smart enough. He liked the ink I made. It was her recipe, but he preferred how I mixed it and it was important to him because at night he sat down to write in his book. It was a book about us but we didn't know that right away. We just thought it was his manner to ask us questions. He commenced to carry round a notebook and write down what we said. I still think it was them questions that tore Sixo up. Tore him up for all time."

She stopped.

Denver knew that her mother was through with it—for now anyway. The single slow blink of her eyes; the bottom lip sliding up slowly to cover the top; and then a nostril sigh, like the snuff of a candle flame—signs that Sethe had reached the point beyond which she would not go.

"Well, I think the baby got plans," said Denver.

"What plans?"

"I don't know, but the dress holding on to you got to mean something."

"Maybe," said Sethe. "Maybe it does have plans."

Whatever they were or might have been, Paul D messed them up for good. With a table and a loud male voice he had rid 124 of its claim to local fame. Denver had taught herself to take pride in the condemnation Negroes heaped on them; the assumption that the haunting was done by an evil thing looking for more. None of them knew the downright pleasure of enchantment, of not suspecting but *knowing* the things behind things. Her brothers had known, but it scared them; Grandma Baby knew, but it saddened her. None could appreciate the safety of ghost company. Even Sethe didn't love it. She just took it for granted—like a sudden change in the weather.

But it was gone now. Whooshed away in the blast of a hazelnut man's shout, leaving Denver's world flat, mostly, with the exception of an emerald closet standing seven feet high in the woods. Her mother had secrets—things she wouldn't tell; things she halfway told. Well, Denver had them too. And hers were sweet—sweet as lily-of-the-valley cologne.

Sethe had given little thought to the white dress until Paul D came, and then she remembered Denver's interpretation: plans. The morning after the first night with Paul D, Sethe smiled just thinking about what the word could mean. It was a luxury she had not had in eighteen years and only that once. Before and since, all her effort was directed not on avoiding pain but on getting through it as quickly as possible. The one set of plans she had made—getting away from Sweet Home—went awry so completely she never dared life by making more.

Yet the morning she woke up next to Paul D, the word her daughter had used a few years ago did cross her mind and she thought about what Denver had seen kneeling next to her, and thought also of the temptation to trust and remember that gripped her as she stood before the cooking stove in his arms. Would it be all right? Would it be all right to go ahead and feel? Go ahead and *count on something*?

She couldn't think clearly, lying next to him listening to his breathing, so carefully, carefully, she had left the bed.

Kneeling in the keeping room where she usually went to talk-think it was clear why Baby Suggs was so starved for color. There wasn't any except for two orange squares in a quilt that made the absence shout. The walls of the room were slate-colored, the floor earth-brown, the wooden dresser the color of itself, curtains white, and the dominating feature, the quilt over an iron cot, was made up of scraps of blue serge, black, brown and gray wool—the full range of the dark and the muted that thrift and modesty allowed. In that sober field, two patches of orange looked wild—like life in the raw.

Sethe looked at her hands, her bottle-green sleeves, and thought how little color there was in the house and how strange that she had not missed it the way Baby did. Deliberate, she thought, it must be deliberate, because the last color she remembered was the pink chips in the headstone of her baby girl. After that she became as color conscious as a hen.

Every dawn she worked at fruit pies, potato dishes and vegetables while the cook did the soup, meat and all the rest. And she could not remember remembering a molly apple or a yellow squash. Every dawn she saw the dawn, but never acknowledged or remarked its color. There was something wrong with that. It was as though one day she saw red baby blood, another day the pink gravestone chips, and that was the last of it.

124 was so full of strong feeling perhaps she was oblivious to the loss of anything at all. There was a time when she scanned the fields every morning and every evening for her boys. When she stood at the open window, unmindful of flies, her head cocked to her left shoulder, her eyes searching to the right for them. Cloud shadow on the road, an old woman, a wandering goat untethered and gnawing bramble—each one looked at first like Howard—no, Buglar. Little by little she stopped and their thirteen-year-old faces faded completely into their baby ones, which came to her only in sleep. When her dreams roamed outside 124, anywhere they wished, she saw them sometimes in beautiful trees, their little legs barely visible in the leaves. Sometimes they ran along the railroad track laughing, too loud, apparently, to hear her because they never did turn around. When she woke the house crowded in on her: there was the door where the soda crackers were lined up in a row; the white stairs her baby girl loved to climb; the corner where Baby Suggs mended shoes, a pile of which were still in the cold room; the exact place on the stove where Denver burned her fingers. And of course the spite of the house itself. There was no room for any other thing or body until Paul D arrived and broke up the place, making room, shifting it, moving it over to someplace else, then standing in the place he had made.

So, kneeling in the keeping room the morning after Paul D

came, she was distracted by the two orange squares that signaled how barren 124 really was.

He was responsible for that. Emotions sped to the surface in his company. Things became what they were: drabness looked drab; heat was hot. Windows suddenly had view. And wouldn't you know he'd be a singing man.

Little rice, little bean,
No meat in between.
Hard work ain't easy,
Dry bread ain't greasy.

He was up now and singing as he mended things he had broken the day before. Some old pieces of song he'd learned on the prison farm or in the War afterward. Nothing like what they sang at Sweet Home, where yearning fashioned every note.

The songs he knew from Georgia were flat-headed nails for pounding and pounding and pounding.

Lay my head on the railroad line,
Train come along, pacify my mind.
If I had my weight in lime,
I'd whip my captain till he went stone blind.
Five-cent nickel,
Ten-cent dime,
Busting rocks is busting time.

But they didn't fit, these songs. They were too loud, had too much power for the little house chores he was engaged in—resetting table legs; glazing.

He couldn't go back to "Storm upon the Waters" that they sang under the trees of Sweet Home, so he contented himself with mmmmmmmmm, throwing in a line if one occurred to him, and what occurred over and over was "Bare feet and chamomile sap,/Took off my shoes; took off my hat."

It was tempting to change the words (Gimme back my shoes; gimme back my hat), because he didn't believe he could live with a woman—any woman—for over two out of three months. That was about as long as he could abide one place. After Delaware and before that Alfred, Georgia, where he slept underground and crawled into sunlight for the sole purpose of breaking rock, walking off when he got ready was the only way he could convince himself that he would no longer have to sleep, pee, eat or swing a sledge hammer in chains.

But this was not a normal woman in a normal house. As soon as he had stepped through the red light he knew that, compared to 124, the rest of the world was bald. After Alfred he had shut down a generous portion of his head, operating on the part that helped him walk, eat, sleep, sing. If he could do those things—with a little work and a little sex thrown in—he asked for no more, for more required him to dwell on Halle's face and Sixo laughing. To recall trembling in a box built into the ground. Grateful for the daylight spent doing mule work in a quarry because he did not tremble when he had a hammer in his hands. The box had done what Sweet Home had not, what working like an ass and living like a dog had not: drove him crazy so he would not lose his mind.

By the time he got to Ohio, then to Cincinnati, then to Halle Suggs' mother's house, he thought he had seen and felt it all. Even now as he put back the window frame he had smashed, he could not account for the pleasure in his surprise at seeing Halle's wife alive, barefoot with uncovered hair—walking around the corner of the house with her shoes and stockings in her hands. The closed portion of his head opened like a greased lock.

"I was thinking of looking for work around here. What you think?"

"Ain't much. River mostly. And hogs."

"Well, I never worked on water, but I can pick up anything heavy as me, hogs included."

"Whitepeople better here than Kentucky but you may have to scramble some."

"It ain't whether I scramble; it's where. You saying it's all right to scramble here?"

"Better than all right."

"Your girl, Denver. Seems to me she's of a different mind."

"Why you say that?"

"She's got a waiting way about her. Something she's expecting and it ain't me."

"I don't know what it could be."

"Well, whatever it is, she believes I'm interrupting it."

"Don't worry about her. She's a charmed child. From the beginning."

"Is that right?"

"Uh huh. Nothing bad can happen to her. Look at it. Everybody I knew dead or gone or dead and gone. Not her. Not my Denver. Even when I was carrying her, when it got clear that I wasn't going to make it—which meant she wasn't going to make it either—she pulled a whitegirl out of the hill. The last thing you'd expect to help. And when the schoolteacher found us and came busting in here with the law and a shotgun—"

"Schoolteacher found you?"

"Took a while, but he did. Finally."

"And he didn't take you back?"

"Oh, no. I wasn't going back there. I don't care who found who. Any life but not that one. I went to jail instead.

Denver was just a baby so she went right along with me. Rats bit everything in there but her."

Paul D turned away. He wanted to know more about it, but jail talk put him back in Alfred, Georgia.

"I need some nails. Anybody around here I can borrow from or should I go to town?"

"May as well go to town. You'll need other things."

One night and they were talking like a couple. They had skipped love and promise and went directly to "You saying it's all right to scramble here?"

To Sethe, the future was a matter of keeping the past at bay. The "better life" she believed she and Denver were living was simply not that other one.

The fact that Paul D had come out of "that other one" into her bed was better too; and the notion of a future with him, or for that matter without him, was beginning to stroke her mind. As for Denver, the job Sethe had of keeping her from the past that was still waiting for her was all that mattered.

PLEASANTLY TROUBLED, Sethe avoided the keeping room and Denver's sidelong looks. As she expected, since life was like that—it didn't do any good. Denver ran a mighty interference and on the third day flat-out asked Paul D how long he was going to hang around.

The phrase hurt him so much he missed the table. The coffee cup hit the floor and rolled down the sloping boards toward the front door.

"Hang around?" Paul D didn't even look at the mess he had made.

"Denver! What's got into you?" Sethe looked at her daughter, feeling more embarrassed than angry.

Paul D scratched the hair on his chin. "Maybe I should make tracks."

"No!" Sethe was surprised by how loud she said it.

"He know what he needs," said Denver.

"Well, you don't," Sethe told her, "and you must not know what you need either. I don't want to hear another word out of you."

"I just asked if—"

"Hush! *You* make tracks. Go somewhere and sit down."

Denver picked up her plate and left the table but not before adding a chicken back and more bread to the heap she was carrying away. Paul D leaned over to wipe the spilled coffee with his blue handkerchief.

"I'll get that." Sethe jumped up and went to the stove. Behind it various cloths hung, each in some stage of drying. In silence she wiped the floor and retrieved the cup. Then she poured him another cupful, and set it carefully before him. Paul D touched its rim but didn't say anything—as though even "thank you" was an obligation he could not meet and the coffee itself a gift he could not take.

Sethe resumed her chair and the silence continued. Finally she realized that if it was going to be broken she would have to do it.

"I didn't train her like that."

Paul D stroked the rim of the cup.

"And I'm as surprised by her manners as you are hurt by em."

Paul D looked at Sethe. "Is there history to her question?"

"History? What you mean?"

"I mean, did she have to ask that, or want to ask it, of anybody else before me?"

Sethe made two fists and placed them on her hips. "You as bad as she is."

"Come on, Sethe."

"Oh, I am coming on. I am!"

"You know what I mean."

"I do and I don't like it."

"Jesus," he whispered.

"Who?" Sethe was getting loud again.

"Jesus! I said Jesus! All I did was sit down for supper! and I get cussed out twice. Once for being here and once for asking why I was cussed in the first place!"

"She didn't cuss."

"No? Felt like it."

"Look here. I apologize for her. I'm real—"

"You can't do that. You can't apologize for nobody. She got to do that."

"Then I'll see that she does." Sethe sighed.

"What I want to know is, is she asking a question that's on your mind too?"

"Oh no. No, Paul D. Oh no."

"Then she's of one mind and you another? If you can call whatever's in her head a mind, that is."

"Excuse me, but I can't hear a word against her. I'll chastise her. You leave her alone."

Risky, thought Paul D, very risky. For a used-to-be-slave woman to love anything that much was dangerous, especially if it was her children she had settled on to love. The best thing, he knew, was to love just a little bit; everything, just a little bit, so when they broke its back, or shoved it in a croaker sack, well, maybe you'd have a little love left over for the next one. "Why?" he asked her. "Why you think you have to take up for her? Apologize for her? She's grown."

"I don't care what she is. Grown don't mean nothing to a mother. A child is a child. They get bigger, older, but grown? What's that supposed to mean? In my heart it don't mean a thing."

"It means she has to take it if she acts up. You can't protect her every minute. What's going to happen when you die?"

"Nothing! I'll protect her while I'm live and I'll protect her when I ain't."

"Oh well, I'm through," he said. "I quit."

"That's the way it is, Paul D. I can't explain it to you no better than that, but that's the way it is. If I have to choose—well, it's not even a choice."

"That's the point. The whole point. I'm not asking you to choose. Nobody would. I thought—well, I thought you could—there was some space for me."

"She's asking me."

"You can't go by that. You got to say it to her. Tell her it's not about choosing somebody over her—it's making space for somebody along with her. You got to say it. And if you say it and mean it, then you also got to know you can't gag me. There's no way I'm going to hurt her or not take care of what she need if I can, but I can't be told to keep my mouth shut if she's acting ugly. You want me here, don't put no gag on me."

"Maybe I should leave things the way they are," she said.

"How are they?"

"We get along."

"What about inside?"

"I don't go inside."

"Sethe, if I'm here with you, with Denver, you can go anywhere you want. Jump, if you want to, 'cause I'll catch you, girl. I'll catch you 'fore you fall. Go as far inside as you need to, I'll hold your ankles. Make sure you get back out. I'm not saying this because I need a place to stay. That's the last thing I need. I told you, I'm a walking man, but I been heading in this direction for seven years. Walking all around this place. Upstate, downstate, east, west; I been in territory ain't got no name, never staying nowhere long. But when I got here and sat out there on the porch, waiting for you, well, I knew it wasn't the place I was heading toward; it was you. We can make a life, girl. A life."

"I don't know. I don't know."

"Leave it to me. See how it goes. No promises, if you don't want to make any. Just see how it goes. All right?"

"All right."

"You willing to leave it to me?"

"Well—some of it."

"Some?" he smiled. "Okay. Here's some. There's a carnival in town. Thursday, tomorrow, is for coloreds and I got two dollars. Me and you and Denver gonna spend every penny of it. What you say?"

"No" is what she said. At least what she started out saying (what would her boss say if she took a day off?), but even when she said it she was thinking how much her eyes enjoyed looking in his face.

The crickets were screaming on Thursday and the sky, stripped of blue, was white hot at eleven in the morning. Sethe was badly dressed for the heat, but this being her first social outing in eighteen years, she felt obliged to wear her one good dress, heavy as it was, and a hat. Certainly a hat. She didn't want to meet Lady Jones or Ella with her head wrapped like she was going to work. The dress, a good-wool castoff, was a Christmas present to Baby Suggs from Miss Bodwin, the whitewoman who loved her. Denver and Paul D fared better in the heat since neither felt the occasion required special clothing. Denver's bonnet knocked against her shoulder blades; Paul D wore his vest open, no jacket and his shirt sleeves rolled above his elbows. They were not holding hands, but their shadows were. Sethe looked to her left and all three of them were gliding over the dust holding hands. Maybe he was right. A life. Watching their hand-holding shadows, she was embarrassed at being dressed for church. The others, ahead and behind them, would think she was putting on airs, letting them know that she was different because she lived in a house with two stories; tougher, because she could do and survive things they believed she should neither do nor survive. She was glad Denver had resisted her urgings to dress up—rebraid her hair at least. But Denver was not doing anything to make this trip a pleasure. She agreed to go—sullenly—but her attitude was "Go 'head. Try and make me happy." The happy one was Paul D. He said howdy to everybody within twenty feet. Made fun of the weather and what it was doing to him, yelled back at the crows, and was the first to smell the doomed roses. All the time, no matter what they were doing—whether Denver wiped perspiration from her forehead or stooped to retie her shoes; whether Paul D kicked a stone or reached over to meddle a child's face leaning on its mother's shoulder—all the time the three shadows that shot out of their feet to the left held hands. Nobody noticed but Sethe and she stopped looking after she decided that it was a good sign. A life. Could be.

Up and down the lumberyard fence old roses were dying. The sawyer who had planted them twelve years ago to give his workplace a friendly feel—something to take the sin out of slicing trees for a living—was amazed by their abundance; how rapidly they crawled all over the stake-and-post fence that separated the lumberyard from the open field next to it where homeless men slept, children ran and, once a year, carnival people pitched tents. The closer the roses got to death, the louder their scent, and everybody who attended the carnival associated it with the stench of the rotten roses. It made them a little dizzy and very thirsty but did nothing to extinguish the eagerness of the coloredpeople filing down the road. Some walked on the grassy shoulders, others dodged the wagons creaking down the road's dusty center. All, like Paul D, were in high spirits, which the smell of dying roses (that Paul D called to everybody's attention) could not dampen. As they pressed to get to the rope entrance they were lit like lamps. Breathless with the excitement of seeing whitepeople loose: doing magic, clowning, without heads or with two heads, twenty feet tall or two feet tall, weighing a ton, completely tattooed, eating glass, swallowing fire, spitting ribbons, twisted into knots, forming pyramids, playing with snakes and beating each other up.

All of this was advertisement, read by those who could and heard by those who could not, and the fact that none of it was true did not extinguish their appetite a bit. The barker called them and their children names ("Pickaninnies free!") but the food on his vest and the hole in his pants rendered it fairly harmless. In any case it was a small price to pay for the fun they might not ever have again. Two pennies and an insult were well spent if it meant seeing the spectacle of whitefolks making a spectacle of themselves. So, although the carnival was a lot less than mediocre (which is why it agreed to a Colored Thursday), it gave the four hundred black people in its audience thrill upon thrill upon thrill.

One-Ton Lady spit at them, but her bulk shortened her aim and they got a big kick out of the helpless meanness in her little eyes. Arabian Nights Dancer cut her performance to three minutes instead of the usual fifteen she normally did—earning the gratitude of the children, who could hardly wait for Abu Snake Charmer, who followed her.

Denver bought horehound, licorice, peppermint and lemonade at a table manned by a little whitegirl in ladies' high-topped shoes. Soothed by sugar, surrounded by a crowd of people who did not find her the main attraction, who, in fact, said, "Hey, Denver," every now and then, pleased her enough to consider the possibility that Paul D wasn't all that bad. In fact there was something about him—when the three of them stood together watching Midget dance—that made the stares of other Negroes kind, gentle, something Denver did not remember seeing in their faces. Several even nodded and smiled at her mother, no one, apparently, able to withstand sharing the pleasure Paul D was having. He slapped his knees when Giant danced with Midget; when Two-Headed Man talked to himself. He bought everything Denver asked for and much she did not. He teased Sethe into tents she was reluctant to enter. Stuck pieces of candy she didn't want between her lips. When Wild African Savage shook his bars and said wa wa, Paul D told everybody he knew him back in

Roanoke. Paul D made a few acquaintances; spoke to them about what work he might find. Sethe returned the smiles she got. Denver was swaying with delight. And on the way home, although leading them now, the shadows of three people still held hands.

A FULLY DRESSED woman walked out of the water. She barely gained the dry bank of the stream before she sat down and leaned against a mulberry tree. All day and all night she sat there, her head resting on the trunk in a position abandoned enough to crack the brim in her straw hat. Everything hurt but her lungs most of all. Sopping wet and breathing shallow she spent those hours trying to negotiate the weight of her eyelids. The day breeze blew her dress dry; the night wind wrinkled it. Nobody saw her emerge or came accidentally by. If they had, chances are they would have hesitated before approaching her. Not because she was wet, or dozing or had what sounded like asthma, but because amid all that she was smiling. It took her the whole of the next morning to lift herself from the ground and make her way through the woods past a giant temple of boxwood to the field and then the yard of the slate-gray house. Exhausted again, she sat down on the first handy place—a stump not far from the steps of 124. By then keeping her eyes open was less of an effort. She could manage it for a full two minutes or more. Her neck, its circumference no wider than a parlor-service saucer, kept bending and her chin brushed the bit of lace edging her dress.

Women who drink champagne when there is nothing to celebrate can look like that: their straw hats with broken brims are often askew; they nod in public places; their shoes are undone. But their skin is not like that of the woman breathing near the steps of 124. She had new skin, lineless and smooth, including the knuckles of her hands.

By late afternoon when the carnival was over, and the Negroes were hitching rides home if they were lucky—walking if they were not—the woman had fallen asleep again. The rays of the sun struck her full in the face, so that when Sethe, Denver and Paul D rounded the curve in the road all they saw was a black dress, two unlaced shoes below it, and Here Boy nowhere in sight.

"Look," said Denver. "What is that?"

And, for some reason she could not immediately account for, the moment she got close enough to see the face, Sethe's bladder filled to capacity. She said, "Oh, excuse me," and ran around to the back of 124. Not since she was a baby girl, being cared for by the eight-year-old girl who pointed out her mother to her, had she had an emergency that unmanageable. She never made the outhouse. Right in front of its door she had to lift her skirts, and the water she voided was endless. Like a horse, she thought, but as it went on and on she thought, No, more like flooding the boat when Denver was born. So much water Amy said, "Hold on, Lu. You going to sink us you keep that up." But there was no stopping water breaking from a breaking womb and there was no stopping now. She hoped Paul D wouldn't take it upon himself to come looking for her and be obliged to see her squatting in front of her own privy making a mudhole too deep to be witnessed without shame. Just about the time she started wondering if the carnival would accept another freak, it stopped. She tidied herself and ran around to the porch. No one was there. All three were inside—Paul D and Denver standing before the stranger, watching her drink cup after cup of water.

"She said she was thirsty," said Paul D. He took off his cap. "Mighty thirsty look like."

The woman gulped water from a speckled tin cup and held it out for more. Four times Denver filled it, and four times the woman drank as though she had crossed a desert. When she was finished a little water was on her chin, but she did not wipe it away. Instead she gazed at Sethe with sleepy eyes. Poorly fed, thought Sethe, and younger than her clothes suggested—good lace at the throat, and a rich woman's hat. Her skin was flawless except for three vertical scratches on her forehead so fine and thin they seemed at first like hair, baby hair before it bloomed and roped into the masses of black yarn under her hat.

"You from around here?" Sethe asked her.

She shook her head no and reached down to take off her shoes. She pulled her dress up to the knees and rolled down her stockings. When the hosiery was tucked into the shoes, Sethe saw that her feet were like her hands, soft and new. She must have hitched a wagon ride, thought Sethe. Probably one of those West Virginia girls looking for something to beat a life of tobacco and sorghum. Sethe bent to pick up the shoes.

"What might your name be?" asked Paul D.

"Beloved," she said, and her voice was so low and rough each one looked at the other two. They heard the voice first—later the name.

"Beloved. You use a last name, Beloved?" Paul D asked her.

"Last?" She seemed puzzled. Then "No," and she spelled it for them, slowly as though the letters were being formed as she spoke them.

Sethe dropped the shoes; Denver sat down and Paul D smiled. He recognized the careful enunciation of letters by those, like himself, who could not read but had memorized the letters of their name. He was about to ask who her people were but thought better of it. A young coloredwoman drifting was drifting from ruin. He had been in Rochester four years ago and seen five women arriving with fourteen female children. All their men—brothers, uncles, fathers, husbands, sons—had been picked off one by one by one. They had a single piece of paper directing them to a preacher on DeVore Street. The War had been over four or five years then, but nobody white or black seemed to know it. Odd clusters and strays of Negroes wandered the back roads and cowpaths from Schenectady to Jackson. Dazed but insistent, they searched each other out for word of a cousin, an aunt, a friend who once said, "Call on me. Anytime you get near Chicago, just call on me." Some of them were running from family that could not support them, some to family; some were running from dead crops, dead kin, life threats, and took-over land. Boys younger than Buglar and Howard; configurations and blends of families of women and children, while elsewhere, solitary, hunted and hunting for, were men, men, men. Forbidden public transportation, chased by debt and filthy "talking sheets," they followed secondary routes, scanned the horizon for signs and counted heavily on each other. Silent, except for social courtesies, when they met one another they neither described nor asked about the sorrow that drove them from one place to another. The whites didn't bear speaking on. Everybody knew.

So he did not press the young woman with the broken hat about where from or how come. If she wanted them to know and was strong enough to get through the telling, she would. What occupied them at the moment was what it might be that she needed. Underneath the major question, each harbored another. Paul D wondered at the newness of her shoes. Sethe was deeply touched by her sweet name; the remembrance of glittering headstone made her feel especially kindly toward her. Denver, however, was shaking. She looked at this sleepy beauty and wanted more.

Sethe hung her hat on a peg and turned graciously toward the girl. "That's a pretty name, Beloved. Take off your hat, why don't you, and I'll make us something. We just got back from the carnival over near Cincinnati. Everything in there is something to see."

Bolt upright in the chair, in the middle of Sethe's welcome, Beloved had fallen asleep again.

"Miss. Miss." Paul D shook her gently. "You want to lay down a spell?"

She opened her eyes to slits and stood up on her soft new feet which, barely capable of their job, slowly bore her to the keeping room. Once there, she collapsed on Baby Suggs' bed. Denver removed her hat and put the quilt with two squares of color over her feet. She was breathing like a steam engine.

"Sounds like croup," said Paul D, closing the door.

"Is she feverish? Denver, could you tell?"

"No. She's cold."

"Then she is. Fever goes from hot to cold."

"Could have the cholera," said Paul D.

"Reckon?"

"All that water. Sure sign."

"Poor thing. And nothing in this house to give her for it. She'll just have to ride it out. That's a hateful sickness if ever there was one."

"She's not sick!" said Denver, and the passion in her voice made them smile.

Four days she slept, waking and sitting up only for water. Denver tended her, watched her sound sleep, listened to her labored breathing and, out of love and a breakneck possessiveness that charged her, hid like a personal blemish Beloved's incontinence. She rinsed the sheets secretly, after Sethe went to the restaurant and Paul D went scrounging for barges to help unload. She boiled the underwear and soaked it in bluing, praying the fever would pass without damage. So intent was her nursing, she forgot to eat or visit the emerald closet.

"Beloved?" Denver would whisper. "Beloved?" and when the black eyes opened a slice all she could say was "I'm here. I'm still here."

Sometimes, when Beloved lay dreamy-eyed for a very long time, saying nothing, licking her lips and heaving deep sighs, Denver panicked. "What is it?" she would ask.

"Heavy," murmured Beloved. "This place is heavy."

"Would you like to sit up?"

"No," said the raspy voice.

It took three days for Beloved to notice the orange patches in the darkness of the quilt. Denver was pleased because it kept her patient awake longer. She seemed totally taken with those faded scraps of orange, even made the effort to lean on her elbow and stroke them. An effort that quickly exhausted her, so Denver rearranged the quilt so its cheeriest part was in the sick girl's sight line.

Patience, something Denver had never known, overtook her. As long as her mother did not interfere, she was a model of compassion, turning waspish, though, when Sethe tried to help.

"Did she take a spoonful of anything today?" Sethe inquired.

"She shouldn't eat with cholera."

"You sure that's it? Was just a hunch of Paul D's."

"I don't know, but she shouldn't eat anyway just yet."

"I think cholera people puke all the time."

"That's even more reason, ain't it?"

"Well she shouldn't starve to death either, Denver."

"Leave us alone, Ma'am. I'm taking care of her."

"She say anything?"

"I'd let you know if she did."

Sethe looked at her daughter and thought, Yes, she has been lonesome. Very lonesome.

"Wonder where Here Boy got off to?" Sethe thought a change of subject was needed.

"He won't be back," said Denver.

"How you know?"

"I just know." Denver took a square of sweet bread off the plate.

Back in the keeping room, Denver was about to sit down when Beloved's eyes flew wide open. Denver felt her heart race. It wasn't that she was looking at that face for the first time with no trace of sleep in it, or that the eyes were big and black. Nor was it that the whites of them were much too white—blue-white. It was that deep down in those big black eyes there was no expression at all.

"Can I get you something?"

Beloved looked at the sweet bread in Denver's hands and Denver held it out to her. She smiled then and Denver's heart stopped bouncing and sat down—relieved and easeful like a traveler who had made it home.

From that moment and through everything that followed, sugar could always be counted on to please her. It was as though sweet things were what she was born for. Honey as well as the wax it came in, sugar sandwiches, the sludgy molasses gone hard and brutal in the can, lemonade, taffy and any type of dessert Sethe brought home from the restaurant. She gnawed a cane stick to flax and kept the strings in her mouth long after the syrup had been sucked away. Denver laughed, Sethe smiled and Paul D said it made him sick to his stomach.

Sethe believed it was a recovering body's need—after an illness—for quick strength. But it was a need that went on and on into glowing health because Beloved didn't go anywhere. There didn't seem anyplace for her to go. She didn't mention one, or have much of an idea of what she was doing in that part of the country or where she had been. They believed the fever had caused her memory to fail just as it kept her slow-moving. A young woman, about nineteen or twenty, and slender, she moved like a heavier one or an older one, holding on to furniture, resting her head in the palm of her hand as though it was too heavy for a neck alone.

"You just gonna feed her? From now on?" Paul D, feeling ungenerous, and surprised by it, heard the irritability in his voice.

"Denver likes her. She's no real trouble. I thought we'd wait till her breath was better. She still sounds a little lumbar to me."

"Something funny 'bout that gal," Paul D said, mostly to himself.

"Funny how?"

"Acts sick, sounds sick, but she don't look sick. Good skin, bright eyes and strong as a bull."

"She's not strong. She can hardly walk without holding on to something."

"That's what I mean. Can't walk, but I seen her pick up the rocker with one hand."

"You didn't."

"Don't tell *me.* Ask Denver. She was right there with her."

"Denver! Come in here a minute."

Denver stopped rinsing the porch and stuck her head in the window.

"Paul D says you and him saw Beloved pick up the rocking chair single-handed. That so?"

Long, heavy lashes made Denver's eyes seem busier than they were; deceptive, even when she held a steady gaze as she did now on Paul D. "No," she said. "I didn't see no such thing."

Paul D frowned but said nothing. If there had been an open latch between them, it would have closed.

RAINWATER held on to pine needles for dear life and Beloved could not take her eyes off Sethe. Stooping to shake the damper, or snapping sticks for kindlin, Sethe was licked, tasted, eaten by Beloved's eyes. Like a familiar, she hovered, never leaving the room Sethe was in unless required and told to. She rose early in the dark to be there, waiting, in the kitchen when Sethe came down to make fast bread before she left for work. In lamplight, and over the flames of the cooking stove, their two shadows clashed and crossed on the ceiling like black swords. She was in the window at two when Sethe returned, or the doorway; then the porch, its steps, the path, the road, till finally, surrendering to the habit, Beloved began inching down Bluestone Road further and further each day to meet Sethe and walk her back to 124. It was as though every afternoon she doubted anew the older woman's return.

Sethe was flattered by Beloved's open, quiet devotion. The same adoration from her daughter (had it been forthcoming) would have annoyed her; made her chill at the thought of having raised a ridiculously dependent child. But the company of this sweet, if peculiar, guest pleased her the way a zealot pleases his teacher.

Time came when lamps had to be lit early because night arrived sooner and sooner. Sethe was leaving for work in the dark; Paul D was walking home in it. On one such evening dark and cool, Sethe cut a rutabaga into four pieces and left them stewing. She gave Denver a half peck of peas to sort and soak overnight. Then she sat herself down to rest. The heat of the stove made her drowsy and she was sliding into sleep when she felt Beloved touch her. A touch no heavier than a feather but loaded, nevertheless, with desire. Sethe stirred and looked around. First at Beloved's soft new hand on her shoulder, then into her eyes. The longing she saw there was bottomless. Some plea barely in control. Sethe patted Beloved's fingers and glanced at Denver, whose eyes were fixed on her pea-sorting task.

"Where your diamonds?" Beloved searched Sethe's face.

"Diamonds? What would I be doing with diamonds?"

"On your ears."

"Wish I did. I had some crystal once. A present from a lady I worked for."

"Tell me," said Beloved, smiling a wide happy smile. "Tell me your diamonds."

It became a way to feed her. Just as Denver discovered and relied on the delightful effect sweet things had on Beloved, Sethe learned the profound satisfaction Beloved got from storytelling. It amazed Sethe (as much as it pleased Beloved) because every mention of her past life hurt. Everything in it was painful or lost. She and Baby Suggs had agreed without saying so that it was unspeakable; to Denver's inquiries Sethe gave short replies or rambling incomplete reveries. Even with Paul D, who had shared some of it and to whom she could talk with at least a measure of calm, the hurt was always there—like a tender place in the corner of her mouth that the bit left.

But, as she began telling about the earrings, she found herself wanting to, liking it. Perhaps it was Beloved's distance from the events itself, or her thirst for hearing it—in any case it was an unexpected pleasure.

Above the patter of the pea sorting and the sharp odor of

cooking rutabaga, Sethe explained the crystal that once hung from her ears.

"That lady I worked for in Kentucky gave them to me when I got married. What they called married back there and back then. I guess she saw how bad I felt when I found out there wasn't going to be no ceremony, no preacher. Nothing. I thought there should be something—something to say it was right and true. I didn't want it to be just me moving over a bit of pallet full of corn husks. Or just me bringing my night bucket into his cabin. I thought there should be some ceremony. Dancing maybe. A little sweet william in my hair." Sethe smiled. "I never saw a wedding, but I saw Mrs. Garner's wedding gown in the press, and heard her go on about what it was like. Two pounds of currants in the cake, she said, and four whole sheep. The people were still eating the next day. That's what I wanted. A meal maybe, where me and Halle and all the Sweet Home men sat down and ate something special. Invite some of the other coloredpeople from over by Covington or High Trees—those places Sixo used to sneak off to. But it wasn't going to be nothing. They said it was all right for us to be husband and wife and that was it. All of it.

"Well, I made up my mind to have at the least a dress that wasn't the sacking I worked in. So I took to stealing fabric, and wound up with a dress you wouldn't believe. The top was from two pillow cases in her mending basket. The front of the skirt was a dresser scarf a candle fell on and burnt a hole in, and one of her old sashes we used to test the flatiron on. Now the back was a problem for the longest time. Seem like I couldn't find a thing that wouldn't be missed right away. Because I had to take it apart afterwards and put all the pieces back where they were. Now Halle was patient, waiting for me to finish it. He knew I wouldn't go ahead without having it. Finally I took the mosquito netting from a nail out the barn. We used it to strain jelly through. I washed it and soaked it best I could and tacked it on for the back of the skirt. And there I was, in the worst-looking gown you could imagine. Only my wool shawl kept me from looking like a haint peddling. I wasn't but fourteen years old, so I reckon that's why I was so proud of myself.

"Anyhow, Mrs. Garner must have seen me in it. I thought I was stealing smart, and she knew everything I did. Even our honeymoon: going down to the cornfield with Halle. That's where we went first. A Saturday afternoon it was. He begged sick so he wouldn't have to go work in town that day. Usually he worked Saturdays and Sundays to pay off Baby Suggs' freedom. But he begged sick and I put on my dress and we walked into the corn holding hands. I can still smell the ears roasting yonder where the Pauls and Sixo was. Next day Mrs. Garner crooked her finger at me and took me upstairs to her bedroom. She opened up a wooden box and took out a pair of crystal earrings. She said, 'I want you to have these, Sethe.' I said, 'Yes, ma'am.' 'Are your ears pierced?' she said. I said, 'No, ma'am.' 'Well do it,' she said, 'so you can wear them. I want you to have them and I want you and Halle to be happy.' I thanked her but I never did put them on till I got away from there. One day after I walked into this here house Baby Suggs unknotted my underskirt and took em out. I sat right here by the stove with Denver in my arms and let her punch holes in my ears for to wear them."

"I never saw you in no earrings," said Denver. "Where are they now?"

"Gone," said Sethe. "Long gone," and she wouldn't say another word. Until the next time when all three of them ran through the wind back into the house with rainsoaked sheets and petticoats. Panting, laughing, they draped the laundry over the chairs and table. Beloved filled herself with water from the bucket and watched while Sethe rubbed Denver's hair with a piece of toweling.

"Maybe we should unbraid it?" asked Sethe.

"Uh uh. Tomorrow." Denver crouched forward at the thought of a fine-tooth comb pulling her hair.

"Today is always here," said Sethe. "Tomorrow, never."

"It hurts," Denver said.

"Comb it every day, it won't."

"Ouch."

"Your woman she never fix up your hair?" Beloved asked.

Sethe and Denver looked up at her. After four weeks they still had not got used to the gravelly voice and the song that seemed to lie in it. Just outside music it lay, with a cadence not like theirs.

"Your woman she never fix up your hair?" was clearly a question for Sethe, since that's who she was looking at.

"My woman? You mean my mother? If she did, I don't remember. I didn't see her but a few times out in the fields and once when she was working indigo. By the time I woke up in the morning, she was in line. If the moon was bright they worked by its light. Sunday she slept like a stick. She must of nursed me two or three weeks—that's the way the others did. Then she went back in rice and I sucked from another woman whose job it was. So to answer you, no. I reckon not. She never fixed my hair nor nothing. She didn't even sleep in the same cabin most nights I remember. Too far from the line-up, I guess. One thing she did do. She picked me up and carried me behind the smokehouse. Back there she opened up her dress front and lifted her breast and pointed under it. Right on her rib was a circle and a cross burnt right in the skin. She said, 'This is your ma'am. This,' and she pointed. 'I am the only one got this mark now. The rest dead. If something happens to me and you can't tell me by my face, you can know me by this mark.' Scared me so. All I could think of was how important this was and how I needed to have something important to say back, but I couldn't think of anything so I just said what I thought. 'Yes, Ma'am,' I said. 'But how will you know me? How will you know me? Mark me, too,' I said. 'Mark the mark on me too.' " Sethe chuckled.

"Did she?" asked Denver.

"She slapped my face."

"What for?"

"I didn't understand it then. Not till I had a mark of my own."

"What happened to her?"

"Hung. By the time they cut her down nobody could tell whether she had a circle and a cross or not, least of all me and I did look." Sethe gathered hair from the comb and leaning back tossed it into the fire. It exploded into stars and the smell infuriated them. "Oh, my Jesus," she said and stood up so suddenly the comb she had parked in Denver's hair fell to the floor.

"Ma'am? What's the matter with you, Ma'am?"

Sethe walked over to a chair, lifted a sheet and stretched it as wide as her arms would go. Then she folded, refolded and double-folded it. She took another. Neither was completely dry but the folding felt too fine to stop. She had to do something with her hands because she was remembering something she had forgotten she knew. Something privately shameful that had seeped into a slit in her mind right behind the slap on her face and the circled cross.

"Why they hang your ma'am?" Denver asked. This was the first time she had heard anything about her mother's mother. Baby Suggs was the only grandmother she knew.

"I never found out. It was a lot of them," she said, but what was getting clear and clearer as she folded and refolded damp laundry was the woman called Nan who took her hand and yanked her away from the pile before she could make out the mark. Nan was the one she knew best, who was around all day, who nursed babies, cooked, had one good arm and half of another. And who used different words. Words Sethe understood then but could neither recall nor repeat now. She believed that must be why she remembered so little before Sweet Home except singing and dancing and how crowded it was. What Nan told her she had forgotten, along with the language she told it in. The same language her ma'am spoke, and which would never come back. But the message—that was and had been there all along. Holding the damp white sheets against her chest, she was picking meaning out of a code she no longer understood. Nighttime. Nan holding her with her good arm, waving the stump of the other in the air. "Telling you. I am telling you, small girl Sethe," and she did that. She told Sethe that her mother and Nan were together from the sea. Both were taken up many times by the crew. "She threw them all away but you. The one from the crew she threw away on the island. The others from more whites she also threw away. Without names, she threw them. You she gave the name of the black man. She put her arms around him. The others she did not put her arms around. Never. Never. Telling you. I am telling you, small girl Sethe."

As small girl Sethe, she was unimpressed. As grown-up woman Sethe she was angry, but not certain at what. A mighty wish for Baby Suggs broke over her like surf. In the quiet following its splash, Sethe looked at the two girls sitting by the stove: her sickly, shallow-minded boarder, her irritable, lonely daughter. They seemed little and far away.

"Paul D be here in a minute," she said.

Denver sighed with relief. For a minute there, while her mother stood folding the wash lost in thought, she clamped her teeth and prayed it would stop. Denver hated the stories her mother told that did not concern herself, which is why Amy was all she ever asked about. The rest was a gleaming, powerful world made more so by Denver's absence from it. Not being in it, she hated it and wanted Beloved to hate it too, although there was no chance of that at all. Beloved took every opportunity to ask some funny question and get Sethe going. Denver noticed how greedy she was to hear Sethe talk. Now she noticed something more. The questions Beloved asked: "Where your diamonds?" "Your woman she never fix up your hair?" And most perplexing: Tell me your earrings.

How did she know?

BELOVED WAS shining and Paul D didn't like it. Women did what strawberry plants did before they shot out their thin vines: the quality of the green changed. Then the vine threads came, then the buds. By the time the white petals died and the mint-colored berry poked out, the leaf shine was gilded tight and waxy. That's how Beloved looked—gilded and shining. Paul D took to having Sethe on waking, so that later, when he went down the white stairs where she made bread under Beloved's gaze, his head was clear.

In the evening when he came home and the three of them were all there fixing the supper table, her shine was so pronounced he wondered why Denver and Sethe didn't see it. Or maybe they did. Certainly women could tell, as men could, when one of their number was aroused. Paul D looked carefully at Beloved to see if she was aware of it but she paid him no attention at all—frequently not even answering a direct question put to her. She would look at him and not open her mouth. Five weeks she had been with them, and they didn't know any more about her than they did when they found her asleep on the stump.

They were seated at the table Paul D had broken the day he arrived at 124. Its mended legs stronger than before. The cabbage was all gone and the shiny ankle bones of smoked pork were pushed in a heap on their plates. Sethe was dishing up bread pudding, murmuring her hopes for it, apologizing in advance the way veteran cooks always do, when something in Beloved's face, some petlike adoration that took hold of her as she looked at Sethe, made Paul D speak.

"Ain't you got no brothers or sisters?"

Beloved diddled her spoon but did not look at him. "I don't have nobody."

"What was you looking for when you came here?" he asked her.

"This place. I was looking for this place I could be in."

"Somebody tell you about this house?"

"She told me. When I was at the bridge, she told me."

"Must be somebody from the old days," Sethe said. The days when 124 was a way station where messages came and then their senders. Where bits of news soaked like dried beans in spring water—until they were soft enough to digest.

"How'd you come? Who brought you?"

Now she looked steadily at him, but did not answer.

He could feel both Sethe and Denver pulling in, holding their stomach muscles, sending out sticky spiderwebs to touch one another. He decided to force it anyway.

"I asked you who brought you here?"

"I walked here," she said. "A long, long, long, long way. Nobody bring me. Nobody help me."

"You had new shoes. If you walked so long why don't your shoes show it?"

"Paul D, stop picking on her."

"I want to know," he said, holding the knife handle in his fist like a pole.

"I take the shoes! I take the dress! The shoe strings don't fix!" she shouted and gave him a look so malevolent Denver touched her arm.

"I'll teach you," said Denver, "how to tie your shoes," and got a smile from Beloved as a reward.

Paul D had the feeling a large, silver fish had slipped from his hands the minute he grabbed hold of its tail. That it was streaming back off into dark water now, gone but for the glistening marking its route. But if her shining was not for him, who then? He had never known a woman who lit up for nobody in particular, who just did it as a general announcement. Always, in his experience, the light appeared when there was focus. Like the Thirty-Mile Woman, dulled to smoke while he waited with her in the ditch, and starlight when Sixo got there. He never knew himself to mistake it. It was there the instant he looked at Sethe's wet legs, otherwise he never would have been bold enough to enclose her in his arms that day and whisper into her back.

This girl Beloved, homeless and without people, beat all, though he couldn't say exactly why, considering the coloredpeople he had run into during the last twenty years. During, before and after the War he had seen Negroes so stunned, or hungry, or tired or bereft it was a wonder they recalled or said anything. Who, like him, had hidden in caves and fought owls for food; who, like him, stole from pigs; who, like him, slept in trees in the day and walked by night; who, like him, had buried themselves in slop and jumped in wells to avoid regulators, raiders, paterollers, veterans, hill men, posses and merrymakers. Once he met a Negro about fourteen years old who lived by himself in the woods and said he couldn't remember living anywhere else. He saw a witless coloredwoman jailed and hanged for stealing ducks she believed were her own babies.

Move. Walk. Run. Hide. Steal and move on. Only once had it been possible for him to stay in one spot—with a woman, or a family—for longer than a few months. That once was almost two years with a weaver lady in Delaware, the meanest place for Negroes he had ever seen outside Pulaski County, Kentucky, and of course the prison camp in Georgia.

From all those Negroes, Beloved was different. Her shining, her new shoes. It bothered him. Maybe it was just the fact that he didn't bother her. Or it could be timing. She had appeared and been taken in on the very day Sethe and he had patched up their quarrel, gone out in public and had a right good time—like a family. Denver had come around, so to speak; Sethe was laughing; he had a promise of steady work, 124 was cleared up from spirits. It had begun to look like a life. And damn! a water-drinking woman fell sick, got took in, healed, and hadn't moved a peg since.

He wanted her out, but Sethe had let her in and he couldn't put her out of a house that wasn't his. It was one thing to beat up a ghost, quite another to throw a helpless coloredgirl out in territory infected by the Klan. Desperately thirsty for black blood, without which it could not live, the dragon swam the Ohio at will.

Sitting at table, chewing on his after-supper broom straw, Paul D decided to place her. Consult with the Negroes in town and find her her own place.

No sooner did he have the thought than Beloved strangled on one of the raisins she had picked out of the bread pudding. She fell backward and off the chair and thrashed around holding her throat. Sethe knocked her on the back while Denver pried her hands away from her neck. Beloved, on her hands and knees, vomited up her food and struggled for breath.

When she was quiet and Denver had wiped up the mess, she said, "Go to sleep now."

"Come in my room," said Denver. "I can watch out for you up there."

No moment could have been better. Denver had worried herself sick trying to think of a way to get Beloved to share her room. It was hard sleeping above her, wondering if she was going to be sick again, fall asleep and not wake, or (God, please don't) get up and wander out of the yard just the way she wandered in. They could have their talks easier there: at night when Sethe and Paul D were asleep; or in the daytime before either came home. Sweet, crazy conversations full of half sentences, daydreams and misunderstandings more thrilling than understanding could ever be.

When the girls left, Sethe began to clear the table. She stacked the plates near a basin of water.

"What is it about her vex you so?"

Paul D frowned, but said nothing.

"We had one good fight about Denver. Do we need one about her too?" asked Sethe.

"I just don't understand what the hold is. It's clear why she holds on to you, but I just can't see why you holding on to her."

Sethe turned away from the plates toward him. "What you care who's holding on to who? Feeding her is no trouble. I pick up a little extra from the restaurant is all. And she's nice girl company for Denver. You know that and I know you know it, so what is it got your teeth on edge?"

"I can't place it. It's a feeling in me."

"Well, feel this, why don't you? Feel how it feels to have a bed to sleep in and somebody there not worrying you to death about what you got to do each day to deserve it. Feel how that feels. And if that don't get it, feel how it feels to be a coloredwoman roaming the roads with anything God made liable to jump on you. Feel that."

"I know every bit of that, Sethe. I wasn't born yesterday and I never mistreated a woman in my life."

"That makes one in the world," Sethe answered.

"Not two?"

"No. Not two."

"What Halle ever do to you? Halle stood by you. He never left you."

"What'd he leave then if not me?"

"I don't know, but it wasn't you. That's a fact."

"Then he did worse; he left his children."

"You don't know that."

"He wasn't there. He wasn't where he said he would be."

"He was there."

"Then why didn't he show himself? Why did I have to pack my babies off and stay behind to look for him?"

"He couldn't get out the loft."

"Loft? What loft?"

"The one over your head. In the barn."

Slowly, slowly, taking all the time allowed, Sethe moved toward the table.

"He saw?"

"He saw."

"He told you?"

"You told me."

"What?"

"The day I came in here. You said they stole your milk. I never knew what it was that messed him up. That was it, I guess. All I knew was that something broke him. Not a one of them years of Saturdays, Sundays and nighttime extra never touched him. But whatever he saw go on in that barn that day broke him like a twig."

"He saw?" Sethe was gripping her elbows as though to keep them from flying away.

"He saw. Must have."

"He saw them boys do that to me and let them keep on breathing air? He saw? He saw? He saw?"

"Hey! Hey! Listen up. Let me tell you something. A man ain't a goddamn ax. Chopping, hacking, busting every goddamn minute of the day. Things get to him. Things he can't chop down because they're inside."

Sethe was pacing up and down, up and down in the lamplight. "The underground agent said, By Sunday. They took my milk and he saw it and didn't come down? Sunday came and he didn't. Monday came and no Halle. I thought he was dead, that's why; then I thought they caught him, that's why. Then I thought, No, he's not dead because if he was I'd know it, and then you come here after all this time and you didn't say he was dead, because you didn't know either, so I thought, Well, he just found him another better way to live. Because if he was anywhere near here, he'd come to Baby Suggs, if not to me. But I never knew he saw."

"What does that matter now?"

"If he is alive, and saw that, he won't step foot in my door. Not Halle."

"It broke him, Sethe." Paul D looked up at her and sighed. "You may as well know it all. Last time I saw him he was sitting by the churn. He had butter all over his face."

Nothing happened, and she was grateful for that. Usually she could see the picture right away of what she heard. But she could not picture what Paul D said. Nothing came to mind. Carefully, carefully, she passed on to a reasonable question.

"What did he say?"

"Nothing."

"Not a word?"

"Not a word."

"Did you speak to him? Didn't you say anything to him? Something!"

"I couldn't, Sethe. I just . . . couldn't."

"Why!"

"I had a bit in my mouth."

Sethe opened the front door and sat down on the porch steps. The day had gone blue without its sun, but she could still make out the black silhouettes of trees in the meadow beyond. She shook her head from side to side, resigned to her rebellious brain. Why was there nothing it refused? No misery, no regret, no hateful picture too rotten to accept? Like a greedy child it snatched up everything. Just once, could it say, No thank you? I just ate and can't hold another bite? I am full God damn it of two boys with mossy teeth, one sucking on my breast the other holding me down, their book-reading teacher watching and writing it up. I am still full of that, God damn it, I can't go back and add more. Add my husband to it, watching, above me in the loft—hiding close by—the one place he thought no one would look for him, looking down on what I couldn't look at at all. And not stopping them—looking and letting it happen. But my greedy brain says, Oh thanks, I'd love more—so I add more. And no sooner than I do, there is no stopping. There is also my husband squatting by the churn smearing the butter as well as its clabber all over his face because the milk they took is on his mind. And as far as he is concerned, the world may as well know it. And if he was that broken then, then he is also and certainly dead now. And if Paul D saw him and could not save or comfort him because the iron bit was in his mouth, then there is still more that Paul D could tell me and my brain would go right ahead and take it and never say, No thank you. I don't want to know or have to remember that. I have other things to do: worry, for example, about tomorrow, about Denver, about Beloved, about age and sickness not to speak of love.

But her brain was not interested in the future. Loaded with the past and hungry for more, it left her no room to imagine, let alone plan for, the next day. Exactly like that afternoon in the wild onions—when one more step was the most she could see of the future. Other people went crazy, why couldn't she? Other people's brains stopped, turned around and went on to something new, which is what must have happened to Halle. And how sweet that would have been: the two of them back by the milk shed, squatting by the churn, smashing cold, lumpy butter into their faces with not a care in the world. Feeling it slippery, sticky—rubbing it in their hair, watching it squeeze through their fingers. What a relief to stop it right there. Close. Shut. Squeeze the butter. But her three children were chewing sugar teat under a blanket on their way to Ohio and no butter play would change that.

Paul D stepped through the door and touched her shoulder.

"I didn't plan on telling you that."

"I didn't plan on hearing it."

"I can't take it back, but I can leave it alone," Paul D said.

He wants to tell me, she thought. He wants me to ask him about what it was like for him—about how offended the tongue is, held down by iron, how the need to spit is so deep you cry for it. She already knew about it, had seen it time after time in the place before Sweet Home. Men, boys, little girls, women. The wildness that shot up into the eye the moment the lips were yanked back. Days after it was taken out, goose fat was rubbed on the corners of the mouth but nothing to soothe the tongue or take the wildness out of the eye.

Sethe looked up into Paul D's eyes to see if there was any trace left in them.

"People I saw as a child," she said, "who'd had the bit always looked wild after that. Whatever they used it on them for, it couldn't have worked, because it put a wildness where before there wasn't any. When I look at you, I don't see it. There ain't no wildness in your eye nowhere."

"There's a way to put it there and there's a way to take it out. I know em both and I haven't figured out yet which is worse." He sat down beside her. Sethe looked at him. In that unlit daylight his face, bronzed and reduced to its bones, smoothed her heart down.

"You want to tell me about it?" she asked him.

"I don't know. I never have talked about it. Not to a soul. Sang it sometimes, but I never told a soul."

"Go ahead. I can hear it."

"Maybe. Maybe you can hear it. I just ain't sure I can say it. Say it right, I mean, because it wasn't the bit—that wasn't it."

"What then?" Sethe asked.

"The roosters," he said. "Walking past the roosters looking at them look at me."

Sethe smiled. "In that pine?"

"Yeah." Paul D smiled with her. "Must have been five of them perched up there, and at least fifty hens."

"Mister, too?"

"Not right off. But I hadn't took twenty steps before I seen him. He come down off the fence post there and sat on the tub."

"He loved that tub," said Sethe, thinking, No, there is no stopping now.

"Didn't he? Like a throne. Was me took him out the shell, you know. He'd a died if it hadn't been for me. The hen had walked on off with all the hatched peeps trailing behind her. There was this one egg left. Looked like a blank, but then I saw it move so I tapped it open and here come Mister, bad feet and all. I watched that son a bitch grow up and whup everything in the yard."

"He always was hateful," Sethe said.

"Yeah, he was hateful all right. Bloody too, and evil. Crooked feet flapping. Comb as big as my hand and some kind of red. He sat right there on the tub looking at me. I swear he smiled. My head was full of what I'd seen of Halle a while back. I wasn't even thinking about the bit. Just Halle and before him Sixo, but when I saw Mister I knew it was me too. Not just them, me too. One crazy, one sold, one missing, one burnt and me licking iron with my hands crossed behind me. The last of the Sweet Home men.

"Mister, he looked so . . . free. Better than me. Stronger, tougher. Son a bitch couldn't even get out the shell by hisself but he was still king and I was . . ." Paul D stopped and squeezed his left hand with his right. He held it that way long enough for it and the world to quiet down and let him go on.

"Mister was allowed to be and stay what he was. But I wasn't allowed to be and stay what I was. Even if you cooked him you'd be cooking a rooster named Mister. But wasn't no way I'd ever be Paul D again, living or dead. Schoolteacher changed me. I was something else and that something was less than a chicken sitting in the sun on a tub."

Sethe put her hand on his knee and rubbed.

Paul D had only begun, what he was telling her was only the beginning when her fingers on his knee, soft and reassuring, stopped him. Just as well. Just as well. Saying more might push them both to a place they couldn't get back from. He would keep the rest where it belonged: in that tobacco tin buried in his chest where a red heart used to be. Its lid rusted shut. He would not pry it loose now in front of this sweet sturdy woman, for if she got a whiff of the contents it would shame him. And it would hurt her to know that there was no red heart bright as Mister's comb beating in him.

Sethe rubbed and rubbed, pressing the work cloth and the stony curves that made up his knee. She hoped it calmed him as it did her. Like kneading bread in the half-light of the restaurant kitchen. Before the cook arrived when she stood in a space no wider than a bench is long, back behind and to the left of the milk cans. Working dough. Working, working dough. Nothing better than that to start the day's serious work of beating back the past.

UPSTAIRS BELOVED was dancing. A little two-step, two-step, make-a-new-step, slide, slide and strut on down.

Denver sat on the bed smiling and providing the music.

She had never seen Beloved this happy. She had seen her pouty lips open wide with the pleasure of sugar or some piece of news Denver gave her. She had felt warm satisfaction radiating from Beloved's skin when she listened to her mother talk about the old days. But gaiety she had never seen. Not ten minutes had passed since Beloved had fallen backward to the floor, pop-eyed, thrashing and holding her throat. Now, after a few seconds lying in Denver's bed, she was up and dancing.

"Where'd you learn to dance?" Denver asked her.

"Nowhere. Look at me do this." Beloved put her fists on her hips and commenced to skip on bare feet. Denver laughed.

"Now you. Come on," said Beloved. "You may as well just come on." Her black skirt swayed from side to side.

Denver grew ice-cold as she rose from the bed. She knew she was twice Beloved's size but she floated up, cold and light as a snowflake.

Beloved took Denver's hand and placed another on Denver's shoulder. They danced then. Round and round the tiny room and it may have been dizziness, or feeling light and icy at once, that made Denver laugh so hard. A catching laugh that Beloved caught. The two of them, merry as kittens, swung to and fro, to and fro, until exhausted they sat on the floor. Beloved let her head fall back on the edge of the bed while she found her breath and Denver saw the tip of the thing she always saw in its entirety when Beloved undressed to sleep. Looking straight at it she whispered, "Why you call yourself Beloved?"

Beloved closed her eyes. "In the dark my name is Beloved."

Denver scooted a little closer. "What's it like over there, where you were before? Can you tell me?"

"Dark," said Beloved. "I'm small in that place. I'm like this here." She raised her head off the bed, lay down on her side and curled up.

Denver covered her lips with her fingers. "Were you cold?"

Beloved curled tighter and shook her head. "Hot. Nothing to breathe down there and no room to move in."

"You see anybody?"

"Heaps. A lot of people is down there. Some is dead."

"You see Jesus? Baby Suggs?"

"I don't know. I don't know the names." She sat up.

"Tell me, how did you get here?"

"I wait; then I got on the bridge. I stay there in the dark, in the daytime, in the dark, in the daytime. It was a long time."

"All this time you were on a bridge?"

"No. After. When I got out."

"What did you come back for?"

Beloved smiled. "To see her face."

"Ma'am's? Sethe?"

"Yes, Sethe."

Denver felt a little hurt, slighted that she was not the main reason for Beloved's return. "Don't you remember we played together by the stream?"

"I was on the bridge," said Beloved. "You see me on the bridge?"

"No, by the stream. The water back in the woods."

"Oh, I was in the water. I saw her diamonds down there. I could touch them."

"What stopped you?"

"She left me behind. By myself," said Beloved. She lifted her eyes to meet Denver's and frowned, perhaps. Perhaps not. The tiny scratches on her forehead may have made it seem so.

Denver swallowed. "Don't," she said. "Don't. You won't leave us, will you?"

"No. Never. This is where I am."

Suddenly Denver, who was sitting cross-legged, lurched forward and grabbed Beloved's wrist. "Don't tell her. Don't let Ma'am know who you are. Please, you hear?"

"Don't tell me what to do. Don't you never never tell me what to do."

"But I'm on your side, Beloved."

"She is the one. She is the one I need. You can go but she is the one I have to have." Her eyes stretched to the limit, black as the all-night sky.

"I didn't do anything to you. I never hurt you. I never hurt anybody," said Denver.

"Me either. Me either."

"What you gonna do?"

"Stay here. I belong here."

"I belong here too."

"Then stay, but don't never tell me what to do. Don't never do that."

"We were dancing. Just a minute ago we were dancing together. Let's."

"I don't want to." Beloved got up and lay down on the bed. Their quietness boomed about on the walls like birds in panic. Finally Denver's breath steadied against the threat of an unbearable loss.

"Tell me," Beloved said. "Tell me how Sethe made you in the boat."

"She never told me all of it," said Denver.

"Tell me."

Denver climbed up on the bed and folded her arms under her apron. She had not been in the tree room once since Beloved sat on their stump after the carnival, and had not remembered that she hadn't gone there until this very desperate moment. Nothing was out there that this sister-girl did not provide in abundance: a racing heart, dreaminess, society, danger, beauty. She swallowed twice to prepare for the telling, to construct out of the strings she had heard all her life a net to hold Beloved.

"She had good hands, she said. The whitegirl, she said, had thin little arms but good hands. She saw that right away, she said. Hair enough for five heads and good hands, she said. I guess the hands made her think she could do it: get us both across the river. But the mouth was what kept her from being scared. She said there ain't nothing to go by with whitepeople. You don't know how they'll jump. Say one thing, do another. But if you looked at the mouth sometimes you could tell by that. She said this girl talked a storm, but there wasn't no meanness around her mouth. She took Ma'am to that lean-to and rubbed her feet for her, so that was one thing. And Ma'am believed she wasn't going to turn her over. You could get money if you turned a runaway over, and she wasn't sure this girl Amy didn't need money more than anything, especially since all she talked about was getting hold of some velvet."

"What's velvet?"

"It's a cloth, kind of deep and soft."

"Go ahead."

"Anyway, she rubbed Ma'am's feet back to life, and she cried, she said, from how it hurt. But it made her think she could make it on over to where Grandma Baby Suggs was and . . ."

"Who is that?"

"I just said it. My grandmother."

"Is that Sethe's mother?"

"No. My father's mother."

"Go ahead."

"That's where the others was. My brothers and . . . the baby girl. She sent them on before to wait for her at Grandma Baby's. So she had to put up with everything to get there. And this here girl Amy helped."

Denver stopped and sighed. This was the part of the story she loved. She was coming to it now, and she loved it because it was all about herself; but she hated it too because it made her feel like a bill was owing somewhere and she, Denver, had to pay it. But who she owed or what to pay it with eluded her. Now, watching Beloved's alert and hungry face, how she took in every word, asking questions about the color of things and their size, her downright craving to know, Denver began to see what she was saying and not just to hear it: there is this nineteen-year-old slavegirl—a year older than herself—walking through the dark woods to get to her children who are far away. She is tired, scared maybe, and maybe even lost. Most of all she is by herself and inside her is another baby she has to think about too. Behind her dogs, perhaps; guns probably; and certainly mossy teeth. She is not so afraid at night because she is the color of it, but in the day every sound is a shot or a tracker's quiet step.

Denver was seeing it now and feeling it—through Beloved. Feeling how it must have felt to her mother. Seeing how it must have looked. And the more fine points she made, the more detail she provided, the more Beloved liked it. So she anticipated the questions by giving blood to the scraps her mother and grandmother had told her—and a heartbeat. The monologue became, in fact, a duet as they lay down together, Denver nursing Beloved's interest like a lover whose pleasure was to overfeed the loved. The dark quilt with two orange patches was there with them because Beloved wanted it near her when she slept. It was smelling like grass and feeling like hands—the unrested hands of busy women: dry, warm, prickly. Denver spoke, Beloved listened, and the two did the best they could to create what really happened, how it really was, something only Sethe knew because she alone had the mind for it and the time afterward to shape it: the quality of Amy's voice, her breath like burning wood. The quick-change weather up in those hills—cool at night, hot in the day, sudden fog. How recklessly she behaved with this whitegirl—a recklessness born of desperation and encouraged by Amy's fugitive eyes and her tenderhearted mouth.

"You ain't got no business walking round these hills, miss."

"Looka here who's talking. I got more business here 'n you got. They catch you they cut your head off. Ain't nobody after me but I know somebody after you." Amy pressed her fingers into the soles of the slavewoman's feet. "Whose baby that?"

Sethe did not answer.

"You don't even know. Come here, Jesus." Amy sighed and shook her head. "Hurt?"

"A touch."

"Good for you. More it hurt more better it is. Can't nothing heal without pain, you know. What you wiggling for?"

Sethe raised up on her elbows. Lying on her back so long had raised a ruckus between her shoulder blades. The fire in her feet and the fire on her back made her sweat.

"My back hurt me," she said.

"Your back? Gal, you a mess. Turn over here and let me see."

In an effort so great it made her sick to her stomach, Sethe turned onto her right side. Amy unfastened the back of her dress and said, "Come here, Jesus," when she saw. Sethe guessed it must be bad because after that call to Jesus Amy didn't speak for a while. In the silence of an Amy struck dumb for a change, Sethe felt the fingers of those good hands lightly touch her back. She could hear her breathing but still the whitegirl said nothing. Sethe could not move. She couldn't lie on her stomach or her back, and to keep on her side meant pressure on her screaming feet. Amy spoke at last in her dreamwalker's voice.

"It's a tree, Lu. A chokecherry tree. See, here's the trunk—it's red and split wide open, full of sap, and this here's the parting for the branches. You got a mighty lot of branches. Leaves, too, look like, and dern if these ain't blossoms. Tiny little cherry blossoms, just as white. Your back got a whole tree on it. In bloom. What God have in mind, I wonder. I had me some whippings, but I don't remember nothing like this. Mr. Buddy had a right evil hand too. Whip you for looking at him straight. Sure would. I looked right at him one time and he hauled off and threw the poker at me. Guess he knew what I was a-thinking."

Sethe groaned and Amy cut her reverie short—long enough to shift Sethe's feet so the weight, resting on leaf-covered stones, was above the ankles.

"That better? Lord what a way to die. You gonna die in here, you know. Ain't no way out of it. Thank your Maker I come along so's you wouldn't have to die outside in them weeds. Snake come along he bite you. Bear eat you up. Maybe you should of stayed where you was, Lu. I can see by your back why you didn't ha ha. Whoever planted that tree beat Mr. Buddy by a mile. Glad I ain't you. Well, spiderwebs is 'bout all I can do for you. What's in here ain't enough. I'll look outside. Could use moss, but sometimes bugs and things is in it. Maybe I ought to break them blossoms open. Get that pus to running, you think? Wonder what God had in mind. You must of did something. Don't run off nowhere now."

Sethe could hear her humming away in the bushes as she hunted spiderwebs. A humming she concentrated on because as soon as Amy ducked out the baby began to stretch. Good question, she was thinking. What did He have in mind? Amy had left the back of Sethe's dress open and now a tail of wind hit it, taking the pain down a step. A relief that let her feel the lesser pain of her sore tongue. Amy returned with two palmfuls of web, which she cleaned of prey and then draped on Sethe's back, saying it was like stringing a tree for Christmas.

"We got a old nigger girl come by our place. She don't know nothing. Sews stuff for Mrs. Buddy—real fine lace but can't barely stick two words together. She don't know nothing, just like you. You don't know a thing. End up dead, that's what. Not me. I'm a get to Boston and get myself some velvet. Carmine. You don't even know about that, do you? Now you never will. Bet you never even sleep with the sun in your face. I did it a couple of times. Most times I'm feeding stock before light and don't get to sleep till way after dark comes. But I was in the back of the wagon once and fell asleep. Sleeping with the sun in your face is the best old feeling. Two times I did it. Once when I was little. Didn't nobody bother me then. Next time, in back of the wagon, it happened again and doggone if the chickens didn't get loose. Mr. Buddy whipped my tail. Kentucky ain't no good place to be in.

Boston's the place to be in. That's where my mother was before she was give to Mr. Buddy. Joe Nathan said Mr. Buddy is my daddy but I don't believe that, you?"

Sethe told her she didn't believe Mr. Buddy was her daddy.

"You know your daddy, do you?"

"No," said Sethe.

"Neither me. All I know is it ain't him." She stood up then, having finished her repair work, and weaving about the lean-to, her slow-moving eyes pale in the sun that lit her hair, she sang:

"When the busy day is done
And my weary little one
Rocketh gently to and fro;
When the night winds softly blow,
And the crickets in the glen
Chirp and chirp and chirp again;
Where 'pon the haunted green
Fairies dance around their queen,
Then from yonder misty skies
Cometh Lady Button Eyes."

Suddenly she stopped weaving and rocking and sat down, her skinny arms wrapped around her knees, her good good hands cupping her elbows. Her slow-moving eyes stopped and peered into the dirt at her feet. "That's my mama's song. She taught me it."

"Through the muck and mist and gloam
To our quiet cozy home,
Where to singing sweet and low
Rocks a cradle to and fro.
Where the clock's dull monotone

Telleth of the day that's done,
Where the moonbeams hover o'er
Playthings sleeping on the floor,
Where my weary wee one lies
Cometh Lady Button Eyes.

"*Layeth she her hands upon*
My dear weary little one,
And those white hands overspread
Like a veil the curly head,
Seem to fondle and caress
Every little silken tress.
Then she smooths the eyelids down
Over those two eyes of brown
In such soothing tender wise
Cometh Lady Button Eyes."

Amy sat quietly after her song, then repeated the last line before she stood, left the lean-to and walked off a little ways to lean against a young ash. When she came back the sun was in the valley below and they were way above it in blue Kentucky light.

"You ain't dead yet, Lu? Lu?"

"Not yet."

"Make you a bet. You make it through the night, you make it all the way." Amy rearranged the leaves for comfort and knelt down to massage the swollen feet again. "Give these one more real good rub," she said, and when Sethe sucked air through her teeth, she said, "Shut up. You got to keep your mouth shut."

Careful of her tongue, Sethe bit down on her lips and let the good hands go to work to the tune of "So bees, sing soft and bees, sing low." Afterward, Amy moved to the other side of the lean-to where, seated, she lowered her head toward her shoulder and braided her hair, saying, "Don't up and die on me in the night, you hear? I don't want to see your ugly black face hankering over me. If you do die, just go on off somewhere where I can't see you, hear?"

"I hear," said Sethe. "I'll do what I can, miss."

Sethe never expected to see another thing in this world, so when she felt toes prodding her hip it took a while to come out of a sleep she thought was death. She sat up, stiff and shivery, while Amy looked in on her juicy back.

"Looks like the devil," said Amy. "But you made it through. Come down here, Jesus, Lu made it through. That's because of me. I'm good at sick things. Can you walk, you think?"

"I have to let my water some kind of way."

"Let's see you walk on em."

It was not good, but it was possible, so Sethe limped, holding on first to Amy, then to a sapling.

"Was me did it. I'm good at sick things ain't I?"

"Yeah," said Sethe, "you good."

"We got to get off this here hill. Come on. I'll take you down to the river. That ought to suit you. Me, I'm going to the Pike. Take me straight to Boston. What's that all over your dress?"

"Milk."

"You one mess."

Sethe looked down at her stomach and touched it. The baby was dead. She had not died in the night, but the baby had. If that was the case, then there was no stopping now. She would get that milk to her baby girl if she had to swim.

"Ain't you hungry?" Amy asked her.

"I ain't nothing but in a hurry, miss."

"Whoa. Slow down. Want some shoes?"

"Say what?"

"I figured how," said Amy and so she had. She tore two

pieces from Sethe's shawl, filled them with leaves and tied them over her feet, chattering all the while.

"How old are you, Lu? I been bleeding for four years but I ain't having nobody's baby. Won't catch me sweating milk cause . . ."

"I know," said Sethe. "You going to Boston."

At noon they saw it; then they were near enough to hear it. By late afternoon they could drink from it if they wanted to. Four stars were visible by the time they found, not a riverboat to stow Sethe away on, or a ferryman willing to take on a fugitive passenger—nothing like that—but a whole boat to steal. It had one oar, lots of holes and two bird nests.

"There you go, Lu. Jesus looking at you."

Sethe was looking at one mile of dark water, which would have to be split with one oar in a useless boat against a current dedicated to the Mississippi hundreds of miles away. It looked like home to her, and the baby (not dead in the least) must have thought so too. As soon as Sethe got close to the river her own water broke loose to join it. The break, followed by the redundant announcement of labor, arched her back.

"What you doing that for?" asked Amy. "Ain't you got a brain in your head? Stop that right now. I said stop it, Lu. You the dumbest thing on this here earth. Lu! Lu!"

Sethe couldn't think of anywhere to go but in. She waited for the sweet beat that followed the blast of pain. On her knees again, she crawled into the boat. It waddled under her and she had just enough time to brace her leaf-bag feet on the bench when another rip took her breath away. Panting under four summer stars, she threw her legs over the sides, because here come the head, as Amy informed her as though she did not know it—as though the rip was a breakup of walnut logs in the brace, or of lightning's jagged tear through a leather sky.

It was stuck. Face up and drowning in its mother's blood. Amy stopped begging Jesus and began to curse His daddy.

"Push!" screamed Amy.

"Pull," whispered Sethe.

And the strong hands went to work a fourth time, none too soon, for river water, seeping through any hole it chose, was spreading over Sethe's hips. She reached one arm back and grabbed the rope while Amy fairly clawed at the head. When a foot rose from the river bed and kicked the bottom of the boat and Sethe's behind, she knew it was done and permitted herself a short faint. Coming to, she heard no cries, just Amy's encouraging coos. Nothing happened for so long they both believed they had lost it. Sethe arched suddenly and the afterbirth shot out. Then the baby whimpered and Sethe looked. Twenty inches of cord hung from its belly and it trembled in the cooling evening air. Amy wrapped her skirt around it and the wet sticky women clambered ashore to see what, indeed, God had in mind.

Spores of bluefern growing in the hollows along the riverbank float toward the water in silver-blue lines hard to see unless you are in or near them, lying right at the river's edge when the sunshots are low and drained. Often they are mistook for insects—but they are seeds in which the whole generation sleeps confident of a future. And for a moment it is easy to believe each one has one—will become all of what is contained in the spore: will live out its days as planned. This moment of certainty lasts no longer than that; longer, perhaps, than the spore itself.

On a riverbank in the cool of a summer evening two women struggled under a shower of silvery blue. They never expected to see each other again in this world and at the moment couldn't care less. But there on a summer night surrounded by bluefern they did something together appropriately and well. A pateroller passing would have sniggered to see two throw-away people, two lawless outlaws—a slave and a barefoot whitewoman with unpinned hair—wrapping a ten-minute-old baby in the rags they wore. But no pateroller came and no preacher. The water sucked and swallowed itself beneath them. There was nothing to disturb them at their work. So they did it appropriately and well.

Twilight came on and Amy said she had to go; that she wouldn't be caught dead in daylight on a busy river with a runaway. After rinsing her hands and face in the river, she stood and looked down at the baby wrapped and tied to Sethe's chest.

"She's never gonna know who I am. You gonna tell her? Who brought her into this here world?" She lifted her chin, looked off into the place where the sun used to be. "You better tell her. You hear? Say Miss Amy Denver. Of Boston."

Sethe felt herself falling into a sleep she knew would be deep. On the lip of it, just before going under, she thought, "That's pretty. Denver. Real pretty."

IT WAS TIME to lay it all down. Before Paul D came and sat on her porch steps, words whispered in the keeping room had kept her going. Helped her endure the chastising ghost; refurbished the baby faces of Howard and Buglar and kept them whole in the world because in her dreams she saw only their parts in trees; and kept her husband shadowy but *there*—somewhere. Now Halle's face between the butter press and the churn swelled larger and larger, crowding her eyes and making her head hurt. She wished for Baby Suggs' fingers molding her nape, reshaping it, saying, "Lay em down, Sethe. Sword and shield. Down. Down. Both of em down. Down by the riverside. Sword and shield. Don't study war no more. Lay all that mess down. Sword and shield." And under the pressing fingers and the quiet instructive voice, she would. Her heavy knives of defense against misery, regret, gall and hurt, she placed one by one on a bank where clear water rushed on below.

Nine years without the fingers or the voice of Baby Suggs was too much. And words whispered in the keeping room were too little. The butter-smeared face of a man God made none sweeter than demanded more: an arch built or a robe sewn. Some fixing ceremony. Sethe decided to go to the Clearing, back where Baby Suggs had danced in sunlight.

Before 124 and everybody in it had closed down, veiled

over and shut away; before it had become the plaything of spirits and the home of the chafed, 124 had been a cheerful, buzzing house where Baby Suggs, holy, loved, cautioned, fed, chastised and soothed. Where not one but two pots simmered on the stove; where the lamp burned all night long. Strangers rested there while children tried on their shoes. Messages were left there, for whoever needed them was sure to stop in one day soon. Talk was low and to the point—for Baby Suggs, holy, didn't approve of extra. "Everything depends on knowing how much," she said, and "Good is knowing when to stop."

It was in front of *that* 124 that Sethe climbed off a wagon, her newborn tied to her chest, and felt for the first time the wide arms of her mother-in-law, who had made it to Cincinnati. Who decided that, because slave life had "busted her legs, back, head, eyes, hands, kidneys, womb and tongue," she had nothing left to make a living with but her heart—which she put to work at once. Accepting no title of honor before her name, but allowing a small caress after it, she became an unchurched preacher, one who visited pulpits and opened her great heart to those who could use it. In winter and fall she carried it to AME's and Baptists, Holinesses and Sanctifieds, the Church of the Redeemer and the Redeemed. Uncalled, unrobed, unanointed, she let her great heart beat in their presence. When warm weather came, Baby Suggs, holy, followed by every black man, woman and child who could make it through, took her great heart to the Clearing—a wide-open place cut deep in the woods nobody knew for what at the end of a path known only to deer and whoever cleared the land in the first place. In the heat of every Saturday afternoon, she sat in the clearing while the people waited among the trees.

After situating herself on a huge flat-sided rock, Baby Suggs bowed her head and prayed silently. The company watched her from the trees. They knew she was ready when she put her stick down. Then she shouted, "Let the children come!" and they ran from the trees toward her.

"Let your mothers hear you laugh," she told them, and the woods rang. The adults looked on and could not help smiling.

Then "Let the grown men come," she shouted. They stepped out one by one from among the ringing trees.

"Let your wives and your children see you dance," she told them, and groundlife shuddered under their feet.

Finally she called the women to her. "Cry," she told them. "For the living and the dead. Just cry." And without covering their eyes the women let loose.

It started that way: laughing children, dancing men, crying women and then it got mixed up. Women stopped crying and danced; men sat down and cried; children danced, women laughed, children cried until, exhausted and riven, all and each lay about the Clearing damp and gasping for breath. In the silence that followed, Baby Suggs, holy, offered up to them her great big heart.

She did not tell them to clean up their lives or to go and sin no more. She did not tell them they were the blessed of the earth, its inheriting meek or its glorybound pure.

She told them that the only grace they could have was the grace they could imagine. That if they could not see it, they would not have it.

"Here," she said, "in this here place, we flesh; flesh that weeps, laughs; flesh that dances on bare feet in grass. Love it. Love it hard. Yonder they do not love your flesh. They despise it. They don't love your eyes; they'd just as soon pick em out. No more do they love the skin on your back. Yonder they flay it. And O my people they do not love your hands. Those they only use, tie, bind, chop off and leave empty. Love your hands! Love them. Raise them up and kiss them. Touch others with them, pat them together, stroke them on your face 'cause they don't love that either. *You* got to love it, *you!* And no, they ain't in love with your mouth. Yonder, out there, they will see it broken and break it again. What you say out of it they will not heed. What you scream from it they do not hear. What you put into it to nourish your body they will snatch away and give you leavins instead. No, they don't love your mouth. *You* got to love it. This is flesh I'm talking about here. Flesh that needs to be loved. Feet that need to rest and to dance; backs that need support; shoulders that need arms, strong arms I'm telling you. And O my people, out yonder, hear me, they do not love your neck unnoosed and straight. So love your neck; put a hand on it, grace it, stroke it and hold it up. And all your inside parts that they'd just as soon slop for hogs, you got to love them. The dark, dark liver—love it, love it, and the beat and beating heart, love that too. More than eyes or feet. More than lungs that have yet to draw free air. More than your life-holding womb and your life-giving private parts, hear me now, love your heart. For this is the prize." Saying no more, she stood up then and danced with her twisted hip the rest of what her heart had to say while the others opened their mouths and gave her the music. Long notes held until the four-part harmony was perfect enough for their deeply loved flesh.

Sethe wanted to be there now. At the least to listen to the spaces that the long-ago singing had left behind. At the most to get a clue from her husband's dead mother as to what she should do with her sword and shield now, dear Jesus, now nine years after Baby Suggs, holy, proved herself a liar, dismissed her great heart and lay in the keeping-room bed roused once in a while by a craving for color and not for another thing.

"Those white things have taken all I had or dreamed," she

said, "and broke my heartstrings too. There is no bad luck in the world but whitefolks." 124 shut down and put up with the venom of its ghost. No more lamp all night long, or neighbors dropping by. No low conversations after supper. No watched barefoot children playing in the shoes of strangers. Baby Suggs, holy, believed she had lied. There was no grace—imaginary or real—and no sunlit dance in a Clearing could change that. Her faith, her love, her imagination and her great big old heart began to collapse twenty-eight days after her daughter-in-law arrived.

Yet it was to the Clearing that Sethe determined to go—to pay tribute to Halle. Before the light changed, while it was still the green blessed place she remembered: misty with plant steam and the decay of berries.

She put on a shawl and told Denver and Beloved to do likewise. All three set out late one Sunday morning, Sethe leading, the girls trotting behind, not a soul in sight.

When they reached the woods it took her no time to find the path through it because big-city revivals were held there regularly now, complete with food-laden tables, banjos and a tent. The old path was a track now, but still arched over with trees dropping buckeyes onto the grass below.

There was nothing to be done other than what she had done, but Sethe blamed herself for Baby Suggs' collapse. However many times Baby denied it, Sethe knew the grief at 124 started when she jumped down off the wagon, her newborn tied to her chest in the underwear of a whitegirl looking for Boston.

Followed by the two girls, down a bright green corridor of oak and horse chestnut, Sethe began to sweat a sweat just like the other one when she woke, mud-caked, on the banks of the Ohio.

Amy was gone. Sethe was alone and weak, but alive, and

so was her baby. She walked a ways downriver and then stood gazing at the glimmering water. By and by a flatbed slid into view, but she could not see if the figures on it were whitepeople or not. She began to sweat from a fever she thanked God for since it would certainly keep her baby warm. When the flatbed was beyond her sight she stumbled on and found herself near three coloredpeople fishing—two boys and an older man. She stopped and waited to be spoken to. One of the boys pointed and the man looked over his shoulder at her—a quick look since all he needed to know about her he could see in no time.

No one said anything for a while. Then the man said, "Headin' 'cross?"

"Yes, sir," said Sethe.

"Anybody know you coming?"

"Yes, sir."

He looked at her again and nodded toward a rock that stuck out of the ground above him like a bottom lip. Sethe walked to it and sat down. The stone had eaten the sun's rays but was nowhere near as hot as she was. Too tired to move, she stayed there, the sun in her eyes making her dizzy. Sweat poured over her and bathed the baby completely. She must have slept sitting up, because when next she opened her eyes the man was standing in front of her with a smoking-hot piece of fried eel in his hands. It was an effort to reach for, more to smell, impossible to eat. She begged him for water and he gave her some of the Ohio in a jar. Sethe drank it all and begged more. The clanging was back in her head but she refused to believe that she had come all that way, endured all she had, to die on the wrong side of the river.

The man watched her streaming face and called one of the boys over.

"Take off that coat," he told him.

"Sir?"

"You heard me."

The boy slipped out of his jacket, whining, "What you gonna do? What I'm gonna wear?"

The man untied the baby from her chest and wrapped it in the boy's coat, knotting the sleeves in front.

"What I'm gonna wear?"

The old man sighed and, after a pause, said, "You want it back, then go head and take it off that baby. Put the baby naked in the grass and put your coat back on. And if you can do it, then go on 'way somewhere and don't come back."

The boy dropped his eyes, then turned to join the other. With eel in her hand, the baby at her feet, Sethe dozed, dry-mouthed and sweaty. Evening came and the man touched her shoulder.

Contrary to what she expected they poled upriver, far away from the rowboat Amy had found. Just when she thought he was taking her back to Kentucky, he turned the flatbed and crossed the Ohio like a shot. There he helped her up the steep bank, while the boy without a jacket carried the baby who wore it. The man led her to a brush-covered hutch with a beaten floor.

"Wait here. Somebody be here directly. Don't move. They'll find you."

"Thank you," she said. "I wish I knew your name so I could remember you right."

"Name's Stamp," he said. "Stamp Paid. Watch out for that there baby, you hear?"

"I hear. I hear," she said, but she didn't. Hours later a woman was right up on her before she heard a thing. A short woman, young, with a croaker sack, greeted her.

"Saw the sign a while ago," she said. "But I couldn't get here no quicker."

"What sign?" asked Sethe.

"Stamp leaves the old sty open when there's a crossing. Knots a white rag on the post if it's a child too."

She knelt and emptied the sack. "My name's Ella," she said, taking a wool blanket, cotton cloth, two baked sweet potatoes and a pair of men's shoes from the sack. "My husband, John, is out yonder a ways. Where you heading?"

Sethe told her about Baby Suggs where she had sent her three children.

Ella wrapped a cloth strip tight around the baby's navel as she listened for the holes—the things the fugitives did not say; the questions they did not ask. Listened too for the unnamed, unmentioned people left behind. She shook gravel from the men's shoes and tried to force Sethe's feet into them. They would not go. Sadly, they split them down the heel, sorry indeed to ruin so valuable an item. Sethe put on the boy's jacket, not daring to ask whether there was any word of the children.

"They made it," said Ella. "Stamp ferried some of that party. Left them on Bluestone. It ain't too far."

Sethe couldn't think of anything to do, so grateful was she, so she peeled a potato, ate it, spit it up and ate more in quiet celebration.

"They be glad to see you," said Ella. "When was this one born?"

"Yesterday," said Sethe, wiping sweat from under her chin. "I hope she makes it."

Ella looked at the tiny, dirty face poking out of the wool blanket and shook her head. "Hard to say," she said. "If anybody was to ask me I'd say, 'Don't love nothing.' " Then, as if to take the edge off her pronouncement, she smiled at Sethe. "You had that baby by yourself?"

"No. Whitegirl helped."

"Then we better make tracks."

. . .

Baby Suggs kissed her on the mouth and refused to let her see the children. They were asleep she said and Sethe was too ugly-looking to wake them in the night. She took the newborn and handed it to a young woman in a bonnet, telling her not to clean the eyes till she got the mother's urine.

"Has it cried out yet?" asked Baby.

"A little."

"Time enough. Let's get the mother well."

She led Sethe to the keeping room and, by the light of a spirit lamp, bathed her in sections, starting with her face. Then, while waiting for another pan of heated water, she sat next to her and stitched gray cotton. Sethe dozed and woke to the washing of her hands and arms. After each bathing, Baby covered her with a quilt and put another pan on in the kitchen. Tearing sheets, stitching the gray cotton, she supervised the woman in the bonnet who tended the baby and cried into her cooking. When Sethe's legs were done, Baby looked at her feet and wiped them lightly. She cleaned between Sethe's legs with two separate pans of hot water and then tied her stomach and vagina with sheets. Finally she attacked the unrecognizable feet.

"You feel this?"

"Feel what?" asked Sethe.

"Nothing. Heave up." She helped Sethe to a rocker and lowered her feet into a bucket of salt water and juniper. The rest of the night Sethe sat soaking. The crust from her nipples Baby softened with lard and then washed away. By dawn the silent baby woke and took her mother's milk.

"Pray God it ain't turned bad," said Baby. "And when you through, call me." As she turned to go, Baby Suggs caught a glimpse of something dark on the bed sheet. She frowned and looked at her daughter-in-law bending toward the baby. Roses of blood blossomed in the blanket covering Sethe's shoulders. Baby Suggs hid her mouth with her hand.

When the nursing was over and the newborn was asleep—its eyes half open, its tongue dream-sucking—wordlessly the older woman greased the flowering back and pinned a double thickness of cloth to the inside of the newly stitched dress.

It was not real yet. Not yet. But when her sleepy boys and crawling-already? girl were brought in, it didn't matter whether it was real or not. Sethe lay in bed under, around, over, among but especially with them all. The little girl dribbled clear spit into her face, and Sethe's laugh of delight was so loud the crawling-already? baby blinked. Buglar and Howard played with her ugly feet, after daring each other to be the first to touch them. She kept kissing them. She kissed the backs of their necks, the tops of their heads and the centers of their palms, and it was the boys who decided enough was enough when she lifted their shirts to kiss their tight round bellies. She stopped when and because they said, "Pappie come?"

She didn't cry. She said "soon" and smiled so they would think the brightness in her eyes was love alone. It was some time before she let Baby Suggs shoo the boys away so Sethe could put on the gray cotton dress her mother-in-law had started stitching together the night before. Finally she lay back and cradled the crawling-already? girl in her arms. She enclosed her left nipple with two fingers of her right hand and the child opened her mouth. They hit home together.

Baby Suggs came in and laughed at them, telling Sethe how strong the baby girl was, how smart, already crawling. Then she stooped to gather up the ball of rags that had been Sethe's clothes.

"Nothing worth saving in here," she said.

Sethe lifted her eyes. "Wait," she called. "Look and see if there's something still knotted up in the petticoat."

Baby Suggs inched the spoiled fabric through her fingers

and came upon what felt like pebbles. She held them out toward Sethe. "Going-away present?"

"Wedding present."

"Be nice if there was a groom to go with it." She gazed into her hand. "What you think happened to him?"

"I don't know," said Sethe. "He wasn't where he said to meet him at. I had to get out. Had to." Sethe watched the drowsy eyes of the sucking girl for a moment then looked at Baby Suggs' face. "He'll make it. If I made it, Halle sure can."

"Well, put these on. Maybe they'll light his way." Convinced her son was dead, she handed the stones to Sethe.

"I need holes in my ears."

"I'll do it," said Baby Suggs. "Soon's you up to it."

Sethe jingled the earrings for the pleasure of the crawling-already? girl, who reached for them over and over again.

In the Clearing, Sethe found Baby's old preaching rock and remembered the smell of leaves simmering in the sun, thunderous feet and the shouts that ripped pods off the limbs of the chestnuts. With Baby Suggs' heart in charge, the people let go.

Sethe had had twenty-eight days—the travel of one whole moon—of unslaved life. From the pure clear stream of spit that the little girl dribbled into her face to her oily blood was twenty-eight days. Days of healing, ease and real-talk. Days of company: knowing the names of forty, fifty other Negroes, their views, habits; where they had been and what done; of feeling their fun and sorrow along with her own, which made it better. One taught her the alphabet; another a stitch. All taught her how it felt to wake up at dawn and *decide* what to do with the day. That's how she got through the waiting for Halle. Bit by bit, at 124 and in the Clearing, along with the others, she had claimed herself. Freeing yourself was one thing; claiming ownership of that freed self was another.

Now she sat on Baby Suggs' rock, Denver and Beloved watching her from the trees. There will never be a day, she thought, when Halle will knock on the door. Not knowing it was hard; knowing it was harder.

Just the fingers, she thought. Just let me feel your fingers again on the back of my neck and I will lay it all down, make a way out of this no way. Sethe bowed her head and sure enough—they were there. Lighter now, no more than the strokes of bird feather, but unmistakably caressing fingers. She had to relax a bit to let them do their work, so light was the touch, childlike almost, more finger kiss than kneading. Still she was grateful for the effort; Baby Suggs' long-distance love was equal to any skin-close love she had known. The desire, let alone the gesture, to meet her needs was good enough to lift her spirits to the place where she could take the next step: ask for some clarifying word; some advice about how to keep on with a brain greedy for news nobody could live with in a world happy to provide it.

She knew Paul D was adding something to her life—something she wanted to count on but was scared to. Now he had added more: new pictures and old rememories that broke her heart. Into the empty space of not knowing about Halle—a space sometimes colored with righteous resentment at what could have been his cowardice, or stupidity or bad luck—that empty place of no definite news was filled now with a brand-new sorrow and who could tell how many more on the way. Years ago—when 124 was alive—she had women friends, men friends from all around to share grief with. Then there was no one, for they would not visit her while the baby ghost filled the house, and she returned their disapproval with the potent pride of the mistreated. But now there was someone to share it, and he had beat the spirit away the very day he entered her house and no sign of it since. A blessing, but in its place he brought another kind of haunting: Halle's face smeared with butter and the clabber too; his own mouth jammed full of iron, and Lord knows what else he could tell her if he wanted to.

The fingers touching the back of her neck were stronger now—the strokes bolder as though Baby Suggs were gathering strength. Putting the thumbs at the nape, while the fingers pressed the sides. Harder, harder, the fingers moved slowly around toward her windpipe, making little circles on the way. Sethe was actually more surprised than frightened to find that she was being strangled. Or so it seemed. In any case, Baby Suggs' fingers had a grip on her that would not let her breathe. Tumbling forward from her seat on the rock, she clawed at the hands that were not there. Her feet were thrashing by the time Denver got to her and then Beloved.

"Ma'am! Ma'am!" Denver shouted. "Ma'ammy!" and turned her mother over on her back.

The fingers left off and Sethe had to swallow huge draughts of air before she recognized her daughter's face next to her own and Beloved's hovering above.

"You all right?"

"Somebody choked me," said Sethe.

"Who?"

Sethe rubbed her neck and struggled to a sitting position. "Grandma Baby, I reckon. I just asked her to *rub* my neck, like she used to and she was doing fine and then just got crazy with it, I guess."

"She wouldn't do that to you, Ma'am. Grandma Baby? Uh uh."

"Help me up from here."

"Look." Beloved was pointing at Sethe's neck.

"What is it? What you see?" asked Sethe.

"Bruises," said Denver.

"On my neck?"

"Here," said Beloved. "Here and here, too." She reached out her hand and touched the splotches, gathering color darker than Sethe's dark throat, and her fingers were mighty cool.

"That don't help nothing," Denver said, but Beloved was leaning in, her two hands stroking the damp skin that felt like chamois and looked like taffeta.

Sethe moaned. The girl's fingers were so cool and knowing. Sethe's knotted, private, walk-on-water life gave in a bit, softened, and it seemed that the glimpse of happiness she caught in the shadows swinging hands on the road to the carnival was a likelihood—if she could just manage the news Paul D brought and the news he kept to himself. Just manage it. Not break, fall or cry each time a hateful picture drifted in front of her face. Not develop some permanent craziness like Baby Suggs' friend, a young woman in a bonnet whose food was full of tears. Like Aunt Phyllis, who slept with her eyes wide open. Like Jackson Till, who slept under the bed. All she wanted was to go on. As she had. Alone with her daughter in a haunted house she managed every damn thing. Why now, with Paul D instead of the ghost, was she breaking up? getting scared? needing Baby? The worst was over, wasn't it? She had already got through, hadn't she? With the ghost in 124 she could bear, do, solve anything. Now a hint of what had happened to Halle and she cut out like a rabbit looking for its mother.

Beloved's fingers were heavenly. Under them and breathing evenly again, the anguish rolled down. The peace Sethe had come there to find crept into her.

We must look a sight, she thought, and closed her eyes to see it: the three women in the middle of the Clearing, at the base of the rock where Baby Suggs, holy, had loved. One seated, yielding up her throat to the kind hands of one of the two kneeling before her.

Denver watched the faces of the other two. Beloved watched the work her thumbs were doing and must have loved what she saw because she leaned over and kissed the tenderness under Sethe's chin.

They stayed that way for a while because neither Denver nor Sethe knew how not to: how to stop and not love the look or feel of the lips that kept on kissing. Then Sethe, grabbing Beloved's hair and blinking rapidly, separated herself. She later believed that it was because the girl's breath was exactly like new milk that she said to her, stern and frowning, "You too old for that."

She looked at Denver, and seeing panic about to become something more, stood up quickly, breaking the tableau apart.

"Come on up! Up!" Sethe waved the girls to their feet. As they left the Clearing they looked pretty much the same as they had when they had come: Sethe in the lead, the girls a ways back. All silent as before, but with a difference. Sethe was bothered, not because of the kiss, but because, just before it, when she was feeling so fine letting Beloved massage away the pain, the fingers she was loving and the ones that had soothed her before they strangled her had reminded her of something that now slipped her mind. But one thing for sure, Baby Suggs had not choked her as first she thought. Denver was right, and walking in the dappled tree-light, clearer-headed now—away from the enchantment of the Clearing—Sethe remembered the touch of those fingers that she knew better than her own. They had bathed her in sections, wrapped her womb, combed her hair, oiled her nipples, stitched her clothes, cleaned her feet, greased her back and dropped just about anything they were doing to massage

Sethe's nape when, especially in the early days, her spirits fell down under the weight of the things she remembered and those she did not: schoolteacher writing in ink she herself had made while his nephews played on her; the face of the woman in a felt hat as she rose to stretch in the field. If she lay among all the hands in the world, she would know Baby Suggs' just as she did the good hands of the whitegirl looking for velvet. But for eighteen years she had lived in a house full of touches from the other side. And the thumbs that pressed her nape were the same. Maybe that was where it had gone to. After Paul D beat it out of 124, maybe it collected itself in the Clearing. Reasonable, she thought.

Why she had taken Denver and Beloved with her didn't puzzle her now—at the time it seemed impulse, with a vague wish for protection. And the girls had saved her, Beloved so agitated she behaved like a two-year-old.

Like a faint smell of burning that disappears when the fire is cut off or the window opened for a breeze, the suspicion that the girl's touch was also exactly like the baby's ghost dissipated. It was only a tiny disturbance anyway—not strong enough to divert her from the ambition welling in her now: she wanted Paul D. No matter what he told and knew, she wanted him in her life. More than commemorating Halle, that is what she had come to the Clearing to figure out, and now it *was* figured. Trust and rememory, yes, the way she believed it could be when he cradled her before the cooking stove. The weight and angle of him; the true-to-life beard hair on him; arched back, educated hands. His waiting eyes and awful human power. The mind of him that knew her own. Her story was bearable because it was his as well—to tell, to refine and tell again. The things neither knew about the other—the things neither had word-shapes for—well, it would come in time: where they led him off to sucking iron; the perfect death of her crawling-already? baby.

She wanted to get back—fast. Set these idle girls to some work that would fill their wandering heads. Rushing through the green corridor, cooler now because the sun had moved, it occurred to her that the two were alike as sisters. Their obedience and absolute reliability shot through with surprise. Sethe understood Denver. Solitude had made her secretive—self-manipulated. Years of haunting had dulled her in ways you wouldn't believe and sharpened her in ways you wouldn't believe either. The consequence was a timid but hard-headed daughter Sethe would die to protect. The other, Beloved, she knew less, nothing, about—except that there was nothing she wouldn't do for Sethe and that Denver and she liked each other's company. Now she thought she knew why. They spent up or held on to their feelings in harmonious ways. What one had to give the other was pleased to take. They hung back in the trees that ringed the Clearing, then rushed into it with screams and kisses when Sethe choked—anyhow that's how she explained it to herself for she noticed neither competition between the two nor domination by one. On her mind was the supper she wanted to fix for Paul D—something difficult to do, something she would do just so—to launch her newer, stronger life with a tender man. Those litty bitty potatoes browned on all sides, heavy on the pepper; snap beans seasoned with rind; yellow squash sprinkled with vinegar and sugar. Maybe corn cut from the cob and fried with green onions and butter. Raised bread, even.

Her mind, searching the kitchen before she got to it, was so full of her offering she did not see right away, in the space under the white stairs, the wooden tub and Paul D sitting in it. She smiled at him and he smiled back.

"Summer must be over," she said.

"Come on in here."

"Uh uh. Girls right behind me."

"I don't hear nobody."

"I have to cook, Paul D."

"Me too." He stood up and made her stay there while he held her in his arms. Her dress soaked up the water from his body. His jaw was near her ear. Her chin touched his shoulder.

"What you gonna cook?"

"I thought some snap beans."

"Oh, yeah."

"Fry up a little corn?"

"Yeah."

There was no question but that she could do it. Just like the day she arrived at 124—sure enough, she had milk enough for all.

Beloved came through the door and they ought to have heard her tread, but they didn't.

Breathing and murmuring, breathing and murmuring. Beloved heard them as soon as the door banged shut behind her. She jumped at the slam and swiveled her head toward the whispers coming from behind the white stairs. She took a step and felt like crying. She had been so close, then closer. And it was so much better than the anger that ruled when Sethe did or thought anything that excluded herself. She could bear the hours—nine or ten of them each day but one—when Sethe was gone. Bear even the nights when she was close but out of sight, behind walls and doors lying next to him. But now—even the daylight time that Beloved had counted on, disciplined herself to be content with, was being reduced, divided by Sethe's willingness to pay attention to other things. Him mostly. Him who said something to her that made her run out into the woods and talk to herself on a rock. Him who kept her hidden at night behind doors. And him who had hold of her now whispering behind the stairs after Beloved had rescued her neck and was ready now to put her hand in that woman's own.

Beloved turned around and left. Denver had not arrived, or else she was waiting somewhere outside. Beloved went to look, pausing to watch a cardinal hop from limb to branch. She followed the blood spot shifting in the leaves until she lost it and even then she walked on, backward, still hungry for another glimpse.

She turned finally and ran through the woods to the stream. Standing close to its edge she watched her reflection there. When Denver's face joined hers, they stared at each other in the water.

"You did it, I saw you," said Denver.

"What?"

"I saw your face. You made her choke."

"I didn't do it."

"You told me you loved her."

"I fixed it, didn't I? Didn't I fix her neck?"

"After. After you choked her neck."

"I kissed her neck. I didn't choke it. The circle of iron choked it."

"I saw you." Denver grabbed Beloved's arm.

"Look out, girl," said Beloved and, snatching her arm away, ran ahead as fast as she could along the stream that sang on the other side of the woods.

Left alone, Denver wondered if, indeed, she had been wrong. She and Beloved were standing in the trees whispering, while Sethe sat on the rock. Denver knew that the Clearing used to be where Baby Suggs preached, but that was when she was a baby. She had never been there herself to remember it. 124 and the field behind it were all the world she knew or wanted.

Once upon a time she had known more and wanted to.

Had walked the path leading to a real other house. Had stood outside the window listening. Four times she did it on her own—crept away from 124 early in the afternoon when her mother and grandmother had their guard down, just before supper, after chores; the blank hour before gears changed to evening occupations. Denver had walked off looking for the house other children visited but not her. When she found it she was too timid to go to the front door so she peeped in the window. Lady Jones sat in a straight-backed chair; several children sat cross-legged on the floor in front of her. Lady Jones had a book. The children had slates. Lady Jones was saying something too soft for Denver to hear. The children were saying it after her. Four times Denver went to look. The fifth time Lady Jones caught her and said, "Come in the front door, Miss Denver. This is not a side show."

So she had almost a whole year of the company of her peers and along with them learned to spell and count. She was seven, and those two hours in the afternoon were precious to her. Especially so because she had done it on her own and was pleased and surprised by the pleasure and surprise it created in her mother and her brothers. For a nickel a month, Lady Jones did what whitepeople thought unnecessary if not illegal: crowded her little parlor with the colored children who had time for and interest in book learning. The nickel, tied to a handkerchief knot, tied to her belt, that she carried to Lady Jones, thrilled her. The effort to handle chalk expertly and avoid the scream it would make; the capital *w*, the little *i*, the beauty of the letters in her name, the deeply mournful sentences from the Bible Lady Jones used as a textbook. Denver practiced every morning; starred every afternoon. She was so happy she didn't even know she was being avoided by her classmates—that they made excuses and altered their pace not to walk with her. It was Nelson Lord—the boy as smart as she was—who put a stop to it; who asked her the question about her mother that put chalk, the little *i* and all the rest that those afternoons held, out of reach forever. She should have laughed when he said it, or pushed him down, but there was no meanness in his face or his voice. Just curiosity. But the thing that leapt up in her when he asked it was a thing that had been lying there all along.

She never went back. The second day she didn't go, Sethe asked her why not. Denver didn't answer. She was too scared to ask her brothers or anyone else Nelson Lord's question because certain odd and terrifying feelings about her mother were collecting around the thing that leapt up inside her. Later on, after Baby Suggs died, she did not wonder why Howard and Buglar had run away. She did not agree with Sethe that they left because of the ghost. If so, what took them so long? They had lived with it as long as she had. But if Nelson Lord was right—no wonder they were sulky, staying away from home as much as they could.

Meanwhile the monstrous and unmanageable dreams about Sethe found release in the concentration Denver began to fix on the baby ghost. Before Nelson Lord, she had been barely interested in its antics. The patience of her mother and grandmother in its presence made her indifferent to it. Then it began to irritate her, wear her out with its mischief. That was when she walked off to follow the children to Lady Jones' house-school. Now it held for her all the anger, love and fear she didn't know what to do with. Even when she did muster the courage to ask Nelson Lord's question, she could not hear Sethe's answer, nor Baby Suggs' words, nor anything at all thereafter. For two years she walked in a silence too solid for penetration but which gave her eyes a power even she found hard to believe. The black nostrils of a sparrow sitting on a branch sixty feet above her head, for instance. For two years she heard nothing at all and then she heard close thunder crawling up the stairs. Baby Suggs thought it was Here Boy padding into places he never went. Sethe thought it was the India-rubber ball the boys played with bounding down the stairs.

"Is that damn dog lost his mind?" shouted Baby Suggs.

"He's on the porch," said Sethe. "See for yourself."

"Well, what's that I'm hearing then?"

Sethe slammed the stove lid. "Buglar! Buglar! I told you all not to use that ball in here." She looked at the white stairs and saw Denver at the top.

"She was trying to get upstairs."

"What?" The cloth she used to handle the stove lid was balled in Sethe's hand.

"The baby," said Denver. "Didn't you hear her crawling?"

What to jump on first was the problem: that Denver heard anything at all or that the crawling-already? baby girl was still at it but more so.

The return of Denver's hearing, cut off by an answer she could not bear to hear, cut on by the sound of her dead sister trying to climb the stairs, signaled another shift in the fortunes of the people of 124. From then on the presence was full of spite. Instead of sighs and accidents there was pointed and deliberate abuse. Buglar and Howard grew furious at the company of the women in the house, and spent in sullen reproach any time they had away from their odd work in town carrying water and feed at the stables. Until the spite became so personal it drove each off. Baby Suggs grew tired, went to bed and stayed there until her big old heart quit. Except for an occasional request for color she said practically nothing—until the afternoon of the last day of her life when she got out of bed, skipped slowly to the door of the keeping room and announced to Sethe and Denver the lesson she had learned from her sixty years a slave and ten years free: that there was no bad luck in the world but whitepeople. "They don't know when to stop," she said, and returned to her bed, pulled up the quilt and left them to hold that thought forever.

Shortly afterward Sethe and Denver tried to call up and reason with the baby ghost, but got nowhere. It took a man, Paul D, to shout it off, beat it off and take its place for himself. And carnival or no carnival, Denver preferred the venomous baby to him any day. During the first days after Paul D moved in, Denver stayed in her emerald closet as long as she could, lonely as a mountain and almost as big, thinking everybody had somebody but her; thinking even a ghost's company was denied her. So when she saw the black dress with two unlaced shoes beneath it she trembled with secret thanks. Whatever her power and however she used it, Beloved was *hers*. Denver was alarmed by the harm she thought Beloved planned for Sethe, but felt helpless to thwart it, so unrestricted was her need to love another. The display she witnessed at the Clearing shamed her because the choice between Sethe and Beloved was without conflict.

Walking toward the stream, beyond her green bush house, she let herself wonder what if Beloved really decided to choke her mother. Would she let it happen? Murder, Nelson Lord had said. "Didn't your mother get locked away for murder? Wasn't you in there with her when she went?"

It was the second question that made it impossible for so long to ask Sethe about the first. The thing that leapt up had been coiled in just such a place: a darkness, a stone, and some other thing that moved by itself. She went deaf rather than hear the answer, and like the little four o'clocks that searched openly for sunlight, then closed themselves tightly when it left, Denver kept watch for the baby and withdrew from everything else. Until Paul D came. But the damage he did came undone with the miraculous resurrection of Beloved.

Just ahead, at the edge of the stream, Denver could see her silhouette, standing barefoot in the water, lifting her black skirts up above her calves, the beautiful head lowered in rapt attention.

Blinking fresh tears Denver approached her—eager for a word, a sign of forgiveness.

Denver took off her shoes and stepped into the water with her. It took a moment for her to drag her eyes from the spectacle of Beloved's head to see what she was staring at.

A turtle inched along the edge, turned and climbed to dry ground. Not far behind it was another one, headed in the same direction. Four placed plates under a hovering motionless bowl. Behind her in the grass the other one moving quickly, quickly to mount her. The impregnable strength of him—earthing his feet near her shoulders. The embracing necks—hers stretching up toward his bending down, the pat pat pat of their touching heads. No height was beyond her yearning neck, stretched like a finger toward his, risking everything outside the bowl just to touch his face. The gravity of their shields, clashing, countered and mocked the floating heads touching.

Beloved dropped the folds of her skirt. It spread around her. The hem darkened in the water.

OUT OF SIGHT of Mister's sight, away, praise His name, from the smiling boss of roosters, Paul D began to tremble. Not all at once and not so anyone could tell. When he turned his head, aiming for a last look at Brother, turned it as much as the rope that connected his neck to the axle of a buckboard allowed, and, later on, when they fastened the iron around his ankles and clamped the wrists as well, there was no outward sign of trembling at all. Nor eighteen days after that when he saw the ditches; the one thousand feet of earth—five feet deep, five feet wide, into which wooden boxes had been fitted. A door of bars that you could lift on hinges like a cage opened into three walls and a roof of scrap lumber and red dirt. Two feet of it over his head; three feet of open trench in front of him with anything that crawled or scurried welcome to share that grave calling itself quarters. And there were forty-five more. He was sent there after trying to kill Brandywine, the man schoolteacher sold him to. Brandywine was leading him, in a coffle with ten others, through Kentucky into Virginia. He didn't know exactly what prompted him to try—other than Halle, Sixo, Paul A, Paul F and Mister. But the trembling was fixed by the time he knew it was there.

Still no one else knew it, because it began inside. A flutter of a kind, in the chest, then the shoulder blades. It felt like rippling—gentle at first and then wild. As though the further south they led him the more his blood, frozen like an ice pond for twenty years, began thawing, breaking into pieces that, once melted, had no choice but to swirl and eddy. Sometimes it was in his leg. Then again it moved to the base of his spine. By the time they unhitched him from the wagon and he saw nothing but dogs and two shacks in a world of sizzling grass, the roiling blood was shaking him to and fro. But no one could tell. The wrists he held out for the bracelets that evening were steady as were the legs he stood on when chains were attached to the leg irons. But when they shoved him into the box and dropped the cage door down, his hands quit taking instruction. On their own, they traveled. Nothing could stop them or get their attention. They would not hold his penis to urinate or a spoon to scoop lumps of lima beans into his mouth. The miracle of their obedience came with the hammer at dawn.

All forty-six men woke to rifle shot. All forty-six. Three whitemen walked along the trench unlocking the doors one by one. No one stepped through. When the last lock was opened, the three returned and lifted the bars, one by one. And one by one the blackmen emerged—promptly and without the poke of a rifle butt if they had been there more than a day; promptly with the butt if, like Paul D, they had just arrived. When all forty-six were standing in a line in the trench, another rifle shot signaled the climb out and up to the ground above, where one thousand feet of the best hand-forged chain in Georgia stretched. Each man bent and waited. The first man picked up the end and threaded it through the loop on his leg iron. He stood up then, and, shuffling a little, brought the chain tip to the next prisoner, who did likewise. As the chain was passed on and each man stood in the other's place, the line of men turned around, facing the boxes they had come out of. Not one spoke to the other. At least not with words. The eyes had to tell what there was to tell: "Help me this mornin; 's bad"; "I'm a make it"; "New man"; "Steady now steady."

Chain-up completed, they knelt down. The dew, more likely than not, was mist by then. Heavy sometimes and if the dogs were quiet and just breathing you could hear doves. Kneeling in the mist they waited for the whim of a guard, or two, or three. Or maybe all of them wanted it. Wanted it from one prisoner in particular or none—or all.

"Breakfast? Want some breakfast, nigger?"

"Yes, sir."

"Hungry, nigger?"

"Yes, sir."

"Here you go."

Occasionally a kneeling man chose gunshot in his head as the price, maybe, of taking a bit of foreskin with him to Jesus. Paul D did not know that then. He was looking at his palsied hands, smelling the guard, listening to his soft grunts so like the doves', as he stood before the man kneeling in mist on his right. Convinced he was next, Paul D retched—vomiting up nothing at all. An observing guard smashed his shoulder with the rifle and the engaged one decided to skip the new man for the time being lest his pants and shoes got soiled by nigger puke.

"Hiiii!"

It was the first sound, other than "Yes, sir," a black man was allowed to speak each morning, and the lead chain gave it everything he had. "Hiiii!" It was never clear to Paul D how he knew when to shout that mercy. They called him Hi Man and Paul D thought at first the guards told him when to give the signal that let the prisoners rise up off their knees and dance two-step to the music of hand-forged iron. Later he doubted it. He believed to this day that the "Hiiii!" at dawn and the "Hoooo!" when evening came were the responsibility Hi Man assumed because he alone knew what was enough, what was too much, when things were over, when the time had come.

They chain-danced over the fields, through the woods to a trail that ended in the astonishing beauty of feldspar, and there Paul D's hands disobeyed the furious rippling of his blood and paid attention. With a sledge hammer in his hands and Hi Man's lead, the men got through. They sang it out and beat it up, garbling the words so they could not be understood; tricking the words so their syllables yielded up other meanings. They sang the women they knew; the children they had been; the animals they had tamed themselves or seen others tame. They sang of bosses and masters and misses; of mules and dogs and the shamelessness of life. They sang lovingly of graveyards and sisters long gone. Of pork in the woods; meal in the pan; fish on the line; cane, rain and rocking chairs.

And they beat. The women for having known them and no more, no more; the children for having been them but never again. They killed a boss so often and so completely they had to bring him back to life to pulp him one more time. Tasting hot mealcake among pine trees, they beat it away. Singing love songs to Mr. Death, they smashed his head. More than the rest, they killed the flirt whom folks called Life for leading them on. Making them think the next sunrise would be worth it; that another stroke of time would do it at last. Only when she was dead would they be safe. The successful ones—the ones who had been there enough years to have maimed, mutilated, maybe even buried her—kept watch over the others who were still in her cock-teasing hug, caring and looking forward, remembering and looking back. They were the ones whose eyes said, "Help me, 's bad"; or "Look out," meaning *this might be the day I bay or eat my own mess or run,* and it was this last that had to be guarded against, for if one pitched and ran—all, all forty-six, would be yanked by the chain that bound them and no telling who or how many would be killed. A man could risk his own life, but not his brother's. So the eyes said, "Steady now," and "Hang by me."

Eighty-six days and done. Life was dead. Paul D beat her butt all day every day till there was not a whimper in her. Eighty-six days and his hands were still, waiting serenely each rat-rustling night for "Hiiii!" at dawn and the eager clench on the hammer's shaft. Life rolled over dead. Or so he thought.

It rained.

Snakes came down from short-leaf pine and hemlock.

It rained.

Cypress, yellow poplar, ash and palmetto drooped under five days of rain without wind. By the eighth day the doves were nowhere in sight, by the ninth even the salamanders were gone. Dogs laid their ears down and stared over their paws. The men could not work. Chain-up was slow, breakfast abandoned, the two-step became a slow drag over soupy grass and unreliable earth.

It was decided to lock everybody down in the boxes till it either stopped or lightened up so a whiteman could walk, damnit, without flooding his gun and the dogs could quit shivering. The chain was threaded through forty-six loops of the best hand-forged iron in Georgia.

It rained.

In the boxes the men heard the water rise in the trench and looked out for cottonmouths. They squatted in muddy water, slept above it, peed in it. Paul D thought he was screaming; his mouth was open and there was this loud throat-splitting sound—but it may have been somebody else. Then he thought he was crying. Something was running down his cheeks. He lifted his hands to wipe away the tears and saw dark brown slime. Above him rivulets of mud slid through the boards of the roof. When it come down, he thought, gonna crush me like a tick bug. It happened so quick he had no time to ponder. Somebody yanked the chain—once—hard enough to cross his legs and throw him into the mud. He never figured out how he knew—how anybody did—but he did know—he did—and he took both hands and yanked the length of chain at his left, so the next man would know too. The water was above his ankles, flowing over the wooden plank he slept on. And then it wasn't water anymore. The ditch was caving in and mud oozed under and through the bars.

They waited—each and every one of the forty-six. Not screaming, although some of them must have fought like the devil not to. The mud was up to his thighs and he held on to the bars. Then it came—another yank—from the left this time and less forceful than the first because of the mud it passed through.

It started like the chain-up but the difference was the power of the chain. One by one, from Hi Man back on down the line, they dove. Down through the mud under the bars, blind, groping. Some had sense enough to wrap their heads in their shirts, cover their faces with rags, put on their shoes. Others just plunged, simply ducked down and pushed out, fighting up, reaching for air. Some lost direction and their neighbors, feeling the confused pull of the chain, snatched them around. For one lost, all lost. The chain that held them would save all or none, and Hi Man was the Delivery. They talked through that chain like Sam Morse and, Great God, they all came up. Like the unshriven dead, zombies on the loose, holding the chains in their hands, they trusted the rain and the dark, yes, but mostly Hi Man and each other.

Past the sheds where the dogs lay in deep depression; past the two guard shacks, past the stable of sleeping horses, past the hens whose bills were bolted into their feathers, they waded. The moon did not help because it wasn't there. The field was a marsh, the track a trough. All Georgia seemed to be sliding, melting away. Moss wiped their faces as they fought the live-oak branches that blocked their way. Georgia took up all of Alabama and Mississippi then, so there was no state line to cross and it wouldn't have mattered anyway. If they had known about it, they would have avoided not only Alfred and the beautiful feldspar, but Savannah too and headed for the Sea Islands on the river that slid down from the Blue Ridge Mountains. But they didn't know.

Daylight came and they huddled in a copse of redbud trees. Night came and they scrambled up to higher ground, praying the rain would go on shielding them and keeping folks at home. They were hoping for a shack, solitary, some distance from its big house, where a slave might be making rope or heating potatoes at the grate. What they found was a camp of sick Cherokee for whom a rose was named.

Decimated but stubborn, they were among those who chose a fugitive life rather than Oklahoma. The illness that swept them now was reminiscent of the one that had killed half their number two hundred years earlier. In between that calamity and this, they had visited George III in London, published a newspaper, made baskets, led Oglethorpe through forests, helped Andrew Jackson fight Creek, cooked maize, drawn up a constitution, petitioned the King of Spain, been experimented on by Dartmouth, established asylums, wrote their language, resisted settlers, shot bear and translated scripture. All to no avail. The forced move to the Arkansas River, insisted upon by the same president they fought for against the Creek, destroyed another quarter of their already shattered number.

That was it, they thought, and removed themselves from those Cherokee who signed the treaty, in order to retire into the forest and await the end of the world. The disease they suffered now was a mere inconvenience compared to the devastation they remembered. Still, they protected each other as best they could. The healthy were sent some miles away; the sick stayed behind with the dead—to survive or join them.

The prisoners from Alfred, Georgia, sat down in semicircle near the encampment. No one came and still they sat. Hours passed and the rain turned soft. Finally a woman stuck her head out of her house. Night came and nothing happened. At dawn two men with barnacles covering their beautiful skin approached them. No one spoke for a moment, then Hi Man raised his hand. The Cherokee saw the chains and went away. When they returned each carried a handful of small axes. Two children followed with a pot of mush cooling and thinning in the rain.

Buffalo men, they called them, and talked slowly to the prisoners scooping mush and tapping away at their chains. Nobody from a box in Alfred, Georgia, cared about the illness the Cherokee warned them about, so they stayed, all forty-six, resting, planning their next move. Paul D had no idea of what to do and knew less than anybody, it seemed. He heard his co-convicts talk knowledgeably of rivers and states, towns and territories. Heard Cherokee men describe the beginning of the world and its end. Listened to tales of other Buffalo men they knew—three of whom were in the healthy camp a few miles away. Hi Man wanted to join them; others wanted to join him. Some wanted to leave; some to stay on. Weeks later Paul D was the only Buffalo man left—without a plan. All he could think of was tracking dogs, although Hi Man said the rain they left in gave that no chance of success. Alone, the last man with buffalo hair among the ailing Cherokee, Paul D finally woke up and, admitting his ignorance, asked how he might get North. Free North. Magical North. Welcoming, benevolent North. The Cherokee smiled and looked around. The flood rains of a month ago had turned everything to steam and blossoms.

"That way," he said, pointing. "Follow the tree flowers,"

he said. "Only the tree flowers. As they go, you go. You will be where you want to be when they are gone."

So he raced from dogwood to blossoming peach. When they thinned out he headed for the cherry blossoms, then magnolia, chinaberry, pecan, walnut and prickly pear. At last he reached a field of apple trees whose flowers were just becoming tiny knots of fruit. Spring sauntered north, but he had to run like hell to keep it as his traveling companion. From February to July he was on the lookout for blossoms. When he lost them, and found himself without so much as a petal to guide him, he paused, climbed a tree on a hillock and scanned the horizon for a flash of pink or white in the leaf world that surrounded him. He did not touch them or stop to smell. He merely followed in their wake, a dark ragged figure guided by the blossoming plums.

The apple field turned out to be Delaware where the weaver lady lived. She snapped him up as soon as he finished the sausage she fed him and he crawled into her bed crying. She passed him off as her nephew from Syracuse simply by calling him that nephew's name. Eighteen months and he was looking out again for blossoms only this time he did the looking on a dray.

It was some time before he could put Alfred, Georgia, Sixo, schoolteacher, Halle, his brothers, Sethe, Mister, the taste of iron, the sight of butter, the smell of hickory, notebook paper, one by one, into the tobacco tin lodged in his chest. By the time he got to 124 nothing in this world could pry it open.

SHE MOVED HIM.

Not the way he had beat off the baby's ghost—all bang and shriek with windows smashed and jelly jars rolled in a heap. But she moved him nonetheless, and Paul D didn't know how to stop it because it looked like he was moving himself. Imperceptibly, downright reasonably, he was moving out of 124.

The beginning was so simple. One day, after supper, he sat in the rocker by the stove, bone-tired, river-whipped, and fell asleep. He woke to the footsteps of Sethe coming down the white stairs to make breakfast.

"I thought you went out somewhere," she said.

Paul D moaned, surprised to find himself exactly where he was the last time he looked.

"Don't tell me I slept in this chair the whole night."

Sethe laughed. "Me? I won't say a word to you."

"Why didn't you rouse me?"

"I did. Called you two or three times. I gave it up around midnight and then I thought you went out somewhere."

He stood, expecting his back to fight it. But it didn't. Not a creak or a stiff joint anywhere. In fact he felt refreshed. Some things are like that, he thought, good-sleep places. The base of certain trees here and there; a wharf, a bench, a rowboat once, a haystack usually, not always bed, and here, now, a rocking chair, which was strange because in his experience furniture was the worst place for a good-sleep sleep.

The next evening he did it again and then again. He was accustomed to sex with Sethe just about every day, and to avoid the confusion Beloved's shining caused him he still made it his business to take her back upstairs in the morning, or lie down with her after supper. But he found a way and a reason to spend the longest part of the night in the rocker. He told himself it must be his back—something supportive it needed for a weakness left over from sleeping in a box in Georgia.

It went on that way and might have stayed that way but one evening, after supper, after Sethe, he came downstairs, sat in the rocker and didn't want to be there. He stood up and realized he didn't want to go upstairs either. Irritable and longing for rest, he opened the door to Baby Suggs' room and dropped off to sleep on the bed the old lady died in. That settled it—so it seemed. It became his room and Sethe didn't object—her bed made for two had been occupied by one for eighteen years before Paul D came to call. And maybe it was better this way, with young girls in the house and him not being her true-to-life husband. In any case, since there was no reduction in his before-breakfast or after-supper appetites, he never heard her complain.

It went on that way and might have stayed that way, except one evening, after supper, after Sethe, he came downstairs and lay on Baby Suggs' bed and didn't want to be there.

He believed he was having house-fits, the glassy anger men sometimes feel when a woman's house begins to bind them, when they want to yell and break something or at least run off. He knew all about that—felt it lots of times—in the Delaware weaver's house, for instance. But always he associated the house-fit with the woman in it. This nervousness had nothing to do with the woman, whom he loved a little bit more every day: her hands among vegetables, her mouth when she licked a thread end before guiding it through a needle or bit it in two when the seam was done, the blood in her eye when she defended her girls (and Beloved was hers now) or any coloredwoman from a slur. Also in this house-fit there was no anger, no suffocation, no yearning to be elsewhere. He just could not, would not, sleep upstairs or in the rocker or, now, in Baby Suggs' bed. So he went to the storeroom.

It went on that way and might have stayed that way except one evening, after supper, after Sethe, he lay on a pallet in the storeroom and didn't want to be there. Then it was the cold house and it was out there, separated from the main part of 124, curled on top of two croaker sacks full of sweet potatoes, staring at the sides of a lard can, that he realized the moving was involuntary. He wasn't being nervous; he was being prevented.

So he waited. Visited Sethe in the morning; slept in the cold room at night and waited.

She came, and he wanted to knock her down.

In Ohio seasons are theatrical. Each one enters like a prima donna, convinced its performance is the reason the world has people in it. When Paul D had been forced out of 124 into a shed behind it, summer had been hooted offstage and autumn with its bottles of blood and gold had everybody's attention. Even at night, when there should have been a restful intermission, there was none because the voices of a dying landscape were insistent and loud. Paul D packed newspaper under himself and over, to give his thin blanket some help. But the chilly night was not on his mind. When he heard the door open behind him he refused to turn and look.

"What you want in here? What you want?" He should have been able to hear her breathing.

"I want you to touch me on the inside part and call me my name."

Paul D never worried about his little tobacco tin anymore. It was rusted shut. So, while she hoisted her skirts and turned her head over her shoulder the way the turtles had, he just looked at the lard can, silvery in moonlight, and spoke quietly.

"When good people take you in and treat you good, you ought to try to be good back. You don't . . . Sethe loves you. Much as her own daughter. You know that."

Beloved dropped her skirts as he spoke and looked at him with empty eyes. She took a step he could not hear and stood close behind him.

"She don't love me like I love her. I don't love nobody but her."

"Then what you come in here for?"

"I want you to touch me on the inside part."

"Go on back in that house and get to bed."

"You have to touch me. On the inside part. And you have to call me my name."

As long as his eyes were locked on the silver of the lard can he was safe. If he trembled like Lot's wife and felt some womanish need to see the nature of the sin behind him; feel a sympathy, perhaps, for the cursing cursed, or want to hold it in his arms out of respect for the connection between them, he too would be lost.

"Call me my name."

"No."

"Please call it. I'll go if you call it."

"Beloved." He said it, but she did not go. She moved closer with a footfall he didn't hear and he didn't hear the whisper that the flakes of rust made either as they fell away from the seams of his tobacco tin. So when the lid gave he didn't know it. What he knew was that when he reached the inside part he was saying, "Red heart. Red heart," over and over again. Softly and then so loud it woke Denver, then Paul D himself. "Red heart. Red heart. Red heart."

TO GO BACK to the original hunger was impossible. Luckily for Denver, looking was food enough to last. But to be looked at in turn was beyond appetite; it was breaking through her own skin to a place where hunger hadn't been discovered. It didn't have to happen often, because Beloved seldom looked right at her, or when she did, Denver could tell that her own face was just the place those eyes stopped while the mind behind it walked on. But sometimes—at moments Denver could neither anticipate nor create—Beloved rested cheek on knuckles and looked at Denver with attention.

It was lovely. Not to be stared at, not seen, but being pulled into view by the interested, uncritical eyes of the other. Having her hair examined as a part of her self, not as material or a style. Having her lips, nose, chin caressed as they might be if she were a moss rose a gardener paused to admire. Denver's skin dissolved under that gaze and became soft and bright like the lisle dress that had its arm around her mother's waist. She floated near but outside her own body, feeling vague and intense at the same time. Needing nothing. Being what there was.

At such times it seemed to be Beloved who needed something—wanted something. Deep down in her wide black eyes, back behind the expressionlessness, was a palm held out for a penny which Denver would gladly give her, if only she knew how or knew enough about her, a knowledge not to be had by the answers to the questions Sethe occasionally put to her: "You disremember everything? I never knew my mother neither, but I saw her a couple of times. Did you never see yours? What kind of whites was they? You don't remember none?"

Beloved, scratching the back of her hand, would say she remembered a woman who was hers, and she remembered being snatched away from her. Other than that, the clearest memory she had, the one she repeated, was the bridge—standing on the bridge looking down. And she knew one whiteman.

Sethe found that remarkable and more evidence to support her conclusions, which she confided to Denver.

"Where'd you get the dress, them shoes?"

Beloved said she took them.

"Who from?"

Silence and a faster scratching of her hand. She didn't know; she saw them and just took them.

"Uh huh," said Sethe, and told Denver that she believed Beloved had been locked up by some whiteman for his own purposes, and never let out the door. That she must have escaped to a bridge or someplace and rinsed the rest out of her mind. Something like that had happened to Ella except it was two men—a father and son—and Ella remembered every bit of it. For more than a year, they kept her locked in a room for themselves.

"You couldn't think up," Ella had said, "what them two done to me."

Sethe thought it explained Beloved's behavior around Paul D, whom she hated so.

Denver neither believed nor commented on Sethe's speculations, and she lowered her eyes and never said a word about the cold house. She was certain that Beloved was the white dress that had knelt with her mother in the keeping room, the true-to-life presence of the baby that had kept her company most of her life. And to be looked at by her, however briefly, kept her grateful for the rest of the time when she was merely the looker. Besides, she had her own set of questions which had nothing to do with the past. The present alone interested Denver, but she was careful to appear uninquisitive about the things she was dying to ask Beloved, for if she pressed too hard, she might lose the penny that the held-out palm wanted, and lose, therefore, the place beyond appetite. It was better to feast, to have permission to be the looker, because the old hunger—the before-Beloved hunger that drove her into boxwood and cologne for just a taste of a life, to feel it bumpy and not flat—was out of the question. Looking kept it at bay.

So she did not ask Beloved how she knew about the earrings, the night walks to the cold house or the tip of the thing she saw when Beloved lay down or came undone in her sleep. The look, when it came, came when Denver had been careful, had explained things, or participated in things, or told stories to keep her occupied when Sethe was at the restaurant. No given chore was enough to put out the licking fire that seemed always to burn in her. Not when they wrung out sheets so tight the rinse water ran back up their arms. Not when they shoveled snow from the path to the outhouse. Or broke three inches of ice from the rain barrel; scoured and boiled last summer's canning jars, packed mud in the cracks of the hen house and warmed the chicks with their skirts. All the while Denver was obliged to talk about what they were doing—the how and why of it. About people Denver knew once or had seen, giving them more life than life had: the sweet-smelling whitewoman who brought her oranges and cologne and good wool skirts; Lady Jones who taught them songs to spell and count by; a beautiful boy as smart as she was with a birthmark like a nickel on his cheek. A white preacher who prayed for their souls while Sethe peeled potatoes and Grandma Baby sucked air. And she told her about Howard and Buglar: the parts of the bed that belonged to each (the top reserved for herself); that before she transferred to Baby Suggs' bed she never knew them to sleep without holding hands. She described them to Beloved slowly, to keep her attention, dwelling on their habits, the games they taught her and not the fright that drove them increasingly out of the house—anywhere—and finally far away.

This day they are outside. It's cold and the snow is hard as packed dirt. Denver has finished singing the counting song Lady Jones taught her students. Beloved is holding her arms steady while Denver unclasps frozen underwear and towels from the line. One by one she lays them in Beloved's arms until the pile, like a huge deck of cards, reaches her chin. The rest, aprons and brown stockings, Denver carries herself. Made giddy by the cold, they return to the house. The clothes will thaw slowly to a dampness perfect for the pressing iron, which will make them smell like hot rain. Dancing around the room with Sethe's apron, Beloved wants to know if there are flowers in the dark. Denver adds sticks to the stovefire and assures her there are. Twirling, her face framed by the neckband, her waist in the apron strings' embrace, she says she is thirsty.

Denver suggests warming up some cider, while her mind races to something she might do or say to interest and entertain the dancer. Denver is a strategist now and has to keep Beloved by her side from the minute Sethe leaves for work until the hour of her return when Beloved begins to hover at the window, then work her way out the door, down the steps and near the road. Plotting has changed Denver markedly. Where she was once indolent, resentful of every task, now she is spry, executing, even extending the assignments Sethe leaves for them. All to be able to say "We got to" and "Ma'am said for us to." Otherwise Beloved gets private and dreamy, or quiet and sullen, and Denver's chances of being looked at by her go down to nothing. She has no control over the evenings. When her mother is anywhere around, Beloved has eyes only for Sethe. At night, in bed, anything might happen. She might want to be told a story in the dark when Denver can't see her. Or she might get up and go into the cold house where Paul D has begun to sleep. Or she might cry, silently. She might even sleep like a brick, her breath sugary from fingerfuls of molasses or sand-cookie crumbs. Denver will turn toward her then, and if Beloved faces her, she will inhale deeply the sweet air from her mouth. If not, she will have to lean up and over her, every once in a while, to catch a sniff. For anything is better than the original hunger—the time when, after a year of the wonderful little *i,* sentences rolling out like pie dough and the company of other children, there was no sound coming through. Anything is better than the silence when she answered to hands gesturing and was indifferent to the movement of lips. When she saw every little thing and colors leaped smoldering into view. She will forgo the most violent of sunsets, stars as fat as dinner plates and all the blood of autumn and settle for the palest yellow if it comes from her Beloved.

The cider jug is heavy, but it always is, even when empty. Denver can carry it easily, yet she asks Beloved to help her. It is in the cold house next to the molasses and six pounds of cheddar hard as bone. A pallet is in the middle of the floor covered with newspaper and a blanket at the foot. It has been slept on for almost a month, even though snow has come and, with it, serious winter.

It is noon, quite light outside; inside it is not. A few cuts of sun break through the roof and walls but once there they are too weak to shift for themselves. Darkness is stronger and swallows them like minnows.

The door bangs shut. Denver can't tell where Beloved is standing.

"Where are you?" she whispers in a laughing sort of way.

"Here," says Beloved.

"Where?"

"Come find me," says Beloved.

Denver stretches out her right arm and takes a step or two. She trips and falls down onto the pallet. Newspaper crackles under her weight. She laughs again. "Oh, shoot. Beloved?"

No one answers. Denver waves her arms and squinches her eyes to separate the shadows of potato sacks, a lard can and a side of smoked pork from the one that might be human.

"Stop fooling," she says and looks up toward the light to check and make sure this is still the cold house and not something going on in her sleep. The minnows of light still swim there; they can't make it down to where she is.

"You the one thirsty. You want cider or don't you?" Denver's voice is mildly accusatory. Mildly. She doesn't want to offend and she doesn't want to betray the panic that is creeping over her like hairs. There is no sight or sound of Beloved. Denver struggles to her feet amid the crackling newspaper. Holding her palm out, she moves slowly toward the door. There is no latch or knob—just a loop of wire to catch a nail. She pushes the door open. Cold sunlight displaces the dark. The room is just as it was when they entered—except Beloved is not there. There is no point in looking further, for everything in the place can be seen at first sight. Denver looks anyway because the loss is ungovernable. She steps back into the shed, allowing the door to close quickly behind her. Darkness or not, she moves rapidly around, reaching, touching cobwebs, cheese, slanting shelves, the pallet interfering with each step. If she stumbles, she is not aware of it because she does not know where her body stops, which part of her is an arm, a foot or a knee. She feels like an ice cake torn away from the solid surface of the stream, floating on darkness, thick and crashing against the edges of things around it. Breakable, meltable and cold.

It is hard to breathe and even if there were light she wouldn't be able to see anything because she is crying. Just as she thought it might happen, it has. Easy as walking into a room. A magical appearance on a stump, the face wiped out by sunlight, and a magical disappearance in a shed, eaten alive by the dark.

"Don't," she is saying between tough swallows. "Don't. Don't go back."

This is worse than when Paul D came to 124 and she cried helplessly into the stove. This is worse. Then it was for herself. Now she is crying because she has no self. Death is a skipped meal compared to this. She can feel her thickness thinning, dissolving into nothing. She grabs the hair at her temples to get enough to uproot it and halt the melting for a while. Teeth clamped shut, Denver brakes her sobs. She doesn't move to open the door because there is no world out there. She decides to stay in the cold house and let the dark swallow her like the minnows of light above. She won't put up with another leaving, another trick. Waking up to find one brother then another not at the bottom of the bed, his foot jabbing her spine. Sitting at the table eating turnips and saving the liquor for her grandmother to drink; her mother's hand on the keeping-room door and her voice saying, "Baby Suggs is gone, Denver." And when she got around to worrying about what would be the case if Sethe died or Paul D took her away, a dream-come-true comes true just to leave her on a pile of newspaper in the dark.

No footfall announces her, but there she is, standing where before there was nobody when Denver looked. And smiling.

Denver grabs the hem of Beloved's skirt. "I thought you left me. I thought you went back."

Beloved smiles, "I don't want that place. This the place I am." She sits down on the pallet and, laughing, lies back looking at the cracklights above.

Surreptitiously, Denver pinches a piece of Beloved's skirt between her fingers and holds on. A good thing she does because suddenly Beloved sits up.

"What is it?" asks Denver.

"Look," she points to the sunlit cracks.

"What? I don't see nothing." Denver follows the pointing finger.

Beloved drops her hand. "I'm like this."

Denver watches as Beloved bends over, curls up and rocks. Her eyes go to no place; her moaning is so small Denver can hardly hear it.

"You all right? Beloved?"

Beloved focuses her eyes. "Over there. Her face."

Denver looks where Beloved's eyes go; there is nothing but darkness there.

"Whose face? Who is it?"

"Me. It's me."

She is smiling again.

THE LAST of the Sweet Home men, so named and called by one who would know, believed it. The other four believed it too, once, but they were long gone. The sold one never returned, the lost one never found. One, he knew, was dead for sure; one he hoped was, because butter and clabber was no life or reason to live it. He grew up thinking that, of all the Blacks in Kentucky, only the five of them were men. Allowed, encouraged to correct Garner, even defy him. To invent ways of doing things; to see what was needed and attack it without permission. To buy a mother, choose a horse or a wife, handle guns, even learn reading if they wanted to—but they didn't want to since nothing important to them could be put down on paper.

Was that it? Is that where the manhood lay? In the naming done by a whiteman who was supposed to know? Who gave them the privilege not of working but of deciding how to? No. In their relationship with Garner was true metal: they were believed and trusted, but most of all they were listened to.

He thought what they said had merit, and what they felt was serious. Deferring to his slaves' opinions did not deprive him of authority or power. It was schoolteacher who taught them otherwise. A truth that waved like a scarecrow in rye: they were only Sweet Home men at Sweet Home. One step off that ground and they were trespassers among the human race. Watchdogs without teeth; steer bulls without horns; gelded workhorses whose neigh and whinny could not be translated into a language responsible humans spoke. His strength had lain in knowing that schoolteacher was wrong. Now he wondered. There was Alfred, Georgia, there was Delaware, there was Sixo and still he wondered. If schoolteacher was right it explained how he had come to be a rag doll—picked up and put back down anywhere any time by a girl young enough to be his daughter. Fucking her when he was convinced he didn't want to. Whenever she turned her behind up, the calves of his youth (was that it?) cracked his resolve. But it was more than appetite that humiliated him and made him wonder if schoolteacher was right. It was being moved, placed where she wanted him, and there was nothing he was able to do about it. For his life he could not walk up the glistening white stairs in the evening; for his life he could not stay in the kitchen, in the keeping room, in the storeroom at night. And he tried. Held his breath the way he had when he ducked into the mud; steeled his heart the way he had when the trembling began. But it was worse than that, worse than the blood eddy he had controlled with a sledge hammer. When he stood up from the supper table at 124 and turned toward the stairs, nausea was first, then repulsion. He, he. He who had eaten raw meat barely dead, who under plum trees bursting with blossoms had crunched through a dove's breast before its heart stopped beating. Because he was a man and a man could do what he would: be still for six hours in a dry well while night dropped; fight raccoon with his hands and win; watch another man, whom he loved better than his brothers, roast without a tear just so the roasters would know what a man was like. And it was he, *that* man, who had walked from Georgia to Delaware, who could not go or stay put where he wanted to in 124—shame.

Paul D could not command his feet, but he thought he could still talk and he made up his mind to break out that way. He would tell Sethe about the last three weeks: catch her alone coming from work at the beer garden she called a restaurant and tell it all.

He waited for her. The winter afternoon looked like dusk as he stood in the alley behind Sawyer's Restaurant. Rehearsing, imagining her face and letting the words flock in his head like kids before lining up to follow the leader.

"Well, ah, this is not the, a man can't, see, but aw listen here, it ain't that, it really ain't, Ole Garner, what I mean is, it ain't a weakness, the kind of weakness I can fight 'cause 'cause something is happening to me, that girl is doing it, I know you think I never liked her nohow, but she is doing it to me. Fixing me. Sethe, she's fixed me and I can't break it."

What? A grown man fixed by a girl? But what if the girl was not a girl, but something in disguise? A lowdown something that looked like a sweet young girl and fucking her or not was not the point, it was not being able to stay or go where he wished in 124, and the danger was in losing Sethe because he was not man enough to break out, so he needed her, Sethe, to help him, to know about it, and it shamed him to have to ask the woman he wanted to protect to help him do it, God damn it to hell.

Paul D blew warm breath into the hollow of his cupped hands. The wind raced down the alley so fast it sleeked the fur of four kitchen dogs waiting for scraps. He looked at the dogs. The dogs looked at him.

Finally the back door opened and Sethe stepped through holding a scrap pan in the crook of her arm. When she saw him, she said Oh, and her smile was both pleasure and surprise.

Paul D believed he smiled back but his face was so cold he wasn't sure.

"Man, you make me feel like a girl, coming by to pick me up after work. Nobody ever did that before. You better watch out, I might start looking forward to it." She tossed the largest bones into the dirt rapidly so the dogs would know there was enough and not fight each other. Then she dumped the skins of some things, heads of other things and the insides of still more things—what the restaurant could not use and she would not—in a smoking pile near the animals' feet.

"Got to rinse this out," she said, "and then I'll be right with you."

He nodded as she returned to the kitchen.

The dogs ate without sound and Paul D thought they at least got what they came for, and if she had enough for them—

The cloth on her head was brown wool and she edged it down over her hairline against the wind.

"You get off early or what?"

"I took off early."

"Anything the matter?"

"In a way of speaking," he said and wiped his lips.

"Not cut back?"

"No, no. They got plenty work. I just—"

"Hm?"

"Sethe, you won't like what I'm 'bout to say."

She stopped then and turned her face toward him and the hateful wind. Another woman would have squinted or at least teared if the wind whipped her face as it did Sethe's. Another woman might have shot him a look of apprehension, pleading, anger even, because what he said sure sounded like part one of Goodbye, I'm gone.

Sethe looked at him steadily, calmly, already ready to accept, release or excuse an in-need-or-trouble man. Agreeing, saying okay, all right, in advance, because she didn't believe any of them—over the long haul—could measure up. And whatever the reason, it was all right. No fault. Nobody's fault.

He knew what she was thinking and even though she was wrong—he was not leaving her, wouldn't ever—the thing he had in mind to tell her was going to be worse. So, when he saw the diminished expectation in her eyes, the melancholy without blame, he could not say it. He could not say to this woman who did not squint in the wind, "I am not a man."

"Well, say it, Paul D, whether I like it or not."

Since he could not say what he planned to, he said something he didn't know was on his mind. "I want you pregnant, Sethe. Would you do that for me?"

Now she was laughing and so was he.

"You came by here to ask me that? You are one crazy-headed man. You right; I don't like it. Don't you think I'm too old to start that all over again?" She slipped her fingers in his hand for all the world like the hand-holding shadows on the side of the road.

"Think about it," he said. And suddenly it was a solution: a way to hold on to her, document his manhood and break out of the girl's spell—all in one. He put the tips of Sethe's fingers on his cheek. Laughing, she pulled them away lest somebody passing the alley see them misbehaving in public, in daylight, in the wind.

Still, he'd gotten a little more time, bought it, in fact, and hoped the price wouldn't wreck him. Like paying for an afternoon in the coin of life to come.

They left off playing, let go hands and hunched forward as they left the alley and entered the street. The wind was quieter there but the dried-out cold it left behind kept pedestrians fast-moving, stiff inside their coats. No men leaned against door frames or storefront windows. The wheels of wagons delivering feed or wood screeched as though they hurt. Hitched horses in front of the saloons shivered and closed their eyes.

Four women, walking two abreast, approached, their shoes loud on the wooden walkway. Paul D touched Sethe's elbow to guide her as they stepped from the slats to the dirt to let the women pass.

Half an hour later, when they reached the city's edge, Sethe and Paul D resumed catching and snatching each other's fingers, stealing quick pats on the behind. Joyfully embarrassed to be that grown-up and that young at the same time.

Resolve, he thought. That was all it took, and no motherless gal was going to break it up. No lazy, stray pup of a woman could turn him around, make him doubt himself, wonder, plead or confess. Convinced of it, that he could do it, he threw his arm around Sethe's shoulders and squeezed. She let her head touch his chest, and since the moment was valuable to both of them, they stopped and stood that way—not breathing, not even caring if a passerby passed them by. The winter light was low. Sethe closed her eyes. Paul D looked at the black trees lining the roadside, their defending arms raised against attack. Softly, suddenly, it began to snow, like a present come down from the sky. Sethe opened her eyes to it and said, "Mercy." And it seemed to Paul D that it was—a little mercy—something given to them on purpose to mark what they were feeling so they would remember it later on when they needed to.

Down came the dry flakes, fat enough and heavy enough to crash like nickels on stone. It always surprised him, how quiet it was. Not like rain, but like a secret.

"Run!" he said.

"You run," said Sethe. "I been on my feet all day."

"Where I been? Sitting down?" and he pulled her along.

"Stop! Stop!" she said. "I don't have the legs for this."

"Then give em to me," he said and before she knew it he had backed into her, hoisted her on his back and was running down the road past brown fields turning white.

Breathless at last, he stopped and she slid back down on her own two feet, weak from laughter.

"You *need* some babies, somebody to play with in the snow." Sethe secured her headcloth.

Paul D smiled and warmed his hands with his breath. "I sure would like to give it a try. Need a willing partner though."

"I'll say," she answered. "Very, very willing."

It was nearly four o'clock now and 124 was half a mile ahead. Floating toward them, barely visible in the drifting snow, was a figure, and although it was the same figure that had been meeting Sethe for four months, so complete was the attention she and Paul D were paying to themselves they both felt a jolt when they saw her close in.

Beloved did not look at Paul D; her scrutiny was for Sethe. She had no coat, no wrap, nothing on her head, but she held in her hands a long shawl. Stretching out her arms she tried to circle it around Sethe.

"Crazy girl," said Sethe. "You the one out here with nothing on." And stepping away and in front of Paul D, Sethe took the shawl and wrapped it around Beloved's head and shoulders. Saying, "You got to learn more sense than that," she enclosed her in her left arm. Snowflakes stuck now. Paul D felt icy cold in the place Sethe had been before Beloved came. Trailing a yard or so behind the women, he fought the anger that shot through his stomach all the way home. When he saw Denver silhouetted in the lamplight at the window, he could not help thinking, "And whose ally you?"

It was Sethe who did it. Unsuspecting, surely, she solved everything with one blow.

"Now I know you not sleeping out there tonight, are you, Paul D?" She smiled at him, and like a friend in need, the chimney coughed against the rush of cold shooting into it from the sky. Window sashes shuddered in a blast of winter air.

Paul D looked up from the stew meat.

"You come upstairs. Where you belong," she said, ". . . and stay there."

The threads of malice creeping toward him from Beloved's side of the table were held harmless in the warmth of Sethe's smile.

Once before (and only once) Paul D had been grateful to a woman. Crawling out of the woods, cross-eyed with hunger and loneliness, he knocked at the first back door he came to in the colored section of Wilmington. He told the woman who opened it that he'd appreciate doing her woodpile, if she could spare him something to eat. She looked him up and down.

"A little later on," she said and opened the door wider. She fed him pork sausage, the worst thing in the world for a starving man, but neither he nor his stomach objected. Later, when he saw pale cotton sheets and two pillows in her bedroom, he had to wipe his eyes quickly, quickly so she would not see the thankful tears of a man's first time. Soil, grass, mud, shucking, leaves, hay, cobs, seashells—all that he'd slept on. White cotton sheets had never crossed his mind. He fell in with a groan and the woman helped him pretend he was making love to her and not her bed linen. He vowed that night, full of pork, deep in luxury, that he would never leave her. She would have to kill him to get him out of that bed. Eighteen months later, when he had been purchased by Northpoint Bank and Railroad Company, he was still thankful for that introduction to sheets.

Now he was grateful a second time. He felt as though he had been plucked from the face of a cliff and put down on sure ground. In Sethe's bed he knew he could put up with two crazy girls—as long as Sethe made her wishes known.

Stretched out to his full length, watching snowflakes stream past the window over his feet, it was easy to dismiss the doubts that took him to the alley behind the restaurant: his expectations for himself were high, too high. What he might call cowardice other people called common sense.

Tucked into the well of his arm, Sethe recalled Paul D's face in the street when he asked her to have a baby for him. Although she laughed and took his hand, it had frightened her. She thought quickly of how good the sex would be if that is what he wanted, but mostly she was frightened by the thought of having a baby once more. Needing to be good enough, alert enough, strong enough, *that* caring—again. Having to stay alive just that much longer. O Lord, she thought, deliver me. Unless carefree, motherlove was a killer. What did he want her pregnant for? To hold on to her? have a sign that he passed this way? He probably had children everywhere anyway. Eighteen years of roaming, he would have to have dropped a few. No. He resented the children she had, that's what. Child, she corrected herself. Child plus Beloved whom she thought of as her own, and that is what he resented. Sharing her with the girls. Hearing the three of them laughing at something he wasn't in on. The code they used among themselves that he could not break. Maybe even the time spent on their needs and not his. They were a family somehow and he was not the head of it.

Can you stitch this up for me, baby?

Um hm. Soon's I finish this petticoat. She just got the one she came here in and everybody needs a change.

Any pie left?

I think Denver got the last of it.

And not complaining, not even minding that he slept all over and around the house now, which she put a stop to this night out of courtesy.

Sethe sighed and placed her hand on his chest. She knew

she was building a case against him in order to build a case against getting pregnant, and it shamed her a little. But she had all the children she needed. If her boys came back one day, and Denver and Beloved stayed on—well, it would be the way it was supposed to be, no? Right after she saw the shadows holding hands at the side of the road hadn't the picture altered? And the minute she saw the dress and shoes sitting in the front yard, she broke water. Didn't even have to see the face burning in the sunlight. She had been dreaming it for years.

Paul D's chest rose and fell, rose and fell under her hand.

DENVER FINISHED washing the dishes and sat down at the table. Beloved, who had not moved since Sethe and Paul D left the room, sat sucking her forefinger. Denver watched her face awhile and then said, "She likes him here."

Beloved went on probing her mouth with her finger. "Make him go away," she said.

"She might be mad at you if he leaves."

Beloved, inserting a thumb in her mouth along with the forefinger, pulled out a back tooth. There was hardly any blood, but Denver said, "Ooooh, didn't that hurt you?"

Beloved looked at the tooth and thought, This is it. Next would be her arm, her hand, a toe. Pieces of her would drop maybe one at a time, maybe all at once. Or on one of those mornings before Denver woke and after Sethe left she would fly apart. It is difficult keeping her head on her neck, her legs attached to her hips when she is by herself. Among the things she could not remember was when she first knew that she could wake up any day and find herself in pieces. She had two dreams: exploding, and being swallowed. When her tooth came out—an odd fragment, last in the row—she thought it was starting.

"Must be a wisdom," said Denver. "Don't it hurt?"

"Yes."

"Then why don't you cry?"

"What?"

"If it hurts, why don't you cry?"

And she did. Sitting there holding a small white tooth in the palm of her smooth smooth hand. Cried the way she wanted to when turtles came out of the water, one behind the other, right after the blood-red bird disappeared back into the leaves. The way she wanted to when Sethe went to him standing in the tub under the stairs. With the tip of her tongue she touched the salt water that slid to the corner of her mouth and hoped Denver's arm around her shoulders would keep them from falling apart.

The couple upstairs, united, didn't hear a sound, but below them, outside, all around 124 the snow went on and on and on. Piling itself, burying itself. Higher. Deeper.

IN THE BACK of Baby Suggs' mind may have been the thought that if Halle made it, God do what He would, it would be a cause for celebration. If only this final son could do for himself what he had done for her and for the three children John and Ella delivered to her door one summer night. When the children arrived and no Sethe, she was afraid and grateful. Grateful that the part of the family that survived was her own grandchildren—the first and only she would know: two boys and a little girl who was crawling already. But she held her heart still, afraid to form questions: What about Sethe and Halle; why the delay? Why didn't Sethe get on board too? Nobody could make it alone. Not only because trappers picked them off like buzzards or netted them like rabbits, but also because you couldn't run if you didn't know how to go. You could be lost forever, if there wasn't nobody to show you the way.

So when Sethe arrived—all mashed up and split open, but with another grandchild in her arms—the idea of a whoop moved closer to the front of her brain. But since there was still no sign of Halle and Sethe herself didn't know what had happened to him, she let the whoop lie—not wishing to hurt his chances by thanking God too soon.

It was Stamp Paid who started it. Twenty days after Sethe got to 124 he came by and looked at the baby he had tied up in his nephew's jacket, looked at the mother he had handed a piece of fried eel to and, for some private reason of his own, went off with two buckets to a place near the river's edge that only he knew about where blackberries grew, tasting so good and happy that to eat them was like being in church. Just one of the berries and you felt anointed. He walked six miles to the riverbank; did a slide-run-slide down into a ravine made almost inaccessible by brush. He reached through brambles lined with blood-drawing thorns thick as knives that cut through his shirt sleeves and trousers. All the while suffering mosquitoes, bees, hornets, wasps and the meanest lady spiders in the state. Scratched, raked and bitten, he maneuvered through and took hold of each berry with fingertips so gentle not a single one was bruised. Late in the afternoon he got back to 124 and put two full buckets down on the porch. When Baby Suggs saw his shredded clothes, bleeding hands, welted face and neck she sat down laughing out loud.

Buglar, Howard, the woman in the bonnet and Sethe came to look and then laughed along with Baby Suggs at the sight of the sly, steely old black man: agent, fisherman, boatman, tracker, savior, spy, standing in broad daylight whipped finally by two pails of blackberries. Paying them no mind he took a berry and put it in the three-week-old Denver's mouth. The women shrieked.

"She's too little for that, Stamp."

"Bowels be soup."

"Sickify her stomach."

But the baby's thrilled eyes and smacking lips made them follow suit, sampling one at a time the berries that tasted like church. Finally Baby Suggs slapped the boys' hands away from the bucket and sent Stamp around to the pump to rinse himself. She had decided to do something with the fruit worthy of the man's labor and his love. That's how it began.

She made the pastry dough and thought she ought to tell

Ella and John to stop on by because three pies, maybe four, were too much to keep for one's own. Sethe thought they might as well back it up with a couple of chickens. Stamp allowed that perch and catfish were jumping into the boat—didn't even have to drop a line.

From Denver's two thrilled eyes it grew to a feast for ninety people. 124 shook with their voices far into the night. Ninety people who ate so well, and laughed so much, it made them angry. They woke up the next morning and remembered the meal-fried perch that Stamp Paid handled with a hickory twig, holding his left palm out against the spit and pop of the boiling grease; the corn pudding made with cream; tired, overfed children asleep in the grass, tiny bones of roasted rabbit still in their hands—and got angry.

Baby Suggs' three (maybe four) pies grew to ten (maybe twelve). Sethe's two hens became five turkeys. The one block of ice brought all the way from Cincinnati—over which they poured mashed watermelon mixed with sugar and mint to make a punch—became a wagonload of ice cakes for a washtub full of strawberry shrug. 124, rocking with laughter, goodwill and food for ninety, made them angry. Too much, they thought. Where does she get it all, Baby Suggs, holy? Why is she and hers always the center of things? How come she always knows exactly what to do and when? Giving advice; passing messages; healing the sick, hiding fugitives, loving, cooking, cooking, loving, preaching, singing, dancing and loving everybody like it was her job and hers alone.

Now to take two buckets of blackberries and make ten, maybe twelve, pies; to have turkey enough for the whole town pretty near, new peas in September, fresh cream but no cow, ice *and* sugar, batter bread, bread pudding, raised bread, shortbread—it made them mad. Loaves and fishes were His powers—they did not belong to an ex-slave who had probably never carried one hundred pounds to the scale, or picked okra with a baby on her back. Who had never been lashed by a ten-year-old whiteboy as God knows they had. Who had not even escaped slavery—had, in fact, been *bought out* of it by a doting son and *driven* to the Ohio River in a wagon—free papers folded between her breasts (driven by the very man who had been her master, who also paid her resettlement fee—name of Garner), and rented a house with *two* floors *and* a well from the Bodwins—the white brother and sister who gave Stamp Paid, Ella and John clothes, goods and gear for runaways because they hated slavery worse than they hated slaves.

It made them furious. They swallowed baking soda, the morning after, to calm the stomach violence caused by the bounty, the reckless generosity on display at 124. Whispered to each other in the yards about fat rats, doom and uncalled-for pride.

The scent of their disapproval lay heavy in the air. Baby Suggs woke to it and wondered what it was as she boiled hominy for her grandchildren. Later, as she stood in the garden, chopping at the tight soil over the roots of the pepper plants, she smelled it again. She lifted her head and looked around. Behind her some yards to the left Sethe squatted in the pole beans. Her shoulders were distorted by the greased flannel under her dress to encourage the healing of her back. Near her in a bushel basket was the three-week-old baby. Baby Suggs, holy, looked up. The sky was blue and clear. Not one touch of death in the definite green of the leaves. She could hear birds and, faintly, the stream way down in the meadow. The puppy, Here Boy, was burying the last bones from yesterday's party. From somewhere at the side of the house came the voices of Buglar, Howard and the crawling girl. Nothing seemed amiss—yet the smell of disapproval was sharp. Back beyond the vegetable garden, closer to the stream but in full sun, she had planted corn. Much as they'd picked for the party, there were still ears ripening, which she could see from where she stood. Baby Suggs leaned back into the peppers and the squash vines with her hoe. Carefully, with the blade at just the right angle, she cut through a stalk of insistent rue. Its flowers she stuck through a split in her hat; the rest she tossed aside. The quiet clok clok clok of wood splitting reminded her that Stamp was doing the chore he promised to the night before. She sighed at her work and, a moment later, straightened up to sniff the disapproval once again. Resting on the handle of the hoe, she concentrated. She was accustomed to the knowledge that nobody prayed for her—but this free-floating repulsion was new. It wasn't whitefolks—that much she could tell—so it must be colored ones. And then she knew. Her friends and neighbors were angry at her because she had overstepped, given too much, offended them by excess.

Baby closed her eyes. Perhaps they were right. Suddenly, behind the disapproving odor, way way back behind it, she smelled another thing. Dark and coming. Something she couldn't get at because the other odor hid it.

She squeezed her eyes tight to see what it was but all she could make out was high-topped shoes she didn't like the look of.

Thwarted yet wondering, she chopped away with the hoe. What could it be? This dark and coming thing. What was left to hurt her now? News of Halle's death? No. She had been prepared for that better than she had for his life. The last of her children, whom she barely glanced at when he was born because it wasn't worth the trouble to try to learn features you would never see change into adulthood anyway. Seven times she had done that: held a little foot; examined the fat fingertips with her own—fingers she never saw become the male or female hands a mother would recognize anywhere. She didn't know to this day what their permanent teeth looked like; or how they held their heads when they walked. Did Patty lose her lisp? What color did Famous' skin finally take? Was that a cleft in Johnny's chin or just a dimple that would disappear soon's his jawbone changed? Four girls, and the last time she saw them there was no hair under their arms. Does Ardelia still love the burned bottom of bread? All seven were gone or dead. What would be the point of looking too hard at that youngest one? But for some reason they let her keep him. He was with her—everywhere.

When she hurt her hip in Carolina she was a real bargain (costing less than Halle, who was ten then) for Mr. Garner, who took them both to Kentucky to a farm he called Sweet Home. Because of the hip she jerked like a three-legged dog when she walked. But at Sweet Home there wasn't a rice field or tobacco patch in sight, and nobody, but nobody, knocked her down. Not once. Lillian Garner called her Jenny for some reason but she never pushed, hit or called her mean names. Even when she slipped in cow dung and broke every egg in her apron, nobody said you-black-bitch-what's-the-matter-with-you and nobody knocked her down.

Sweet Home was tiny compared to the places she had been. Mr. Garner, Mrs. Garner, herself, Halle, and four boys, over half named Paul, made up the entire population. Mrs. Garner hummed when she worked; Mr. Garner acted like the world was a toy he was supposed to have fun with. Neither wanted her in the field—Mr. Garner's boys, including Halle, did all of that—which was a blessing since she could not have managed it anyway. What she did was stand beside the humming Lillian Garner while the two of them cooked, preserved, washed, ironed, made candles, clothes, soap and cider; fed chickens, pigs, dogs and geese; milked cows, churned butter, rendered fat, laid fires. . . . Nothing to it. And nobody knocked her down.

Her hip hurt every single day—but she never spoke of it.

Only Halle, who had watched her movements closely for the last four years, knew that to get in and out of bed she had to lift her thigh with both hands, which was why he spoke to Mr. Garner about buying her out of there so she could sit down for a change. Sweet boy. The one person who did something hard for her: gave her his work, his life and now his children, whose voices she could just make out as she stood in the garden wondering what was the dark and coming thing behind the scent of disapproval. Sweet Home was a marked improvement. No question. And no matter, for the sadness was at her center, the desolated center where the self that was no self made its home. Sad as it was that she did not know where her children were buried or what they looked like if alive, fact was she knew more about them than she knew about herself, having never had the map to discover what she was like.

Could she sing? (Was it nice to hear when she did?) Was she pretty? Was she a good friend? Could she have been a loving mother? A faithful wife? Have I got a sister and does she favor me? If my mother knew me would she like me?

In Lillian Garner's house, exempted from the field work that broke her hip and the exhaustion that drugged her mind; in Lillian Garner's house where nobody knocked her down (or up), she listened to the whitewoman humming at her work; watched her face light up when Mr. Garner came in and thought, It's better here, but I'm not. The Garners, it seemed to her, ran a special kind of slavery, treating them like paid labor, listening to what they said, teaching what they wanted known. And he didn't stud his boys. Never brought them to her cabin with directions to "lay down with her," like they did in Carolina, or rented their sex out on other farms. It surprised and pleased her, but worried her too. Would he pick women for them or what did he think was going to happen when those boys ran smack into their nature? Some danger he was courting and he surely knew it. In fact, his order for them not to leave Sweet Home, except in his company, was not so much because of the law, but the danger of men-bred slaves on the loose.

Baby Suggs talked as little as she could get away with because what was there to say that the roots of her tongue could manage? So the whitewoman, finding her new slave excellent if silent help, hummed to herself while she worked.

When Mr. Garner agreed to the arrangements with Halle, and when Halle looked like it meant more to him that she go free than anything in the world, she let herself be taken 'cross the river. Of the two hard things—standing on her feet till she dropped or leaving her last and probably only living child—she chose the hard thing that made him happy, and never put to him the question she put to herself: What for? What does a sixty-odd-year-old slavewoman who walks like a three-legged dog need freedom for? And when she stepped foot on free ground she could not believe that Halle knew what she didn't; that Halle, who had never drawn one free breath, knew that there was nothing like it in this world. It scared her.

Something's the matter. What's the matter? What's the matter? she asked herself. She didn't know what she looked like and was not curious. But suddenly she saw her hands and thought with a clarity as simple as it was dazzling, "These hands belong to me. These *my* hands." Next she felt a knocking in her chest and discovered something else new: her own heartbeat. Had it been there all along? This pounding thing? She felt like a fool and began to laugh out loud. Mr. Garner looked over his shoulder at her with wide brown eyes and smiled himself. "What's funny, Jenny?"

She couldn't stop laughing. "My heart's beating," she said.

And it was true.

Mr. Garner laughed. "Nothing to be scared of, Jenny. Just keep your same ways, you'll be all right."

She covered her mouth to keep from laughing too loud.

"These people I'm taking you to will give you what help you need. Name of Bodwin. A brother and a sister. Scots. I been knowing them for twenty years or more."

Baby Suggs thought it was a good time to ask him something she had long wanted to know.

"Mr. Garner," she said, "why you all call me Jenny?"

"'Cause that what's on your sales ticket, gal. Ain't that your name? What you call yourself?"

"Nothing," she said. "I don't call myself nothing."

Mr. Garner went red with laughter. "When I took you out of Carolina, Whitlow called you Jenny and Jenny Whitlow is what his bill said. Didn't he call you Jenny?"

"No, sir. If he did I didn't hear it."

"What did you answer to?"

"Anything, but Suggs is what my husband name."

"You got married, Jenny? I didn't know it."

"Manner of speaking."

"You know where he is, this husband?"

"No, sir."

"Is that Halle's daddy?"

"No, sir."

"Why you call him Suggs, then? His bill of sale says Whitlow too, just like yours."

"Suggs is my name, sir. From my husband. He didn't call me Jenny."

"What he call you?"

"Baby."

"Well," said Mr. Garner, going pink again, "if I was you I'd stick to Jenny Whitlow. Mrs. Baby Suggs ain't no name for a freed Negro."

Maybe not, she thought, but Baby Suggs was all she had left of the "husband" she claimed. A serious, melancholy man who taught her how to make shoes. The two of them made a pact: whichever one got a chance to run would take it; together if possible, alone if not, and no looking back. He got his chance, and since she never heard otherwise she believed he made it. Now how could he find or hear tell of her if she was calling herself some bill-of-sale name?

She couldn't get over the city. More people than Carolina and enough whitefolks to stop the breath. Two-story buildings everywhere, and walkways made of perfectly cut slats of wood. Roads wide as Garner's whole house.

"This is a city of water," said Mr. Garner. "Everything travels by water and what the rivers can't carry the canals take. A queen of a city, Jenny. Everything you ever dreamed of, they make it right here. Iron stoves, buttons, ships, shirts, hairbrushes, paint, steam engines, books. A sewer system make your eyes bug out. Oh, this is a city, all right. If you have to live in a city—this is it."

The Bodwins lived right in the center of a street full of houses and trees. Mr. Garner leaped out and tied his horse to a solid iron post.

"Here we are."

Baby picked up her bundle and with great difficulty, caused by her hip and the hours of sitting in a wagon, climbed down. Mr. Garner was up the walk and on the porch before she touched ground, but she got a peep at a Negro girl's face at the open door before she followed a path to the back of the house. She waited what seemed a long time before this same girl opened the kitchen door and offered her a seat by the window.

"Can I get you anything to eat, ma'am?" the girl asked.

"No, darling. I'd look favorable on some water though."

The girl went to the sink and pumped a cupful of water. She placed it in Baby Suggs' hand. "I'm Janey, ma'am."

Baby, marveling at the sink, drank every drop of water although it tasted like a serious medicine. "Suggs," she said, blotting her lips with the back of her hand. "Baby Suggs."

"Glad to meet you, Mrs. Suggs. You going to be staying here?"

"I don't know where I'll be. Mr. Garner—that's him what brought me here—he say he arrange something for me." And then, "I'm free, you know."

Janey smiled. "Yes, ma'am."

"Your people live around here?"

"Yes, ma'am. All us live out on Bluestone."

"We scattered," said Baby Suggs, "but maybe not for long."

Great God, she thought, where do I start? Get somebody to write old Whitlow. See who took Patty and Rosa Lee. Somebody name Dunn got Ardelia and went West, she heard. No point in trying for Tyree or John. They cut thirty years ago and, if she searched too hard and they were hiding, finding them would do them more harm than good. Nancy and Famous died in a ship off the Virginia coast before it set sail for Savannah. That much she knew. The overseer at Whitlow's place brought her the news, more from a wish to have his way with her than from the kindness of his heart. The captain waited three weeks in port, to get a full cargo before setting off. Of the slaves in the hold who didn't make it, he said, two were Whitlow pickaninnies name of . . .

But she knew their names. She knew, and covered her ears with her fists to keep from hearing them come from his mouth.

Janey heated some milk and poured it in a bowl next to a plate of cornbread. After some coaxing, Baby Suggs came to the table and sat down. She crumbled the bread into the hot milk and discovered she was hungrier than she had ever been in her life and that was saying something.

"They going to miss this?"

"No," said Janey. "Eat all you want; it's ours."

"Anybody else live here?"

"Just me. Mr. Woodruff, he does the outside chores. He comes by two, three days a week."

"Just you two?"

"Yes, ma'am. I do the cooking and washing."

"Maybe your people know of somebody looking for help."

"I be sure to ask, but I know they take women at the slaughterhouse."

"Doing what?"

"I don't know."

"Something men don't want to do, I reckon."

"My cousin say you get all the meat you want, plus twenty-five cents the hour. She make summer sausage."

Baby Suggs lifted her hand to the top of her head. Money? Money? They would pay her money every single day? Money?

"Where is this here slaughterhouse?" she asked.

Before Janey could answer, the Bodwins came in to the kitchen with a grinning Mr. Garner behind. Undeniably brother and sister, both dressed in gray with faces too young for their snow-white hair.

"Did you give her anything to eat, Janey?" asked the brother.

"Yes, sir."

"Keep your seat, Jenny," said the sister, and that good news got better.

When they asked what work she could do, instead of reeling off the hundreds of tasks she had performed, she asked about the slaughterhouse. She was too old for that, they said.

"She's the best cobbler you ever see," said Mr. Garner.

"Cobbler?" Sister Bodwin raised her black thick eyebrows. "Who taught you that?"

"Was a slave taught me," said Baby Suggs.

"New boots, or just repair?"

"New, old, anything."

"Well," said Brother Bodwin, "that'll be something, but you'll need more."

"What about taking in wash?" asked Sister Bodwin.

"Yes, ma'am."

"Two cents a pound."

"Yes, ma'am. But where's the in?"

"What?"

"You said 'take in wash.' Where is the 'in'? Where I'm going to be."

"Oh, just listen to this, Jenny," said Mr. Garner. "These two angels got a house for you. Place they own out a ways."

It had belonged to their grandparents before they moved in town. Recently it had been rented out to a whole parcel of Negroes, who had left the state. It was too big a house for Jenny alone, they said (two rooms upstairs, two down), but it was the best and the only thing they could do. In return for laundry, some seamstress work, a little canning and so on (oh shoes, too), they would permit her to stay there. Provided she was clean. The past parcel of colored wasn't. Baby Suggs agreed to the situation, sorry to see the money go but excited about a house with steps—never mind she couldn't climb them. Mr. Garner told the Bodwins that she was a right fine cook as well as a fine cobbler and showed his belly and the sample on his feet. Everybody laughed.

"Anything you need, let us know," said the sister. "We don't hold with slavery, even Garner's kind."

"Tell em, Jenny. You live any better on any place before mine?"

"No, sir," she said. "No place."

"How long was you at Sweet Home?"

"Ten year, I believe."

"Ever go hungry?"

"No, sir."

"Cold?"

"No, sir."

"Anybody lay a hand on you?"

"No, sir."

"Did I let Halle buy you or not?"

"Yes, sir, you did," she said, thinking, But you got my boy and I'm all broke down. You be renting him out to pay for me way after I'm gone to Glory.

Woodruff, they said, would carry her out there, they said, and all three disappeared through the kitchen door.

"I have to fix the supper now," said Janey.

"I'll help," said Baby Suggs. "You too short to reach the fire."

It was dark when Woodruff clicked the horse into a trot. He was a young man with a heavy beard and a burned place on his jaw the beard did not hide.

"You born up here?" Baby Suggs asked him.

"No, ma'am. Virginia. Been here a couple years."

"I see."

"You going to a nice house. Big too. A preacher and his family was in there. Eighteen children."

"Have mercy. Where they go?"

"Took off to Illinois. Bishop Allen gave him a congregation up there. Big."

"What churches around here? I ain't set foot in one in ten years."

"How come?"

"Wasn't none. I dislike the place I was before this last one, but I did get to church every Sunday some kind of way. I bet the Lord done forgot who I am by now."

"Go see Reverend Pike, ma'am. He'll reacquaint you."

"I won't need him for that. I can make my own acquaintance. What I need him for is to reacquaint me with my children. He can read and write, I reckon?"

"Sure."

"Good, 'cause I got a lot of digging up to do." But the news they dug up was so pitiful she quit. After two years of messages written by the preacher's hand, two years of washing, sewing, canning, cobbling, gardening, and sitting in churches, all she found out was that the Whitlow place was gone and that you couldn't write to "a man named Dunn" if all you knew was that he went West. The good news, however, was that Halle got married and had a baby coming. She fixed on that and her own brand of preaching, having made up her mind about what to do with the heart that started beating the minute she crossed the Ohio River. And it worked out, worked out just fine, until she got proud and let herself be overwhelmed by the sight of her daughter-in-law and Halle's children—one of whom was born on the way—and have a celebration of blackberries that put Christmas to shame. Now she stood in the garden smelling disapproval, feeling a dark and coming thing, and seeing high-topped shoes that she didn't like the look of at all. At all.

WHEN THE four horsemen came—schoolteacher, one nephew, one slave catcher and a sheriff—the house on Bluestone Road was so quiet they thought they were too late. Three of them dismounted, one stayed in the saddle, his rifle ready, his eyes trained away from the house to the left and to the right, because likely as not the fugitive would make a dash for it. Although sometimes, you could never tell, you'd find them folded up tight somewhere: beneath floorboards, in a pantry—once in a chimney. Even then care was taken, because the quietest ones, the ones you pulled from a press, a hayloft, or, that once, from a chimney, would go along nicely for two or three seconds. Caught red-handed, so to speak, they would seem to recognize the futility of outsmarting a whiteman and the hopelessness of outrunning a rifle. Smile even, like a child caught dead with his hand in the jelly jar, and when you reached for the rope to tie him, well, even then you couldn't tell. The very nigger with his head hanging and a little jelly-jar smile on his face could all of a sudden roar, like a bull or some such, and commence to do disbelievable things. Grab the rifle at its mouth; throw himself at the one holding it—anything. So you had to keep back a pace, leave the tying to another. Otherwise you ended up killing what you were paid to bring back alive. Unlike a snake or a bear, a dead nigger could not be skinned for profit and was not worth his own dead weight in coin.

Six or seven Negroes were walking up the road toward the house: two boys from the slave catcher's left and some women from his right. He motioned them still with his rifle and they stood where they were. The nephew came back from peeping inside the house, and after touching his lips for silence, pointed his thumb to say that what they were looking for was round back. The slave catcher dismounted then and joined the others. Schoolteacher and the nephew moved to the left of the house; himself and the sheriff to the right. A crazy old nigger was standing in the woodpile with an ax. You could tell he was crazy right off because he was grunting—making low, cat noises like. About twelve yards beyond that nigger was another one—a woman with a flower in her hat. Crazy too, probably, because she too was standing stock-still—but fanning her hands as though pushing cobwebs out of her way. Both, however, were staring at the same place—a shed. Nephew walked over to the old nigger boy and took the ax from him. Then all four started toward the shed.

Inside, two boys bled in the sawdust and dirt at the feet of a nigger woman holding a blood-soaked child to her chest with one hand and an infant by the heels in the other. She did not look at them; she simply swung the baby toward the wall planks, missed and tried to connect a second time, when out of nowhere—in the ticking time the men spent staring at what there was to stare at—the old nigger boy, still mewing, ran through the door behind them and snatched the baby from the arc of its mother's swing.

Right off it was clear, to schoolteacher especially, that there was nothing there to claim. The three (now four—because she'd had the one coming when she cut) pickaninnies they had hoped were alive and well enough to take back to Kentucky, take back and raise properly to do the work Sweet Home desperately needed, were not. Two were lying open-eyed in sawdust; a third pumped blood down the dress of the main one—the woman schoolteacher bragged about, the one he said made fine ink, damn good soup, pressed his collars the way he liked besides having at least ten breeding years left. But now she'd gone wild, due to the mishandling of the nephew who'd overbeat her and made her cut and run. Schoolteacher had chastised that nephew, telling him to think—just think—what would his own horse do if you beat it beyond the point of education. Or Chipper, or Samson. Suppose you beat the hounds past that point thataway. Never again could you trust them in the woods or anywhere else. You'd be feeding them maybe, holding out a piece of rabbit in your hand, and the animal would revert—bite your hand clean off. So he punished that nephew by not letting him come on the hunt. Made him stay there, feed stock, feed himself, feed Lillian, tend crops. See how he liked it; see what happened when you overbeat creatures God had given you the responsibility of—the trouble it was, and the loss. The whole lot was lost now. Five. He could claim the baby struggling in the arms of the mewing old man, but who'd tend her? Because the woman—something was wrong with her. She was looking at him now, and if his other nephew could see that look he would learn the lesson for sure: you just can't mishandle creatures and expect success.

The nephew, the one who had nursed her while his brother held her down, didn't know he was shaking. His uncle had warned him against that kind of confusion, but the warning didn't seem to be taking. What she go and do that for? On account of a beating? Hell, he'd been beat a million times and he was white. Once it hurt so bad and made him so mad he'd smashed the well bucket. Another time he took it out on Samson—a few tossed rocks was all. But no beating ever made him . . . I mean no way he could have . . . What she go and do that for? And that is what he asked the sheriff, who was standing there amazed like the rest of them, but not shaking. He was swallowing hard, over and over again. "What she want to go and do that for?"

The sheriff turned, then said to the other three, "You all better go on. Look like your business is over. Mine's started now."

Schoolteacher beat his hat against his thigh and spit before leaving the woodshed. Nephew and the catcher backed out with him. They didn't look at the woman in the pepper plants with the flower in her hat. And they didn't look at the seven or so faces that had edged closer in spite of the catcher's rifle warning. Enough nigger eyes for now. Little nigger-boy eyes open in sawdust; little nigger-girl eyes staring between the wet fingers that held her face so her head wouldn't fall off; little nigger-baby eyes crinkling up to cry in the arms of the old nigger whose own eyes were nothing but slivers looking down at his feet. But the worst ones were those of the nigger woman who looked like she didn't have any. Since the whites in them had disappeared and since they were as black as her skin, she looked blind.

They unhitched from schoolteacher's horse the borrowed mule that was to carry the fugitive woman back to where she belonged, and tied it to the fence. Then, with the sun straight up over their heads, they trotted off, leaving the sheriff behind among the damnedest bunch of coons they'd ever seen. All testimony to the results of a little so-called freedom imposed on people who needed every care and guidance in the world to keep them from the cannibal life they preferred.

The sheriff wanted to back out too. To stand in the sunlight outside of that place meant for housing wood, coal, kerosene—fuel for cold Ohio winters, which he thought of now, while resisting the urge to run into the August sunlight.

Not because he was afraid. Not at all. He was just cold. And he didn't want to touch anything. The baby in the old man's arms was crying, and the woman's eyes with no whites were gazing straight ahead. They all might have remained that way, frozen till Thursday, except one of the boys on the floor sighed. As if he were sunk in the pleasure of a deep sweet sleep, he sighed the sigh that flung the sheriff into action.

"I'll have to take you in. No trouble now. You've done enough to last you. Come on now."

She did not move.

"You come quiet, hear, and I won't have to tie you up."

She stayed still and he had made up his mind to go near her and some kind of way bind her wet red hands when a shadow behind him in the doorway made him turn. The nigger with the flower in her hat entered.

Baby Suggs noticed who breathed and who did not and went straight to the boys lying in the dirt. The old man moved to the woman gazing and said, "Sethe. You take my armload and gimme yours."

She turned to him, and glancing at the baby he was holding, made a low sound in her throat as though she'd made a mistake, left the salt out of the bread or something.

"I'm going out here and send for a wagon," the sheriff said and got into the sunlight at last.

But neither Stamp Paid nor Baby Suggs could make her put her crawling-already? girl down. Out of the shed, back in the house, she held on. Baby Suggs had got the boys inside and was bathing their heads, rubbing their hands, lifting their lids, whispering, "Beg your pardon, I beg your pardon," the whole time. She bound their wounds and made them breathe camphor before turning her attention to Sethe. She took the crying baby from Stamp Paid and carried it on her shoulder for a full two minutes, then stood in front of its mother.

"It's time to nurse your youngest," she said.

Sethe reached up for the baby without letting the dead one go.

Baby Suggs shook her head. "One at a time," she said and traded the living for the dead, which she carried into the keeping room. When she came back, Sethe was aiming a bloody nipple into the baby's mouth. Baby Suggs slammed her fist on the table and shouted, "Clean up! Clean yourself up!"

They fought then. Like rivals over the heart of the loved, they fought. Each struggling for the nursing child. Baby Suggs lost when she slipped in a red puddle and fell. So Denver took her mother's milk right along with the blood of her sister. And that's the way they were when the sheriff returned, having commandeered a neighbor's cart, and ordered Stamp to drive it.

Outside a throng, now, of black faces stopped murmuring. Holding the living child, Sethe walked past them in their silence and hers. She climbed into the cart, her profile knife-clean against a cheery blue sky. A profile that shocked them with its clarity. Was her head a bit too high? Her back a little too straight? Probably. Otherwise the singing would have begun at once, the moment she appeared in the doorway of the house on Bluestone Road. Some cape of sound would have quickly been wrapped around her, like arms to hold and steady her on the way. As it was, they waited till the cart turned about, headed west to town. And then no words. Humming. No words at all.

Baby Suggs meant to run, skip down the porch steps after the cart, screaming, No. No. Don't let her take that last one too. She meant to. Had started to, but when she got up from the floor and reached the yard the cart was gone and a wagon was rolling up. A red-haired boy and a yellow-haired girl jumped down and ran through the crowd toward her. The boy had a half-eaten sweet pepper in one hand and a pair of shoes in the other.

"Mama says Wednesday." He held them together by their tongues. "She says you got to have these fixed by Wednesday."

Baby Suggs looked at him, and then at the woman holding a twitching lead horse to the road.

"She says Wednesday, you hear? Baby? Baby?"

She took the shoes from him—high-topped and muddy—saying, "I beg your pardon. Lord, I beg your pardon. I sure do."

Out of sight, the cart creaked on down Bluestone Road. Nobody in it spoke. The wagon rock had put the baby to sleep. The hot sun dried Sethe's dress, stiff, like rigor mortis.

THAT AIN'T her mouth.

Anybody who didn't know her, or maybe somebody who just got a glimpse of her through the peephole at the restaurant, might think it was hers, but Paul D knew better. Oh well, a little something around the forehead—a quietness—that kind of reminded you of her. But there was no way you could take that for her mouth and he said so. Told Stamp Paid, who was watching him carefully.

"I don't know, man. Don't look like it to me. I know Sethe's mouth and this ain't it." He smoothed the clipping with his fingers and peered at it, not at all disturbed. From the solemn air with which Stamp had unfolded the paper, the tenderness in the old man's fingers as he stroked its creases and flattened it out, first on his knees, then on the split top of the piling, Paul D knew that it ought to mess him up. That whatever was written on it should shake him.

Pigs were crying in the chute. All day Paul D, Stamp Paid and twenty more had pushed and prodded them from canal to shore to chute to slaughterhouse. Although, as grain farmers moved west, St. Louis and Chicago now ate up a lot of the business, Cincinnati was still pig port in the minds of Ohioans. Its main job was to receive, slaughter and ship up the river the hogs that Northerners did not want to live without. For a month or so in the winter any stray man had work, if he could breathe the stench of offal and stand up for twelve hours, skills in which Paul D was admirably trained.

A little pig shit, rinsed from every place he could touch, remained on his boots, and he was conscious of it as he stood there with a light smile of scorn curling his lips. Usually he left his boots in the shed and put his walking shoes on along with his day clothes in the corner before he went home. A route that took him smack dab through the middle of a cemetery as old as sky, rife with the agitation of dead Miami no longer content to rest in the mounds that covered them. Over their heads walked a strange people; through their earth pillows roads were cut; wells and houses nudged them out of eternal rest. Outraged more by their folly in believing land was holy than by the disturbances of their peace, they growled on the banks of Licking River, sighed in the trees on Catherine Street and rode the wind above the pig yards. Paul D heard them but he stayed on because all in all it wasn't a bad job, especially in winter when Cincinnati reassumed its status of slaughter and riverboat capital. The craving for pork was growing into a mania in every city in the country. Pig farmers were cashing in, provided they could raise enough and get them sold farther and farther away. And the Germans who flooded southern Ohio brought and developed swine cooking to its highest form. Pig boats jammed the Ohio River, and their captains' hollering at one another over the grunts of the stock was as common a water sound as that of the ducks flying over their heads. Sheep, cows and fowl too floated up and down that river, and all a Negro had to do was show up and there was work: poking, killing, cutting, skinning, case packing and saving offal.

A hundred yards from the crying pigs, the two men stood behind a shed on Western Row and it was clear why Stamp had been eyeing Paul D this last week of work; why he paused when the evening shift came on, to let Paul D's movements catch up to his own. He had made up his mind to show him this piece of paper—newspaper—with a picture drawing of a woman who favored Sethe except that was not her mouth. Nothing like it.

Paul D slid the clipping out from under Stamp's palm. The print meant nothing to him so he didn't even glance at it. He simply looked at the face, shaking his head no. No. At the mouth, you see. And no at whatever it was those black scratches said, and no to whatever it was Stamp Paid wanted him to know. Because there was no way in hell a black face could appear in a newspaper if the story was about something anybody wanted to hear. A whip of fear broke through the heart chambers as soon as you saw a Negro's face in a paper, since the face was not there because the person had a healthy baby, or outran a street mob. Nor was it there because the person had been killed, or maimed or caught or burned or jailed or whipped or evicted or stomped or raped or cheated, since that could hardly qualify as news in a newspaper. It would have to be something out of the ordinary—something whitepeople would find interesting, truly different, worth a few minutes of teeth sucking if not gasps. And it must have been hard to find news about Negroes worth the breath catch of a white citizen of Cincinnati.

So who was this woman with a mouth that was not Sethe's, but whose eyes were almost as calm as hers? Whose head was turned on her neck in the manner he loved so well it watered his eye to see it.

And he said so. "This ain't her mouth. I know her mouth and this ain't it." Before Stamp Paid could speak he said it and even while he spoke Paul D said it again. Oh, he heard all the old man was saying, but the more he heard, the stranger the lips in the drawing became.

Stamp started with the party, the one Baby Suggs gave, but stopped and backed up a bit to tell about the berries—where they were and what was in the earth that made them grow like that.

"They open to the sun, but not the birds, 'cause snakes down in there and the birds know it, so they just grow—fat and sweet—with nobody to bother em 'cept me because don't nobody go in that piece of water but me and ain't too many legs willing to glide down that bank to get them. Me neither. But I was willing that day. Somehow or 'nother I was willing. And they whipped me, I'm telling you. Tore me up. But I filled two buckets anyhow. And took em over to Baby Suggs' house. It was on from then on. Such a cooking you never see no more. We baked, fried and stewed everything God put down here. Everybody came. Everybody stuffed. Cooked so much there wasn't a stick of kindlin left for the next day. I volunteered to do it. And next morning I come over, like I promised, to do it."

"But this ain't her mouth," Paul D said. "This ain't it at all."

Stamp Paid looked at him. He was going to tell him about how restless Baby Suggs was that morning, how she had a listening way about her; how she kept looking down past the corn to the stream so much he looked too. In between ax swings, he watched where Baby was watching. Which is why they both missed it: they were looking the wrong way—toward water—and all the while it was coming down the road. Four. Riding close together, bunched-up like, and righteous. He was going to tell him that, because he thought it was important: why he and Baby Suggs both missed it. And about the party too, because that explained why nobody ran on ahead; why nobody sent a fleet-footed son to cut 'cross a field soon as they saw the four horses in town hitched for watering while the riders asked questions. Not Ella, not John, not anybody ran down or to Bluestone Road, to say some new whitefolks with the Look just rode in. The righteous

Look every Negro learned to recognize along with his ma'am's tit. Like a flag hoisted, this righteousness telegraphed and announced the faggot, the whip, the fist, the lie, long before it went public. Nobody warned them, and he'd always believed it wasn't the exhaustion from a long day's gorging that dulled them, but some other thing—like, well, like meanness—that let them stand aside, or not pay attention, or tell themselves somebody else was probably bearing the news already to the house on Bluestone Road where a pretty woman had been living for almost a month. Young and deft with four children, one of which she delivered herself the day before she got there and who now had the full benefit of Baby Suggs' bounty and her big old heart. Maybe they just wanted to know if Baby really was special, blessed in some way they were not. He was going to tell him that, but Paul D was laughing, saying, "Uh uh. No way. A little semblance round the forehead maybe, but this ain't her mouth."

So Stamp Paid did not tell him how she flew, snatching up her children like a hawk on the wing; how her face beaked, how her hands worked like claws, how she collected them every which way: one on her shoulder, one under her arm, one by the hand, the other shouted forward into the woodshed filled with just sunlight and shavings now because there wasn't any wood. The party had used it all, which is why he was chopping some. Nothing was in that shed, he knew, having been there early that morning. Nothing but sunlight. Sunlight, shavings, a shovel. The ax he himself took out. Nothing else was in there except the shovel—and of course the saw.

"You forgetting I knew her before," Paul D was saying. "Back in Kentucky. When she was a girl. I didn't just make her acquaintance a few months ago. I been knowing her a long time. And I can tell you for sure: this ain't her mouth. May look like it, but it ain't."

So Stamp Paid didn't say it all. Instead he took a breath and leaned toward the mouth that was not hers and slowly read out the words Paul D couldn't. And when he finished, Paul D said with a vigor fresher than the first time, "I'm sorry, Stamp. It's a mistake somewhere 'cause that ain't her mouth."

Stamp looked into Paul D's eyes and the sweet conviction in them almost made him wonder if it had happened at all, eighteen years ago, that while he and Baby Suggs were looking the wrong way, a pretty little slavegirl had recognized a hat, and split to the woodshed to kill her children.

"SHE WAS crawling already when I got here. One week, less, and the baby who was sitting up and turning over when I put her on the wagon was crawling already. Devil of a time keeping her off the stairs. Nowadays babies get up and walk soon's you drop em, but twenty years ago when I was a girl, babies stayed babies longer. Howard didn't pick up his own head till he was nine months. Baby Suggs said it was the food, you know. If you ain't got nothing but milk to give em, well they don't do things so quick. Milk was all I ever had. I thought teeth meant they was ready to chew. Wasn't nobody to ask. Mrs. Garner never had no children and we was the only women there."

She was spinning. Round and round the room. Past the jelly cupboard, past the window, past the front door, another window, the sideboard, the keeping-room door, the dry sink, the stove—back to the jelly cupboard. Paul D sat at the table watching her drift into view then disappear behind his back, turning like a slow but steady wheel. Sometimes she crossed her hands behind her back. Other times she held her ears, covered her mouth or folded her arms across her breasts. Once in a while she rubbed her hips as she turned, but the wheel never stopped.

"Remember Aunt Phyllis? From out by Minnowville? Mr. Garner sent one a you all to get her for each and every one of my babies. That'd be the only time I saw her. Many's the time I wanted to get over to where she was. Just to talk. My plan was to ask Mrs. Garner to let me off at Minnowville whilst she went to meeting. Pick me up on her way back. I believe she would a done that if I was to ask her. I never did, 'cause that's the only day Halle and me had with sunlight in it for the both of us to see each other by. So there wasn't nobody. To talk to, I mean, who'd know when it was time to chew up a little something and give it to em. Is that what make the teeth come on out, or should you wait till the teeth came and then solid food? Well, I know now, because Baby Suggs fed her right, and a week later, when I got here, she was crawling already. No stopping her either. She loved those steps so much we painted them so she could see her way to the top."

Sethe smiled then, at the memory of it. The smile broke in two and became a sudden suck of air, but she did not shudder or close her eyes. She wheeled.

"I wish I'd a known more, but, like I say, there wasn't nobody to talk to. Woman, I mean. So I tried to recollect what I'd seen back where I was before Sweet Home. How the women did there. Oh they knew all about it. How to make that thing you use to hang the babies in the trees—so you could see them out of harm's way while you worked the fields. Was a leaf thing too they gave em to chew on. Mint, I believe, or sassafras. Comfrey, maybe. I still don't know how they constructed that basket thing, but I didn't need it anyway, because all my work was in the barn and the house, but I forgot what the leaf was. I could have used that. I tied Buglar when we had all that pork to smoke. Fire everywhere and he was getting into everything. I liked to lost him so many times. Once he got up on the well, right on it. I flew. Snatched him just in time. So when I knew we'd be rendering and smoking and I couldn't see after him, well, I got a rope and tied it round his ankle. Just long enough to play round a little, but not long enough to reach the well or the fire. I didn't like the look of it, but I didn't know what else to do. It's hard, you know what I mean? by yourself and no woman to help you get through. Halle was good, but he was debt-working all over the place. And when he did get down to a little sleep, I didn't want to be bothering him with all that. Sixo was the biggest help. I don't 'spect you rememory this, but Howard got in the milk parlor and Red Cora I believe it was mashed his hand. Turned his thumb backwards. When I got to him, she was getting ready to bite it. I don't know to this day how I got him out. Sixo heard him screaming and come running. Know what he did? Turned the thumb right back and tied it cross his palm to his little finger. See, I never would have thought of that. Never. Taught me a lot, Sixo."

It made him dizzy. At first he thought it was her spinning. Circling him the way she was circling the subject. Round and round, never changing direction, which might have helped his head. Then he thought, No, it's the sound of her voice; it's too near. Each turn she made was at least three yards from where he sat, but listening to her was like having a child whisper into your ear so close you could feel its lips form the words you couldn't make out because they were too close. He caught only pieces of what she said—which was fine, because she hadn't gotten to the main part—the answer to the question he had not asked outright, but which lay in the clipping he showed her. And lay in the smile as well. Because he smiled too, when he showed it to her, so when she burst out laughing at the joke—the mix-up of her face put where some other coloredwoman's ought to be—well, he'd be ready to laugh right along with her. "Can you beat it?" he would ask. And "Stamp done lost his mind," she would giggle. "Plumb lost it."

But his smile never got a chance to grow. It hung there, small and alone, while she examined the clipping and then handed it back.

Perhaps it was the smile, or maybe the ever-ready love she saw in his eyes—easy and upfront, the way colts, evangelists and children look at you: with love you don't have to deserve—that made her go ahead and tell him what she had not told Baby Suggs, the only person she felt obliged to explain anything to. Otherwise she would have said what the newspaper said she said and no more. Sethe could recognize only seventy-five printed words (half of which appeared in the newspaper clipping), but she knew that the words she did not understand hadn't any more power than she had to explain. It was the smile and the upfront love that made her try.

"I don't have to tell you about Sweet Home—what it was—but maybe you don't know what it was like for me to get away from there."

Covering the lower half of her face with her palms, she paused to consider again the size of the miracle; its flavor.

"I did it. I got us all out. Without Halle too. Up till then it was the only thing I ever did on my own. Decided. And it came off right, like it was supposed to. We was here. Each and every one of my babies and me too. I birthed them and I got em out and it wasn't no accident. I did that. I had help, of course, lots of that, but still it was me doing it; me saying, *Go on,* and *Now.* Me having to look out. Me using my own head. But it was more than that. It was a kind of selfishness I never knew nothing about before. It felt good. Good and right. I was big, Paul D, and deep and wide and when I stretched out my arms all my children could get in between. I was *that* wide. Look like I loved em more after I got here. Or maybe I couldn't love em proper in Kentucky because they wasn't mine to love. But when I got here, when I jumped down off that wagon—there wasn't nobody in the world I couldn't love if I wanted to. You know what I mean?"

Paul D did not answer because she didn't expect or want him to, but he did know what she meant. Listening to the doves in Alfred, Georgia, and having neither the right nor the permission to enjoy it because in that place mist, doves, sunlight, copper dirt, moon—everything belonged to the men who had the guns. Little men, some of them, big men too, each one of whom he could snap like a twig if he wanted to. Men who knew their manhood lay in their guns and were not even embarrassed by the knowledge that without gunshot fox would laugh at them. And these "men" who made even vixen laugh could, if you let them, stop you from hearing doves or loving moonlight. So you protected yourself and loved small. Picked the tiniest stars out of the sky to own; lay down with head twisted in order to see the loved one over the rim of the trench before you slept. Stole shy glances at her between the trees at chain-up. Grass blades, salamanders, spiders, woodpeckers, beetles, a kingdom of ants. Anything bigger wouldn't do. A woman, a child, a brother—a big love like that would split you wide open in Alfred, Georgia. He knew exactly what she meant: to get to a place where you could love anything you chose—not to need permission for desire—well now, *that* was freedom.

Circling, circling, now she was gnawing something else instead of getting to the point.

"There was this piece of goods Mrs. Garner gave me. Calico. Stripes it had with little flowers in between. 'Bout a yard—not enough for more 'n a head tie. But I been wanting to make a shift for my girl with it. Had the prettiest colors. I don't even know what you call that color: a rose but with yellow in it. For the longest time I been meaning to make it for her and do you know like a fool I left it behind? No more than a yard, and I kept putting it off because I was tired or didn't have the time. So when I got here, even before they let me get out of bed, I stitched her a little something from a piece of cloth Baby Suggs had. Well, all I'm saying is that's a selfish pleasure I never had before. I couldn't let all that go back to where it was, and I couldn't let her nor any of em live under schoolteacher. That was out."

Sethe knew that the circle she was making around the room, him, the subject, would remain one. That she could never close in, pin it down for anybody who had to ask. If they didn't get it right off—she could never explain. Because the truth was simple, not a long-drawn-out record of flowered shifts, tree cages, selfishness, ankle ropes and wells. Simple: she was squatting in the garden and when she saw them coming and recognized schoolteacher's hat, she heard wings. Little hummingbirds stuck their needle beaks right through her headcloth into her hair and beat their wings. And if she thought anything, it was No. No. Nono. Nonono. Simple. She just flew. Collected every bit of life she had made, all the parts of her that were precious and fine and beautiful, and carried, pushed, dragged them through the veil, out, away, over there where no one could hurt them. Over there. Outside this place, where they would be safe. And the hummingbird wings beat on. Sethe paused in her circle again and looked out the window. She remembered when the yard had a fence with a gate that somebody was always latching and unlatching in the time when 124 was busy as a way station. She did not see the whiteboys who pulled it down, yanked up the posts and smashed the gate leaving 124 desolate and exposed at the very hour when everybody stopped dropping by. The shoulder weeds of Bluestone Road were all that came toward the house.

When she got back from the jail house, she was glad the fence was gone. That's where they had hitched their horses—

where she saw, floating above the railing as she squatted in the garden, schoolteacher's hat. By the time she faced him, looked him dead in the eye, she had something in her arms that stopped him in his tracks. He took a backward step with each jump of the baby heart until finally there were none.

"I stopped him," she said, staring at the place where the fence used to be. "I took and put my babies where they'd be safe."

The roaring in Paul D's head did not prevent him from hearing the pat she gave to the last word, and it occurred to him that what she wanted for her children was exactly what was missing in 124: safety. Which was the very first message he got the day he walked through the door. He thought he had made it safe, had gotten rid of the danger; beat the shit out of it; run it off the place and showed it and everybody else the difference between a mule and a plow. And because she had not done it before he got there her own self, he thought it was because she could not do it. That she lived with 124 in helpless, apologetic resignation because she had no choice; that minus husband, sons, mother-in-law, she and her slow-witted daughter had to live there all alone making do. The prickly, mean-eyed Sweet Home girl he knew as Halle's girl was obedient (like Halle), shy (like Halle), and work-crazy (like Halle). He was wrong. This here Sethe was new. The ghost in her house didn't bother her for the very same reason a room-and-board witch with new shoes was welcome. This here Sethe talked about love like any other woman; talked about baby clothes like any other woman, but what she meant could cleave the bone. This here Sethe talked about safety with a handsaw. This here new Sethe didn't know where the world stopped and she began. Suddenly he saw what Stamp Paid wanted him to see: more important than what Sethe had done was what she claimed. It scared him.

"Your love is too thick," he said, thinking, That bitch is

looking at me; she is right over my head looking down through the floor at me.

"Too thick?" she said, thinking of the Clearing where Baby Suggs' commands knocked the pods off horse chestnuts. "Love is or it ain't. Thin love ain't love at all."

"Yeah. It didn't work, did it? Did it work?" he asked.

"It worked," she said.

"How? Your boys gone you don't know where. One girl dead, the other won't leave the yard. How did it work?"

"They ain't at Sweet Home. Schoolteacher ain't got em."

"Maybe there's worse."

"It ain't my job to know what's worse. It's my job to know what is and to keep them away from what I know is terrible. I did that."

"What you did was wrong, Sethe."

"I should have gone on back there? Taken my babies back there?"

"There could have been a way. Some other way."

"What way?"

"You got two feet, Sethe, not four," he said, and right then a forest sprang up between them; trackless and quiet.

Later he would wonder what made him say it. The calves of his youth? or the conviction that he was being observed through the ceiling? How fast he had moved from his shame to hers. From his cold-house secret straight to her too-thick love.

Meanwhile the forest was locking the distance between them, giving it shape and heft.

He did not put his hat on right away. First he fingered it, deciding how his going would be, how to make it an exit not an escape. And it was very important not to leave without looking. He stood up, turned and looked up the white stairs. She was there all right. Standing straight as a line with her back to him. He didn't rush to the door. He moved slowly and when he got there he opened it before asking Sethe to put supper aside for him because he might be a little late getting back. Only then did he put on his hat.

Sweet, she thought. He must think I can't bear to hear him say it. That after all I have told him and after telling me how many feet I have, "goodbye" would break me to pieces. Ain't that sweet.

"So long," she murmured from the far side of the trees.

II

124 WAS LOUD. Stamp Paid could hear it even from the road. He walked toward the house holding his head as high as possible so nobody looking could call him a sneak, although his worried mind made him feel like one. Ever since he showed that newspaper clipping to Paul D and learned that he'd moved out of 124 that very day, Stamp felt uneasy. Having wrestled with the question of whether or not to tell a man about his woman, and having convinced himself that he should, he then began to worry about Sethe. Had he stopped the one shot she had of the happiness a good man could bring her? Was she vexed by the loss, the free and unasked-for revival of gossip by the man who had helped her cross the river and who was her friend as well as Baby Suggs'?

"I'm too old," he thought, "for clear thinking. I'm too old and I seen too much." He had insisted on privacy during the revelation at the slaughter yard—now he wondered whom he was protecting. Paul D was the only one in town who didn't know. How did information that had been in the newspaper become a secret that needed to be whispered in a pig yard? A secret from whom? Sethe, that's who. He'd gone behind her back, like a sneak. But sneaking was his job—his life; though always for a clear and holy purpose. Before the War all he did was sneak: runaways into hidden places, secret information to public places. Underneath his legal vegetables were the contraband humans that he ferried across the river. Even the pigs he worked in the spring served his purposes. Whole families lived on the bones and guts he distributed to them. He wrote their letters and read to them the ones they received. He knew who had dropsy and who needed stovewood; which children had a gift and which needed correction. He knew the secrets of the Ohio River and its banks; empty houses and full; the best dancers, the worst speakers, those with beautiful voices and those who could not carry a tune. There was nothing interesting between his legs, but he remembered when there had been—when that drive drove the driven—and that was why he considered long and hard before opening his wooden box and searching for the eighteen-year-old clipping to show Paul D as proof.

Afterward—not before—he considered Sethe's feelings in the matter. And it was the lateness of this consideration that made him feel so bad. Maybe he should have left it alone; maybe Sethe would have gotten around to telling him herself; maybe he was not the high-minded Soldier of Christ he thought he was, but an ordinary, plain meddler who had interrupted something going along just fine for the sake of truth and forewarning, things he set much store by. Now 124 was back like it was before Paul D came to town—worrying Sethe and Denver with a pack of haunts he could hear from the road. Even if Sethe could deal with the return of the spirit, Stamp didn't believe her daughter could. Denver needed somebody normal in her life. By luck he had been there at her very birth almost—before she knew she was alive—and it made him partial to her. It was seeing her, alive, don't you know, and looking healthy four weeks later that pleased him so much he gathered all he could carry of the best blackberries in the county and stuck two in her mouth first, before he presented the difficult harvest to Baby Suggs. To this day he believed his berries (which sparked the feast and the wood chopping that followed) were the reason Denver was still alive. Had he not been there, chopping firewood, Sethe would have spread her baby brains on the planking. Maybe he should have thought of Denver, if not Sethe, before he gave Paul D the news that ran him off, the one normal somebody in the girl's life since Baby Suggs died. And right there was the thorn.

Deeper and more painful than his belated concern for Denver or Sethe, scorching his soul like a silver dollar in a fool's pocket, was the memory of Baby Suggs—the mountain to his sky. It was the memory of her and the honor that was her due that made him walk straight-necked into the yard of 124, although he heard its voices from the road.

He had stepped foot in this house only once after the Misery (which is what he called Sethe's rough response to the Fugitive Bill) and that was to carry Baby Suggs, holy, out of it. When he picked her up in his arms, she looked to him like a girl, and he took the pleasure she would have knowing she didn't have to grind her hipbone anymore—that at last somebody carried *her*. Had she waited just a little she would have seen the end of the War, its short, flashy results. They could have celebrated together; gone to hear the great sermons preached on the occasion. As it was, he went alone from house to joyous house drinking what was offered. But she hadn't waited and he attended her funeral more put out with her than bereaved. Sethe and her daughter were dry-eyed on that occasion. Sethe had no instructions except "Take her to the Clearing," which he tried to do, but was prevented by some rule the whites had invented about where the dead should rest. Baby Suggs went down next to the baby with its throat cut—a neighborliness that Stamp wasn't sure had Baby Suggs' approval.

The setting-up was held in the yard because nobody besides himself would enter 124—an injury Sethe answered with another by refusing to attend the service Reverend Pike presided over. She went instead to the gravesite, whose silence she competed with as she stood there not joining in the hymns the others sang with all their hearts. That insult spawned another by the mourners: back in the yard of 124, they ate the food they brought and did not touch Sethe's, who did not touch theirs and forbade Denver to. So Baby Suggs, holy, having devoted her freed life to harmony, was buried amid a regular dance of pride, fear, condemnation and spite. Just about everybody in town was longing for Sethe to come on difficult times. Her outrageous claims, her self-sufficiency seemed to demand it, and Stamp Paid, who had not felt a trickle of meanness his whole adult life, wondered if some of the "pride goeth before a fall" expectations of the townsfolk had rubbed off on him anyhow—which would explain why he had not considered Sethe's feelings or Denver's needs when he showed Paul D the clipping.

He hadn't the vaguest notion of what he would do or say when and if Sethe opened the door and turned her eyes on his. He was willing to offer her help, if she wanted any from him, or receive her anger, if she harbored any against him. Beyond that, he trusted his instincts to right what he may have done wrong to Baby Suggs' kin, and to guide him in and through the stepped-up haunting 124 was subject to, as evidenced by the voices he heard from the road. Other than that, he would rely on the power of Jesus Christ to deal with things older, but not stronger, than He Himself was.

What he heard, as he moved toward the porch, he didn't understand. Out on Bluestone Road he thought he heard a conflagration of hasty voices—loud, urgent, all speaking at once so he could not make out what they were talking about or to whom. The speech wasn't nonsensical, exactly, nor was it tongues. But something was wrong with the order of the words and he couldn't describe or cipher it to save his life. All he could make out was the word *mine.* The rest of it stayed outside his mind's reach. Yet he went on through. When he got to the steps, the voices drained suddenly to less than a whisper. It gave him pause. They had become an occasional mutter—like the interior sounds a woman makes when she believes she is alone and unobserved at her work: a *sth* when she misses the needle's eye; a soft moan when she sees another chip in her one good platter; the low, friendly argument with which she greets the hens. Nothing fierce or startling. Just that eternal, private conversation that takes place between women and their tasks.

Stamp Paid raised his fist to knock on the door he had never knocked on (because it was always open to or for him) and could not do it. Dispensing with that formality was all the pay he expected from Negroes in his debt. Once Stamp Paid brought you a coat, got the message to you, saved your life, or fixed the cistern he took the liberty of walking in your door as though it were his own. Since all his visits were beneficial, his step or holler through a doorway got a bright welcome. Rather than forfeit the one privilege he claimed for himself, he lowered his hand and left the porch.

Over and over again he tried it: made up his mind to visit Sethe; broke through the loud hasty voices to the mumbling beyond it and stopped, trying to figure out what to do at the door. Six times in as many days he abandoned his normal route and tried to knock at 124. But the coldness of the gesture—its sign that he was indeed a stranger at the gate—overwhelmed him. Retracing his steps in the snow, he sighed. Spirit willing; flesh weak.

While Stamp Paid was making up his mind to visit 124 for Baby Suggs' sake, Sethe was trying to take her advice: *to lay it all down, sword and shield.* Not just to acknowledge the advice Baby Suggs gave her, but actually to take it. Four days after Paul D reminded her of how many feet she had, Sethe rummaged among the shoes of strangers to find the ice skates she was sure were there. Digging in the heap she despised herself for having been so trusting, so quick to surrender at the stove while Paul D kissed her back. She should have known that he would behave like everybody else in town once he knew. The twenty-eight days of having women friends, a mother-in-law, and all her children together; of being part of a neighborhood; of, in fact, having neighbors at all to call her own—all that was long gone and would never come back. No more dancing in the Clearing or happy feeds. No more discussions, stormy or quiet, about the true meaning of the Fugitive Bill, the Settlement Fee, God's Ways and Negro pews; antislavery, manumission, skin voting, Republicans, Dred Scott, book learning, Sojourner's high-wheeled buggy, the Colored Ladies of Delaware, Ohio, and the other weighty issues that held them in chairs, scraping the floorboards or pacing them in agony or exhilaration. No anxious wait for the *North Star* or news of a beat-off. No sighing at a new betrayal or handclapping at a small victory.

Those twenty-eight happy days were followed by eighteen years of disapproval and a solitary life. Then a few months of the sun-splashed life that the shadows holding hands on the road promised her; tentative greetings from other coloredpeople in Paul D's company; a bed life for herself. Except for Denver's friend, every bit of it had disappeared. Was that the pattern? she wondered. Every eighteen or twenty years her unlivable life would be interrupted by a short-lived glory?

Well, if that's the way it was—that's the way it was.

She had been on her knees, scrubbing the floor, Denver trailing her with the drying rags, when Beloved appeared saying, "What these do?" On her knees, scrub brush in hand, she looked at the girl and the skates she held up. Sethe couldn't skate a lick but then and there she decided to take Baby

Suggs' advice: *lay it all down.* She left the bucket where it was. Told Denver to get out the shawls and started searching for the other skates she was certain were in that heap somewhere. Anybody feeling sorry for her, anybody wandering by to peep in and see how she was getting on (including Paul D) would discover that the woman junkheaped for the third time because she loved her children—that woman was sailing happily on a frozen creek.

Hurriedly, carelessly she threw the shoes about. She found one blade—a man's.

"Well," she said. "We'll take turns. Two skates on one; one skate on one; and shoe slide for the other."

Nobody saw them falling.

Holding hands, bracing each other, they swirled over the ice. Beloved wore the pair; Denver wore one, step-gliding over the treacherous ice. Sethe thought her two shoes would hold and anchor her. She was wrong. Two paces onto the creek, she lost her balance and landed on her behind. The girls, screaming with laughter, joined her on the ice. Sethe struggled to stand and discovered not only that she could do a split, but that it hurt. Her bones surfaced in unexpected places and so did laughter. Making a circle or a line, the three of them could not stay upright for one whole minute, but nobody saw them falling.

Each seemed to be helping the other two stay upright, yet every tumble doubled their delight. The live oak and soughing pine on the banks enclosed them and absorbed their laughter while they fought gravity for each other's hands. Their skirts flew like wings and their skin turned pewter in the cold and dying light.

Nobody saw them falling.

Exhausted finally they lay down on their backs to recover breath. The sky above them was another country. Winter stars, close enough to lick, had come out before sunset. For a moment, looking up, Sethe entered the perfect peace they offered. Then Denver stood up and tried for a long, independent glide. The tip of her single skate hit an ice bump, and as she fell, the flapping of her arms was so wild and hopeless that all three—Sethe, Beloved and Denver herself—laughed till they coughed. Sethe rose to her hands and knees, laughter still shaking her chest, making her eyes wet. She stayed that way for a while, on all fours. But when her laughter died, the tears did not and it was some time before Beloved or Denver knew the difference. When they did they touched her lightly on the shoulders.

Walking back through the woods, Sethe put an arm around each girl at her side. Both of them had an arm around her waist. Making their way over hard snow, they stumbled and had to hold on tight, but nobody saw them fall.

Inside the house they found out they were cold. They took off their shoes, wet stockings, and put on dry woolen ones. Denver fed the fire. Sethe warmed a pan of milk and stirred cane syrup and vanilla into it. Wrapped in quilts and blankets before the cooking stove, they drank, wiped their noses, and drank again.

"We could roast some taters," said Denver.

"Tomorrow," said Sethe. "Time to sleep."

She poured them each a bit more of the hot sweet milk. The stovefire roared.

"You finished with your eyes?" asked Beloved.

Sethe smiled. "Yes, I'm finished with my eyes. Drink up. Time for bed."

But none of them wanted to leave the warmth of the blankets, the fire and the cups for the chill of an unheated bed. They went on sipping and watching the fire.

When the click came Sethe didn't know what it was. Afterward it was clear as daylight that the click came at the very beginning—a beat, almost, before it started; before she heard three notes; before the melody was even clear. Leaning forward a little, Beloved was humming softly.

It was then, when Beloved finished humming, that Sethe recalled the click—the settling of pieces into places designed and made especially for them. No milk spilled from her cup because her hand was not shaking. She simply turned her head and looked at Beloved's profile: the chin, mouth, nose, forehead, copied and exaggerated in the huge shadow the fire threw on the wall behind her. Her hair, which Denver had braided into twenty or thirty plaits, curved toward her shoulders like arms. From where she sat Sethe could not examine it, not the hairline, nor the eyebrows, the lips, nor . . .

"All I remember," Baby Suggs had said, "is how she loved the burned bottom of bread. Her little hands I wouldn't know em if they slapped me."

. . . the birthmark, nor the color of the gums, the shape of her ears, nor . . .

"Here. Look here. This is your ma'am. If you can't tell me by my face, look here."

. . . the fingers, nor their nails, nor even . . .

But there would be time. The click had clicked; things were where they ought to be or poised and ready to glide in.

"I made that song up," said Sethe. "I made it up and sang it to my children. Nobody knows that song but me and my children."

Beloved turned to look at Sethe. "I know it," she said.

A hobnail casket of jewels found in a tree hollow should be fondled before it is opened. Its lock may have rusted or broken away from the clasp. Still you should touch the nail heads, and test its weight. No smashing with an ax head before it is decently exhumed from the grave that has hidden it all this time. No gasp at a miracle that is truly miraculous because the magic lies in the fact that you knew it was there for you all along.

Sethe wiped the white satin coat from the inside of the pan, brought pillows from the keeping room for the girls' heads. There was no tremor in her voice as she instructed them to keep the fire—if not, come on upstairs.

With that, she gathered her blanket around her elbows and ascended the lily-white stairs like a bride. Outside, snow solidified itself into graceful forms. The peace of winter stars seemed permanent.

Fingering a ribbon and smelling skin, Stamp Paid approached 124 again.

My marrow is tired, he thought. I been tired all my days, bone-tired, but now it's in the marrow. Must be what Baby Suggs felt when she lay down and thought about color for the rest of her life. When she told him what her aim was, he thought she was ashamed and too shamed to say so. Her authority in the pulpit, her dance in the Clearing, her powerful Call (she didn't deliver sermons or preach—insisting she was too ignorant for that—she *called* and the hearing heard)—all that had been mocked and rebuked by the bloodspill in her backyard. God puzzled her and she was too ashamed of Him to say so. Instead she told Stamp she was going to bed to think about the colors of things. He tried to dissuade her. Sethe was in jail with her nursing baby, the one he had saved. Her sons were holding hands in the yard, terrified of letting go. Strangers and familiars were stopping by to hear how it went one more time, and suddenly Baby declared peace. She just up and quit. By the time Sethe was released she had exhausted blue and was well on her way to yellow.

At first he would see her in the yard occasionally, or delivering food to the jail, or shoes in town. Then less and less. He believed then that shame put her in the bed. Now, eight years after her contentious funeral and eighteen years after the Misery, he changed his mind. Her marrow was tired and it was a testimony to the heart that fed it that it took eight years to meet finally the color she was hankering after. The onslaught of her fatigue, like his, was sudden, but lasted for years. After sixty years of losing children to the people who chewed up her life and spit it out like a fish bone; after five years of freedom given to her by her last child, who bought her future with his, exchanged it, so to speak, so she could have one whether he did or not—to lose him too; to acquire a daughter and grandchildren and see that daughter slay the children (or try to); to belong to a community of other free Negroes—to love and be loved by them, to counsel and be counseled, protect and be protected, feed and be fed—and then to have that community step back and hold itself at a distance—well, it could wear out even a Baby Suggs, holy.

"Listen here, girl," he told her, "you can't quit the Word. It's given to you to speak. You can't quit the Word, I don't care what all happen to you."

They were standing in Richmond Street, ankle deep in leaves. Lamps lit the downstairs windows of spacious houses and made the early evening look darker than it was. The odor of burning leaves was brilliant. Quite by chance, as he pocketed a penny tip for a delivery, he had glanced across the street and recognized the skipping woman as his old friend. He had not seen her in weeks. Quickly he crossed the street, scuffing red leaves as he went. When he stopped her with a greeting, she returned it with a face knocked clean of interest. She could have been a plate. A carpetbag full of shoes in her hand, she waited for him to begin, lead or share a conversation. If there had been sadness in her eyes he would have understood it; but indifference lodged where sadness should have been.

"You missed the Clearing three Saturdays running," he told her.

She turned her head away and scanned the houses along the street.

"Folks came," he said.

"Folks come; folks go," she answered.

"Here, let me carry that." He tried to take her bag from her but she wouldn't let him.

"I got a delivery someplace long in here," she said. "Name of Tucker."

"Yonder," he said. "Twin chestnuts in the yard. Sick, too."

They walked a bit, his pace slowed to accommodate her skip.

"Well?"

"Well, what?"

"Saturday coming. You going to Call or what?"

"If I call them and they come, what on earth I'm going to say?"

"Say the Word!" He checked his shout too late. Two whitemen burning leaves turned their heads in his direction. Bending low he whispered into her ear, "The Word. The Word."

"That's one other thing took away from me," she said, and that was when he exhorted her, pleaded with her not to quit, no matter what. The Word had been given to her and she had to speak it. Had to.

They had reached the twin chestnuts and the white house that stood behind them.

"See what I mean?" he said. "Big trees like that, both of em together ain't got the leaves of a young birch."

"I see what you mean," she said, but she peered instead at the white house.

"You got to do it," he said. "You got to. Can't nobody Call like you. You have to be there."

"What I have to do is get in my bed and lay down. I want to fix on something harmless in this world."

"What world you talking about? Ain't nothing harmless down here."

"Yes it is. Blue. That don't hurt nobody. Yellow neither."

"You getting in the bed to think about yellow?"

"I likes yellow."

"Then what? When you get through with blue and yellow, then what?"

"Can't say. It's something can't be planned."

"You blaming God," he said. "That's what you doing."

"No, Stamp. I ain't."

"You saying the whitefolks won? That what you saying?"

"I'm saying they came in my yard."

"You saying nothing counts."

"I'm saying they came in my yard."

"Sethe's the one did it."

"And if she hadn't?"

"You saying God give up? Nothing left for us but pour out our own blood?"

"I'm saying they came in my yard."

"You punishing Him, ain't you."

"Not like He punish me."

"You can't do that, Baby. It ain't right."

"Was a time I knew what that was."

"You still know."

"What I know is what I see: a nigger woman hauling shoes."

"Aw, Baby." He licked his lips searching with his tongue for the words that would turn her around, lighten her load. "We have to be steady. 'These things too will pass.' What you looking for? A miracle?"

"No," she said. "I'm looking for what I was put here to look for: the back door," and skipped right to it. They didn't let her in. They took the shoes from her as she stood on the steps and she rested her hip on the railing while the whitewoman went looking for the dime.

Stamp Paid rearranged his way. Too angry to walk her home and listen to more, he watched her for a moment and turned to go before the alert white face at the window next door had come to any conclusion.

Trying to get to 124 for the second time now, he regretted that conversation: the high tone he took; his refusal to see the effect of marrow weariness in a woman he believed was a mountain. Now, too late, he understood her. The heart that pumped out love, the mouth that spoke the Word, didn't count. They came in her yard anyway and she could not approve or condemn Sethe's rough choice. One or the other might have saved her, but beaten up by the claims of both, she went to bed. The whitefolks had tired her out at last.

And him. Eighteen seventy-four and whitefolks were still on the loose. Whole towns wiped clean of Negroes; eighty-seven lynchings in one year alone in Kentucky; four colored schools burned to the ground; grown men whipped like children; children whipped like adults; black women raped by the crew; property taken, necks broken. He smelled skin, skin and hot blood. The skin was one thing, but human blood cooked in a lynch fire was a whole other thing. The stench stank. Stank up off the pages of the *North Star,* out of the mouths of witnesses, etched in crooked handwriting in letters delivered by hand. Detailed in documents and petitions full of *whereas* and presented to any legal body who'd read it, it stank. But none of that had worn out his marrow. None of that. It was the ribbon. Tying his flatbed up on the bank of the Licking River, securing it the best he could, he caught sight of something red on its bottom. Reaching for it, he thought it was a cardinal feather stuck to his boat. He tugged and what came loose in his hand was a red ribbon knotted around a curl of wet woolly hair, clinging still to its bit of scalp. He untied the ribbon and put it in his pocket, dropped the curl in the weeds. On the way home, he stopped, short of breath and dizzy. He waited until the spell passed before continuing on his way. A moment later, his breath left him again. This time he sat down by a fence. Rested, he got to his feet, but before he took a step he turned to look back down the road he was traveling and said, to its frozen mud and the river beyond, "What *are* these people? You tell me, Jesus. What *are* they?"

When he got to his house he was too tired to eat the food his sister and nephews had prepared. He sat on the porch in the cold till way past dark and went to his bed only because his sister's voice calling him was getting nervous. He kept the ribbon; the skin smell nagged him, and his weakened marrow made him dwell on Baby Suggs' wish to consider what in the world was harmless. He hoped she stuck to blue, yellow, maybe green, and never fixed on red.

Mistaking her, upbraiding her, owing her, now he needed to let her know he knew, and to get right with her and her kin. So, in spite of his exhausted marrow, he kept on through the voices and tried once more to knock at the door of 124. This time, although he couldn't cipher but one word, he believed he knew who spoke them. The people of the broken necks, of fire-cooked blood and black girls who had lost their ribbons.

What a roaring.

Sethe had gone to bed smiling, eager to lie down and unravel the proof for the conclusion she had already leapt to. Fondle the day and circumstances of Beloved's arrival and the meaning of that kiss in the Clearing. She slept instead and woke, still smiling, to a snow-bright morning, cold enough to see her breath. She lingered a moment to collect the courage to throw off the blankets and hit a chilly floor. For the first time, she was going to be late for work.

Downstairs she saw the girls sleeping where she'd left them, but back to back now, each wrapped tight in blankets, breathing into their pillows. The pair and a half of skates were lying by the front door, the stockings hung on a nail behind the cooking stove to dry had not.

Sethe looked at Beloved's face and smiled.

Quietly, carefully she stepped around her to wake the fire. First a bit of paper, then a little kindlin—not too much—just a taste until it was strong enough for more. She fed its dance until it was wild and fast. When she went outside to collect more wood from the shed, she did not notice the man's frozen footprints. She crunched around to the back, to the cord piled high with snow. After scraping it clean, she filled her arms with as much dry wood as she could. She even looked straight at the shed, smiling, smiling at the things she would not have to remember now. Thinking, She ain't even mad with me. Not a bit.

Obviously the hand-holding shadows she had seen on the road were not Paul D, Denver and herself, but "us three." The three holding on to each other skating the night before; the three sipping flavored milk. And since that was so—if her daughter could come back home from the timeless place—certainly her sons could, and would, come back from wherever they had gone to.

Sethe covered her front teeth with her tongue against the cold. Hunched forward by the burden in her arms, she walked back around the house to the porch—not once noticing the frozen tracks she stepped in.

Inside, the girls were still sleeping, although they had changed positions while she was gone, both drawn to the fire. Dumping the armload into the woodbox made them stir but not wake. Sethe started the cooking stove as quietly as she could, reluctant to wake the sisters, happy to have them asleep at her feet while she made breakfast. Too bad she would be late for work—too, too bad. Once in sixteen years? That's just too bad.

She had beaten two eggs into yesterday's hominy, formed it into patties and fried them with some ham pieces before Denver woke completely and groaned.

"Back stiff?"

"Ooh yeah."

"Sleeping on the floor's supposed to be good for you."

"Hurts like the devil," said Denver.

"Could be that fall you took."

Denver smiled. "That was fun." She turned to look down at Beloved snoring lightly. "Should I wake her?"

"No, let her rest."

"She likes to see you off in the morning."

"I'll make sure she does," said Sethe, and thought, Be nice to think first, before I talk to her, let her know I know. Think about all I ain't got to remember no more. Do like Baby said: Think on it then lay it down—for good. Paul D convinced me there was a world out there and that I could live in it. Should have known better. *Did* know better. Whatever is going on outside my door ain't for me. The world is in this room. This here's all there is and all there needs to be.

They ate like men, ravenous and intent. Saying little, content with the company of the other and the opportunity to look in her eyes.

When Sethe wrapped her head and bundled up to go to town, it was already midmorning. And when she left the house she neither saw the prints nor heard the voices that ringed 124 like a noose.

Trudging in the ruts left earlier by wheels, Sethe was

excited to giddiness by the things she no longer had to remember.

I don't have to remember nothing. I don't even have to explain. She understands it all. I can forget how Baby Suggs' heart collapsed; how we agreed it was consumption without a sign of it in the world. Her eyes when she brought my food, I can forget that, and how she told me that Howard and Buglar were all right but wouldn't let go each other's hands. Played that way: stayed that way especially in their sleep. She handed me the food from a basket; things wrapped small enough to get through the bars, whispering news: Mr. Bodwin going to see the judge—in chambers, she kept on saying, in chambers, like I knew what it meant or she did. The Colored Ladies of Delaware, Ohio, had drawn up a petition to keep me from being hanged. That two white preachers had come round and wanted to talk to me, pray for me. That a newspaperman came too. She told me the news and I told her I needed something for the rats. She wanted Denver out and slapped her palms when I wouldn't let her go. "Where your earrings?" she said. "I'll hold em for you." I told her the jailer took them, to protect me from myself. He thought I could do some harm with the wire. Baby Suggs covered her mouth with her hand. "Schoolteacher left town," she said. "Filed a claim and rode on off. They going to let you out for the burial," she said, "not the funeral, just the burial," and they did. The sheriff came with me and looked away when I fed Denver in the wagon. Neither Howard nor Buglar would let me near them, not even to touch their hair. I believe a lot of folks were there, but I just saw the box. Reverend Pike spoke in a real loud voice, but I didn't catch a word—except the first two, and three months later when Denver was ready for solid food and they let me out for good, I went and got you a gravestone, but I didn't have money enough for the carving so I exchanged (bartered, you might say) what I did have and I'm sorry to this day I never thought to ask him for the whole thing: all I heard of what Reverend Pike said. Dearly Beloved, which is what you are to me and I don't have to be sorry about getting only one word, and I don't have to remember the slaughterhouse and the Saturday girls who worked its yard. I can forget that what I did changed Baby Suggs' life. No Clearing, no company. Just laundry and shoes. I can forget it all now because as soon as I got the gravestone in place you made your presence known in the house and worried us all to distraction. I didn't understand it then. I thought you were mad with me. And now I know that if you was, you ain't now because you came back here to me and I was right all along: there is no world outside my door. I only need to know one thing. How bad is the scar?

As Sethe walked to work, late for the first time in sixteen years and wrapped in a timeless present, Stamp Paid fought fatigue and the habit of a lifetime. Baby Suggs refused to go to the Clearing because she believed *they* had won; he refused to acknowledge any such victory. Baby had no back door; so he braved the cold and a wall of talk to knock on the one she did have. He clutched the red ribbon in his pocket for strength. Softly at first, then harder. At the last he banged furiously—disbelieving it could happen. That the door of a house with coloredpeople in it did not fly open in his presence. He went to the window and wanted to cry. Sure enough, there they were, not a one of them heading for the door. Worrying his scrap of ribbon to shreds, the old man turned and went down the steps. Now curiosity joined his shame and his debt. Two backs curled away from him as he looked in the window. One had a head he recognized; the other troubled him. He didn't know her and didn't know anybody it could be. Nobody, but nobody visited that house.

After a disagreeable breakfast he went to see Ella and John to find out what they knew. Perhaps there he could find out if, after all these years of clarity, he had misnamed himself and there was yet another debt he owed. Born Joshua, he renamed himself when he handed over his wife to his master's son. Handed her over in the sense that he did not kill anybody, thereby himself, because his wife demanded he stay alive. Otherwise, she reasoned, where and to whom could she return when the boy was through? With that gift, he decided that he didn't owe anybody anything. Whatever his obligations were, that act paid them off. He thought it would make him rambunctious, renegade—a drunkard even, the debtlessness, and in a way it did. But there was nothing to do with it. Work well; work poorly. Work a little; work not at all. Make sense; make none. Sleep, wake up; like somebody, dislike others. It didn't seem much of a way to live and it brought him no satisfaction. So he extended this debtlessness to other people by helping them pay out and off whatever they owed in misery. Beaten runaways? He ferried them and rendered them paid for; gave them their own bill of sale, so to speak. "You paid it; now life owes you." And the receipt, as it were, was a welcome door that he never had to knock on, like John and Ella's in front of which he stood and said, "Who in there?" only once and she was pulling on the hinge.

"Where you been keeping yourself? I told John must be cold if Stamp stay inside."

"Oh, I been out." He took off his cap and massaged his scalp.

"Out where? Not by here." Ella hung two suits of underwear on a line behind the stove.

"Was over to Baby Suggs' this morning."

"What you want in there?" asked Ella. "Somebody invite you in?"

"That's Baby's kin. I don't need no invite to look after her people."

"Sth." Ella was unmoved. She had been Baby Suggs'

friend and Sethe's too till the rough time. Except for a nod at the carnival, she hadn't given Sethe the time of day.

"Somebody new in there. A woman. Thought you might know who is she."

"Ain't no new Negroes in this town I don't know about," she said. "What she look like? You sure that wasn't Denver?"

"I know Denver. This girl's narrow."

"You sure?"

"I know what I see."

"Might see anything at all at 124."

"True."

"Better ask Paul D," she said.

"Can't locate him," said Stamp, which was the truth although his efforts to find Paul D had been feeble. He wasn't ready to confront the man whose life he had altered with his graveyard information.

"He's sleeping in the church," said Ella.

"The church!" Stamp was shocked and very hurt.

"Yeah. Asked Reverend Pike if he could stay in the cellar."

"It's cold as charity in there!"

"I expect he knows that."

"What he do that for?"

"He's a touch proud, seem like."

"He don't have to do that! Any number'll take him in."

Ella turned around to look at Stamp Paid. "Can't nobody read minds long distance. All he have to do is ask somebody."

"Why? Why he have to ask? Can't nobody offer? What's going on? Since when a blackman come to town have to sleep in a cellar like a dog?"

"Unrile yourself, Stamp."

"Not me. I'm going to stay riled till somebody gets some sense and leastway act like a Christian."

"It's only a few days he been there."

"Shouldn't be no days! You know all about it and don't

give him a hand? That don't sound like you, Ella. Me and you been pulling coloredfolk out the water more'n twenty years. Now you tell me you can't offer a man a bed? A working man, too! A man what can pay his own way."

"He ask, I give him anything."

"Why's that necessary all of a sudden?"

"I don't know him all that well."

"You know he's colored!"

"Stamp, don't tear me up this morning. I don't feel like it."

"It's her, ain't it?"

"Her who?"

"Sethe. He took up with her and stayed in there and you don't want nothing to—"

"Hold on. Don't jump if you can't see bottom."

"Girl, give it up. We been friends too long to act like this."

"Well, who can tell what all went on in there? Look here, I don't know who Sethe is or none of her people."

"What?!"

"All I know is she married Baby Suggs' boy and I ain't sure I know that. Where is *he*, huh? Baby never laid eyes on her till John carried her to the door with a baby I strapped on her chest."

"*I* strapped that baby! And you way off the track with that wagon. Her children know who she was even if you don't."

"So what? I ain't saying she wasn't their ma'ammy, but who's to say they was Baby Suggs' grandchildren? How she get on board and her husband didn't? And tell me this, how she have that baby in the woods by herself? Said a whitewoman come out the trees and helped her. Shoot. You believe that? A *white*woman? Well, I know what kind of white that was."

"Aw, no, Ella."

"Anything white floating around in the woods—if it ain't got a shotgun, it's something I don't want *no* part of!"

"You all was friends."

"Yeah, till she showed herself."

"Ella."

"I ain't got no friends take a handsaw to their own children."

"You in deep water, girl."

"Uh uh. I'm on dry land and I'm going to stay there. You the one wet."

"What's any of what you talking got to do with Paul D?"

"What run him off? Tell me that."

"I run him off."

"You?"

"I told him about—I showed him the newspaper, about the—what Sethe did. Read it to him. He left that very day."

"You didn't tell me that. I thought he knew."

"He didn't know nothing. Except her, from when they was at that place Baby Suggs was at."

"He knew Baby Suggs?"

"Sure he knew her. Her boy Halle too."

"And left when he found out what Sethe did?"

"Look like he might have a place to stay after all."

"What you say casts a different light. I thought—"

But Stamp Paid knew what she thought.

"You didn't come here asking about him," Ella said. "You came about some new girl."

"That's so."

"Well, Paul D must know who she is. Or *what* she is."

"Your mind is loaded with spirits. Everywhere you look you see one."

"You know as well as I do that people who die bad don't stay in the ground."

He couldn't deny it. Jesus Christ Himself didn't, so Stamp

ate a piece of Ella's head cheese to show there were no bad feelings and set out to find Paul D. He found him on the steps of Holy Redeemer, holding his wrists between his knees and looking red-eyed.

Sawyer shouted at her when she entered the kitchen, but she just turned her back and reached for her apron. There was no entry now. No crack or crevice available. She had taken pains to keep them out, but knew full well that at any moment they could rock her, rip her from her moorings, send the birds twittering back into her hair. Drain her mother's milk, they had already done. Divided her back into plant life—that too. Driven her fat-bellied into the woods—they had done that. All news of them was rot. They buttered Halle's face; gave Paul D iron to eat; crisped Sixo; hanged her own mother. She didn't want any more news about whitefolks; didn't want to know what Ella knew and John and Stamp Paid, about the world done up the way whitefolks loved it. All news of them should have stopped with the birds in her hair.

Once, long ago, she was soft, trusting. She trusted Mrs. Garner and her husband too. She knotted the earrings into her underskirt to take along, not so much to wear but to hold. Earrings that made her believe she could discriminate among them. That for every schoolteacher there would be an Amy; that for every pupil there was a Garner, or Bodwin, or even a sheriff, whose touch at her elbow was gentle and who looked away when she nursed. But she had come to believe every one of Baby Suggs' last words and buried all recollection of them and luck. Paul D dug it up, gave her back her body, kissed her divided back, stirred her rememory and brought her more news: of clabber, of iron, of roosters' smiling, but when he heard *her* news, he counted her feet and didn't even say goodbye.

"Don't talk to me, Mr. Sawyer. Don't say nothing to me this morning."

"What? What? What? You talking back to me?"

"I'm telling you don't say nothing to me."

"You better get them pies made."

Sethe touched the fruit and picked up the paring knife.

When pie juice hit the bottom of the oven and hissed, Sethe was well into the potato salad. Sawyer came in and said, "Not too sweet. You make it too sweet they don't eat it."

"Make it the way I always did."

"Yeah. Too sweet."

None of the sausages came back. The cook had a way with them and Sawyer's Restaurant never had leftover sausage. If Sethe wanted any, she put them aside soon as they were ready. But there was some passable stew. Problem was, all her pies were sold too. Only rice pudding left and half a pan of gingerbread that didn't come out right. Had she been paying attention instead of daydreaming all morning, she wouldn't be picking around looking for her dinner like a crab. She couldn't read clock time very well, but she knew when the hands were closed in prayer at the top of the face she was through for the day. She got a metal-top jar, filled it with stew and wrapped the gingerbread in butcher paper. These she dropped in her outer skirt pockets and began washing up. None of it was anything like what the cook and the two waiters walked off with. Mr. Sawyer included midday dinner in the terms of the job—along with $3.40 a week—and she made him understand from the beginning she would take her dinner home. But matches, sometimes a bit of kerosene, a little salt, butter too—these things she took also, once in a while, and felt ashamed because she could afford to buy them; she just didn't want the embarrassment of waiting out back of Phelps store with the others till every white in Ohio was served before the keeper turned to the cluster of Negro faces looking through a hole in his back door. She was ashamed, too, because it was stealing and Sixo's argument on the subject amused her but didn't change the way she felt; just as it didn't change schoolteacher's mind.

"Did you steal that shoat? You stole that shoat." Schoolteacher was quiet but firm, like he was just going through the motions—not expecting an answer that mattered. Sixo sat there, not even getting up to plead or deny. He just sat there, the streak-of-lean in his hand, the gristle clustered in the tin plate like gemstones—rough, unpolished, but loot nevertheless.

"You stole that shoat, didn't you?"

"No. Sir," said Sixo, but he had the decency to keep his eyes on the meat.

"You telling me you didn't steal it, and I'm looking right at you?"

"No, sir. I didn't steal it."

Schoolteacher smiled. "Did you kill it?"

"Yes, sir. I killed it."

"Did you butcher it?"

"Yes, sir."

"Did you cook it?"

"Yes, sir."

"Well, then. Did you eat it?"

"Yes, sir. I sure did."

"And you telling me that's not stealing?"

"No, sir. It ain't."

"What is it then?"

"Improving your property, sir."

"What?"

"Sixo plant rye to give the high piece a better chance. Sixo take and feed the soil, give you more crop. Sixo take and feed Sixo give you more work."

Clever, but schoolteacher beat him anyway to show him that definitions belonged to the definers—not the defined. After Mr. Garner died with a hole in his ear that Mrs. Garner said was an exploded ear drum brought on by stroke and Sixo said was gunpowder, everything they touched was looked on as stealing. Not just a rifle of corn, or two yard eggs the hen herself didn't even remember, everything. Schoolteacher took away the guns from the Sweet Home men and, deprived of game to round out their diet of bread, beans, hominy, vegetables and a little extra at slaughter time, they began to pilfer in earnest, and it became not only their right but their obligation.

Sethe understood it then, but now with a paying job and an employer who was kind enough to hire an ex-convict, she despised herself for the pride that made pilfering better than standing in line at the window of the general store with all the other Negroes. She didn't want to jostle them or be jostled by them. Feel their judgment or their pity, especially now. She touched her forehead with the back of her wrist and blotted the perspiration. The workday had come to a close and already she was feeling the excitement. Not since that other escape had she felt so alive. Slopping the alley dogs, watching their frenzy, she pressed her lips. Today would be a day she would accept a lift, if anybody on a wagon offered it. No one would, and for sixteen years her pride had not let her ask. But today. Oh, today. Now she wanted speed, to skip over the long walk home and *be* there.

When Sawyer warned her about being late again, she barely heard him. He used to be a sweet man. Patient, tender in his dealings with his help. But each year, following the death of his son in the War, he grew more and more crotchety. As though Sethe's dark face was to blame.

"Un huh," she said, wondering how she could hurry time along and get to the no-time waiting for her.

She needn't have worried. Wrapped tight, hunched forward, as she started home her mind was busy with the things she could forget.

Thank God I don't have to rememory or say a thing because you know it. All. You know I never would a left you. Never. It was all I could think of to do. When the train came I had to be ready. Schoolteacher was teaching us things we couldn't learn. I didn't care nothing about the measuring string. We all laughed about that—except Sixo. He didn't laugh at nothing. But I didn't care. Schoolteacher'd wrap that string all over my head, 'cross my nose, around my behind. Number my teeth. I thought he was a fool. And the questions he asked was the biggest foolishness of all.

Then me and your brothers come up from the second patch. The first one was close to the house where the quick things grew: beans, onions, sweet peas. The other one was further down for long-lasting things, potatoes, pumpkin, okra, pork salad. Not much was up yet down there. It was early still. Some young salad maybe, but that was all. We pulled weeds and hoed a little to give everything a good start. After that we hit out for the house. The ground raised up from the second patch. Not a hill exactly but kind of. Enough for Buglar and Howard to run up and roll down, run up and roll down. That's the way I used to see them in my dreams, laughing, their short fat legs running up the hill. Now all I see is their backs walking down the railroad tracks. Away from me. Always away from me. But that day they was happy, running up and rolling down. It was early still—the growing season had took hold but not much was up. I remember the peas still had flowers. The grass was long though, full of white buds and those tall red blossoms people call Diane and something there with the leastest little bit of blue—light, like a cornflower but pale, pale. Real pale. I maybe should have hurried because I left you back at the house in a basket in the yard. Away from where the chickens scratched but you never know. Anyway I took my time getting back but your brothers didn't have patience with me staring at flowers and sky every two or three steps. They ran on ahead and I let em. Something sweet lives in the air that time of year, and if the breeze is right, it's hard to stay indoors. When I got back I could hear Howard and Buglar laughing down by the quarters. I put my hoe down and cut across the side yard to get to you. The shade moved so by the time I got back the sun was shining right on you. Right in your face, but you wasn't woke at all. Still asleep. I wanted to pick you up in my arms and I wanted to look at you sleeping too. Didn't know which; you had the sweetest face. Yonder, not far, was a grape arbor Mr. Garner made. Always full of big plans, he wanted to make his own wine to get drunk off. Never did get more than a kettle of jelly from it. I don't think the soil was right for grapes. Your daddy believed it was the rain, not the soil. Sixo said it was bugs. The grapes so little and tight. Sour as vinegar too. But there was a little table in there. So I picked up your basket and carried you over to the grape arbor. Cool in there and shady. I set you down on the little table and figured if I got a piece of muslin the bugs and things wouldn't get to you. And if Mrs. Garner didn't need me right there in the kitchen, I could get a chair and you and me could set out there while I did the vegetables. I headed for the back door to get the clean muslin we kept in the kitchen press. The grass felt good on my feet. I got near the door and I heard voices. Schoolteacher made his pupils sit and learn books for a spell every afternoon. If it was nice enough weather, they'd sit on the side porch. All three of em. He'd talk and they'd write. Or he would read and they would write down what he said. I never told nobody this. Not your pap, not nobody. I almost told Mrs. Garner, but she was so weak then and getting weaker. This is the first time I'm telling it and I'm telling it to you because it might help explain something to you although I know you don't need me to do it. To tell it or even think over it. You don't have to listen either, if you don't want to. But I couldn't help listening to what I heard that day. He was talking to his pupils and I heard him say, "Which one are you doing?" And one of the boys said, "Sethe." That's when I stopped because I heard my name, and then I took a few steps to where I could see what they was doing. Schoolteacher was standing over one of them with one hand behind his back. He licked a forefinger a couple of times and turned a few pages. Slow. I was about to turn around and keep on my way to where the muslin was, when I heard him say, "No, no. That's not the way. I told you to put her human characteristics on the left; her animal ones on the right. And don't forget to line them up." I commenced to walk backward, didn't even look behind me to find out where I was headed. I just kept lifting my feet and pushing back. When I bumped up against a tree my scalp was prickly. One of the dogs was licking out a pan in the yard. I got to the grape arbor fast enough, but I didn't have the muslin. Flies settled all over your face, rubbing their hands. My head itched like the devil. Like somebody was sticking fine needles in my scalp. I never told Halle or nobody. But that very day I asked Mrs. Garner a part of it. She was low then. Not as low as she ended up, but failing. A kind of bag grew under her jaw. It didn't seem to hurt her, but it made her weak. First she'd be up and spry in the morning and by the second milking she couldn't stand up. Next she took to sleeping late. The day I went up there she was in bed the whole day, and I thought to carry her some bean soup and ask her then. When I opened the bedroom door she looked at me from underneath her nightcap. Already it was hard to catch life in her eyes. Her shoes and stockings were on the floor so I knew she had tried to get dressed.

"I brung you some bean soup," I said.

She said, "I don't think I can swallow that."

"Try a bit," I told her.

"Too thick. I'm sure it's too thick."

"Want me to loosen it up with a little water?"

"No. Take it away. Bring me some cool water, that's all."

"Yes, ma'am. Ma'am? Could I ask you something?"

"What is it, Sethe?"

"What do characteristics mean?"

"What?"

"A word. Characteristics."

"Oh." She moved her head around on the pillow. "Features. Who taught you that?"

"I heard the schoolteacher say it."

"Change the water, Sethe. This is warm."

"Yes, ma'am. Features?"

"Water, Sethe. Cool water."

I put the pitcher on the tray with the white bean soup and went downstairs. When I got back with the fresh water I held her head while she drank. It took her a while because that lump made it hard to swallow. She laid back and wiped her mouth. The drinking seemed to satisfy her but she frowned and said, "I don't seem able to wake up, Sethe. All I seem to want is sleep."

"Then do it," I told her. "I'm take care of things."

Then she went on: what about this? what about that? Said she knew Halle was no trouble, but she wanted to know if schoolteacher was handling the Pauls all right and Sixo.

"Yes, ma'am," I said. "Look like it."

"Do they do what he tells them?"

"They don't need telling."

"Good. That's a mercy. I should be back downstairs in a day or two. I just need more rest. Doctor's due back. Tomorrow, is it?"

"You said features, ma'am?"

"What?"

"Features?"

"Umm. Like, a feature of summer is heat. A characteristic is a feature. A thing that's natural to a thing."

"Can you have more than one?"

"You can have quite a few. You know. Say a baby sucks its thumb. That's one, but it has others too. Keep Billy away from Red Cora. Mr. Garner never let her calve every other year. Sethe, you hear me? Come away from that window and listen."

"Yes, ma'am."

"Ask my brother-in-law to come up after supper."

"Yes, ma'am."

"If you'd wash your hair you could get rid of that lice."

"Ain't no lice in my head, ma'am."

"Whatever it is, a good scrubbing is what it needs, not scratching. Don't tell me we're out of soap."

"No, ma'am."

"All right now. I'm through. Talking makes me tired."

"Yes, ma'am."

"And thank you, Sethe."

"Yes, ma'am."

You was too little to remember the quarters. Your brothers slept under the window. Me, you and your daddy slept by the wall. The night after I heard why schoolteacher measured me, I had trouble sleeping. When Halle came in I asked him what he thought about schoolteacher. He said there wasn't nothing to think about. Said, He's white, ain't he? I said, But I mean is he like Mr. Garner?

"What you want to know, Sethe?"

"Him and her," I said, "they ain't like the whites I seen before. The ones in the big place I was before I came here."

"How these different?" he asked me.

"Well," I said, "they talk soft for one thing."

"It don't matter, Sethe. What they say is the same. Loud or soft."

"Mr. Garner let you buy out your mother," I said.

"Yep. He did."

"Well?"

"If he hadn't of, she would of dropped in his cooking stove."

"Still, he did it. Let you work it off."

"Uh huh."

"Wake up, Halle."

"I said, Uh huh."

"He could of said no. He didn't tell you no."

"No, he didn't tell me no. She worked here for ten years. If she worked another ten you think she would've made it out? I pay him for her last years and in return he got you, me and three more coming up. I got one more year of debt work; one more. Schoolteacher in there told me to quit it. Said the reason for doing it don't hold. I should do the extra but here at Sweet Home."

"Is he going to pay you for the extra?"

"Nope."

"Then how you going to pay it off? How much is it?"

"$123.70."

"Don't he want it back?"

"He want something."

"What?"

"I don't know. Something. But he don't want me off Sweet Home no more. Say it don't pay to have my labor somewhere else while the boys is small."

"What about the money you owe?"

"He must have another way of getting it."

"What way?"

"I don't know, Sethe."

"Then the only question is how? How he going get it?"

"No. That's one question. There's one more."

"What's that?"

He leaned up and turned over, touching my cheek with his knuckles. "The question now is, Who's going buy you out? Or me? Or her?" He pointed over to where you was laying.

"What?"

"If all my labor is Sweet Home, including the extra, what I got left to sell?"

He turned over then and went back to sleep and I thought I wouldn't but I did too for a while. Something he said, maybe, or something he didn't say woke me. I sat up like somebody hit me, and you woke up too and commenced to cry. I rocked you some, but there wasn't much room, so I stepped outside the door to walk you. Up and down I went. Up and down. Everything dark but lamplight in the top window of the house. She must've been up still. I couldn't get out of my head the thing that woke me up: "While the boys is small." That's what he said and it snapped me awake. They tagged after me the whole day weeding, milking, getting firewood. For now. For now.

That's when we should have begun to plan. But we didn't. I don't know what we thought—but getting away was a money thing to us. Buy out. Running was nowhere on our minds. All of us? Some? Where to? How to go? It was Sixo who brought it up, finally, after Paul F. Mrs. Garner sold him, trying to keep things up. Already she lived two years off his price. But it ran out, I guess, so she wrote schoolteacher to come take over. Four Sweet Home men and she still believed she needed her brother-in-law and two boys 'cause people said she shouldn't be alone out there with nothing but Negroes. So he came with a big hat and spectacles and a coach box full of paper. Talking soft and watching hard. He beat Paul A. Not hard and not long, but it was the first time anyone had, because Mr. Garner disallowed it. Next time I saw him he had company in the prettiest trees you ever saw. Sixo started watching the sky. He was the only one who crept at night and Halle said that's how he learned about the train.

"That way." Halle was pointing over the stable. "Where he took my ma'am. Sixo say freedom is that way. A whole train is going and if we can get there, don't need to be no buy-out."

"Train? What's that?" I asked him.

They stopped talking in front of me then. Even Halle. But they whispered among themselves and Sixo watched the sky. Not the high part, the low part where it touched the trees. You could tell his mind was gone from Sweet Home.

The plan was a good one, but when it came time, I was big with Denver. So we changed it a little. A little. Just enough to butter Halle's face, so Paul D tells me, and make Sixo laugh at last.

But I got you out, baby. And the boys too. When the signal for the train come, you all was the only ones ready. I couldn't find Halle or nobody. I didn't know Sixo was burned up and Paul D dressed in a collar you wouldn't believe. Not till later. So I sent you all to the wagon with the woman who waited in the corn. Ha ha. No notebook for my babies and no measuring string neither. What I had to get through later I got through because of you. Passed right by those boys hanging in the trees. One had Paul A's shirt on but not his feet or his head. I walked right on by because only me had your milk, and God do what He would, I was going to get it to you. You remember that, don't you; that I did? That when I got here I had milk enough for all?

One more curve in the road, and Sethe could see her chimney; it wasn't lonely-looking anymore. The ribbon of smoke was from a fire that warmed a body returned to her—just like it never went away, never needed a headstone. And the heart that beat inside it had not for a single moment stopped in her hands.

She opened the door, walked in and locked it tight behind her.

The day Stamp Paid saw the two backs through the window and then hurried down the steps, he believed the undecipherable language clamoring around the house was the mumbling of the black and angry dead. Very few had died in bed, like Baby Suggs, and none that he knew of, including Baby, had lived a livable life. Even the educated colored: the long-school people, the doctors, the teachers, the paper-writers and businessmen had a hard row to hoe. In addition to having to use their heads to get ahead, they had the weight of the whole race sitting there. You needed two heads for that. Whitepeople believed that whatever the manners, under every dark skin was a jungle. Swift unnavigable waters, swinging screaming baboons, sleeping snakes, red gums ready for their sweet white blood. In a way, he thought, they were right. The more coloredpeople spent their strength trying to convince them how gentle they were, how clever and loving, how human, the more they used themselves up to persuade whites of something Negroes believed could not be questioned, the deeper and more tangled the jungle grew inside. But it wasn't the jungle blacks brought with them to this place from the other (livable) place. It was the jungle whitefolks planted in them. And it grew. It spread. In, through and after life, it spread, until it invaded the whites who had made it. Touched them every one. Changed and altered them. Made them bloody, silly, worse than even they wanted to be, so scared were they of the jungle they had made. The screaming baboon lived under their own white skin; the red gums were their own.

Meantime, the secret spread of this new kind of whitefolks' jungle was hidden, silent, except once in a while when you could hear its mumbling in places like 124.

Stamp Paid abandoned his efforts to see about Sethe, after the pain of knocking and not gaining entrance, and when he did, 124 was left to its own devices. When Sethe locked the door, the women inside were free at last to be what they liked, see whatever they saw and say whatever was on their minds.

Almost. Mixed in with the voices surrounding the house, recognizable but undecipherable to Stamp Paid, were the thoughts of the women of 124, unspeakable thoughts, unspoken.

BELOVED, she my daughter. She mine. See. She come back to me of her own free will and I don't have to explain a thing. I didn't have time to explain before because it had to be done quick. Quick. She had to be safe and I put her where she would be. But my love was tough and she back now. I knew she would be. Paul D ran her off so she had no choice but to come back to me in the flesh. I bet you Baby Suggs, on the other side, helped. I won't never let her go. I'll explain to her, even though I don't have to. Why I did it. How if I hadn't killed her she would have died and that is something I could not bear to happen to her. When I explain it she'll understand, because she understands everything already. I'll tend her as no mother ever tended a child, a daughter. Nobody will ever get my milk no more except my own children. I never had to give it to nobody else—and the one time I did it was took from me—they held me down and took it. Milk that belonged to my baby. Nan had to nurse whitebabies and me too because Ma'am was in the rice. The little whitebabies got it first and I got what was left. Or none. There was no nursing milk to call my own. I know what it is to be without the milk that belongs to you; to have to fight and holler for it, and to have so little left. I'll tell Beloved about that; she'll understand. She my daughter. The one I managed to have milk for and to get it to her even after they stole it; after they handled me like I was the cow, no, the goat, back behind the stable because it was too nasty to stay in with the horses. But I wasn't too nasty to cook their food or take care of Mrs. Garner. I tended her like I would have tended my own mother if she needed me. If they had let her out the rice field, because I was the one she didn't throw away. I couldn't have done more for that woman than I would my own ma'am if she was to take sick and need me and I'd have stayed with her till she got well or died. And I would have stayed after that except Nan snatched me back. Before I could check for the sign. It was her all right, but for a long time I didn't believe it. I looked everywhere for that hat. Stuttered after that. Didn't stop it till I saw Halle. Oh, but that's all over now. I'm here. I lasted. And my girl come home. Now I can look at things again because she's here to see them too. After the shed, I stopped. Now, in the morning, when I light the fire I mean to look out the window to see what the sun is doing to the day. Does it hit the pump handle first or the spigot? See if the grass is gray-green or brown or what. Now I know why Baby Suggs pondered color her last years. She never had time to see, let alone enjoy it before. Took her a long time to finish with blue, then yellow, then green. She was well into pink when she died. I don't believe she wanted to get to red and I understand why because me and Beloved outdid ourselves with it. Matter of fact, that and her pinkish headstone was the last color I recall. Now I'll be on the lookout. Think what spring will be for us! I'll plant carrots just so she can see them, and turnips. Have you ever seen one, baby? A prettier thing God never made. White and purple with a tender tail and a hard head. Feels good when you hold it in your hand and smells like the creek when it floods, bitter but happy. We'll smell them together, Beloved. Beloved. Because you mine and I have to show you these things, and teach you what a mother should. Funny how you lose sight of some things and memory others. I never will forget that whitegirl's hands. Amy. But I forget the color of all that hair on her head. Eyes must have been gray, though. Seem like I do rememory that. Mrs. Garner's was light brown—while she was well. Got dark when she took sick. A strong woman, used to be. And when she talked off her head, she'd say it. "I used to be strong as a mule, Jenny." Called me "Jenny" when she was babbling, and I can bear witness to that. Tall and strong. The two of us on a cord of wood was as good as two men. Hurt her like the devil not to be able to raise her head off the pillow. Still can't figure why she thought she needed schoolteacher, though. I wonder if she lasted, like I did. Last time I saw her she couldn't do nothing but cry, and I couldn't do a thing for her but wipe her face when I told her what they done to me. Somebody had to know it. Hear it. Somebody. Maybe she lasted. Schoolteacher wouldn't treat her the way he treated me. First beating I took was the last. Nobody going to keep me from my children. Hadn't been for me taking care of her maybe I would have known what happened. Maybe Halle was trying to get to me. I stood by her bed waiting for her to finish with the slop jar. When I got her back in the bed she said she was cold. Hot as blazes and she wanted quilts. Said to shut the window. I told her no. She needed the cover; I needed the breeze. Long as those yellow curtains flapped, I was all right. Should have heeded her. Maybe what sounded like shots really was. Maybe I would have seen somebody or something. Maybe. Anyhow I took my babies to the corn, Halle or no. Jesus. When I heard that woman's rattle. She said, Any more? I told her I didn't know. She said, I been here all night. Can't wait. I tried to make her. She said, Can't do it. Come on. Hoo! Not a man around. Boys scared. You asleep on my back. Denver sleep in my stomach. Felt like I was split in two. I told her to take you all; I had to go back. In case. She just looked at me. Said, Woman? Bit a piece of my tongue off when they opened my back. It was hanging by a shred. I didn't mean to. Clamped down on it, it come right off. I thought, Good God, I'm going to eat myself up. They dug a hole for my stomach so as not to hurt the baby. Denver don't like for me to talk about it. She hates anything about Sweet Home except how she was born. But you was there and even if you too young to memory it, I can tell it to you. The grape arbor. You memory that? I ran so fast. Flies beat me to you. I would have known right away who you was when the sun blotted out your face the way it did when I took you to the grape arbor. I would have known at once when my water broke. The minute I saw you sitting on the stump, it broke. And when I did see your face it had more than a hint of what you would look like after all these years. I would have known who you were right away because the cup after cup of water you drank proved and connected to the fact that you dribbled clear spit on my face the day I got to 124. I would have known right off, but Paul D distracted me. Otherwise I would have seen my fingernail prints right there on your forehead for all the world to see. From when I held your head up, out in the shed. And later on, when you asked me about the earrings I used to dangle for you to play with, I would have recognized you right off, except for Paul D. Seems to me he wanted you out from the beginning, but I wouldn't let him. What you think? And look how he ran when he found out about me and you in the shed. Too rough for him to listen to. Too thick, he said. My love was too thick. What he know about it? Who in the world is he willing to die for? Would he give his privates to a stranger in return for a carving? Some other way, he said. There must have been some other way. Let schoolteacher haul us away, I guess, to measure your behind before he tore it up? I have felt what it felt like and nobody walking or stretched out is going to make you feel it too. Not you, not none of mine, and when I tell you you mine, I also mean I'm yours. I wouldn't draw breath without my children. I told Baby Suggs that and she got down on her knees to beg God's pardon for me. Still, it's so. My plan was to take us all to the other side where my own ma'am is. They stopped me from getting us there, but they didn't stop you from getting here. Ha ha. You came right on back like a good girl, like a daughter, which is what I wanted to be and would have been if my ma'am had been able to get out of the rice long enough before they hanged her and let me be one. You know what? She'd had the bit so many times she smiled. When she wasn't smiling she smiled, and I never saw her own smile. I wonder what they was doing when they was caught. Running, you think? No. Not that. Because she was my ma'am and nobody's ma'am would run off and leave her daughter, would she? Would she, now? Leave her in the yard with a one-armed woman? Even if she hadn't been able to suckle the daughter for more than a week or two and had to turn her over to another woman's tit that never had enough for all. They said it was the bit that made her smile when she didn't want to. Like the Saturday girls working the slaughterhouse yard. When I came out of jail I saw them plain. They came when the shift changed on Saturday when the men got paid and worked behind the fences, back of the outhouse. Some worked standing up, leaning on the toolhouse door. They gave some of their nickels and dimes to the foreman as they left but by then their smiles was over. Some of them drank liquor to keep from feeling what they felt. Some didn't drink a drop—just beat it on over to Phelps to pay for what their children needed, or their ma'ammies. Working a pig yard. That has got to be something for a woman to do, and I got close to it myself when I got out of jail and bought, so to speak, your name. But the Bodwins got me the cooking job at Sawyer's and left me able to smile on my own like now when I think about you.

But you know all that because you smart like everybody

said because when I got here you was crawling already. Trying to get up the stairs. Baby Suggs had them painted white so you could see your way to the top in the dark where lamplight didn't reach. Lord, you loved the stairsteps.

I got close. I got close. To being a Saturday girl. I had already worked a stone mason's shop. A step to the slaughterhouse would have been a short one. When I put that headstone up I wanted to lay in there with you, put your head on my shoulder and keep you warm, and I would have if Buglar and Howard and Denver didn't need me, because my mind was homeless then. I couldn't lay down with you then. No matter how much I wanted to. I couldn't lay down nowhere in peace, back then. Now I can. I can sleep like the drowned, have mercy. She come back to me, my daughter, and she is mine.

BELOVED is my sister. I swallowed her blood right along with my mother's milk. The first thing I heard after not hearing anything was the sound of her crawling up the stairs. She was my secret company until Paul D came. He threw her out. Ever since I was little she was my company and she helped me wait for my daddy. Me and her waited for him. I love my mother but I know she killed one of her own daughters, and tender as she is with me, I'm scared of her because of it. She missed killing my brothers and they knew it. They told me die-witch! stories to show me the way to do it, if ever I needed to. Maybe it was getting that close to dying made them want to fight the War. That's what they told me they were going to do. I guess they rather be around killing men than killing women, and there sure is something in her that makes it all right to kill her own. All the time, I'm afraid the thing that happened that made it all right for my mother to kill my sister could happen again. I don't know what it is, I don't know who it is, but maybe there is something else terrible enough to make her do it again. I need to know what that thing might be, but I don't want to. Whatever it is, it comes from outside this house, outside the yard, and it can come right on in the yard if it wants to. So I never leave this house and I watch over the yard, so it can't happen again and my mother won't have to kill me too. Not since Miss Lady Jones' house have I left 124 by myself. Never. The only other times—two times in all—I was with my mother. Once to see Grandma Baby put down next to Beloved, she's my sister. The other time Paul D went too and when we came back I thought the house would still be empty from when he threw my sister's ghost out. But no. When I came back to 124, there she was. Beloved. Waiting for me. Tired from her long journey back. Ready to be taken care of; ready for me to protect her. This time I have to keep my mother away from her. That's hard, but I have to. It's all on me. I've seen my mother in a dark place, with scratching noises. A smell coming from her dress. I have been with her where something little watched us from the corners. And touched. Sometimes they touched. I didn't remember it for a long time until Nelson Lord made me. I asked her if it was true but couldn't hear what she said and there was no point in going back to Lady Jones if you couldn't hear what anybody said. So quiet. Made me have to read faces and learn how to figure out what people were thinking, so I didn't need to hear what they said. That's how come me and Beloved could play together. Not talking. On the porch. By the creek. In the secret house. It's all on me, now, but she can count on me. I thought she was trying to kill her that day in the Clearing. Kill her back. But then she kissed her neck and I have to warn her about that. Don't love her too much. Don't. Maybe it's still in her the thing that makes it all right to kill her children. I have to tell her. I have to protect her.

She cut my head off every night. Buglar and Howard told me she would and she did. Her pretty eyes looking at me like I was a stranger. Not mean or anything, but like I was somebody she found and felt sorry for. Like she didn't want to do it but she had to and it wasn't going to hurt. That it was just a thing grown-up people do—like pull a splinter out your hand; touch the corner of a towel in your eye if you get a cinder in it. She looks over at Buglar and Howard—see if they all right. Then she comes over to my side. I know she'll be good at it, careful. That when she cuts it off it'll be done right; it won't hurt. After she does it I lie there for a minute with just my head. Then she carries it downstairs to braid my hair. I try not to cry but it hurts so much to comb it. When she finishes the combing and starts the braiding, I get sleepy. I want to go to sleep but I know if I do I won't wake up. So I have to stay awake while she finishes my hair, then I can sleep. The scary part is waiting for her to come in and do it. Not when she does it, but when I wait for her to. Only place she can't get to me in the night is Grandma Baby's room. The room we sleep in upstairs used to be where the help slept when whitepeople lived here. They had a kitchen outside, too. But Grandma Baby turned it into a woodshed and toolroom when she moved in. And she boarded up the back door that led to it because she said she didn't want to make that journey no more. She built around it to make a storeroom, so if you want to get in 124 you have to come by her. Said she didn't care what folks said about her fixing a two-story house up like a cabin where you cook inside. She said they told her visitors with nice dresses don't want to sit in the same room with the cook stove and the peelings and the grease and the smoke. She wouldn't pay them no mind, she said. I was safe at night in there with her. All I could hear was me breathing but sometimes in the day I couldn't tell whether it was me breathing or somebody next to me. I used to watch Here Boy's stomach go in and out, in and out, to see if it matched mine, holding my breath to get off his rhythm, releasing it to get on. Just to see whose it was—that sound like when you blow soft in a bottle only regular, regular. Am I making that sound? Is Howard? Who is? That was when everybody was quiet and I couldn't hear anything they said. I didn't care either because the quiet let me dream my daddy better. I always knew he was coming. Something was holding him up. He had a problem with the horse. The river flooded; the boat sank and he had to make a new one. Sometimes it was a lynch mob or a windstorm. He was coming and it was a secret. I spent all of my outside self loving Ma'am so she wouldn't kill me, loving her even when she braided my head at night. I never let her know my daddy was coming for me. Grandma Baby thought he was coming, too. For a while she thought so, then she stopped. I never did. Even when Buglar and Howard ran away. Then Paul D came in here. I heard his voice downstairs, and Ma'am laughing, so I thought it was him, my daddy. Nobody comes to this house anymore. But when I got downstairs it was Paul D and he didn't come for me; he wanted my mother. At first. Then he wanted my sister, too, but she got him out of here and I'm so glad he's gone. Now it's just us and I can protect her till my daddy gets here to help me watch out for Ma'am and anything come in the yard.

My daddy do anything for runny fried eggs. Dip his bread in it. Grandma used to tell me his things. She said anytime she could make him a plate of soft fried eggs was Christmas, made him so happy. She said she was always a little scared of my daddy. He was too good, she said. From the beginning, she said, he was too good for the world. Scared her. She thought, He'll never make it through nothing. Whitepeople must have thought so too, because they never got split up. So she got the chance to know him, look after him, and he scared her the way he loved things. Animals and tools and crops and the alphabet. He could count on paper. The boss taught him. Offered to teach the other boys but only my daddy wanted it. She said the other boys said no. One of them with a number for a name said it would change his mind—make him forget things he shouldn't and memorize things he shouldn't and he didn't want his mind messed up. But my daddy said, If you can't count they can cheat you. If you can't read they can beat you. They thought that was funny. Grandma said she didn't know, but it was because my daddy could count on paper and figure that he bought her away from there. And she said she always wished she could read the Bible like real preachers. So it was good for me to learn how, and I did until it got quiet and all I could hear was my own breathing and one other who knocked over the milk jug while it was sitting on the table. Nobody near it. Ma'am whipped Buglar but he didn't touch it. Then it messed up all the ironed clothes and put its hands in the cake. Look like I was the only one who knew right away who it was. Just like when she came back I knew who she was too. Not right away, but soon as she spelled her name—not her given name, but the one Ma'am paid the stonecutter for—I knew. And when she wondered about Ma'am's earrings—something I didn't know about—well, that just made the cheese more binding: my sister come to help me wait for my daddy.

My daddy was an angel man. He could look at you and tell where you hurt and he could fix it too. He made a hanging thing for Grandma Baby, so she could pull herself up from the floor when she woke up in the morning, and he made a step so when she stood up she was level. Grandma said she was always afraid a whiteman would knock her down in front of her children. She behaved and did everything right in front of her children because she didn't want them to see her knocked down. She said it made children crazy to see that. At Sweet Home nobody did or said they would, so my daddy never saw it there and never went crazy and even now I bet he's trying to get here. If Paul D could do it my daddy could too. Angel man. We should all be together. Me, him and Beloved. Ma'am could stay or go off with Paul D if she wanted to. Unless Daddy wanted her himself, but I don't think he would now, since she let Paul D in her bed. Grandma Baby said people look down on her because she had eight children with different men. Coloredpeople and whitepeople both look down on her for that. Slaves not supposed to have pleasurable feelings on their own; their bodies not supposed to be like that, but they have to have as many children as they can to please whoever owned them. Still, they were not supposed to have pleasure deep down. She said for me not to listen to all that. That I should always listen to my body and love it.

The secret house. When she died I went there. Ma'am wouldn't let me go outside in the yard and eat with the others. We stayed inside. That hurt. I know Grandma Baby would have liked the party and the people who came to it, because she got low not seeing anybody or going anywhere—just grieving and thinking about colors and how she made a mistake. That what she thought about what the heart and the body could do was wrong. The whitepeople came anyway. In her yard. She had done everything right and they came in her yard anyway. And she didn't know what to think. All she had left was her heart and they busted it so even the War couldn't rouse her.

She told me all my daddy's things. How hard he worked to buy her. After the cake was ruined and the ironed clothes all messed up, and after I heard my sister crawling up the stairs to get back to her bed, she told me my things too. That I was charmed. My birth was and I got saved all the time. And that I shouldn't be afraid of the ghost. It wouldn't harm me because I tasted its blood when Ma'am nursed me. She said the ghost was after Ma'am and her too for not doing anything to stop it. But it would never hurt me. I just had to watch out for it because it was a greedy ghost and needed a lot of love, which was only natural, considering. And I do. Love her. I do. She played with me and always came to be with me whenever I needed her. She's mine, Beloved. She's mine.

I AM BELOVED and she is mine. I see her take flowers away from leaves she puts them in a round basket the leaves are not for her she fills the basket she opens the grass I would help her but the clouds are in the way how can I say things that are pictures I am not separate from her there is no place where I stop her face is my own and I want to be there in the place where her face is and to be looking at it too a hot thing

All of it is now it is always now there will never be a time when I am not crouching and watching others who are crouching too I am always crouching the man on my face is dead his face is not mine his mouth smells sweet but his eyes are locked

some who eat nasty themselves I do not eat the men without skin bring us their morning water to drink we have none at night I cannot see the dead man on my face daylight comes through the cracks and I can see his locked eyes I am not big small rats do not wait for us to sleep someone is thrashing but there is no room to do it in if we had more to drink we could make tears we cannot make sweat or morning water so the men without skin bring us theirs one time they bring us sweet rocks to suck we are all trying to leave our bodies behind the man on my face has done it it is hard to make yourself die forever you sleep short and then return in the beginning we could vomit now we do not

now we cannot his teeth are pretty white points someone is trembling I can feel it over here he is fighting hard to leave his body which is a small bird trembling there is no room to tremble so he is not able to die my own dead man is pulled away from my face I miss his pretty white points

We are not crouching now we are standing but my legs are like my dead man's eyes I cannot fall because there is no room to the men without skin are making loud noises I am not dead the bread is sea-colored I am too hungry to eat it the sun closes my eyes those able to die are in a pile I cannot find my man the one whose teeth I have loved a hot thing the little hill of dead people a hot thing the men without skin push them through with poles the woman is there with the face I want the face that is mine they fall into the sea which is the color of the bread she has nothing in her ears if I had the teeth of the man who died on my face I would bite the circle around her neck bite it away I know she does not like it now there is room to crouch and to watch the crouching others it is the crouching that is now always now inside the woman with my face is in the sea a hot thing

In the beginning I could see her I could not help her because the clouds were in the way in the beginning I could see her the shining in her ears she does not like the circle around her neck I know this I look hard at her so she will know that the clouds are in the way I am sure she saw me I am looking at her see me she empties out her eyes I am there in the place where her face is and telling her the noisy clouds were in my way she wants her earrings she wants her round basket I want her face a hot thing

in the beginning the women are away from the men and the men are away from the women storms rock us and mix the men into the women and the women into the men that is when I begin to be on the back of the man for a long time I see only his neck and his wide shoulders above me I am small I love him because he has a song when he turned around to die I see the teeth he sang through his singing was soft his singing is of the place where a woman takes flowers away from their leaves and puts them in a round basket before the clouds she is crouching near us but I do not see her until he locks his eyes and dies on my face we are that way there is no breath coming from his mouth and the place where breath should be is sweet-smelling the others do not know he is dead I know his song is gone now I love his pretty little teeth instead

I cannot lose her again my dead man was in the way like the noisy clouds when he dies on my face I can see hers she is going to smile at me she is going to her sharp earrings are gone the men without skin are making loud noises they push my own man through they do not push the woman with my face through she goes in they do not push her she goes in the little hill is gone she was going to smile at me she was going to a hot thing

They are not crouching now we are they are floating on the water they break up the little hill and push it through I cannot find my pretty teeth I see the dark face that is going to smile at me it is my dark face that is going to smile at me the iron circle is around our neck she does not have sharp earrings in her ears or a round basket she goes in the water with my face

I am standing in the rain falling the others are taken I am not taken I am falling like the rain is I watch him eat inside I am crouching to keep from falling with the rain I am going to be in pieces he hurts where I sleep he puts his finger there I drop the food and break into pieces she took my face away

there is no one to want me to say me my name I wait on the bridge because she is under it there is night and there is day

again again night day night day I am waiting no iron circle is around my neck no boats go on this water no men without skin my dead man is not floating here his teeth are down there where the blue is and the grass so is the face I want the face that is going to smile at me it is going to in the day diamonds are in the water where she is and turtles in the night I hear chewing and swallowing and laughter it belongs to me she is the laugh I am the laugher I see her face which is mine it is the face that was going to smile at me in the place where we crouched now she is going to her face comes through the water a hot thing her face is mine she is not smiling she is chewing and swallowing I have to have my face I go in the grass opens she opens it I am in the water and she is coming there is no round basket no iron circle around her neck she goes up where the diamonds are I follow her we are in the diamonds which are her earrings now my face is coming I have to have it I am looking for the join I am loving my face so much my dark face is close to me I want to join she whispers to me she whispers I reach for her chewing and swallowing she touches me she knows I want to join she chews and swallows me   I am gone   now I am her face my own face has left me   I see me swim away   a hot thing I see the bottoms of my feet   I am alone   I want to be the two of us   I want the join

I come out of blue water   after the bottoms of my feet swim   away from me I come up   I need to find a place to be the air is heavy   I am not dead   I am not   there is a house there is what she whispered to me   I am where she told me I am not dead   I sit   the sun closes my eyes   when I open them I see the face I lost   Sethe's is the face that left me Sethe sees me see her and I see the smile   her smiling face is the place for me   it is the face I lost   she is my face smiling at me   doing it at last   a hot thing   now we can join   a hot thing

I AM BELOVED and she is mine. Sethe is the one that picked flowers, yellow flowers in the place before the crouching. Took them away from their green leaves. They are on the quilt now where we sleep. She was about to smile at me when the men without skin came and took us up into the sunlight with the dead and shoved them into the sea. Sethe went into the sea. She went there. They did not push her. She went there. She was getting ready to smile at me and when she saw the dead people pushed into the sea she went also and left me there with no face or hers. Sethe is the face I found and lost in the water under the bridge. When I went in, I saw her face coming to me and it was my face too. I wanted to join. I tried to join, but she went up into the pieces of light at the top of the water. I lost her again, but I found the house she whispered to me and there she was, smiling at last. It's good, but I cannot lose her again. All I want to know is why did she go in the water in the place where we crouched? Why did she do that when she was just about to smile at me? I wanted to join her in the sea but I could not move; I wanted to help her when she was picking the flowers, but the clouds of gunsmoke blinded me and I lost her. Three times I lost her: once with the flowers because of the noisy clouds of smoke; once when she went into the sea instead of smiling at me; once under the bridge when I went in to join her and she came toward me but did not smile. She whispered to me, chewed me, and swam away. Now I have found her in this house. She smiles at me and it is my own face smiling. I will not lose her again. She is mine.

Tell me the truth. Didn't you come from the other side?
Yes. I was on the other side.
You came back because of me?
Yes.
You rememory me?
Yes. I remember you.
You never forgot me?
Your face is mine.
Do you forgive me? Will you stay? You safe here now.
Where are the men without skin?
Out there. Way off.
Can they get in here?
No. They tried that once, but I stopped them. They won't ever come back.
One of them was in the house I was in. He hurt me.
They can't hurt us no more.
Where are your earrings?
They took them from me.
The men without skin took them?
Yes.
I was going to help you but the clouds got in the way.
There're no clouds here.
If they put an iron circle around your neck I will bite it away.
Beloved.
I will make you a round basket.
You're back. You're back.
Will we smile at me?

Can't you see I'm smiling?
I love your face.

We played by the creek.
I was there in the water.
In the quiet time, we played.
The clouds were noisy and in the way.
When I needed you, you came to be with me.
I needed her face to smile.
I could only hear breathing.
The breathing is gone; only the teeth are left.
She said you wouldn't hurt me.
She hurt me.
I will protect you.
I want her face.
Don't love her too much.
I am loving her too much.
Watch out for her; she can give you dreams.
She chews and swallows.
Don't fall asleep when she braids your hair.
She is the laugh; I am the laughter.
I watch the house; I watch the yard.
She left me.
Daddy is coming for us.
A hot thing.

Beloved
You are my sister
You are my daughter
You are my face; you are me
I have found you again; you have come back to me
You are my Beloved
You are mine

You are mine
You are mine

I have your milk
I have your smile
I will take care of you

You are my face; I am you. Why did you leave me who am you?
I will never leave you again
Don't ever leave me again
You will never leave me again
You went in the water
I drank your blood
I brought your milk
You forgot to smile
I loved you
You hurt me
You came back to me
You left me

I waited for you
You are mine
You are mine
You are mine

IT WAS a tiny church no bigger than a rich man's parlor. The pews had no backs, and since the congregation was also the choir, it didn't need a stall. Certain members had been assigned the construction of a platform to raise the preacher a few inches above his congregation, but it was a less than urgent task, since the major elevation, a white oak cross, had already taken place. Before it was the Church of the Holy Redeemer, it was a dry-goods shop that had no use for side windows, just front ones for display. These were papered over while members considered whether to paint or curtain them—how to have privacy without losing the little light that might want to shine on them. In the summer the doors were left open for ventilation. In winter an iron stove in the aisle did what it could. At the front of the church was a sturdy porch where customers used to sit, and children laughed at the boy who got his head stuck between the railings. On a sunny and windless day in January it was actually warmer out there than inside, if the iron stove was cold. The damp cellar was fairly warm, but there was no light lighting the pallet or the washbasin or the nail from which a man's clothes could be hung. And an oil lamp in a cellar was sad, so Paul D sat on the porch steps and got additional warmth from a bottle of liquor jammed in his coat pocket. Warmth and red eyes. He held his wrist between his knees, not to keep his hands still but because he had nothing else to hold on to. His tobacco tin, blown open, spilled contents that floated freely and made him their play and prey.

He couldn't figure out why it took so long. He may as well have jumped in the fire with Sixo and they both could have had a good laugh. Surrender was bound to come anyway, why not meet it with a laugh, shouting Seven-O! Why not? Why the delay? He had already seen his brother wave goodbye from the back of a dray, fried chicken in his pocket, tears in his eyes. Mother. Father. Didn't remember the one. Never saw the other. He was the youngest of three half-brothers (same mother—different fathers) sold to Garner and kept there, forbidden to leave the farm, for twenty years. Once, in Maryland, he met four families of slaves who had all been together for a hundred years: great-grands, grands, mothers, fathers, aunts, uncles, cousins, children. Half white, part white, all black, mixed with Indian. He watched them with awe and envy, and each time he discovered large families of black people he made them identify over and over who each was, what relation, who, in fact, belonged to who.

"That there's my auntie. This here's her boy. Yonder is my pap's cousin. My ma'am was married twice—this my half-sister and these her two children. Now, my wife . . ."

Nothing like that had ever been his and growing up at Sweet Home he didn't miss it. He had his brothers, two friends, Baby Suggs in the kitchen, a boss who showed them how to shoot and listened to what they had to say. A mistress who made their soap and never raised her voice. For twenty years they had all lived in that cradle, until Baby left, Sethe came, and Halle took her. He made a family with her, and Sixo was hell-bent to make one with the Thirty-Mile Woman. When Paul D waved goodbye to his oldest brother, the boss was dead, the mistress nervous and the cradle already split. Sixo said the doctor made Mrs. Garner sick. Said he was giving her to drink what stallions got when they broke a leg and no gunpowder could be spared, and had it not been for schoolteacher's new rules, he would have told her so. They laughed at him. Sixo had a knowing tale about everything. Including Mr. Garner's stroke, which he said was a shot in his ear put there by a jealous neighbor.

"Where's the blood?" they asked him.

There was no blood. Mr. Garner came home bent over his mare's neck, sweating and blue-white. Not a drop of blood. Sixo grunted, the only one of them not sorry to see him go. Later, however, he was mighty sorry; they all were.

"Why she call on him?" Paul D asked. "Why she need the schoolteacher?"

"She need somebody can figure," said Halle.

"You can do figures."

"Not like that."

"No, man," said Sixo. "She need another white on the place."

"What for?"

"What you think? What you think?"

Well, that's the way it was. Nobody counted on Garner dying. Nobody thought he could. How 'bout that? Everything rested on Garner being alive. Without his life each of theirs fell to pieces. Now ain't that slavery or what is it? At the peak of his strength, taller than tall men, and stronger than most, they clipped him, Paul D. First his shotgun, then his thoughts, for schoolteacher didn't take advice from Negroes. The information they offered he called backtalk and developed a variety of corrections (which he recorded in his notebook) to reeducate them. He complained they ate too much, rested too much, talked too much, which was certainly true compared to him, because schoolteacher ate little, spoke less and rested not at all. Once he saw them playing—a pitching game—and his look of deeply felt hurt was enough to make Paul D blink. He was as hard on his pupils as he was on them—except for the corrections.

For years Paul D believed schoolteacher broke into children what Garner had raised into men. And it was that that made them run off. Now, plagued by the contents of his tobacco tin, he wondered how much difference there really was between before schoolteacher and after. Garner called and announced them men—but only on Sweet Home, and by his leave. Was he naming what he saw or creating what he did not? That was the wonder of Sixo, and even Halle; it was always clear to Paul D that those two were men whether Garner said so or not. It troubled him that, concerning his own manhood, he could not satisfy himself on that point. Oh, he did manly things, but was that Garner's gift or his own will? What would he have been anyway—before Sweet Home—without Garner? In Sixo's country, or his mother's? Or, God help him, on the boat? Did a whiteman saying it make it so? Suppose Garner woke up one morning and changed his mind? Took the word away. Would they have run then? And if he didn't, would the Pauls have stayed there all their lives? Why did the brothers need the one whole night to decide? To discuss whether they would join Sixo and Halle. Because they had been isolated in a wonderful lie, dismissing Halle's and Baby Suggs' life before Sweet Home as bad luck. Ignorant of or amused by Sixo's dark stories. Protected and convinced they were special. Never suspecting the problem of Alfred, Georgia; being so in love with the look of the world, putting up with anything and everything, just to stay alive in a place where a moon he had no right to was nevertheless there. Loving small and in secret. His little love was a tree, of course, but not like Brother—old, wide and beckoning.

In Alfred, Georgia, there was an aspen too young to call sapling. Just a shoot no taller than his waist. The kind of thing a man would cut to whip his horse. Song-murder and the aspen. He stayed alive to sing songs that murdered life, and watched an aspen that confirmed it, and never for a minute did he believe he could escape. Until it rained. Afterward, after the Cherokee pointed and sent him running toward blossoms, he wanted simply to move, go, pick up one day and be somewhere else the next. Resigned to life without aunts, cousins, children. Even a woman, until Sethe.

And then she moved him. Just when doubt, regret and every single unasked question was packed away, long after he believed he had willed himself into being, at the very time and place he wanted to take root—she moved him. From room to room. Like a rag doll.

Sitting on the porch of a dry-goods church, a little bit drunk and nothing much to do, he could have these thoughts. Slow, what-if thoughts that cut deep but struck nothing solid a man could hold on to. So he held his wrists. Passing by that woman's life, getting in it and letting it get in him had set him up for this fall. Wanting to live out his life with a whole woman was new, and losing the feeling of it made him want to cry and think deep thoughts that struck nothing solid. When he was drifting, thinking only about the next meal and night's sleep, when everything was packed tight in his chest, he had no sense of failure, of things not working out. Anything that worked at all worked out. Now he wondered whatall went wrong, and starting with the Plan, everything had. It was a good plan, too. Worked out in detail with every possibility of error eliminated.

Sixo, hitching up the horses, is speaking English again and tells Halle what his Thirty-Mile Woman told him. That seven Negroes on her place were joining two others going North. That the two others had done it before and knew the way. That one of the two, a woman, would wait for them in the corn when it was high—one night and half of the next day she would wait, and if they came she would take them to the caravan, where the others would be hidden. That she would rattle, and that would be the sign. Sixo was going, his woman was going, and Halle was taking his whole family. The two Pauls say they need time to think about it. Time to wonder where they will end up; how they will live. What work; who will take them in; should they try to get to Paul F, whose owner, they remember, lived in something called the "trace"? It takes them one evening's conversation to decide.

Now all they have to do is wait through the spring, till the corn is as high as it ever got and the moon as fat.

And plan. Is it better to leave in the dark to get a better start, or go at daybreak to be able to see the way better? Sixo spits at the suggestion. Night gives them more time and the protection of color. He does not ask them if they are afraid. He manages some dry runs to the corn at night, burying blankets and two knives near the creek. Will Sethe be able to swim the creek? they ask him. It will be dry, he says, when the corn is tall. There is no food to put by, but Sethe says she will get a jug of cane syrup or molasses, and some bread when it is near the time to go. She only wants to be sure the blankets are where they should be, for they will need them to tie her baby on her back and to cover them during the journey. There are no clothes other than what they wear. And of course no shoes. The knives will help them eat, but they bury rope and a pot as well. A good plan.

They watch and memorize the comings and goings of schoolteacher and his pupils: what is wanted when and where; how long it takes. Mrs. Garner, restless at night, is sunk in sleep all morning. Some days the pupils and their teacher do lessons until breakfast. One day a week they skip breakfast completely and travel ten miles to church, expecting a large dinner upon their return. Schoolteacher writes in his notebook after supper; the pupils clean, mend or sharpen tools. Sethe's work is the most uncertain because she is on call for Mrs. Garner anytime, including nighttime when the pain or the weakness or the downright loneliness is too much for her. So: Sixo and the Pauls will go after supper and wait in the creek for the Thirty-Mile Woman. Halle will bring Sethe and the three children before dawn—before the sun, before the chickens and the milking cow need attention, so by the time smoke should be coming from the cooking stove, they will be in or near the creek with the others. That way, if Mrs. Garner needs Sethe in the night and calls her, Sethe will be there to answer. They only have to wait through the spring.

But. Sethe was pregnant in the spring and by August is so heavy with child she may not be able to keep up with the men, who can carry the children but not her.

But. Neighbors discouraged by Garner when he was alive now feel free to visit Sweet Home and might appear in the right place at the wrong time.

But. Sethe's children cannot play in the kitchen anymore, so she is dashing back and forth between house and quarters—fidgety and frustrated trying to watch over them. They are too young for men's work and the baby girl is nine months old. Without Mrs. Garner's help her work increases as do schoolteacher's demands.

But. After the conversation about the shoat, Sixo is tied up with the stock at night, and locks are put on bins, pens, sheds, coops, the tackroom and the barn door. There is no place to dart into or congregate. Sixo keeps a nail in his mouth now, to help him undo the rope when he has to.

But. Halle is told to work his extra on Sweet Home and has no call to be anywhere other than where schoolteacher tells him. Only Sixo, who has been stealing away to see his woman, and Halle, who has been hired away for years, know what lies outside Sweet Home and how to get there.

It is a good plan. It can be done right under the watchful pupils and their teacher.

But. They had to alter it—just a little. First they change the leaving. They memorize the directions Halle gives them. Sixo, needing time to untie himself, break open the door and not disturb the horses, will leave later, joining them at the creek with the Thirty-Mile Woman. All four will go straight to the corn. Halle, who also needs more time now, because of Sethe, decides to bring her and the children at night; not wait till first light. They will go straight to the corn and not assemble at the creek. The corn stretches to their shoulders—it will never be higher. The moon is swelling. They can hardly harvest, or chop, or clear, or pick, or haul for listening for a rattle that is not bird or snake. Then one midmorning, they hear it. Or Halle does and begins to sing it to the others: "Hush, hush. Somebody's calling my name. Hush, hush. Somebody's calling my name. O my Lord, O my Lord, what shall I do?"

On his dinner break he leaves the field. He has to. He has to tell Sethe that he has heard the sign. For two successive nights she has been with Mrs. Garner and he can't chance it that she will not know that this night she cannot be. The Pauls see him go. From underneath Brother's shade where they are chewing corn cake, they see him, swinging along. The bread tastes good. They lick sweat from their lips to give it a saltier flavor. Schoolteacher and his pupils are already at the house eating dinner. Halle swings along. He is not singing now.

Nobody knows what happened. Except for the churn, that was the last anybody ever saw of Halle. What Paul D knew was that Halle disappeared, never told Sethe anything, and was next seen squatting in butter. Maybe when he got to the gate and asked to see Sethe, schoolteacher heard a tint of anxiety in his voice—the tint that would make him pick up his ever-ready shotgun. Maybe Halle made the mistake of saying "my wife" in some way that would put a light in schoolteacher's eye. Sethe says now that she heard shots, but did not look out the window of Mrs. Garner's bedroom. But Halle was not killed or wounded that day because Paul D saw him later, after she had run off with no one's help; after Sixo laughed and his brother disappeared. Saw him greased and flat-eyed as a fish. Maybe schoolteacher shot after him, shot at his feet, to remind him of the trespass. Maybe Halle got in the barn, hid there and got locked in with the rest of schoolteacher's stock. Maybe anything. He disappeared and everybody was on his own.

Paul A goes back to moving timber after dinner. They are to meet at quarters for supper. He never shows up. Paul D leaves for the creek on time, believing, hoping, Paul A has gone on ahead; certain schoolteacher has learned something. Paul D gets to the creek and it is as dry as Sixo promised. He waits there with the Thirty-Mile Woman for Sixo and Paul A. Only Sixo shows up, his wrists bleeding, his tongue licking his lips like a flame.

"You see Paul A?"

"No."

"Halle?"

"No."

"No sign of them?"

"No sign. Nobody in quarters but the children."

"Sethe?"

"Her children sleep. She must be there still."

"I can't leave without Paul A."

"I can't help you."

"Should I go back and look for them?"

"I can't help you."

"What you think?"

"I think they go straight to the corn."

Sixo turns, then, to the woman and they clutch each other and whisper. She is lit now with some glowing, some shining that comes from inside her. Before when she knelt on creek pebbles with Paul D, she was nothing, a shape in the dark breathing lightly.

Sixo is about to crawl out to look for the knives he buried. He hears something. He hears nothing. Forget the knives. Now. The three of them climb up the bank and schoolteacher, his pupils and four other whitemen move toward them. With lamps. Sixo pushes the Thirty-Mile Woman and she runs further on in the creekbed. Paul D and Sixo run the other way toward the woods. Both are surrounded and tied.

The air gets sweet then. Perfumed by the things honeybees love. Tied like a mule, Paul D feels how dewy and inviting the grass is. He is thinking about that and where Paul A might be when Sixo turns and grabs the mouth of the nearest pointing rifle. He begins to sing. Two others shove Paul D and tie him to a tree. Schoolteacher is saying, "Alive. Alive. I want him alive." Sixo swings and cracks the ribs of one, but with bound hands cannot get the weapon in position to use it in any other way. All the whitemen have to do is wait. For his song, perhaps, to end? Five guns are trained on him while they listen. Paul D cannot see them when they step away from lamplight. Finally one of them hits Sixo in the head with his rifle, and when he comes to, a hickory fire is in front of him and he is tied at the waist to a tree. Schoolteacher has changed his mind: "This one will never be suitable." The song must have convinced him.

The fire keeps failing and the whitemen are put out with themselves at not being prepared for this emergency. They came to capture, not kill. What they can manage is only enough for cooking hominy. Dry faggots are scarce and the grass is slick with dew.

By the light of the hominy fire Sixo straightens. He is through with his song. He laughs. A rippling sound like Sethe's sons make when they tumble in hay or splash in rainwater. His feet are cooking; the cloth of his trousers smokes.

He laughs. Something is funny. Paul D guesses what it is when Sixo interrupts his laughter to call out, "Seven-O! Seven-O!"

Smoky, stubborn fire. They shoot him to shut him up. Have to.

Shackled, walking through the perfumed things honeybees love, Paul D hears the men talking and for the first time learns his worth. He has always known, or believed he did, his value—as a hand, a laborer who could make profit on a farm—but now he discovers his worth, which is to say he learns his price. The dollar value of his weight, his strength, his heart, his brain, his penis, and his future.

As soon as the whitemen get to where they have tied their horses and mount them, they are calmer, talking among themselves about the difficulty they face. The problems. Voices remind schoolteacher about the spoiling these particular slaves have had at Garner's hands. There's laws against what he done: letting niggers hire out their own time to buy themselves. He even let em have guns! And you think he mated them niggers to get him some more? Hell no! He planned for them to marry! if that don't beat all! Schoolteacher sighs, and says doesn't he know it? He had come to put the place aright. Now it faced greater ruin than what Garner left for it, because of the loss of two niggers, at the least, and maybe three because he is not sure they will find the one called Halle. The sister-in-law is too weak to help out and doggone if now there ain't a full-scale stampede on his hands. He would have to trade this here one for $900 if he could get it, and set out to secure the breeding one, her foal and the other one, if he found him. With the money from "this here one" he could get two young ones, twelve or fifteen years old. And maybe with the breeding one, her three pickaninnies and whatever the foal might be, he and his nephews would have seven niggers and Sweet Home would be worth the trouble it was causing him.

"Look to you like Lillian gonna make it?"

"Touch and go. Touch and go."

"You was married to her sister-in-law, wasn't you?"

"I was."

"She frail too?"

"A bit. Fever took her."

"Well, you don't need to stay no widower in these parts."

"My cogitation right now is Sweet Home."

"Can't say as I blame you. That's some spread."

They put a three-spoke collar on him so he can't lie down and they chain his ankles together. The number he heard with his ear is now in his head. Two. Two? Two niggers lost? Paul D thinks his heart is jumping. They are going to look for Halle, not Paul A. They must have found Paul A and if a whiteman finds you it means you are surely lost.

Schoolteacher looks at him for a long time before he closes the door of the cabin. Carefully, he looks. Paul D does not look back. It is sprinkling now. A teasing August rain that raises expectations it cannot fill. He thinks he should have sung along. Loud, something loud and rolling to go with Sixo's tune, but the words put him off—he didn't understand the words. Although it shouldn't have mattered because he understood the sound: hatred so loose it was juba.

The warm sprinkle comes and goes, comes and goes. He thinks he hears sobbing that seems to come from Mrs. Garner's window, but it could be anything, anyone, even a she-cat making her yearning known. Tired of holding his head up, he lets his chin rest on the collar and speculates on how he can hobble over to the grate, boil a little water and throw in a handful of meal. That's what he is doing when Sethe comes in, rain-wet and big-bellied, saying she is going to cut. She has just come back from taking her children to the corn. The whites were not around. She couldn't find Halle. Who was caught? Did Sixo get away? Paul A?

He tells her what he knows: Sixo is dead; the Thirty-Mile Woman ran, and he doesn't know what happened to Paul A or Halle. "Where could he be?" she asks.

Paul D shrugs because he can't shake his head.

"You saw Sixo die? You sure?"

"I'm sure."

"Was he woke when it happened? Did he see it coming?"

"He was woke. Woke and laughing."

"Sixo laughed?"

"You should have heard him, Sethe."

Sethe's dress steams before the little fire over which he is boiling water. It is hard to move about with shackled ankles and the neck jewelry embarrasses him. In his shame he avoids her eyes, but when he doesn't he sees only black in them—no whites. She says she is going, and he thinks she will never make it to the gate, but he doesn't dissuade her. He knows he will never see her again, and right then and there his heart stopped.

The pupils must have taken her to the barn for sport right afterward, and when she told Mrs. Garner, they took down the cowhide. Who in hell or on this earth would have thought that she would cut anyway? They must have believed, what with her belly and her back, that she wasn't going anywhere. He wasn't surprised to learn that they had tracked her down in Cincinnati, because, when he thought about it now, her price was greater than his; property that reproduced itself without cost.

Remembering his own price, down to the cent, that schoolteacher was able to get for him, he wondered what Sethe's would have been. What had Baby Suggs' been? How much did Halle owe, still, besides his labor? What did Mrs. Garner get for Paul F? More than nine hundred dollars? How much more? Ten dollars? Twenty? Schoolteacher would know. He knew the worth of everything. It accounted for the real sorrow in his voice when he pronounced Sixo unsuitable. Who could be fooled into buying a singing nigger with a gun? Shouting Seven-O! Seven-O! because his Thirty-Mile Woman got away with his blossoming seed. What a laugh. So rippling and full of glee it put out the fire. And it was Sixo's laughter that was on his mind, not the bit in his mouth, when they hitched him to the buckboard. Then he saw Halle, then the rooster, smiling as if to say, You ain't seen nothing yet. How could a rooster know about Alfred, Georgia?

"HOWDY."

Stamp Paid was still fingering the ribbon and it made a little motion in his pants pocket.

Paul D looked up, noticed the side pocket agitation and snorted. "I can't read. You got any more newspaper for me, just a waste of time."

Stamp withdrew the ribbon and sat down on the steps.

"No. This here's something else." He stroked the red cloth between forefinger and thumb. "Something else."

Paul D didn't say anything so the two men sat in silence for a few moments.

"This is hard for me," said Stamp. "But I got to do it. Two things I got to say to you. I'm a take the easy one first."

Paul D chuckled. "If it's hard for you, might kill me dead."

"No, no. Nothing like that. I come looking for you to ask your pardon. Apologize."

"For what?" Paul D reached in his coat pocket for his bottle.

"You pick any house, any house where colored live. In all of Cincinnati. Pick any one and you welcome to stay there. I'm apologizing because they didn't offer or tell you. But you welcome anywhere you want to be. My house is your house too. John and Ella, Miss Lady, Able Woodruff, Willie Pike—

anybody. You choose. You ain't got to sleep in no cellar, and I apologize for each and every night you did. I don't know how that preacher let you do it. I knowed him since he was a boy."

"Whoa, Stamp. He offered."

"Did? Well?"

"Well. I wanted, I didn't want to, I just wanted to be off by myself a spell. He offered. Every time I see him he offers again."

"That's a load off. I thought everybody gone crazy."

Paul D shook his head. "Just me."

"You planning to do anything about it?"

"Oh, yeah. I got big plans." He swallowed twice from the bottle.

Any planning in a bottle is short, thought Stamp, but he knew from personal experience the pointlessness of telling a drinking man not to. He cleared his sinuses and began to think how to get to the second thing he had come to say. Very few people were out today. The canal was frozen so that traffic too had stopped. They heard the clop of a horse approaching. Its rider sat a high Eastern saddle but everything else about him was Ohio Valley. As he rode by he looked at them and suddenly reined his horse, and came up to the path leading to the church. He leaned forward.

"Hey," he said.

Stamp put his ribbon in his pocket. "Yes, sir?"

"I'm looking for a gal name of Judy. Works over by the slaughterhouse."

"Don't believe I know her. No, sir."

"Said she lived on Plank Road."

"Plank Road. Yes, sir. That's up a ways. Mile, maybe."

"You don't know her? Judy. Works in the slaughterhouse."

"No, sir, but I know Plank Road. 'Bout a mile up thataway."

Paul D lifted his bottle and swallowed. The rider looked at him and then back at Stamp Paid. Loosening the right rein, he turned his horse toward the road, then changed his mind and came back.

"Look here," he said to Paul D. "There's a cross up there, so I guess this here's a church or used to be. Seems to me like you ought to show it some respect, you follow me?"

"Yes, sir," said Stamp. "You right about that. That's just what I come over to talk to him about. Just that."

The rider clicked his tongue and trotted off. Stamp made small circles in the palm of his left hand with two fingers of his right. "You got to choose," he said. "Choose anyone. They let you be if you want em to. My house. Ella. Willie Pike. None of us got much, but all of us got room for one more. Pay a little something when you can, don't when you can't. Think about it. You grown. I can't make you do what you won't, but think about it."

Paul D said nothing.

"If I did you harm, I'm here to rectify it."

"No need for that. No need at all."

A woman with four children walked by on the other side of the road. She waved, smiling. "Hoo-oo. I can't stop. See you at meeting."

"I be there," Stamp returned her greeting. "There's another one," he said to Paul D. "Scripture Woodruff, Able's sister. Works at the brush and tallow factory. You'll see. Stay around here long enough, you'll see ain't a sweeter bunch of colored anywhere than what's right here. Pride, well, that bothers em a bit. They can get messy when they think somebody's too proud, but when it comes right down to it, they good people and anyone will take you in."

"What about Judy? She take me in?"

"Depends. What you got in mind?"

"You know Judy?"

"Judith. I know everybody."

"Out on Plank Road?"

"Everybody."

"Well? She take me in?"

Stamp leaned down and untied his shoe. Twelve black buttonhooks, six on each side at the bottom, led to four pairs of eyes at the top. He loosened the laces all the way down, adjusted the tongue carefully and wound them back again. When he got to the eyes he rolled the lace tips with his fingers before inserting them.

"Let me tell you how I got my name." The knot was tight and so was the bow. "They called me Joshua," he said. "I renamed myself," he said, "and I'm going to tell you why I did it," and he told him about Vashti. "I never touched her all that time. Not once. Almost a year. We was planting when it started and picking when it stopped. Seemed longer. I should have killed him. She said no, but I should have. I didn't have the patience I got now, but I figured maybe somebody else didn't have much patience either—his own wife. Took it in my head to see if she was taking it any better than I was. Vashti and me was in the fields together in the day and every now and then she be gone all night. I never touched her and damn me if I spoke three words to her a day. I took any chance I had to get near the great house to see her, the young master's wife. Nothing but a boy. Seventeen, twenty maybe. I caught sight of her finally, standing in the backyard by the fence with a glass of water. She was drinking out of it and just gazing out over the yard. I went over. Stood back a ways and took off my hat. I said, 'Scuse me, miss. Scuse me?' She turned to look. I'm smiling. 'Scuse me. You seen Vashti? My wife Vashti?' A little bitty thing, she was. Black hair. Face no bigger than my hand. She said, 'What? Vashti?' I say, 'Yes'm, Vashti. My wife. She say she owe you all some eggs. You know if she brung em? You know her if you see her. Wear a black ribbon on her neck.' She got rosy then and I knowed she knowed. He give Vashti that to wear. A cameo on a black ribbon. She used to put it on every time she went to him. I put my hat back on. 'You see her tell her I need her. Thank you. Thank you, ma'am.' I backed off before she could say something. I didn't dare look back till I got behind some trees. She was standing just as I left her, looking in her water glass. I thought it would give me more satisfaction than it did. I also thought she might stop it, but it went right on. Till one morning Vashti came in and sat by the window. A Sunday. We worked our own patches on Sunday. She sat by the window looking out of it. 'I'm back,' she said. 'I'm back, Josh.' I looked at the back of her neck. She had a real small neck. I decided to break it. You know, like a twig—just snap it. I been low but that was as low as I ever got."

"Did you? Snap it?"

"Uh uh. I changed my name."

"How you get out of there? How you get up here?"

"Boat. On up the Mississippi to Memphis. Walked from Memphis to Cumberland."

"Vashti too?"

"No. She died."

"Aw, man. Tie your other shoe!"

"What?"

"Tie your goddamn shoe! It's sitting right in front of you! Tie it!"

"That make you feel better?"

"No." Paul D tossed the bottle on the ground and stared at the golden chariot on its label. No horses. Just a golden coach draped in blue cloth.

"I said I had two things to say to you. I only told you one. I have to tell you the other."

"I don't want to know it. I don't want to know nothing. Just if Judy will take me in or won't she."

"I was there, Paul D."

"You was where?"

"There in the yard. When she did it."

"Judy?"

"Sethe."

"Jesus."

"It ain't what you think."

"You don't know what I think."

"She ain't crazy. She love those children. She was trying to out-hurt the hurter."

"Leave off."

"And spread it."

"Stamp, let me off. I knew her when she was a girl. She scares me and I knew her when she was a girl."

"You ain't scared of Sethe. I don't believe you."

"Sethe scares me. I scare me. And that girl in her house scares me the most."

"Who is that girl? Where she come from?"

"I don't know. Just shot up one day sitting on a stump."

"Huh. Look like you and me the only ones outside 124 lay eyes on her."

"She don't go nowhere. Where'd you see her?"

"Sleeping on the kitchen floor. I peeped in."

"First minute I saw her I didn't want to be nowhere around her. Something funny about her. Talks funny. Acts funny." Paul D dug his fingers underneath his cap and rubbed the scalp over his temple. "She reminds me of something. Something, look like, I'm supposed to remember."

"She never say where she was from? Where's her people?"

"She don't know, or says she don't. All I ever heard her

say was something about stealing her clothes and living on a bridge."

"What kind of bridge?"

"Who you asking?"

"No bridges around here I don't know about. But don't nobody live on em. Under em neither. How long she been over there with Sethe?"

"Last August. Day of the carnival."

"That's a bad sign. Was she at the carnival?"

"No. When we got back, there she was—'sleep on a stump. Silk dress. Brand-new shoes. Black as oil."

"You don't say? Huh. Was a girl locked up in the house with a whiteman over by Deer Creek. Found him dead last summer and the girl gone. Maybe that's her. Folks say he had her in there since she was a pup."

"Well, now she's a bitch."

"Is she what run you off? Not what I told you 'bout Sethe?"

A shudder ran through Paul D. A bone-cold spasm that made him clutch his knees. He didn't know if it was bad whiskey, nights in the cellar, pig fever, iron bits, smiling roosters, fired feet, laughing dead men, hissing grass, rain, apple blossoms, neck jewelry, Judy in the slaughterhouse, Halle in the butter, ghost-white stairs, chokecherry trees, cameo pins, aspens, Paul A's face, sausage or the loss of a red, red heart.

"Tell me something, Stamp." Paul D's eyes were rheumy. "Tell me this one thing. How much is a nigger supposed to take? Tell me. How much?"

"All he can," said Stamp Paid. "All he can."

"Why? Why? Why? Why? Why?"

III

124 WAS QUIET. Denver, who thought she knew all about silence, was surprised to learn hunger could do that: quiet you down and wear you out. Neither Sethe nor Beloved knew or cared about it one way or another. They were too busy rationing their strength to fight each other. So it was she who had to step off the edge of the world and die because if she didn't, they all would. The flesh between her mother's forefinger and thumb was thin as china silk and there wasn't a piece of clothing in the house that didn't sag on her. Beloved held her head up with the palms of her hands, slept wherever she happened to be, and whined for sweets although she was getting bigger, plumper by the day. Everything was gone except two laying hens, and somebody would soon have to decide whether an egg every now and then was worth more than two fried chickens. The hungrier they got, the weaker; the weaker they got, the quieter they were—which was better than the furious arguments, the poker slammed up against the wall, all the shouting and crying that followed that one happy January when they played. Denver had joined in the play, holding back a bit out of habit, even though it was the most fun she had ever known. But once Sethe had seen the scar, the tip of which Denver had been looking at whenever Beloved undressed—the little curved shadow of a smile in the kootchy-kootchy-coo place under her chin—once Sethe saw it, fingered

it and closed her eyes for a long time, the two of them cut Denver out of the games. The cooking games, the sewing games, the hair and dressing-up games. Games her mother loved so well she took to going to work later and later each day until the predictable happened: Sawyer told her not to come back. And instead of looking for another job, Sethe played all the harder with Beloved, who never got enough of anything: lullabies, new stitches, the bottom of the cake bowl, the top of the milk. If the hen had only two eggs, she got both. It was as though her mother had lost her mind, like Grandma Baby calling for pink and not doing the things she used to. But different because, unlike Baby Suggs, she cut Denver out completely. Even the song that she used to sing to Denver she sang for Beloved alone: "High Johnny, wide Johnny, don't you leave my side, Johnny."

At first they played together. A whole month and Denver loved it. From the night they ice-skated under a star-loaded sky and drank sweet milk by the stove, to the string puzzles Sethe did for them in afternoon light, and shadow pictures in the gloaming. In the very teeth of winter and Sethe, her eyes fever bright, was plotting a garden of vegetables and flowers—talking, talking about what colors it would have. She played with Beloved's hair, braiding, puffing, tying, oiling it until it made Denver nervous to watch her. They changed beds and exchanged clothes. Walked arm in arm and smiled all the time. When the weather broke, they were on their knees in the backyard designing a garden in dirt too hard to chop. The thirty-eight dollars of life savings went to feed themselves with fancy food and decorate themselves with ribbon and dress goods, which Sethe cut and sewed like they were going somewhere in a hurry. Bright clothes—with blue stripes and sassy prints. She walked the four miles to John Shillito's to buy yellow ribbon, shiny buttons and bits of black lace. By the end of March the three of them looked like carnival women with nothing to do. When it became clear that they were only interested in each other, Denver began to drift from the play, but she watched it, alert for any sign that Beloved was in danger. Finally convinced there was none, and seeing her mother that happy, that smiling—how could it go wrong?—she let down her guard and it did. Her problem at first was trying to find out who was to blame. Her eye was on her mother, for a signal that the thing that was in her was out, and she would kill again. But it was Beloved who made demands. Anything she wanted she got, and when Sethe ran out of things to give her, Beloved invented desire. She wanted Sethe's company for hours to watch the layer of brown leaves waving at them from the bottom of the creek, in the same place where, as a little girl, Denver played in the silence with her. Now the players were altered. As soon as the thaw was complete Beloved gazed at her gazing face, rippling, folding, spreading, disappearing into the leaves below. She flattened herself on the ground, dirtying her bold stripes, and touched the rocking faces with her own. She filled basket after basket with the first things warmer weather let loose in the ground—dandelions, violets, forsythia—presenting them to Sethe, who arranged them, stuck them, wound them all over the house. Dressed in Sethe's dresses, she stroked her skin with the palm of her hand. She imitated Sethe, talked the way she did, laughed her laugh and used her body the same way down to the walk, the way Sethe moved her hands, sighed through her nose, held her head. Sometimes coming upon them making men and women cookies or tacking scraps of cloth on Baby Suggs' old quilt, it was difficult for Denver to tell who was who.

Then the mood changed and the arguments began. Slowly at first. A complaint from Beloved, an apology from Sethe. A reduction of pleasure at some special effort the older woman made. Wasn't it too cold to stay outside? Beloved gave a look that said, So what? Was it past bedtime, the light no good for sewing? Beloved didn't move; said, "Do it," and Sethe complied. She took the best of everything—first. The best chair, the biggest piece, the prettiest plate, the brightest ribbon for her hair, and the more she took, the more Sethe began to talk, explain, describe how much she had suffered, been through, for her children, waving away flies in grape arbors, crawling on her knees to a lean-to. None of which made the impression it was supposed to. Beloved accused her of leaving her behind. Of not being nice to her, not smiling at her. She said they were the same, had the same face, how could she have left her? And Sethe cried, saying she never did, or meant to—that she had to get them out, away, that she had the milk all the time and had the money too for the stone but not enough. That her plan was always that they would all be together on the other side, forever. Beloved wasn't interested. She said when she cried there was no one. That dead men lay on top of her. That she had nothing to eat. Ghosts without skin stuck their fingers in her and said beloved in the dark and bitch in the light. Sethe pleaded for forgiveness, counting, listing again and again her reasons: that Beloved was more important, meant more to her than her own life. That she would trade places any day. Give up her life, every minute and hour of it, to take back just one of Beloved's tears. Did she know it hurt her when mosquitoes bit her baby? That to leave her on the ground to run into the big house drove her crazy? That before leaving Sweet Home Beloved slept every night on her chest or curled on her back? Beloved denied it. Sethe never came to her, never said a word to her, never smiled and worst of all never waved goodbye or even looked her way before running away from her.

When once or twice Sethe tried to assert herself—be the unquestioned mother whose word was law and who knew what was best—Beloved slammed things, wiped the table clean of plates, threw salt on the floor, broke a windowpane.

She was not like them. She was wild game, and nobody said, Get on out of here, girl, and come back when you get some sense. Nobody said, You raise your hand to me and I will knock you into the middle of next week. Ax the trunk, the limb will die. Honor thy mother and father that thy days may be long upon the land which the Lord thy God giveth thee. I will wrap you round that doorknob, don't nobody work for you and God don't love ugly ways.

No, no. They mended the plates, swept the salt, and little by little it dawned on Denver that if Sethe didn't wake up one morning and pick up a knife, Beloved might. Frightened as she was by the thing in Sethe that could come out, it shamed her to see her mother serving a girl not much older than herself. When she saw her carrying out Beloved's night bucket, Denver raced to relieve her of it. But the pain was unbearable when they ran low on food, and Denver watched her mother go without—pick-eating around the edges of the table and stove: the hominy that stuck on the bottom; the crusts and rinds and peelings of things. Once she saw her run her longest finger deep in an empty jam jar before rinsing and putting it away.

They grew tired, and even Beloved, who was getting bigger, seemed nevertheless as exhausted as they were. In any case she substituted a snarl or a tooth-suck for waving a poker around and 124 was quiet. Listless and sleepy with hunger Denver saw the flesh between her mother's forefinger and thumb fade. Saw Sethe's eyes bright but dead, alert but vacant, paying attention to everything about Beloved—her lineless palms, her forehead, the smile under her jaw, crooked and much too long—everything except her basket-fat stomach. She also saw the sleeves of her own carnival shirtwaist cover her fingers; hems that once showed her ankles now swept the floor. She saw themselves beribboned, decked-out, limp and starving but locked in a love that wore everybody out. Then Sethe spit up something she had not eaten and it rocked Denver like gunshot. The job she started out with, protecting Beloved from Sethe, changed to protecting her mother from Beloved. Now it was obvious that her mother could die and leave them both and what would Beloved do then? Whatever was happening, it only worked with three—not two—and since neither Beloved nor Sethe seemed to care what the next day might bring (Sethe happy when Beloved was; Beloved lapping devotion like cream), Denver knew it was on her. She would have to leave the yard; step off the edge of the world, leave the two behind and go ask somebody for help.

Who would it be? Who could she stand in front of who wouldn't shame her on learning that her mother sat around like a rag doll, broke down, finally, from trying to take care of and make up for. Denver knew *about* several people, from hearing her mother and grandmother talk. But she knew, personally, only two: an old man with white hair called Stamp and Lady Jones. Well, Paul D, of course. And that boy who told her about Sethe. But they wouldn't do at all. Her heart kicked and an itchy burning in her throat made her swallow all her saliva away. She didn't even know which way to go. When Sethe used to work at the restaurant and when she still had money to shop, she turned right. Back when Denver went to Lady Jones' school, it was left.

The weather was warm; the day beautiful. It was April and everything alive was tentative. Denver wrapped her hair and her shoulders. In the brightest of the carnival dresses and wearing a stranger's shoes, she stood on the porch of 124 ready to be swallowed up in the world beyond the edge of the porch. Out there where small things scratched and sometimes touched. Where words could be spoken that would close your ears shut. Where, if you were alone, feeling could overtake you and stick to you like a shadow. Out there where there were places in which things so bad had happened that when you went near them it would happen again. Like Sweet Home where time didn't pass and where, like her mother said, the bad was waiting for her as well. How would she know these places? What was more—much more—out there were whitepeople and how could you tell about them? Sethe said the mouth and sometimes the hands. Grandma Baby said there was no defense—they could prowl at will, change from one mind to another, and even when they thought they were behaving, it was a far cry from what real humans did.

"They got me out of jail," Sethe once told Baby Suggs.

"They also put you in it," she answered.

"They drove you 'cross the river."

"On my son's back."

"They gave you this house."

"Nobody *gave* me nothing."

"I got a job from them."

"He got a cook from them, girl."

"Oh, some of them do all right by us."

"And every time it's a surprise, ain't it?"

"You didn't used to talk this way."

"Don't box with me. There's more of us they drowned than there is all of them ever lived from the start of time. Lay down your sword. This ain't a battle; it's a rout."

Remembering those conversations and her grandmother's last and final words, Denver stood on the porch in the sun and couldn't leave it. Her throat itched; her heart kicked—and then Baby Suggs laughed, clear as anything. "You mean I never told you nothing about Carolina? About your daddy? You don't remember nothing about how come I walk the way I do and about your mother's feet, not to speak of her back? I never told you all that? Is that why you can't walk down the steps? My Jesus my."

But you said there was no defense.

"There ain't."

Then what do I do?

"Know it, and go on out the yard. Go on."

It came back. A dozen years had passed and the way came back. Four houses on the right, sitting close together in a line like wrens. The first house had two steps and a rocking chair on the porch; the second had three steps, a broom propped on the porch beam, two broken chairs and a clump of forsythia at the side. No window at the front. A little boy sat on the ground chewing a stick. The third house had yellow shutters on its two front windows and pot after pot of green leaves with white hearts or red. Denver could hear chickens and the knock of a badly hinged gate. At the fourth house the buds of a sycamore tree had rained down on the roof and made the yard look as though grass grew there. A woman, standing at the open door, lifted her hand halfway in greeting, then froze it near her shoulder as she leaned forward to see whom she waved to. Denver lowered her head. Next was a tiny fenced plot with a cow in it. She remembered the plot but not the cow. Under her headcloth her scalp was wet with tension. Beyond her, voices, male voices, floated, coming closer with each step she took. Denver kept her eyes on the road in case they were whitemen; in case she was walking where they wanted to; in case they said something and she would have to answer them. Suppose they flung out at her, grabbed her, tied her. They were getting closer. Maybe she should cross the road—now. Was the woman who half waved at her still there in the open door? Would she come to her rescue, or, angry at Denver for not waving back, would she withhold her help? Maybe she should turn around, get closer to the waving woman's house. Before she could make up her mind, it was too late—they were right in front of her. Two men, Negro. Denver breathed. Both men touched their caps and murmured, "Morning. Morning." Denver believed her eyes spoke gratitude but she never got her mouth open in time to reply. They moved left of her and passed on.

Braced and heartened by that easy encounter, she picked up speed and began to look deliberately at the neighborhood surrounding her. She was shocked to see how small the big things were: the boulder by the edge of the road she once couldn't see over was a sitting-on rock. Paths leading to houses weren't miles long. Dogs didn't even reach her knees. Letters cut into beeches and oaks by giants were eye level now.

She would have known it anywhere. The post and scrap-lumber fence was gray now, not white, but she would have known it anywhere. The stone porch sitting in a skirt of ivy, pale yellow curtains at the windows; the laid brick path to the front door and wood planks leading around to the back, passing under the windows where she had stood on tiptoe to see above the sill. Denver was about to do it again, when she realized how silly it would be to be found once more staring into the parlor of Mrs. Lady Jones. The pleasure she felt at having found the house dissolved, suddenly, in doubt. Suppose she didn't live there anymore? Or remember her former student after all this time? What would she say? Denver shivered inside, wiped the perspiration from her forehead and knocked.

Lady Jones went to the door expecting raisins. A child, probably, from the softness of the knock, sent by its mother with the raisins she needed if her contribution to the supper was to be worth the trouble. There would be any number of plain cakes, potato pies. She had reluctantly volunteered her own special creation, but said she didn't have raisins, so raisins is what the president said would be provided—early enough so there would be no excuses. Mrs. Jones, dreading the fatigue of beating batter, had been hoping she had forgotten. Her bake oven had been cold all week—getting it to the right temperature would be awful. Since her husband died and her eyes grew dim, she had let up-to-snuff housekeeping fall away. She was of two minds about baking something for the church. On the one hand, she wanted to remind everybody of what she was able to do in the cooking line; on the other, she didn't want to have to. When she heard the tapping at the door, she sighed and went to it hoping the raisins had at least been cleaned.

She was older, of course, and dressed like a chippy, but the girl was immediately recognizable to Lady Jones. Everybody's child was in that face: the nickel-round eyes, bold yet mistrustful; the large powerful teeth between dark sculptured lips that did not cover them. Some vulnerability lay across the bridge of the nose, above the cheeks. And then the skin. Flawless, economical—just enough of it to cover the bone and not a bit more. She must be eighteen or nineteen by now, thought Lady Jones, looking at the face young enough to be twelve. Heavy eyebrows, thick baby lashes and the unmistakable love call that shimmered around children until they learned better.

"Why, Denver," she said. "Look at you."

Lady Jones had to take her by the hand and pull her in, because the smile seemed all the girl could manage. Other people said this child was simple, but Lady Jones never believed it. Having taught her, watched her eat up a page, a rule, a figure, she knew better. When suddenly she had stopped coming, Lady Jones thought it was the nickel. She approached the ignorant grandmother one day on the road, a woods preacher who mended shoes, to tell her it was all right if the money was owed. The woman said that wasn't it; the child was deaf, and deaf Lady Jones thought she still was until she offered her a seat and Denver heard that.

"It's nice of you to come see me. What brings you?"

Denver didn't answer.

"Well, nobody needs a reason to visit. Let me make us some tea."

Lady Jones was mixed. Gray eyes and yellow woolly hair, every strand of which she hated—though whether it was the color or the texture even she didn't know. She had married the blackest man she could find, had five rainbow-colored children and sent them all to Wilberforce, after teaching them all she knew right along with the others who sat in her parlor. Her light skin got her picked for a coloredgirls' normal school in Pennsylvania and she paid it back by teaching the unpicked. The children who played in dirt until they were old enough for chores, these she taught. The colored population of Cincinnati had two graveyards and six churches, but since no school or hospital was obliged to serve them, they learned and died at home. She believed in her heart that, except for her husband, the whole world (including her children) despised her and her hair. She had been listening to "all that yellow gone to waste" and "white nigger" since she was a girl in a houseful of silt-black children, so she disliked everybody a little bit because she believed they hated her hair as much as she did. With that education pat and firmly set, she dispensed with rancor, was indiscriminately polite, saving her real affection for the unpicked children of Cincinnati, one of whom sat before her in a dress so loud it embarrassed the needlepoint chair seat.

"Sugar?"

"Yes. Thank you." Denver drank it all down.

"More?"

"No, ma'am."

"Here. Go ahead."

"Yes, ma'am."

"How's your family, honey?"

Denver stopped in the middle of a swallow. There was no way to tell her how her family was, so she said what was at the top of her mind.

"I want work, Miss Lady."

"Work?"

"Yes, ma'am. Anything."

Lady Jones smiled. "What can you do?"

"I can't do anything, but I would learn it for you if you have a little extra."

"Extra?"

"Food. My ma'am, she doesn't feel good."

"Oh, baby," said Mrs. Jones. "Oh, baby."

Denver looked up at her. She did not know it then, but it was the word "baby," said softly and with such kindness, that inaugurated her life in the world as a woman. The trail she followed to get to that sweet thorny place was made up of paper scraps containing the handwritten names of others. Lady Jones gave her some rice, four eggs and some tea. Denver said she couldn't be away from home long because of her mother's condition. Could she do chores in the morning? Lady Jones told her that no one, not herself, not anyone she knew, could pay anybody anything for work they did themselves. "But if you all need to eat until your mother is well, all you have to do is say so." She mentioned her church's committee invented so nobody had to go hungry. That agitated her guest who said, "No, no," as though asking for help from strangers was worse than hunger. Lady Jones said goodbye to her and asked her to come back anytime. "Anytime at all."

Two days later Denver stood on the porch and noticed something lying on the tree stump at the edge of the yard. She went to look and found a sack of white beans. Another time a plate of cold rabbit meat. One morning a basket of eggs sat there. As she lifted it, a slip of paper fluttered down. She picked it up and looked at it. "M. Lucille Williams" was written in big crooked letters. On the back was a blob of flour-water paste. So Denver paid a second visit to the world outside the porch, although all she said when she returned the basket was "Thank you."

"Welcome," said M. Lucille Williams.

Every now and then, all through the spring, names appeared near or in gifts of food. Obviously for the return of the pan or plate or basket; but also to let the girl know, if she cared to, who the donor was, because some of the parcels were wrapped in paper, and though there was nothing to return, the name was nevertheless there. Many had X's with designs about them, and Lady Jones tried to identify the plate or pan or the covering towel. When she could only guess, Denver followed her directions and went to say thank you anyway—whether she had the right benefactor or not. When she was wrong, when the person said, "No, darling. That's not my bowl. Mine's got a blue ring on it," a small conversation took place. All of them knew her grandmother and some had even danced with her in the Clearing. Others remembered the days when 124 was a way station, the place they assembled to catch news, taste oxtail soup, leave their children, cut out a skirt. One remembered the tonic mixed there that cured a relative. One showed her the border of a pillowslip, the stamens of its pale blue flowers French-knotted in Baby Suggs' kitchen by the light of an oil lamp while arguing the Settlement Fee. They remembered the party with twelve turkeys and tubs of strawberry smash. One said she wrapped Denver when she was a single day old and cut shoes to fit her mother's blasted feet. Maybe they were sorry for her. Or for Sethe. Maybe they were sorry for the years of their own disdain. Maybe they were simply nice people who could hold meanness toward each other for just so long and when trouble rode bareback among them, quickly, easily they did what they could to trip him up. In any case, the personal pride, the arrogant claim staked out at 124 seemed to them to have run its course. They whispered, naturally, wondered, shook their heads. Some even laughed outright at Denver's clothes of a hussy, but it didn't stop them caring whether she ate and it didn't stop the pleasure they took in her soft "Thank you."

At least once a week, she visited Lady Jones, who perked up enough to do a raisin loaf especially for her, since Denver was set on sweet things. She gave her a book of Bible verse and listened while she mumbled words or fairly shouted them. By June Denver had read and memorized all fifty-two pages—one for each week of the year.

As Denver's outside life improved, her home life deteriorated. If the whitepeople of Cincinnati had allowed Negroes into their lunatic asylum they could have found candidates in 124. Strengthened by the gifts of food, the source of which neither Sethe nor Beloved questioned, the women had arrived at a doomsday truce designed by the devil. Beloved sat around, ate, went from bed to bed. Sometimes she screamed, "Rain! Rain!" and clawed her throat until rubies of blood opened there, made brighter by her midnight skin. Then Sethe shouted, "No!" and knocked over chairs to get to her and wipe the jewels away. Other times Beloved curled up on the floor, her wrists between her knees, and stayed there for hours. Or she would go to the creek, stick her feet in the water and whoosh it up her legs. Afterward she would go to Sethe, run her fingers over the woman's teeth while tears slid from her wide black eyes. Then it seemed to Denver the thing was done: Beloved bending over Sethe looked the mother, Sethe the teething child, for other than those times when Beloved needed her, Sethe confined herself to a corner chair. The bigger Beloved got, the smaller Sethe became; the brighter

Beloved's eyes, the more those eyes that used never to look away became slits of sleeplessness. Sethe no longer combed her hair or splashed her face with water. She sat in the chair licking her lips like a chastised child while Beloved ate up her life, took it, swelled up with it, grew taller on it. And the older woman yielded it up without a murmur.

Denver served them both. Washing, cooking, forcing, cajoling her mother to eat a little now and then, providing sweet things for Beloved as often as she could to calm her down. It was hard to know what she would do from minute to minute. When the heat got hot, she might walk around the house naked or wrapped in a sheet, her belly protruding like a winning watermelon.

Denver thought she understood the connection between her mother and Beloved: Sethe was trying to make up for the handsaw; Beloved was making her pay for it. But there would never be an end to that, and seeing her mother diminished shamed and infuriated her. Yet she knew Sethe's greatest fear was the same one Denver had in the beginning—that Beloved might leave. That before Sethe could make her understand what it meant—what it took to drag the teeth of that saw under the little chin; to feel the baby blood pump like oil in her hands; to hold her face so her head would stay on; to squeeze her so she could absorb, still, the death spasms that shot through that adored body, plump and sweet with life—Beloved might leave. Leave before Sethe could make her realize that worse than that—far worse—was what Baby Suggs died of, what Ella knew, what Stamp saw and what made Paul D tremble. That anybody white could take your whole self for anything that came to mind. Not just work, kill, or maim you, but dirty you. Dirty you so bad you couldn't like yourself anymore. Dirty you so bad you forgot who you were and couldn't think it up. And though she and others lived through and got over it, she could never let it happen to her own. The best thing she was, was her children. Whites might dirty *her* all right, but not her best thing, her beautiful, magical best thing—the part of her that was clean. No undreamable dreams about whether the headless, feetless torso hanging in the tree with a sign on it was her husband or Paul A; whether the bubbling-hot girls in the colored-school fire set by patriots included her daughter; whether a gang of whites invaded her daughter's private parts, soiled her daughter's thighs and threw her daughter out of the wagon. *She* might have to work the slaughterhouse yard, but not her daughter.

And no one, nobody on this earth, would list her daughter's characteristics on the animal side of the paper. No. Oh no. Maybe Baby Suggs could worry about it, live with the likelihood of it; Sethe had refused—and refused still.

This and much more Denver heard her say from her corner chair, trying to persuade Beloved, the one and only person she felt she had to convince, that what she had done was right because it came from true love.

Beloved, her fat new feet propped on the seat of a chair in front of the one she sat in, her unlined hands resting on her stomach, looked at her. Uncomprehending everything except that Sethe was the woman who took her face away, leaving her crouching in a dark, dark place, forgetting to smile.

Her father's daughter after all, Denver decided to do the necessary. Decided to stop relying on kindness to leave something on the stump. She would hire herself out somewhere, and although she was afraid to leave Sethe and Beloved alone all day not knowing what calamity either one of them would create, she came to realize that her presence in that house had no influence on what either woman did. She kept them alive and they ignored her. Growled when they chose; sulked, explained, demanded, strutted, cowered, cried and provoked each other to the edge of violence, then over. She had begun to notice that even when Beloved was quiet, dreamy, minding her own business, Sethe got her going again. Whispering, muttering some justification, some bit of clarifying information to Beloved to explain what it had been like, and why, and how come. It was as though Sethe didn't really want forgiveness given; she wanted it refused. And Beloved helped her out.

Somebody had to be saved, but unless Denver got work, there would be no one to save, no one to come home to, and no Denver either. It was a new thought, having a self to look out for and preserve. And it might not have occurred to her if she hadn't met Nelson Lord leaving his grandmother's house as Denver entered it to pay a thank you for half a pie. All he did was smile and say, "Take care of yourself, Denver," but she heard it as though it were what language was made for. The last time he spoke to her his words blocked up her ears. Now they opened her mind. Weeding the garden, pulling vegetables, cooking, washing, she plotted what to do and how. The Bodwins were most likely to help since they had done it twice. Once for Baby Suggs and once for her mother. Why not the third generation as well?

She got lost so many times in the streets of Cincinnati it was noon before she arrived, though she started out at sunrise. The house sat back from the sidewalk with large windows looking out on a noisy, busy street. The Negro woman who answered the front door said, "Yes?"

"May I come in?"

"What you want?"

"I want to see Mr. and Mrs. Bodwin."

"Miss Bodwin. They brother and sister."

"Oh."

"What you want em for?"

"I'm looking for work. I was thinking they might know of some."

"You Baby Suggs' kin, ain't you?"

"Yes, ma'am."

"Come on in. You letting in flies." She led Denver toward the kitchen, saying, "First thing you have to know is what door to knock on." But Denver only half heard her because she was stepping on something soft and blue. All around her was thick, soft and blue. Glass cases crammed full of glistening things. Books on tables and shelves. Pearl-white lamps with shiny metal bottoms. And a smell like the cologne she poured in the emerald house, only better.

"Sit down," the woman said. "You know my name?"

"No, ma'am."

"Janey. Janey Wagon."

"How do you do?"

"Fairly. I heard your mother took sick, that so?"

"Yes, ma'am."

"Who's looking after her?"

"I am. But I have to find work."

Janey laughed. "You know what? I've been here since I was fourteen, and I remember like yesterday when Baby Suggs, holy, came here and sat right there where you are. Whiteman brought her. That's how she got that house you all live in. Other things, too."

"Yes, ma'am."

"What's the trouble with Sethe?" Janey leaned against an indoor sink and folded her arms.

It was a little thing to pay, but it seemed big to Denver. Nobody was going to help her unless she told it—told all of it. It was clear Janey wouldn't and wouldn't let her see the Bodwins otherwise. So Denver told this stranger what she hadn't told Lady Jones, in return for which Janey admitted the Bodwins needed help, although they didn't know it. She was alone there, and now that her employers were getting older, she couldn't take care of them like she used to. More and more she was required to sleep the night there. Maybe she could talk them into letting Denver do the night shift, come right after supper, say, maybe get the breakfast. That way Denver could care for Sethe in the day and earn a little something at night, how's that?

Denver had explained the girl in her house who plagued her mother as a cousin come to visit, who got sick too and bothered them both. Janey seemed more interested in Sethe's condition, and from what Denver told her it seemed the woman had lost her mind. That wasn't the Sethe she remembered. This Sethe had lost her wits, finally, as Janey knew she would—trying to do it all alone with her nose in the air. Denver squirmed under the criticism of her mother, shifting in the chair and keeping her eyes on the inside sink. Janey Wagon went on about pride until she got to Baby Suggs, for whom she had nothing but sweet words. "I never went to those woodland services she had, but she was always nice to me. Always. Never be another like her."

"I miss her too," said Denver.

"Bet you do. Everybody miss her. That was a good woman."

Denver didn't say anything else and Janey looked at her face for a while. "Neither one of your brothers ever come back to see how you all was?"

"No, ma'am."

"Ever hear from them?"

"No, ma'am. Nothing."

"Guess they had a rough time in that house. Tell me, this here woman in your house. The cousin. She got any lines in her hands?"

"No," said Denver.

"Well," said Janey. "I guess there's a God after all."

The interview ended with Janey telling her to come back in a few days. She needed time to convince her employers what they needed: night help because Janey's own family needed her. "I don't want to quit these people, but they can't have all my days and nights too."

What did Denver have to do at night?

"Be here. In case."

In case what?

Janey shrugged. "In case the house burn down." She smiled then. "Or bad weather slop the roads so bad I can't get here early enough for them. Case late guests need serving or cleaning up after. Anything. Don't ask me what whitefolks need at night."

"They used to be good whitefolks."

"Oh, yeah. They good. Can't say they ain't good. I wouldn't trade them for another pair, tell you that."

With those assurances, Denver left, but not before she had seen, sitting on a shelf by the back door, a blackboy's mouth full of money. His head was thrown back farther than a head could go, his hands were shoved in his pockets. Bulging like moons, two eyes were all the face he had above the gaping red mouth. His hair was a cluster of raised, widely spaced dots made of nail heads. And he was on his knees. His mouth, wide as a cup, held the coins needed to pay for a delivery or some other small service, but could just as well have held buttons, pins or crab-apple jelly. Painted across the pedestal he knelt on were the words "At Yo Service."

The news that Janey got hold of she spread among the other coloredwomen. Sethe's dead daughter, the one whose throat she cut, had come back to fix her. Sethe was worn down, speckled, dying, spinning, changing shapes and generally bedeviled. That this daughter beat her, tied her to the bed and pulled out all her hair. It took them days to get the story properly blown up and themselves agitated and then to calm down and assess the situation. They fell into three groups:

those that believed the worst; those that believed none of it; and those, like Ella, who thought it through.

"Ella. What's all this I'm hearing about Sethe?"

"Tell me it's in there with her. That's all I know."

"The daughter? The killed one?"

"That's what they tell me."

"How they know that's her?"

"It's sitting there. Sleeps, eats and raises hell. Whipping Sethe every day."

"I'll be. A baby?"

"No. Grown. The age it would have been had it lived."

"You talking about flesh?"

"I'm talking about flesh."

"Whipping her?"

"Like she was batter."

"Guess she had it coming."

"Nobody got that coming."

"But, Ella—"

"But nothing. What's fair ain't necessarily right."

"You can't just up and kill your children."

"No, and the children can't just up and kill the mama."

It was Ella more than anyone who convinced the others that rescue was in order. She was a practical woman who believed there was a root either to chew or avoid for every ailment. Cogitation, as she called it, clouded things and prevented action. Nobody loved her and she wouldn't have liked it if they had, for she considered love a serious disability. Her puberty was spent in a house where she was shared by father and son, whom she called "the lowest yet." It was "the lowest yet" who gave her a disgust for sex and against whom she measured all atrocities. A killing, a kidnap, a rape—whatever, she listened and nodded. Nothing compared to "the lowest yet." She understood Sethe's rage in the shed twenty years ago, but not her reaction to it, which Ella thought was prideful, misdirected, and Sethe herself too complicated. When she got out of jail and made no gesture toward anybody, and lived as though she were alone, Ella junked her and wouldn't give her the time of day.

The daughter, however, appeared to have some sense after all. At least she had stepped out the door, asked for the help she needed and wanted work. When Ella heard 124 was occupied by something-or-other beating up on Sethe, it infuriated her and gave her another opportunity to measure what could very well be the devil himself against "the lowest yet." There was also something very personal in her fury. Whatever Sethe had done, Ella didn't like the idea of past errors taking possession of the present. Sethe's crime was staggering and her pride outstripped even that; but she could not countenance the possibility of sin moving on in the house, unleashed and sassy. Daily life took as much as she had. The future was sunset; the past something to leave behind. And if it didn't stay behind, well, you might have to stomp it out. Slave life; freed life—every day was a test and a trial. Nothing could be counted on in a world where even when you were a solution you were a problem. "Sufficient unto the day is the evil thereof," and nobody needed more; nobody needed a grown-up evil sitting at the table with a grudge. As long as the ghost showed out from its ghostly place—shaking stuff, crying, smashing and such—Ella respected it. But if it took flesh and came in her world, well, the shoe was on the other foot. She didn't mind a little communication between the two worlds, but this was an invasion.

"Shall we pray?" asked the women.

"Uh huh," said Ella. "First. Then we got to get down to business."

The day Denver was to spend her first night at the Bodwins', Mr. Bodwin had some business on the edge of the city and told Janey he would pick the new girl up before supper. Denver sat on the porch steps with a bundle in her lap, her carnival dress sun-faded to a quieter rainbow. She was looking to the right, in the direction Mr. Bodwin would be coming from. She did not see the women approaching, accumulating slowly in groups of twos and threes from the left. Denver was looking to the right. She was a little anxious about whether she would prove satisfactory to the Bodwins, and uneasy too because she woke up crying from a dream about a running pair of shoes. The sadness of the dream she hadn't been able to shake, and the heat oppressed her as she went about the chores. Far too early she wrapped a nightdress and hairbrush into a bundle. Nervous, she fidgeted the knot and looked to the right.

Some brought what they could and what they believed would work. Stuffed in apron pockets, strung around their necks, lying in the space between their breasts. Others brought Christian faith—as shield and sword. Most brought a little of both. They had no idea what they would do once they got there. They just started out, walked down Bluestone Road and came together at the agreed-upon time. The heat kept a few women who promised to go at home. Others who believed the story didn't want any part of the confrontation and wouldn't have come no matter what the weather. And there were those like Lady Jones who didn't believe the story and hated the ignorance of those who did. So thirty women made up that company and walked slowly, slowly toward 124.

It was three in the afternoon on a Friday so wet and hot Cincinnati's stench had traveled to the country: from the canal, from hanging meat and things rotting in jars; from small animals dead in the fields, town sewers and factories. The stench, the heat, the moisture—trust the devil to make his presence known. Otherwise it looked almost like a regular workday. They could have been going to do the laundry at the orphanage or the insane asylum; corn shucking at the mill; or to clean fish, rinse offal, cradle whitebabies, sweep stores, scrape hog skin, press lard, case-pack sausage or hide in tavern kitchens so whitepeople didn't have to see them handle their food.

But not today.

When they caught up with each other, all thirty, and arrived at 124, the first thing they saw was not Denver sitting on the steps, but themselves. Younger, stronger, even as little girls lying in the grass asleep. Catfish was popping grease in the pan and they saw themselves scoop German potato salad onto the plate. Cobbler oozing purple syrup colored their teeth. They sat on the porch, ran down to the creek, teased the men, hoisted children on their hips or, if they were the children, straddled the ankles of old men who held their little hands while giving them a horsey ride. Baby Suggs laughed and skipped among them, urging more. Mothers, dead now, moved their shoulders to mouth harps. The fence they had leaned on and climbed over was gone. The stump of the butternut had split like a fan. But there they were, young and happy, playing in Baby Suggs' yard, not feeling the envy that surfaced the next day.

Denver heard mumbling and looked to the left. She stood when she saw them. They grouped, murmuring and whispering, but did not step foot in the yard. Denver waved. A few waved back but came no closer. Denver sat back down wondering what was going on. A woman dropped to her knees. Half of the others did likewise. Denver saw lowered heads, but could not hear the lead prayer—only the earnest syllables of agreement that backed it: Yes, yes, yes, oh yes. Hear me. Hear me. Do it, Maker, do it. Yes. Among those not on their knees, who stood holding 124 in a fixed glare, was Ella, trying to see through the walls, behind the door, to what was really in there. Was it true the dead daughter come back? Or a pretend? Was it whipping Sethe? Ella had been beaten every way but down. She remembered the bottom teeth she had lost to the brake and the scars from the belt were thick as rope around her waist. She had delivered, but would not nurse, a hairy white thing, fathered by "the lowest yet." It lived five days never making a sound. The idea of that pup coming back to whip her too set her jaw working, and then Ella hollered.

Instantly the kneelers and the standers joined her. They stopped praying and took a step back to the beginning. In the beginning there were no words. In the beginning was the sound, and they all knew what that sound sounded like.

Edward Bodwin drove a cart down Bluestone Road. It displeased him a bit because he preferred his figure astride Princess. Curved over his own hands, holding the reins made him look the age he was. But he had promised his sister a detour to pick up a new girl. He didn't have to think about the way—he was headed for the house he was born in. Perhaps it was his destination that turned his thoughts to time—the way it dripped or ran. He had not seen the house for thirty years. Not the butternut in front, the stream at the rear nor the block house in between. Not even the meadow across the road. Very few of the interior details did he remember because he was three years old when his family moved into town. But he did remember that the cooking was done behind the house, the well was forbidden to play near, and that women died there: his mother, grandmother, an aunt and an older sister before he was born. The men (his father and grandfather) moved with himself and his baby sister to Court Street sixty-seven years ago. The land, of course, eighty acres of it on both sides of Bluestone, was the central thing, but he felt something sweeter and deeper about the house which is why he rented it for a little something if he could get it, but it didn't trouble him to get no rent at all since the tenants at least kept it from the disrepair total abandonment would permit.

There was a time when he buried things there. Precious things he wanted to protect. As a child every item he owned was available and accountable to his family. Privacy was an adult indulgence, but when he got to be one, he seemed not to need it.

The horse trotted along and Edward Bodwin cooled his beautiful mustache with his breath. It was generally agreed upon by the women in the Society that, except for his hands, it was the most attractive feature he had. Dark, velvety, its beauty was enhanced by his strong clean-shaven chin. But his hair was white, like his sister's—and had been since he was a young man. It made him the most visible and memorable person at every gathering, and cartoonists had fastened onto the theatricality of his white hair and big black mustache whenever they depicted local political antagonism. Twenty years ago when the Society was at its height in opposing slavery, it was as though his coloring was itself the heart of the matter. The "bleached nigger" was what his enemies called him, and on a trip to Arkansas, some Mississippi rivermen, enraged by the Negro boatmen they competed with, had caught him and shoe-blackened his face and his hair. Those heady days were gone now; what remained was the sludge of ill will; dashed hopes and difficulties beyond repair. A tranquil Republic? Well, not in his lifetime.

Even the weather was getting to be too much for him. He was either too hot or freezing, and this day was a blister. He pressed his hat down to keep the sun from his neck, where heatstroke was a real possibility. Such thoughts of mortality were not new to him (he was over seventy now), but they still had the power to annoy. As he drew closer to the old homestead, the place that continued to surface in his dreams, he was even more aware of the way time moved. Measured by the wars he had lived through but not fought in (against the Miami, the Spaniards, the Secessionists), it was slow. But measured by the burial of his private things it was the blink of an eye. Where, exactly, was the box of tin soldiers? The watch chain with no watch? And who was he hiding them from? His father, probably, a deeply religious man who knew what God knew and told everybody what it was. Edward Bodwin thought him an odd man, in so many ways, yet he had one clear directive: human life is holy, all of it. And that his son still believed, although he had less and less reason to. Nothing since was as stimulating as the old days of letters, petitions, meetings, debates, recruitment, quarrels, rescue and downright sedition. Yet it had worked, more or less, and when it had not, he and his sister made themselves available to circumvent obstacles. As they had when a runaway slavewoman lived in his homestead with her mother-in-law and got herself into a world of trouble. The Society managed to turn infanticide and the cry of savagery around, and build a further case for abolishing slavery. Good years, they were, full of spit and conviction. Now he just wanted to know where his soldiers were and his watchless chain. That would be enough for this day of unbearable heat: bring back the new girl and recall exactly where his treasure lay. Then home, supper, and God willing, the sun would drop once more to give him the blessing of a good night's sleep.

The road curved like an elbow, and as he approached it he heard the singers before he saw them.

When the women assembled outside 124, Sethe was breaking a lump of ice into chunks. She dropped the ice pick into her apron pocket to scoop the pieces into a basin of water. When the music entered the window she was wringing a cool cloth to put on Beloved's forehead. Beloved, sweating profusely, was sprawled on the bed in the keeping room, a salt rock in her hand. Both women heard it at the same time and both lifted their heads. As the voices grew louder, Beloved sat up, licked the salt and went into the bigger room. Sethe and she exchanged glances and started toward the window. They saw Denver sitting on the steps and beyond her, where the yard met the road, they saw the rapt faces of thirty neighborhood women. Some had their eyes closed; others looked at the hot, cloudless sky. Sethe opened the door and reached for Beloved's hand. Together they stood in the doorway. For Sethe it was as though the Clearing had come to her with all its heat and simmering leaves, where the voices of women searched for the right combination, the key, the code, the sound that broke the back of words. Building voice upon voice until they found it, and when they did it was a wave of sound wide enough to sound deep water and knock the pods off chestnut trees. It broke over Sethe and she trembled like the baptized in its wash.

The singing women recognized Sethe at once and surprised themselves by their absence of fear when they saw what stood next to her. The devil-child was clever, they thought. And beautiful. It had taken the shape of a pregnant woman, naked and smiling in the heat of the afternoon sun. Thunderblack and glistening, she stood on long straight legs, her belly big and tight. Vines of hair twisted all over her head. Jesus. Her smile was dazzling.

Sethe feels her eyes burn and it may have been to keep them clear that she looks up. The sky is blue and clear. Not one touch of death in the definite green of the leaves. It is when she lowers her eyes to look again at the loving faces before her that she sees him. Guiding the mare, slowing down, his black hat wide-brimmed enough to hide his face but not his purpose. He is coming into her yard and he is coming for her best thing. She hears wings. Little hummingbirds stick needle beaks right through her headcloth into her hair and beat their wings. And if she thinks anything, it is no. No no. Nonono. She flies. The ice pick is not in her hand; it is her hand.

Standing alone on the porch, Beloved is smiling. But now her hand is empty. Sethe is running away from her, running, and she feels the emptiness in the hand Sethe has been holding. Now she is running into the faces of the people out there, joining them and leaving Beloved behind. Alone. Again. Then Denver, running too. Away from her to the pile of people out there. They make a hill. A hill of black people, falling. And above them all, rising from his place with a whip in his hand, the man without skin, looking. He is looking at her.

Bare feet and chamomile sap.
Took off my shoes; took off my hat.
Bare feet and chamomile sap.
Gimme back my shoes; gimme back my hat.

Lay my head on a potato sack,
Devil sneak up behind my back.
Steam engine got a lonesome whine;
Love that woman till you go stone blind.

Stone blind; stone blind.
Sweet Home gal make you lose your mind.

HIS COMING is the reverse route of his going. First the cold house, the storeroom, then the kitchen before he tackles the beds. Here Boy, feeble and shedding his coat in patches, is asleep by the pump, so Paul D knows Beloved is truly gone. Disappeared, some say, exploded right before their eyes. Ella is not so sure. "Maybe," she says, "maybe not. Could be hiding in the trees waiting for another chance." But when Paul D sees the ancient dog, eighteen years if a day, he is certain 124 is clear of her. But he opens the door to the cold house halfway expecting to hear her. "Touch me. Touch me. On the inside part and call me my name."

There is the pallet spread with old newspapers gnawed at the edges by mice. The lard can. The potato sacks too, but empty now, they lie on the dirt floor in heaps. In daylight he can't imagine it in darkness with moonlight seeping through the cracks. Nor the desire that drowned him there and forced him to struggle up, up into that girl like she was the clear air at the top of the sea. Coupling with her wasn't even fun. It was more like a brainless urge to stay alive. Each time she came, pulled up her skirts, a life hunger overwhelmed him and he had no more control over it than over his lungs. And afterward, beached and gobbling air, in the midst of repulsion and personal shame, he was thankful too for having been escorted to some ocean-deep place he once belonged to.

Sifting daylight dissolves the memory, turns it into dust motes floating in light. Paul D shuts the door. He looks toward the house and, surprisingly, it does not look back at him. Unloaded, 124 is just another weathered house needing repair. Quiet, just as Stamp Paid said.

"Used to be voices all round that place. Quiet, now," Stamp said. "I been past it a few times and I can't hear a thing. Chastened, I reckon, 'cause Mr. Bodwin say he selling it soon's he can."

"That the name of the one she tried to stab? That one?"

"Yep. His sister say it's full of trouble. Told Janey she was going to get rid of it."

"And him?" asked Paul D.

"Janey say he against it but won't stop it."

"Who they think want a house out there? Anybody got the money don't want to live out there."

"Beats me," Stamp answered. "It'll be a spell, I guess, before it get took off his hands."

"He don't plan on taking her to the law?"

"Don't seem like it. Janey say all he wants to know is who was the naked blackwoman standing on the porch. He was looking at her so hard he didn't notice what Sethe was up to. All he saw was some coloredwomen fighting. He thought Sethe was after one of them, Janey say."

"Janey tell him any different?"

"No. She say she so glad her boss ain't dead. If Ella hadn't clipped her, she say she would have. Scared her to death have that woman kill her boss. She *and* Denver be looking for a job."

"Who Janey tell him the naked woman was?"

"Told him she didn't see none."

"You believe they saw it?"

"Well, they saw something. I trust Ella anyway, and she say she looked it in the eye. It was standing right next to Sethe. But from the way they describe it, don't seem like it was the girl I saw in there. The girl I saw was narrow. This one was big. She say they was holding hands and Sethe looked like a little girl beside it."

"Little girl with a ice pick. How close she get to him?"

"Right up on him, they say. Before Denver and them grabbed her and Ella put her fist in her jaw."

"He got to know Sethe was after him. He got to."

"Maybe. I don't know. If he did think it, I reckon he decided not to. That be just like him, too. He's somebody never turned us down. Steady as a rock. I tell you something, if she had got to him, it'd be the worst thing in the world for us. You know, don't you, he's the main one kept Sethe from the gallows in the first place."

"Yeah. Damn. That woman is crazy. Crazy."

"Yeah, well, ain't we all?"

They laughed then. A rusty chuckle at first and then more, louder and louder until Stamp took out his pocket handkerchief and wiped his eyes while Paul D pressed the heel of his hand in his own. As the scene neither one had witnessed took shape before them, its seriousness and its embarrassment made them shake with laughter.

"Every time a whiteman come to the door she got to kill somebody?"

"For all she know, the man could be coming for the rent."

"Good thing they don't deliver mail out that way."

"Wouldn't nobody get no letter."

"Except the postman."

"Be a mighty hard message."

"And his last."

When their laughter was spent, they took deep breaths and shook their heads.

"And he still going to let Denver spend the night in his house? Ha!"

"Aw no. Hey. Lay off Denver, Paul D. That's my heart. I'm proud of that girl. She was the first one wrestle her mother down. Before anybody knew what the devil was going on."

"She saved his life then, you could say."

"You could. You could," said Stamp, thinking suddenly of the leap, the wide swing and snatch of his arm as he rescued the little curly-headed baby from within inches of a split skull. "I'm proud of her. She turning out fine. Fine."

It was true. Paul D saw her the next morning when he was on his way to work and she was leaving hers. Thinner, steady in the eyes, she looked more like Halle than ever.

She was the first to smile. "Good morning, Mr. D."

"Well, it is now." Her smile, no longer the sneer he remembered, had welcome in it and strong traces of Sethe's mouth. Paul D touched his cap. "How you getting along?"

"Don't pay to complain."

"You on your way home?"

She said no. She had heard about an afternoon job at the shirt factory. She hoped that with her night work at the Bodwins' and another one, she could put away something and help her mother too. When he asked her if they treated her all right over there, she said more than all right. Miss Bodwin taught her stuff. He asked her what stuff and she laughed and said book stuff. "She says I might go to Oberlin. She's experimenting on me." And he didn't say, "Watch out. Watch out. Nothing in the world more dangerous than a white schoolteacher." Instead he nodded and asked the question he wanted to.

"Your mother all right?"

"No," said Denver. "No. No, not a bit all right."

"You think I should stop by? Would she welcome it?"

"I don't know," said Denver. "I think I've lost my mother, Paul D."

They were both silent for a moment and then he said, "Uh, that girl. You know. Beloved?"

"Yes?"

"You think she sure 'nough your sister?"

Denver looked at her shoes. "At times. At times I think she was—more." She fiddled with her shirtwaist, rubbing a spot of something. Suddenly she leveled her eyes at his. "But who would know that better than you, Paul D? I mean, you sure 'nough knew her."

He licked his lips. "Well, if you want my opinion—"

"I don't," she said. "I have my own."

"You grown," he said.

"Yes, sir."

"Well. Well, good luck with the job."

"Thank you. And, Paul D, you don't have to stay 'way, but be careful how you talk to my ma'am, hear?"

"Don't worry," he said and left her then, or rather she left him because a young man was running toward her, saying, "Hey, Miss Denver. Wait up."

She turned to him, her face looking like someone had turned up the gas jet.

He left her unwillingly because he wanted to talk more, make sense out of the stories he had been hearing: whiteman came to take Denver to work and Sethe cut him. Baby ghost came back evil and sent Sethe out to get the man who kept her from hanging. One point of agreement is: first they saw it and then they didn't. When they got Sethe down on the ground and the ice pick out of her hands and looked back to the house, it was gone. Later, a little boy put it out how he had been looking for bait back of 124, down by the stream, and saw, cutting through the woods, a naked woman with fish for hair.

As a matter of fact, Paul D doesn't care how It went or even why. He cares about how he left and why. When he looks at himself through Garner's eyes, he sees one thing. Through Sixo's, another. One makes him feel righteous. One makes him feel ashamed. Like the time he worked both sides of the War. Running away from the Northpoint Bank and Railway to join the 44th Colored Regiment in Tennessee, he thought he had made it, only to discover he had arrived at another colored regiment forming under a commander in New Jersey. He stayed there four weeks. The regiment fell apart before it got started on the question of whether the soldiers should have weapons or not. Not, it was decided, and the white commander had to figure out what to command them to do instead of kill other whitemen. Some of the ten thousand stayed there to clean, haul and build things; others drifted away to another regiment; most were abandoned, left to their own devices with bitterness for pay. He was trying to make up his mind what to do when an agent from Northpoint

Bank caught up with him and took him back to Delaware, where he slave-worked a year. Then Northpoint took $300 in exchange for his services in Alabama, where he worked for the Rebellers, first sorting the dead and then smelting iron. When he and his group combed the battlefields, their job was to pull the Confederate wounded away from the Confederate dead. Care, they told them. Take good care. Coloredmen and white, their faces wrapped to their eyes, picked their way through the meadows with lamps, listening in the dark for groans of life in the indifferent silence of the dead. Mostly young men, some children, and it shamed him a little to feel pity for what he imagined were the sons of the guards in Alfred, Georgia.

In five tries he had not had one permanent success. Every one of his escapes (from Sweet Home, from Brandywine, from Alfred, Georgia, from Wilmington, from Northpoint) had been frustrated. Alone, undisguised, with visible skin, memorable hair and no whiteman to protect him, he never stayed uncaught. The longest had been when he ran with the convicts, stayed with the Cherokee, followed their advice and lived in hiding with the weaver woman in Wilmington, Delaware: three years. And in all those escapes he could not help being astonished by the beauty of this land that was not his. He hid in its breast, fingered its earth for food, clung to its banks to lap water and tried not to love it. On nights when the sky was personal, weak with the weight of its own stars, he made himself not love it. Its graveyards and low-lying rivers. Or just a house—solitary under a chinaberry tree; maybe a mule tethered and the light hitting its hide just so. Anything could stir him and he tried hard not to love it.

After a few months on the battlefields of Alabama, he was impressed to a foundry in Selma along with three hundred captured, lent or taken coloredmen. That's where the War's end found him, and leaving Alabama when he had been declared free should have been a snap. He should have been able to walk from the foundry in Selma straight to Philadelphia, taking the main roads, a train if he wanted to, or passage on a boat. But it wasn't like that. When he and two colored soldiers (who had been captured from the 44th he had looked for) walked from Selma to Mobile, they saw twelve dead blacks in the first eighteen miles. Two were women, four were little boys. He thought this, for sure, would be the walk of his life. The Yankees in control left the Rebels out of control. They got to the outskirts of Mobile, where blacks were putting down tracks for the Union that, earlier, they had torn up for the Rebels. One of the men with him, a private called Keane, had been with the Massachusetts 54th. He told Paul D they had been paid less than white soldiers. It was a sore point with him that, as a group, they had refused the offer Massachusetts made to make up the difference in pay. Paul D was so impressed by the idea of being paid money to fight he looked at the private with wonder and envy.

Keane and his friend, a Sergeant Rossiter, confiscated a skiff and the three of them floated in Mobile Bay. There the private hailed a Union gunboat, which took all three aboard. Keane and Rossiter disembarked at Memphis to look for their commanders. The captain of the gunboat let Paul D stay aboard all the way to Wheeling, West Virginia. He made his own way to New Jersey.

By the time he got to Mobile, he had seen more dead people than living ones, but when he got to Trenton the crowds of alive people, neither hunting nor hunted, gave him a measure of free life so tasty he never forgot it. Moving down a busy street full of whitepeople who needed no explanation for his presence, the glances he got had to do with his disgusting clothes and unforgivable hair. Still, nobody raised an alarm. Then came the miracle. Standing in a street in front of a row of brick houses, he heard a whiteman call him ("Say there!

Yo!") to help unload two trunks from a coach cab. Afterward the whiteman gave him a coin. Paul D walked around with it for hours—not sure what it could buy (a suit? a meal? a horse?) and if anybody would sell him anything. Finally he saw a greengrocer selling vegetables from a wagon. Paul D pointed to a bunch of turnips. The grocer handed them to him, took his one coin and gave him several more. Stunned, he backed away. Looking around, he saw that nobody seemed interested in the "mistake" or him, so he walked along, happily chewing turnips. Only a few women looked vaguely repelled as they passed. His first earned purchase made him glow, never mind the turnips were withered dry. That was when he decided that to eat, walk and sleep anywhere was life as good as it got. And he did it for seven years till he found himself in southern Ohio, where an old woman and a girl he used to know had gone.

Now his coming is the reverse of his going. First he stands in the back, near the cold house, amazed by the riot of late-summer flowers where vegetables should be growing. Sweet william, morning glory, chrysanthemums. The odd placement of cans jammed with the rotting stems of things, the blossoms shriveled like sores. Dead ivy twines around bean poles and door handles. Faded newspaper pictures are nailed to the outhouse and on trees. A rope too short for anything but skip-jumping lies discarded near the washtub; and jars and jars of dead lightning bugs. Like a child's house; the house of a very tall child.

He walks to the front door and opens it. It is stone quiet. In the place where once a shaft of sad red light had bathed him, locking him where he stood, is nothing. A bleak and minus nothing. More like absence, but an absence he had to get through with the same determination he had when he trusted Sethe and stepped through the pulsing light. He glances quickly at the lightning-white stairs. The entire railing is wound with ribbons, bows, bouquets. Paul D steps inside. The outdoor breeze he brings with him stirs the ribbons. Carefully, not quite in a hurry but losing no time, he climbs the luminous stairs. He enters Sethe's room. She isn't there and the bed looks so small he wonders how the two of them had lain there. It has no sheets, and because the roof windows do not open the room is stifling. Brightly colored clothes lie on the floor. Hanging from a wall peg is the dress Beloved wore when he first saw her. A pair of ice skates nestles in a basket in the corner. He turns his eyes back to the bed and keeps looking at it. It seems to him a place he is not. With an effort that makes him sweat he forces a picture of himself lying there, and when he sees it, it lifts his spirit. He goes to the other bedroom. Denver's is as neat as the other is messy. But still no Sethe. Maybe she has gone back to work, gotten better in the days since he talked to Denver. He goes back down the stairs, leaving the image of himself firmly in place on the narrow bed. At the kitchen table he sits down. Something is missing from 124. Something larger than the people who lived there. Something more than Beloved or the red light. He can't put his finger on it, but it seems, for a moment, that just beyond his knowing is the glare of an outside thing that embraces while it accuses.

To the right of him, where the door to the keeping room is ajar, he hears humming. Someone is humming a tune. Something soft and sweet, like a lullaby. Then a few words. Sounds like "high Johnny, wide Johnny. Sweet William bend down low." Of course, he thinks. That's where she is—and she is. Lying under a quilt of merry colors. Her hair, like the dark delicate roots of good plants, spreads and curves on the pillow. Her eyes, fixed on the window, are so expressionless he is not sure she will know who he is. There is too much light here in this room. Things look sold.

"Jackweed raise up high," she sings. "Lambswool over my

shoulder, buttercup and clover fly." She is fingering a long clump of her hair.

Paul D clears his throat to interrupt her. "Sethe?"

She turns her head. "Paul D."

"Aw, Sethe."

"I made the ink, Paul D. He couldn't have done it if I hadn't made the ink."

"What ink? Who?"

"You shaved."

"Yeah. Look bad?"

"No. You looking good."

"Devil's confusion. What's this I hear about you not getting out of bed?"

She smiles, lets it fade and turns her eyes back to the window.

"I need to talk to you," he tells her.

She doesn't answer.

"I saw Denver. She tell you?"

"She comes in the daytime. Denver. She's still with me, my Denver."

"You got to get up from here, girl." He is nervous. This reminds him of something.

"I'm tired, Paul D. So tired. I have to rest a while."

Now he knows what he is reminded of and he shouts at her, "Don't you die on me! This is Baby Suggs' bed! Is that what you planning?" He is so angry he could kill her. He checks himself, remembering Denver's warning, and whispers, "What you planning, Sethe?"

"Oh, I don't have no plans. No plans at all."

"Look," he says, "Denver be here in the day. I be here in the night. I'm a take care of you, you hear? Starting now. First off, you don't smell right. Stay there. Don't move. Let me heat up some water." He stops. "Is it all right, Sethe, if I heat up some water?"

"And count my feet?" she asks him.

He steps closer. "Rub your feet."

Sethe closes her eyes and presses her lips together. She is thinking: No. This little place by a window is what I want. And rest. There's nothing to rub now and no reason to. Nothing left to bathe, assuming he even knows how. Will he do it in sections? First her face, then her hands, her thighs, her feet, her back? Ending with her exhausted breasts? And if he bathes her in sections, will the parts hold? She opens her eyes, knowing the danger of looking at him. She looks at him. The peachstone skin, the crease between his ready, waiting eyes and sees it—the thing in him, the blessedness, that has made him the kind of man who can walk in a house and make the women cry. Because with him, in his presence, they could. Cry and tell him things they only told each other: that time didn't stay put; that she called, but Howard and Buglar walked on down the railroad track and couldn't hear her; that Amy was scared to stay with her because her feet were ugly and her back looked so bad; that her ma'am had hurt her feelings and she couldn't find her hat anywhere and "Paul D?"

"What, baby?"

"She left me."

"Aw, girl. Don't cry."

"She was my best thing."

Paul D sits down in the rocking chair and examines the quilt patched in carnival colors. His hands are limp between his knees. There are too many things to feel about this woman. His head hurts. Suddenly he remembers Sixo trying to describe what he felt about the Thirty-Mile Woman. "She is a friend of my mind. She gather me, man. The pieces I am, she gather them and give them back to me in all the right order. It's good, you know, when you got a woman who is a friend of your mind."

He is staring at the quilt but he is thinking about her

wrought-iron back; the delicious mouth still puffy at the corner from Ella's fist. The mean black eyes. The wet dress steaming before the fire. Her tenderness about his neck jewelry—its three wands, like attentive baby rattlers, curving two feet into the air. How she never mentioned or looked at it, so he did not have to feel the shame of being collared like a beast. Only this woman Sethe could have left him his manhood like that. He wants to put his story next to hers.

"Sethe," he says, "me and you, we got more yesterday than anybody. We need some kind of tomorrow."

He leans over and takes her hand. With the other he touches her face. "You your best thing, Sethe. You are." His holding fingers are holding hers.

"Me? Me?"

THERE IS a loneliness that can be rocked. Arms crossed, knees drawn up; holding, holding on, this motion, unlike a ship's, smooths and contains the rocker. It's an inside kind—wrapped tight like skin. Then there is a loneliness that roams. No rocking can hold it down. It is alive, on its own. A dry and spreading thing that makes the sound of one's own feet going seem to come from a far-off place.

Everybody knew what she was called, but nobody anywhere knew her name. Disremembered and unaccounted for, she cannot be lost because no one is looking for her, and even if they were, how can they call her if they don't know her name? Although she has claim, she is not claimed. In the place where long grass opens, the girl who waited to be loved and cry shame erupts into her separate parts, to make it easy for the chewing laughter to swallow her all away.

It was not a story to pass on.

They forgot her like a bad dream. After they made up their tales, shaped and decorated them, those that saw her that day on the porch quickly and deliberately forgot her. It took longer for those who had spoken to her, lived with her, fallen in love with her, to forget, until they realized they couldn't remember or repeat a single thing she said, and began to believe that, other than what they themselves were thinking, she hadn't said anything at all. So, in the end, they forgot her too. Remembering seemed unwise. They never knew where or why she crouched, or whose was the underwater face she needed like that. Where the memory of the smile under her chin might have been and was not, a latch latched and lichen attached its apple-green bloom to the metal. What made her think her fingernails could open locks the rain rained on?

It was not a story to pass on.

So they forgot her. Like an unpleasant dream during a troubling sleep. Occasionally, however, the rustle of a skirt hushes when they wake, and the knuckles brushing a cheek in sleep seem to belong to the sleeper. Sometimes the photograph of a close friend or relative—looked at too long—shifts, and something more familiar than the dear face itself moves there. They can touch it if they like, but don't, because they know things will never be the same if they do.

This is not a story to pass on.

Down by the stream in back of 124 her footprints come and go, come and go. They are so familiar. Should a child, an adult place his feet in them, they will fit. Take them out and they disappear again as though nobody ever walked there.

By and by all trace is gone, and what is forgotten is not only the footprints but the water too and what it is down there. The rest is weather. Not the breath of the disremembered and unaccounted for, but wind in the eaves, or spring ice thawing too quickly. Just weather. Certainly no clamor for a kiss.

Beloved.

ALSO BY

Toni Morrison

GOD HELP THE CHILD

At the center: a young woman who calls herself Bride, whose stunning blue-black skin is only one element of her beauty, her boldness and confidence, her success in life, but which caused her light-skinned mother to deny her even the simplest forms of love. There is Booker, the man Bride loves and loses to anger. Rain, the mysterious white child with whom she crosses paths. And finally, Bride's mother herself, Sweetness, who takes a lifetime to come to understand that "what you do to children matters. And they might never forget." A fiery and provocative novel, *God Help the Child* weaves a tale about the way the sufferings of childhood can shape, and misshape, the life of the adult.

Fiction

PARADISE

"They shoot the white girl first. With the rest they can take their time." So begins *Paradise*, which opens with a horrifying scene of mass violence and chronicles its genesis in an all-black small town in rural Oklahoma. Founded by the descendants of freed slaves and survivors in exodus from a hostile world, the patriarchal community of Ruby is built on righteousness, rigidly enforced moral law, and fear. But seventeen miles away, another group of exiles has gathered in a promised land of their own. And it is upon these women in flight from death and despair that nine male citizens of Ruby will lay their pain, terror, and murderous rage. In prose that soars with the rhythms, grandeur, and tragic arc of an epic poem, Toni Morrison challenges our most fiercely held beliefs as she weaves folklore and history, memory and myth into an unforgettable meditation on race, religion, gender, and a far-off past that is ever present.

Fiction

HOME

When Frank Money joined the army to escape his too-small world, he left behind his cherished little sister, Cee. After the war, his shattered life has no purpose until he hears that Cee is in danger. Frank is a modern Odysseus returning to a 1950s America mined with lethal pitfalls for a black man. As he journeys to his native Georgia in search of Cee, it becomes clear that their troubles began before their wartime separation. Together, they return to their hometown of Lotus, where buried secrets are unearthed and where Frank learns at last what it means to be a man, what it takes to heal, and—above all—what it means to come home.

Fiction

VINTAGE INTERNATIONAL

Available wherever books are sold.

www.vintagebooks.com

Acclaim for Toni Morrison's

SONG OF SOLOMON

"It places Toni Morrison in the front rank of contemporary American writers. She has written a novel that will endure."

—*The Washington Post*

"Lovely. . . . A delight, full of lyrical variety and allusiveness. . . . [An] exceptionally diverse novel." —*The Atlantic Monthly*

"A rich, full novel. . . . It lifts us up [and] impresses itself upon us like a love affair." —*The New York Times Book Review*

"Morrison dazzles. . . . She creates a black community strangely unto itself yet never out of touch with the white world. . . . With an ear as sharp as glass she has listened to the music of black talk and uses it as a palette knife to create black lives and to provide some of the best fictional dialogue around today." —*The Nation*

"A marvelous novel, the most moving I have read in ten years of reviewing." —*The Plain Dealer*

"Toni Morrison has created a fanciful world here. . . . She has an impeccable sense of emotional detail. She's the most sensible lyrical writer around today." —*The Philadelphia Inquirer*

"A fine novel exuberantly constructed. . . . So rich in its use of common speech, so sophisticated in its use of literary traditions and language from the Bible to Faulkner . . . it is also extremely funny."

—*The Hudson Review*

"Toni Morrison is an extraordinarily good writer. Two pages into anything she writes one feels the power of her language and the emotional authority behind that language. . . . One closes the book warmed through by the richness of its sympathy, and by its breathtaking feel for the nature of sexual sorrow." —*The Village Voice*

"Morrison moves easily in and out of the lives and thoughts of her characters, luxuriating in the diversity of circumstances and personality, and revelling in the sound of their voices and of her own, which echoes and elaborates theirs." —*The New Yorker*

Also by Toni Morrison

FICTION

God Help the Child

Home

A Mercy

Love

Paradise

Jazz

Beloved

Tar Baby

Sula

The Bluest Eye

NONFICTION

The Source of Self-Regard

The Dancing Mind

Playing in the Dark: Whiteness and the Literary Imagination

The Origin of Others

Toni Morrison

SONG OF SOLOMON

Toni Morrison is the author of eleven novels, from *The Bluest Eye* (1970) to *God Help the Child* (2015). She received the National Book Critics Circle Award, the Pulitzer Prize, and in 1993 she was awarded the Nobel Prize in Literature. She died in 2019.

VINTAGE INTERNATIONAL

SONG OF

SOLOMON

Toni Morrison

VINTAGE INTERNATIONAL

Vintage Books • A Division of Penguin Random House LLC • New York

FIRST VINTAGE INTERNATIONAL EDITION, JUNE 2004

 Published in the United States by Vintage Books, a division of Penguin Random House LLC, New York, and distributed in Canada by Penguin Random House Canada Limited, Toronto. Originally published in slightly different form in hardcover in the United States by Alfred A. Knopf, a division of Penguin Random House LLC, New York, in 1977.

The Library of Congress has cataloged the Knopf edition as follows:
Morrison, Toni.
Song of Solomon.
I. Title.
PZ4.M883So [PS3563.08749]
813'.5'4
77-874

Vintage International Trade Paperback ISBN: 978-1-4000-3342-3
eBook ISBN: 978-0-307-38812-4

Book design by Gwen Townsend

www.vintagebooks.com

Printed in the United States of America
40 39 38 37 36

Daddy

The fathers may soar
And the children may know their names

Foreword

I have long despised artists' chatter about muses—"voices" that speak to them and enable a vision, the source of which they could not otherwise name. I thought of muses as inventions to protect one's insight, to avoid questions like "Where do your ideas come from?" Or to escape inquiry into the fuzzy area between autobiography and fiction. I regarded the "mystery" of creativity as a shield erected by artists to avoid articulating, analyzing, or even knowing the details of their creative process—for fear it would fade away.

Writing *Song of Solomon* destroyed all that. I had no access to what I planned to write about until my father died. In the unmanageable sadness that followed, there was none of the sibling wrangling, guilt or missed opportunities, or fights for this or that memento. Each of his four children was convinced that he loved her or him best. He had sacrificed greatly for one, risking his house and his job; he took another to baseball games over whole summers where they lay in the grass listening to a portable radio, talking, evaluating the players on the field. In the company of one, his firstborn, he always beamed and preferred her cooking over everyone else's, including his wife's. He carried a letter from me in his coat pocket for years and years, and drove through blinding snowstorms to help me. Most important, he talked to each of us in language cut to our different understandings. He had a flattering view of me as someone interesting, capable, witty, smart, high-spirited. I did not share that view of myself, and wondered why he held it. But it was the death of that girl—the one who lived in his head—that I mourned when he died. Even more than I mourned him, I suffered the loss of the person he thought I was. I think it was because I felt closer to him than to myself that, after his death, I deliberately sought his advice for writing the novel that continued to elude me. "What are the men you have known really like?"

He answered.

Whatever it is called—muse, insight, inspiration, "the dark finger that guides," "bright angel"—it exists and, in many forms, I have trusted it ever since.

The challenge of *Song of Solomon* was to manage what was for me a radical shift in imagination from a female locus to a male one. To get out of the house, to de-domesticate the landscape that had so far been the site of my work. To travel. To fly. In such an overtly, stereotypically male narrative, I thought that straightforward chronology would be more suitable than the kind of play with sequence and time I had employed in my previous novels. A journey, then, with the accomplishment of flight, the triumphant end of a trip through earth, to its surface, on into water, and finally into air. All very saga-like. Old-school heroic, but with other meanings. Opening the novel with the suicidal leap of the insurance agent, ending it with the protagonist's confrontational soar into danger, was meant to enclose the mystical but problematic one taken by the Solomon of the title.

I have written, elsewhere and at some length, details of how certain sentences get written and the work I hope they do. Let me extrapolate an example here.

"The North Carolina Mutual Life Insurance agent promised to fly from Mercy to the other side of Lake Superior at 3:00."

This declarative sentence is designed to mock a journalistic style. With a minor alteration it could be the opening of an item in a small town newspaper. It has the tone of an everyday event of minimal local interest, yet I wanted it to contain important signs and crucial information. The name of the insurance company is that of a well-known black-owned company dependent on black clients, and in its corporate name are "life" and "mutual." The sentence starts with "North Carolina" and closes with "Lake Superior"—geographical locations that suggest a journey from south to north—a direction common for black immigration and in the literature about it, but which is reversed here since the protagonist has to go south to mature. Two other words of significance are "fly" and "mercy." Both terms are central to the narrative: flight as escape or confrontation; mercy the unspoken wish of the novel's population. Some grant it; some despise it; one makes it the sole cry of her extemporaneous sermon upon the death of her granddaughter. Mercy touches, turns, and returns to Guitar at the end of the book, and moves him to make it his own final gift to his former friend. Mercy is what one wishes for Hagar; what is unavailable to and unsought by Macon Dead, senior; what his wife learns to demand from him, and what the townsfolk believe can never come from the white world, as is signified by the inversion of the name of the hospital from Mercy to "No-Mercy." But the sentence turns, as all sentences do, on its verb. "Promise." The insurance agent does not declare, announce, or threaten his act; he promises, as though a contract is being executed between himself and others. He hopes his flight, like that of the character in the title, toward asylum (Canada, or freedom, or the company of the welcoming dead), or home, is interpreted as a radical gesture demanding change, an alternative way, a cessation of things as they are. He does not want it understood as a simple desperate act, the end of a fruitless life, a life without examination, but as a deep commitment to his people. And in their response to his decision there is a tenderness, some contrition, and mounting respect ("They didn't know he had it in him"), an awareness that his suicide enclosed, rather than repudiated them. The note he leaves asks for forgiveness. It is tacked on his door as a modest invitation to whoever might pass by.

Of the flights in the novel, Solomon's is the most magical, the most theatrical, and, for Milkman, the most satisfying. Unlike most mythical flights, which clearly imply triumph, in the attempt if not the success, Solomon's escape, the insurance man's jump, and Milkman's leap are ambiguous, disturbing. Solomon's escape from slavery is also the abandonment of his family; the insurance man leaves a message saying his suicide is a gesture of love, but guilt and despair also inform his decision. Milkman believes he is risking his life in return for Pilate's, yet he knows his enemy has disarmed himself. These flights, these erstwhile heroics, are viewed rather differently by the women left behind. Both the quotation and the song of the title fairly shout that different understanding. To praise a woman whose attention was focused solely on family and domestic responsibilities, Milkman summons a conundrum: that without ever leaving the ground she could fly. My father laughed.

Part I

Chapter 1

The North Carolina Mutual Life Insurance agent promised to fly from Mercy to the other side of Lake Superior at three o'clock. Two days before the event was to take place he tacked a note on the door of his little yellow house:

> At 3:00 p.m. on Wednesday the 18th of February, 1931, I will take off from Mercy and fly away on my own wings. Please forgive me. I loved you all.
>
> (signed) Robert Smith,
> Ins. agent

Mr. Smith didn't draw as big a crowd as Lindbergh had four years earlier—not more than forty or fifty people showed up—because it was already eleven o'clock in the morning, on the very Wednesday he had chosen for his flight, before anybody read the note. At that time of day, during the middle of the week, word-of-mouth news just lumbered along. Children were in school; men were at work; and most of the women were fastening their corsets and getting ready to go see what tails or entrails the butcher might be giving away. Only the unemployed, the self-employed, and the very young were available—deliberately available because they'd heard about it, or accidentally available because they happened to be walking at that exact moment in the shore end of Not Doctor Street, a name the post office did not recognize. Town maps registered the street as Mains Avenue, but the only colored doctor in the city had lived and died on that street, and when he moved there in 1896 his patients took to calling the street, which none of them lived in or near, Doctor Street. Later, when other Negroes moved there, and when the postal service became a popular means of transferring messages among them, envelopes from Louisiana, Virginia, Alabama, and Georgia began to arrive addressed to people at house numbers on Doctor Street. The post office workers returned these envelopes or passed them on to the Dead Letter Office. Then in 1918, when colored men were being drafted, a few gave their address at the recruitment office as Doctor Street. In that way, the name acquired a quasi-official status. But not for long. Some of the city legislators, whose concern for appropriate names and the maintenance of the city's landmarks was the principal part of their political life, saw to it that "Doctor Street" was never used in any official capacity. And since they knew that only Southside residents kept it up, they had notices posted in the stores, barbershops, and restaurants in that part of the city saying that the avenue running northerly and southerly from Shore Road fronting the lake to the junction of routes 6 and 2 leading to Pennsylvania, and also running parallel to and between Rutherford Avenue and Broadway, had always been and would always be known as Mains Avenue and not Doctor Street.

It was a genuinely clarifying public notice because it gave Southside residents a way to keep their memories alive and please the city legislators as well. They called it Not Doctor Street, and were inclined to call the charity hospital at its northern end No Mercy Hospital since it was 1931, on the day following Mr. Smith's leap from its cupola, before the first colored expectant mother was allowed to give birth inside its wards and not on its steps. The reason for the hospital's generosity to that particular woman was not the fact that she was the only child of this Negro doctor, for during his entire professional life he had never been granted hospital privileges and only two of his patients were ever admitted to Mercy, both white. Besides, the doctor had been dead a long time by 1931. It must have been Mr. Smith's leap from the roof over their heads that made them admit her. In any case, whether or not the little insurance agent's conviction that he could fly contributed to the place of her delivery, it certainly contributed to its time.

When the dead doctor's daughter saw Mr. Smith emerge as promptly as he had promised from behind the cupola, his wide blue silk wings curved forward around his chest, she dropped her covered peck basket, spilling red velvet rose petals. The wind blew them about, up, down, and into small mounds of snow. Her half-grown daughters scrambled about trying to catch them, while their mother moaned and held the underside of her stomach. The rose-petal scramble got a lot of attention, but the pregnant lady's moans did not. Everyone knew the girls had spent hour after hour tracing, cutting, and stitching the costly velvet, and that Gerhardt's Department Store would be quick to reject any that were soiled.

It was nice and gay there for a while. The men joined in trying to collect the scraps before the snow soaked through them—snatching them from a gust of wind or plucking them delicately from the snow. And the very young children couldn't make up their minds whether to watch the man circled in blue on the roof or the bits of red flashing around on the ground. Their dilemma was solved when a woman suddenly burst into song. The singer, standing at the back of the crowd, was as poorly dressed as the doctor's daughter was well dressed. The latter had on a neat gray coat with the traditional pregnant-woman bow at her navel, a black cloche, and a pair of four-button ladies' galoshes. The singing woman wore a knitted navy cap pulled far down over her forehead. She had wrapped herself up in an old quilt instead of a winter coat. Her head cocked to one side, her eyes fixed on Mr. Robert Smith, she sang in a powerful contralto:

O Sugarman done fly away
Sugarman done gone
Sugarman cut across the sky
Sugarman gone home. . . .

A few of the half a hundred or so people gathered there nudged each other and sniggered. Others listened as though it were the helpful and defining piano music in a silent movie. They stood this way for some time, none of them crying out to Mr. Smith, all of them preoccupied with one or the other of the minor events about them, until the hospital people came.

They had been watching from the windows—at first with mild curiosity, then, as the crowd seemed to swell to the very walls of the hospital, they watched with apprehension. They wondered if one of those things that racial-uplift groups were always organizing was taking place. But when they saw neither placards nor speakers, they ventured outside into the cold: white-coated surgeons, dark-jacketed business and personnel clerks, and three nurses in starched jumpers.

The sight of Mr. Smith and his wide blue wings transfixed them for a few seconds, as did the woman's singing and the roses strewn about. Some of them thought briefly that this was probably some form of worship. Philadelphia, where Father Divine reigned, wasn't all that far away. Perhaps the young girls holding baskets of flowers were two of his virgins. But the laughter of a gold-toothed man brought them back to their senses. They stopped daydreaming and swiftly got down to business, giving orders. Their shouts and bustling caused great confusion where before there had been only a few men and some girls playing with pieces of velvet and a woman singing.

One of the nurses, hoping to bring some efficiency into the disorder, searched the faces around her until she saw a stout woman who looked as though she might move the earth if she wanted to.

"You," she said, moving toward the stout woman. "Are these your children?"

The stout woman turned her head slowly, her eyebrows lifted at the carelessness of the address. Then, seeing where the voice came from, she lowered her brows and veiled her eyes.

"Ma'am?"

"Send one around back to the emergency office. Tell him to tell the guard to get over here quick. That boy there can go. That one." She pointed to a cat-eyed boy about five or six years old.

The stout woman slid her eyes down the nurse's finger and looked at the child she was pointing to.

"Guitar, ma'am."

"What?"

"Guitar."

The nurse gazed at the stout woman as though she had spoken Welsh. Then she closed her mouth, looked again at the cat-eyed boy, and lacing her fingers, spoke her next words very slowly to him.

"Listen. Go around to the back of the hospital to the guard's office. It will say 'Emergency Admissions' on the door. A-D-M-I-S-I-O-N-S. But the guard will be there. Tell him to get over here—on the double. Move now. Move!" She unlaced her fingers and made scooping motions with her hands, the palms pushing against the wintry air.

A man in a brown suit came toward her, puffing little white clouds of breath. "Fire truck's on its way. Get back inside. You'll freeze to death."

The nurse nodded.

"You left out a *s*, ma'am," the boy said. The North was new to him and he had just begun to learn he could speak up to white people. But she'd already gone, rubbing her arms against the cold.

"Granny, she left out a *s*."

"And a 'please.' "

"You reckon he'll jump?"

"A nutwagon do anything."

"Who is he?"

"Collects insurance. A nutwagon."

"Who is that lady singing?"

"That, baby, is the very last thing in pea-time." But she smiled when she looked at the singing woman, so the cat-eyed boy listened to the musical performance with at least as much interest as he devoted to the man flapping his wings on top of the hospital.

The crowd was beginning to be a little nervous now that the law was being called in. They each knew Mr. Smith. He came to their houses twice a month to collect one dollar and sixty-eight cents and write down on a little yellow card both the date and their eighty-four cents a week payment. They were always half a month or so behind, and talked endlessly to him about paying ahead—after they had a preliminary discussion about what he was doing back so soon anyway.

"You back in here already? Look like I just got rid of you."

"I'm tired of seeing your face. Really tired."

"I knew it. Soon's I get two dimes back to back, here you come. More regular than the reaper. Do Hoover know about you?"

They kidded him, abused him, told their children to tell him they were out or sick or gone to Pittsburgh. But they held on to those little yellow cards as though they meant something—laid them gently in the shoe box along with the rent receipts, marriage licenses, and expired factory identification badges. Mr. Smith smiled through it all, managing to keep his eyes focused almost the whole time on his customers' feet. He wore a business suit for his work, but his house was no better than theirs. He never had a woman that any of them knew about and said nothing in church but an occasional "Amen." He never beat anybody up and he wasn't seen after dark, so they thought he was probably a nice man. But he was heavily associated with illness and death, neither of which was distinguishable from the brown picture of the North Carolina Mutual Life Building on the back of their yellow cards. Jumping from the roof of Mercy was the most interesting thing he had done. None of them had suspected he had it in him. Just goes to show, they murmured to each other, you never really do know about people.

The singing woman quieted down and, humming the tune, walked through the crowd toward the rose-petal lady, who was still cradling her stomach.

"You should make yourself warm," she whispered to her, touching her lightly on the elbow. "A little bird'll be here with the morning."

"Oh?" said the rose-petal lady. "Tomorrow morning?"

"That's the only morning coming."

"It can't be," the rose-petal lady said. "It's too soon."

"No it ain't. Right on time."

The women were looking deep into each other's eyes when a loud roar went up from the crowd—a kind of wavy *oo* sound. Mr. Smith had lost his balance for a second, and was trying gallantly to hold on to a triangle of wood that jutted from the cupola. Immediately the singing woman began again:

O Sugarman done fly
O Sugarman done gone . . .

Downtown the firemen pulled on their greatcoats, but when they arrived at Mercy, Mr. Smith had seen the rose petals, heard the music, and leaped on into the air.

The next day a colored baby was born inside Mercy for the first time. Mr. Smith's blue silk wings must have left their mark, because when the little boy discovered, at four, the same thing Mr. Smith had learned earlier—that only birds and airplanes could fly—he lost all interest in himself. To have to live without that single gift saddened him and left his imagination so bereft that he appeared dull even to the women who did not hate his mother. The ones who did, who accepted her invitations to tea and envied the doctor's big dark house of twelve rooms and the green sedan, called him "peculiar." The others, who knew that the house was more prison than palace, and that the Dodge sedan was for Sunday drives only, felt sorry for Ruth Foster and her dry daughters, and called her son "deep." Even mysterious.

"Did he come with a caul?"

"You should have dried it and made him some tea from it to drink. If you don't he'll see ghosts."

"You believe that?"

"I don't, but that's what the old people say."

"Well, he's a deep one anyway. Look at his eyes."

And they pried pieces of baked-too-fast sunshine cake from the roofs of their mouths and looked once more into the boy's eyes. He met their gaze as best he could until, after a pleading glance toward his mother, he was allowed to leave the room.

It took some planning to walk out of the parlor, his back washed with the hum of their voices, open the heavy double doors leading to the dining room, slip up the stairs past all those bedrooms, and not arouse the attention of Lena and Corinthians sitting like big baby dolls before a table heaped with scraps of red velvet. His sisters made roses in the afternoon. Bright, lifeless roses that lay in peck baskets for months until the specialty buyer at Gerhardt's sent Freddie the janitor over to tell the girls that they could use another gross. If he did manage to slip by his sisters and avoid their casual malice, he knelt in his room at the window sill and wondered again and again why he had to stay level on the ground. The quiet that suffused the doctor's house then, broken only by the murmur of the women eating sunshine cake, was only that: quiet. It was not peaceful, for it was preceded by and would soon be terminated by the presence of Macon Dead.

Solid, rumbling, likely to erupt without prior notice, Macon kept each member of his family awkward with fear. His hatred of his wife glittered and sparked in every word he spoke to her. The disappointment he felt in his daughters sifted down on them like ash, dulling their buttery complexions and choking the lilt out of what should have been girlish voices. Under the frozen heat of his glance they tripped over doorsills and dropped the salt cellar into the yolks of their poached eggs. The way he mangled their grace, wit, and self-esteem was the single excitement of their days. Without the tension and drama he ignited, they might not have known what to do with themselves. In his absence his daughters bent their necks over blood-red squares of velvet and waited eagerly for any hint of him, and his wife, Ruth, began her days stunned into stillness by her husband's contempt and ended them wholly animated by it.

When she closed the door behind her afternoon guests, and let the quiet smile die from her lips, she began the preparation of food her husband found impossible to eat. She did not try to make her meals nauseating; she simply didn't know how not to. She would notice that the sunshine cake was too haggled to put before him and decide on a rennet dessert. But the grinding of the veal and beef for a meat loaf took so long she not only forgot the pork, settling for bacon drippings poured over the meat, she had no time to make a dessert at all. Hurriedly, then, she began to set the table. As she unfolded the white linen and let it billow over the fine mahogany table, she would look once more at the large water mark. She never set the table or passed through the dining room without looking at it. Like a lighthouse keeper drawn to his window to gaze once again at the sea, or a prisoner automatically searching out the sun as he steps into the yard for his hour of exercise, Ruth looked for the water mark several times during the day. She knew it was there, would always be there, but she needed to confirm its presence. Like the keeper of the lighthouse and the prisoner, she regarded it as a mooring, a checkpoint, some stable visual object that assured her that the world was still there; that this was life and not a dream. That she was alive somewhere, inside, which she acknowledged to be true only because a thing she knew intimately was out there, outside herself.

Even in the cave of sleep, without dreaming of it or thinking of it at all, she felt its presence. Oh, she talked endlessly to her daughters and her guests about how to get rid of it—what might hide this single flaw on the splendid wood: Vaseline, tobacco juice, iodine, a sanding followed by linseed oil. She had tried them all. But her glance was nutritious; the spot became, if anything, more pronounced as the years passed.

The cloudy gray circle identified the place where the bowl filled every day during the doctor's life with fresh flowers had stood. Every day. And when there were no flowers, it held a leaf arrangement, a gathering of twigs and berries, pussy willow, Scotch pine. . . . But always something to grace the dinner table in the evening.

It was for her father a touch that distinguished his own family from the people among whom they lived. For Ruth it was the summation of the affectionate elegance with which she believed her childhood had been surrounded. When Macon married her and moved into Doctor's house, she kept up the centerpiece-arranging. Then came the time she walked down to the shore through the roughest part of the city to get some driftwood. She had seen an arrangement of driftwood and dried seaweed in the homemakers section of the newspaper. It was a damp November day, and Doctor was paralyzed even then and taking liquid food in his bedroom. The wind had lifted her skirt from around her ankles and cut through her laced shoes. She'd had to rub her feet down with warm olive oil when she got back. At dinner, where just the two of them sat, she turned toward her husband and asked him how he liked the centerpiece. "Most people overlook things like that. They see it, but they don't see anything beautiful in it. They don't see that nature has already made it as perfect as it can be. Look at it from the side. It is pretty, isn't it?"

Her husband looked at the driftwood with its lacy beige seaweed, and without moving his head, said, "Your chicken is red at the bone. And there is probably a potato dish that is supposed to have lumps in it. Mashed ain't the dish."

Ruth let the seaweed disintegrate, and later, when its veins and stems dropped and curled into brown scabs on the table, she removed the bowl and brushed away the scabs. But the water mark, hidden by the bowl all these years, was exposed. And once exposed, it behaved as though it were itself a plant and flourished into a huge suede-gray flower that throbbed like fever, and sighed like the shift of sand dunes. But it could also be still. Patient, restful, and still.

But there was nothing you could do with a mooring except acknowledge it, use it for the verification of some idea you wanted to keep alive. Something else is needed to get from sunup to sundown: a balm, a gentle touch or nuzzling of some sort. So Ruth rose up and out of her guileless inefficiency to claim her bit of balm right after the preparation of dinner and just before the return of her husband from his office. It was one of her two secret indulgences—the one that involved her son—and part of the pleasure it gave her came from the room in which she did it. A damp greenness lived there, made by the evergreen that pressed against the window and filtered the light. It was just a little room that Doctor had called a study, and aside from a sewing machine that stood in the corner along with a dress form, there was only a rocker and tiny footstool. She sat in this room holding her son on her lap, staring at his closed eyelids and listening to the sound of his sucking. Staring not so much from maternal joy as from a wish to avoid seeing his legs dangling almost to the floor.

In late afternoon, before her husband closed his office and came home, she called her son to her. When he came into the little room she unbuttoned her blouse and smiled. He was too young to be dazzled by her nipples, but he was old enough to be bored by the flat taste of mother's milk, so he came reluctantly, as to a chore, and lay as he had at least once each day of his life in his mother's arms, and tried to pull the thin, faintly sweet milk from her flesh without hurting her with his teeth.

She felt him. His restraint, his courtesy, his indifference, all of which pushed her into fantasy. She had the distinct impression that his lips were pulling from her a thread of light. It was as though she were a cauldron issuing spinning gold. Like the miller's daughter—the one who sat at night in a straw-filled room, thrilled with the secret power Rumpelstiltskin had given her: to see golden thread stream from her very own shuttle. And that was the other part of her pleasure, a pleasure she hated to give up. So when Freddie the janitor, who liked to pretend he was a friend of the family and not just their flunky as well as their tenant, brought his rent to the doctor's house late one day and looked in the window past the evergreen, the terror that sprang to Ruth's eyes came from the quick realization that she was to lose fully half of what made her daily life bearable. Freddie, however, interpreted her look as simple shame, but that didn't stop him from grinning.

"Have mercy. I be damn."

He fought the evergreen for a better look, hampered more by his laughter than by the branches. Ruth jumped up as quickly as she could and covered her breast, dropping her son on the floor and confirming for him what he had begun to suspect—that these afternoons were strange and wrong.

Before either mother or son could speak, rearrange themselves properly, or even exchange looks, Freddie had run around the house, climbed the porch steps, and was calling them between gulps of laughter.

"Miss Rufie. Miss Rufie. Where you? Where you all at?" He opened the door to the green room as though it were his now.

"I be damn, Miss Rufie. When the last time I seen that? I don't even know the last time I seen that. I mean, ain't nothing wrong with it. I mean, old folks swear by it. It's just, you know, you don't see it up here much. . . ." But his eyes were on the boy. Appreciative eyes that communicated some complicity she was excluded from. Freddie looked the boy up and down, taking in the steady but secretive eyes and the startling contrast between Ruth's lemony skin and the boy's black skin. "Used to be a lot of womenfolk nurse they kids a long time down South. Lot of 'em. But you don't see it much no more. I knew a family—the mother wasn't too quick, though—nursed hers till the boy, I reckon, was near 'bout thirteen. But that's a bit much, ain't it?" All the time he chattered, he rubbed his chin and looked at the boy. Finally he stopped, and gave a long low chuckle. He'd found the phrase he'd been searching for. "A milkman. That's what you got here, Miss Rufie. A natural milkman if ever I seen one. Look out, womens. Here he come. Huh!"

Freddie carried his discovery not only into the homes in Ruth's neighborhood, but to Southside, where he lived and where Macon Dead owned rent houses. So Ruth kept close to home and had no afternoon guests for the better part of two months, to keep from hearing that her son had been rechristened with a name he was never able to shake and that did nothing to improve either one's relationship with his father.

Macon Dead never knew how it came about—how his only son acquired the nickname that stuck in spite of his own refusal to use it or acknowledge it. It was a matter that concerned him a good deal, for the giving of names in his family was always surrounded by what he believed to be monumental foolishness. No one mentioned to him the incident out of which the nickname grew because he was a difficult man to approach—a hard man, with a manner so cool it discouraged casual or spontaneous conversation. Only Freddie the janitor took liberties with Macon Dead, liberties he purchased with the services he rendered, and Freddie was the last person on earth to tell him. So Macon Dead neither heard of nor visualized Ruth's sudden terror, her awkward jump from the rocking chair, the boy's fall broken by the tiny footstool, or Freddie's amused, admiring summation of the situation.

Without knowing any of the details, however, he guessed, with the accuracy of a mind sharpened by hatred, that the name he heard schoolchildren call his son, the name he overheard the ragman use when he paid the boy three cents for a bundle of old clothes—he guessed that this name was not clean. Milkman. It certainly didn't sound like the honest job of a dairyman, or bring to his mind cold bright cans standing on the back porch, glittering like captains on guard. It sounded dirty, intimate, and hot. He knew that wherever the name came from, it had something to do with his wife and was, like the emotion he always felt when thinking of her, coated with disgust.

This disgust and the uneasiness with which he regarded his son affected everything he did in that city. If he could have felt sad, simply sad, it would have relieved him. Fifteen years of regret at not having a son had become the bitterness of finally having one in the most revolting circumstances.

There had been a time when he had a head full of hair and when Ruth wore lovely complicated underwear that he deliberately took a long time to undo. When all of his foreplay was untying, unclasping, unbuckling the snaps and strings of what must have been the most beautiful, the most delicate, the whitest and softest underwear on earth. Each eye of her corset he toyed with (and there were forty–twenty on each side); each grosgrain ribbon that threaded its pale-blue way through the snowy top of her bodice he unlaced. He not only undid the blue bow; he pulled it all the way out of the hem, so she had to rethread it afterward with a safety pin. The elastic bands that connected her perspiration shields to her slip he unsnapped and snapped again, teasing her and himself with the sound of the snaps and the thrill of his fingertips on her shoulders. They never spoke during these undressings. But they giggled occasionally, and as when children play "doctor," undressing of course was the best part.

When Ruth was naked and lying there as moist and crumbly as unbleached sugar, he bent to unlace her shoes. That was the final delight, for once he had undressed her feet, had peeled her stockings down over her ankles and toes, he entered her and ejaculated quickly. She liked it that way. So did he. And in almost twenty years during which he had not laid eyes on her naked feet, he missed only the underwear.

Once he believed that the sight of her mouth on the dead man's fingers would be the thing he would remember always. He was wrong. Little by little he remembered fewer and fewer of the details, until finally he had to imagine them, even fabricate them, guess what they must have been. The image left him, but the odiousness never did. For the nourishment of his outrage he depended on the memory of her underwear; those round, innocent corset eyes now lost to him forever.

So if the people were calling his son Milkman, and if she was lowering her eyelids and dabbing at the sweat on her top lip when she heard it, there was definitely some filthy connection and it did not matter at all to Macon Dead whether anyone gave him the details or not.

And they didn't. Nobody both dared enough and cared enough to tell him. The ones who cared enough, Lena and Corinthians, the living proof of those years of undressing his wife, did not dare. And the one person who dared to but didn't care to was the one person in the world he hated more than his wife in spite of the fact that she was his sister. He had not crossed the tracks to see her since his son was born and he had no intention of renewing their relationship now.

Macon Dead dug in his pocket for his keys, and curled his fingers around them, letting their bunchy solidity calm him. They were the keys to all the doors of his houses (only four true houses; the rest were really shacks), and he fondled them from time to time as he walked down Not Doctor Street to his office. At least he thought of it as his office, had even painted the word OFFICE on the door. But the plate-glass window contradicted him. In peeling gold letters arranged in a semicircle, his business establishment was declared to be Sonny's Shop. Scraping the previous owner's name off was hardly worth the trouble since he couldn't scrape it from anybody's mind. His storefront office was never called anything but Sonny's Shop, although nobody now could remember thirty years back, when, presumably, Sonny did something or other there.

He walked there now—strutted is the better word, for he had a high behind and an athlete's stride—thinking of names. Surely, he thought, he and his sister had some ancestor, some lithe young man with onyx skin and legs as straight as cane stalks, who had a name that was real. A name given to him at birth with love and seriousness. A name that was not a joke, nor a disguise, nor a brand name. But who this lithe young man was, and where his cane-stalk legs carried him from or to, could never be known. No. Nor his name. His own parents, in some mood of perverseness or resignation, had agreed to abide by a naming done to them by somebody who couldn't have cared less. Agreed to take and pass on to all their issue this heavy name scrawled in perfect thoughtlessness by a drunken Yankee in the Union Army. A literal slip of the pen handed to his father on a piece of paper and which he handed on to his only son, and his son likewise handed on to his; Macon Dead who begat a second Macon Dead who married Ruth Foster (Dead) and begat Magdalene called Lena Dead and First Corinthians Dead and (when he least expected it) another Macon Dead, now known to the part of the world that mattered as Milkman Dead. And as if that were not enough, a sister named Pilate Dead, who would never mention to her brother the circumstances or the details of this foolish misnaming of his son because the whole thing would have delighted her. She would savor it, maybe fold it too in a brass box and hang it from her other ear.

He had cooperated as a young father with the blind selection of names from the Bible for every child other than the first male. And abided by whatever the finger pointed to, for he knew every configuration of the naming of his sister. How his father, confused and melancholy over his wife's death in childbirth, had thumbed through the Bible, and since he could not read a word, chose a group of letters that seemed to him strong and handsome; saw in them a large figure that looked like a tree hanging in some princely but protective way over a row of smaller trees. How he had copied the group of letters out on a piece of brown paper; copied, as illiterate people do, every curlicue, arch, and bend in the letters, and presented it to the midwife.

"That's the baby's name."

"You want this for the baby's name?"

"I want that for the baby's name. Say it."

"You can't name the baby this."

"Say it."

"It's a man's name."

"Say it."

"Pilate."

"What?"

"Pilate. You wrote down Pilate."

"Like a riverboat pilot?"

"No. Not like no riverboat pilot. Like a Christ-killing Pilate. You can't get much worse than that for a name. And a baby girl at that."

"That's where my finger went down at."

"Well, your brain ain't got to follow it. You don't want to give this motherless child the name of the man that killed Jesus, do you?"

"I asked Jesus to save me my wife."

"Careful, Macon."

"I asked him all night long."

"He give you your baby."

"Yes. He did. Baby name Pilate."

"Jesus, have mercy."

"Where you going with that piece of paper?"

"It's going back where it came from. Right in the Devil's flames."

"Give it here. It come from the Bible. It stays in the Bible."

And it did stay there, until the baby girl turned twelve and took it out, folded it up into a tiny knot and put it in a little brass box, and strung the entire contraption through her left earlobe. Fluky about her own name at twelve, how much more fluky she'd become since then Macon could only guess. But he knew for certain that she would treat the naming of the third Macon Dead with the same respect and awe she had treated the boy's birth.

Macon Dead remembered when his son was born, how she seemed to be more interested in this first nephew of hers than she was in her own daughter, and even that daughter's daughter. Long after Ruth was up and about, as capable as she ever would be—and that wasn't much—of running the house again, Pilate continued to visit, her shoelaces undone, a knitted cap pulled down over her forehead, bringing her foolish earring and sickening smell into the kitchen. He had not seen her since he was sixteen years old, until a year before the birth of his son, when she appeared in his city. Now she was acting like an in-law, like an aunt, dabbling at helping Ruth and the girls, but having no interest in or knowledge of decent housekeeping, she got in the way. Finally she just sat in a chair near the crib, singing to the baby. That wasn't so bad, but what Macon Dead remembered most was the expression on her face. Surprise, it looked like, and eagerness. But so intense it made him uneasy. Or perhaps it was more than that. Perhaps it was seeing her all those years after they had separated outside that cave, and remembering his anger and her betrayal. How far down she had slid since then. She had cut the last thread of propriety. At one time she had been the dearest thing in the world to him. Now she was odd, murky, and worst of all, unkempt. A regular source of embarrassment, if he would allow it. But he would not allow it.

Finally he had told her not to come again until she could show some respect for herself. Could get a real job instead of running a wine house.

"Why can't you dress like a woman?" He was standing by the stove. "What's that sailor's cap doing on your head? Don't you have stockings? What are you trying to make me look like in this town?" He trembled with the thought of the white men in the bank—the men who helped him buy and mortgage houses—discovering that this raggedy bootlegger was his sister. That the propertied Negro who handled his business so well and who lived in the big house on Not Doctor Street had a sister who had a daughter but no husband, and that daughter had a daughter but no husband. A collection of lunatics who made wine and sang in the streets "like common street women! Just like common street women!"

Pilate had sat there listening to him, her wondering eyes resting on his face. Then she said, "I been worried sick about you too, Macon."

Exasperated, he had gone to the kitchen door. "Go 'head,

Pilate. Go on now. I'm on the thin side of evil and trying not to break through."

Pilate stood up, wrapped her quilt around her, and with a last fond look at the baby, left through the kitchen door. She never came back.

When Macon Dead got to the front door of his office he saw a stout woman and two young boys standing a few feet away. Macon unlocked his door, walked over to his desk, and settled himself behind it. As he was thumbing through his accounts book, the stout woman entered, alone.

"Afternoon Mr. Dead, sir. I'm Mrs. Bains. Live over at number three on Fifteenth Street."

Macon Dead remembered—not the woman, but the circumstances at number three. His tenant's grandmother or aunt or something had moved in there and the rent was long overdue.

"Yes, Mrs. Bains. You got something for me?"

"Well, that's what I come to talk to you about. You know Cency left all them babies with me. And my relief check ain't no more'n it take to keep a well-grown yard dog alive—half alive, I should say."

"Your rent is four dollars a month, Mrs. Bains. You two months behind already."

"I do know that, Mr. Dead, sir, but babies can't make it with nothing to put in they stomach."

Their voices were low, polite, without any hint of conflict.

"Can they make it in the street, Mrs. Bains? That's where they gonna be if you don't figure out some way to get me my money."

"No, sir. They can't make it in the street. We need both, I reckon. Same as yours does."

"Then you better rustle it up, Mrs. Bains. You got till"—he swiveled around to consult the calendar on the wall—"till Saturday coming. Saturday, Mrs. Bains. Not Sunday. Not Monday. Saturday."

If she had been younger and had more juice, the glitter in her eyes would have washed down onto her cheeks. Now, at her time of life, it simply gleamed. She pressed the flat of her hand on Macon Dead's desk and, holding the gleam steady in her eyes, pushed herself up from the chair. She turned her head a little to look out the plate-glass window, and then back at him.

"What's it gonna profit you, Mr. Dead, sir, to put me and them children out?"

"Saturday, Mrs. Bains."

Lowering her head, Mrs. Bains whispered something and walked slowly and heavily from the office. As she closed the door to Sonny's Shop, her grandchildren moved out of the sunlight into the shadow where she stood.

"What he say, Granny?"

Mrs. Bains put a hand on the taller boy's hair and fingered it lightly, absently searching with her nails for tetter spots.

"He must've told her no," said the other boy.

"Do we got to move?" The tall boy tossed his head free of her fingers and looked at her sideways. His cat eyes were gashes of gold.

Mrs. Bains let her hand fall to her side. "A nigger in business is a terrible thing to see. A terrible, terrible thing to see."

The boys looked at each other and back at their grandmother. Their lips were parted as though they had heard something important.

When Mrs. Bains closed the door, Macon Dead went back to the pages of his accounts book, running his fingertips over the figures and thinking with the unoccupied part of his mind about the first time he called on Ruth Foster's father. He had only two keys in his pocket then, and if he had let people like the woman who just left have their way, he wouldn't have had any keys at all. It was because of those keys that he could dare to walk over to that part of Not Doctor Street (it was still Doctor Street then) and approach the most important Negro in the city. To lift the lion's paw knocker, to entertain thoughts of marrying the doctor's daughter was possible because each key represented a house which he owned at the time. Without those keys he would have floated away at the doctor's first word: "Yes?" Or he would have melted like new wax under the heat of that pale eye. Instead he was able to say that he had been introduced to his daughter, Miss Ruth Foster, and would appreciate having the doctor's permission to keep her company now and then. That his intentions were honorable and that he himself was certainly worthy of the doctor's consideration as a gentleman friend for Miss Foster since, at twenty-five, he was already a colored man of property.

"I don't know anything about you," the doctor said, "other than your name, which I don't like, but I will abide by my daughter's preference."

In fact the doctor knew a good deal about him and was more grateful to this tall young man than he ever allowed himself to show. Fond as he was of his only child, useful as she was in his house since his wife had died, lately he had begun to chafe under her devotion. Her steady beam of love was unsettling, and she had never dropped those expressions of affection that had been so lovable in her childhood. The good-night kiss was itself a masterpiece of slow-wittedness on her part and discomfort on his. At sixteen, she still insisted on having him come to her at night, sit on her bed, exchange a few pleasantries, and plant a kiss on her lips. Perhaps it was the loud silence of his dead wife, perhaps it was Ruth's disturbing resemblance to her mother. More probably it was the ecstasy that always seemed to be shining in Ruth's face when he bent to kiss her—an ecstasy he felt inappropriate to the occasion.

None of that, of course, did he describe to the young man who came to call. Which is why Macon Dead still believed the magic had lain in the two keys.

In the middle of his reverie, Macon was interrupted by rapid tapping on the window. He looked up, saw Freddie peeping through the gold lettering, and nodded for him to enter. A gold-toothed bantamweight, Freddie was as much of a town crier as Southside had. It was this same rapid tapping on the windowpane, the same flash-of-gold smile that had preceded his now-famous scream to Macon: "Mr. Smith went splat!" It was obvious to Macon that Freddie now had news of another calamity.

"Porter gone crazy drunk again! Got his shotgun!"

"Who's he out for?" Macon began closing books and opening desk drawers. Porter was a tenant and tomorrow was collection day.

"Ain't out for nobody in particular. Just perched himself up in the attic window and commenced to waving a shotgun. Say he gotta kill him somebody before morning."

"He go to work today?"

"Yep. Caught the eagle too."

"Drunk it all up?"

"Not all of it. He only got one bottle, and he still got a fist fulla money."

"Who's crazy enough to sell him any liquor?"

Freddie showed a few gold teeth but said nothing, so Macon knew it was Pilate. He locked all his drawers save one—the one he unlocked and took a small .32 from.

"Police warn every bootlegger in the county, and he still gets it somehow." Macon went on with the charade, pretending he didn't know his sister was the one Porter and anybody else—adult, child, or beast—could buy wine from. He thought for the hundredth time that she needed to be in jail and that he would be willing to put her there if he could be sure she wouldn't loudmouth him and make him seem trashy in the eyes of the law—and the banks.

"You know how to use that thing, Mr. Dead, sir?"

"I know how."

"Porter's crazy when he drunk."

"I know what he is."

"How you aiming to get him down?"

"I ain't aiming to get him down. I'm aiming to get my money down. He can go on and die up there if he wants to. But if he don't toss me my rent, I'm going to blow him out of that window."

Freddie's giggle was soft, but his teeth strengthened its impact. A born flunky, he loved gossip and the telling of it. He was the ear that heard every murmur of complaint, every name-calling; and his was the eye that saw everything: the secret loving glances, the fights, the new dresses.

Macon knew Freddie as a fool and a liar, but a reliable liar. He was always right about his facts and always wrong about the motives that produced the facts. Just as now he was right about Porter having a shotgun, being in the attic window, and being drunk. But Porter was not waiting to kill somebody, meaning anybody, before morning. In fact he was very specific about whom he wanted to kill—himself. However, he did have a precondition which he shouted down, loud and clear, from the attic. "I want to fuck! Send me up somebody to fuck! Hear me? Send me up somebody, I tell ya, or I'ma blow my brains out!"

As Macon and Freddie approached the yard, the women from the rooming house were hollering answers to Porter's plea.

"What kinda bargain is that?"

"Kill yourself first and then we'll send you somebody."

"Do it have to be a woman?"

"Do it got to be human?"

"Do it got to be alive?"

"Can it be a piece of liver?"

"Put that thing down and throw me my goddam money!" Macon's voice cut through the women's fun. "Float those dollars down here, nigger, then blow yourself up!"

Porter turned and aimed his shotgun at Macon.

"If you pull that trigger," shouted Macon, "you better not miss. If you take a shot you better make sure I'm dead, cause if you don't I'm gonna shoot your balls up in your throat!" He pulled out his own weapon. "Now get the hell outta that window!"

Porter hesitated for only a second, before turning the barrel of the shotgun toward himself—or trying to. Its length made it difficult; his drunkenness made it impossible. Struggling to get the right angle, he was suddenly distracted. He leaned his shotgun on the window sill, pulled out his penis and in a high arc, peed over the heads of the women, making them scream and run in a panic that the shotgun had not been able to create. Macon rubbed the back of his head while Freddie bent double with laughter.

For more than an hour Porter held them at bay: cowering, screaming, threatening, urinating, and interspersing all of it with pleas for a woman.

He would cry great shoulder-heaving sobs, followed by more screams.

"I love ya! I love ya all. Don't act like that. You women. Stop it. Don't act like that. Don't you see I love ya? I'd die for ya, kill for ya. I'm saying I love ya. I'm telling ya. Oh, God have mercy. What I'm gonna do? What in this fuckin world am I gonna dooooo?"

Tears streamed down his face and he cradled the barrel of the shotgun in his arms as though it were the woman he had been begging for, searching for, all his life. "Gimme hate, Lord," he whimpered. "I'll take hate any day. But don't give me love. I can't take no more love, Lord. I can't carry it. Just like Mr. Smith. He couldn't carry it. It's too heavy. Jesus, *you* know. You know all about it. Ain't it heavy? Jesus? Ain't love heavy? Don't you see, Lord? You own son couldn't carry it. If it killed Him, what You think it's gonna do to me? Huh? Huh?" He was getting angry again.

"Come down outta there, nigger!" Macon's voice was still loud, but it was getting weary.

"And you, you baby-dicked baboon"—he tried to point at Macon—"you the worst. You need killin, you really *need* killin. You know why? Well, I'm gonna tell you why. I *know* why. Everybody . . ."

Porter slumped down in the window, muttering, "Everybody know why," and fell fast asleep. As he sank deeper into it, the shotgun slipped from his hand, rattled down the roof, and hit the ground with a loud explosion. The shot zipped past a bystander's shoe and blew a hole in the tire of a stripped Dodge parked in the road.

"Go get my money," Macon said.

"Me?" Freddie asked. "Suppose he . . ."

"Go get me my money."

Porter was snoring. Through the blast of the gun and the picking of his pocket he slept like a baby.

When Macon walked out of the yard, the sun had disappeared behind the bread company. Tired, irritable, he walked down Fifteenth Street, glancing up as he passed one of his other houses, its silhouette melting in the light that trembled between dusk and twilight. Scattered here and there, his houses stretched up beyond him like squat ghosts with hooded eyes. He didn't like to look at them in this light. During the day they were reassuring to see; now they did not seem to belong to him at all—in fact he felt as though the houses were in league with one another to make him feel like the outsider, the propertyless, landless wanderer. It was this feeling of loneliness that made him decide to take a shortcut back to Not Doctor Street, even though to do so would lead him past his sister's house. In the gathering darkness, he was sure his passing would be unnoticed by her. He crossed a yard and followed a fence that led into Darling Street where Pilate lived in a narrow single-story house whose basement seemed to be rising from rather than settling into the ground. She had no electricity because she would not pay for the service. Nor for gas. At night she and her daughter lit the house with candles and kerosene lamps; they warmed themselves and cooked with wood and coal, pumped kitchen water into a dry sink through a pipeline from a well and lived pretty much as though progress was a word that meant walking a little farther on down the road.

Her house sat eighty feet from the sidewalk and was backed by four huge pine trees, from which she got the needles she stuck into her mattress. Seeing the pine trees started him thinking about her mouth; how she loved, as a girl, to chew pine needles and as a result smelled even then like a forest. For a dozen years she had been like his own child. After their mother died, she had come struggling out of the womb without help from throbbing muscles or the pressure of swift womb water. As a result, for all the years he knew her, her stomach was as smooth and sturdy as her back, at no place interrupted by a navel. It was the absence of a navel that convinced people that she had not come into this world through normal channels; had never lain, floated, or grown in some warm and liquid place connected by a tissue-thin tube to a reliable source of human nourishment. Macon knew otherwise, because he was there and had seen the eyes of the midwife as his mother's legs collapsed. And heard as well her shouts when the baby, who they had believed was dead also, inched its way headfirst out of a still, silent, and indifferent cave of flesh, dragging her own cord and her own afterbirth behind her. But the rest was true. Once the new baby's lifeline was cut, the cord stump shriveled, fell off, and left no trace of having ever existed, which, as a young boy taking care of his baby sister, he thought no more strange than a bald head. He was seventeen years old, irreparably separated from her and already pressing forward in his drive for wealth, when he learned that there was probably not another stomach like hers on earth.

Now, nearing her yard, he trusted that the dark would keep anyone in her house from seeing him. He did not even look to his left as he walked by it. But then he heard the music. They were singing. All of them. Pilate, Reba, and Reba's daughter, Hagar. There was no one on the street that he could see; people were at supper, licking their fingers, blowing into saucers of coffee, and no doubt chattering about Porter's escapade and Macon's fearless confrontation of the wild man in the attic. There were no street lights in this part of town; only the moon directed the way of a pedestrian. Macon walked on, resisting as best he could the sound of the voices that followed him. He was rapidly approaching a part of the road where the music could not follow, when he saw, like a scene on the back of a postcard, a picture of where he was headed—his own home; his wife's narrow unyielding back; his daughters, boiled dry from years of yearning; his son, to whom he could speak only if his words held some command or criticism. "Hello, Daddy." "Hello, son, tuck your shirt in." "I found a dead bird, Daddy." "Don't bring that mess in this house. . . ." There was no music there, and tonight he wanted just a bit of music—from the person who had been his first caring for.

He turned back and walked slowly toward Pilate's house. They were singing some melody that Pilate was leading. A phrase that the other two were taking up and building on. Her powerful contralto, Reba's piercing soprano in counterpoint, and the soft voice of the girl, Hagar, who must be about ten or eleven now, pulled him like a carpet tack under the influence of a magnet.

Surrendering to the sound, Macon moved closer. He wanted no conversation, no witness, only to listen and perhaps to see the three of them, the source of that music that made him think of fields and wild turkey and calico. Treading as lightly as he could, he crept up to the side window where the candlelight flickered lowest, and peeped in. Reba was cutting her toenails with a kitchen knife or a switchblade, her long neck bent almost to her knees. The girl, Hagar, was braiding her hair, while Pilate, whose face he could not see because her back was to the window, was stirring something in a pot. Wine pulp, perhaps. Macon knew it was not food she was stirring, for she and her daughters ate like children. Whatever they had a taste for. No meal was ever planned or balanced or served. Nor was there any gathering at the table. Pilate might bake hot bread and each one of them would eat it with butter whenever she felt like it. Or there might be grapes, left over from the winemaking, or peaches for days on end. If one of them bought a gallon of milk they drank it until it was gone. If another got a half bushel of tomatoes or a dozen ears of corn, they ate them until they were gone too. They ate what they had or came across or had a craving for. Profits from their wine-selling evaporated like sea water in a hot wind—going for junk jewelry for Hagar, Reba's gifts to men, and he didn't know what all.

Near the window, hidden by the dark, he felt the irritability of the day drain from him and relished the effortless beauty of the women singing in the candlelight. Reba's soft profile, Hagar's hands moving, moving in her heavy hair, and Pilate. He knew her face better than he knew his own. Singing now, her face would be a mask; all emotion and passion would have left her features and entered her voice. But he knew that when she was neither singing nor talking, her face was animated by her constantly moving lips. She chewed things. As a baby, as a very young girl, she kept things in her mouth—straw from brooms, gristle, buttons, seeds, leaves, string, and her favorite, when he could find some for her, rubber bands and India rubber erasers. Her lips were alive with small movements. If you were close to her, you wondered if she was about to smile or was she merely shifting a straw from the baseline of her gums to her tongue. Perhaps she was dislodging a curl of rubber band from inside her cheek, or was she really smiling? From a distance she appeared to be whispering to herself, when she was only nibbling or splitting tiny seeds with her front teeth. Her lips were darker than her skin, wine-stained, blueberry-dyed, so her face had a cosmetic look—as though she had applied a very dark lipstick neatly and blotted away its shine on a scrap of newspaper.

As Macon felt himself softening under the weight of memory and music, the song died down. The air was quiet and yet Macon Dead could not leave. He liked looking at them freely this way. They didn't move. They simply stopped singing and Reba went on paring her toenails, Hagar threaded and unthreaded her hair, and Pilate swayed like a willow over her stirring.

Chapter 2

Only Magdalene called Lena and First Corinthians were genuinely happy when the big Packard rolled evenly and silently out of the driveway. They alone had a sense of adventure and were flagrant in their enjoyment of the automobile's plushness. Each had a window to herself and commanded an unobstructed view of the summer day flying past them. And each was both old enough and young enough to actually believe she was a princess riding in a regal chariot driven by a powerful coachman. In the back seat, away from the notice of Macon and Ruth, they slipped off their patent leather pumps, rolled their stockings down over their knees, and watched the men walking down the streets.

These rides that the family took on Sunday afternoons had become rituals and much too important for Macon to enjoy. For him it was a way to satisfy himself that he was indeed a successful man. It was a less ambitious ritual for Ruth, but a way, nevertheless, for her to display her family. For the little boy it was simply a burden. Pressed in the front seat between his parents, he could see only the winged woman careening off the nose of the car. He was not allowed to sit on his mother's lap during the drive—not because she wouldn't have it, but because his father objected to it. So it was only by kneeling on the dove gray seat and looking out the back window that he could see anything other than the laps, feet, and hands of his parents, the dashboard, or the silver winged woman poised at the tip of the Packard. But riding backward made him uneasy. It was like flying blind, and not knowing where he was going—just where he had been—troubled him. He did not want to see trees that he had passed, or houses and children slipping into the space the automobile had left behind.

Macon Dead's Packard rolled slowly down Not Doctor Street, through the rough part of town (later known as the Blood Bank because blood flowed so freely there), over the bypass downtown, and headed for the wealthy white neighborhoods. Some of the black people who saw the car passing by sighed with good-humored envy at the classiness, the dignity of it. In 1936 there were very few among them who lived as well as Macon Dead. Others watched the family gliding by with a tiny bit of jealousy and a whole lot of amusement, for Macon's wide green Packard belied what they thought a car was for. He never went over twenty miles an hour, never gunned his engine, never stayed in first gear for a block or two to give pedestrians a thrill. He never had a blown tire, never ran out of gas and needed twelve grinning raggle-tailed boys to help him push it up a hill or over to a curb. No rope ever held the door to its frame, and no teen-agers leaped on his running board for a lift down the street. He hailed no one and no one hailed him. There was never a sudden braking and backing up to shout or laugh with a friend. No beer bottles or ice cream cones poked from the open windows. Nor did a baby boy stand up to pee out of them. He never let rain fall on it if he could help it and he walked to Sonny's Shop—taking the car out only on these occasions. What's more, they doubted that he had ever taken a woman into the back seat, because rumor was that he went to "bad houses" or lay, sometimes, with a slack or lonely female tenant. Other than the bright and roving eyes of Magdalene called Lena and First Corinthians, the Packard had no real lived life at all. So they called it Macon Dead's hearse.

First Corinthians pulled her fingers through her hair. It was long, lightweight hair, the color of wet sand. "Are you going anyplace special, or are we just driving around?" She kept her eyes on the street, watching the men and women walking by.

"Careful, Macon. You always take the wrong turn here." Ruth spoke softly from the right side of the car.

"Do you want to drive?" Macon asked her.

"You know I don't drive," she answered.

"Then let me do it."

"All right, but don't blame me if . . ."

Macon pulled smoothly into the left fork of the road that led through downtown and into a residential area.

"Daddy? Are we going any special place?"

"Honoré," Macon said.

Magdalene called Lena pushed her stockings farther down on her legs. "On the lake? What's out there? There's nothing out there, nobody."

"There's a beach community out there, Lena. Your father wants to look at it." Ruth reasserted herself into the conversation.

"What for? Those are white people's houses," said Lena.

"All of it's not white people's houses. Some of it's nothing. Just land. Way over on the other side. It could be a nice summer place for colored people. Beach houses. You understand what I mean?" Macon glanced at his daughter through the rear-view mirror.

"Who's going to live in them? There's no colored people who can afford to have two houses," Lena said.

"Reverend Coles can, and Dr. Singleton," Corinthians corrected her.

"And that lawyer—what's his name?" Ruth looked around at Corinthians, who ignored her.

"And Mary, I suppose." Lena laughed.

Corinthians stared coldly at her sister. "Daddy wouldn't sell property to a barmaid. Daddy, would you let us live next to a barmaid?"

"She owns that place, Corinthians," Ruth said.

"I don't care what she owns. I care about what she is. Daddy?" Corinthians leaned toward her father for confirmation.

"You're going too fast, Macon." Ruth pressed the toe of her shoe against the floorboard.

"If you say one more thing to me about the way I drive, you're going to walk back home. I mean it."

Magdalene called Lena sat forward and put her hand on her mother's shoulder. Ruth was quiet. The little boy kicked his feet against the underside of the dashboard.

"Stop that!" Macon told him.

"I have to go to the bathroom," said his son.

Corinthians held her head. "Oh, Lord."

"But you went before we left," said Ruth.

"I have to *go!*" He was beginning to whine.

"Are you sure?" his mother asked him. He looked at her. "I guess we better stop," Ruth said to nobody in particular. Her eyes grazed the countryside they were entering.

Macon didn't alter his speed.

"Are *we* going to have a summer place, or are you just selling property?"

"I'm not selling anything. I'm thinking of buying and then renting," Macon answered her.

"But are *we*—"

"I have to go," said the little boy.

"—going to live there too?"

"Maybe."

"By ourselves? Who else?" Corinthians was very interested.

"I can't tell you that. But in a few years—five or ten—a whole lot of coloreds will have enough to afford it. A whole lot. Take my word for it."

Magdalene called Lena took a deep breath. "Up ahead you could pull over, Daddy. He might mess up the seat."

Macon glanced at her in the mirror and slowed down. "Who's going to take him?" Ruth fiddled with the door handle. "Not you," Macon said to her.

Ruth looked at her husband. She parted her lips but didn't say anything.

"Not me," said Corinthians. "I have on high heels."

"Come on," Lena sighed. They left the car, little boy and big sister, and disappeared into the trees that reared up off the shoulder of the road.

"You really think there'll be enough colored people—I mean nice colored people—in this city to live there?"

"They don't have to be from this city, Corinthians. People will drive to a summer house. White people do it all the time." Macon drummed his fingers on the steering wheel, which trembled a little as the car idled.

"Negroes don't like the water." Corinthians giggled.

"They'll like it if they own it," said Macon. He looked out the window and saw Magdalene called Lena coming out of the trees. A large colorful bouquet of flowers was in her hand, but her face was crumpled in anger. Over her pale-blue dress dark wet stains spread like fingers.

"He wet on me," she said. "He wet me, Mama." She was close to tears.

Ruth clucked her tongue.

Corinthians laughed. "I told you Negroes didn't like water."

He didn't mean it. It happened before he was through. She'd stepped away from him to pick flowers, returned, and at the sound of her footsteps behind him, he'd turned around before he was through. It was becoming a habit—this concentration on things behind him. Almost as though there were no future to be had.

But if the future did not arrive, the present did extend itself, and the uncomfortable little boy in the Packard went to school and at twelve met the boy who not only could liberate him, but could take him to the woman who had as much to do with his future as she had his past.

Guitar said he knew her. Had even been inside her house.

"What's it like in there?" Milkman asked him.

"Shiny," Guitar answered. "Shiny and brown. With a smell."

"A bad smell?"

"I don't know. Her smell. You'll see."

All those unbelievable but entirely possible stories about his father's sister—the woman his father had forbidden him to go near—had both of them spellbound. Neither wished to live one more day without finding out the truth, and they believed they were the legitimate and natural ones to do so. After all, Guitar already knew her, and Milkman was her nephew.

They found her on the front steps sitting wide-legged in a long-sleeved, long-skirted black dress. Her hair was wrapped in black too, and from a distance, all they could really see beneath her face was the bright orange she was peeling. She was all angles, he remembered later, knees, mostly, and elbows. One foot pointed east and one pointed west.

As they came closer and saw the brass box dangling from her ear, Milkman knew that what with the earring, the orange, and the angled black cloth, nothing—not the wisdom of his father nor the caution of the world—could keep him from her.

Guitar, being older and already in high school, had none of the reluctance that his young buddy still struggled with, and was the first one to speak.

"Hi."

The woman looked up. First at Guitar and then at Milkman.

"What kind of word is that?" Her voice was light but gravel-sprinkled. Milkman kept on staring at her fingers, manipulating the orange. Guitar grinned and shrugged. "It means hello."

"Then say what you mean."

"Okay. Hello."

"That's better. What you want?"

"Nothin. We just passin by."

"Look like you standin by."

"If you don't want us here, Miss Pilate, we'll go." Guitar spoke softly.

"I ain't the one with the wants. You the one want something."

"We wanna ask you something." Guitar stopped feigning indifference. She was too direct, and to keep up with her he had to pay careful attention to his language.

"Ask it."

"Somebody said you ain't got no navel."

"That the question?"

"Yes."

"Don't sound like a question. Sound like an answer. Gimme the question."

"Do you?"

"Do I what?"

"Do you have a navel?"

"No."

"What happened to it?"

"Beats me." She dropped a bright peeling into her lap and separated an orange section slowly. "Now do I get to ask a question?"

"Sure."

"Who's your little friend?"

"This here's Milkman."

"Do he talk?" Pilate swallowed a piece of the fruit.

"Yeah. He talk. Say something." Guitar shoved an elbow at Milkman without taking his eyes off Pilate.

Milkman took a breath, held it, and said, "Hi."

Pilate laughed. "You all must be the dumbest unhung Negroes on earth. What they telling you in them schools? You say 'Hi' to pigs and sheep when you want 'em to move. When you tell a human being 'Hi,' he ought to get up and knock you down."

Shame had flooded him. He had expected to feel it, but not that kind; to be embarrassed, yes, but not that way. She was the one who was ugly, dirty, poor, and drunk. The queer aunt whom his sixth-grade schoolmates teased him about and whom he hated because he felt personally responsible for her ugliness, her poverty, her dirt, and her wine.

Instead she was making fun of his school, of his teachers, of him. And while she looked as poor as everyone said she was, something was missing from her eyes that should have confirmed it. Nor was she dirty; unkempt, yes, but not dirty. The whites of her fingernails were like ivory. And unless he knew absolutely nothing, this woman was definitely not drunk. Of course she was anything but pretty, yet he knew he could have watched her all day: the fingers pulling thread veins from the orange sections, the berry-black lips that made her look as though she wore make-up, the earring. . . . And when she stood up, he all but gasped. She was as tall as his father, head and shoulders taller than himself. Her dress wasn't as long as he had thought; it came to just below her calf and now he could see her unlaced men's shoes and the silvery-brown skin of her ankles.

She held the peelings precisely as they had fallen in her lap, and as she walked up the steps she looked as though she were holding her crotch.

"Your daddy wouldn't like that. He don't like dumb peoples." Then she looked right at Milkman, one hand holding the peelings, the other on the doorknob. "I know your daddy. I know you too."

Again Guitar spoke up. "You his daddy's sister?"

"The only one he got. Ain't but three Deads alive."

Milkman, who had been unable to get one word out of his mouth after the foolish "Hi," heard himself shouting: "I'm a Dead! My mother's a Dead! My sisters. You and him ain't the only ones!"

Even while he was screaming he wondered why he was suddenly so defensive—so possessive about his name. He had always hated that name, all of it, and until he and Guitar became friends, he had hated his nickname too. But in Guitar's mouth it sounded clever, grown up. Now he was behaving with this strange woman as though having the name was a matter of deep personal pride, as though she had tried to expel him from a very special group, in which he not only belonged, but had exclusive rights.

In the heartbeat of silence that followed his shouts, Pilate laughed.

"You all want a soft-boiled egg?" she asked.

The boys looked at each other. She'd changed rhythm on them. They didn't want an egg, but they did want to be with her, to go inside the wine house of this lady who had one earring, no navel, and looked like a tall black tree.

"No, thanks, but we'd like a drink of water." Guitar smiled back at her.

"Well. Step right in." She opened the door and they followed her into a large sunny room that looked both barren and cluttered. A moss-green sack hung from the ceiling. Candles were stuck in bottles everywhere; newspaper articles and magazine pictures were nailed to the walls. But other than a rocking chair, two straight-backed chairs, a large table, a sink and stove, there was no furniture. Pervading everything was the odor of pine and fermenting fruit.

"You ought to try one. I know how to do them just right. I don't like my whites to move, you know. The yolk I want soft, but not runny. Want it like wet velvet. How come you don't just try one?"

She had dumped the peelings in a large crock, which like most everything in the house had been made for some other purpose. Now she stood before the dry sink, pumping water into a blue-and-white wash basin which she used for a saucepan.

"Now, the water and the egg have to meet each other on a kind of equal standing. One can't get the upper hand over the other. So the temperature has to be the same for both. I knock the chill off the water first. Just the chill. I don't let it get warm because the egg is room temperature, you see. Now then, the real secret is right here in the boiling. When the tiny bubbles come to the surface, when they as big as peas and just before they get big as marbles. Well, right then you take the pot off the fire. You don't just put the fire out; you take the pot off. Then you put a folded newspaper over the pot and do one small obligation. Like answering the door or emptying the bucket and bringing it in off the front porch. I generally go to the toilet. Not for a long stay, mind you. Just a short one. If you do all that, you got yourself a perfect soft-boiled egg.

"I remember the messes I used to make for my father when I cooked. Your father"—she directed a thumb at Milkman—"he couldn't cook worth poot. Once I made a cherry pie for him, or tried to. Macon was a nice boy and awful good to me. Be nice if you could have known him then. He would have been a real good friend to you too, like he was to me."

Her voice made Milkman think of pebbles. Little round pebbles that bumped up against each other. Maybe she was hoarse, or maybe it was the way she said her words, with both a drawl and a clip. The piny-winy smell was narcotic, and so was the sun streaming in, strong and unfettered because there were no curtains or shades at the windows that were all around the room, two in each of three walls, one on each side of the door, one on either side of the sink and the stove, and two on the farther wall. The fourth wall must back on the bedrooms, Milkman thought. The pebbly voice, the sun, and the narcotic wine smell weakened both the boys, and they sat in a pleasant semi-stupor, listening to her go on and on. . . .

"Hadn't been for your daddy, I wouldn't be here today. I would have died in the womb. And died again in the woods. Those woods and the dark would have surely killed me. But he saved me and here I am boiling eggs. Our papa was dead, you see. They blew him five feet up into the air. He was sitting on his fence waiting for 'em, and they snuck up from behind and blew him five feet into the air. So when we left Circe's big house we didn't have no place to go, so we just walked around and lived in them woods. Farm country. But Papa came back one day. We didn't know it was him at first, cause we both saw him blowed five feet into the air. We were lost then. And talking about dark! You think dark is just one color, but it ain't. There're five or six kinds of black. Some silky, some woolly.

Some just empty. Some like fingers. And it don't stay still. It moves and changes from one kind of black to another. Saying something is pitch black is like saying something is green. What kind of green? Green like my bottles? Green like a grasshopper? Green like a cucumber, lettuce, or green like the sky is just before it breaks loose to storm? Well, night black is the same way. May as well be a rainbow.

"Now, we lost and there was this wind and in front of us was the back of our daddy. We were some scared children. Macon kept telling me that the things we was scared of wasn't real. What difference do it make if the thing you scared of is real or not? I remember doing laundry for a man and his wife once, down in Virginia. The husband came into the kitchen one afternoon shivering and saying did I have any coffee made. I asked him what was it that had grabbed hold of him, he looked so bad. He said he couldn't figure it out, but he felt like he was about to fall off a cliff. Standing right there on that yellow and white and red linoleum, as level as a flatiron. He was holding on to the door first, then the chair, trying his best not to fall down. I opened my mouth to tell him wasn't no cliff in that kitchen. Then I remembered how it was being in those woods. I felt it all over again. So I told the man did he want me to hold on to him so he couldn't fall. He looked at me with the most grateful look in the world. 'Would you?' he said. I walked around back of him and locked my fingers in front of his chest and held on to him. His heart was kicking under his vest like a mule in heat. But little by little it calmed down."

"You saved his life," said Guitar.

"No such thing. His wife come in before it was time to let go. She asked me what I was doing and I told her."

"Told her what? What'd you say?"

"The truth. That I was trying to keep him from falling off a cliff."

"I bet he wished he had jumped off then. She believe you? Don't tell me she believed you."

"Not right away she didn't. But soon's I let go he fell dead-weight to the floor. Smashed his glasses and everything. Fell right on his face. And you know what? He went down so slow. I swear it took three minutes, three whole minutes to go from a standing upright position to when he mashed his face on the floor. I don't know if the cliff was real or not, but it took him three minutes to fall down it."

"Was he dead?" asked Guitar.

"Stone dead."

"Who shot your daddy? Did you say somebody shot him?" Guitar was fascinated, his eyes glittering with lights.

"Five feet into the air . . ."

"Who?"

"I don't know who and I don't know why. I just know what I'm telling you: what, when, and where."

"You didn't say where." He was insistent.

"I did too. Off a fence."

"Where was the fence?"

"On our farm."

Guitar laughed, but his eyes were too shiny to convey much humor. "Where was the farm?"

"Montour County."

He gave up on "where." "Well, when then?"

"When he sat there—on the fence."

Guitar felt like a frustrated detective. "What year?"

"The year they shot them Irish people down in the streets. Was a good year for guns and gravediggers, I know that." Pilate put a barrel lid on the table. Then she lifted the eggs from the wash basin and began to peel them. Her lips moved as she played an orange seed around in her mouth. Only after the eggs were split open, revealing moist reddish-yellow centers, did she return to her story. "One morning we woke up when the sun was nearly a quarter way cross the sky. Bright as anything. And blue. Blue like the ribbons on my mother's bonnet. See that streak of sky?" She pointed out the window. "Right behind them hickories. See? Right over there."

They looked and saw the sky stretching back behind the houses and the trees. "That's the same color," she said, as if she had discovered something important. "Same color as my mama's ribbons. I'd know her ribbon color anywhere, but I don't know her name. After she died Papa wouldn't let anybody say it. Well, before we could get the sand rubbed out of our eyes and take a good look around, we saw him sitting there on a stump. Right in the sunlight. We started to call him but he looked on off, like he was lookin at us and not lookin at us at the same time. Something in his face scared us. It was like looking at a face under water. Papa got up after a while and moved out of the sun on back into the woods. We just stood there looking at the stump. Shaking like leaves."

Pilate scraped the eggshells together into a little heap, her fingers fanning out over and over again in a gentle sweeping. The boys watched, afraid to say anything lest they ruin the next part of her story, and afraid to remain silent lest she not go on with its telling.

"Shaking like leaves," she murmured, "just like leaves."

Suddenly she lifted her head and made a sound like a hoot owl. "Ooo! Here I come!"

Neither Milkman nor Guitar saw or heard anyone approaching, but Pilate jumped up and ran toward the door. Before she reached it, a foot kicked it open and Milkman saw the bent back of a girl. She was dragging a large five-bushel basket of what looked like brambles, and a woman was pushing the other side of it, saying, "Watch the doorsill, baby."

"I got it," the girl answered. "Push."

"About time," said Pilate. "The light be gone before you know it."

"Tommy's truck broke down," the girl said, panting. When the two had managed to get the basket into the room, the girl stretched her back and turned around, facing them. But Milkman had no need to see her face; he had already fallen in love with her behind.

"Hagar." Pilate looked around the room. "This here's your brother, Milkman. And this is his friend. What's your name again, pretty?"

"Guitar."

"Guitar? You play any?" she asked.

"That ain't her brother, Mama. They cousins." The older woman spoke.

"Same thing."

"No it ain't. Is it, baby?"

"No," said Hagar. "It's different."

"See there. It's different."

"Well, what is the difference, Reba? You know so much."

Reba looked at the ceiling. "A brother is a brother if you both got the same mother or if you both—"

Pilate interrupted her. "I mean what's the difference in the way you act toward 'em? Don't you have to act the same way to both?"

"That's not the point, Mama."

"Shut up, Reba. I'm talking to Hagar."

"Yes, Mama. You treat them both the same."

"Then why they got two words for it 'stead of one, if they ain't no difference?" Reba put her hands on her hips and opened her eyes wide.

"Pull that rocker over here," said Pilate. "You boys have to give up your seats unless you gonna help."

The women circled the basket, which was full of blackberries still on their short, thorny branches.

"What we have to do?" Guitar asked.

"Get them little berries off them hateful branches without popping 'em. Reba, get that other crock."

Hagar looked around, all eyes and hair. "Why don't we pull a bed out the back room? Then we can all sit down."

"Floor's good enough for me," said Pilate, and she squatted down on her haunches and lifted a branch gently from the basket. "This all you got?"

"No." Reba was side-rolling a huge crock. "Two more outside."

"Better bring them in. Draw too many flies out there."

Hagar started for the door and motioned to Milkman. "Come on, brother. You can help."

Milkman jumped up, knocking his chair backward, and trotted after Hagar. She was, it seemed to him, as pretty a girl as he'd ever seen. She was much much older than he was. She must be as old as Guitar, maybe even seventeen. He seemed to be floating. More alive than he'd ever been, and floating. Together he and Hagar dragged two baskets up the porch stairs and into the house. She was as strong and muscular as he was.

"Careful, Guitar. Go slow. You keep on busting 'em."

"Leave him alone, Reba. He got to get the feel first. I asked you did you play any. That why they call you Guitar?"

"Not cause I do play. Because I wanted to. When I was real little. So they tell me."

"Where'd you ever see a guitar?"

"It was a contest, in a store down home in Florida. I saw it when my mother took me downtown with her. I was just a baby. It was one of those things where you guess how many beans in the big glass jar and you win a guitar. I cried for it, they said. And always asked about it."

"You should of called Reba. She'd get it for you."

"No, you couldn't buy it. You had to give the number of jellybeans."

"I heard you. Reba would of known how many. Reba wins things. She ain't never lost nothing."

"Really?" Guitar smiled, but he was doubtful. "She lucky?"

"Sure I'm lucky." Reba grinned. "People come from everywhere to get me to stand in for 'em at drawings and give them numbers to play. It works pretty well for them, and it always works for me. I win everything I try to win and lots of things I don't even try to win."

"Got to where won't nobody sell her a raffle ticket. They just want her to hold theirs."

"See this?" Reba put her hand down in the top of her dress and pulled out a diamond ring attached to a string. "I won this last year. I was the . . . what was it, Mama?"

"Five hundred thousandth."

"Five hundred . . . no it wasn't. That ain't what they said."

"Half a million is what they said."

"That's right. The half a millionth person to walk into Sears and Roebuck." Her laughter was gay and proud.

"They didn't want to give it to her," said Hagar, "cause she looked so bad."

Guitar was astonished. "I remember that contest, but I don't remember hearing nothing 'bout no colored person winning it." Guitar, a habitual street roamer, believed he knew every public thing going on in the city.

"Nobody did. They had picture-taking people and everything waiting for the next person to walk in the door. But they never did put my picture in the paper. Me and Mama looked, too, didn't we?" She glanced at Pilate for confirmation and went on. "But they put the picture of the man who won second prize in. He won a war bond. He was white."

"Second prize?" Guitar asked. "What kind of 'second prize'? Either you the half-millionth person or you ain't. Can't be no next-to-the-half-millionth."

"Can if the winner is Reba," Hagar said. "The only reason they got a second was cause she was the first. And the only reason they gave it to her was because of them cameras."

"Tell 'em why you was in Sears, Reba."

"Looking for a toilet." Reba threw her head back to let the laughter escape. Her hands were stained with blackberry juice, and when she wiped the tears from her eyes she streaked the purple from her nose to her cheekbone. Much lighter than Pilate or Hagar, Reba had the simple eyes of an infant. All of them had a guileless look about them, but complication and something more lurked behind Pilate's and Hagar's faces. Only Reba, with her light pimply skin and deferential manner, looked as though her simplicity might also be vacuousness.

"Ain't but two toilets downtown they let colored in: Mayflower Restaurant and Sears. Sears was closer. Good thing nature wasn't in a hurry. They kept me there fifteen minutes gettin my name and address to send the diamond over to me. But I wouldn't let 'em send it to me. I kept asking them, Is this a real contest? I don't believe you."

"It was worth a diamond ring to get you out of there. Drawing a crowd and getting ready to draw flies," said Hagar.

"What're you going to do with the ring?" Milkman asked her.

"Wear it. Seldom I win something I like."

"Everything she win, she give away," Hagar said.

"To a man," said Pilate.

"She don't never keep none of it. . . ."

"That's what she want to win—a man. . . ."

"Worse'n Santa Claus. . . ."

"Funny kind of luck ain't no luck at all. . . ."

"*He* comes just once a year. . . ."

Hagar and Pilate pulled the conversation apart, each yanking out some thread of comment more to herself than to Milkman or Guitar—or even Reba, who had dropped her ring back inside her dress and was smiling sweetly, and deftly separating the royal-purple berries from their twigs.

Milkman was five feet seven then but it was the first time in his life that he remembered being completely happy. He was with his friend, an older boy—wise and kind and fearless. He was sitting comfortably in the notorious wine house; he was surrounded by women who seemed to enjoy him and who laughed out loud. And he was in love. No wonder his father was afraid of them.

"When will this wine be ready?" he asked.

"This batch? Few weeks," Pilate said.

"You gonna let us have some?" Guitar smiled.

"Sure. You want some now? Plenty wine in the cellar."

"I don't want that. I want some of this. Some of the wine I made."

"You think you made this?" Pilate laughed at him. "You think this all there is to it? Picking a few berries?"

"Oh." Guitar scratched his head. "I forgot. We got to mash them in our bare feet."

"Feet? Feet?" Pilate was outraged. "Who makes wine with they feet?"

"Might taste good, Mama," said Hagar.

"Couldn't taste no worse," Reba said.

"Your wine any good, Pilate?" asked Guitar.

"Couldn't tell you."

"Why not?"

"Never tasted it."

Milkman laughed. "You sell wine you don't even taste?"

"Folks don't buy it for the taste. Buy it to get drunk."

Reba nodded. "Used to anyway. Ain't buying nothing now."

"Don't nobody want no cheap home brew. The Depression's over," Hagar said. "Everybody got work now. They can afford to buy Four Roses."

"Plenty still buy," Pilate told her.

"Where you get the sugar for it?" Guitar asked.

"Black market," said Reba.

"What 'plenty'? Tell the truth, Mama. If Reba hadn't won that hundred pounds of groceries, we'd have starved last winter."

"Would not." Pilate put a fresh piece of twig in her mouth.

"We *would* have."

"Hagar, don't contradict your mama," Reba whispered.

"Who was gonna feed us?" Hagar was insistent. "Mama can go for months without food. Like a lizard."

"Lizard live that long without food?" asked Reba.

"Girl, ain't nobody gonna let you starve. You ever had a hungry day?" Pilate asked her granddaughter.

"Course she ain't," said her mother.

Hagar tossed a branch to the heap on the floor and rubbed her fingers. The tips were colored a deep red. "Some of my days were hungry ones."

With the quickness of birds, the heads of Pilate and Reba shot up. They peered at Hagar, then exchanged looks.

"Baby?" Reba's voice was soft. "You been hungry, baby? Why didn't you say so?" Reba looked hurt. "We get you anything you want, baby. Anything. You *been* knowing that."

Pilate spit her twig into the palm of her hand. Her face went still. Without those moving lips her face was like a mask. It seemed to Milkman that somebody had just clicked off a light.

He looked at the faces of the women. Reba's had crumpled. Tears were streaming down her cheeks. Pilate's face was still as death, but alert as though waiting for some signal. Hagar's profile was hidden by her hair. She leaned forward, her elbows on her thighs, rubbing fingers that looked bloodstained in the lessening light. Her nails were very very long.

The quiet held. Even Guitar didn't dare break it.

Then Pilate spoke. "Reba. She don't mean food."

Realization swept slowly across Reba's face, but she didn't answer. Pilate began to hum as she returned to plucking the berries. After a moment, Reba joined her, and they hummed together in perfect harmony until Pilate took the lead:

O Sugarman don't leave me here
Cotton balls to choke me
O Sugarman don't leave me here
Buckra's arms to yoke me. . . .

When the two women got to the chorus, Hagar raised her head and sang too.

Sugarman done fly away
Sugarman done gone
Sugarman cut across the sky
Sugarman gone home.

Milkman could hardly breathe. Hagar's voice scooped up what little pieces of heart he had left to call his own. When he thought he was going to faint from the weight of what he was feeling, he risked a glance at his friend and saw the setting sun gilding Guitar's eyes, putting into shadow a slow smile of recognition.

Delicious as the day turned out to be for Milkman, it was even more so because it included secrecy and defiance, both of which dissipated within an hour of his father's return. Freddie had let Macon Dead know that his son had spent the afternoon "drinking in the wine house."

"He's lying! We didn't drink nothing. Nothing. Guitar didn't even get the glass of water he asked for."

"Freddie never lies. He misrepresents, but he never lies."

"He lied to you."

"About the wine-drinking? Maybe. But not about you being there, huh?"

"No, sir. Not about that." Milkman softened his tone a bit, but succeeded in keeping the edge of defiance in his voice.

"Now, what were your instructions from me?"

"You told me to stay away from there. To stay away from Pilate."

"Right."

"But you never told me why. They're our cousins. She's your own sister."

"And you're my own son. And you will do what I tell you to do. With or without explanations. As long as your feet are under my table, you'll do in this house what you are told."

At fifty-two, Macon Dead was as imposing a man as he had been at forty-two, when Milkman thought he was the biggest thing in the world. Bigger even than the house they lived in. But today he had seen a woman who was just as tall and who had made him feel tall too.

"I know I'm the youngest one in this family, but I ain't no baby. You treat me like I was a baby. You keep saying you don't have to explain nothing to me. How do you think that makes me feel? Like a baby, that's what. Like a twelve-year-old baby!"

"Don't you raise your voice to me."

"Is that the way your father treated you when you were twelve?"

"Watch your mouth!" Macon roared. He took his hands out of his pockets but didn't know what to do with them. He was momentarily confused. His son's question had shifted the scenery. He was seeing himself at twelve, standing in Milkman's shoes and feeling what he himself had felt for his own father. The numbness that had settled on him when he saw the man he loved and admired fall off the fence; something wild ran through him when he watched the body twitching in the dirt. His father had sat for five nights on a split-rail fence cradling a shotgun and in the end died protecting his property. Was that what this boy felt for him? Maybe it was time to tell him things.

"Well, did he?"

"I worked right alongside my father. Right alongside him. From the time I was four or five we worked together. Just the two of us. Our mother was dead. Died when Pilate was born. Pilate was just a baby. She stayed over at another farm in the daytime. I carried her over there myself in my arms every morning. Then I'd go back across the fields and meet my father. We'd hitch President Lincoln to the plow and . . . That's what we called her: President Lincoln. Papa said Lincoln was a good plow hand before he was President and you shouldn't take a good plow hand away from his work. He called our farm Lincoln's Heaven. It was a little bit a place. But it looked big to me then. I know now it must a been a little bit a place, maybe a hundred and fifty acres. We tilled fifty. About eighty of it was woods. Must of been a fortune in oak and pine; maybe that's what they wanted—the lumber, the oak and the pine. We had a pond that was four acres. And a stream, full of fish. Right down in the heart of a valley. Prettiest mountain you ever saw, Montour Ridge. We lived in Montour County. Just north of the Susquehanna. We had a four-stall hog pen. The big barn was forty feet by a hundred and forty—hip-roofed too. And all around in the mountains was deer and wild turkey. You ain't tasted nothing till you taste wild turkey the way Papa cooked it. He'd burn it real fast in the fire. Burn it black all over. That sealed it. Sealed the juices in. Then he'd let it roast on a spit for twenty-four hours. When you cut the black burnt part off, the meat underneath was tender, sweet, juicy. And we had fruit trees. Apple, cherry. Pilate tried to make me a cherry pie once."

Macon paused and let the smile come on. He had not said any of this for years. Had not even reminisced much about it recently. When he was first married he used to talk about Lincoln's Heaven to Ruth. Sitting on the porch swing in the dark, he would re-create the land that was to have been his. Or when he was just starting out in the business of buying houses, he would lounge around the barbershop and swap stories with the men there. But for years he hadn't had that kind of time, or interest. But now he was doing it again, with his son, and every detail of that land was clear in his mind: the well, the apple orchard, President Lincoln; her foal, Mary Todd; Ulysses S. Grant, their cow; General Lee, their hog. That was the way he knew what history he remembered. His father couldn't read, couldn't write; knew only what he saw and heard tell of. But he had etched in Macon's mind certain historical figures, and as a boy in school, Macon thought of the personalities of his horse, his hog, when he read about these people. His father may have called their plow horse President Lincoln as a joke, but Macon always thought of Lincoln with fondness since he had loved him first as a strong, steady, gentle, and obedient horse. He even liked General Lee, for one spring they slaughtered him and ate the best pork outside Virginia, "from the butt to the smoked ham to the ribs to the sausage to the jowl to the feet to the tail to the head cheese"—for eight months. And there was cracklin in November.

"General Lee was all right by me," he told Milkman, smiling. "Finest general I ever knew. Even his balls was tasty. Circe made up the best pot of maws she ever cooked. Huh! I'd forgotten that woman's name. That was it, Circe. Worked at a big farm some white people owned in Danville, Pennsylvania. Funny how things get away from you. For years you can't remember nothing. Then just like that, it all comes back to you. Had a dog run, they did. That was the big sport back then. Dog races. White people did love their dogs. Kill a nigger and comb their hair at the same time. But I've seen grown white men cry about their dogs."

His voice sounded different to Milkman. Less hard, and his speech was different. More southern and comfortable and soft. Milkman spoke softly too. "Pilate said somebody shot your father. Five feet into the air."

"Took him sixteen years to get that farm to where it was paying. It's all dairy country up there now. Then it wasn't. Then it was . . . nice."

"Who shot him, Daddy?"

Macon focused his eyes on his son. "Papa couldn't read, couldn't even sign his name. Had a mark he used. They tricked him. He signed something, I don't know what, and they told him they owned his property. He never read nothing. I tried to teach him, but he said he couldn't remember those little marks from one day to the next. Wrote one word in his life—Pilate's name; copied it out of the Bible. That's what she got folded up in that earring. He should have let me teach him. Everything bad that ever happened to him happened because he couldn't read. Got his name messed up cause he couldn't read."

"His name? How?"

"When freedom came. All the colored people in the state had to register with the Freedmen's Bureau."

"Your father was a slave?"

"What kind of foolish question is that? Course he was. Who hadn't been in 1869? They all had to register. Free and not free. Free and used-to-be-slaves. Papa was in his teens and went to sign up, but the man behind the desk was drunk. He asked Papa where he was born. Papa said Macon. Then he asked him who his father was. Papa said, 'He's dead.' Asked him who owned him, Papa said, 'I'm free.' Well, the Yankee wrote it all down, but in the wrong spaces. Had him born in Dunfrie, wherever the hell that is, and in the space for his name the fool wrote, 'Dead' comma 'Macon.' But Papa couldn't read so he never found out what he was registered as till Mama told him. They met on a wagon going North. Started talking about one thing and another, told her about being a freedman and showed off his papers to her. When she looked at his paper she read him out what it said."

"He didn't have to keep the name, did he? He could have used his real name, couldn't he?"

"Mama liked it. Liked the name. Said it was new and would wipe out the past. Wipe it all out."

"What was his real name?"

"I don't remember my mother too well. She died when I was four. Light-skinned, pretty. Looked like a white woman to me. Me and Pilate don't take nothing after her. If you ever have a doubt we from Africa, look at Pilate. She look just like Papa and he looked like all them pictures you ever see of Africans. A Pennsylvania African. Acted like one too. Close his face up like a door."

"I saw Pilate's face like that." Milkman felt close and confidential now that his father had talked to him in a relaxed and intimate way.

"I haven't changed my mind, Macon. I don't want you over there."

"Why? You still haven't said why."

"Just listen to what I say. That woman's no good. She's a snake, and can charm you like a snake, but still a snake."

"You talking about your own sister, the one you carried in your arms to the fields every morning."

"That was a long time ago. You seen her. What she look like to you? Somebody nice? Somebody normal?"

"Well, she . . ."

"Or somebody cut your throat?"

"She didn't look like that, Daddy."

"Well she *is* like that."

"What'd she do?"

"It ain't what she did; it's what she is."

"What is she?"

"A snake, I told you. Ever hear the story about the snake? The man who saw a little baby snake on the ground? Well, the man saw this baby snake bleeding and hurt. Lying there in the dirt. And the man felt sorry for it and picked it up and put it in his basket and took it home. And he fed it and took care of it till it was big and strong. Fed it the same thing he ate. Then one day, the snake turned on him and bit him. Stuck his poison tongue right in the man's heart. And while he was laying there dying, he turned to the snake and asked him, 'What'd you do that for?' He said, 'Didn't I take good care of you? Didn't I save your life?' The snake said, 'Yes.' 'Then what'd you do it for? What'd you kill me for?' Know what the snake said? Said, 'But you knew I was a snake, didn't you?' Now, I mean for you to stay out of that wine house and as far away from Pilate as you can."

Milkman lowered his head. His father had explained nothing to him.

"Boy, you got better things to do with your time. Besides, it's time you started learning how to work. You start Monday. After school come to my office; work a couple of hours there and learn what's real. Pilate can't teach you a thing you can use in this world. Maybe the next, but not this one. Let me tell you right now the one important thing you'll ever need to know: Own things. And let the things you own own other things. Then you'll own yourself and other people too. Starting Monday, I'm going to teach you how."

Chapter 3

Life improved for Milkman enormously after he began working for Macon. Contrary to what his father hoped, there was more time to visit the wine house. Running errands for Macon's rent houses gave him leave to be in Southside and get to know the people Guitar knew so well. Milkman was young and he was friendly—just the opposite of his father—and the tenants felt at ease enough with him to tease him, feed him, confide in him. But it was hard to see much of Guitar. Saturdays were the only days he was certain to find him. If Milkman got up early enough on Saturday morning, he could catch his friend before Guitar went roaming the streets and before he himself had to help Macon collect rents. But there were days in the week when they agreed to skip school and hang out, and on one of those days Guitar took him to Feather's pool hall on Tenth Street, right in the middle of the Blood Bank area.

It was eleven o'clock in the morning when Guitar pushed open the door and shouted, "Hey, Feather! Give us a couple of Red Caps."

Feather, a short squat man with sparse but curly hair, looked up at Guitar, then at Milkman, and frowned.

"Get him out of here."

Guitar stopped short and followed the little man's gaze to Milkman's face and back again. The half-dozen men there playing pool turned around at the sound of Feather's voice. Three of them were air force pilots, part of the 332nd Fighter Group. Their beautiful hats and gorgeous leather jackets were carefully arranged on chairs. Their hair was cut close to the skull; their shirt cuffs were turned neatly back on their forearms; their white scarves hung in snowy rectangles from their hip pockets. Silver chains glistened at their necks and they looked faintly amused as they worked chalk into the tips of their cues.

Guitar's face shone with embarrassment. "He's with me," he said.

"I said get him outta here."

"Come on, Feather, he's my friend."

"He's Macon Dead's boy, ain't he?"

"So what?"

"So get him outta here."

"He can't help who his daddy is." Guitar had his voice under control.

"Neither can I. Out."

"What his daddy do to you?"

"Nothing yet. That's why I want him outta here."

"He ain't like his daddy."

"He ain't got to be like him—*from* him is enough."

"I'll be responsible for—"

"Stop messing with me, Guitar. Get him out. He ain't old enough to have wet dreams."

The pilots laughed and a man in a gray straw hat with a white band said, "Aw, let the boy stay, Feather."

"You shut your mouth. I'm running this."

"What harm can he do? A twelve-year-old kid." He smiled at Milkman, who stopped himself from saying, No, thirteen.

"But it ain't your problem, is it?" asked Feather. "His daddy ain't your landlord, is he, and you ain't got no operating license to hang on to either. You ain't got nothing. . . ."

Feather turned on the man with the white hatband the same acid manner he'd used with the boys. Guitar took the opportunity offered by Feather's new target to shoot his hand out like a double-edged hatchet slamming into a tree, and shout, "Later for you, man. Come on. Let's shake this place." His voice now was loud and deep—loud enough and deep enough for two. Milkman slid his hands into his back pockets and followed his friend to the door. He stretched his neck a little to match the chilly height he hoped the soldiers had seen in his eyes.

Silently they ambled down Tenth Street until they reached a stone bench that jutted from the sidewalk near the curb. They stopped there and sat down, their backs to the eyes of two men in white smocks who were watching them. One of the men leaned in the doorway of a barbershop. The other sat in a chair tilted back to the plate-glass window of the shop. They were the owners of the barbershop, Railroad Tommy and Hospital Tommy. Neither boy spoke, not to the men nor to each other. They sat and watched the traffic go by.

"Have all the halls of academe crumbled, Guitar?" Hospital Tommy spoke from his chair. His eyes were milky, like those of very old people, but the rest of him was firm, lithe, and young-looking. His tone was casual but suggested authority nonetheless.

"No, sir." Guitar answered him over his shoulder.

"Then what, pray, are you doing out here in the streets at this time of day?"

Guitar shrugged. "We just took a day off, Mr. Tommy."

"And your companion? Is he on sabbatical too?"

Guitar nodded. Hospital Tommy talked like an encyclopedia and Guitar had to guess at most of his words. Milkman kept looking at the cars going by.

"Neither one of you appears to be having much fun on your holiday. You could have stayed in the halls of academe and looked evil."

Guitar fished for a cigarette and offered one to Milkman. "Feather made me mad is all."

"Feather?"

"Yeah. He wouldn't let us in. I go in there all the time. All the time and he don't say nothing. But today he throws us out. Said my friend here is too young. Can you beat that? Feather? Worrying about somebody's age?"

"I didn't know Feather had so much as a brain cell to worry with."

"He don't. Just showing off is all. He wouldn't even let me have a bottle of beer."

Railroad Tommy laughed softly from the doorway. "Is that all? He wouldn't let you have a beer?" He rubbed the back of his neck and then crooked a finger at Guitar. "Come over here, boy, and let me tell you about some other stuff you are not going to have. Come on over here."

Reluctantly they stood up and sidled closer to the laughing man.

"You think that's something? Not having a beer? Well, let me ask you something. You ever stood stock still in the galley of the Baltimore and Ohio dining car in the middle of the night when the kitchen closed down and everything's neat and ready for the next day? And the engine's highballing down the track and three of your buddies is waiting for you with a brand-new deck of cards?"

Guitar shook his head. "No, I never . . ."

"That's right, you never. And you never going to. That's one more thrill you not going to have, let alone a bottle of beer."

Guitar smiled. "Mr. Tommy," he began, but Tommy cut him off.

"You ever pull fourteen days straight and come home to a sweet woman, clean sheets, and a fifth of Wild Turkey? Eh?" He looked at Milkman. "Did you?"

Milkman smiled and said, "No, sir."

"No? Well, don't look forward to it, cause you not going to have that either."

Hospital Tommy drew a pinfeather toothpick from under his smock. "Don't tease the boy, Tommy."

"Who's teasing? I'm telling him the truth. He ain't going to have it. Neither one of 'em going to have it. And I'll tell you something else you not going to have. You not going to have no private coach with four red velvet chairs that swivel around in one place whenever you want 'em to. No. And you not going to have your own special toilet and your own special-made eight-foot bed either. And a valet and a cook and a secretary to travel with you and do everything you say. Everything: get the right temperature in your hot-water bottle and make sure the smoking tobacco in the silver humidor is fresh each and *every* day. That's something else you not going to have. You ever have five thousand dollars of cold cash money in your pocket and walk into a bank and tell the bank man you want such and such a house on such and such a street and he sell it to you right then? Well, you won't ever have it. And you not going to have a governor's mansion, or eight thousand acres of timber to sell. And you not going to have no ship under your command to sail on, no train to run, and you can join the 332nd if you want to and shoot down a thousand German planes all by yourself and land in Hitler's backyard and whip him with your own hands, but you never going to have four stars on your shirt front, or even three. And you not going to have no breakfast tray brought in to you early in the morning with a red rose on it and two warm croissants and a cup of hot chocolate. Nope. Never. And no pheasant buried in coconut leaves for twenty days and stuffed with wild rice and cooked over a wood fire so tender and delicate it make you cry. And no Rothschild '29 or even Beaujolais to go with it."

A few men passing by stopped to listen to Tommy's lecture. "What's going on?" they asked Hospital Tommy.

"Feather refused them a beer," he said. The men laughed.

"And *no* baked Alaska!" Railroad Tommy went on. "None! You never going to have that."

"No baked Alaska?" Guitar opened his eyes wide with horror and grabbed his throat. "You breaking my heart!"

"Well, now. That's something you will have—a broken heart." Railroad Tommy's eyes softened, but the merriment in them died suddenly. "And folly. A whole lot of folly. You can count on it."

"Mr. Tommy, suh," Guitar sang in mock humility, "we just wanted a bottle of beer is all."

"Yeah," said Tommy. "Yeah, well, welcome aboard."

"What's a baked Alaska?" They left the Tommys just as they had found them and continued down Tenth Street.

"Something sweet," answered Guitar. "A dessert."

"Taste good?"

"I don't know. I can't eat sweets."

"You can't?" Milkman was amazed. "Why not?"

"Makes me sick."

"You don't like nothing sweet?"

"Fruit, but nothing with sugar. Candy, cake, stuff like that. I don't even like to smell it. Makes me want to throw up."

Milkman searched for a physical cause. He wasn't sure he trusted anybody who didn't like sweets. "You must have sugar diabetes."

"You don't get sugar diabetes from not eating sugar. You get it from eating too much sugar."

"Then what is it, then?"

"I don't know. It makes me think of dead people. And white people. And I start to puke."

"Dead people?"

"Yeah. And white people."

"I don't get it."

Guitar said nothing, so Milkman continued, "How long you been like that?"

"Since I was little. Since my father got sliced up in a sawmill and his boss came by and gave us kids some candy. Divinity. A big sack of divinity. His wife made it special for us. It's sweet, divinity is. Sweeter than syrup. Real sweet. Sweeter than . . ." He stopped walking and wiped from his forehead the beads of sweat that were collecting there. His eyes paled and wavered. He spit on the sidewalk. "Ho—hold it," he whispered, and stepped into a space between a fried-fish restaurant and Lilly's Beauty Parlor.

Milkman waited on the sidewalk, staring at the curtained window of the beauty shop. Beauty shops always had curtains or shades up. Barbershops didn't. The women didn't want anybody on the street to be able to see them getting their hair done. They were ashamed.

When Guitar emerged, his eyes were teary from the effort of dry heaving. "Come on," he said. "Let's get us some weed. That's one thing I can have."

By the time Milkman was fourteen he had noticed that one of his legs was shorter than the other. When he stood barefoot and straight as a pole, his left foot was about half an inch off the floor. So he never stood straight; he slouched or leaned or stood with a hip thrown out, and he never told anybody about it—ever. When Lena said, "Mama, what is he walking like *that* for?" he said, "I'll walk any way I want to, including over your ugly face." Ruth said, "Be quiet, you two. It's just growing pains, Lena." Milkman knew better. It wasn't a limp—not at all—just the suggestion of one, but it looked like an affected walk, the strut of a very young man trying to appear more sophisticated than he was. It bothered him and he acquired movements and habits to disguise what to him was a burning defect. He sat with his left ankle on his right knee, never the other way around. And he danced each new dance with a curious stiff-legged step that the girls loved and other boys eventually copied. The deformity was mostly in his mind. Mostly, but not completely, for he did have shooting pains in that leg after several hours on a basketball court. He favored it, believed it was polio, and felt secretly connected to the late President Roosevelt for that reason. Even when everybody was raving about Truman because he had set up a Committee on Civil Rights,

Milkman secretly preferred FDR and felt very very close to him. Closer, in fact, to him than to his own father, for Macon had no imperfection and age seemed to strengthen him. Milkman feared his father, respected him, but knew, because of the leg, that he could never emulate him. So he differed from him as much as he dared. Macon was clean-shaven; Milkman was desperate for a mustache. Macon wore bow ties; Milkman wore four-in-hands. Macon didn't part his hair; Milkman had a part shaved into his. Macon hated tobacco; Milkman tried to put a cigarette in his mouth every fifteen minutes. Macon hoarded his money; Milkman gave his away. But he couldn't help sharing with Macon his love of good shoes and fine thin socks. And he did try, as his father's employee, to do the work the way Macon wanted it done.

Macon was delighted. His son belonged to him now and not to Ruth, and he was relieved at not having to walk all over town like a peddler collecting rents. It made his business more dignified, and he had time to think, to plan, to visit the bank men, to read the public notices, auctions, to find out what plots were going for taxes, unclaimed heirs' property, where roads were being built, what supermarkets, schools; and who was trying to sell what to the government for the housing projects that were going to be built. The quickie townlets that were springing up around war plants. He knew as a Negro he wasn't going to get a big slice of the pie. But there were properties nobody wanted yet, or little edges of property somebody didn't want Jews to have, or Catholics to have, or properties nobody knew were of any value yet. There was quite a bit of pie filling oozing around the edge of the crust in 1945. Filling that could be his. Everything had improved for Macon Dead during the war. Except Ruth. And years later when the war was over and that pie filling had spilled over into his very lap, had stickied his hands and weighed his stomach down into a sagging paunch, he still wished he had strangled her back in 1921. She hadn't stopped spending occasional nights out of the house, but she was fifty years old now and what lover could she have kept so long? What lover could there be that even Freddie didn't know about? Macon decided it was of no importance, and less and less often did he get angry enough to slap her. Particularly after the final time, which became final because his son jumped up and knocked him back into the radiator.

Milkman was twenty-two then and since he had been fucking for six years, some of them with the same woman, he'd begun to see his mother in a new light. She was no longer the person who worried him about galoshes and colds and food, who stood in the way of most of the little pleasures he could take at home because they all involved some form of dirt, noise, or disarray. Now he saw her as a frail woman content to do tiny things; to grow and cultivate small life that would not hurt her if it died: rhododendron, goldfish, dahlias, geraniums, imperial tulips. Because these little lives did die. The goldfish floated to the top of the water and when she tapped the side of the bowl with her fingernail they did not flash away in a lightning arc of terror. The rhododendron leaves grew wide and green and when their color was at its deepest and waxiest, they suddenly surrendered it and lapsed into limp yellow hearts. In a way she was jealous of death. Inside all that grief she felt when the doctor died, there had been a bit of pique too, as though he had chosen a more interesting subject than life—a more provocative companion than she was—and had deliberately followed death when it beckoned. She was fierce in the presence of death, heroic even, as she was at no other time. Its threat gave her direction, clarity, audacity. Regardless of what Macon had done, she'd always suspected that the doctor didn't have to die if he hadn't wanted to. And it may have been that suspicion of personal failure and rejection (plus a smidgen of revenge against Macon) that made her lead her husband down paths from which there was no exit save violence. Lena thought Macon's rages unaccountable. But Corinthians began to see a plan. To see how her mother had learned to bring her husband to a point, not of power (a nine-year-old girl could slap Ruth and get away with it), but of helplessness. She would begin by describing some incident in which she was a sort of honest buffoon. It began as a piece of pleasant dinner conversation, harmless on the surface because no one at the table was required to share her embarrassment; but all were able to admire her honesty and to laugh at her ignorance.

She had gone to the wedding of Mrs. Djvorak's granddaughter. Anna Djvorak was an old Hungarian woman who had been one of her father's patients. He'd had many working-class white patients and some middle-class white women who thought he was handsome. Anna Djvorak was convinced that the doctor had miraculously saved her son's life by not sending him to the tuberculosis sanatorium back in 1903. Almost everybody who did go to the "san," as they called it, died in it. Anna didn't know that the doctor had no practicing privileges there, just as he had none at Mercy. Nor did she know that the cure for tuberculosis in 1903 was precisely the one most detrimental to the patients. All she knew was that the doctor had prescribed a certain diet, hours of rest to be rigidly adhered to, and cod-liver oil twice a day. The boy survived. It was natural that she would want the miracle doctor's daughter at the wedding of this son's youngest daughter. Ruth went and when the congregation went to the altar to receive the host, she went also. Kneeling there with her head bowed, she was not aware that the priest was left with the choice of placing the wafer on her hat or skipping her. He knew immediately that she was not Catholic since she did not raise her head at his words and push out her tongue for the wafer to be carefully placed there.

"Corpus Domini Nostri Jesu Christi," said the priest, and then, to her, a sharp whisper: "Ssss. Raise your head!" She looked up, saw the wafer and the acolyte holding a little silver tray under it. "Corpus Domini Nostri Jesu Christi custodiat animam tuam . . ." The priest held the host toward her and she opened her mouth.

Later, at the reception, the priest asked her point-blank whether she was Catholic.

"No. I'm Methodist," she said.

"I see," he said. "Well, the sacraments of the Church are reserved for—" Just then old Mrs. Djvorak interrupted him.

"Father," she said, "I want you to meet one of my dearest

friends. Dr. Foster's daughter. Her father saved Ricky's life. Ricky wouldn't be here today if . . ."

Father Padrew smiled and shook Ruth's hand. "Very pleased to meet you, Miss Foster."

It was a simple occurrence, elaborately told. Lena listened and experienced each phrase of her mother's emotion from religious ecstasy to innocent confidence to embarrassment. Corinthians listened analytically, expectantly–wondering how her mother would develop this anecdote into a situation in which Macon would either lash out at her verbally or hit her. Milkman was only half listening.

" 'Are you Catholic?' he asked me. Well, I was embarrassed for a minute, but then I said, 'No. I'm Methodist.' And he started to tell me that only Catholics could take communion in a Catholic church. Well, I never heard of that. Anybody can take communion, I thought. At our church anybody can come up on the first Sunday. Well, before he could get it out, Anna came up and said, 'Father, I want you to meet one of my dearest friends. Dr. Foster's daughter.' Well, the priest was all smiles then. And shook my hand and said he was *very* pleased and honored to make my acquaintance. So it all turned out all right. But honestly, I didn't know. I went up there as innocent as a lamb."

"You didn't know that only Catholics take communion in a Catholic church?" Macon Dead asked her, his tone making it clear that he didn't believe her.

"No, Macon. How would I know?"

"You see them put up their own school, keep their kids out of public schools, and you still think their religious stuff is open to anybody who wants to drop in?"

"Communion is communion."

"You're a silly woman."

"Father Padrew didn't think so."

"You made a fool of yourself."

"Mrs. Djvorak didn't think so."

"She was just trying to keep the wedding going, keep you from fucking it up."

"Macon, please don't use that language in front of the children."

"What goddam children? Everybody in here is old enough to vote."

"There is no call for an argument."

"You make a fool of yourself in a Catholic church, embarrass everybody at the reception, and come to the table to gloat about how wonderful you were?"

"Macon . . ."

"And sit there lying, saying you didn't know any better?"

"Anna Djvorak wasn't the least bit–"

"Anna Djvorak don't even know your name! She called you *Dr. Foster's daughter!* I bet you one hundred dollars she still don't know your name! You by yourself ain't nobody. You your daddy's daughter!"

"That's so," said Ruth in a thin but steady voice. "I certainly am my daddy's daughter." She smiled.

Macon didn't wait to put his fork down. He dropped it on the table while his hand was on its way across the bread plate becoming the fist he smashed into her jaw.

Milkman hadn't planned any of it, but he had to know that one day, after Macon hit her, he'd see his mother's hand cover her lips as she searched with her tongue for any broken teeth, and discovering none, tried to adjust the partial plate in her mouth without anyone noticing–and that on that day he would not be able to stand it. Before his father could draw his hand back, Milkman had yanked him by the back of his coat collar, up out of his chair, and knocked him into the radiator. The window shade flapped and rolled itself up.

"You touch her again, one more time, and I'll kill you."

Macon was so shocked at being assaulted he could not speak. He had come to believe, after years of creating respect and fear wherever he put his foot down, after years of being the tallest man in every gathering, that he was impregnable. Now he crept along the wall looking at a man who was as tall as he was–and forty years younger.

Just as the father brimmed with contradictory feelings as he crept along the wall—humiliation, anger, and a grudging feeling of pride in his son—so the son felt his own contradictions. There was the pain and shame of seeing his father crumple before any man—even himself. Sorrow in discovering that the pyramid was not a five-thousand-year wonder of the civilized world, mysteriously and permanently constructed by generation after generation of hardy men who had died in order to perfect it, but that it had been made in the back room at Sears, by a clever window dresser, of papier-mâché, guaranteed to last for a mere lifetime.

He also felt glee. A snorting, horse-galloping glee as old as desire. He had won something and lost something in the same instant. Infinite possibilities and enormous responsibilities stretched out before him, but he was not prepared to take advantage of the former, or accept the burden of the latter. So he cock-walked around the table and asked his mother, "Are you all right?"

She was looking at her fingernails. "Yes, I'm fine."

Milkman looked at his sisters. He had never been able to really distinguish them (or their roles) from his mother. They were in their early teens when he was born; they were thirty-five and thirty-six now. But since Ruth was only sixteen years older than Lena, all three had always looked the same age to him. Now when he met his sisters' eyes over the table, they returned him a look of hatred so fresh, so new, it startled him. Their pale eyes no longer appeared to blur into their even paler skin. It seemed to him as though charcoal lines had been drawn around their eyes; that two drag lines had been smudged down their cheeks, and their rosy lips were swollen in hatred so full it was about to burst through. Milkman had to blink twice before their faces returned to the vaguely alarmed blandness he was accustomed to. Quickly he left the room, realizing there was no one to thank him—or abuse him. His action was his alone. It would change nothing between his parents. It would change nothing inside them. He had knocked his father down and perhaps there were some new positions on the chessboard, but the game would go on.

Sleeping with Hagar had made him generous. Or so he thought. Wide-spirited. Or so he imagined. Wide-spirited and generous enough to defend his mother, whom he almost never thought about, and to deck his father, whom he both feared and loved.

Back in his bedroom, Milkman fiddled with things on his dresser. There was a pair of silver-backed brushes his mother had given him when he was sixteen, engraved with his initials, the abbreviated degree designation of a doctor. He and his mother had joked about it and she hinted strongly that he ought to consider going to medical school. He'd foisted her off with "How would that look? M.D., M.D. If you were sick, would you go see a man called Dr. Dead?"

She laughed but reminded him that his middle name was Foster. Couldn't he use Foster as a last name? Dr. Macon Foster. Didn't that sound fine? He had to admit that it did. The silver-backed brushes were a constant reminder of what her wishes for him were—that he not stop his education at high school, but go on to college and medical school. She had as little respect for her husband's work as Macon had for college graduates. To Milkman's father, college was time spent in idleness, far away from the business of life, which was learning to own things. He was eager for his daughters to go to college—where they could have found suitable husbands—and one, Corinthians, did go. But it was pointless for Milkman, particularly since his son's presence was a real help to him in the office. So much so that he had been able to get his bank friends to speak to some of their friends and get his son moved out of 1-A draft classification and into a "necessary to support family" status.

Milkman stood before his mirror and glanced, in the low light of the wall lamp, at his reflection. He was, as usual, unimpressed with what he saw. He had a fine enough face. Eyes women complimented him on, a firm jaw line, splendid teeth. Taken apart, it looked all right. Even better than all right. But it lacked coherence, a coming together of the features into a total self. It was all very tentative, the way he looked, like a man peeping around a corner of someplace he is not supposed to be, trying to make up his mind whether to go forward or to turn back. The decision he made would be extremely important, but the way in which he made the decision would be careless, haphazard, and uninformed.

Standing there in the lamplight, trying not to think of how his father had looked creeping along the wall, he heard a knock at his door. He didn't want to see the face of Lena or Corinthians, nor to have any secret talk with his mother. But he was not any happier to see his father looming there in the hall. A line of blood was still visible in the thin cut at the corner of Macon's mouth. But he stood straight, and his eyes were steady.

"Look, Daddy," Milkman began, "I–"

"Don't say anything," Macon said, pushing past him. "Sit down."

Milkman moved toward the bed. "Look here, let's try to forget this. If you promise–"

"I told you to sit down. And down is what I mean." Macon's voice was low, but his face looked like Pilate's. He closed the door. "You a big man now, but big ain't nearly enough. You have to be a whole man. And if you want to be a whole man, you have to deal with the whole truth."

"You don't have to do any of this, you know. I don't need to know everything between you and Mama."

"I do have to do it and you do need to know it. If you're in the business of raising your fist at your father, you better have some intelligence behind that fist the next time you throw it. Nothing I'm about to say is by way of apology or excuse. It's just information.

"I married your mother in 1917. She was sixteen, living alone with her father. I can't tell you I was in love with her. People didn't require that as much as they do now. Folks were expected to be civilized to one another, honest, and–and clear. You relied on people being what they said they were, because there was no other way to survive. The important thing, when you took a wife, was that the two of you agreed on what was important.

"Your mother's father never liked me and I have to say I was very disappointed in him. He was just about the biggest Negro in this city. Not the richest, but the most respected. But a bigger hypocrite never lived. Kept all his money in four different banks. Always calm and dignified. I thought he was naturally that way until I found out he sniffed ether. Negroes in this town worshipped him. He didn't give a damn about them, though. Called them cannibals. He delivered both your sisters himself and each time all he was interested in was the color of their skin. He would have disowned you. I didn't like the notion of his being his own daughter's doctor, especially since she was also my wife. Mercy wouldn't take colored then. Anyway, Ruth wouldn't go to any other doctor. I tried to get a midwife for her, but the doctor said midwives were dirty. I told him a midwife delivered me, and if a midwife was good enough for my mother, a midwife was good enough for his daughter. Well, we had some words between us about it, and I ended up telling him that nothing could be nastier than a father delivering his own daughter's baby. That stamped it. We had very little to say after that, but they did it anyway. Both Lena and Corinthians. They let me do the naming by picking a word blind, but that was all. Your sisters are just a little over a year apart, you know. And both times he was there. She had her legs wide open and he was there. I know he was a doctor and doctors not supposed to be bothered by things like that, but he was a man before he was a doctor. I knew then they'd ganged up on me forever—the both of them—and no matter what I did, they managed to have things their way. They made sure I remembered whose house I was in, where the china came from, how he sent to England for the Waterford bowl, and again for the table they put it on. That table was so big they had to take it apart to get it in the door. He was always bragging about how he was the second man in the city to have a two-horse carriage.

"Where I'd come from, the farm we had, that was nothing to them. And what I was trying to do—they didn't have any interest in that. Buying shacks in shacktown, they called it.

'How's shacktown?' That's the way he'd greet me in the evenings.

"But it wasn't that. I could put up with that, because I knew what I wanted, and pretty much how to get it. So I could put up with that. Did put up with it. It was something else, something I couldn't put my finger on. I tried to get him to spend some of that money out of those four banks once. Some track land was going for a lot of money—railroad money. Erie Lackawanna was buying. I had a good hunch where the track would be laid. I walked all around over there, the Shore Road, the docks, the fork in routes 6 and 2. I figured out just where the tracks would have to go. And found land I could have got cheap and sold back to the railroad agents. He wouldn't lend me a dime. If he had, he would have died a rich man, instead of a fair-to-middling one. And I would have been way ahead. I asked your mother to talk him into it. I told her exactly where the Erie was headed. She said it had to be *his* decision; she couldn't influence him. She told me, her husband, that. Then I began to wonder who she was married to—me or him.

"Well, he took sick." Macon stopped, as though the mention of illness reminded him of his own frailty, and pulled a large white handkerchief out of his pocket. Gingerly he pressed it against the thin cut on his lip. He looked at the faint stain it made on his handkerchief. "All that ether," he said, "must have got in his blood. They had another name for it, but I know it was that ether. He just lay down and started swelling up. His body did; his legs and arms just wasted away. He couldn't see patients anymore, and for the first time in his life the pompous donkey found out what it was like to have to be sick and pay another donkey to make you well. One of them doctors, the one that was taking care of him—one of the same ones wouldn't let him set foot in their hospital, and who, if he had delivered *their* daughter's or wife's baby, had even thought of it, would have run him out of here on a rail—one of them, the ones he thought worth his attention, well, he came in here with some magic potion, Radiathor, and told him it would cure him. Ruth was all excited. And for a few days he was better. Then he got sicker. Couldn't move, holes were forming in his scalp. And he just lay there in that bed where your mother still sleeps and then he died there. Helpless, fat stomach, skinny arms and legs, looking like a white rat. He couldn't digest his food, you know. Had to drink all his meals and swallow something after every meal. I believe to this day that was ether too.

"The night he died, I'd been over on the other side of town, fixing a porch that fell down. Mr. Bradlee's house. Porch had been leaning for twenty years, and then just fell down, split clean away from the foundation. I got some men to help me and went over there to get it back up so the people wouldn't have to jump to get out the house and climb up three feet to get in it. Somebody tiptoed up to me and said, 'Doctor died.' Ruth, they said, was upstairs with him. I figured she was upset and went up right away to comfort her. I didn't have time to change clothes from working on the porch, but I went up anyway. She was sitting in a chair next to his bed, and the minute she saw me she jumped up and screamed at me, 'You dare come in here like that? Clean yourself! Clean up before you come in here!' It vexed me some, but I do respect the dead. I went and washed up. Took a bath, put on a clean shirt and collar, and went back in." Macon paused again and touched his cut lip as though that were where the pain that showed in his eyes was coming from.

"In the bed," he said, and stopped for so long Milkman was not sure he was going to continue. "In the bed. That's where she was when I opened the door. Laying next to him. Naked as a yard dog, kissing him. Him dead and white and puffy and skinny, and she had his fingers in her mouth.

"Now, I want you to know I had a terrible time after that. I started thinking all sorts of things. If Lena and Corinthians were my children. I come to know pretty quick they were, cause it was clear that bastard couldn't fuck nothing. Ether took care of whatever he had in that area long before I got there. And he wouldn't have been so worried about what color skin they had unless they were coming from me. Then I thought about his delivering Ruth's babies. I'm not saying that they had contact. But there's lots of things a man can do to please a woman, even if he can't fuck. Whether or not, the fact is she was in that bed sucking his fingers, and if she do that when he was dead, what'd she do when he was alive? Nothing to do but kill a woman like that. I swear, many's the day I regret she talked me out of killing her. But I wasn't looking forward to spending the rest of my days on some rock pile. But you see, Macon, sometimes I can't catch hold of myself quick enough. It just gets out. Tonight, when she said, 'Yes, I am my daddy's daughter,' and gave that little smirk . . ." Macon looked up at his son. The door of his face had opened; his skin looked iridescent. With only a minor break in his voice, he told him, "I am not a bad man. I want you to know that. Or believe it. No man ever took his responsibilities more seriously than I have. I'm not making claims to sainthood, but you have to know it all. I'm forty years older than you and I don't have another forty in me. Next time you take it into your head to jump me, I want you to think about the man you think you whipping. And think about the fact that next time I might not let you. Old as I am, I might not let you."

He stood up and pushed his handkerchief into his back pocket.

"Don't say anything now. But think about everything I've said."

Macon turned the doorknob, and without a backward glance, left the room.

Milkman sat on the edge of his bed; everything was still except for the light buzzing in his head. He felt curiously dis-associated from all that he had heard. As though a stranger that he'd sat down next to on a park bench had turned to him and begun to relate some intimacy. He was entirely sympathetic to the stranger's problems—understood perfectly his view of what had happened to him—but part of his sympathy came from the fact that he himself was not involved or in any way threatened by the stranger's story. It was quite the opposite from the feeling he'd had an hour or less ago. The alien who had just walked out of his room was also the man he felt passionately enough about to strike with all the fervor he could summon up. Even now he could feel the tingle in his shoulder that had signaled the uncontrollable urge to smash his father's face. On the way upstairs to his room he had felt isolated, but righteous. He was a man who saw another man hit a helpless person. And he had interfered. Wasn't that the history of the world? Isn't that what men did? Protected the frail and confronted the King of the Mountain? And the fact that the frail was his mother and the King of the Mountain his father made it more poignant, but did not change the essential facts. No. He would not pretend that it was love for his mother. She was too insubstantial, too shadowy for love. But it was her vaporishness that made her more needful of defense. She was not a maternal drudge, her mind pressed flat, her shoulders hunched under the burden of housework and care of others, brutalized by a bear of a man. Nor was she the acid-tongued shrew who defended herself with a vicious vocabulary and a fast lip. Ruth was a pale but complicated woman given to deviousness and ultra-fine manners. She seemed to know a lot and understand very little. It was an interesting train of thought, and new for him. Never had he thought of his mother as a person, a separate individual, with a life apart from allowing or interfering with his own.

Milkman put on his jacket and left the house. It was seven-thirty in the evening and not yet dark. He wanted to walk and breathe some other air. He wouldn't know what to feel until he knew what to think. And it was difficult thinking in that room where the silver-backed brushes with the M.D. initials shone in the light and where the chair his father had just sat in still held the imprint of his buttocks in the cushion. As the stars made themselves visible, Milkman tried to figure what was true and what part of what was true had anything to do with him. What was he supposed to do with this new information his father had dumped on him? Was it an effort to cop a plea? How was he supposed to feel about the two of them now? Was it *true*, first of all? Did his mother . . . had his mother made it with her own father? Macon had said no. That the doctor was impotent. How did he know? Well, he must have known what he was talking about, because he was much too eager for it to be true to let it go if there were any possibility it could have taken place. Still, he had admitted there were "other things" a man could do to please a woman. "Goddam," Milkman said aloud. "What the fuck did he tell me all that shit for?" He didn't want to know any of it. There was nothing he could do about it. The doctor was dead. You can't do the past over.

Milkman's confusion was rapidly turning to anger. "Strange motherfuckers," he whispered. "Strange." If he wanted me to lay off, he thought, why didn't he just say that? Just come to me like a man and say, Cool it. You cool it and I'll cool it. We'll both cool it. And I'd say, Okay, you got it. But no. He comes to me with some way-out tale about how come and why.

Milkman was heading toward Southside. Maybe he could find Guitar. A drink with Guitar would be just the thing. Or if he couldn't find Guitar, he'd go see Hagar. No. He didn't want to talk to Hagar, to any woman, just yet. Talk about strange. Now, that was a really strange bunch. His whole family was a bunch of crazies. Pilate singing all day and talking off the wall. Reba turning on for everything in pants. And Hagar . . . well, she was just fine, but still, she wasn't regular. She had some queer ways. But at least they were fun and not full of secrets.

Where would Guitar be? Never anywhere when you really needed him. A real pop-up. Popped up anywhere, anytime, but never on time. Milkman realized he was whispering every now and then and that people on the street were looking at him. Suddenly it seemed to him that there were a lot of people out for that time of day. Where the hell was everybody going? He made an effort not to vocalize his thoughts.

"You want to be a whole man, you have to deal with the whole truth," his father had said. Couldn't I be a whole man without knowing all that? "You better have some intelligence behind that fist." Okay. What intelligence? That my mama screwed her daddy. That my grandfather was a high-yellow nigger who loved ether and hated black skin. So what did he let you marry his daughter for? So he could screw her without the neighbors knowing it? Did you ever catch them doing it? No. You just felt something you couldn't put your finger on. His money, probably. He wouldn't let you put your finger on that, would he? And his daughter wouldn't help you, would she? So you figured they must be gettin it on the operating table. If he'd given you those four bankbooks to do what you liked, to buy up the Erie Lackawanna Railroad, he could have had her all he liked, right? He could have come right in your bed, and the three of you could have had a ball. He'd get one tit and you'd get . . . the . . . other. . . .

Milkman stopped dead in his tracks. Cold sweat broke out on his neck. People jostled him trying to get past the solitary man standing in their way. He had remembered something. Or believed he remembered something. Maybe he'd dreamed it and it was the dream he remembered. The picture was developing, of the two men in the bed with his mother, each nibbling on a breast, but the picture cracked and in the crack another picture emerged. There was this green room, a very small green room, and his mother was sitting in the green room and her breasts were uncovered and somebody was sucking them and the somebody was himself. So? So what? My mother nursed me. Mothers nurse babies. Why the sweat? He walked on, hardly noticing the people pushing past him, their annoyed, tight faces. He tried to see more of the picture, but couldn't. Then he heard something that he knew was related to the picture. Laughter. Somebody he couldn't see, in the room laughing . . . at him and at his mother, and his mother is ashamed. She lowers her eyes and won't look at him. "Look at me, Mama. Look at me." But she doesn't and the laughter is loud now. Everybody is laughing. Did he wet his pants? Is his mother ashamed because while he was nursing he wet his pants? What pants? He didn't wear pants then. He wore diapers. Babies always wet their diapers. Why does he think he has pants on? Blue pants with elastic around the calf. Little blue corduroy knickers. Why is he dressed that way?

Is that what the man is laughing at? Because he is a tiny baby dressed in blue knickers? He sees himself standing there. "Look at me, Mama," is all he can think of to say. "Please look at me." Standing? He is a tiny baby. Nursing in his mother's arms. He can't stand up.

"I couldn't stand up," he said aloud, and turned toward a shop window. There was his face leaning out of the upturned collar of his jacket, and he knew. "My mother nursed me when I was old enough to talk, stand up, and wear knickers, and somebody saw it and laughed and–and that is why they call me Milkman and that is why my father never does and that is why my mother never does, but everybody else does. And how did I forget that? And why? And if she did that to me when there was no reason for it, when I also drank milk and Ovaltine and everything else from a glass, then maybe she did other things with her father?"

Milkman closed his eyes and then opened them. The street was even more crowded with people, all going in the direction he was coming from. All walking hurriedly and bumping against him. After a while he realized that nobody was walking on the other side of the street. There were no cars and the street lights were on, now that darkness had come, but the sidewalk on the other side of the street was completely empty. He turned around to see where everybody was going, but there was nothing to see except their backs and hats pressing forward into the night. He looked again at the other side of Not Doctor Street. Not a soul.

He touched the arm of a man in a cap who was trying to get past him. "Why is everybody on this side of the street?" he asked him.

"Watch it, buddy," the man snapped, and moved on with the crowd.

Milkman walked on, still headed toward Southside, never once wondering why he himself did not cross over to the other side of the street, where no one was walking at all.

He believed he was thinking coldly, clearly. He had never

loved his mother, but had always known that she had loved him. And that had always seemed right to him, the way it should be. Her confirmed, eternal love of him, love that he didn't even have to earn or deserve, seemed to him natural. And now it was decomposing. He wondered if there was anyone in the world who liked him. Liked him for himself alone. His visits to the wine house seemed (before his talk with his father) an extension of the love he had come to expect from his mother. Not that Pilate or Reba felt the possessive love for him that his mother did, but they had accepted him without question and with all the ease in the world. They took him seriously too. Asked him questions and thought all his responses to things were important enough to laugh at or quarrel with him about. Everything he did at home was met with quiet understanding from his mother and his sisters (or indifference and criticism from his father). The women in the wine house were indifferent to nothing and understood nothing. Every sentence, every word, was new to them and they listened to what he said like bright-eyed ravens, trembling in their eagerness to catch and interpret every sound in the universe. Now he questioned them. Questioned everybody. His father had crept along the wall and then come upstairs with a terrible piece of news. His mother had been portrayed not as a mother who simply adored her only son, but as an obscene child playing dirty games with whatever male was near—be it her father or her son. Even his sisters, the most tolerant and accommodating of all the women he knew, had changed their faces and rimmed their eyes with red and charcoal dust.

Where was Guitar? He needed to find the one person left whose clarity never failed him, and unless he was out of the state, Milkman was determined to find him.

His first stop, Tommy's Barbershop, was fruitful. Guitar was there with several other men, leaning in various attitudes, but all listening to something.

As Milkman entered and spotted Guitar's back, he was so relieved he shouted, "Hey, Guitar!"

"Sh!" said Railroad Tommy. Guitar turned around and motioned him to come in but to be quiet. They were listening to the radio and muttering and shaking their heads. It was some time before Milkman discovered what they were so tense about. A young Negro boy had been found stomped to death in Sunflower County, Mississippi. There were no questions about who stomped him—his murderers had boasted freely—and there were no questions about the motive. The boy had whistled at some white woman, refused to deny he had slept with others, and was a Northerner visiting the South. His name was Till.

Railroad Tommy was trying to keep the noise down so he could hear the last syllable of the newscaster's words. In a few seconds it was over, since the announcer had only a few speculations and even fewer facts. The minute he went on to another topic of news, the barbershop broke into loud conversation. Railroad Tommy, the one who had tried to maintain silence, was himself completely silent now. He moved to his razor strop while Hospital Tommy tried to keep his customer in the chair. Porter, Guitar, Freddie the janitor, and three or four other men were exploding, shouting angry epithets all over the room. Apart from Milkman, only Railroad Tommy and Empire State were quiet—Railroad Tommy because he was preoccupied with his razor and Empire State because he was simple, and probably mute, although nobody seemed sure about that. There was no question whatever about his being simple.

Milkman tried to focus on the crisscrossed conversations.

"It'll be in the morning paper."

"Maybe it will, and maybe it won't," said Porter.

"It was on the radio! Got to be in the paper!" said Freddie.

"They don't put that kind of news in no white paper. Not unless he raped somebody."

"What you bet? What you bet it'll be in there?" said Freddie.

"Bet anything you can lose," Porter answered.

"You on for five."

"Wait a minute," Porter shouted. "Say where."

"What you mean, 'where'? I got five says it'll be in the morning paper."

"On the sports page?" asked Hospital Tommy.

"Or the funny papers?" said Nero Brown.

"No, man. Front page. I bet five dollars on front page."

"What the fuck is the difference?" shouted Guitar. "A kid is stomped and you standin round fussin about whether some cracker put it in the paper. He stomped, ain't he? Dead, ain't he? Cause he whistled at some Scarlett O'Hara cunt."

"What'd he do it for?" asked Freddie. "He knew he was in Mississippi. What he think that was? Tom Sawyer Land?"

"So he whistled! So what!" Guitar was steaming. "He supposed to die for that?"

"He from the North," said Freddie. "Acting big down in Bilbo country. Who the hell he think he is?"

"Thought he was a man, that's what," said Railroad Tommy.

"Well, he thought wrong," Freddie said. "Ain't no black men in Bilbo country."

"The hell they ain't," said Guitar.

"Who?" asked Freddie.

"Till. That's who."

"He dead. A dead man ain't no man. A dead man is a corpse. That's all. A corpse."

"A living coward ain't a man either," said Porter.

"Who you talking to?" Freddie was quick to get the personal insult.

"Calm down, you two," said Hospital Tommy.

"You!" shouted Porter.

"You calling me a coward?" Freddie wanted to get the facts first.

"If the shoe fits, put your rusty foot in it."

"You all gonna keep that up, you have to get out of my shop."

"Tell that nigger somethin," said Porter.

"I'm serious now," Hospital Tommy went on. "There is no cause for all this. The boy's dead. His mama's screaming. Won't let them bury him. That ought to be enough colored blood on the streets. You want to spill blood, spill the crackers' blood that bashed his face in."

"Oh, they'll catch them," said Walters.

"Catch 'em? Catch 'em?" Porter was astounded. "You out of your fuckin mind? They'll catch 'em, all right, and give 'em a big party and a medal."

"Yeah. The whole town planning a parade," said Nero.

"They got to catch 'em."

"So they catch 'em. You think they'll get any time? Not on your life!"

"How can they *not* give 'em time?" Walters' voice was high and tight.

"How? Just *don't*, that's how." Porter fidgeted with his watch chain.

"But everybody knows about it now. It's all over. Everywhere. The law is the law."

"You wanna bet? This is sure money!"

"You stupid, man. Real stupid. Ain't no law for no colored man except the one sends him to the chair," said Guitar.

"They say Till had a knife," Freddie said.

"They always say that. He could of had a wad of bubble gum, they'd swear it was a hand grenade."

"I still say he shoulda kept his mouth shut," said Freddie.

"You should keep yours shut," Guitar told him.

"Hey, man!" Again Freddie felt the threat.

"South's bad," Porter said. "Bad. Don't nothing change in the good old U.S. of A. Bet his daddy got his balls busted off in the Pacific somewhere."

"If they ain't busted already, them crackers will see to it. Remember them soldiers in 1918?"

"Ooooo. Don't bring all that up. . . ."

The men began to trade tales of atrocities, first stories they had heard, then those they'd witnessed, and finally the things that had happened to themselves. A litany of personal humiliation, outrage, and anger turned sicklelike back to themselves as humor. They laughed then, uproariously, about the speed with which they had run, the pose they had assumed, the ruse they had invented to escape or decrease some threat to their manliness, their humanness. All but Empire State, who stood, broom in hand and drop-lipped, with the expression of a very intelligent ten-year-old.

And Guitar. His animation had died down, leaving its traces in his eyes.

Milkman waited until he could get his attention. Then they both left, walking silently down the street.

"What is it? You looked pissed when you came in."

"Nothing," said Milkman. "Where can we get a drink?"

"Mary's?"

"Naw. Too many broads hasslin you."

"It's just eight-thirty. Cedar Lounge don't open till nine."

"Shit. *You* think. I'm tired."

"I got a taste at the pad," Guitar offered.

"Solid. Your box working?"

"Uh uh. Still broke."

"I need some music. Music and a taste."

"Then it'll have to be Miss Mary. I'll keep the ladies working elsewhere."

"Yeah? I want to see you tell those ladies what to do."

"Come on, Milk. This ain't New York; choices are limited."

"Okay. Mary's."

They walked a few blocks to the corner of Rye and Tenth streets. When they passed a tiny bakery, Guitar swallowed hard and quickened his steps. Mary's was the bar/lounge that did the best business in the Blood Bank—although each of the three other corners had a similar place—because of Mary herself, a pretty but overpainted barmaid/part-owner, who was sassy, funny, and good company for the customers. Whores worked her bar in safety; lonely drunks could drink there in peace; cruisers found chickens or hawks—whichever they preferred, even jailbait; restless housewives were flattered there and danced their heels off; teen-agers learned "life rules" there; and everybody found excitement there. For in Mary's the lights made everybody beautiful, or if not beautiful, then fascinating. The music gave tone and texture to conversations that would put you to sleep anywhere else. And the food and drink provoked people into behavior that resembled nothing less than high drama.

But all that began around eleven o'clock. It was practically empty at eight-thirty in the evening, when Guitar and Milkman arrived. They slid into a booth and ordered Scotch and water. Milkman drank his up quickly and ordered another before asking Guitar, "How come they call me Milkman?"

"How the fuck would I know? That's your name, ain't it?"

"My name is Macon Dead."

"You drag me all the way over here to tell me your name?"

"I need to know it."

"Aw, drink up, man."

"You know your name, don't you?"

"Cut the shit. What's on your mind?"

"I decked my old man."

"Decked?"

"Yeah. Hit him. Knocked him into the fuckin radiator."

"What'd he do to you?"

"Nothin."

"Nothin? You just up and popped him?"

"Yeah."

"For no reason?"

"He hit my mother."

"Oh."

"He hit her. I hit him."

"That's tough."

"Yeah."

"I mean it."

"I know." Milkman sighed heavily. "I know."

"Listen. I can understand how you feel."

"Uh uh. You can't understand. Unless it happens to you, you can't understand."

"Yes I can. You know I used to hunt a lot. When I was a kid down home—"

"Oh, shit, do we have to hear about Alabama again?"

"Not Alabama. Florida."

"Whatever."

"Just listen, Milkman. Listen to me. I used to hunt a lot. From the time I could walk almost and I was good at it. Everybody said I was a natural. I could hear anything, smell anything, and see like a cat. You know what I mean? A natural. And I was never scared—not of the dark or shadows or funny sounds, and I was never afraid to kill. Anything. Rabbit, bird, snakes, squirrels, deer. And I was little. It never bothered me. I'd take a shot at anything. The grown men used to laugh about it. Said I was a natural-born hunter. After we moved up here with my grandmother, that was the only thing about the South I missed. So when my grandmother used to send us kids back home in the summer, all I thought about was hunting again. They'd pile us on the bus and we'd spend the summer with my grandmother's sister, Aunt Florence. Soon's I got there I looked for my uncles, to go out in the woods. And one summer—I was about ten or eleven, I guess—we all went out and I went off on my own. I thought I saw deer tracks. It wasn't the season for deer, but that didn't bother me any. If I saw one I killed one. I was right about the tracks; it was a deer, but spaced funny—not wide apart like I thought they should be, but still a deer. You know they step in their own prints. If you never saw them before you'd think a two-legged creature was jumping. Anyway, I stayed on the trail until I saw some bushes. The light was good and all of a sudden I saw a rump between the branches. I dropped it with the first shot and finished it with the next. Now, I want to tell you I was feeling good. I saw myself showing my uncles what I'd caught. But when I got up to it—and I was going real slow because I thought I might have to shoot it again—I saw it was a doe. Not a young one; she was old, but she was still a doe. I felt . . . bad. You know what I mean? I killed a doe. A doe, man."

Milkman was gazing at Guitar with the wide steady eyes of a man trying to look sober.

"So I know how you felt when you saw your father hit your mother. It's like that doe. A man shouldn't do that. You couldn't help what you felt."

Milkman nodded his head, but it was clear to Guitar that nothing he had said had made any difference. Chances were Milkman didn't even know what a doe was, and whatever it was, it wasn't his mother. Guitar ran his finger around the rim of his glass.

"What'd she do, Milk?"

"Nothin. Smiled. He didn't like her smile."

"You're not making sense. Talk sense. And slow down. You know you can't hold liquor."

"What you mean, I can't hold liquor?"

" 'Scuse me. Help yourself."

"I'm trying to have a serious conversation and you talking shit, Guitar."

"I'm listening."

"And I'm talking."

"Yes, you talking, but what are you saying? Your papa clips your mama cause she smiles at him. You clip him cause he clipped her. Now, is that the way you all spend the evening in your house or is there something else you're trying to say?"

"Came up to talk to me afterwards."

"Who?"

"My old man."

"What'd he say?"

"Said I had to be a whole man and know the whole thing."

"Go on."

"He was gonna buy the Erie Lackawanna, but my mother wouldn't let him."

"Oh, yeah? Maybe she needs beatin."

"That's very funny, man."

"Why ain't you laughing, then?"

"I am laughing. Inside."

"Milk?"

"Yeah?"

"Your daddy slapped your mama, right?"

"Right. Right."

"You hit him, right?"

"Right."

"Nobody appreciates what you did. Right?"

"Hey, Guitar. You right again."

"Not your mother, not your sisters, and your daddy appreciates it least of all."

"Least of all. Right."

"So he bawls you out."

"Yep. No. No. He . . ."

"He talks quiet to you?"

"Right!"

"Explains things to you."

"Yeah."

"About why he hit her."

"Uh huh."

"And it's all about something that happened a long time ago? Before you were born?"

"You got it! You are a very smart little colored boy. And I am going to tell Oxford University about you."

"And you wish he'd kept it to himself because it don't concern you and you can't do nothin about it anyway."

"You have just passed the course. Guitar Bains, Ph.D."

"But it bothers you just the same?"

"Let me think." Milkman closed his eyes and tried to prop his chin on his hand, but it was too difficult. He was trying to get as drunk as possible as rapidly as possible. "Yes. Well, it did bother me. Before I came in here it did. I don't know, Guitar." He became serious and his face had the still and steady look of a grown man trying not to vomit . . . or cry.

"Forget it, Milk. Whatever it is, forget it. It ain't nothin. Whatever he told you, forget it."

"I hope I can. I sure hope I can."

"Listen, baby, people do funny things. Specially us. The cards are stacked against us and just trying to stay in the game, stay alive and in the game, makes us do funny things. Things we can't help. Things that make us hurt one another. We don't even know why. But look here, don't carry it inside and don't give it to nobody else. Try to understand it, but if you can't, just forget it and keep yourself strong, man."

"I don't know, Guitar. Things seem to be getting to me, you know?"

"Don't let 'em. Unless you got a plan. Look at Till. They got to him too. Now he's just an item on WJR's evening news."

"He was crazy."

"No. Not crazy. Young, but not crazy."

"Who cares if he fucks a white girl? Anybody can do that. What's he bragging for? Who cares?"

"Crackers care."

"Then they're crazier'n he is."

"Of course. But they're alive and crazy."

"Yeah, well, fuck Till. I'm the one in trouble."

"Did I hear you right, brother?"

"All right. I didn't mean that. I . . ."

"What's your trouble? You don't like your name?"

"No." Milkman let his head fall to the back of the booth. "No, I don't like my name."

"Let me tell you somethin, baby. Niggers get their names the way they get everything else—the best way they can. The best way they can."

Milkman's eyes were blurred now and so were his words. "Why can't we get our stuff the right way?"

"The best way is the right way. Come on. I'll take you home."

"No, I can't go back there."

"No? Where then?"

"Let me stay in your pad."

"Oh, man, you know my situation. One of us'll have to sleep on the floor. Besides . . ."

"I'll sleep on the floor."

"Besides, I may have company."

"No shit?"

"No shit. Come on, let's go."

"I ain't going home, Guitar. Hear me?"

"Want me to take you over to Hagar's?" Guitar motioned to the waitress for the check.

"Hagar's. Yeah. Sweet Hagar. Wonder what her name is."

"You just said it."

"I mean her last name. Her daddy's name."

"Ask Reba." Guitar paid their bar bill and helped Milkman negotiate to the door. The wind had risen and cooled. Guitar flapped his elbows against the cold.

"Ask anybody *but* Reba," said Milkman. "Reba don't know her own last name."

"Ask Pilate."

"Yeah. I'll ask Pilate. Pilate knows. It's in that dumb-ass box hanging from her ear. Her own name and everybody else's. Bet mine's in there too. I'm gonna ask her what my name is. Say, you know how my old man's daddy got his name?"

"Uh uh. How?"

"Cracker gave it to him."

"Sho 'nough?"

"Yep. And he took it. Like a fuckin sheep. Somebody should have shot him."

"What for? He was already Dead."

Chapter 4

Once again he did his Christmas shopping in a Rexall drugstore. It was late, the day before Christmas Eve, and he hadn't had the spirit or energy or presence of mind to do it earlier or thoughtfully. Boredom, which had begun as a mild infection, now took him over completely. No activity seemed worth the doing, no conversation worth having. The fluttery preparations at home seemed fake and dingy. His mother was going on as she did every year about the incredible price of trees and butter. As though their tree would be anything other than it had always been: the huge shadowy thing in a corner burdened with decorations she had had since she was a girl. As if her fruitcakes were edible, or her turkey done all the way to the bone. His father gave them all envelopes of varying amounts of money, never thinking that just once they might like something he actually went into a department store and selected.

The gifts Milkman had to buy were few and easily chosen in a drugstore. Cologne and dusting powder for Magdalene called Lena; a compact for Corinthians; a five-pound box of chocolates for his mother. And some shaving equipment for his father. In fifteen minutes he was done. The only problem gift was Hagar's. It was hard to select something hurriedly for her since she liked everything but preferred nothing. More important, he wasn't sure he wanted to keep it up. Keep up the whole business of "going with" Hagar. He seldom took her anywhere except to the movies and he never took her to parties where people of his own set danced and laughed and developed intrigues among themselves. Everybody who knew him knew about Hagar, but she was considered his private honey pot, not a real or legitimate girl friend—not someone he might marry. And only one or two of the various women he dated "seriously" ever put up a fight about her since they believed she was less than a rival.

Now, after more than a dozen years, he was getting tired of her. Her eccentricities were no longer provocative and the stupefying ease with which he had gotten and stayed between her legs had changed from the great good fortune he'd considered it, to annoyance at her refusal to make him hustle for it, work for it, do something difficult for it. He didn't even have to pay for it. It was so free, so abundant, it had lost its fervor. There was no excitement, no galloping of blood in his neck or his heart at the thought of her.

She was the third beer. Not the first one, which the throat receives with almost tearful gratitude; nor the second, that confirms and extends the pleasure of the first. But the third, the one you drink because it's there, because it can't hurt, and because what difference does it make?

Perhaps the end of the year was a good time to call it off. It wasn't going anywhere and it was keeping him lazy, like a pampered honey bear who had only to stick out his paw for another scoop, and so had lost the agility of the tree-climbers, the bee-fighters, but not the recollection of how thrilling the search had been.

He would buy her something for Christmas, of course, something nice to remember him by, but nothing that would give her any ideas about marriage. There was some costume jewelry on display. She might like that, but it would pale before the diamond ring Reba had stuck down in her dress. A Timex? She would never look at it. Staring at the glass tube that housed the watches, he found himself getting angry. All this indecision about what to get for Hagar was new. At Christmases past he simply chose (or had his sisters choose) from a long list of things that Hagar had mentioned specifically. Things quite out of place in her household: a navy-blue satin bathrobe (this for a woman who lived in a house that had no bathroom); a chubby; a snood with a velvet bow; a rhinestone bracelet with earrings to match; patent leather pumps; White Shoulders cologne. Milkman used to wonder at her specificity and her acquisitiveness until he reminded himself that Pilate and Reba celebrated no holidays. Yet their generosity was so wholehearted it looked like carelessness, and they did their best to satisfy every whim Hagar had. When he first took her in his arms, Hagar was a vain and somewhat distant creature. He liked to remember it that way—that he took her in his arms—but in truth it was she who called him back into the bedroom and stood there smiling while she unbuttoned her blouse.

From the time he first saw her, when he was twelve and she was seventeen, he was deeply in love with her, alternately awkward and witty in her presence. She babied him, ignored him, teased him—did anything she felt like, and he was grateful just to see her do anything or be any way. A good part of the enthusiasm with which he collected his father's rents was because of the time it gave him to visit the wine house and, hopefully, find Hagar there. He was free to drop in anytime and after school he tried to make sure he saw her.

Years passed and his puppy breath came as fast as ever in Hagar's presence. It slowed finally, after Guitar took him to his first Southside party, and after he found himself effortlessly popular with girls of his own age and in his own neighborhood. But while his breath was no longer that of a puppy, Hagar could still whip it into a pant when he was seventeen and she was twenty-two. Which she did on the dullest flattest day he could remember, a throw-away day in March when he drove his father's two-tone Ford over to her house for two bottles of wine. Milkman was much sought after and depended upon to secure the liquor he and his under-twenty-one friends believed vital to a party. When he got to Pilate's he walked in on a domestic crisis.

Reba's new man friend had asked her for a small loan and she had told him that she didn't have any money at all. The man, who had received two or three nice presents from her unasked, thought she was lying and was trying to tell him to shove off. They were quarreling in the backyard—that is, the man was quarreling. Reba was crying and trying to convince him that what she'd said was true. Just after Milkman opened the door, Hagar came running from the bedroom, where she'd been looking out the back window. She screamed to Pilate, "Mama! He's hitting her! I saw him! With his fist, Mama!"

Pilate looked up from a fourth-grade geography book she was reading and closed it. Slowly, it seemed to Milkman, she walked over to a shelf that hung over the dry sink, put the geography book on it, and removed a knife. Slowly still, she walked out the front door—there was no back door—and as soon as she did, Milkman could hear Reba's screams and the man's curses.

It didn't occur to him to stop Pilate—her mouth was not moving and her earring flashed fire—but he did follow her, as did Hagar, around to the back of the house, where, approaching the man from the back, she whipped her right arm around his neck and positioned the knife at the edge of his heart. She waited until the man felt the knife point before she jabbed it skillfully, about a quarter of an inch through his shirt into the skin. Still holding his neck, so he couldn't see but could feel the blood making his shirt sticky, she talked to him.

"Now, I'm not going to kill you, honey. Don't you worry none. Just be still a minute, the heart's right here, but I'm not going to stick it in any deeper. Cause if I stick it in any deeper, it'll go straight through your heart. So you have to be real still, you hear? You can't move a inch cause I might lose control. It's just a little hole now, honey, no more'n a pin scratch. You might lose about two tablespoons of blood, but no more. And if you're real still, honey, I can get it back out without no mistake. But before I do that, I thought we'd have a little talk."

The man closed his eyes. Sweat ran from his temples down the sides of his face. A few neighbors who had heard Reba's screams had gathered in Pilate's backyard. They knew right away that the man was a newcomer to the city. Otherwise he would have known a few things about Reba, one of which was that she gave away everything she had and if there was a case quarter in that house she'd have given it to him; and more important, he would have known not to fool with anything that belonged to Pilate, who never bothered anybody, was helpful to everybody, but who also was believed to have the power to step out of her skin, set a bush afire from fifty yards, and turn a man into a ripe rutabaga—all on account of the fact that she had no navel. So they didn't have much sympathy for him. They just craned their necks to hear better what Pilate was telling him.

"You see, darlin, that there is the only child I got. The first baby I ever had, and if you could turn around and see my face, which of course you can't cause my hand might slip, you'd know she's also the last. Women are foolish, you know, and mamas are the most foolish of all. And you know how mamas are, don't you? You got a mama, ain't you? Sure you have, so you know what I'm talking about. Mamas get hurt and nervous when somebody don't like they children. First real misery I ever had in my life was when I found out somebody—a little teeny tiny boy it was—didn't like my little girl. Made me so mad, I didn't know what to do. We do the best we can, but we ain't got the strength you men got. That's why it makes us so sad if a grown man start beating up on one of us. You know what I mean? I'd hate to pull this knife out and have you try some other time to act mean to my little girl. Cause one thing I know for sure: whatever she done, she's been good to *you*. Still, I'd hate to push it in more and have your mama feel like I do now. I confess, I don't know what to do. Maybe you can help me. Tell me, what should I do?"

The man struggled for breath and Pilate eased up on his throat but not his heart.

"Lemme go," he whispered.

"Hmmmmm?"

"Lemme go. I . . . won't never . . . put a hand on her. I promise."

"A real promise, sugar?"

"Yeah. I promise. You won't never see me no more."

Reba sat on the ground, her arms around her knees, staring through her unswollen eye at the scene as though she were at a picture show. Her lip was split and her cheek was badly bruised, and though her skirt and hands were stained with her effort to stop the blood pouring from her nose, a little still trickled down.

Pilate plucked the knife out of the man's shirt and took her arm away. He lurched a little, looked down at the blood on his clothes and up at Pilate, and licking his lips, backed all the way to the side of the house under Pilate's gaze. Her lips didn't start moving again until he was out of sight and running down the road.

All attention turned to Reba, who was having difficulty trying to stand up. She said she thought something was broken inside in the place where he'd kicked her. Pilate felt her ribs and said nothing was broken. But Reba said she wanted to go to the hospital. (It was her dream to be a patient in a hospital; she was forever trying to get admitted, since in her picture-show imagination, it was a nice hotel. She gave blood there as often as they would let her, and stopped only when the blood bank was moved to an office-type clinic some distance away from Mercy.) She was insistent now, and Pilate surrendered her judgment to Reba's. A neighbor offered to drive them and off they went, leaving Milkman to buy his wine from Hagar.

He was delighted with the performance and followed Hagar into the house to laugh and talk excitedly about it. She was as tranquil as he was agitated, as monosyllabic as he was garrulous.

"Was that something? Wow! She's two inches taller than he is, and she's talking about weak."

"We are weak."

"Compared to what? A B-52?"

"Every woman's not as strong as she is."

"I hope not. Half as strong is too much."

"Well, muscle strength is one thing. I meant women are weak in other ways."

"Name some. I want you to name some for me. Where are you weak?"

"I don't mean me. I mean other women."

"You don't have any weakness?"

"I haven't found any."

"I suppose you think you can whip me." It was the seventeen-year-old's constant preoccupation—who could whip him.

"Probably," said Hagar.

"Ha! Well, I guess I better not try to prove you wrong. Pilate might be back with her knife."

"Pilate scare you?"

"Yeah. Don't she scare you?"

"No. Nobody scares me."

"Yeah. You tough. I know you tough."

"Not tough. I just don't let people tell me what to do. I do what I want."

"Pilate tells you what to do."

"But I don't have to do it, if I don't want to."

"Wish I could say the same for my mother."

"Your mother boss you?"

"Well . . . not boss exactly." Milkman floundered for a word to describe the nagging he thought he was a victim of.

"How old are you now?" asked Hagar. She lifted her eyebrows like a woman mildly interested in the age of a small child.

"Seventeen."

"You old enough to be married." Hagar said it with the strong implication that he should not allow his mother to have any say about what he did.

"I'm waiting for you," he said, trying to regain (or acquire) some masculine flippancy.

"Be a long wait."

"Why?"

Hagar sighed as if her patience was being tried. "I'd like to be in love with the man I marry."

"Try me. You could learn if you'd try."

"You're too young for me."

"State of mind," he said.

"Uh huh. My mind."

"You're like all women. Waiting for Prince Charming to come trotting down the street and pull up in front of your door. Then you'll sweep down the steps and powie! Your eyes meet and he'll yank you up on his horse and the two of you ride off into the wind. Violins playing and 'courtesy of MGM' stamped on the horse's butt. Right?"

"Right," she said.

"What you going to do in the meantime?"

"Watch the lump grow in a little boy's pants."

Milkman smiled, but he was not amused. Hagar laughed. He jumped up to grab her, but she ran into the bedroom and shut the door. He rubbed his chin with the back of his hand and looked at the door. Then he shrugged and picked up the two bottles of wine.

"Milkman?" Hagar stuck her head out the door. "Come in here."

He turned around and put the bottles down on the table. The door was open, but he couldn't see her, could only hear her laughing, a low private laugh as though she had won a bet. He moved so quickly he forgot to duck the green sack hanging from the ceiling. A hickey was forming on his forehead by the time he got to her. "What you all got in there?" he asked her.

"That's Pilate's stuff. She calls it her inheritance." Hagar was unbuttoning her blouse.

"What'd she inherit? Bricks?" Then he saw her breasts.

"This is what I do in the meantime," she said.

Their tossing and giggling had been free and open then and they began to spend as much time in Guitar's room when he was at work as Guitar himself did when he was home. She became a quasi-secret but permanent fixture in his life. Very much a tease, sometimes accommodating his appetites, sometimes refusing. He never knew when or why she would do either. He assumed Reba and Pilate knew, but they never made any reference to the change in his relationship to Hagar. While he had lost some of his twelve-year-old's adoration of her, he was delighted to be sleeping with her and she was odd, funny, quirky company, spoiled, but artlessly so and therefore more refreshing than most of the girls his own age. There were months when Hagar would not see him, and then he'd appear one day and she was all smiles and welcome.

After about three years or so of Hagar's on-again-off-again passion, her refusals dwindled until finally, by the time he'd hit his father, they were nonexistent. Furthermore, she began to wait for him, and the more involved he got with the other part of his social life, the more reliable she became. She began to pout, sulk, and accuse him of not loving her or wanting to see her anymore. And though he seldom thought about his age, she was very aware of hers. Milkman had stretched his carefree boyhood out for thirty-one years. Hagar was thirty-six—and nervous. She placed duty squarely in the middle of their relationship; he tried to think of a way out.

He paid the clerk for the presents he had chosen and left the drugstore, having made up his mind to call it off.

I'll remind her that we are cousins, he thought. He would not buy her a present at all; instead he would give her a nice piece of money. Explain that he wanted her to get something really nice for herself, but that his gift-giving was compromising her. That he was not what she needed. She needed a steady man who could marry her. He was standing in her way. And since they were related and all, she should start looking for someone else. It hurt him, he would say, deeply hurt him, after all these years, but if you loved somebody as he did her, you had to think of them first. You couldn't be selfish with somebody you loved.

Having thought so carefully of what he would say to her, he felt as though he had already had the conversation and had settled everything. He went back to his father's office, got some cash out of the safe, and wrote Hagar a nice letter which ended: "Also, I want to thank you. Thank you for all you have meant to me. For making me happy all these years. I am signing this letter with love, of course, but more than that, with gratitude."

And he did sign it with love, but it was the word "gratitude" and the flat-out coldness of "thank you" that sent Hagar spinning into a bright blue place where the air was thin and it was silent all the time, and where people spoke in whispers or did not make sounds at all, and where everything was frozen except for an occasional burst of fire inside her chest that crackled away until she ran out into the streets to find Milkman Dead.

Long after he'd folded the money and the letter into an envelope, Milkman sat on at his father's desk. He added and re-added columns of figures, always eighty cents too little or eighty cents too much. He was still distracted and edgy, and all of it was not because of the problem of Hagar. He'd had a conversation with Guitar some time ago about the dragnet. A young boy, about sixteen years old, on his way home from school, had been strangled with what was believed to be a rope, and his head was bashed in. The state troopers cooperating with the local police said the way in which the boy had been killed was similar to the way another boy had been killed on New Year's Eve in 1953, and the way four grown men had been killed in 1955—the strangulation, the smashing of the face. In the poolrooms and in Tommy's Barbershop, the word was that Winnie Ruth Judd had struck again. The men laughed about it and repeated for the benefit of newcomers the story of how, in 1932, Winnie Ruth, a convicted murderer, who axed and dismembered her victims and stuffed them in trunks, was committed to a state asylum for the criminally insane, and escaped two or three times each year.

Once she had walked two hundred miles through two states before they caught her. Because there was a brutal killing in the city in December of that year, during the time Winnie Ruth was at large, Southside people were convinced that she had done it. From then on when some particularly nasty murder was reported, the Negroes said it was Winnie Ruth. They said that because Winnie Ruth was white and so were the victims. It was their way of explaining what they believed was white madness—crimes planned and executed in a truly lunatic manner against total strangers. Such murders could only be committed by a fellow lunatic of the race and Winnie Ruth Judd fit the description. They believed firmly that members of their own race killed one another for good reasons: violation of another's turf (a man is found with somebody else's wife); refusal to observe the laws of hospitality (a man reaches into his friend's pot of mustards and snatches out the meat); or verbal insults impugning their virility, honesty, humanity, and mental health. More important, they believed the crimes they committed were legitimate because they were committed in the heat of passion: anger, jealousy, loss of face, and so on. Bizarre killings amused them, unless of course the victim was one of their own.

They speculated about Winnie Ruth's motives for this recent murder. Somebody said she was raunchy from being cooped up and went looking for a lay. But she knew better than to expect a grown man to want her, so she went for a schoolboy. Another said she probably didn't like saddle shoes and when she got out of the loony bin and walked four hundred miles to safety, the first thing she saw was a kid wearing saddle shoes and she couldn't take it—ran amok.

Amid the jokes, however, was a streak of unspoken terror. The police said there had been a witness who thought he saw a "bushy-haired Negro" running from the schoolyard where the body was found.

"The same bushy-haired Negro they saw when Sam Sheppard axed his wife," said Porter.

"Hammered, man," said Guitar. "Twenty-seven hammer blows."

"Great Jesus. Why he do twenty-seven? That's a hard killin."

"Every killing is a hard killing," said Hospital Tommy. "Killing anybody is hard. You see those movies where the hero puts his hands around somebody's neck and the victim coughs a little bit and expires? Don't believe it, my friends. The human body is robust. It can gather strength when it's in mortal danger."

"You kill anybody in the war, Tommy?"

"I put my hand to a few."

"With your hands?"

"Bayonet, friend. The men of the Ninety-second used bayonets. Belleau Wood glittered with them. Fairly glittered."

"How'd it feel?"

"Unpleasant. Extremely unpleasant. Even when you know he'll do the same to you, it's still a very indelicate thing to do."

They laughed as usual at Tommy's proper way of speaking.

"That's because you didn't want to be in the army no way," said a fat man. "What about if you was roaming the streets and met up with Orval Faubus?"

"Boy, I'd love to kill that sucker," a heavy-set man said.

"Keep saying that. They'll soon have your ass downtown."

"My hair ain't bushy."

"They'll make it bushy."

"They'll take some brass knuckles and make your *head* bushy and call it hair."

Aside from Empire State's giggle, which was wholehearted, it had seemed to Milkman then that the laughter was wan and nervous. Each man in that room knew he was subject to being picked up as he walked the street and whatever his proof of who he was and where he was at the time of the murder, he'd have a very uncomfortable time being questioned.

And there was one more thing. For some time Milkman had been picking up hints that one or more of these murders had in fact been either witnessed or committed by a Negro. Some slip, someone knowing some detail about the victim. Like whether or not Winnie Ruth couldn't stand saddle shoes. Did the boy have on saddle shoes? Did the newspaper say so? Or was that just one of the fanciful details a good jokester would think of.

The two Tommys were cleaning up. "Closed," they said to a

man who poked his face in the door. "Shop's closing." The conversation died down and the men who were just hanging around seemed reluctant to go. Guitar too, but finally he slipped on his jacket, shadow-boxed with Empire State, and joined Milkman at the door. Southside shops were featuring feeble wreaths and lights, made more feeble by the tacky Yuletide streamers and bells the city had strung up on the lampposts. Only downtown were the lights large, bright, festive, and full of hope.

The two men walked down Tenth Street, headed for Guitar's room.

"Freaky," said Milkman. "Some freaky shit."

"Freaky world," said Guitar. "A freaky, fucked-up world."

Milkman nodded. "Railroad Tommy said the boy had on saddle shoes."

"Did he?" Guitar asked.

"Did he? You know he did. You were laughing right along with the rest of us."

Guitar glanced at him. "What you opening your nose for?"

"I know when I'm being put off."

"Then that's what it is, man. Nothing else. Maybe I don't feel like discussing it."

"You mean you don't feel like discussing it with me. You were full of discussion in Tommy's."

"Look, Milk, we've been tight a long time, right? But that don't mean we're not different people. We can't always think the same way about things. Can't we leave it like that? There are all kinds of people in this world. Some are curious, some ain't; some talk, some scream; some are kickers and other people are kicked. Take your daddy, now. He's a kicker. First time I laid eyes on him, he was kicking us out of our house. That was a difference right there between you and me, but we got to be friends anyway. . . ."

Milkman stopped and forced Guitar to stop too and turn around. "I know you're not going to give me a bullshit lecture."

"No lecture, man. I'm trying to tell you something."

"Well, tell me. Don't give me no fuckin bullshit lecture."

"What do you call a lecture?" asked Guitar. "When *you* don't talk for two seconds? When you have to listen to somebody else instead of talk? Is that a lecture?"

"A lecture is when somebody talks to a thirty-one-year-old man like he's a ten-year-old kid."

"You want me to talk or not?"

"Go ahead. Talk. Just don't talk to me in that funny tone. Like you a teacher and I'm some snot-nosed kid."

"That's the problem, Milkman. You're more interested in my tone than in what I'm saying. I'm trying to say that we don't have to agree on everything; that you and me are different; that—"

"You mean you got some secret shit you don't want me to know about."

"I mean there are things that interest me that don't interest you."

"How you know they don't interest me?"

"I know you. Been knowing you. You got your high-tone friends and your picnics on Honoré Island and you can afford to spend fifty percent of your brainpower thinking about a piece of ass. You got that red-headed bitch and you got a Southside bitch and no telling what in between."

"I don't believe it. After all these years you putting me down because of where I live?"

"Not where you live—where you hang out. You don't live nowhere. Not Not Doctor Street *or* Southside."

"You begrudge me—"

"I don't begrudge you a thing."

"You're welcome everywhere I go. I've tried to get you to come to Honoré—"

"Fuck Honoré! You hear me? The only way I'll go to that nigger heaven is with a case of dynamite and a book of matches."

"You used to like it."

"I never liked it! I went with you, but I never liked it. Never."

"What's wrong with Negroes owning beach houses? What

do you want, Guitar? You mad at every Negro who ain't scrubbing floors and picking cotton. This ain't Montgomery, Alabama."

Guitar looked at him, first in rage, and then he began to laugh. "You're right, Milkman. You have never in your life said a truer word. This definitely is not Montgomery, Alabama. Tell me. What would you do if it was? If this turned out to be another Montgomery?"

"Buy a plane ticket."

"Exactly. Now you know something about yourself you didn't know before: who you are and what you are."

"Yeah. A man that refuses to live in Montgomery, Alabama."

"No. A man that can't live there. If things ever got tough, you'd melt. You're not a serious person, Milkman."

"Serious is just another word for miserable. I know all about serious. My old man is serious. My sisters are serious. And nobody is more serious than my mother. She's so serious, she wasting away. I was looking at her in the backyard the other day. It was as cold as a witch's tit out there, but she had to get some bulbs in the ground before the fifteenth of December, she said. So there she was on her knees, digging holes in the ground."

"So? I miss the point."

"The point is that she wanted to put those bulbs in. She didn't have to. She likes to plant flowers. She really likes it. But you should have seen her face. She looked like the unhappiest woman in the world. The most miserable. So where's the fun? I've never in my whole life heard my mother laugh. She smiles sometimes, even makes a little sound. But I don't believe she has ever laughed out loud."

Without the least transition and without knowing he was going to, he began to describe to Guitar a dream he had had about his mother. He called it a dream because he didn't want to tell him it had really happened, that he had really seen it.

He was standing at the kitchen sink pouring the rest of his coffee down the drain when he looked through the window and saw Ruth digging in the garden. She made little holes and tucked something that looked like a small onion in them. As he stood there, mindlessly watching her, tulips began to grow out of the holes she had dug. First a solitary thin tube of green, then two leaves opened up from the stem—one on each side. He rubbed his eyes and looked again. Now several stalks were coming out of the ground behind her. Either they were bulbs she had already planted or they had been in the sack so long they had germinated. The tubes were getting taller and taller and soon there were so many of them they were pressing up against each other and up against his mother's dress. And still she didn't notice them or turn around. She just kept digging. Some of the stems began to sprout heads, bloody red heads that bobbed over and touched her back. Finally she noticed them, growing and nodding and touching her. Milkman thought she would jump up in fear—at least surprise. But she didn't. She leaned back from them, even hit out at them, but playfully, mischievously. The flowers grew and grew, until he could see only her shoulders above them and her flailing arms high above those bobbing, snapping heads. They were smothering her, taking away her breath with their soft jagged lips. And she merely smiled and fought them off as though they were harmless butterflies.

He knew they were dangerous, that they would soon suck up all the air around her and leave her limp on the ground. But she didn't seem to guess this at all. Eventually they covered her and all he could see was a mound of tangled tulips bent low over her body, which was kicking to the last.

He described all of that to Guitar as though the dream emphasized his point about the dangers of seriousness. He tried to be as light-hearted as possible in the telling, but at the end, Guitar looked him in the eyes and said, "Why didn't you go help her?"

"What?"

"Help her. Pull her out from underneath."

"But she liked it. She was having fun. She liked it."

"Are you sure?" Guitar was smiling.

"Sure I'm sure. It was my dream."

"It was *your* mother too."

"Aw, man, why you making something out of it that ain't there? You're making the whole thing into something superserious, just to prove your point. First I'm wrong for not living in Alabama. Then I'm wrong for not behaving right in my own dream. Now I'm wrong for dreaming it. You see what I mean? The least little thing is a matter of life and death to you. You're getting to be just like my old man. He thinks if a paper clip is in the wrong drawer, I should apologize. What's happening to everybody?"

"Looks like everybody's going in the wrong direction but you, don't it?"

Milkman swallowed. He remembered that long-ago evening after he hit his father how everybody was crammed on one side of the street, going in the direction he was coming from. Nobody was going his way. It was as though Guitar had been in that dream too.

"Maybe," he said. "But I know where I'm going."

"Where?"

"Wherever the party is."

Guitar smiled. His teeth were as white as the snowflakes that were settling on his jacket. "Merry Christmas," he said, "and Happy New Year." He waved his hand and cut around the corner to his street. He was lost in the snowy shadows of Southside before Milkman could ask him where he was going or tell him to wait.

Now he closed the accounts book in Sonny's Shop and gave up on the column of numbers. Something was happening to Guitar, had already happened to him. He was constantly chafing Milkman about how he lived, and that conversation was just one more example of how he'd changed. No more could Milkman run up the stairs to his room to drag him off to a party or a bar. And he didn't want to talk about girls or getting high. Sports were about the only things he was still enthusiastic about, and music. Other than that, he was all gloom and golden eyes. And politics.

It was that atmosphere of earnestness he provoked that led Milkman to talking about his family more than he would normally do and that also led him to defend with flippant remarks the kind of life he led. Pussy and Honoré parties. Guitar knew that wasn't all he was interested in, didn't he? He knew Milkman had other interests. Such as? he asked himself. Well, he was very good in his father's business, for one thing. Excellent, in fact. But he had to admit right away that real estate was of no real interest to him. If he had to spend the rest of his life thinking about rents and property, he'd lose his mind. But he was going to spend the rest of his life doing just that, wasn't he? That's what his father assumed and he supposed that was what he had assumed as well.

Maybe Guitar was right—partly. His life was pointless, aimless, and it was true that he didn't concern himself an awful lot about other people. There was nothing he wanted bad enough to risk anything for, inconvenience himself for. Still, what right had Guitar to talk? He didn't live in Montgomery either; all he did was work at that automobile factory and sneak off places—nobody knew where—and hang around Tommy's Barbershop. He never kept a woman more than a few months—the time span that he said was average before she began to make "permanent-arrangement-type noises."

He ought to get married, Milkman thought. Maybe I should too. Who? There were lots of women around and he was very much the eligible bachelor to the Honoré crowd. Maybe he'd pick one—the redhead. Get a nice house. His father would help him find one. Go into a real partnership with his father and . . . And what? There had to be something better to look forward to. He couldn't get interested in money. No one had ever denied him any, so it had no exotic attraction. Politics—at least barbershop politics and Guitar's brand—put him to sleep. He was bored. Everybody bored him. The city was boring. The racial problems that consumed Guitar were the most boring of all. He wondered what they would do if they didn't have black and white problems to talk about. Who would they be if they couldn't describe the insults, violence, and oppression that their lives (and the television news) were made up of? If they didn't have Kennedy or Elijah to quarrel about? They excused themselves for everything. Every job of work undone, every bill unpaid, every illness, every death was The Man's fault. And Guitar was becoming just like them—except he made no excuses for himself—just agreed, it seemed to Milkman, with every grievance he heard.

Milkman went into the bathroom, which served also as a pantry, and plugged in the hot plate to make himself some instant coffee. While he was there, he heard a rapid tapping on the windowpane. He stepped back into the office and saw Freddie's eyes through the lettering. Milkman unlocked the door.

"Hey, Freddie. What's up?"

"Looking for a warm spot. They got me runnin tonight. Christmas comin and all, all I do is run up and down the street." Freddie's janitor duties at the department store were supplemented by his function as a messenger and package deliverer.

"They give you a new truck yet?" Milkman asked him.

"You crazy? The engine have to fall out on the ground before they give me a decent one."

"I put some coffee water on. Have a cup?"

"Just what I'm lookin for. Saw your lights and thought there's got to be a hot cup a coffee in there. You wouldn't happen to have a little taste to go in it, would ya?"

"Just so happens I do."

"Atta boy."

Milkman went into the bathroom, lifted the lid from the toilet tank, and took out the half-pint bottle he kept hidden from Macon, who wouldn't have alcohol on the premises. He brought the bottle into the office, put it on the desk, and went back to make up two cups of coffee. When he reentered, Freddie was trying to look as though he hadn't already turned the pint up to his mouth. They laced their coffee and Milkman looked around for his cigarettes.

"Hard times, boy," Freddie said absently, after his first sip. "Hard times." Then, as though he noticed something missing, he asked, "Where's your buddy?"

"You mean Guitar?"

"Yeah. Guitar. Where's he?"

"Haven't seen him in a few days. You know Guitar. He'll disappear on you in a minute." Milkman noticed how white Freddie's hair was.

"How old are you, Freddie?"

"Who knows? They made dirt in the morning and me that afternoon." He giggled. "But I been around a long long time."

"You born here?"

"Naw. Down south. Jacksonville, Florida. Bad country, boy. Bad, bad country. You know they ain't even got an orphanage in Jacksonville where colored babies can go? They have to put 'em in jail. I tell people that talk about them sit-ins I was *raised* in jail, and it don't scare me none."

"I didn't know you were an orphan."

"Well, not a regular orphan. I had people and all, but my mama died and nobody would take me in. It was on account of the way she died that nobody would take me."

"How'd she die?"

"Ghosts."

"Ghosts?"

"You don't believe in ghosts?"

"Well"—Milkman smiled—"I'm willing to, I guess."

"You better believe, boy. They're here."

"Here?" Milkman didn't glance around the office, but he wanted to. The wind howled outside in the blackness and Freddie, looking like a gnome, flashed his gold teeth. "I don't mean in this room necessarily. Although they could be." He cocked his head and listened. "No. I mean they in the world."

"You've seen some?"

"Plenty. Plenty. Ghosts killed my mother. I didn't see that, of course, but I seen 'em since."

"Tell me about them."

"No I ain't. I don't do no talkin 'bout the ghosts I seen. They don't like that."

"Well, tell me about the one you didn't see. The one killed your mother."

"Oh. Well. That one. She was walking cross the yard with this neighbor friend of hers and they both looked up and saw a woman comin down the road. They stopped and waited to see who she was. When the woman got near, the neighbor called out howdy and soon's she said the word, the woman turned into a white bull. Right before their eyes. My mama fell down on the ground in labor pain right then and there. When I was born and they showed me to her, she screamed and passed out. Never *did* come to. My father died two months before I was born, and they couldn't get none of my people and nobody else to take a baby brought here by a white bull."

Milkman started laughing. He didn't mean to hurt Freddie's feelings, but he couldn't stop the laughter, and the more he tried, the more it came.

Freddie looked more surprised than hurt. "You don't believe me, do you?"

Milkman couldn't answer, he was laughing so hard.

"Okay," Freddie said, and threw up his hands. "Okay, laugh on. But they's a lot of strange things you don't know nothin about, boy. You'll learn. Lot of strange things. Strange stuff goin on right in this here town."

Milkman's laughter was under control now. "What? What strange stuff is happening in this town? I haven't seen any white bulls lately."

"Open your eyes. Ask your buddy. He knows."

"What buddy?"

"Your buddy Guitar. Ask him what strange stuff been happenin. Ask him how come he runnin round with Empire State all of a sudden."

"Empire State?"

"That's right. Empire State."

"Nobody runs around with Empire State. He's a nut. He just stands around with a broom, dribbling spit. He can't even talk."

"He *don't* talk. That don't mean he can't. Only reason he don't is cause he found his wife in bed with another man long time ago, and ain't found nothing to say since then."

"Well, what's Guitar doing with him?"

"Good question. Police would like to know the answer to that too."

"How'd you get from Empire State to the police?"

"You ain't heard? People say the police is lookin for a colored man what killed that white boy in the schoolyard."

"I know that. Everybody knows that."

"Well, the description fits State. And Guitar been takin him places. Hidin him, I believe."

"What's so strange about that? You know Guitar is like that. He'll hide anybody the law is looking for. He hates white people, especially cops, and anybody they're after can count on him for help."

"You don't understand. Him and State ain't actin like they just hidin him. They actin like he did it."

"You a little drunk, Freddie?"

"Yeah, I'm a little drunk, but that don't change nothin. Look here. Remember when Emmet Till was killed? Back in fifty-three? Well, right after that, a white boy was killed in the schoolyard, wasn't he?"

"I don't know. I can't remember the dates of murders I haven't committed."

"You don't know?" Freddie was incredulous.

"No. Are you saying State did it?"

"I'm sayin he acts like it and I'm sayin Guitar knows, and I'm sayin somethin strange is goin on. That's what I'm sayin."

He's mad at me, thought Milkman, because I laughed at his mother and that white bull story. So he's trying to get back at me.

"Keep your eyes open," Freddie went on. "Just keep them open." He looked in the pint bottle, saw it was empty, and got up to leave. "Yep. Some strange goings on round here. But don't put my name in it if you hear anything. Was just like this when that insurance man jumped off the roof. Ever hear tell of him?"

"Seems like I did."

"That must a been when you was a little bitty baby, 1931.

Well, it was some strange stuff then too." Freddie buttoned his coat and pulled his flap-eared cap down as far as it would go. "Well, thanks for the coffee, boy. Did me a lot of good. A lot of good." He took his gloves out of his pocket and moved to the door.

"You're welcome, Freddie. Merry Christmas if I don't see you before that."

"Same to you. And your folks. Tell Mr. Dead and your mother I said Merry Christmas." He was smiling again. When he reached the door he put on his gloves. Then he turned his head slowly and faced Milkman. "Tell you somebody else might know about what's goin on. Corinthians. Ask Corinthians."

He flashed his gold merrily and was gone.

Chapter 5

Nothing happened to the fear. He lay in Guitar's bed face-up in the sunlight, trying to imagine how it would feel when the ice pick entered his neck. But picturing a spurt of wine-red blood and wondering if the ice pick would make him cough didn't help. Fear lay like a pair of crossed paws on his chest.

He closed his eyes and threw his arm over his face to keep the light from overexposing his thoughts. In the darkness that his arm made he could see ice picks coming down faster than raindrops had when he tried as a little boy to catch them with his tongue.

Five hours ago, before he knocked on Guitar's door, he had stood on the top step, dripping in the summer rain that still patted the window, imagining that the drops were tiny steely picks. Then he knocked on the door.

"Yeah?" The voice was lightly aggressive; Guitar never opened his door to a knock anymore before finding out who it was.

"Me–Milkman," he answered, and waited for the clicking sounds of three locks being released.

Milkman walked in, hunching his shoulders under his wet suit jacket. "Anything to drink?"

"Now, you know better'n that." Guitar was smiling, his golden eyes dimmed for the moment. They had not seen much of each other since that argument about Honoré versus Alabama, but the quarrel had been cleansing for both of them. They were easy with each other now that they didn't have to pretend. When in conversation they came to the battleground of difference, their verbal sparring was full of good humor. Furthermore, their friendship had been tested in more immediate ways. The last six months had been dangerous for Milkman, and Guitar had come to his aid over and over again.

"Coffee, then," said Milkman. He sat on the bed with the heaviness of a very old man. "How long you gonna keep that up?"

"Forever. It's over, man. No booze. How about some tea?"

"Jesus."

"Loose too. Bet you thought tea grew in little bags."

"Oh, Christ."

"Like Louisiana cotton. Except the black men picking it wear diapers and turbans. All over India that's all you see. Bushes with little bitsy white tea bags blossoming. Right?"

"Gimme the tea, Guitar. Just the tea. No geography."

"No geography? Okay, no geography. What about some history in your tea? Or some sociopolitico– No. That's still geography. Goddam, Milk, I do believe my whole life's geography."

"Don't you wash pots out for people before you cook water in them?"

"For example, I live in the North now. So the first question come to mind is North of what? Why, north of the South. So North exists because South does. But does that mean North is different from South? No way! South is just south of North. . . ."

"You don't put the fuckin leaves in the boiling water. You pour the water *over* the leaves. In a pot, man. In a teapot!"

"But there is some slight difference worth noticing. Northerners, for example—born and bred ones, that is—are picky about their food. Well, not about the food. They actually don't give a shit about the food. What they're picky about is the trappings. You know what I mean? The pots and shit. Now, they're real funny about pots. But tea? They don't know Earl Grey from old man Lipton's instant."

"I want tea, man. Not won-ton shredded wheat."

"Old man Lipton dye him up some shredded *New York Times* and put it in a cute little white bag and northern Negroes run amok. Can't contain themselves. Ever notice that? How they love them little white bags?"

"Oh, Jesus."

"He's a Northerner too. Lived in Israel, but a Northerner in His heart. His bleeding heart. His cute little old bleeding red heart. Southerners think they own Him, but that's just because the first time they laid eyes on Him, He was strung up on a tree. They can relate to that, see. Both the stringer and the strung. But Northerners know better. . . ."

"Who you talking about? Black people or white people?"

"Black? White? Don't tell me you're one of those racial Negroes? Who said anything about black people? This is just a geography lesson." Guitar handed Milkman a steaming cup of tea.

"Yeah, well, if this is tea, I'm a soft-fried egg."

"See what I mean? Picky. Why you got to be a *soft*-fried egg? Why can't you be just a fried egg? Or just a plain old egg? And why a egg anyway? Negro's been a lotta things, but he ain't never been no egg."

Milkman began to laugh. Guitar had done it again. He'd come to the door sopping wet, ready to roll over and die, and now he was laughing, spilling tea, and choking out his reply: "How come? How come a nigger can't be a egg? He can be a egg if he wants to."

"Nope. Can't be no egg. It ain't in him. Something about his genes. His genes won't let him be no egg no matter how hard he tries. Nature says no. 'No, you can't be no egg, nigger. Now, you can be a crow if you wanna. Or a big baboon. But not no egg. Eggs is difficult, complicated. Fragile too. And white.' "

"They got brown eggs."

"Miscegenation. Besides, don't nobody want 'em."

"French people do."

"In France, yeah. But not in the Congo. Frenchman in the Congo won't touch a brown egg."

"Why won't he?"

"Scared of 'em. Might do something to his skin. Like the sun."

"French people love the sun. They're always trying to get in the sun. On the Riviera—"

"They try to get in the French sun, but not the Congo sun. In the Congo they hate the sun."

"Well, I got a right to be what I want to be, and I want to be a egg."

"Fried?"

"Fried."

"Then somebody got to bust your shell."

Quicker than a pulse beat, Guitar had changed the air. Milkman wiped his mouth, avoiding Guitar's eyes because he knew the phosphorus was back in them. The little room stood at attention in the quiet. It was a second-story porch walled in to make a room-for-rent so the landlady could get an income from it and have a watchman too. Its outside stairway made it perfect for a bachelor. Especially a secretive one like Guitar Bains.

"Can I have the pad tonight?" Milkman asked him. He examined his fingernails.

"To cop?"

Milkman shook his head.

Guitar didn't believe him. Didn't believe his friend really wanted to be alone the night before the day of his own murder. "That's scary, man. Very scary."

Milkman didn't answer.

"You're not obliged to go through no number, you know. Not for me. Everybody knows you're brave when you want to be."

Milkman looked up but still did not answer.

"Still and all," Guitar went on carefully, "you might get your heart cut out. Then you'll be just another brave nigger what got wasted."

Milkman reached for the Pall Mall package. It was empty, so he pulled a longish butt from the Planter's peanut butter jar top that was Guitar's ashtray for the day. He stretched out on the bed, letting his long fingers rub the pocket places in his clothes where matches might be. "Everything's cool," he said.

"Shit," said Guitar. "Ain't nothing cool. Nothing, nowhere. Even the North Pole ain't cool. You think so, go on up there and watch them fuckin glaciers ice your ass. And what the glaciers don't get the polar bears will." Guitar stood up, his head almost touching the ceiling. Annoyed by Milkman's indifference, he relieved his agitation by straightening up the room. He pulled an empty crate from underneath the straight-backed chair leaning in the corner, and started dumping trash into the box: dead matches from the window sill, pork bones from the barbecue he had eaten the day before. He crumpled the pleated paper cups that had been overflowing with cole slaw and fired them into the crate. "Every nigger I know wants to be cool. There's nothing wrong with controlling yourself, but can't nobody control other people." He looked sideways at Milkman's face, alert for any sign, any opening. This kind of silence was new. Something must have happened. Guitar was genuinely worried about his friend, but he also didn't want anything to happen in his room that would bring the police there. He picked up the peanut-butter-top ashtray.

"Wait. There's still some good butts in there." Milkman spoke softly.

Guitar dumped the whole ashtray into the box.

"What'd you do that for? You know we don't have no cigarettes."

"Then move your ass and go get some."

"Come on, Guitar. Cut the shit." Milkman rose from the bed and reached for the crate. He would have gotten it except Guitar stepped back and flung it all the way across the room, letting the mess settle right back where it came from. Graceful and economical as a cat, he arced his arm out of the swing and slammed his fist up against the wall, forming a barrier to any move Milkman might make.

"Pay attention." Guitar's voice was low. "Pay attention when I'm trying to tell you something."

Head to head, toe to toe they stood. Milkman's left foot hovered above the floor, and Guitar's eyes with their phosphorous lights singed his heart a little, but he took the stare. "And if I don't? What then, man? You gonna do me in? My name is Macon, remember? I'm already Dead."

Guitar didn't smile at the familiar joke, but there was enough recognition of it in his face to soften the glare in his eyes.

"Somebody ought to tell your murderer that," said Guitar.

Milkman gave a short laugh and moved back toward the bed. "You worry too much, Guitar."

"I worry just enough. But right now I need to know how come you ain't worried at all. You come up here knowing it's the thirtieth day. Knowing if anybody wants to find you they come here if not first then last. And you ask me to leave you by yourself. Just tell me what you doing."

"Look," Milkman said. "Out of all those times, I was scared just twice: the first time and the third. I've been handling it ever since, right?"

"Yeah, but something's funny this time."

"Ain't nothing funny."

"Yeah, it is. You. You funny."

"No I'm not. Just tired. Tired of dodging crazy people, tired of this jive town, of running up and down these streets getting nowhere. . . ."

"Well, you're home free if tired is all you are. Soon you'll have all the rest you ever need. Can't promise you the bed's comfortable, but morticians don't make mattresses."

"Maybe she won't come this time."

"She ain't missed in six months. You countin on her taking a holiday or something?"

"I can't hide from that bitch no more. I got to stop it. I don't want to go through this again a month from now."

"Why don't you get her people to do something?"

"I am her people."

"Listen, Milk, I'll split if you say so. But just listen to me a minute. That broad had a Carlson skinning knife last time. You know how sharp a Carlson skinning knife is? Cut you like a laser, man."

"I know."

"No, you don't know. You was up under the bar when me and Moon grabbed her."

"I know what she had."

"Won't be no Moon in this room tomorrow. And no Guitar either, if I listen to you. This time she might have a pistol."

"What fool is gonna give a colored woman a pistol?"

"Same fool that gave Porter a shotgun."

"That was years ago."

"It ain't even that that bothers me. It's the way you acting. Like you want it. Like you looking forward to it."

"Where'd you think that up?"

"Look at you. You all dressed up."

"I had to work in Sonny's Shop. You know my old man makes me dress up like this when I'm behind the desk."

"You had time to change. It's past midnight."

"Okay. So I'm clean. So I'm looking forward to it. I just got through telling you I don't want to hide no more. . . ."

"It's a secret, ain't it? You got yourself a secret."

"That makes two of us."

"Two? You and her?"

"No. You and me. You've been making some funny smoke screens lately." Milkman looked up at Guitar and smiled. "Just so you don't think I ain't noticed."

Guitar grinned back. Now that he knew there was a secret, he settled down into the groove of their relationship.

"Okay, Mr. Dead, sir. You on your own. Would you ask your visitor to kind of neaten things up a little before she goes? I don't want to come back and have to look through a pile of cigarette butts for your head. Be nice if it was laying somewhere I could spot it right off. And if it's her head that's left behind, well, there's some towels in the closet on the shelf in the back."

"Rest your mind, boy. Ain't nobody giving up no head."

They laughed then at the suitableness of the unintended pun, and it was in the sound of this laughter that Guitar picked up his brown leather jacket and started out the door.

"Cigarettes!" Milkman called after him. "Bring me some cigarettes before you disappear."

"Gotcha!" Guitar was halfway down the stairs. Already his thoughts had left Milkman and had flown ahead to the house where six old men waited for him.

He didn't come back that night.

Milkman lay quietly in the sunlight, his mind a blank, his lungs craving smoke. Gradually his fear of and eagerness for death returned. Above all he wanted to escape what he knew, escape the implications of what he had been told. And all he knew in the world about the world was what other people had told him. He felt like a garbage pail for the actions and hatreds of other people. He himself did nothing. Except for the one time he had hit his father, he had never acted independently, and that act, his only one, had brought unwanted knowledge too, as well as some responsibility for that knowledge. When his father told him about Ruth, he joined him in despising her, but he felt put upon; felt as though some burden had been given to him and that he didn't deserve it. None of that was his fault, and he didn't want to have to think or be or do something about any of it.

In that mood of lazy righteousness he wallowed in Guitar's bed, the same righteousness that had made him tail his mother like a secret agent when she left the house a week or so ago.

Returning home from a party, he had hardly pulled Macon's Buick up to the curb and turned off the car lights when he saw his mother walking a little ahead of him down Not Doctor Street. It was one-thirty in the morning, but in spite of the hour and her turned-up coat collar, there was no air of furtiveness about her at all. She was walking in what seemed to him a determined manner. Neither hurried nor aimless. Just the even-paced walk of a woman on her way to some modest but respectable work.

When Ruth turned the corner, Milkman waited a minute and started up the car. Creeping, not letting the engine slide into high gear, he drove around the corner. She was standing at the bus stop, so Milkman waited in the shadows until the bus came and she boarded it.

Surely this was no meeting of lovers. The man would have picked her up nearby somewhere. No man would allow a woman he had any affection for to come to him on public transportation in the middle of the night, especially a woman as old as Ruth. And what man wanted a woman over sixty anyway?

Following the bus was a nightmare; it stopped too often, too long, and it was difficult to tail it, hide, and watch to see if she got off. Milkman turned on the car radio, but the music, which he hoped would coat his nerve ends, only splayed them. He was very nervous and thought seriously about turning back.

Finally the bus pulled up at the intracounty train station. Its last stop. There, among the few remaining passengers, he saw her go into the lobby of the station. He believed he'd lost her. He'd never find out what train she was taking. He thought again of going back home. It was late, he was exhausted, and he wasn't sure he wanted to know any more about his mother. But having come this far, he realized it was foolish to turn back now and leave things forever up in the air. He parked in the lot and walked slowly toward the station. Maybe she's not taking a train, he thought. Maybe he meets her in the station.

He looked around carefully before pushing open the doors. There was no sign of her inside. It was a small, plain building. Old but well lit. Looming over the modest waiting room was the Great Seal of Michigan, in vivid Technicolor, painted, probably, by some high school art class. Two pink deer reared up on their hind legs, facing each other, and an eagle perched at eye level between them. The eagle's wings were open and looked like raised shoulders. Its head was turned to the left; one fierce eye bored into that of a deer. Purple Latin words stretched in a long ribbon beneath the seal: *Si Quaeris Peninsulam Amoenam Circumspice.* Milkman didn't understand the Latin and he didn't understand why the wolverine state had a buck painted on the seal. Or were they does? He remembered Guitar's story about killing one. "A man shouldn't do that." Milkman felt a quick beat of something like remorse, but he shook it off and resumed his search for his mother. He walked to the back of the station. Still no sight of her. Then he noticed that there was an upper platform, stairs leading to it, and an arrow with the words FAIRFIELD AND NORTHEASTERN SUBURBS painted on it. Perhaps she was up there. He moved cautiously toward the stairs, glancing up and all around lest he see her or miss her. A loudspeaker broke the silence, announcing the arrival of the two-fifteen train to Fairfield Heights, leaving from the upper platform. He dashed up the stairs then just in time to see Ruth step into a car, and to jump into another car himself.

The train made ten stops at about ten-minute intervals. He leaned out between the cars at each stop to see if she was getting off. After the sixth stop, he asked the conductor when the next train returned to the city. "Five forty-five a.m.," he said.

Milkman looked at his watch. It was already three o'clock. When the conductor called out, "Fairfield Heights. Last stop," a half hour later, Milkman looked out again and this time he saw her disembark. He darted behind the three-sided wooden structure that sheltered waiting passengers from the wind until he heard her wide rubber heels padding down the steps.

Beyond the shelter along the street below were stores—all closed now: newsstands, coffee shops, stationery shops, but no houses. The wealthy people of Fairfield did not live near a train station and very few of their houses could even be seen from the road. Nevertheless, Ruth walked in her even-paced way down the street and in just a few minutes was at the wide winding lane that led into Fairfield Cemetery.

As Milkman stared at the ironwork arched over the entrance, he remembered snatches of his mother's chatter about having looked so very carefully for a cemetery for the doctor's body—someplace other than the one where Negroes were all laid together in one area. And forty years ago Fairfield was farm country with a county cemetery too tiny for anybody to care whether its dead were white or black.

Milkman leaned against a tree and waited at the entrance. Now he knew, if he'd had any doubts, that all his father had told him was true. She was a silly, selfish, queer, faintly obscene woman. Again he felt abused. Why couldn't anybody in his whole family just be normal?

He waited for an hour before she came out.

"Hello, Mama," he said. He tried to make his voice sound as coolly cruel as he felt; just as he tried to frighten her by stepping out suddenly from behind the tree.

He succeeded. She stumbled in alarm and took a great gulp of air into her mouth.

"Macon! Is that you? You're here? Oh, my goodness. I . . ." She tried desperately to normalize the situation, smiling wanly and blinking her eyes, searching for words and manners and civilization.

Milkman stopped her. "You come to lay down on your father's grave? Is that what you've been doing all these years? Spending a night every now and then with your father?"

Ruth's shoulders seemed to slump, but she said in a surprisingly steady voice, "Let's walk toward the train stop."

Neither said a word during the forty-five minutes they waited in the little shelter for the train back to the city. The sun came up and pointed out the names of young lovers painted on the wall. A few men were walking up the stairs to the platform.

When the train backed in from its siding they still had not spoken. Only when the wheels were actually turning and the engine had cleared its throat did Ruth begin, and she began in the middle of a sentence as though she had been thinking it all through since she and her son left the entrance to Fairfield Cemetery.

". . . because the fact is that I am a small woman. I don't mean little; I mean small, and I'm small because I was pressed small. I lived in a great big house that pressed me into a small package. I had no friends, only schoolmates who wanted to touch my dresses and my white silk stockings. But I didn't think I'd ever need a friend because I had him. I was small, but he was big. The only person who ever really cared whether I lived or died. Lots of people were *interested* in whether I lived or died, but he cared. He was not a good man, Macon. Certainly he was an arrogant man, and often a foolish and destructive one. But he cared whether and he cared how I lived, and there was, and is, no one else in the world who ever did. And for that I would do anything. It was important for me to be in his presence, among his things, the things he used, had touched. Later it was just important for me to know that he was in the world. When he left it, I kept on reigniting that cared-for feeling that I got from him.

"I am not a strange woman. I am a small one.

"I don't know what all your father has told you about me down in that shop you all stay in. But I know, as well as I know my own name, that he told you only what was flattering to him. I know he never told you that he killed my father and that he tried to kill you. Because both of you took my attention away from him. I know he never told you that. And I know he never told you that he threw my father's medicine away, but it's true. And I couldn't save my father. Macon took away his medicine and I just didn't know it, and I wouldn't have been able to save you except for Pilate. Pilate was the one brought you here in the first place."

"Pilate?" Milkman was coming awake. He had begun listening to his mother with the dulled ear of someone who was about to be conned and knew it.

"Pilate. Old, crazy, sweet Pilate. Your father and I hadn't had physical relations since my father died, when Lena and Corinthians were just toddlers. We had a terrible quarrel. He threatened to kill me. I threatened to go to the police about what he had done to my father. We did neither. I guess my father's money was more important to him than the satisfaction of killing me. And I would have happily died except for my babies. But he did move into another room and that's the way things stayed until I couldn't stand it anymore. Until I thought I'd really die if I had to live that way. With nobody touching me, or even looking as though they'd like to touch me. That's when I started coming to Fairfield. To talk. To talk to somebody who wanted to listen and not laugh at me. Somebody I could trust. Somebody who trusted me. Somebody who was . . . interested in me. For my own self. I didn't care if that somebody was under the ground. You know, I was twenty years old when your father stopped sleeping in the bed with me. That's hard, Macon. Very hard. By the time I was thirty . . . I think I was just afraid I'd die that way.

"Then Pilate came to town. She came into this city like she owned it. Pilate, Reba, and Reba's little baby. Hagar. Pilate came to see Macon right away and soon as she saw me she knew what my trouble was. And she asked me one day, 'Do you want him?' 'I want somebody,' I told her. 'He's as good as anybody,' she said. 'Besides, you'll get pregnant and your baby ought to be his. He ought to have a son. Otherwise this be the end of us.'

"She gave me funny things to do. And some greenish-gray grassy-looking stuff to put in his food." Ruth laughed. "I felt like a doctor, like a chemist doing some big important scientific experiment. It worked too. Macon came to me for four days. He even came home from his office in the middle of the day to be with me. He looked puzzled, but he came. Then it was over. And two months later I was pregnant. When he found out about it, he immediately suspected Pilate and he told me to get rid of the baby. But I wouldn't and Pilate helped me stand him off. I wouldn't have been strong enough without her. She saved my life. And yours, Macon. She saved yours too. She watched you like you were her own. Until your father threw her out."

Milkman leaned his head against the cold handbar that was attached to the seat in front of him. He held it there, letting its chill circle his head. Then he turned to his mother. "Were you in the bed with your father when he was dead? Naked?"

"No. But I did kneel there in my slip at his bedside and kiss his beautiful fingers. They were the only part of him that wasn't . . ."

"You nursed me."

"Yes."

"Until I was . . . old. Too old."

Ruth turned toward her son. She lifted her head and looked deep into his eyes. "And I also prayed for you. Every single night and every single day. On my knees. Now you tell me. What harm did I do you on my knees?"

That was the beginning. Now it was all going to end. In a little while she would walk in the door and this time he would let her do it. Afterward there would be no remembrance of who he was or where. Of Magdalene called Lena and First Corinthians, of his father trying to stop him dead before he was born. Of the brilliant bitterness between his father and his mother, a bitterness as smooth and fixed as steel. And he wouldn't have those waking dreams or hear those awful words his mother had spoken to him: What harm? What harm did I do you on my knees?

He could hear her footsteps, and then the sound of the doorknob turning, sticking, and turning again. He knew, without uncovering his eyes, that she was right there, looking at him through the window.

Hagar. Killing, ice-pick-wielding Hagar, who, shortly after a Christmas thank-you note, found herself each month searching the barrels and cupboards and basement shelves for some comfortably portable weapon with which to murder her true love.

The "thank you" cut her to the quick, but it was not the

reason she ran scurrying into cupboards looking for weapons. That had been accomplished by the sight of Milkman's arms around the shoulders of a girl whose silky copper-colored hair cascaded over the sleeve of his coat. They were sitting in Mary's, smiling into glasses of Jack Daniel's on the rocks. The girl looked a little like Corinthians or Lena from the back, and when she turned, laughing, toward Milkman, and Hagar saw her gray eyes, the fist that had been just sitting in her chest since Christmas released its forefinger like the blade of a skinning knife. As regularly as the new moon searched for the tide, Hagar looked for a weapon and then slipped out of her house and went to find the man for whom she believed she had been born into the world. Being five years older than he was and his cousin as well did nothing to dim her passion. In fact her maturity and blood kinship converted her passion to fever, so it was more affliction than affection. It literally knocked her down at night, and raised her up in the morning, for when she dragged herself off to bed, having spent another day without his presence, her heart beat like a gloved fist against her ribs. And in the morning, long before she was fully awake, she felt a longing so bitter and tight it yanked her out of a sleep swept clean of dreams.

She moved around the house, onto the porch, down the streets, to the fruit stalls and the butchershop, like a restless ghost, finding peace nowhere and in nothing. Not in the first tomato off the vine, split open and salted lightly, which her grandmother put before her. Not the six-piece set of pink glass dishes Reba won at the Tivoli Theater. And not the carved wax candle that the two of them made for her, Pilate dipping the wick and Reba scratching out tiny flowers with a nail file, and put in a genuine store-bought candleholder next to her bed. Not even the high fierce sun at noon, nor the ocean-dark evenings. Nothing could pull her mind away from the mouth Milkman was not kissing, the feet that were not running toward him, the eye that no longer beheld him, the hands that were not touching him.

She toyed, sometimes, with her unsucked breasts, but at some point her lethargy dissipated of its own accord and in its place was wilderness, the focused meanness of a flood or an avalanche of snow which only observers, flying in a rescue helicopter, believed to be an indifferent natural phenomenon, but which the victims, in their last gulp of breath, knew was both directed and personal. The calculated violence of a shark grew in her, and like every witch that ever rode a broom straight through the night to a ceremonial infanticide as thrilled by the black wind as by the rod between her legs; like every fed-up-to-the-teeth bride who worried about the consistency of the grits she threw at her husband as well as the potency of the lye she had stirred into them; and like every queen and every courtesan who was struck by the beauty of her emerald ring as she tipped its poison into the old red wine, Hagar was energized by the details of her mission. She stalked him. Whenever the fist that beat in her chest became that pointing finger, when any contact with him at all was better than none, she stalked him. She could not get his love (and the possibility that he did not think of her at all was intolerable), so she settled for his fear.

On those days, her hair standing out from her head like a thundercloud, she haunted Southside and Not Doctor Street until she found him. Sometimes it took two days, or three, and the people who saw her passed the word along that Hagar "done took off after Milkman again." Women watched her out of their windows. Men looked up from their checker games and wondered if she'd make it this time. The lengths to which lost love drove men and women never surprised them. They had seen women pull their dresses over their heads and howl like dogs for lost love. And men who sat in doorways with pennies in their mouths for lost love. "Thank God," they whispered to themselves, "thank God I ain't never had one of them graveyard loves." Empire State himself was a good example of one. He'd married a white girl in France and brought her home. Happy as a fly and just as industrious, he lived with her for six years until he came home to find her with another man. Another black man. And when he discovered that his white wife loved not only him, not only this other black man, but the whole race, he sat down, closed his mouth, and never said another word. Railroad Tommy had given him a janitor's job to save him from the poorhouse, workhouse, or nuthouse, one.

So Hagar's forays were part and parcel of the mystery of having been "lifed" by love, and while the manifestation it took was a source of great interest to them, the consequences were not. After all, it served him right, messing with his own cousin.

Luckily for Milkman, she had proved, so far, to be the world's most incept killer. Awed (even in the midst of her anger) by the very presence of her victim, she trembled violently and her knife thrusts and hammer swings and ice-pick jabs were clumsy. As soon as the attempt had been thwarted by a wrist grab from behind or a body tackle from the front or a neat clip on the jaw, she folded up into herself and wept cleansing tears right there and later under Pilate's strap—to which she submitted with relief. Pilate beat her, Reba cried, and Hagar crouched. Until the next time. Like this time when she turned the doorknob of Guitar's little bachelor room.

It was locked. So she swung one leg over the porch railing and fiddled with the window. Milkman heard the noises, heard the window shake, but refused to move or take his arm away from his eyes. Even when he heard the tinkle and clatter of glass he did not move.

Hagar put her shoe back on before reaching into the window hole she had made and turning the catch. It took her the longest time to raise the window. She was hanging lopsided over the railing, one leg supporting her weight. The window slid in a crooked path up its jamb.

Milkman refused to look. Perspiration collected in the small of his back and ran out of his armpit down his side. But the fear was gone. He lay there as still as the morning light, and sucked the world's energy up into his own will. And willed her dead. Either she will kill me or she will drop dead. Either I am to live in this world on my terms or I will die out of it. If I am to live in it, then I want her dead. One or the other. Me or her. Choose.

Die, Hagar. Die. Die. Die.

But she didn't. She crawled into the room and walked over to the little iron bed. In her hand was a butcher knife, which she raised high over her head and brought down heavily toward the smooth neck flesh that showed above his shirt collar. The knife struck his collarbone and angled off to his shoulder. A small break in the skin began to bleed. Milkman jerked, but did not move his arm nor open his eyes. Hagar raised the knife again, this time with both hands, but found she could not get her arms down. Try as she might, the ball joint in her shoulders would not move. Ten seconds passed. Fifteen. The paralyzed woman and the frozen man.

At the thirtieth second Milkman knew he had won. He moved his arm and opened his eyes. His gaze traveled to her strung-up, held-up arms.

Oh, she thought, when she saw his face, I had forgotten how beautiful he is.

Milkman sat up, swung his legs over the side of the bed, and stood.

"If you keep your hands just that way," he said, "and then bring them down straight, straight and fast, you can drive that knife right smack in your cunt. Why don't you do that? Then all your problems will be over." He patted her cheek and turned away from her wide, dark, pleading, hollow eyes.

She stood that way for a long time, and it was an even longer time before anybody found her. They could have guessed where she was, though. If anybody missed her for a while they could guess. Even Ruth knew now. A week earlier she had learned from Freddie that Hagar had tried to kill Milkman six times in as many months. She stared at his golden teeth and said, "Hagar?" She hadn't laid eyes on her in years; had been to Pilate's house only once in her life—a very long time ago.

"Hagar?"

"Hagar. Shore Hagar."

"Does Pilate know?"

"Course she do. Whip her every time, but it don't do no good."

Ruth was relieved. For a moment she imagined that Pilate, who had brought her son to life in the first place, was now bound to see him dead. But right after that moment of relief, she felt hurt because Milkman had not told her himself. Then she realized that he really didn't tell her anything, and hadn't for years. Her son had never been a person to her, a separate real person. He had always been a passion. Because she had been so desperate to lie with her husband and have another baby by him, the son she bore was first off a wished-for bond between herself and Macon, something to hold them together and reinstate their sex lives. Even before his birth he was a strong feeling—a feeling about the nasty greenish-gray powder Pilate had given her to be stirred into rain water and put into food. But Macon came out of his few days of sexual hypnosis in a rage and later when he discovered her pregnancy, tried to get her to abort. Then the baby became the nausea caused by the half ounce of castor oil Macon made her drink, then a hot pot recently emptied of scalding water on which she sat, then a soapy enema, a knitting needle (she inserted only the tip, squatting in the bathroom, crying, afraid of the man who paced outside the door), and finally, when he punched her stomach (she had been about to pick up his breakfast plate, when he looked at her stomach and punched it), she ran to Southside looking for Pilate. She had never walked through that part of town, but she knew the street Pilate lived on, though not the house. Pilate had no telephone and no number on her house. Ruth had asked some passer-by where Pilate lived and was directed to a lean brown house set back from the unpaved road. Pilate was sitting on a chair; Reba was cutting Pilate's hair with a barber's clippers. That was the first time she saw Hagar, who was four or five years old then. Chubby, with four long braids, two like horns over each ear, two like tails at the back of her neck. Pilate comforted Ruth, gave her a peach, which Ruth could not eat because the fuzz made her sick. She listened to what Ruth said and sent Reba to the store for a box of Argo cornstarch. She sprinkled a little of it into her hand and offered it to Ruth, who obediently took a lump and put it in her mouth. As soon as she tasted it, felt its crunchiness, she asked for more, and ate half a box before she left. (From then on she ate cornstarch, cracked ice, nuts, and once in a fit she put a few tiny pebbles of gravel in her mouth. "When you expectin, you have to eat what the baby craves," Pilate said, " 'less it come in the world hongry for what you denied it." Ruth could not bite enough. Her teeth were on edge with the yearning. Like the impulse of a cat to claw, she searched for crunchy things, and when there was nothing, she would grind her teeth.)

Gnashing the cornstarch, Ruth let Pilate lead her into the bedroom, where the woman wrapped her in a homemade-on-the-spot girdle—tight in the crotch—and told her to keep it on until the fourth month and "don't take no more mess off Macon and don't ram another thing up in your womb." She also told her not to worry. Macon wouldn't bother her no more; she, Pilate, would see to it. (Years later Ruth learned that Pilate put a small doll on Macon's chair in his office. A male doll with a small painted chicken bone stuck between its legs and a round red circle painted on its belly. Macon knocked it out of the chair and with a yardstick pushed it into the bathroom, where he doused it with alcohol and burned it. It took nine separate burnings before the fire got down to the straw and cotton ticking of its insides. But he must have remembered the round fire-red stomach, for he left Ruth alone after that.)

When the baby was born the day after she stood in the snow, with cloth roses at her feet and a man with blue wings above her head, she regarded him as a beautiful toy, a respite, a distraction, a physical pleasure as she nursed him—until Freddie (again Freddie) caught her at it; then he was no longer her velveteened toy. He became a plain on which, like the cowboys and Indians in the movies, she and her husband fought. Each one befuddled by the values of the other. Each one convinced of his own purity and outraged by the idiocy he saw in the other. She was the Indian, of course, and lost her land, her customs, her integrity to the cowboy and became a spread-eagled footstool resigned to her fate and holding fast to tiny irrelevant defiances.

But who was this son of hers? This tall man who had flesh on the outside and feelings on the inside that she knew nothing of, but somebody did, knew enough about him to want to kill him. Suddenly, the world opened up for her like one of her imperial tulips and revealed its evil yellow pistil. She had been husbanding her own misery, shaping it, making of it an art and a Way. Now she saw a larger, more malevolent world outside her own. Outside the fourposter bed where Doctor had bubbled and rotted (all but his beautiful hands, which were the only things his grandson had inherited). Outside her garden and the fishbowl where her goldfish died. She had thought it was all done. That she had won out over the castor oil, and the pot of steam that had puckered and burned her skin so she could not bear to urinate or sit with her daughters at the table where they cut and sewed. She had had the baby anyway, and although it did nothing to close the break between herself and Macon, there he was, her single triumph.

Now Freddie was telling her that it wasn't done and over yet. Somebody was still trying to kill him. To deprive her of the one aggressive act brought to royal completion. And the person who was threatening his life was someone who shared Macon's blood.

"That hurts," she said aloud to Freddie as she folded into her pocket the rent money he handed her. "That hurts, you know."

She climbed the porch steps and went into the kitchen. Without knowing what her foot was planning to do, she kicked the cabinet door with the worn lock under the sink. It answered her kick with a tiny whine before it sneaked open again. Ruth looked at it and kicked it closed once more. Again it whined and opened right back up.

"I want you closed," she whispered. "Closed."

The door stayed open.

"Closed. You hear me? Closed. Closed. Closed." She was screaming by now.

Magdalene called Lena, hearing her shouts, ran down the stairs and into the kitchen. She found her mother staring at the sink and commanding it.

"Mother?" Lena was frightened.

Ruth looked up at her. "What is it?"

"I don't know. . . . I thought I heard you saying something."

"Get somebody to fix that door. I want it shut. Tight."

Lena stared as Ruth hurried past and when she heard her mother running up the stairs, she put her fingers to her lips in disbelief. Ruth was sixty-two years old. Lena had no idea she could move that fast.

Her passions were narrow but deep. Long deprived of sex, long dependent on self-manipulation, she saw her son's imminent death as the annihilation of the last occasion she had been made love to.

With the same determined tread that took her to the graveyard six or seven times a year, Ruth left the house and caught the number 26 bus and sat down right in back of the driver. She took her glasses off and wiped them on the hem of her skirt. She was serene and purposeful as always when death turned his attention to someone who belonged to her, as she was when death breathed in her father's wispy hair and blew the strands about. She had the same calmness and efficiency with which she cared for the doctor, putting her hand on death's chest and holding him back, denying him, keeping her father alive even past the point where he wanted to be alive, past pain on into disgust and horror at having to smell himself in his next breath. Past that until he was too sick to fight her efforts to keep him alive, lingering in absolute hatred of this woman who would not grant him peace, but kept her shining lightish eyes fixed on him like magnets holding him from the narrow earth he longed for.

Ruth wiped her glasses clean so she could see the street signs as they passed ("Eat cherries," Pilate had told her, "and you won't have to wear them little windows over your eyes"), her mind empty except for getting there—to Darling Street, where Pilate lived and where, she supposed, Hagar lived too. How had that chubby little girl weighed down with hair become a knife-wielding would-be killer out to get her son? Maybe Freddie lied. Maybe. She'd see.

When the banks disappeared and small shops in between rickety houses came into view, Ruth pulled the cord. She stepped down and walked toward the underpass that cut across Darling Street. It was a long walk and she was sweating by the time she got to Pilate's house. The door was open, but nobody was inside. The house smelled fruity and she remembered how the peach had nauseated her the last time she was there. Here was the chair she had collapsed in. There the candlemaker's rack, the pan where Pilate's homemade soap hardened into a yellowish-brown slab. This house had been a haven then, and in spite of the cold anger she felt now, it still looked like an inn, a safe harbor. A flypaper roll entirely free of flies curled down from the ceiling not far from a sack that hung there too. Ruth looked into the bedroom and saw three little beds, and like Goldilocks, she walked over to the nearest one and sat down. There was no back door to this two-room house, just a big room where they lived and this bedroom. It had a cellar that one could enter only from the outside under a metal door that slanted away from the house and opened onto stone stairs.

Ruth sat still, letting the anger and determination jell. She wondered whose bed it was and lifted up the blanket and saw only mattress ticking. The same was true of the next bed, but not of the third. It had sheets, a pillow, and a pillow slip. That would be Hagar's, she thought. The anger unjelled and flooded through her. She left the room, pressing her fury back so she would be able to wait and wait until somebody returned. Pacing the floor of the outer room, her elbows in the palms of her hands, she suddenly heard humming that seemed to be coming from the back of the house. Pilate, she thought. Pilate hummed and chewed things all the time. Ruth would ask her first if what Freddie said was true. She needed Pilate's calm view, her honesty and equilibrium. Then she would know what to do. Whether to unfold her arms and let the rage out to do whatever it might, or . . . She tasted again the Argo cornstarch and felt the marvelous biting and crunching it allowed her. Now she merely ground her teeth as she stepped out to the porch and made her way around the side of the house through the nicotiana growing all wild and out of control.

A woman sat on a bench, her hands clasped between her knees. It was not Pilate. Ruth stood still and looked at the woman's back. It didn't look like death's back at all. It looked vulnerable, soft, like an easily wounded shin, full of bone but susceptible to the slightest pain.

"Reba?" she said.

The woman turned around and fastened on her the most sorrowful eyes Ruth had ever seen.

"Reba's gone," she said, the second word sounding as if the going were permanent. "Can I do something for you?"

"I'm Ruth Foster."

Hagar stiffened. A lightning shot of excitement ran through her. Milkman's mother: the silhouette she had seen through the curtains in an upstairs window on evenings when she stood across the street hoping at first to catch him, then hoping just to see him, finally just to be near the things he was familiar with. Private vigils held at night, made more private because they were expressions of public lunacy. The outline she'd seen once or twice when the side door opened and a woman shook crumbs from a tablecloth or dust from a small rug onto the ground. Whatever Milkman had told her about his mother, whatever she had heard from Pilate and Reba, she could not remember, so overwhelmed was she in the presence of *his* mother. Hagar let her morbid pleasure spread across her face in a smile.

Ruth was not impressed. Death always smiled. And breathed. And looked helpless like a shinbone, or a tiny speck of black on the Queen Elizabeth roses, or film on the eye of a dead goldfish.

"You are trying to kill him." Ruth's voice was matter-of-fact. "If you so much as bend a hair on his head, so help me Jesus, I will tear your throat out."

Hagar looked surprised. She loved nothing in the world except this woman's son, wanted him alive more than anybody, but hadn't the least bit of control over the predator that lived inside her. Totally taken over by her anaconda love, she had no self left, no fears, no wants, no intelligence that was her own. So it was with a great deal of earnestness that she replied to Ruth. "I'll try not to. But I can't make you a for-certain promise."

Ruth heard the supplication in her words and it seemed to her that she was not looking at a person but at an impulse, a cell, a red corpuscle that neither knows nor understands why it is driven to spend its whole life in one pursuit: swimming up a dark tunnel toward the muscle of a heart or an eye's nerve end that it both nourished and fed from.

Hagar lowered her eyelids and gazed hungrily down the figure of the woman who had been only a silhouette to her. The woman who slept in the same house with him, and who could call him home and he would come, who knew the mystery of his flesh, had memory of him as long as his life. The woman who knew him, had watched his teeth appear, stuck her finger in his mouth to soothe his gums. Cleaned his behind, Vaselined his penis, and caught his vomit in a fresh white diaper. Had fed him from her own nipples, carried him close and warm and safe under her heart, and who had opened her legs far far wider than she herself ever had for him. Who even now could walk freely into his room if she wanted to and smell his clothes, stroke his shoes, and lay her head on the very spot where he had lain his. But what was more, so much more, this thin lemon-yellow woman knew with absolute certainty what Hagar would willingly have her throat torn out to know: that she would see him this very day. Jealousy loomed so large in her it made her tremble. Maybe you, she thought. Maybe it's you I should be killing. Maybe then he will come to me and let me come to him. He is my home in this world. And then, aloud, "He is my home in this world."

"And I am his," said Ruth.

"And he wouldn't give a pile of swan shit for either one of you."

They turned then and saw Pilate leaning on the window sill. Neither knew how long she'd been there.

"Can't say as I blame him neither. Two growed-up women

talkin 'bout a man like he was a house or needed one. He ain't a house, he's a man, and whatever he need, don't none of you got it."

"Leave me alone, Mama. Just leave me alone."

"You already alone. If you want more alone, I can knock you into the middle of next week, and leave you there."

"You're botherin me!" Hagar was shouting and digging her fingers in her hair. It was an ordinary gesture of frustration, but its awkwardness made Ruth know that there was something truly askew in this girl. That here was the wilderness of Southside. Not the poverty or dirt or noise, not just extreme unregulated passion where even love found its way with an ice pick, but the absence of control. Here one lived knowing that at any time, anybody might do anything. Not wilderness where there was system, or the logic of lions, trees, toads, and birds, but wild wilderness where there was none.

She had not recognized it in Pilate, whose equilibrium overshadowed all her eccentricities and who was, in any case, the only person she knew of strong enough to counter Macon. Although Ruth had been frightened of her the first time she saw her—when she knocked on the kitchen door way back then, looking, as she said, for her brother Macon. (Ruth was still frightened of her a little. Not just her short hair cut regularly like a man's, or her large sleepy eyes and busy lips, or the smooth smooth skin, hairless, scarless, and wrinkleless. For Ruth had actually seen it. The place on her stomach where a navel should have been and was not. Even if you weren't frightened of a woman who had no navel, you certainly had to take her very seriously.)

Now she held up her hand, imperiously, and silenced Hagar's whines.

"Sit down there. Sit down and don't leave this yard."

Hagar slumped and moved slowly back to her bench.

Pilate turned her eyes to Ruth. "Come on in. Rest yourself before you hop on that bus again."

They sat down at the table facing each other.

"Peaches kind of dried up on me in this heat," said Pilate, and she reached for a peck basket which held about a half dozen. "But there should be some good ones left in here. Can I slice you up some?"

"No, thank you," said Ruth. She was trembling a little now. After the tension, the anger, the bravado of her earlier state of mind, followed by the violence of Pilate's words to her granddaughter, this quiet social-tea tone disarmed her, threw her too soon and too suddenly back into the mannered dignity that was habitual for her. Ruth pressed her hands together in her lap to stop the shaking.

They were so different, these two women. One black, the other lemony. One corseted, the other buck naked under her dress. One well read but ill traveled. The other had read only a geography book, but had been from one end of the country to another. One wholly dependent on money for life, the other indifferent to it. But those were the meaningless things. Their similarities were profound. Both were vitally interested in Macon Dead's son, and both had close and supportive posthumous communication with their fathers.

"The last time I was here you offered me a peach. My visit was about my son then too."

Pilate nodded her head and with her right thumbnail slit the peach open.

"You won't never be able to forgive her. For just tryin to do it you won't never be able to forgive her. But it looks to me like you ought to be able to understand her. Think on it a minute. You ready now to kill her—well, maim her anyway—because she's tryin to take him away from you. She's the enemy to you because she wants to take him out of your life. Well, in her eyes there's somebody who wants to take him out of her life too—him. So he's her enemy. He's the one who's tryin to take himself out of her life. And she'll kill him before she lets him do that. What I'm sayin is that you both got the same idea.

"I do my best to keep her from it. She's my baby too, you know, but I tear her up every time she try. Just for the tryin, mind you, because I know one thing sure: she'll never pull it off. He come in the world tryin to keep from gettin killed. Layin in your stomach, his own papa was tryin to do it. And you helped some too. He had to fight off castor oil and knittin needles and being blasted with hot steam and I don't know what all you and Macon did. But he made it. When he was at his most helpless, he made it. Ain't nothin goin to kill him but his own ignorance, and won't no woman ever kill him. What's likelier is that it'll be a woman save his life."

"Nobody lives forever, Pilate."

"Don't?"

"Of course not."

"Nobody?"

"Of course, nobody."

"I don't see why not."

"Death is as natural as life."

"Ain't nothin natural about death. It's the most unnatural thing they is."

"You think people should live forever?"

"Some people. Yeah."

"Who's to decide? Which ones should live and which ones shouldn't?"

"The people themselves. Some folks want to live forever. Some don't. I believe they decide on it anyway. People die when they want to and if they want to. Don't nobody have to die if they don't want to."

Ruth felt a chill. She'd always believed that her father wanted to die. "I wish I could count on your faith as far as my son was concerned. But I think I'd be a really foolish woman if I did that. You saw your own father die, just like I did; you saw him killed. Do you think he wanted to die?"

"I saw Papa shot. Blown off a fence five feet into the air. I saw him wigglin on the ground, but not only did I not see him die, I seen him since he was shot."

"Pilate. You all buried him yourselves." Ruth spoke as if she were talking to a child.

"Macon did."

"It's the same thing."

"Macon seen him too. After he buried him, after he was blown off that fence. We both seen him. I see him still. He's helpful to me, real helpful. Tells me things I need to know."

"What things?"

"All kinds of things. It's a good feelin to know he's around. I tell you he's a person I can always rely on. I tell you somethin else. He's the *only* one. I was cut off from people early. You can't know what that was like. After my papa was blown off that fence, me and Macon wandered around for a few days until we had a fallin out and I went off on my own. I was about twelve, I think. When I cut out by myself, I headed for Virginia. I thought I remembered that was where my papa had people. Or my mother did. Seemed to me like I remembered somebody sayin that. I don't remember my mother because she died before I was born."

"*Before* you were born? How could she . . . ?"

"She died and the next minute I was born. But she was dead by the time I drew air. I never saw her face. I don't even know what her name was. But I do remember thinkin she come from Virginia. Anyways, that's where I struck out for. I looked around for somebody to take me in, give me a little work for a while so I could earn some money to get on down there. I walked for seven days before I found a place with a preacher's family. A nice place except they made me wear shoes. They sent me to school, though. A one-room place, where everybody sat. I was twelve, but since this was my first school I had to sit over there with the little bitty children. I didn't mind it too much; matter of fact, I liked a lot of it. I loved the geography part. Learning about that made me want to read. And the teacher was tickled at how much I liked geography. She let me have the book and I took it home with me to look at. But then the preacher started pattin on me. I was so dumb I didn't know enough to stop him. But his wife caught him at it, thumbin my breasts, and put me out. I took my geography book off with me.

I could of stayed in that town cause they was plenty of colored people to take me in. In them days, anybody too old to work kept the children. Grown folks worked and left their kids in other people's houses. But him being the preacher and all like that, I figured I ought to make tracks. I was broke as a haint cause the place didn't carry no wages. Just room and board. So I just took my geography book and a rock I picked up for a souvenir and lit out.

"It was a Sunday when I met up with some pickers. Folks call 'em migrants nowadays; then they was just called pickers. They took me in and treated me fine. I worked up in New York State pickin beans, then we'd move to another place and pick a different crop. Everyplace I went I got me a rock. They was about four or five families all together in the crew. All of them related one way or another. But they was good people and treated me fine. I stayed with them for three years, I believe, and the main reason I stayed on was a woman there I took to. A root worker. She taught me a lot and kept me from missin my own family, Macon and Papa. I didn't have a thought in my head of ever leavin them, but I did. I had to. After a while they didn't want me around no more." Pilate sucked a peach stone and her face was dark and still with the memory of how she was "cut off" so early from other people.

The boy. The nephew, or was it the cousin, of the woman who worked roots. When she was fifteen, and the rain was so heavy they had to stay in the shacks (those who had them–the others had tents) because nothing could be harvested in that pouring rain, the boy and Pilate lay down together. He was no older than she was and while everything about her delighted him, nothing about her surprised him. So it was with no malice whatsoever that one evening after supper he mentioned to some of the men (but within listening distance of the women) that he didn't know that some folks had navels and some didn't. The men and the women raised their eyes at his remark, and asked him to explain what he meant. He got it out, finally, after many false starts–he thought they were alarmed because he had taken the pretty girl with the single earring to bed—but he soon discovered that the navel thing was what bothered them.

The root woman was assigned the job of finding out if what he said was true or not. She called Pilate into her shack one day later. "Lay down," she said. "I want to check on something." Pilate lay down on the straw pallet. "Now lift up your dress," the woman said. "More. All the way up. Higher." And then her eyes flew open wide and she put her hand over her mouth. Pilate leaped up. "What? What is it?" She looked down at herself, thinking a snake or a poisonous spider had crawled over her legs.

"Nothin," the woman said. Then, "Child, where's your navel?"

Pilate had never heard the word "navel" and didn't know what the woman was talking about. She looked down at her legs, parted on the rough ticking. "Navel?" she asked.

"You know. This." And the woman pulled up her own dress and slipped the elastic of her bloomers down over her fat stomach. Pilate saw the little corkscrew thing right in the middle, the little piece of skin that looked like it was made for water to drain down into, like the little whirlpools along the edges of a creek. It was just like the thing her brother had on his stomach. He had one. She did not. He peed standing up. She squatting down. He had a penis like a horse did. She had a vagina like the mare. He had a flat chest with two nipples. She had teats like the cow. He had a corkscrew in his stomach. She did not. She thought it was one more way in which males and females were different. The boy she went to bed with had one too. But until now she had never seen another woman's stomach. And from the horror on the older woman's face she knew there was something wrong with not having it.

"What's it for?" she asked.

The woman swallowed. "It's for . . . it's for people who were born natural."

Pilate didn't understand that, but she did understand the conversation she had later with the root worker and some other women in the camp. She was to leave. They were very sorry, they liked her and all, and she was such a good worker and a big help to everybody. But she had to leave just the same.

"On account of my stomach?" But the women would not answer her. They looked at the ground.

Pilate left with more than her share of earnings, because the women did not want her to go away angry. They thought she might hurt them in some way if she got angry, and they also felt pity along with their terror of having been in the company of something God never made.

Pilate went away. Again she headed for Virginia. But now she knew how to harvest in a team and looked for another migrant crew, or a group of women who had followed their men to some seasonal work as brickmakers, iron workers, shipyard workers. In her three years picking, she had seen a number of these women, their belongings stuffed into wagons heading for the towns and cities that sought out and transported black men to various crafts that could be practiced only when the weather permitted. The companies did not encourage the women to come—they did not want an influx of poor colored settlers in those towns—but the women came anyway and took jobs as domestics and farm helpers in the towns, and lived wherever housing was free or dirt cheap. But Pilate did not want a steady job in a town where a lot of colored people lived. All her encounters with Negroes who had established themselves in businesses or trades in those small midwestern towns had been unpleasant. Their wives did not like the trembling unhampered breasts under her dress, and told her so. And though the men saw many raggedy black children, Pilate was old enough to disgrace them. Besides, she wanted to keep moving.

Finally she was taken on by some pickers heading home, stopping for a week's work here and there, wherever they could find it. Again she took a man to bed, and again she was expelled. Only this time there was no polite but firm pronouncement, nor any generous share of profits. They simply left her one day, moved out while she was in the town buying thread. She got back to campground to find nothing but a dying fire, a bag of rocks, and her geography book propped up on a tree. They even took her tin cup.

She had six copper pennies, five rocks, the geography book, and two spools of black thread—heavyweight No. 30. Right there she knew she must decide on whether to get to Virginia or settle in a town where she would probably have to wear shoes. So she did both—the latter to make the former possible. With the six pennies, the book, the rocks, and the thread, she walked back to town. Black women worked in numbers at two places in that town: the laundry and, across the street from it, the hotel/whorehouse. Pilate chose the laundry and walked in, saying to the three young girls elbow deep in water there, "Can I stay here tonight?"

"Nobody in here at night."

"I know. Can I stay?"

They shrugged. The next day Pilate was hired as a washerwoman at ten cents a day. She worked there, ate there, slept there, and saved her dimes. Her hands, well calloused from years of harvesting, were stripped of their toughness and became soft in the wash water. Before her hands could get the different but equally tough skin of a laundress, her knuckles split with the rubbing and wringing, and ran blood into the rinse tubs. She almost ruined an entire batch of sheets, but the other girls covered for her, giving the sheets a second rinse.

One day she noticed a train steaming away from the town. "Where does it go to?" she asked.

"South," they said.

"How much does it cost?"

They laughed. "They freight trains," they told her. Only two passenger cars, and no colored allowed.

"Well, how do colored people get where they want to go?"

"Ain't supposed to go nowhere," they said, "but if they do, have to go by wagon. Ask at the livery stable when the next wagon is going down. The livery people always know when somebody is getting ready to take off."

She did, and by the end of October, just before cold weather set in, she was on her way to West Virginia, which was close anyway, according to her geography book. When she got to Virginia itself, she realized that she didn't know in what part of the state to look for her people. There were more Negroes there than she'd ever seen, and the comfort she felt in their midst she kept all her life.

Pilate had learned, whenever she was asked her name, to give only her first name. The last name had a bad effect on people. Now she was forced to ask if anybody knew of a family called Dead. People frowned and said, "No, never heard of any such."

She was in Culpeper, Virginia, washing clothes in a hotel, when she learned that there was a colony of Negro farmers on an island off the coast of Virginia. They grew vegetables, had cattle, made whiskey, and sold a little tobacco. They did not mix much with other Negroes, but were respected by them and self-sustaining. And you could get to them only by boat. On a Sunday, she convinced the ferryman to take her there, when his work was done, in his skiff.

"What you want over there?" he asked.

"Work."

"You don't want to work over there," he said.

"Why not?"

"Them folks keep to theyselves too much."

"Take me. I'll pay."

"How much?"

"A nickel."

"Great Jesus! You on. Be here at nine-thirty."

There were twenty-five or thirty families on that island and when Pilate made it clear that she wasn't afraid of work, but didn't like the mainland and the confinement of town, she was taken in. She worked there for three months, hoeing, fishing, plowing, planting, and helping out at the stills. All she had to do, she thought, was keep her belly covered. And it was true. At sixteen now, she took a lover from one of the island families and managed to keep direct light from ever hitting her stomach. She also managed to get pregnant, and to the great consternation of the island women, who were convinced their menfolk were the most desirable on earth—which accounted for so much intermarrying among them—Pilate refused to marry the man, who was eager to take her for his wife. Pilate was afraid that she wouldn't be able to hide her stomach from a husband forever. And once he saw that uninterrupted flesh, he would respond the same way everybody else had. Yet, incredible as they found her decision, nobody asked her to leave. They watched over her and gave her fewer and lighter chores as her time drew near. When her baby was born, a girl, the two midwives in attendance were so preoccupied with what was going on between her legs they never even noticed her smooth balloon of a stomach.

The first thing the new mother looked for in her baby girl was the navel, which she was relieved to see. Remembering how she got the name that was folded in her ear, when the nine days' waiting was done she asked one of the women for a Bible. There was a hymnal, they said, but not a Bible on the island. Everybody who wanted to go to services had to go to the mainland.

"Can you tell me a nice name for a girl that's in the Bible?" Pilate asked.

"Oh, plenty," they said, and reeled off a score, from which she chose Rebecca and shortened it to Reba.

It was right after Reba was born that her father came to her again. Pilate had become extremely depressed and lonely after the birth. The baby's father was forbidden to see her, since she had not "healed" yet, and she spent some dark lonely hours along with the joyous ones with the baby. Clear as day, her father said, "Sing. Sing," and later he leaned in at the window and said, "You just can't fly on off and leave a body."

Pilate understood all of what he told her. To sing, which she did beautifully, relieved her gloom immediately. And she knew he was telling her to go back to Pennsylvania and collect what was left of the man she and Macon had murdered. (The fact that she had struck no blow was irrelevant. She was part of her brother's act, because, then, she and he were one.) When the child was six months old, she asked the mother of the baby's father to keep it, and left the island for Pennsylvania. They tried to discourage her because it was getting to be winter, but she paid them no attention.

A month later she returned with a sack, the contents of which she never discussed, which she added to her geography book and the rocks and the two spools of thread.

When Reba was two years old, Pilate was seized with restlessness. It was as if her geography book had marked her to roam the country, planting her feet in each pink, yellow, blue or green state. She left the island and began the wandering life that she kept up for the next twenty-some-odd years, and stopped only after Reba had a baby. No place was like the island ever again. Having had one long relationship with a man, she sought another, but no man was like that island man ever again either.

After a while, she stopped worrying about her stomach, and stopped trying to hide it. It occurred to her that although men fucked armless women, one-legged women, hunchbacks and blind women, drunken women, razor-toting women, midgets, small children, convicts, boys, sheep, dogs, goats, liver, each other, and even certain species of plants, they were terrified of fucking her—a woman with no navel. They froze at the sight of that belly that looked like a back; became limp even, or cold, if she happened to undress completely and walked straight toward them, showing them, deliberately, a stomach as blind as a knee.

"What are you? Some kinda *mer*maid?" one man had shouted, and reached hurriedly for his socks.

It isolated her. Already without family, she was further isolated from her people, for, except for the relative bliss on the island, every other resource was denied her: partnership in marriage, confessional friendship, and communal religion. Men frowned, women whispered and shoved their children behind them. Even a traveling side show would have rejected her, since her freak quality lacked that important ingredient—the grotesque. There was really nothing to see. Her defect, frightening and exotic as it was, was also a theatrical failure. It needed intimacy, gossip, and the time it took for curiosity to become drama.

Finally Pilate began to take offense. Although she was hampered by huge ignorances, but not in any way unintelligent, when she realized what her situation in the world was and would probably always be she threw away every assumption she had learned and began at zero. First off, she cut her hair. That was one thing she didn't want to have to think about anymore. Then she tackled the problem of trying to decide how she wanted to live and what was valuable to her. When am I happy and when am I sad and what is the difference? What do I need to know to stay alive? What is true in the world? Her mind traveled crooked streets and aimless goat paths, arriving sometimes at profundity, other times at the revelations of a three-year-old. Throughout this fresh, if common, pursuit of knowledge, one conviction crowned her efforts: since death held no terrors for her (she spoke often to the dead), she knew there was nothing to fear. That plus her alien's compassion for troubled people ripened her and—the consequence of the knowledge she had made up or acquired—kept her just barely within the boundaries of the elaborately socialized world of black people. Her dress might be outrageous to them, but her respect for other people's privacy—which they were all very intense about—was balancing. She stared at people, and in those days looking straight into another person's eyes was considered among black people the height of rudeness, an act acceptable only with and among children and certain kinds of outlaws—but she never made an impolite observation. And true to the palm oil that flowed in her veins, she never had a visitor to whom she did not offer food before one word of conversation—business or social—began. She laughed but never smiled and in 1963, when she was sixty-eight years old, she had not shed a tear since Circe had brought her cherry jam for breakfast.

She gave up, apparently, all interest in table manners or hygiene, but acquired a deep concern for and about human relationships. Those twelve years in Montour County, where she had been treated gently by a father and a brother, and where she herself was in a position to help farm animals under her care, had taught her a preferable kind of behavior. Preferable to that of the men who called her mermaid and the women who swept up her footprints or put mirrors on her door.

She was a natural healer, and among quarreling drunks and fighting women she could hold her own, and sometimes mediated a peace that lasted a good bit longer than it should have because it was administered by someone not like them. But most important, she paid close attention to her mentor—the father who appeared before her sometimes and told her things. After Reba was born, he no longer came to Pilate dressed as he had been on the woods' edge and in the cave, when she and Macon had left Circe's house. Then he had worn the coveralls and heavy shoes he was shot in. Now he came in a white shirt, a blue collar, and a brown peaked cap. He wore no shoes (they were tied together and slung over his shoulder), probably because his feet hurt, since he rubbed his toes a lot as he sat near her bed or on the porch, or rested against the side of the still. Along with winemaking, cooking whiskey became the way Pilate began to make her steady living. That skill allowed her more freedom hour by hour and day by day than any other work a woman of no means whatsoever and no inclination to make love for money could choose. Once settled in as a small-time bootlegger in the colored section of a town, she had only occasional police or sheriff problems, for she allowed none of the activities that often accompanied wine houses—women, gambling—and she more often than not refused to let her customers drink what they bought from her on the premises. She made and sold liquor. Period.

After Reba grew up and began to live from one orgasm to another, taking time out to produce one child, Hagar, Pilate thought it might be time for a change. Not because of Reba, who was quite content with the life her mother and she lived, but because of her granddaughter. Hagar was prissy. She hated, even as a two-year-old, dirt and disorganization. At three she was already vain and beginning to be proud. She liked pretty clothes. Astonished as Pilate and Reba were by her wishes, they enjoyed trying to fulfill them. They spoiled her, and she, as a favor to their indulgence, hid as best she could the fact that they embarrassed her.

Pilate decided to find her brother, if he was still alive, for the child, Hagar, needed family, people, a life very different from what she and Reba could offer, and if she remembered anything about Macon, he would be different. Prosperous, conventional, more like the things and people Hagar seemed to admire. In addition, Pilate wanted to make peace between them. She asked her father where he was, but he just rubbed his feet and shook his head. So for the first time, Pilate went voluntarily to the police, who sent her to the Red Cross, who sent her to the Salvation Army, who sent her to the Society of Friends, who sent her back to the Salvation Army, who wrote to their command posts in large cities from New York to St. Louis and from Detroit to Louisiana and asked them to look in the telephone directory, where in fact one captain's secretary found him listed. Pilate was surprised that they were successful, but the captain was not, because there could hardly be many people with such a name.

They made the trip in style (one train and two buses), for Pilate had a lot of money; the crash of 1929 had produced so many buyers of cheap home brew she didn't even need the collection the Salvation Army took up for her. She arrived with suitcases, a green sack, a full-grown daughter, and a granddaughter, and found her brother truculent, inhospitable, embarrassed, and unforgiving. Pilate would have moved on immediately except for her brother's wife, who was dying of lovelessness then, and seemed to be dying of it now as she sat at the table across from her sister-in-law listening to her life story, which Pilate was making deliberately long to keep Ruth's mind off Hagar.

Chapter 6

"I took her home. She was standing in the middle of the room when I got there. So I just took her home. Pitiful. Really pitiful."

Milkman shrugged. He didn't want to talk about Hagar, but it was a way to sit Guitar down and get around to asking him something else.

"What'd you do to her?" asked Guitar.

"What'd I do to *her?* You saw her with a butcher knife and you ask me that?"

"I mean before. That's a messed-up lady."

"I did what you do to some woman every six months—called the whole thing off."

"I don't believe you."

"It's the truth."

"No. It had to be something more."

"You calling me a liar?"

"Take it any way you want. But that girl's hurt—and the hurt came from you."

"What's the matter with you? You've been watching her try

to kill me for months and I never laid a hand on her. Now you sit there worried about her. All of a sudden you're police. You've been wearing a halo a lot lately. You got a white robe too?"

"What's that supposed to mean?"

"It means I'm tired of being criticized by you. I know we don't see eye to eye on a lot of things. I know you think I'm lazy—not serious, you say—but if we're friends . . . I don't meddle you, do I?"

"No. Not at all."

Several minutes passed while Milkman played with his beer and Guitar sipped tea. They were sitting in Mary's Place on a Sunday afternoon a few days after Hagar's latest attempt on his life.

"You're not smoking?" asked Milkman.

"No. I quit. Feel a hell of a lot better too." There was another pause before Guitar continued. "You ought to stop yourself."

Milkman nodded. "Yeah. If I stay around you I will. I'll stop smoking, fucking, drinking—everything. I'll take up a secret life and hanging out with Empire State."

Guitar frowned. "Now who's meddling?"

Milkman sighed and looked straight at his friend. "I am. I want to know why you were running around with Empire State last Christmas."

"He was in trouble. I helped him."

"That's all?"

"What else?"

"I don't know what else. But I know there is something else. Now, if it's something I can't know, okay, say so. But something's going on with you. And I'd like to know what it is."

Guitar didn't answer.

"We've been friends a long time, Guitar. There's nothing you don't know about me. I can tell you anything—whatever our differences, I know I can trust you. But for some time now it's been a one-way street. You know what I mean? I talk to you, but you don't talk to me. You don't think I can be trusted?"

"I don't know if you can or not."

"Try me."

"I can't. Other people are involved."

"Then don't tell me about other people; tell me about you."

Guitar looked at him for a long time. Maybe, he thought. Maybe I can trust you. Maybe not, but I'll risk it anyway because one day . . .

"Okay," he said aloud, "but you have to know that what I tell you can't go any further. And if it does, you'll be dropping a rope around my neck. Now do you still want to know it?"

"Yeah."

"You sure?"

"I'm sure."

Guitar poured some more hot water over his tea. He looked into his cup for a minute while the leaves settled slowly to the bottom. "I suppose you know that white people kill black people from time to time, and most folks shake their heads and say, 'Eh, eh, eh, ain't that a shame?' "

Milkman raised his eyebrows. He thought Guitar was going to let him in on some deal he had going. But he was slipping into his race bag. He was speaking slowly, as though each word had to count, and as though he were listening carefully to his own words. "I can't suck my teeth or say 'Eh, eh, eh.' I had to do something. And the only thing left to do is balance it; keep things on an even keel. Any man, any woman, or any child is good for five to seven generations of heirs before they're bred out. So every death is the death of five to seven generations. You can't stop them from killing us, from trying to get rid of us. And each time they succeed, they get rid of five to seven generations. I help keep the numbers the same.

"There is a society. It's made up of a few men who are willing to take some risks. They don't initiate anything; they don't even choose. They are as indifferent as rain. But when a Negro child, Negro woman, or Negro man is killed by whites and nothing is done about it by *their* law and *their* courts, this society selects a similar victim at random, and they execute him or her in a similar manner if they can. If the Negro was hanged, they hang; if a Negro was burnt, they burn; raped and murdered, they rape and murder. If they can. If they can't do it precisely in the same manner, they do it any way they can, but they do it. They call themselves the Seven Days. They are made up of seven men. Always seven and only seven. If one of them dies or leaves or is no longer effective, another is chosen. Not right away, because that kind of choosing takes time. But they don't seem to be in a hurry. Their secret is time. To take the time, to last. Not to grow; that's dangerous because you might become known. They don't write their names in toilet stalls or brag to women. Time and silence. Those are their weapons, and they go on forever.

"It got started in 1920, when that private from Georgia was killed after his balls were cut off and after that veteran was blinded when he came home from France in World War I. And it's been operating ever since. I am one of them now."

Milkman had held himself very still all the time Guitar spoke. Now he felt tight, shriveled, and cold.

"You? You're going to kill people?"

"Not people. White people."

"But why?"

"I just told you. It's necessary; it's got to be done. To keep the ratio the same."

"And if it isn't done? If it just goes on the way it has?"

"Then the world is a zoo, and I can't live in it."

"Why don't you just hunt down the ones who did the killing? Why kill innocent people? Why not just those who did it?"

"It doesn't matter who did it. Each and every one of them could do it. So you just get any one of them. There are no innocent white people, because every one of them is a potential nigger-killer, if not an actual one. You think Hitler surprised them? You think just because they went to war they thought he was a freak? Hitler's the most natural white man in the world. He killed Jews and Gypsies because he didn't have us. Can you see those Klansmen shocked by him? No, you can't."

"But people who lynch and slice off people's balls—they're crazy, Guitar, crazy."

"Every time somebody does a thing like that to one of us,

they say the people who did it were crazy or ignorant. That's like saying they were drunk. Or constipated. Why isn't cutting a man's eyes out, cutting his nuts off, the kind of thing you never get too drunk or ignorant to do? Too crazy to do? Too constipated to do? And more to the point, how come Negroes, the craziest, most ignorant people in America, don't get that crazy and that ignorant? No. White people are unnatural. As a race they are unnatural. And it takes a strong effort of the will to overcome an unnatural enemy."

"What about the nice ones? Some whites made sacrifices for Negroes. Real sacrifices."

"That just means there are one or two natural ones. But they haven't been able to stop the killing either. They are outraged, but that doesn't stop it. They might even speak out, but that doesn't stop it either. They might even inconvenience themselves, but the killing goes on and on. So will we."

"You're missing the point. There're not just one or two. There're a lot."

"Are there? Milkman, if Kennedy got drunk and bored and was sitting around a potbellied stove in Mississippi, he might join a lynching party just for the hell of it. Under those circumstances his unnaturalness would surface. But I know I wouldn't join one no matter how drunk I was or how bored, and I know you wouldn't either, nor any black man I know or ever heard tell of. Ever. In any world, at any time, just get up and go find somebody white to slice up. But they *can* do it. And they don't even do it for profit, which is why they do most things. They do it for fun. Unnatural."

"What about . . ." Milkman searched his memory for some white person who had shown himself unequivocally supportive of Negroes. "Schweitzer. Albert Schweitzer. Would he do it?"

"In a minute. He didn't care anything about those Africans. They could have been rats. He was in a laboratory testing *himself*—proving he could work on human dogs."

"What about Eleanor Roosevelt?"

"I don't know about the women. I can't say what their women would do, but I do remember that picture of those white mothers holding up their babies so they could get a good look at some black men burning on a tree. So I have my suspicions about Eleanor Roosevelt. But *none* about Mr. Roosevelt. You could've taken him and his wheelchair and put him in a small dusty town in Alabama and given him some tobacco, a checkerboard, some whiskey, and a rope and he'd have done it too. What I'm saying is, under certain conditions they would *all* do it. And under the same circumstances we would not. So it doesn't matter that some of them *haven't* done it. I listen. I read. And now I know that they know it too. They know they are unnatural. Their writers and artists have been saying it for years. Telling them they are unnatural, telling them they are depraved. They call it tragedy. In the movies they call it adventure. It's just depravity that they try to make glorious, natural. But it ain't. The disease they have is in their blood, in the structure of their chromosomes."

"You can prove this, I guess. Scientifically?"

"No."

"Shouldn't you be able to prove it before you act on something like that?"

"Did they prove anything scientifically about us before they killed us? No. They killed us first and then tried to get some scientific proof about why we should die."

"Wait a minute, Guitar. If they are as bad, as unnatural, as you say, why do you want to be like them? Don't you want to be better than they are?"

"I am better."

"But now you're doing what the worst of them do."

"Yes, but I am reasonable."

"Reasonable? How?"

"I am not, one, having fun; two, trying to gain power or public attention or money or land; three, angry at anybody."

"You're not angry? You must be!"

"Not at all. I hate doing it. I'm afraid to do it. It's hard to do it when you aren't angry or drunk or doped up or don't have a personal grudge against the person."

"I can't see how it helps. I can't see how it helps anybody."

"I told you. Numbers. Balance. Ratio. And the earth, the land."

"I'm not understanding you."

"The earth is soggy with black people's blood. And before us Indian blood. Nothing can cure them, and if it keeps on there won't be any of us left and there won't be any land for those who are left. So the numbers have to remain static."

"But there are more of them than us."

"Only in the West. But still the ratio can't widen in their favor."

"But you should want everybody to know that the society exists. Then maybe that would help stop it. What's the secrecy for?"

"To keep from getting caught."

"Can't you even let other Negroes know about it? I mean to give us hope?"

"No."

"Why not?"

"Betrayal. The possibility of betrayal."

"Well, let *them* know. Let white people know. Like the Mafia or the Klan; frighten them into behaving."

"You're talking foolishness. How can you let one group know and not the other? Besides, we are not like them. The Mafia is unnatural. So is the Klan. One kills for money, the other kills for fun. And they have huge profits and protection at their disposal. We don't. But it's not about other people knowing. We don't even tell the victims. We just whisper to him, 'Your Day has come.' The beauty of what we do is its secrecy, its smallness. The fact that nobody needs the unnatural satisfaction of talking about it. Telling about it. We don't discuss it among ourselves, the details. We just get an assignment. If the Negro was killed on a Wednesday, the Wednesday man takes it; if he was killed on Monday, the Monday man takes that one. And we just notify one another when it's completed, not how or who. And if it ever gets to be too much, like it was for Robert Smith, we do *that* rather than crack and tell somebody. Like Porter. It was getting him down. They thought somebody would have to take over his day. He just needed a rest and he's okay now."

Milkman stared at his friend and then let the spasm he had been holding back run through him. "I can't buy it, Guitar."

"I know that."

"There's too much wrong with it."

"Tell me."

"Well, for one thing, you'll get caught eventually."

"Maybe. But if I'm caught I'll just die earlier than I'm supposed to—not better than I'm supposed to. And how I die or when doesn't interest me. What I die *for* does. It's the same as what I live for. Besides, if I'm caught they'll accuse me and kill me for one crime, maybe two, never for all. And there are still six other days in the week. We've been around for a long long time. And believe me, we'll be around for a long long time to come."

"You can't marry."

"No."

"Have children."

"No."

"What kind of life is that?"

"Very satisfying."

"There's no love in it."

"No love? No love? Didn't you hear me? What I'm doing ain't about hating white people. It's about loving us. About loving you. My whole life is love."

"Man, you're confused."

"Am I? When those concentration camp Jews hunt down Nazis, are they hating Nazis or loving dead Jews?"

"It's not the same thing."

"Only because they have money and publicity."

"No; because they turn them over to the courts. You kill and you don't kill the killers. You kill innocent people."

"I told you there are no—"

"And you don't correct a thing by—"

"We poor people, Milkman. I work at an auto plant. The rest

of us barely eke out a living. Where's the money, the state, the country to finance our justice? You say Jews try their catches in a court. Do we have a court? Is there one courthouse in one city in the country where a jury would convict them? There are places right now where a Negro still can't testify against a white man. Where the judge, the jury, the court, are legally bound to ignore anything a Negro has to say. What that means is that a black man is a victim of a crime only when a white man says he is. Only then. If there was anything like or near justice or courts when a cracker kills a Negro, there wouldn't have to be no Seven Days. But there ain't; so we are. And we do it without money, without support, without costumes, without newspapers, without senators, without lobbyists, and without illusions!"

"You sound like that red-headed Negro named X. Why don't you join him and call yourself Guitar X?"

"X, Bains—what difference does it make? I don't give a damn about names."

"You miss his point. His point is to let white people know you don't accept your slave name."

"I don't give a shit what white people know or even think. Besides, I do accept it. It's part of who I am. Guitar is *my* name. Bains is the slave master's name. And I'm all of that. Slave names don't bother me; but slave status does."

"And knocking off white folks changes your slave status?"

"Believe it."

"Does it do anything for my slave status?"

Guitar smiled. "Well, doesn't it?"

"Hell, no." Milkman frowned. "Am I going to live any longer because you all read the newspaper and then ambush some poor old white man?"

"It's not about you living longer. It's about how you live and why. It's about whether your children can make other children. It's about trying to make a world where one day white people will think before they lynch."

"Guitar, none of that shit is going to change how I live or how any other Negro lives. What you're doing is crazy. And something else: it's a habit. If you do it enough, you can do it to anybody. You know what I mean? A torpedo is a torpedo, I don't care what his reasons. You can off anybody you don't like. You can off me."

"We don't off Negroes."

"You hear what you said? *Negroes*. Not Milkman. Not 'No, I can't touch *you*, Milkman,' but 'We don't off Negroes.' Shit, man, suppose you all change your parliamentary rules?"

"The Days are the Days. It's been that way a long time."

Milkman thought about that. "Any other young dudes in it? Are all the others older? You the only young one?"

"Why?"

"Cause young dudes are subject to change the rules."

"You worried about yourself, Milkman?" Guitar looked amused.

"No. Not really." Milkman put his cigarette out and reached for another one. "Tell me, what's your day?"

"Sunday. I'm the Sunday man."

Milkman rubbed the ankle of his short leg. "I'm scared for you, man."

"That's funny. I'm scared for you too."

Chapter 7

Truly landlocked people know they are. Know the occasional Bitter Creek or Powder River that runs through Wyoming; that the large tidy Salt Lake of Utah is all they have of the sea and that they must content themselves with *bank*, *shore*, and *beach* because they cannot claim a coast. And having none, seldom dream of flight. But the people living in the Great Lakes region are confused by their place on the country's edge—an edge that is border but not coast. They seem to be able to live a long time believing, as coastal people do, that they are at the frontier where final exit and total escape are the only journeys left. But those five Great Lakes which the St. Lawrence feeds with memories of the sea are themselves landlocked, in spite of the wandering river that connects them to the Atlantic. Once the people of the lake region discover this, the longing to leave becomes acute, and a break from the area, therefore, is necessarily dream-bitten, but necessary nonetheless. It might be an appetite for other streets, other slants of light. Or a yearning to be surrounded by strangers. It may even be a wish to hear the solid click of a door closing behind their backs.

For Milkman it was the door click. He wanted to feel the heavy white door on Not Doctor Street close behind him and know that he might be hearing the catch settle into its groove for the last time.

"You'll own it all. All of it. You'll be free. Money is freedom, Macon. The only real freedom there is."

"I know, Daddy, I know. But I have to get away just the same. I'm not leaving the country; I just want to be on my own. Get a job on my own, live on my own. You did it at sixteen. Guitar at seventeen. Everybody. I'm still living at home, working for you—not because I sweated for the job, but because I'm your son. I'm over thirty years old."

"I need you here, Macon. If you were going to go, you should have gone five years ago. Now I've come to depend on you." It was difficult for him to beg, but he came as close to it as he could.

"Just a year. One year. Stake me for a year and let me go. When I come back, I'll work a year for nothing and pay you back."

"It's not the money. It's you being here, taking care of this. Taking care of all I'm going to leave you. Getting to know it, know how to handle it."

"Let me use some of it now, when I need it. Don't do like Pilate, put it in a green sack and hang it from the wall so nobody can get it. Don't make me wait until—"

"What did you say?" As suddenly as an old dog drops a shoe when he smells raw meat, Macon Dead dropped his pleading look and flared his nostrils with some new interest.

"I said give me a little bit—"

"No. Not that. About Pilate and a sack."

"Yeah. Her sack. You've seen it, haven't you? That green sack she got hanging from the ceiling? She calls it her inheritance. You can't get from one side of the room to the other without cracking your head on it. Don't you remember it?"

Macon was blinking rapidly, but he managed to calm himself and say, "I've never set foot in Pilate's house in my life. I looked in there once, but it was dark and I didn't see anything hanging down from the ceiling. When's the last time you saw it?"

"Maybe nine or ten months ago. What about it?"

"You think it's still there?"

"Why wouldn't it be?"

"You say it's green. You know for sure it's green?"

"Yeah, green. Grass green. What is it? What's bothering you?"

"She told you it was her inheritance, huh?" Macon was smiling, but so craftily that Milkman could hardly recognize it as a smile.

"No. She didn't; Hagar did. I was walking across the room toward the . . . uh . . . toward the other side and I'm tall enough for it to be in my way. I bumped my head on it. Made a hickey too. When I asked Hagar what it was she said, 'Pilate's inheritance.' "

"And it made a hickey on your head?"

"Yeah. Felt like bricks. What're you going to do, sue her?"

"You had any lunch?"

"It's ten-thirty, Daddy."

"Go to Mary's. Get us a couple of orders of barbecue. Meet me in the park across from Mercy. We'll eat lunch there."

"Daddy . . ."

"Go on now. Do what I say. Go on, Macon."

They met in the little public park across the street from Mercy Hospital. It was full of pigeons, students, drunks, dogs, squirrels, children, trees, and secretaries. The two colored men sat down on an iron bench a little away from the most crowded part, but not the edge. They were very well dressed, too well dressed to be eating pork out of a box, but on that warm September day it seemed natural, a perfect addition to the mellowness that pervaded the park.

Milkman was curious about his father's agitation, but not alarmed. So much had been going on, so many changes. Besides, he knew whatever was making his father fidget and look around to see if anyone was too near had to do with something his father wanted, not something he wanted himself. He could look at his father coolly now that he had sat on that train and listened to his mother's sad sad song. Her words still danced around in his head. "What harm did I do you on my knees?"

Deep down in that pocket where his heart hid, he felt used. Somehow everybody was using him for something or as something. Working out some scheme of their own on him, making him the subject of their dreams of wealth, or love, or martyrdom. Everything they did seemed to be about him, yet nothing he wanted was part of it. Once before he had had a long talk with his father, and it ended up with his being driven further from his mother. Now he had had a confidential talk with his mother, only to discover that before he was born, before the first nerve end had formed in his mother's womb, he was the subject of great controversy and strife. And now the one woman who claimed to love him more than life, more than her life, actually loved him more than *his* life, for she had spent half a year trying to relieve him of it. And Guitar. The one sane and constant person he knew had flipped, had ripped open and was spilling blood and foolishness instead of conversation. He was a fit companion for Empire State. So now he waited with curiosity, but without excitement or hope, for this latest claim.

"Listen to me. Just eat your meat and listen to me. Don't interrupt, because I might lose my train of thought.

"A long time ago, I told you about when I was a boy on the farm. About Pilate and me. About my father getting killed. I never finished the story; I never told you all of it. The part I left out was about me and Pilate. I tried to keep you away from her and said she was a snake. Now I'm going to tell you why."

A red ball rolled to his feet, and Macon picked it up and threw it back to a little girl. He made sure she was safely back in her mother's view before he began his story.

Six days after the first Macon Dead died, his children, a twelve-year-old Pilate and a sixteen-year-old Macon Dead, found themselves homeless. Bewildered and grieving, they went to the house of the closest colored person they knew: Circe, the midwife who had delivered them both and who was there when their mother died and when Pilate was named. She worked in a large house—a mansion—outside Danville, for a family of what was then called gentlemen farmers. The orphans called to Circe from the vegetable garden early in the morning as soon as they saw the smoke from the cook stove rising. Circe let them in, pressing her hands together with relief, and saying how glad she was to see them alive. She hadn't known what had happened to them after the killing. Macon explained that he had buried his father himself, down by that part of the stream on Lincoln's Heaven where they used to fish together, the place where he had caught that nine-pound trout. The grave was shallower than it ought to be, but he'd piled rocks there.

Circe told them to stay with her until they could all figure out what to do, someplace for them to go. She hid them in that house easily. There were rooms the family seldom went into, but if they weren't safe, she was prepared to share her own room (which was off limits to everybody in the house). It was small, though, so they agreed to stay in a pair of rooms on the third floor that were used only for storage. Circe would bring them food, water to wash in, and she would empty their slop jar.

Macon asked if they couldn't work there; would her mistress take them on as kitchen help, yard help, anything?

Circe bit her tongue trying to get the words out. "You crazy? You say you saw the men what killed him. You think they don't know you saw them? If they kill a growed man, what you think they do to you? Be sensible. We got to plan and figure this thing out."

Macon and Pilate stayed there two weeks, not a day longer. He had been working hard on a farm since he was five or six years old and she was born wild. They couldn't bear the stillness, the walls, the boredom of having nothing to do but wait for the day's excitement of eating and going to the toilet. Anything was better than walking all day on carpeting, than eating the soft bland food white people ate, than having to sneak a look at the sky from behind ivory curtains.

Pilate began to cry the day Circe brought her white toast and cherry jam for breakfast. She wanted her own cherries, from her own cherry tree, with stems and seeds; not some too-sweet mashed mush. She thought she would die if she couldn't hold her mouth under Ulysses S. Grant's teat and squirt the warm milk into her mouth, or pull a tomato off its vine and eat it where she stood. Craving certain specific foods had almost devastated her. That, plus the fact that her earlobe was sore from the operation she had performed on herself, had her near hysteria. Before they left the farm, she'd taken the scrap of brown paper with her name on it from the Bible, and after a long time trying to make up her mind between a snuffbox and a sunbonnet with blue ribbons on it, she took the little brass box that had belonged to her mother. Her miserable days in the mansion were spent planning how to make an earring out of the box which would house her name. She found a piece of wire, but couldn't get it through. Finally, after much begging and whining, Circe got a Negro blacksmith to solder a bit of gold wire to the box. Pilate rubbed her ear until it was numb, burned the end of the wire, and punched it through her earlobe. Macon fastened the wire ends into a knot, but the lobe was swollen and running pus. At Circe's instruction she put cobwebs on it to draw the pus out and stop the bleeding.

On the night of the day she cried so about the cherries, the two of them decided that when her ear got better, they would leave. It was too much of a hardship on Circe anyway for them to stay there, and if her white folks found out about them, they might let her go.

One morning Circe climbed all the way to the third floor with a covered plate of scrapple and found two empty rooms. They didn't even take a blanket. Just a knife and a tin cup.

The first day out was joyous for them. They ate raspberries and apples; they took off their shoes and let the dewy grass and sun-warmed dirt soothe their feet. At night they slept in a haystack, so grateful for open air even the field mice and the ticks were welcome bedmates.

The next day was pleasant but less exciting. They bathed in a curve of the Susquehanna and then wandered in a southerly direction, keeping to fields, woods, stream beds, and little-used paths, headed, they thought, for Virginia, where Macon believed they had people.

On the third day they woke to find a man that looked just like their father sitting on a stump not fifty yards away. He was not looking at them; he was just sitting there. They would have called out to him or run toward him except he was staring right past them with such distance in his eyes, he frightened them. So they ran away. All day long at various intervals they saw him: staring down into duck ponds; framed by the Y of a sycamore tree; shading his eyes from the sun as he peered over a rock at the wide valley floor beneath them. Each time they saw him they backed off and went in the opposite direction. Now the land itself, the only one they knew and knew intimately, began to terrify them. The sun was blazing down, the air was sweet, but every leaf that the wind lifted, every rustle of a pheasant hen in a clump of ryegrass, sent needles of fear through their veins. The cardinals, the gray squirrels, the garden snakes, the butterflies, the ground hogs and rabbits—all the affectionate things that had peopled their lives ever since they were born became ominous signs of a presence that was searching for them, following them. Even the river's babbling sounded like the call of a liquid throat waiting, just waiting for them. That was in the daylight. How much more terrible was the night.

Just before dark, when the sun had left them alone, when they were coming out of some woods looking around for the crest of the hill where they could see, perhaps, a farm, an abandoned shed—anyplace where they could spend the night—they saw a cave, and at its mouth stood their father. This time he motioned for them to follow him. Faced with the choice of the limitless nighttime woods and a man who looked like their father, they chose the latter. After all, if it was their father, he wouldn't hurt them, would he?

Slowly they approached the mouth of the cave, following their father's beckoning hand and his occasional backward glance.

They looked into the cave and saw nothing but a great maw of darkness. Their father had disappeared. If they stayed near the lip, they thought, it was as good a place as any to spend the night; perhaps he was simply looking out for them, showing them what to do and where to go. They made themselves as comfortable as they could on a rock formation that jutted out like a shelf from a hip-high mass of stone. There was nothing behind them that they could see and only the certainty of bats to disturb them. Yet it was nothing to that other darkness—outside.

Toward morning, Macon woke from a light and fitful sleep, with a terrific urge to relieve his bowels, the consequence of three days' diet of wild fruit. Without waking his sister, he climbed off the shelf, and shy of squatting on the crown of a hill in a new sun, he walked a little farther back into the cave. When he was finished, the darkness had disintegrated somewhat, and he saw, some fifteen feet in front of him, a man stirring in his sleep. Macon tried to button his pants and get away without waking him, but the leaves and twigs crunching under his feet pulled the man all the way out of his sleep. He raised his head, turned over, and smiled. Macon saw that he was very old, very white, and his smile was awful.

Macon stepped back, one hand outstretched behind him, thinking all the while of how his father's body had twitched and danced for whole minutes in the dirt. He touched the cave's wall and a piece of it gave way in his hand. Closing his fingers around it, he threw it at the grinning man's head, hitting him just above the eye. Blood spurted out and knocked the smile off the pale face, but did not stop the man from coming and coming, all the time wiping blood from his face and smearing it on his shirt.

Macon got hold of another rock, but missed that time. The man kept coming.

The scream that boomed down the cave tunnel and woke the bats came just when Macon thought he had taken his last living breath. The bleeding man turned toward the direction of the scream and looked at the colored girl long enough for Macon to pull out his knife and bring it down on the old man's back. He crashed forward, then turned his head to look up at them. His mouth moved and he mumbled something that sounded like "What for?" Macon stabbed him again and again until he stopped moving his mouth, stopped trying to talk, and stopped jumping and twitching on the ground.

Panting with the exertion of slashing through an old man's rib cage, Macon ran back to get the blanket the man had been sleeping on. He wanted the dead man to disappear, to be covered, hidden, to be gone. When he snatched the blanket, a large tarpaulin came with it and he saw three boards positioned across what looked like a shallow pit. He paused and then kicked the boards aside. Underneath were little gray bags, their necks tied with wire, arranged like nest eggs. Macon picked one of them up and was amazed at its weight.

"Pilate," he called. "Pilate."

But she was growing roots where she stood, and staring open-mouthed at the dead man. Macon had to pull her by the arm over to the hole where the bags lay. After some difficulty with the wire (he ended up having to use his teeth), he got one open and shook the gold nuggets it held out into the leaves and twigs that lay on the floor of the cave.

"Gold," he whispered, and immediately, like a burglar out on his first job, stood up to pee.

Life, safety, and luxury fanned out before him like the tail-spread of a peacock, and as he stood there trying to distinguish each delicious color, he saw the dusty boots of his father standing just on the other side of the shallow pit.

"It *is* Papa!" said Pilate. And as if in answer to her recognition, he took a deep breath, rolled his eyes back, and whispered, "Sing. Sing," in a hollow voice before he melted away again.

Pilate darted around the cave calling him, looking for him, while Macon piled the sacks of gold into the tarpaulin.

"Let's go, Pilate. Let's get out of here."

"We can't take that." She pointed a finger at his bundle.

"What? Not take it? You lost your mind?"

"That's stealing. We killed a man. They'll be after us, all over. If we take his money, then they'll think that's why we did it. We got to leave it, Macon. We can't get caught with no bags of money."

"This ain't money; it's gold. It'll keep us for life, Pilate. We can get us another farm. We can—"

"Leave it, Macon! Leave it! Let them find it just where it was!" Then she began to shout, "Papa! Papa!"

Macon slapped her and the little brass box dangled on her ear. She cupped it in her hands for a moment and then leaped on her brother like an antelope. They fought right there in front of the dead man's staring eyes. Pilate was almost as strong as Macon, but no real match for him, and he probably would have beaten her unconscious had she not got his knife, not yet dry from the old man's blood, and held it ready for his heart.

Macon stood very still and watched her eyes. He began calling her ugly names, but she didn't answer. He backed out of the cave and walked a little distance away.

All day he waited for her to come out. All day she stayed there. When night came he just sat, at the foot of a tree, unafraid of all the night things that had terrified him before, eyes wide open, waiting for her to stick her woolly head out of the cave. There was no sound from her direction and he waited the whole night. At dawn he crept forward a foot at a time, hoping he would catch her asleep. Just then he heard some dogs and knew hunters were walking nearby. He ran as fast as he could through the woods until he couldn't hear the dogs anymore.

Another day and a night he spent trying to work his way back to the cave and avoid the hunters if they were still about. Finally he got there, three days and two nights later. Inside the cave the dead man was still looking placidly up at him, but the tarpaulin and the gold were gone.

The secretaries went away. So did the children and the dogs. Only the pigeons, the drunks, and the trees were left in the little park.

Milkman had eaten almost none of his barbecue. He was watching his father's face, shining with perspiration and the emotions of memory.

"She took it, Macon. After all that, she took the gold."

"How do you know? You didn't see her take it," said Milkman.

"The tarpaulin was green." Macon Dead rubbed his hands together. "Pilate came to this city in 1930. Two years later they call back all the gold. I figured she spent it all in the twenty or so years since I'd seen her, since she was living like poor trash when she got here. It was natural for me to believe she'd got rid of it all. Now you tell me she got a green sack full of something hard enough to give you a hickey on your head when you bumped into it. That's the gold, boy. That's it!"

He turned to his son full face and licked his lips. "Macon, get it and you can have half of it; go wherever you want. Get it. For both of us. Please get it, son. Get the gold."

Chapter 8

Every night now Guitar was seeing little scraps of Sunday dresses—white and purple, powder blue, pink and white, lace and voile, velvet and silk, cotton and satin, eyelet and grosgrain. The scraps stayed with him all night and he remembered Magdalene called Lena and Corinthians bending in the wind to catch the heart-red pieces of velvet that had floated under the gaze of Mr. Robert Smith. Only Guitar's scraps were different. The bits of Sunday dresses that he saw did not fly; they hung in the air quietly, like the whole notes in the last measure of an Easter hymn.

Four little colored girls had been blown out of a church, and his mission was to approximate as best he could a similar death of four little white girls some Sunday, since he was the Sunday man. He couldn't do it with a piece of wire, or a switchblade. For this he needed explosives, or guns, or hand grenades. And that would take money. He knew that the assignments of the Days would more and more be the killing of white people in groups, since more and more Negroes were being killed in groups. The single, solitary death was going rapidly out of fashion, and the Days might as well prepare themselves for it.

So when Milkman came to him with a proposal to steal and share a cache of gold, Guitar smiled. "Gold?" He could hardly believe it.

"Gold."

"Nobody got gold, Milkman."

"Pilate does."

"It's against the law to have gold."

"That's why she got it. She can't use it, and she can't report its being stolen since she wasn't supposed to have it in the first place."

"How do we get rid of it—get greenbacks for it?"

"Leave that to my father. He knows bank people who know other bank people. They'll give him legal tender for it."

"Legal tender." Guitar laughed softly. "How much legal tender will it bring?"

"That's what we have to find out."

"What's the split?"

"Three ways."

"Your papa know that?"

"Not yet. He thinks it's two ways."

"When you gonna tell him?"

"Afterwards."

"Will he go for it?"

"How can he *not* go for it?"

"When do we get it?"

"Whenever we want to."

Guitar spread his palm. "My man." Milkman slapped his hand. "Legal tender. Legal tender. I love it. Sounds like a virgin bride." Guitar rubbed the back of his neck and lifted his face to the sun in a gesture of expansiveness and luxury.

"Now we have to come up with something. A way to get it," said Milkman.

"Be a breeze. A cool cool breeze," Guitar continued, smiling at the sun, his eyes closed as though to ready himself for the gold by trying out a little bit of the sun's.

"A breeze?" Now that Guitar was completely enthusiastic, Milkman's own excitement was blunted. Something perverse made him not want to hand the whole score to his friend on a platter. There should be some difficulty, some complication in this adventure. "We just walk over there and snatch it off the wall, right? And if Pilate or Reba say anything, we just knock them out the way. That what you have in mind?" He summoned as much irony as he could into his voice.

"Defeatism. That's what you got. Defeatism."

"Common sense is what I got."

"Come on, old dude. Your pappy give you a good thing and you want to fight it."

"I'm not fighting. I just want to get out alive and breathing so what I snatch does me some good. I don't want to have to give it to a brain surgeon to pull an ice pick out the back of my head."

"Can't no ice pick get through the back of your head, nigger."

"Can get through my heart."

"What you doin with a heart anyway?"

"Pumping blood. And I'd like to keep on pumping it."

"Okay. We got us a problem. A little bitty problem: how can two big men get a fifty-pound sack out of a house with three women in it—women who all together don't weigh three hundred pounds."

"What you have to weigh to pull a trigger?"

"What trigger? Nobody in that house got a gun."

"You don't know what Hagar's got."

"Look, Milk. She's been trying to kill you for almost a year. Used everything she could get her hands on and never once did she use a gun."

"So? Maybe she's thinking. Wait till next month."

"Next month she'll be too late, won't she?" Guitar leaned his head over to the side and smiled at Milkman, an engaging boyish smile. Milkman hadn't seen him this relaxed and cordial in a long

long time. He wondered if that's why he had let him in on it. Obviously he could pull it off alone, but maybe he wanted to see Guitar warm and joking again, his face open and smiling instead of with that grim reaper look.

They met again on Sunday on route 6 away from the colored part of town. A road consisting of used-car lots, Dairy Queens, and White Castle hamburger places. It was empty of shoppers that morning–nothing but the occasional sound of automobiles breaking the graveyard silence of the cars in the lots, lined up like tombstones.

Since that last conversation–the important one in which Guitar explained his work, not the brief chancy talks they'd had afterward–Milkman wished he had the nerve to ask Guitar the question that was bothering him. "Has he?" He could hardly phrase the question in his own mind, and certainly could never say it aloud. Guitar had impressed him with the seriousness and the dread of the work of the Days, and the danger. He had said that the Days never even talked about the details among themselves, so Milkman was sure any inquiry from him would only make Guitar sullen again. And cold. But the question was there. "Has he done it? Has he really killed somebody?" Like the old men on Tenth Street, now he bought the morning and evening papers, and once every two weeks the black newspaper, and read nervously, looking for reports of murders that appeared suspicious, pointless. When he found one, he followed the news stories until a suspect was found. Then he had to see if there were any black people murdered by someone other than their own.

"Did you do it yet?" He was like a teen-age girl wondering about the virginity of her friend, the friend who has a look, a manner newly minted–different, separate, focused somehow. "Did you do it yet? Do you know something both exotic and ordinary that I have not felt? Do you now know what it's like to risk your one and only self? How did it feel? Were you afraid? Did it change you? And if I do it, will it change me too?"

Maybe he could ask him one day, but not this day when it was so much like old times. Taking risks together the way they did when Milkman was twelve and Guitar was a teen-ager and they swaggered, haunched, leaned, straddled, ran all over town trying to pick fights or at least scare somebody: other boys, girls, dogs, pigeons, old women, school principals, drunks, ice cream vendors, and the horses of junkyard men. When they succeeded they rode the wind and covered their mouths to aggravate their laughter. And when they didn't, when somebody out-insulted them, or ignored them, or sent them running, they wisecracked and name-called until the sweat of embarrassment evaporated from the palms of their hands. Now they were men, and the terror they needed to provoke in others, if for no other reason than to feel it themselves, was rarer but not lighter. Dominion won by fear and secured by fear was still sweeter than any that could be got another way. (Except for women, whom they liked to win with charm but keep with indifference.)

It was like that again now, and Milkman didn't want to lose it.

There was something else too. Guitar had placed himself willingly and eagerly in a life cause that would always provide him with a proximity to knife-cold terror. Milkman knew his own needs were milder, for he could thrive in the presence of someone who inspired fear. His father, Pilate, Guitar. He gravitated toward each one, envious of their fearlessness now, even Hagar's, in spite of the fact that she was no longer a threat, but a fool who wanted not his death so much as his attention. Guitar could still create the sense of danger and life lived on the cutting edge. So Milkman had brought him into this scheme only partially for his help. Mostly because this escapade cried out for a cutting edge to go with its larklike quality. With Guitar as his co-conspirator, Milkman could look forward to both fun and fear.

They sauntered on down route 6, stopping frequently to examine the cars, gesticulating, bantering each other about the best way to burglarize a shack that, as Guitar said, "didn't have a door or window with a lock."

"But it's got people," Milkman insisted. "Three. All crazy."

"Women."

"Crazy women."

"Women."

"You're forgetting, Guitar, how Pilate got the gold in the first place. She waited in a cave with a dead man for three days to haul it out, and that was when she was twelve. If she did that at twelve to get it, what you think she'll do now when she's almost seventy to keep it?"

"We don't have to be rough. Cunning is all we need to be."

"Okay. Tell me how you gonna cunning them out of the house."

"Well, let's see now." Guitar stopped to scratch his back on a telephone pole. He closed his eyes, in either the ecstasy of relief or the rigors of concentration. Milkman stared off into the sky for inspiration, and while glancing toward the rooftops of the used-car places, he saw a white peacock poised on the roof of a long low building that served as headquarters for Nelson Buick. He was about to accept the presence of the bird as one of those waking dreams he was subject to whenever indecisiveness was confronted with reality, when Guitar opened his eyes and said, "Goddam! Where'd that come from?"

Milkman was relieved. "Must of come from the zoo."

"That raggedy-ass zoo? Ain't nothing in there but two tired monkeys and some snakes."

"Well, where then?"

"Beats me."

"Look—she's flying down." Milkman felt again his unrestrained joy at anything that could fly. "Some jive flying, but look at her strut."

"He."

"Huh?"

"He. That's a he. The male is the only one got that tail full of jewelry. Son of a bitch. Look at that." The peacock opened its tail wide. "Let's catch it. Come on, Milk," and Guitar started to run toward the fence.

"What for?" asked Milkman, running behind him. "What we gonna do if we catch him?"

"Eat him!" Guitar shouted. He swung easily over the double pipes that bordered the lot and began to circle the bird at a distance, holding his head a little to the side to fool the peacock, which was strutting around a powder-blue Buick. It closed its tail and let the tips trail in the gravel. The two men stood still, watching.

"How come it can't fly no better than a chicken?" Milkman asked.

"Too much tail. All that jewelry weighs it down. Like vanity. Can't nobody fly with all that shit. Wanna fly, you got to give up the shit that weighs you down."

The peacock jumped onto the hood of the Buick and once more spread its tail, sending the flashy Buick into oblivion.

"Faggot." Guitar laughed softly. "White faggot."

Milkman laughed too, and they watched a while more before leaving the used cars and the pure white peacock.

But the bird had set them up. Instead of continuing the argument about how they would cop, they began to fantasize about what the gold could buy when it became legal tender. Guitar, eschewing his recent asceticism, allowed himself the pleasure of waking up old dreams: what he would buy for his grandmother and her brother, Uncle Billy, the one who had come up from Florida to help raise them all after his father died; the marker he would buy for his father's grave, "pink with lilies carved on it"; then stuff for his brother and sisters, and his sisters' children. Milkman fantasized too, but not for the stationary things Guitar described. Milkman wanted boats, cars, airplanes, and the command of a large crew. He would be whimsical, generous, mysterious with his money. But all the time he was laughing and going on about what he would do and how he planned to live, he was aware of a falseness in his voice. He wanted the money—desperately, he believed—but other than making tracks out of the city, far away from Not Doctor Street, and Sonny's Shop, and Mary's Place, and Hagar, he could not visualize a life that much different from the one he had. New people. New places. Command. That was what he wanted in his life. And he couldn't get deep into Guitar's talk of elegant clothes for himself and his brother, sumptuous meals for Uncle Billy, and week-long card games in which the stakes would be a yard and a half and then a deuce and a quarter. He screamed and shouted "Wooeeeee!" at Guitar's list, but because his life was not unpleasant and even had a certain amount of luxury in addition to its comfort, he felt off center. He just wanted to beat a path away from his parents' past, which was also their present and which was threatening to become his present as well. He hated the acridness in his mother's and father's relationship, the conviction of righteousness they each held on to with both hands. And his efforts to ignore it, transcend it, seemed to work only when he spent his days looking for whatever was light-hearted and without grave consequences. He avoided commitment and strong feelings, and shied away from decisions. He wanted to know as little as possible, to feel only enough to get through the day amiably and to be interesting enough to warrant the curiosity of other people—but not their all-consuming devotion. Hagar had given him this last and more drama than he could ever want again. He'd always believed his childhood was sterile, but the knowledge Macon and Ruth had given him wrapped his memory of it in septic sheets, heavy with the odor of illness, misery, and unforgiving hearts. His rebellions, minor as they were, had all been in the company of, or shared with, Guitar. And this latest Jack and the Beanstalk bid for freedom, even though it had been handed to him by his father—assigned almost—stood some chance of success.

He had half expected his friend to laugh at him, to refuse with some biting comment that would remind Milkman that Guitar was a mystery man now, a man with blood-deep responsibilities. But when he watched Guitar's face as he described what could be had almost for the asking, he knew right away he hadn't guessed wrong. Maybe the professional assassin had had enough, or had changed his mind. Had he . . . ? "Did you . . . ?" As he listened to him go over each detail of meals, clothes, tombstones, he wondered if Guitar simply could not resist the lure of something he had never had—money.

Guitar smiled at the sun, and talked lovingly of televisions, and brass beds, and week-long card games, but his mind was on the wonders of TNT.

By the time they'd exhausted their imaginative spending, it was almost noon and they were back on the edge of Southside. They picked up where they'd left off in the discussion of the scheme. Guitar was ready now; Milkman was still cautious. Too cautious for Guitar.

"I don't understand you. You come running after me with a dynamite proposition, and for three days we talk about it, the best news I've had since pussy, but when we get down to business, you come up with some shit about how it can't be done. You shucking me or what?"

"What would I be shucking for? I didn't have to tell you about it."

"I don't know. I don't even know why you doing it. You know about me—you can guess why I'm in it. But money ain't never been what you needed or couldn't get."

Milkman ignored the reference to why Guitar was "in it," and said as calmly as he could, "I need it to get away. I told you, man. I got to get out of here. Be on my own."

"On *your* own? With a million-dollar wallet, you call that on your own?"

"Fuck you. What difference does it make why I want it?"

"Cause I'm not sure you do want it. At least not bad enough to go ahead and cop."

"I just want it right. No hassles. No . . . You know, burglary is a serious crime. I don't want to end up in—"

"What burglary? This ain't no burglary. This is Pilate."

"So?"

"So! They're your people."

"They're still people, and people scream."

"What's the worst? What's the worst thing can happen? We

bust in, right? Suppose all three of them are there. They're women. What can they do? Whip us?"

"Maybe."

"Come on! Who? Hagar? Right up in your face she blows it. Pilate? She loves you, boy. She wouldn't touch you."

"You believe that?"

"Yeah, I believe it! Look. You got qualms, tell me about them. Because you related? Your daddy's more related than you are, and it's his idea."

"It's not that."

"Then what?"

"They're crazy, Guitar. Nobody knows what they'll do; *they* don't even know."

"I know they're crazy. Anybody live like they do, selling fifty-cent wine and peeing in a bucket, with one million dollars hanging over their nappy heads, has to be. You scared of craziness? If you are, *you're* crazy."

"I don't want to be caught, that's all. I don't want to do time. I want to plan it so neither one happens. How come that's too much to ask? To plan."

"It don't look like planning. Looks like stalling."

"It is planning. Planning how to get them out the house. How to get us in the house. How to cut that sack off the ceiling and then get back out the house and on down the street. And it's hard to plan with them. They're not regular. They don't have regular habits. And then there's the wineheads. One of them liable to drop in any old time. They're not clock people, Guitar. I don't believe Pilate knows how to tell time except by the sun."

"They sleep at night."

"Anybody sleep can wake up."

"Anybody woke up can be knocked down."

"I don't want to knock nobody down. I want them gone when we hit."

"And what's gonna make them leave?"

Milkman shook his head. "An earthquake, maybe."

"Then let's make an earthquake."

"How?"

"Set the house on fire. Put a skunk in there. A bear. Something. Anything."

"Be serious, man."

"I'm trying, baby. I'm trying. Don't they go nowhere?"

"All together?"

"All together."

Milkman shrugged. "Funerals. They go to funerals. And circuses."

"Oh, man! We have to wait for somebody to die? Or for Ringling Brothers to come to town?"

"I'm trying to figure it out is all. At the moment we don't have a chance."

"Well, if a man don't *have* a chance, then he has to *take* a chance!"

"Be reasonable."

"Reasonable? You can't get no pot of gold being reasonable. Can't nobody get no gold being reasonable. You have to be unreasonable. How come you don't know that?"

"Listen to me. . . ."

"I just quit listening. You listen! You got a life? Live it! Live the motherfuckin life! Live it!"

Milkman's eyes opened wide. He tried hard not to swallow, but the clarion call in Guitar's voice filled his mouth with salt. The same salt that lay in the bottom of the sea and in the sweat of a horse's neck. A taste so powerful and necessary that stallions galloped miles and days for it. It was new, it was delicious, and it was his own. All the tentativeness, doubt, and inauthenticity that plagued him slithered away without a trace, a sound.

Now he knew what his hesitation had been all about. It was not to give an unnatural complexity to a simple job; nor was it to keep Guitar on hold. He had simply not believed in it before. When his father told him that long story, it really seemed like Jack and the Beanstalk . . . some fairy tale mess. He hadn't believed it was really there, or really gold, or that he could really have it just for the taking. It was too simple. But Guitar believed it, gave it a crisp concreteness, and what's more, made it into an act, an important, real, and daring thing to do. He felt a self inside himself emerge, a clean-lined definite self. A self that could join the chorus at Railroad Tommy's with more than laughter. He could tell this. The only other real confrontation he'd had was hitting his father, but that wasn't the kind of story that stirred the glitter up in the eyes of the old men in Tommy's.

Milkman didn't think through any of this clearly. He only tasted the salt and heard the hunter's horn in Guitar's voice.

"Tomorrow," he said. "Tomorrow night."

"What time?"

"One-thirty. I'll pick you up."

"Beautiful."

Far down the road, a long way from Milkman and Guitar, the peacock spread its tail.

On autumn nights, in some parts of the city, the wind from the lake brings a sweetish smell to shore. An odor like crystallized ginger, or sweet iced tea with a dark clove floating in it. There is no explanation for the smell either, since the lake, on September 19, 1963, was so full of mill refuse and the chemical wastes of a plastics manufacturer that the hair of the willows that stood near the shore was thin and pale. Carp floated belly up onto the beach, and the doctors at Mercy knew, but did not announce, that ear infections were a certainty for those who swam in those waters.

Yet there was this heavy spice-sweet smell that made you think of the East and striped tents and the *sha-sha-sha* of leg bracelets. The people who lived near the lake hadn't noticed the smell for a long time now because when air conditioners came, they shut their windows and slept a light surface sleep under the motor's drone.

So the ginger sugar blew unnoticed through the streets, around the trees, over roofs, until, thinned out and weakened a little, it reached Southside. There, where some houses didn't even have screens, let alone air conditioners, the windows were thrown wide open to whatever the night had to offer. And there the ginger smell was sharp, sharp enough to distort dreams and make the sleeper believe the things he hungered for were right at hand. To the Southside residents who were awake on such nights, it gave all their thoughts and activity a quality of being both intimate and far away. The two men standing near the pines on Darling Street—right near the brown house where wine drinkers went—could smell the air, but they didn't think of ginger. Each thought it was the way freedom smelled, or justice, or luxury, or vengeance.

Breathing the air that could have come straight from a marketplace in Accra, they stood for what seemed to them a very long time. One leaned against a tree, his foot hovering off the ground. Finally one touched the elbow of the other and they both moved toward an open window. With no trouble at all, they entered. Although they had stood deliberately in the dark of the pine trees, they were unprepared for the deeper darkness that met them there in that room. Neither had seen that kind of blackness, not even behind their own eyelids. More unsettling than the darkness, however, was the fact that in contrast to the heat outside (the slumbering ginger-laden heat that had people wiping sweat from their neck folds), it was as cold as ice in Pilate's house.

Suddenly the moon came out and shone like a flashlight right into the room. They both saw it at the same time. It hung heavy, hung green like the green of Easter eggs left too long in the dye. And like Easter, it promised everything: the Risen Son and the heart's lone desire. Complete power, total freedom, and perfect justice. Guitar knelt down before it and wove his fingers together into a footstep. Milkman hoisted himself up, one hand on Guitar's head, and shifted himself until he sat on Guitar's shoulders. Slowly Guitar stood up. Milkman felt upward along the sack until he found its neck. He thought the rope would have to be cut, and was annoyed to find the sack hung by wire instead.

He hoped the knife would be enough, because they hadn't figured on wire and had brought neither pincers nor a wire cutter. The sound of the grating knife filled the room. No one, he thought, could sleep through that. At last some few strands broke and it was only a moment before the entire blackness was severed. They'd figured on the weight of the sack being enough to tumble them the minute it was cut free, and planned that at a whispered signal, Guitar would bend his knees and sink down so Milkman's feet would hit the floor almost immediately. But there was no need for this graceful footwork; the bag was much lighter than they had anticipated, and Milkman made it down quite easily. As soon as they both regained balance, there was a huge airy sigh that each one believed was made by the other. Milkman handed his knife to Guitar, who closed it and tucked it in his back pocket. There was the deep sigh again and an even more piercing chill. Holding the sack by its neck and its bottom, Milkman followed Guitar to the window. Once Guitar had cleared the sill, he reached back to help Milkman over. The moonlight was playing tricks on him, for he thought he saw the figure of a man standing right behind his friend. Enveloped by the heat they'd left a few minutes earlier, they walked swiftly away from the house and out onto the road.

At another open window on the same side of the house, the one next to the sink where Hagar washed her hair and where Reba put pintos to soak, a woman's face appeared. "What the devil they want that for?" she wondered. Then she picked at the window sill until she had a splinter of wood and put it in her mouth.

Chapter 9

Amanuensis. That was the word she chose, and since it was straight out of the nineteenth century, her mother approved, relishing the blank stares she received when she told her lady guests what position her daughter had acquired with the State Poet Laureate. "She's Michael-Mary Graham's amanuensis." The rickety Latin word made the work her daughter did (she, after all, wasn't required to work) sound intricate, demanding, and totally in keeping with her education. And the women didn't dare ask for further details (they tried to remember its sound, but still couldn't find it in the dictionary), for they were suitably impressed by the name of Michael-Mary Graham. It was a lie, of course, even as the simpler word "secretary" was a lie, but Ruth repeated it with confidence because she believed it was true. She did not know then, and never found out, that Corinthians was Miss Graham's maid.

Unfit for any work other than the making of red velvet roses, she had a hard time finding employment befitting her degree. The three years she had spent in college, a junior year in France, and being the granddaughter of the eminent Dr. Foster should have culminated in something more elegant than the two uniforms that hung on Miss Graham's basement door. That all these advantages didn't was still incredible to her. It had been assumed that she and Magdalene called Lena would marry well—but hopes for Corinthians were especially high since she'd gone to college. Her education had taught her how to be an enlightened mother and wife, able to contribute to the civilization—or in her case, the civilizing—of her community. And if marriage was not achieved, there were alternative roles: teacher, librarian, or . . . well, something intelligent and public-spirited. When neither of these fates tapped her on the forehead right away, she simply waited. High toned and high yellow, she believed what her mother was also convinced of: that she was a prize for a professional man of color. So there were vacations and weekends in other cities as well as visits and teas in her own, where and when such men appeared. The first of the black doctors to move there, in the forties when she graduated, had a son five years her junior. The second, a dentist, had two infant girls; the third was a very old physician (rumored to be an alcoholic), whose two sons were already raising families. Then there were teachers, two lawyers, a mortician—but on the few occasions when eligible bachelors were among them, Corinthians was not their choice. She was pretty enough, pleasant enough, and her father had the money they could rely on if needed, but she lacked drive. These men wanted wives who could manage, who were not so well accustomed to middle-class life that they had no ambition, no hunger, no hustle in them. They wanted their wives to like the climbing, the acquiring, and the work it took to maintain status once it was achieved. They wanted wives who would sacrifice themselves and appreciate the hard work and sacrifice of their husbands. Corinthians was a little too elegant. Bryn Mawr in 1940. France in 1939. That was a bit much. Fisk, Howard, Talledega, Tougaloo—that was their hunting territory. A woman who spoke French and who had traveled on the *Queen Mary* might not have the proper attitude toward future patients or clients, and if the man was a teacher, he steered clear of a woman who had a better education than he did. At one point post office workers were even being considered suitable for Lena and Corinthians, but that was long after they had reached thirty-five, and after Ruth came to terms with the savage fact that her daughters were not going to marry doctors. It was a shock to them all, which they managed to withstand by not accepting a more complete truth: that they probably were not going to marry anybody.

Magdalene called Lena seemed resigned to her life, but when Corinthians woke up one day to find herself a forty-two-year-old maker of rose petals, she suffered a severe depression which lasted until she made up her mind to get out of the house. So her search for work—which was shock number two—was intense. The twenty-one years that she had been out of college worked against her for a teaching job. She had none of the "new" courses now required by the board of education. She considered going to the state teachers' school to take the required courses, even went to the administration building to register. But the sight of those torpedo breasts under fuzzy blue sweaters, the absolute nakedness of those young faces, drove her out of the building and off the campus like a leaf before a hailstorm. Which was too bad, because she had no real skills. Bryn Mawr had done what a four-year dose of liberal education was designed to do: unfit her for eighty percent of the useful work of the world. First, by training her for leisure time, enrichments, and domestic mindlessness. Second, by a clear implication that she was too good for such work. After graduation she returned to a work world in which colored girls, regardless of their background, were in demand for one and only one kind of work. And by 1963, Corinthians' main concern was simply that her family not know that she had been doing it for two years.

She avoided the other maids on the street, and those whom she saw regularly on the bus assumed that she had some higher household position than theirs since she came to work in high-heeled shoes and only a woman who didn't have to be on her feet all day could stand the pressure of heels on the long ride home. Corinthians was careful; she carried no shopping bag of shoes, aprons, or uniforms. Instead she had a book. A small gray book on which *Contes de Daudet* was printed in gold lettering on its cover. Once she was inside Miss Graham's house she changed into her uniform (which was a discreet blue anyway, not white) and put on a pair of loafers before she dropped to her knees with the pail of soapy water.

Miss Graham was delighted with Corinthians' dress and slightly uppity manners. It gave her house the foreign air she liked to affect, for she was the core, the very heartbeat, of the city's literary world. Michael-Mary Graham was very considerate of Corinthians. When she had large dinner parties, a Swedish cook was hired and the heavy work was done by the old white rummy she shared with the Goodwill Industries. Nor was she impatient with Corinthians' undistinguished everyday cooking, for Michael-Mary ate several small plain meals. It was also a pleasure and a relief to have a maid who read and who seemed to be acquainted with some of the great masters of literature. So nice to give a maid a copy of *Walden* for Christmas rather than that dreary envelope, and to be able to say so to her friends. In the world Michael-Mary Graham inhabited, her mild liberalism, a residue of her Bohemian youth, and her posture of sensitive lady poet passed for anarchy.

Corinthians was naïve, but she was not a complete fool. She never let her mistress know she had ever been to college or Europe or could recognize one word of French that Miss Graham had not taught her (*entrez*, for example). Actually, the work Corinthians did was good for her. In that house she had what she never had in her own: responsibility. She flourished in a way, and exchanged arrogance occasionally for confidence. The humiliation of wearing a uniform, even if it was blue, and deceiving people was tempered by the genuine lift which came of having her own money rather than receiving an allowance like a child. And she was surprised to discover that the amount of neatly folded bills Michael-Mary handed her each Saturday at noon was within two dollars of the amount real secretaries took home each week.

Other than scrubbing the kitchen tile and keeping a hard shine on the wooden floors, the work was not hard. The poetess lived alone and shaped her time and activities carefully in order to meet the heavy demands of artistic responsibility. Being a poet she could, of course, do little else. Marriage, children—all had been sacrificed to the Great Agony and her home was a tribute to the fastidiousness of her dedication (and the generosity of her father's will). Colors, furnishings, and appointments had been selected for their inspirational value. And she was fond of saying, in deprecating some item, "I couldn't write a line with *that* in the house." *That* might be a vase, the new toilet bowl the plumbers hauled in, a plant, or even the Christmas wreath St. John's third-grade class presented to her in gratitude for the moving reading she'd given at their holiday assembly. Every morning between ten and noon she wrote, and every afternoon between three and four-fifteen. Evenings were often given over to discussions and meetings with local poets, painters, musicians, and writers of fiction, at which they praised or condemned other artists, scorned the marketplace and courted it. Of this group Michael-Mary Graham was the queen, for her poetry had been published—first in 1938, in a volume called *Seasons of My Soul;* there was a second collection in 1941, called *Farther Shores.* What was more, her poems had appeared in at least twenty small literary magazines, two "slicks," six college journals, and the Sunday supplements of countless newspapers. She was also the winner, between 1938 and 1958, of nine Poet of the Year awards, culminating finally in the much-coveted State Poet Laureateship. At the ceremony, her most famous poem, "Watchword," was performed by the Choral Speech Society of St. John's High School. None of that, however, had mitigated the reluctance of her publishers to bring out her complete collected works (tentatively called *The Farthest Shore*). But there was no question in her mind that they would come around.

When Miss Graham first saw Corinthians, she was not at all

impressed with her. First, because the prospective employee came ten minutes early for the interview and Michael-Mary, who adhered to her schedule to the minute, was forced to answer the door in a print peignoir. Already irritated by this lapse, she was further disenchanted by the woman's delicate frame. Obviously she could not put up the screens, take down the storm windows, or endure any sustained heavy cleaning. But when she learned the woman's name, Michael-Mary was so charmed by the sound of "Corinthians Dead," she hired her on the spot. As she told friends later, her poetic sensibility overwhelmed her good judgment.

They got on well together, mistress and maid, and by the sixth month of her stay, Michael-Mary suggested that she learn how to type. So Corinthians was almost on her way to becoming an amanuensis after all.

Shortly after Miss Graham encouraged her to take typing so she might be helpful with some of her mistress's work, a black man sat down next to Corinthians on the bus. She took little notice of him—only that he was ill-dressed and appeared elderly. But soon she became aware that he was staring at her. A quick corner-of-the-eye peek to verify this was met by his radiant smile. Corinthians turned her head and kept it so until he got off.

The next day he was there again. Once more she made her disdain clear. The rest of the week passed without his watchful eyes. But on the following Monday he was back, looking at her with an expression that stopped just short of a leer. These occasional meetings went on for a month or so. Corinthians thought she should be afraid of him, for something in his manner suggested waiting—a confident, assured waiting. Then one morning he dropped a white envelope on the seat beside her just before he got off the bus. She let it lie there all the way to her stop, but couldn't resist scooping it up as surreptitiously as possible when she stood to pull the cord.

Standing at the stove, waiting for Michael-Mary's milk to skim, she opened the envelope and withdrew a greeting card.

Raised letters of the word "Friendship" hung above a blue and yellow bouquet of flowers and were repeated inside above a verse.

Friendship is an outstretched hand,
A smile of warm devotion.
I offer both to you this day,
With all the heart's emotion.

A white hand of no particular sex held another, smaller, blue and yellow bouquet. There was no signature.

Corinthians threw it in the brown paper bag opened for the day's garbage. It stayed there all day, but it also stayed on her mind. When evening came, she reached down through the grapefruit rind, the tea leaves, and the salami casing to find it, brush it clean, and transfer it to her purse. She couldn't explain to herself why. The man was a complete nuisance and his flirtation an insult. But no one, not anyone at all, had made any attempt (any serious attempt) to flirt with her in a long time. At the very least the card was good for conversation. She wished he had signed it, not because she wanted to know his name, but so it would look more authentic—otherwise somebody might think she bought it herself.

For two weeks afterward the man was not on the bus. When he did appear, it was hard for Corinthians not to speak or acknowledge his presence. As they neared the place where he usually got off, he leaned over to her and said, "I truly hope you didn't mind." She looked up, gave him a small smile, and shook her head. He said nothing more.

But on subsequent days they did exchange greetings and finally they began to talk. In a while they were chatting (carefully, guardedly) and she, at least, was looking forward to his being there. By the time she knew that his name was Henry Porter and that he had occasional yard work in that part of town, she was glad she had never shown or mentioned either the card or the man to anyone.

Pleasant as their conversations were, they were also curious.

Each took care not to ask the other certain questions—for fear he or she would have to volunteer the same information. What part of town do you live in? Do you know Mr. So-and-so?

Eventually Mr. Porter offered to pick Corinthians up after work. He didn't own a car, he said, but borrowed a friend's sometimes. Corinthians agreed, and the result was a pair of middle-aged lovers who behaved like teen-agers—afraid to be caught by their parents in a love relationship they were too young for. He took her for rides in an old gray Oldsmobile—to the country, to drive-in movies—and they sat over bad coffee in certain dime stores where they were not likely to be recognized.

Corinthians knew she was ashamed of him, that she would have to add him to the other secret, the nature of her work, that he could never set foot in her house. And she hated him a lot for the shame she felt. Hated him sometimes right in the middle of his obvious adoration of her, his frequent compliments about her looks, her manners, her voice. But those swift feelings of contempt never lasted long enough for her to refuse those drive-in movie sessions where she was the sole object of someone's hunger and satisfaction.

At some point Corinthians began to suspect that Porter's discretion was not only in deference to who she was (her position and all), but also because he too didn't want to be discovered. Her first thought was that he was married. His denials, accompanied by a wistful smile which she interpreted as a sly one, only aggravated her suspicions. Finally, to prove his bachelorhood as well as to indulge himself in a real bed, he invited her to his room. She declined immediately and repeatedly for several days until he accused her of the very thing that was absolutely true: that she was ashamed of him.

"Ashamed of you?" Her eyes and mouth went wide with surprise (genuine surprise, because she never thought he would guess it). "If I were ashamed I wouldn't see you at all, let alone *this* way." Her hand pointed toward the world outside the car they sat in: the row upon row of automobiles in the hot drive-in movie lot.

Porter traced her cheek line with his knuckle. "Well, then? The things you tell me can't be true and not true at the same time."

"I've never told you anything except what was true. I thought we both knew . . . understood . . . the problem."

"Maybe," he said. "Let's hear it, Corrie." His knuckles stroked her jaw line. "Let's hear the problem."

"My father. It's only my father . . . the way he is."

"How is he?"

Corinthians shrugged. "You know as well as I do. He never wanted us to mix with . . . people. He's very strict."

"And that's the reason you won't come home with me?"

"I'm sorry. I have to live there. I can't let him know about us. Not yet." But when? she thought. If not at forty-four, then when? If not now, when even my pubic hair is turning gray and when my breasts have dropped of their own accord–then when?

Porter spoke her own question aloud. "When, then?" And she could not answer him right away. She put her fingers to her forehead and said, "I don't know. I honestly don't know."

It was such a fake gesture to go along with her fake feelings of moral and filial commitment that she knew right away how foolish she seemed. The things they did in that old car, the things she'd let her tongue say, as recently as five minutes ago . . . and now to caress her temples and say in Michael-Mary's reading voice, "I don't know," embarrassed her and must have disgusted Porter, for he took his hand from her face and put it on the steering wheel. Right at the beginning of the second feature, he started the car and moved it slowly down the gravel aisle.

Neither spoke until the car entered downtown traffic. It was ten-thirty. She'd told her mother she would be typing manuscript for Miss Graham until very late. "In this heat?" was all her mother said. Corinthians sat quietly, feeling shame but not thinking the word, until she realized that he was driving her to the bus stop where he always let her out to walk home the way she normally would. In a sudden flash she knew he was never going to see her again, and the days rolled out before her like a dingy gray carpet in an unfurnished, unpeopled hall-for-rent.

"Are you taking me home?" She succeeded in keeping the anxiety out of her voice—succeeded too well, for her words sounded arrogant and careless.

He nodded and said, "I don't want a doll baby. I want a woman. A grown-up woman that's not scared of her daddy. I guess you don't want to be a grown-up woman, Corrie."

She stared through the windshield. A grown-up woman? She tried to think of some. Her mother? Lena? The dean of women at Bryn Mawr? Michael-Mary? The ladies who visited her mother and ate cake? Somehow none of them fit. She didn't know any grown-up women. Every woman she knew was a doll baby. Did he mean like the women who rode on the bus? The other maids, who were not hiding what they were? Or the black women who walked the streets at night?

"You mean like those women on the bus? You can have one of *them*, you know. Why don't you drop a greeting card in one of *their* laps?" His words had hit home; she had been compared —unfavorably, she believed—with the only people she knew for certain she was superior to. "They'd love to have a greeting card dropped in their lap. Just love it. But oh, I forgot. You couldn't do that, could you, because they wouldn't be able to read it. They'd have to take it home and wait till Sunday and give it to the preacher to read it to them. Of course when they heard it they might not know what it meant. But it wouldn't matter—they'd see the flowers and the curlicues all over the words and they'd be happy. It wouldn't matter a bit that it was the most ridiculous, most clichéd, most commercial piece of tripe the drugstore world has to offer. They wouldn't know mediocrity if it punched them right in their fat faces. They'd laugh and slap their fat thighs and take you right on into their kitchens. Right up on the breakfast table. But you wouldn't give them a fifteen-cent greeting card, would you?—no matter how silly and stupid it was—because they're grown-up women and you don't have to court *them*. You can just come right out and say, 'Hello there, come on to my room tonight.' Right? Isn't that so? Isn't that so?" She was close to screaming. "But no. You wanted a lady. Somebody who knows how to sit down, how to dress, how to eat the food on her plate. Well, there is a difference between a woman and a lady, and I know you know which one I am."

Porter pulled the car over to the curb, and without shutting off the motor, leaned across her and opened the door. Corinthians got out and did her best to slam it, but the rusty hinges of the borrowed Oldsmobile did not accommodate her. She had to settle for the gesture.

By the time she reached number 12 Not Doctor Street, her trembling had become uncontrollable. Suddenly the shaking stopped and she froze at the steps. Two seconds later she turned on her heel and ran back down the street to where Porter had stopped the car. The moment she had put her foot on the step leading up to the porch, she saw her ripeness mellowing and rotting before a heap of red velvet scraps on a round oak table. The car was still there, its motor purring. Corinthians ran toward it faster than she had ever run in her life, faster than she'd cut across the grass on Honoré Island when she was five and the whole family went there for a holiday. Faster even than the time she flew down the stairs having seen for the first time what the disease had done to her grandfather. She put her hand on the door handle and found it locked. Porter was sitting pretty much the way he was when she'd tried to slam the door. Bending down, she rapped on the window. Porter's profile did not move. She rapped again, louder, mindless of who might see her under the gray beech tree just around the corner from home. So close and yet so far, she felt as though she were in a dream; there, but not there, within a hair's breadth but not reaching it.

She was First Corinthians Dead, daughter of a wealthy property owner and the elegant Ruth Foster, granddaughter of the magnificent and worshipped Dr. Foster, who had been the second man in the city to have a two-horse carriage, and a woman who had turned heads on every deck of the *Queen Mary* and had Frenchmen salivating all over Paris. Corinthians Dead, who had held herself pure all these years (well, almost all, and almost pure), was now banging on the car-door window of a yardman. But she would bang forever to escape the velvet. The red velvet that had flown all over the snow that day when she and Lena and her mother had walked past the hospital on their way to the department store. Her mother was pregnant—a fact that had embarrassed Corinthians when first she learned of it. All she could think of was how her friends would laugh when they found out she had a pregnant mother. Her relief was sweet when she discovered that it was too soon to show. But by February her mother was heavy and needed to get out of the house, to exercise a little. They'd walked slowly through the snow, watching carefully for icy places. Then as they passed Mercy, there was a crowd watching a man on the roof. Corinthians had seen him before her mother did, but when Ruth looked up she was so startled she dropped the basket, scattering the roses everywhere. Corinthians and Lena busied themselves picking them up, wiping the snow from the cloth on their coats, all the while peeping at the man in blue wings on the hospital roof. They were laughing, Lena and she; collecting the roses, looking up at the man, and laughing from fear, embarrassment, and giddiness. It was all mixed together—the red velvet, the screams, and the man crashing down on the pavement. She had seen his body quite clearly, and to her astonishment, there was no blood. The only red in view was in their own hands and in the basket. Her mother's moans were getting louder and she seemed to be sinking into the ground. A stretcher came at last for the doll-broken body (all the more doll-like because there was no blood), and finally a wheelchair for her mother, who was moving straight into labor.

Corinthians continued to make roses, but she hated that stupid hobby and gave Lena any excuse to avoid it. They spoke to her of death. First the death of the man in the blue wings. Now her own. For if Porter did not turn his head and lean toward the door to open it for her, Corinthians believed she would surely die. She banged her knuckles until they ached to get the attention of the living flesh behind the glass, and would have smashed her fist through the window just to touch him, feel his heat, the only thing that could protect her from a smothering death of dry roses.

He did not move. In a panic, lest he shift gears and drive away, leaving her alone in the street, Corinthians climbed up on the fender and lay full out across the hood of the car. She didn't look through the windshield at him. She just lay there, stretched across the car, her fingers struggling for a grip on steel. She thought of nothing. Nothing except what her body needed to do to hang on, to never let go. Even if he drove off at one hundred miles an hour, she would hang on. Her eyes were shut tight with the effort of clinging to the hood, and she didn't hear the door open and shut, nor Porter's footsteps as he moved around to the front of the car. She screamed at first when he put his hand on her shoulders and began pulling her gently into his arms. He carried her to the passenger's side of the car, stood her on her feet while he opened the door and helped her ease into the seat. In the car, he pressed her head onto his shoulder and waited for her soft crying to wane before he left the driver's seat to pick up the purse she had let fall on the sidewalk. He drove away then to number 3 Fifteenth Street, a house owned by Macon Dead, where sixteen tenants lived, and where there was an attic window, from which this same Henry Porter had screamed, wept, waved a shotgun, and urinated over the heads of the women in the yard.

It was not yet midnight and hot—hot enough to make people angry, had it not been for a pleasant smell in the air, like sweet ginger. Corinthians and Porter entered the hall that opened off the front door. Except for a hem of light under the kitchen door, where a card game was in progress, there was no sign of any other tenant.

Corinthians saw only the bed, an iron bed painted hospital white. She sank down on it as soon as she got into the room and stretched out, feeling bathed, scoured, vacuumed, and for the first time simple. Porter undressed after she did and lay down beside her. They were quiet for a minute, then he turned over and parted her legs with his.

Corinthians looked down at him. "Is this for me?" she asked.

"Yes," he said. "Yes, this is for you."

"Porter."

"This is . . . for you. Instead of roses. And silk underwear and bottles of perfume."

"Porter."

"Instead of chocolate creams in a heart-shaped box. Instead of a big house and a great big car. Instead of long trips . . ."

"Porter."

". . . in a clean white boat."

"No."

"Instead of picnics . . ."

"No."

". . . and fishing . . ."

"No."

". . . and being old together on a porch."

"No."

"This is for you, girl. Oh, yes. This is for you."

They woke at four o'clock in the morning, or rather she did. When she opened her eyes she saw him staring at her and those were either tears in his eyes or sweat. It was very hot in that room in spite of the open window.

"The bathroom," she murmured. "Where is the bathroom?"

"Down the hall," he said. Then, apologetically, "Can I get you something?"

"Oh." She pushed a few strands of matted damp hair from her forehead. "Something to drink, please. Something cold."

He dressed quickly, leaving off his shirt and his socks, and left the room. Corinthians got up too and began to put her clothes on. Since there seemed to be no mirror in the room, she stood in front of the open window and used the upper part of the pane, dark enough to show her reflection, to smooth her hair. Then she noticed the walls. What she had assumed to be wallpaper as she entered and fell on the bed was in fact calendars. Row after row of calendars: S. &. J. Automobile Parts, featuring a 1939 Hudson; the Cuyahoga River Construction Company ("We build to please–We're pleased to build"); Lucky Hart Beauty Products (a wavy-haired lady smiling out of a heavily powdered face); the *Call and Post* newspaper. But most of them were from the North Carolina Mutual Life Insurance Company. They literally covered the walls, each one turned to December. It was as though he'd kept every calendar since 1939. Some of them were large cards displaying all twelve months and on those she noticed circles drawn around dates.

Porter came in while she was gazing at them. He held a glass of iced water, the cubes jammed to the rim.

"Why do you keep calendars?" she asked.

He smiled. "Passes the time. Here. Drink your drink. It'll cool you."

She took the glass and sipped a little from it, trying to keep the ice from touching her teeth as she looked at him over the rim. Standing there, barefoot, her hair damp with sweat and sticking to her cheeks like paint, she felt easy. In place of vanity she now felt a self-esteem that was quite new. She was grateful to him, this man who rented a tiny room from her father, who ate with a knife and did not even own a pair of dress shoes. A perfect example of the men her parents had kept her from (and whom she had also kept herself from) all her life because such a man was known to beat his woman, betray her, shame her, and leave her. Corinthians moved close to him, tilted his chin up with her fingers, and planted a feathery kiss on his throat. He held her head in his hands until she closed her eyes and tried to set the glass down on a tiny table.

"Uh uh. It'll be light soon. Gotta get you home."

She obeyed and finished dressing herself. They walked as softly as possible down the stairs and past the wide triangle of light that lay on the floor in front of the kitchen door. The men were still at their card game, but the door was partially open now. Porter and Corinthians moved quickly past, just out of the light.

Still a voice called, "Who that? Mary?"

"No. Just me. Porter."

"Porter?" The voice was incredulous. "What shift you on?"

"Catch you later," said Porter and opened the front door before the speaker's curiosity could propel him into the hall.

Corinthians slid as close to Porter as the floor gear of the car allowed, her head resting on the seat back. She closed her eyes once more and took deep breaths of the sweet air her brother had been inhaling three hours ago.

"Hadn't you better fix your hair?" Porter asked. He thought she was beautiful like that, girlish, but he didn't want her excuse to her parents, if they were still awake, to sound ridiculous.

She shook her head. She wouldn't have collected her hair into a ball at her nape now for anything in the world.

Porter parked under the same tree where Corinthians had thrown herself across the hood of the car. Now, after a whispered confession, she walked the four blocks, no longer afraid to mount the porch steps.

As soon as she closed the door she heard voices and instinctively touched her loose hair. The voices came from beyond the dining room, from behind the closed kitchen door. Men's voices. Corinthians blinked. She had just come from a house in which men sat in a lit kitchen talking in loud excited voices, only to meet an identical scene at home. She wondered if this part of the night, a part she was unfamiliar with, belonged, had always belonged, to men. If perhaps it was a secret hour in which men rose like giants from dragon's teeth and, while the women slept, clustered in their kitchens. On tiptoe she approached the door. Her father was speaking.

"You still haven't explained to me why you brought him along."

"What difference does it make now?" That was her brother's voice.

"He knows about it," said her father. "That's what difference."

"About what? There's nothing to know. It was a bust." Milkman's voice swelled like a blister.

"It was a mistake, not a bust. It just means it's somewhere else. That's all."

"Yeah. The mint. You want me to go to the mint?"

"No!" Macon struck the table. "It's got to be there. It's got to."

Corinthians couldn't make sense out of what they were talking about with so much passion, and she didn't want to stay there and learn, lest it distract her from the contentment she was feeling. She left them and climbed the stairs to her own bed.

Downstairs in the kitchen, Milkman folded his arms on the table and put his head down. "I don't care. I don't care where it is."

"It was just a mistake," said his father. "One little mess-up. That don't mean we have to pull out."

"You call being thrown in jail a little mess-up?"

"You out, ain't you? You was only there twenty minutes."

"Two hours."

"Wouldn't have been two minutes if you had called me soon's you got there. Sooner. Should have called me soon's they picked you up."

"Police cars don't have telephones in them." Milkman was weary. He lifted his head and let it rest in his hand, directing his words into his shirt sleeve.

"They would have let you, if it had just been you. Soon as you told them your name they would have let you go. But you was with that Southside nigger. That's what did it."

"That is *not* what did it. It was riding around with a sack of rocks and human bones that did it. Human bones. Which is, if you're a halfway intelligent cop, a hint that there must have been a human being connected to them bones at one time."

"Of course at one time. But not tonight. There couldn't have been a human attached to the bones yesterday. It takes time for a body to be a skeleton. They know that. And don't tell me it wasn't Guitar they was suspicious of. That yellow-eyed nigger looks like he might do anything."

"They didn't see his eyes when they told us to pull over. They didn't see nothing. They just sideswiped us, and told us to get out. Now, what was that for? What'd they stop us for? We wasn't speeding. Just driving along." Milkman searched for cigarettes. He got angry again when he thought about bending over the car, his legs spread, his hands on the hood, while the policeman fingered his legs, his back, his ass, his arms. "What business they got stopping cars that ain't speeding?"

"They stop anybody they want to. They saw you was colored, that's all. And they're looking for the Negro that killed that boy."

"Who said it was a Negro?"

"Paper said it."

"They always say that. Every time . . ."

"What difference does it make? If you'd been alone and told them your name they never would have hauled you in, never would have searched the car, and never would have opened that sack. They know me. You saw how they acted when I got there."

"They didn't act any different when you got there. . . ."

"What?"

"They acted different when you took that sucker off in the corner and opened your wallet."

"You better be thankful I got a wallet."

"I am. God knows I am."

"And that would have been the end of it, except for that Southside nigger. Hadn't been for him, they wouldn't of had to get Pilate down there." Macon rubbed his knees. The idea of having to depend on Pilate to get his son out of jail humiliated him. "Raggedy bootlegging bitch."

"She's still a bitch?" Milkman began to chuckle. Exhaustion and the slow release of tension made him giddy. "You thought she stole it. All these years . . . all these years you've been holding that against her." He was laughing out right now. "How she sneaked out of some cave with a big bag of gold that must have weighed a hundred pounds over her shoulder, all over the country for fifty years and didn't spend none of it, just hung it from the ceiling like a fuckin sack of onions." Milkman put his head back and let the laughter fill the kitchen. Macon was silent. "Fifty years . . . You been thinking about that gold for fifty years! Oh, shit. This is some crazy shit. . . ." Tears of laughter were running from his eyes. "Crazy. All of you. Just straight-out, laid-back crazy. I should of known. The whole thing was crazy; everything about it was crazy—the whole idea."

"What's crazier? Her hauling a sack of gold around all this time, or hauling a dead man's bones around? Huh? Which one?" Macon asked.

"I don't know. I really don't know."

"If she do one, she could do the other. She's the one they should have kept. When you all told them the bones belonged to her, they should have locked her up soon's she walked in the door."

Milkman wiped the tears on his sleeve. "Lock her up for what? After that story she told?" He started laughing again. "She came in there like Louise Beaver and Butterfly McQueen all rolled up in one. 'Yassuh, boss. Yassuh, boss. . . .'"

"She didn't say that."

"Almost. She even changed her voice."

"I told you she was a snake. Drop her skin in a split second."

"She didn't even look the same. She looked short. Short and pitiful."

"That's cause she wanted it back. She wanted them to let her have the bones back."

"Her poor husband's bones, that she didn't have no money to bury. Pilate got a husband somewhere?"

"Does the Pope?"

"Well, she got 'em back. They gave 'em to her."

"She knew what she was doing, all right."

"Yeah, she knew. But how did she know so fast? I mean she came in there . . . you know . . . prepared. She had it all together when she got there. Cop must have told her everything when he picked her up and brought her to the station."

"Uh uh. They don't do that."

"Then how did she know?"

"Who knows what Pilate knows?"

Milkman shook his head. "Only The Shadow knows." He was still amused, but earlier, when he and Guitar had sat handcuffed on a wooden bench, his neck skin had crawled with fear.

"White man's bones," Macon said. He stood up and yawned. The dark of the sky was softened now. "Nigger bitch roaming around with a white man's bones." He yawned again. "I'll never understand that woman. I'm seventy-two years old and I'm going to die not understanding one thing about her." Macon walked toward the kitchen door and opened it. Then he turned around and said to Milkman, "But you know what that means, don't you? If she took the white man's bones and left the gold, then the gold must still be there." He shut the door before his son could protest.

Well, it would rot there, thought Milkman. If anybody even mentions the word "gold," I'm going to have to take his teeth out. He sat on there in the kitchen, wishing for more coffee, but too tired to get up and fix it. In a minute his mother would be downstairs; she had got up when he and Macon had come in, but Macon sent her back upstairs. Milkman fished for another cigarette and watched dawn eclipse the electric light over the sink. It was a cheery sun, which suggested another hot day. But the stronger it got, the more desolate he became. Alone, without Macon, he let the events of the night come back to him—he remembered little things, details, and yet he wasn't sure these details had really happened. Perhaps he made them up. Pilate *had* been shorter. As she stood there in the receiving room of the jail, she didn't even come up to the sergeant's shoulder—and the sergeant's head barely reached Milkman's own chin. But Pilate was as tall as he was. When she whined to the policeman, verifying Milkman's and Guitar's lie that they had ripped off the sack as a joke on an old lady, she had to look up at him. And her hands were shaking as she described how she didn't know the sack was gone until the officer woke her up; that she couldn't imagine why anybody would want to run off with her husband's bones; that her husband had been lynched in Mississippi fifteen years ago, and that they wouldn't let her cut him down, and that she left town then and that when she went back the body had dropped off the rope of its own accord, so she collected it and tried to bury it, but the "funeral peoples" wanted fifty dollars for a coffin, and the carpenter wanted twelve-fifty for a pine box and she just didn't have no twelve dollars and fifty cents so she just carried what was left of Mr. Solomon (she always called him Mr. Solomon cause he was such a dignified colored man) and put it in a sack and kept it with her. "Bible say what so e'er the Lord hath brought together, let no man put asunder—Matthew Twenty-one: Two. We was bony fide and legal wed, suh," she pleaded. Even her eyes, those big sleepy old eyes, were small as she went on: "So I thought I just as well keep him near me and when I die they can put him in the same hole as me. We'll raise up to Judgment Day together. Hand in hand."

Milkman was astonished. He thought Pilate's only acquaintance with the Bible was the getting of names out of it, but she quoted it, apparently, verse and chapter. Furthermore, she had looked at Milkman and Guitar and Macon like she didn't know who exactly they were. In fact, when asked if she knew them, she pointedly said, "Not this man, here," looking at her brother, "but I do believe I've noticed this fella around the neighborhood." Here she motioned toward Guitar, who sat there like marble with the eyes of a dead man. Later, as Macon drove them all home—Pilate sitting in front, Guitar and himself in the back—Guitar never said a word. His anger was like heat shimmering out of his skin, making the hot air blowing in through the open window seem refreshing by comparison.

And again there was a change. Pilate was tall again. The top of her head, wrapped in a silk rag, almost touched the roof of the car, as did theirs. And her own voice was back. She spoke, but to Macon only, and nobody else spoke at all. In a conversational tone, like somebody picking up a story that had been interrupted in the telling, she told her brother something quite different from what she told the policemen.

"I spent that whole day and night in there, and when I looked out the next morning you was gone. I was scared I would run into you, but I didn't see hide nor hair of you. It was three years or more 'fore I went back. The winter it was. Snow was everywhere and I couldn't hardly find my way. I looked up Circe first, then went looking for the cave. It was a hard trek, I can tell you, and I was in frail condition. Snow piled up every which way. But you should of known better than to think I'd go back there for them little old bags. I wasn't stuttin 'em when I first laid eyes on 'em, I sure wasn't thinking about them three years later. I went cause Papa told me to. He kept coming to see me, off and on. Tell me things to do. First he just told me to sing, to keep on singing. 'Sing,' he'd whisper. 'Sing, sing.' Then right after Reba was born he came and told me outright: 'You just can't fly on off and leave a body,' he tole me. A human life is precious. You shouldn't fly off and leave it. So I knew right away what he meant cause he was right there when we did it. He meant that if you take a life, then you own it. You responsible for it. You can't get rid of nobody by killing them. They still there, and they yours now. So I had to go back for it. And I did find the cave. And there he was. Some wolves or something must have drug it cause it was right in the mouth of the cave, laying up, sitting up almost, on that very rock we slept on. I put him in my sack, piece by piece. Some cloth was still on him, but his bones was clean and dry. I've had it every since. Papa told me to, and he was right, you know. You can't take a life and walk off and leave it. Life is life. Precious. And the dead you kill is yours. They stay with you anyway, in your mind. So it's a better thing, a more better thing to have the bones right there with you wherever you go. That way, it frees up your mind."

Fucks up your mind, thought Milkman, fucks it up for good. He pulled himself up from the table. He had to get some sleep before he went looking for Guitar.

Staggering up the stairs, he remembered Pilate's back as she got out of the Buick—not bent at all under the weight of the sack. And he remembered how Guitar glared at her as she walked away from the car. When Macon dropped him off, he neither answered nor turned his head at Milkman's "See y' later."

Milkman woke at noon. Somebody had come into his room and placed a small fan on the floor near the foot of his bed. He listened to the whirring for a long time before he got up and went into the bathroom to fill the tub. He lay there in lukewarm water, still sweating, too hot and tired to soap himself. Every now and then he flicked water on his face, letting it wet his two-day-old beard. He wondered if he could shave without slicing his chin open. The tub was uncomfortable, too short for him to stretch out, though he remembered when he could almost swim in it. Now he looked down at his legs. The left one looked just as long as the other. His eyes traveled up his body. The touch of the policeman's hand was still there—a touch that made his flesh jump like the tremor of a horse's flank when flies light on it. And something more. Something like shame stuck to his skin. Shame at being spread-eagled, fingered, and handcuffed. Shame at having stolen a skeleton, like a kid on a Halloween trick-or-treat prank rather than a grown man making a hit. Shame at needing both his father and his aunt to get him off. Then more shame at seeing his father—with an accommodating "we all understand how it is" smile—buckle before the policemen. But nothing was like the shame he felt as he watched and listened to Pilate. Not just her Aunt Jemima act, but the fact that she was both adept at it and willing to do it—for him. For the one who had just left her house carrying what he believed was her inheritance. It didn't matter that he also believed she had "stolen" it. . . . From whom? From a dead man? From his father, who was also stealing it? Then and now? He had stolen it too, and what's more, he had been prepared—at least he told himself he had been prepared—to knock her down if she had come into the room while he was in the act of stealing it. To knock down an old black lady who had cooked him his first perfect egg, who had shown him the sky, the blue of it, which was like her mother's ribbons, so that from then on when he looked at it, it had no distance, no remoteness, but was intimate, familiar, like a room that he lived in, a place where he belonged. She had told him stories, sung him songs, fed him bananas and corn bread and, on the first cold day of the year, hot nut soup. And if his mother was right, this old black lady—in her late sixties, but with the skin and agility of a teen-aged girl—had brought him into the world when only a miracle could have. It was this woman, whom he would have knocked senseless, who shuffled into the police station and did a little number for the cops—opening herself up wide for their amusement, their pity, their scorn, their mockery, their disbelief, their meanness, their whimsy, their annoyance, their power, their anger, their boredom—whatever would be useful to her and to himself.

Milkman sloshed his legs in the water. He thought again of how Guitar had looked at Pilate—the jeweled hatred in his eyes. He had no right to that look. Suddenly, Milkman knew the answer to the question he had never been able to ask Guitar. Guitar could kill, would kill, and probably had killed. The Seven Days was the consequence of this ability, but not its origin. No. He had no cause to look at her like that, Milkman thought, and heaving himself upright in the tub, he soaped himself hurriedly.

The September heat blasted him as soon as he got outside, and wiped out the pleasant effects of his bath. Macon had taken the Buick—age forced him to walk less—so Milkman went on foot to Guitar's house. As he rounded the corner, he noticed a familiar-looking gray Oldsmobile, a jagged crack in the rear window, parked in front of the house. Several men were inside and two were standing outside: Guitar and Railroad Tommy. Milkman slowed his steps. Tommy was talking, while Guitar nodded his head. Then the two men shook hands—a handshake Milkman had never seen before: first Tommy held Guitar's hand in both his own, then Guitar held Tommy's hand in his two. Tommy got in the car and Guitar dashed around the house to the side stairs that led to his room. The Oldsmobile—Milkman figured it was a 1953 or 1954 model—made a tight U-turn and headed toward him. When it passed by, all the occupants looked straight ahead. Porter was driving, with Empire State in the middle and Railroad Tommy on the far side, and in the back seat was Hospital Tommy and a man named Nero. Milkman didn't know the other man.

That must be *them*, he thought. His heart beat wildly. Six men, one of them Porter, and Guitar. Those are the Days. And that car. That was the car that let Corinthians off near the house sometimes. Milkman had first assumed his sister had an occasional lift home from her job. Later, since she never mentioned it, and also because she seemed quieter and rounder lately, he decided she was seeing some man on the sly. He thought it funny, sweet and a little sad. But now he knew that whoever she was seeing belonged to that car and belonged to the Seven Days. Foolish woman, he thought. Of all the people to pick. She was so silly. So silly. Jesus!

He wasn't up to Guitar now. He would see him later.

People behaved much better, were more polite, more understanding when Milkman was drunk. The alcohol didn't change him at all, but it had a tremendous impact on whomever he saw while he was under its influence. They looked better, never spoke above a whisper, and when they touched him, even to throw him out of the house party because he had peed in the kitchen sink, or when they picked his pockets as he dozed on a bench at the bus station, they were gentle, loving.

He stayed that way, swaying from light buzz to stoned, for two days and a night, and would have extended it to at least another day but for a sobering conversation with Magdalene called Lena, to whom he had not said more than four consecutive sentences since he was in the ninth grade.

She was waiting for him at the top of the stairs when he came home early one morning. Wrapped in a rayon robe and without her glasses, she looked unreal yet kind, like the man who had picked his pocket a short while ago.

"Come here. I want to show you something. Can you come in here for a minute?" She was whispering.

"Can't it wait?" He was kind too; and he was proud of the civility in his voice, considering how tired he was.

"No," she said. "No. You have to see it now. Today. Just look at it."

"Lena, I'm really beat out . . ." he began in sweet reasonableness.

"It won't take more'n a minute. It's important."

He sighed and followed her down the hall into her bedroom. She walked to the window and pointed. "Look down there."

In what seemed to him like elegant if slow motion, Milkman went to the window, parted the curtain, and followed her pointing finger with his eyes. All he saw was the lawn at the side of the house. Not a thing was moving there, but in the light of early day he thought he might have missed it.

"What?"

"That little maple. Right there." She pointed to a tiny maple tree about four feet high. "The leaves should be turning red now. September is almost over. But they're not; they're just shriveling and falling down green."

He turned to her and smiled. "You said it was important." He was not angry, not even irritated, and he enjoyed his equanimity.

"It is important. Very important." Her voice was soft; she kept on staring at the tree.

"Then tell me. I've got to go to work in a few minutes."

"I know. But you can spare me a minute, can't you?"

"Not to stare at a dead bush, I can't."

"It's not dead yet. But it will be soon. The leaves aren't turning this year."

"Lena, you been in the sherry?"

"Don't make fun of me," she said, and there was a hint of steel in her voice.

"But you have, haven't you?"

"You're not paying any attention to me."

"I am. I'm standing here listening to you tell me the news of the day—that a bush is dying."

"You don't remember it, do you?"

"Remember it?"

"You peed on it."

"I what?"

"You peed on it."

"Lena, maybe we can discuss this later. . . ."

"And on me."

"Uh . . . Lena, I have done some things in my life. Some things I don't feel too good about. But I swear to God I never peed on you."

"It was summer. The year Daddy had that Packard. We went for a ride and you had to go to the bathroom. Remember?"

Milkman shook his head. "No. I don't remember that."

"I took you. We were in the country and there was no place else to go. So they made me take you. Mama wanted to, but Daddy wouldn't let her. And he wouldn't go himself. Corinthians turned up her nose and refused outright, so they made me go. I had on heels too. I was a girl too, but they made me go. You and I had to slide down a little slope off the shoulder of the road. It was pretty back in there. I unbuttoned your pants and turned away so you could be private. Some purple violets were growing all over the grass, and wild jonquil. I picked them and took some twigs from a tree. When I got home I stuck them in the ground right down there." She nodded toward the window. "Just made a hole and stuck them in. I always liked flowers, you know. I was the one who started making artificial roses. Not Mama. Not Corinthians. Me. I loved to do it. It kept me . . . quiet. That's why they make those people in the asylum weave baskets and make rag rugs. It keeps them quiet. If they didn't have the baskets they might find out what's really wrong and . . . do something. Something terrible. After you peed on me, I wanted to kill you. I even tried to once or twice. In little ways:

leaving soap in your tub, things like that. But you never slipped and broke your neck, or fell down the stairs or anything." She laughed a little. "But then I saw something. The flowers I'd stuck in the ground, the ones you peed on—well, they died, of course, but not the twig. It lived. It's that maple. So I wasn't mad about it anymore—the pee, I mean—because the tree was growing. But it's dying now, Macon."

Milkman rubbed the corner of his eye with his ring finger. He was so sleepy. "Yeah, well, that was a helluva piss, wouldn't you say? You want me to give it another shot?"

Magdalene called Lena drew one hand out of the pocket of her robe and smashed it across his mouth. Milkman stiffened and made an incomplete gesture toward her. She ignored it and said, "As surely as my name is Magdalene, you are the line I will step across. I thought because that tree was alive that it was all right. But I forgot that there are all kinds of ways to pee on people."

"You listen here." Milkman was sober now and he spoke as steadily as he could. "I'm going to make some allowance for your sherry—up to a point. But you keep your hands off me. What is all this about peeing on people?"

"You've been doing it to us all your life."

"You're crazy. When have I ever messed over anybody in this house? When did you ever see me telling anybody what to do or giving orders? I don't carry no stick; I live and let live, you know that."

"I know you told Daddy about Corinthians, that she was seeing a man. Secretly. And—"

"I *had* to. I'd love for her to find somebody, but I *know* that man. I—I've been around him. And I don't think he . . ." Milkman stopped, unable to explain. About the Days, about what he suspected.

"Oh?" Her voice was thick with sarcasm. "You have somebody else in mind for her?"

"No."

"No? But he's Southside, and not good enough for her? It's good enough for you, but not for her, right?"

"Lena . . ."

"What do you know about somebody not being good enough for somebody else? And since when did you care whether Corinthians stood up or fell down? You've been laughing at us all your life. Corinthians. Mama. Me. Using us, ordering us, and judging us: how we cook your food; how we keep your house. But now, all of a sudden, you have Corinthians' welfare at heart and break her up from a man you don't approve of. Who are you to approve or disapprove anybody or anything? I was breathing air in the world thirteen years before your lungs were even formed. Corinthians, twelve. You don't know a single thing about either one of us—we made roses; that's all you knew—but now you know what's best for the very woman who wiped the dribble from your chin because you were too young to know how to spit. Our girlhood was spent like a found nickel on you. When you slept, we were quiet; when you were hungry, we cooked; when you wanted to play, we entertained you; and when you got grown enough to know the difference between a woman and a two-toned Ford, everything in this house stopped for you. You have yet to wash your own underwear, spread a bed, wipe the ring from your tub, or move a fleck of your dirt from one place to another. And to this day, you have never asked one of us if we were tired, or sad, or wanted a cup of coffee. You've never picked up anything heavier than your own feet, or solved a problem harder than fourth-grade arithmetic. Where do you get the *right* to decide our lives?"

"Lena, cool it. I don't want to hear it."

"I'll tell you where. From that hog's gut that hangs down between your legs. Well, let me tell you something, baby brother: you will need more than that. I don't know where you will get it or who will give it to you, but mark my words, you will need more than that. He has forbidden her to leave the house, made her quit her job, evicted the man, garnisheed his wages, and it is all because of you. You are exactly like him. Exactly. I didn't go to college because of him. Because I was afraid of what he might do to Mama. You think because you hit him once that we all believe you were protecting her. Taking her side. It's a lie. You were taking over, letting us know you had the right to tell her and all of us what to do."

She stopped suddenly and Milkman could hear her breathing. When she started up again, her voice had changed; the steel was gone and in its place was a drifting, breezy music. "When we were little girls, before you were born, he took us to the ice-house once. Drove us there in his Hudson. We were all dressed up, and we stood there in front of those sweating black men, sucking ice out of our handkerchiefs, leaning forward a little so as not to drip water on our dresses. There were other children there. Barefoot, naked to the waist, dirty. But we stood apart, near the car, in white stockings, ribbons, and gloves. And when he talked to the men, he kept glancing at us, us and the car. The car and us. You see, he took us there so they could see us, envy us, envy him. Then one of the little boys came over to us and put his hand on Corinthians' hair. She offered him her piece of ice and before we knew it, *he* was running toward us. He knocked the ice out of her hand into the dirt and shoved us both into the car. First he displayed us, then he splayed us. All our lives were like that: he would parade us like virgins through Babylon, then humiliate us like whores in Babylon. Now he has knocked the ice out of Corinthians' hand again. And you are to blame." Magdalene called Lena was crying. "You are to blame. You are a sad, pitiful, stupid, selfish, hateful man. I hope your little hog's gut stands you in good stead, and that you take good care of it, because you don't have anything else. But I want to give you notice." She pulled her glasses out of her pocket and put them on. Her eyes doubled in size behind the lenses and were very pale and cold. "I don't make roses anymore, and you have pissed your last in this house."

Milkman said nothing.

"Now," she whispered, "get out of my room."

Milkman turned and walked across the room. It was good advice, he thought. Why not take it? He closed the door.

Part II

Chapter 10

When Hansel and Gretel stood in the forest and saw the house in the clearing before them, the little hairs at the nape of their necks must have shivered. Their knees must have felt so weak that blinding hunger alone could have propelled them forward. No one was there to warn or hold them; their parents, chastened and grieving, were far away. So they ran as fast as they could to the house where a woman older than death lived, and they ignored the shivering nape hair and the softness in their knees. A grown man can also be energized by hunger, and any weakness in his knees or irregularity in his heartbeat will disappear if he thinks his hunger is about to be assuaged. Especially if the object of his craving is not gingerbread or chewy gumdrops, but gold.

Milkman ducked under the boughs of black walnut trees and walked straight toward the big crumbling house. He knew that an old woman had lived in it once, but he saw no signs of life there now. He was oblivious to the universe of wood life that did live there in layers of ivy grown so thick he could have sunk his arm in it up to the elbow. Life that crawled, life that slunk and crept and never closed its eyes. Life that burrowed and scurried, and life so still it was indistinguishable from the ivy stems on which it lay. Birth, life, and death—each took place on the hidden side of a leaf. From where he stood, the house looked as if it had been eaten by a galloping disease, the sores of which were dark and fluid.

One mile behind him were macadam and the reassuring sounds of an automobile or two—one of which was Reverend Cooper's car, driven by his thirteen-year-old nephew.

Noon, Milkman had told him. Come back at noon. He could just as easily have said twenty minutes, and now that he was alone, assaulted by what city people regard as raucous silence, he wished he had said five minutes. But even if the boy hadn't had chores to do, it would be foolish to be driven fifteen miles outside Danville on "business" and stay a hot minute.

He should never have made up that elaborate story to disguise his search for the cave; somebody might ask him about it. Besides, lies should be very simple, like the truth. Excessive detail was simply excess. But he was so tired after the long bus ride from Pittsburgh, coming right after the luxury of the flight, he was afraid he wouldn't be convincing.

The airplane ride exhilarated him, encouraged illusion and a feeling of invulnerability. High above the clouds, heavy yet light, caught in the stillness of speed ("Cruise," the pilot said), sitting in intricate metal become glistening bird, it was not possible to believe he had ever made a mistake, or could. Only one small thought troubled him—that Guitar was not there too. He would have loved it—the view, the food, the stewardesses. But Milkman wanted to do this by himself, with no input from anybody. This one time he wanted to go solo. In the air, away from real life, he felt free, but on the ground, when he talked to Guitar just before he left, the wings of all those other people's nightmares flapped in his face and constrained him. Lena's anger, Corinthians' loose and uncombed hair, matching her slack lips, Ruth's stepped-up surveillance, his father's bottomless greed, Hagar's hollow eyes—he did not know whether he deserved any of that, but he knew he was fed up and he knew he had to leave quickly. He told Guitar of his decision before he told his father.

"Daddy thinks the stuff is still in the cave."

"Could be." Guitar sipped his tea.

"Anyway, it's worth checking out. At least we'll know once and for all."

"I couldn't agree more."

"So I'm going after it."

"By yourself?"

Milkman sighed. "Yeah. Yeah. By myself. I need to get out of here. I mean I really have to go away somewhere."

Guitar put his cup down and folded his hands in front of his mouth. "Wouldn't it be easier with the two of us? Suppose you have trouble?"

"It might be easier, but it might look more suspicious with two men instead of one roaming around the woods. If I find it, I'll haul it back and we'll split it up just like we agreed. If I don't, well, I'll be back anyway."

"When you leaving?"

"Tomorrow morning."

"What's your father say about you going alone?"

"I haven't told him yet. You're the only one knows so far." Milkman stood up and went to the window that looked out on Guitar's little porch. "Shit."

Guitar was watching him carefully. "What's the matter?" he asked. "Why you so low? You don't act like a man on his way to the end of the rainbow."

Milkman turned around and sat on the sill. "I hope it *is* a rainbow, and nobody has run off with the pot, cause I need it."

"Everybody needs it."

"Not as bad as me."

Guitar smiled. "Look like you really got the itch now. More than before."

"Yeah, well, everything's worse than before, or maybe it's the same as before. I don't know. I just know that I want to live my own life. I don't want to be my old man's office boy no more. And as long as I'm in this place I will be. Unless I have my own money. I have to get out of that house and I don't want to owe anybody when I go. My family's driving me crazy. Daddy wants me to be like him and hate my mother. My mother wants me to think like her and hate my father. Corinthians won't speak to me; Lena wants me out. And Hagar wants me chained to her bed or dead. Everybody wants something from me, you know what I mean? Something they think they can't get anywhere else. Something they think I got. I don't know what it is—I mean what it is they really want."

Guitar stretched his legs. "They want your life, man."

"My life?"

"What else?"

"No. Hagar wants my life. My family . . . they want—"

"I don't mean that way. I don't mean they want your dead life; they want your living life."

"You're losing me," said Milkman.

"Look. It's the condition our condition is in. Everybody wants the life of a black man. Everybody. White men want us dead or quiet—which is the same thing as dead. White women, same thing. They want us, you know, 'universal,' human, no 'race consciousness.' Tame, except in bed. They like a little racial loincloth in the bed. But outside the bed they want us to be individuals. You tell them, 'But they lynched my papa,' and they say, 'Yeah, but you're better than the lynchers are, so forget it.' And black women, they want your whole self. Love, they call it, and understanding. 'Why don't you *understand* me?' What they mean is, Don't love anything on earth except me. They say, 'Be responsible,' but what they mean is, Don't go anywhere where I ain't. You try to climb Mount Everest, they'll tie up your ropes. Tell them you want to go to the bottom of the sea—just for a look—they'll hide your oxygen tank. Or you don't even have to go that far. Buy a horn and say you want to play. Oh, they love the music, but only after you pull eight at the post office. Even if you make it, even if you stubborn and mean and you get to the top of Mount Everest, or you do play and you good, real good—that still ain't enough. You blow your lungs out on the horn and they want what breath you got left to hear about how you love them. They want your full attention. Take a risk and they say you not for real. That you don't love them. They won't even let you risk your own life, man, your *own* life—unless it's over them. You can't even die unless it's about them. What good is a man's life if he can't even choose what to die for?"

"Nobody can choose what to die for."

"Yes you can, and if you can't, you can damn well try to."

"You sound bitter. If that's what you feel, why are you playing your numbers game? Keeping the racial ratio the same and all? Every time I ask you what you doing it for, you talk about love. Loving Negroes. Now you say—"

"It *is* about love. What else but love? Can't I love what I criticize?"

"Yeah, but except for skin color, I can't tell the difference between what the white women want from us and what the colored women want. You say they all want our life, our living life. So if a colored woman is raped and killed, why do the Days rape and kill a white woman? Why worry about the colored woman at all?"

Guitar cocked his head and looked sideways at Milkman. His nostrils flared a little. "Because she's *mine*."

"Yeah. Sure." Milkman didn't try to keep disbelief out of his voice. "So everybody wants to kill us, except black men, right?"

"Right."

"Then why did my father—who is a very black man—try to kill me before I was even born?"

"Maybe he thought you were a little girl; I don't know. But I don't have to tell you that your father is a very strange Negro. He'll reap the benefits of what we sow, and there's nothing we can do about that. He behaves like a white man, thinks like a white man. As a matter of fact, I'm glad you brought him up. Maybe you can tell me how, after losing everything his own father worked for to some crackers, after *seeing* his father shot down by them, how can he keep his knees bent? Why does he love them so? And Pilate. She's worse. She saw it too and, first, goes back to get a cracker's bones for some kind of crazy self-punishment, and second, leaves the cracker's gold right where it was! Now, is that voluntary slavery or not? She slipped into those Jemima shoes cause they fit."

"Look, Guitar. First of all, my father doesn't care whether a white man lives or swallows lye. He just wants what they have. And Pilate is a little nuts, but she wanted us out of there. If she hadn't been smart, both our asses would be cooling in the joint right now."

"My ass. Not yours. She wanted you out, not me."

"Come on. That ain't even fair."

"No. Fair is one more thing I've given up."

"But to Pilate? What for? She knew what we did and still she bailed us out. Went down for us, clowned and crawled for us. You saw her face. You ever see anything like it in your life?"

"Once. Just once," said Guitar. And he remembered anew how his mother smiled when the white man handed her the four ten-dollar bills. More than gratitude was showing in her eyes. More than that. Not love, but a willingness to love. Her husband was sliced in half and boxed backward. He'd heard the mill men tell how the two halves, not even fitted together, were placed cut side down, skin side up, in the coffin. Facing each other. Each eye looking deep into its mate. Each nostril inhaling the breath the other nostril had expelled. The right cheek facing the left. The right elbow crossed over the left elbow. And he had worried then, as a child, that when his father was wakened on Judgment Day his first sight would not be glory or the magnificent head of God—or even the rainbow. It would be his own other eye.

Even so, his mother had smiled and shown that willingness to love the man who was responsible for dividing his father up throughout eternity. It wasn't the divinity from the foreman's wife that made him sick. That came later. It was the fact that instead of life insurance, the sawmill owner gave his mother forty dollars "to tide you and them kids over," and she took it happily and bought each of them a big peppermint stick on the very day of the funeral. Guitar's two sisters and baby brother sucked away at the bone-white and blood-red stick, but Guitar couldn't. He held it in his hand until it stuck there. All day he held it. At the graveside, at the funeral supper, all the sleepless night. The others made fun of what they believed was his miserliness, but he could not eat it or throw it away, until finally, in the outhouse, he let it fall into the earth's stinking hole.

"Once," he said. "Just once." And felt the nausea all over again. "The crunch is here," he said. "The big crunch. Don't let them Kennedys fool you. And I'll tell you the truth: I hope your daddy's right about what's in that cave. And I sure hope you don't have no second thoughts about getting it back here."

"What's that supposed to mean?"

"It means I'm nervous. Real nervous. I need the bread."

"If you're in a hurt, I can let you have—"

"Not *me*. *Us*. We have work to do, man. And just recently"—Guitar squinted his eyes at Milkman—"just recently one of us was put out in the streets, by somebody I don't have to name. And his wages were garnisheed cause this somebody said two months rent was owing. This somebody needs two months rent on a twelve-by-twelve hole in the wall like a fish needs side pockets. Now we have to take care of this man, get him a place to stay, pay the so-called back rent, and—"

"That was my fault. Let me tell you what happened. . . ."

"No. Don't tell me nothing. You ain't the landlord and you didn't put him out. You may have handed him the gun, but you didn't pull the trigger. I'm not blaming you."

"Why not? You talk about my father, my father's sister, and you'll talk about my sister too if I let you. Why you trust me?"

"Baby, I hope I never have to ask myself that question."

It ended all right, that gloomy conversation. There was no real anger and nothing irrevocable was said. When Milkman left, Guitar opened his palm as usual and Milkman slapped it. Maybe it was fatigue, but the touching of palms seemed a little weak.

At the Pittsburgh airport he discovered that Danville was 240 miles northeast, and not accessible by any public transportation other than a Greyhound bus. Reluctantly, unwilling to give up the elegance he had felt on the flight, he taxied from the airport to the bus station and settled himself for two idle hours before the Greyhound left. By the time he boarded, the inactivity, the picture magazines he'd read, the strolls in the streets near the station, had exhausted him. He fell asleep fifteen minutes outside Pittsburgh. When he woke it was late in the afternoon, with an hour more to go before he reached Danville. His father had raved about the beauty of this part of the country, but Milkman saw it as merely green, deep into its Indian summer but cooler than his own city, although it was farther south. The mountains, he thought, must make for the difference in temperature. For a few minutes he tried to enjoy the scenery running past his window, then the city man's boredom with nature's repetition overtook him. Some places had lots of trees, some did not; some fields were green, some were not, and the hills in the distance were like the hills in every distance. Then he watched signs—the names of towns that lay twenty-two miles ahead, seventeen miles to the east, five miles to the northeast. And the names of junctions, counties, crossings, bridges, stations, tunnels, mountains, rivers, creeks, landings, parks, and lookout points. Everybody had to do his act, he thought, for surely anybody who was interested in Dudberry Point already knew where it was.

He had two bottles of Cutty Sark in his suitcase, along with two shirts and some underwear. The large suitcase, he thought, would have its real load on the return trip. Now he wished he had not checked it under the bus, for he wanted a drink right then. According to his watch, the gold Longines his mother had given him, it would be another twenty minutes before a stop. He lay back on the headrest and tried to fall asleep. His eyes were creasing from the sustained viewing of uneventful countryside.

In Danville he was astonished to learn that the bus depot was a diner on route 11 where the counterman sold bus tickets, hamburgers, coffee, cheese and peanut butter crackers, cigarettes, candy and a cold-cut plate. No lockers, no baggage room, no taxi, and now he realized no men's room either.

Suddenly he felt ridiculous. What was he supposed to do? Put his suitcase down and ask the man: Where is the cave near the farm where my father lived fifty-eight years ago? He knew nobody, had no names except the first name of an old lady who was now dead. And rather than call any more attention to himself in this tiny farming town than his beige three-piece suit, his button-down light-blue shirt and black string tie, and his beautiful Florsheim shoes had already brought, he asked the counterman if he could check his bag there. The man gazed at the suitcase and seemed to be turning the request over in his mind.

"I'll pay," said Milkman.

"Leave 'er here. Back a the pop crates," the man said. "When you wanna pick 'er up?"

"This evening," he said.

"Fine. She'll be right here."

Milkman left the diner/bus station with a small satchel of shaving things and walked out into the streets of Danville, Pennsylvania. He'd seen places like this in Michigan, of course, but he never had to do anything in them other than buy gas. The three stores on the street were closing up for the night. It was five-fifteen and about a dozen people, all told, were walking on the sidewalks. One of them was a Negro. A tall man, elderly, with a brown peaked cap and an old-fashioned collar. Milkman followed him for a while, then caught up to him and said, "Say, I wonder if you could help me." He smiled as he spoke.

The man turned around but did not answer. Milkman wondered if he had offended him in some way. Finally the man nodded and said, "Do what I can." He had a slight country lilt, like that of the white man at the counter.

"I'm looking for . . . Circe, a lady named Circe. Well, not

her, but her house. Do you know where she used to live? I'm from out of town. I just got off the bus. I have some business to take care of here, an insurance policy, and I need to check on some property out there."

The man was listening and apparently not going to interrupt him, so Milkman ended his sentence lamely with: "Can you help me?"

"Reverend Cooper would know," said the man.

"Where can I find him?" Milkman felt something missing from the conversation.

"Stone Lane. Follow this here street till you come to the post office. Go on around the post office and that'll be Windsor. The next street is Stone Lane. He lives in there."

"Will there be a church there?" Milkman assumed a preacher lived next door to his church.

"No. No. Church ain't got no parsonage. Reverend Cooper lives in Stone Lane. Yella house, I believe."

"Thanks," said Milkman. "Thanks a lot."

"Mighty welcome," said the man. "Good evenin'." And he walked away.

Milkman considered whether to go back for his suitcase, abandoned the idea, and followed the directions given him. An American flag identified the post office, a frame structure next to a drugstore that served also as the Western Union office. He turned left at the corner, but noticed there were no street signs anywhere. How could he find Windsor or Stone Lane if there were no signs? He walked through a residential street, another and another, and he was just about to go back to the drugstore and look under "A.M.E." or "A.M.E. Zion" in the telephone directory when he saw a yellow-and-white house. Maybe this is it, he thought. He climbed the steps, determined to mind his manners. A thief should be polite and win goodwill.

"Good evening. Is Reverend Cooper here?"

A woman was standing in the doorway. "Yes, he's here. Would you like to come in? I'll call him."

"Thank you." Milkman entered a tiny hall and waited.

A short chubby man appeared, fingering his glasses. "Yes, sir? You wanted to see me?" His eyes ran rapidly over Milkman's clothes, but his voice betrayed no excessive curiosity.

"Yes. Uh . . . how are you?"

"Fine. Fine. And you?"

"Pretty good." Milkman felt as awkward as he sounded. He had never had to try to make a pleasant impression on a stranger before, never needed anything from a stranger before, and did not remember ever asking anybody in the world how they were. I might as well say it all, he thought. "I could use your help, sir. My name is Macon Dead. My father is from around—"

"Dead? Macon Dead, you say?"

"Yes." Milkman smiled apologetically for the name. "My father—"

"Well, I'll be." Reverend Cooper took off his glasses. "Well, I'll be! Esther!" He threw his voice over his shoulder without taking his eyes off his guest. "Esther, come here!" Then to Milkman: "I know your people!"

Milkman smiled and let his shoulders slump a little. It was a good feeling to come into a strange town and find a stranger who knew your people. All his life he'd heard the tremor in the word: "I live here, but my *people* . . ." or: "She acts like she ain't got no *people*," or: "Do any of your *people* live there?" But he hadn't known what it meant: links. He remembered Freddie sitting in Sonny's Shop just before Christmas, saying, "None of my people would take me in." Milkman beamed at Reverend Cooper and his wife. "You do?"

"Sit on down here, boy. You the son of the Macon Dead I knew. Oh, well, now, I don't mean to say I knew him all that well. Your daddy was four or five years older than me, and they didn't get to town much, but everybody round here remembers the old man. Old Macon Dead, your granddad. My daddy and him was good friends. A blacksmith, my daddy was. I'm the only one got the call. Well well well." Reverend Cooper grinned and massaged his knees. "Oh, Lord, I'm forgetting myself. You must be hungry. Esther, get him something to fill himself up on."

"Oh, no. No, thank you, sir. Maybe a little something to drink. I mean if you do drink, that is."

"Sure. Sure. Nothing citified, I'm sorry to say, but– Esther!" She was on her way to the kitchen. "Bring some glasses and get that whiskey out the cupboard. This here's Macon Dead's boy and he's tired and needs a drink. Tell me, how'd you find me? Don't tell me your daddy remembered me?"

"He probably does, but I met a man in the street and he told me how to find you."

"You asked him for me?" Reverend Cooper wanted to get all the facts straight. Already he was framing the story for his friends: how the man came to his house first, how he asked for him. . . .

Esther returned with a Coca-Cola tray, two glasses, and a large mayonnaise jar of what looked like water. Reverend Cooper poured it warm and neat into the two glasses. No ice, no water–just pure rye whiskey that almost tore Milkman's throat when he swallowed it.

"No. I didn't ask for you by name. I asked him if he knew where a woman named Circe used to live."

"Circe? Yes. Lord, old Circe!"

"He told me to talk to you."

Reverend Cooper smiled and poured more whiskey. "Everybody round here knows me and I know everybody."

"Well, I know my father stayed with her awhile, after they . . . when they . . . after his father died."

"They had a fine place. Mighty fine. Some white folks own it now. Course that's what they wanted. That's why they shot him. Upset a lot of people here, a whole lot of people. Scared 'em too. But didn't your daddy have a sister name of Pilate?"

"Yes, sir. Pilate."

"Still living, is she?"

"Oh, yes. Very much living."

"Issat so? Pretty girl, real pretty. My daddy was the one made the earring for her. That's how we knew they was alive. After Old Macon Dead was killed, nobody knew whether the children was dead too or what. Then a few weeks passed and Circe came to my daddy's shop. Right across from where the post office is now—that's where my daddy's blacksmith shop was. She came in there with this little metal box with a piece of paper bag folded up in it. Pilate's name was written on it. Circe didn't tell Daddy anything, but that he was to make a earring out of it. She stole a brooch from the folks she worked for. My daddy took the gold pin off it and soldered it to the box. So we knew they was alive and Circe was taking care of 'em. They'd be all right with Circe. She worked for the Butlers—rich white folks, you know—but she was a good midwife in those days. Delivered everybody. Me included."

Maybe it was the whiskey, which always made other people gracious when he drank it, but Milkman felt a glow listening to a story come from this man that he'd heard many times before but only half listened to. Or maybe it was being there in the place where it happened that made it seem so real. Hearing Pilate talk about caves and woods and earrings on Darling Street, or his father talk about cooking wild turkey over the automobile noise of Not Doctor Street, seemed exotic, something from another world and age, and maybe not even true. Here in the parsonage, sitting in a cane-bottomed chair near an upright piano and drinking homemade whiskey poured from a mayonnaise jar, it was real. Without knowing it, he had walked right by the place where Pilate's earring had been fashioned, the earring that had fascinated him when he was little, the fixing of which informed the colored people here that the children of the murdered man were alive. And this was the living room of the son of the man who made the earring.

"Did anybody ever catch the men who did it—who killed him?"

Reverend Cooper raised his eyebrows. "Catch?" he asked, his face full of wonder. Then he smiled again. "Didn't have to catch 'em. They never went nowhere."

"I mean did they have a trial; were they arrested?"

"Arrested for what? Killing a nigger? Where did you say you was from?"

"You mean nobody did anything? Didn't even try to find out who did it?"

"Everybody knew who did it. Same people Circe worked for—the Butlers."

"And nobody did anything?" Milkman wondered at his own anger. He hadn't felt angry when he first heard about it. Why now?

"Wasn't nothing to do. White folks didn't care, colored folks didn't dare. Wasn't no police like now. Now we got a county sheriff handles things. Not then. Then the circuit judge came through just once or twice a year. Besides, the people what did it owned half the county. Macon's land was in their way. Folks just was thankful the children escaped."

"You said Circe worked for the people who killed him. Did she know that?"

"Course she did."

"And she let them stay there?"

"Not out in the open. She hid them."

"Still, they were in the same house, right?"

"Yep. Best place, I'd say. If they came to town somebody'd see 'em. Nobody would think of looking there."

"Did Daddy—did my father know that?"

"I don't know what he knew, if Circe ever told him. I never saw him after the murder. None of us did."

"Where are they? The Butlers. They still live here?"

"Dead now. Every one of 'em. The last one, the girl Elizabeth, died a couple years back. Barren as a rock and just as old. Things work out, son. The ways of God are mysterious, but if you live it out, just live it out, you see that it always works out. Nothing they stole or killed for did 'em a bit a good. Not one bit."

"I don't care whether it did them good. The fact is they did somebody else harm."

Reverend Cooper shrugged. "White folks different up your way?"

"No, I guess not. . . . Sometimes, though, you can do something."

"What?" The preacher looked genuinely interested.

Milkman couldn't answer except in Guitar's words, so he said nothing.

"See this here?" The reverend turned around and showed Milkman a knot the size of a walnut that grew behind his ear. "Some of us went to Philly to try and march in an Armistice Day parade. This was after the First World War. We were invited and had a permit, but the people, the white people, didn't like us being there. They started a fracas. You know, throwing rocks and calling us names. They didn't care nothing 'bout the uniform. Anyway, some police on horseback came—to quiet them down, we thought. They ran *us* down. Right under their horses. This here's what a hoof can do. Ain't that something?"

"Jesus God."

"You wouldn't be here to even things up, would you?" The preacher leaned over his stomach.

"No. I'm passing through, that's all. Just thought I'd look around. I wanted to see the farm. . . ."

"Cause any evening up left to do, Circe took care of."

"What'd she do?"

"Hah! What didn't she do?"

"Sorry I didn't come out here long time ago. I would have liked to meet her. She must have been a hundred years old when she died."

"Older. Was a hundred when I was a boy."

"Is the farm nearby?" Milkman appeared mildly interested.

"Not too far."

"I sort of wanted to see where it was since I'm out this way. Daddy talked so much about it."

"It's right back of the Butler place, about fifteen miles out. I can take you there. My old piece of car's in the shop, but it was supposed to be ready yesterday. I'll check on it."

Milkman waited four days for the car to be ready. Four days at Reverend Cooper's house as his guest, and the purpose of long visits from every old man in the town who remembered his father or his grandfather, and some who'd only heard. They all repeated various aspects of the story, all talked about how beautiful Lincoln's Heaven was. Sitting in the kitchen, they looked at Milkman with such rheumy eyes, and spoke about his grandfather with such awe and affection, Milkman began to miss him too. His own father's words came back to him: "I worked right alongside my father. Right alongside him." Milkman thought then that his father was boasting of his manliness as a child. Now he knew he had been saying something else. That he loved his father; had an intimate relationship with him; that his father loved him, trusted him, and found him worthy of working "right alongside" him. "Something went wild in me," he'd said, "when I saw him on the ground."

His was the genuine feeling that Milkman had faked when Reverend Cooper described the hopelessness of "doing anything." These men remembered both Macon Deads as extraordinary men. Pilate they remembered as a pretty woods-wild girl "that couldn't nobody put shoes on." Only one of them remembered his grandmother. "Good-lookin, but looked like a white woman. Indian, maybe. Black hair and slanted-up eyes. Died in childbirth, you know." The more the old men talked—the more he heard about the only farm in the county that grew peaches, real peaches like they had in Georgia, the feasts they had when hunting was over, the pork kills in the winter and the work, the backbreaking work of a going farm—the more he missed something in his life. They talked about digging a well, fashioning traps, felling trees, warming orchards with fire when spring weather was bad, breaking young horses, training dogs. And in it all was his own father, the second Macon Dead, their contemporary, who was strong as an ox, could ride bareback and barefoot, who, they agreed, outran, outplowed, outshot, outpicked, outrode them all. He could not recognize that stern, greedy, unloving man in the boy they talked about, but he loved the boy they described and loved that boy's father, with his hip-roofed barn, his peach trees, and Sunday break-of-dawn fishing parties in a fish pond that was two acres wide.

They talked on and on, using Milkman as the ignition that gunned their memories. The good times, the hard times, things that changed, things that stayed the same—and head and shoulders above all of it was the tall, magnificent Macon Dead, whose death, it seemed to him, was the beginning of their own dying even though they were young boys at the time. Macon Dead was the farmer they wanted to be, the clever irrigator, the peach-tree grower, the hog slaughterer, the wild-turkey roaster, the man who could plow forty in no time flat and sang like an angel while he did it. He had come out of nowhere, as ignorant as a hammer and broke as a convict, with nothing but free papers, a Bible, and a pretty black-haired wife, and in one year he'd leased ten acres, the next ten more. Sixteen years later he had one of the best farms in Montour County. A farm that colored their lives like a paintbrush and spoke to them like a sermon. "You see?" the farm said to them. "See? See what you can do? Never mind you can't tell one letter from another, never mind you born a slave, never mind you lose your name, never mind your daddy dead, never mind nothing. Here, this here, is what a man can do if he puts his mind to it and his back in it. Stop sniveling," it said. "Stop picking around the edges of the world. Take advantage, and if you can't take advantage, take disadvantage. We live here. On this planet, in this nation, in this county right here. *No*where else! We got a home in this rock, don't you see! Nobody starving in my home; nobody crying in my home, and if I got a home you got one too! Grab it. Grab this land! Take it, hold it, my brothers, make it, my brothers, shake it, squeeze it, turn it, twist it, beat it, kick it, kiss it, whip it, stomp it, dig it, plow it, seed it, reap it, rent it, buy it, sell it, own it, build it, multiply it, and pass it on—can you hear me? Pass it on!"

But they shot the top of his head off and ate his fine Georgia peaches. And even as boys these men began to die and were dying still. Looking at Milkman in those nighttime talks, they yearned for something. Some word from him that would rekindle the dream and stop the death they were dying. That's why Milkman began to talk about his father, the boy they knew, the son of the fabulous Macon Dead. He bragged a little and they came alive. How many houses his father owned (they grinned); the new car every two years (they laughed); and when he told them how his father tried to buy the Erie Lackawanna (it sounded better that way), they hooted with joy. That's him! That's Old Macon Dead's boy, all right! They wanted to know everything and Milkman found himself rattling off assets like an accountant, describing deals, total rents income, bank loans, and this new thing his father was looking into—the stock market.

Suddenly, in the midst of his telling, Milkman wanted the gold. He wanted to get up right then and there and go get it. Run to where it was and snatch every grain of it from under the noses of the Butlers, who were dumb enough to believe that if they killed one man his whole line died. He glittered in the light of their adoration and grew fierce with pride.

"Who'd your daddy marry?"

"The daughter of the richest Negro doctor in town."

"That's him! That's Macon Dead!"

"Send you all to college?"

"Sent my sisters. I work right alongside him in our office."

"Hah! Keep you home to get that money! Macon Dead gonna always make him some money!"

"What kinda car he drive?"

"Buick. Two-twenty-five."

"Great God, a deuce and a quarter! What year?"

"This year!"

"That's him! That's Macon Dead! He gonna buy the Erie Lackawanna! If he want it, he'll get it! Bless my soul. Bet he worry them white folks to death. Can't nobody keep him down! Not no Macon Dead! Not in this world! And not in the next! Haw! Goddam! The Erie Lacka*wan*na!"

After all the waiting, Reverend Cooper couldn't go. His preaching income was supplemented by freightyard work and he was called for an early shift. His nephew, called Nephew since he was their only one, was assigned to drive Milkman out to the farm—as close as they could get. Nephew was thirteen and barely able to see over the steering wheel.

"Does he have a license?" Milkman asked Mrs. Cooper.

"Not yet," she said, and when she saw his consternation she explained that farm kids drove early—they had to.

Milkman and Nephew started out right after breakfast. It took them the better part of an hour because the roads were curving two-lanes and they spent twenty minutes behind a light truck they couldn't pull around. Nephew spoke very little. He seemed interested only in Milkman's clothes, which he took every opportunity to examine. Milkman decided to give him one of his shirts, and asked him to stop by the bus station to pick up the suitcase he'd left there.

Finally Nephew slowed down on a stretch of road that showed no houses at all. He stopped.

"What's the matter? You want me to drive?"

"No, sir. This is it."

"What's it? Where?"

"Back in there." He pointed to some bushes. "The road to the Butler place is in there and the farm's back behind it. You got to walk it. Car won't make it."

Nothing was truer; as it turned out, Milkman's feet could hardly make it over the stony road covered with second growth. He had asked Nephew to wait, thinking he would survey the area quickly and come back later on his own. But the boy had chores, he said, and would be back whenever Milkman wanted him to be there.

"An hour," said Milkman.

"Take me an hour just to get back to town," said Nephew.

"Reverend Cooper said you were to take me. Not leave me stranded."

"My mama whip me, I don't do my chores."

Milkman was annoyed, but because he didn't want the boy to think he was nervous about being left out there alone, he agreed to having him come back at—he glanced at his heavy, overdesigned watch—at noon. It was nine o'clock then.

His hat had been knocked off by the first branches of the old walnut trees, so he held it in his hand. His cuffless pants were darkened by the mile-long walk over moist leaves. The quiet fairly roared in his ears. He was uncomfortable and a little anxious, but the gold loomed large in his mind, as did the faces of the men he'd drunk with last night, and he stepped firmly onto the gravel and leaves of the driveway which circled the biggest house he'd ever seen.

This is where they stayed, he thought, where Pilate cried when given cherry jam. He stood still a moment. It must have been beautiful, must have seemed like a palace to them, but neither had ever spoken of it in any terms but how imprisoned they felt, how difficult it was to see the sky from their room, how repelled they were by the carpets, the draperies. Without knowing who killed their father, they instinctively hated the murderers' house. And it did look like a murderer's house. Dark, ruined, evil. Never, not since he knelt by his window sill wishing he could fly, had he felt so lonely. He saw the eyes of a child peer at him over the sill of the one second-story window the ivy had not covered. He smiled. Must be myself I'm seeing—thinking about how I used to watch the sky out the window. Or maybe it's the light trying to get through the trees. Four graceful columns supported the portico, and the huge double door featured a heavy, brass knocker. He lifted it and let it fall; the sound was soaked up like a single raindrop in cotton. Nothing stirred. He looked back down the path and saw the green maw out of which he had come, a greenish-black tunnel, the end of which was nowhere in sight.

The farm, they said, was right in back of the Butler place, but knowing how different their concept of distance was, he thought he'd better get moving. If he found what he was looking for he would have to come back at night—with equipment, of course, but also with some familiarity with the area. On impulse he reached out his hand and tried to turn the doorknob. It didn't budge. Half turning to leave—literally as an afterthought—he pushed the door and it swung open with a sigh. He leaned in. The smell prevented him from seeing anything more than the absence of light did. A hairy animal smell, ripe, rife, suffocating. He coughed and looked for somewhere to spit, for the odor was in his mouth, coating his teeth and tongue. He pulled a handkerchief from his back pocket, held it over his nose, backed away from the open door, and had just begun to spill the little breakfast he'd eaten when the odor disappeared and, quite suddenly, in its place was a sweet spicy perfume. Like ginger root—pleasant, clean, seductive. Surprised and charmed by it, he retraced his steps and went inside. After a second or two he was able to see the hand-laid and hand-finished wooden floor in a huge hall, and at its farther end a wide staircase spiraling up into the dark. His eyes traveled up the stairs.

He had had dreams as a child, dreams every child had, of the witch who chased him down dark alleys, between lawn trees, and finally into rooms from which he could not escape. Witches in black dresses and red underskirts; witches with pink eyes and green lips, tiny witches, long rangy witches, frowning witches, smiling witches, screaming witches and laughing witches, witches that flew, witches that ran, and some that merely glided on the ground. So when he saw the woman at the top of the stairs there was no way for him to resist climbing up toward her outstretched hands, her fingers spread wide for him, her mouth gaping open for him, her eyes devouring him. In a dream you climb the stairs. She grabbed him, grabbed his shoulders and pulled him right up against her and tightened her arms around him. Her head came to his chest and the feel of that hair under his chin, the dry bony hands like steel springs rubbing his back, her floppy mouth babbling into his vest, made him dizzy, but he knew that always, always at the very instant of the pounce or the gummy embrace he would wake with a scream and an erection. Now he had only the erection.

Milkman closed his eyes, helpless to pull away before the completion of the dream. What made him surface from it was a humming sound around his knees. He looked down and there, surrounding him, was a pack of golden-eyed dogs, each of which had the intelligent child's eyes he had seen from the window. Abruptly the woman let him go and he looked down at her too. Beside the calm, sane, appraising eyes of the dogs, her eyes looked crazy. Beside their combed, brushed gun-metal hair, hers was wild and filthy.

She spoke to the dogs. "Go on away. Helmut, go on. Horst, move." She waved her hands and the dogs obeyed.

"Come, come," she said to Milkman. "In here." She took his hand in both of hers, and he followed her—his arm outstretched, his hand in hers—like a small boy being dragged reluctantly to bed. Together they weaved among the bodies of the dogs that floated around his legs. She led him into a room, made him sit on a gray velvet sofa, and dismissed all the dogs but two that lay at her feet.

"Remember the Weimaraners?" she asked, settling herself, pulling her chair close to him.

She was old. So old she was colorless. So old only her mouth and eyes were distinguishable features in her face. Nose, chin, cheekbones, forehead, neck all had surrendered their identity to the pleats and crochetwork of skin committed to constant change.

Milkman struggled for a clear thought, so hard to come by in a dream: Perhaps this woman is Circe. But Circe is dead. This woman is alive. That was as far as he got, because although the woman was talking to him, she might in any case still be dead—as a matter of fact, she *had* to be dead. Not because of the wrinkles, and the face so old it could not be alive, but because out of the toothless mouth came the strong, mellifluent voice of a twenty-year-old girl.

"I knew one day you would come back. Well, that's not entirely true. Some days I doubted it and some days I didn't think about it at all. But you see, I was right. You did come."

It was awful listening to that voice come from that face. Maybe something was happening to his ears. He wanted to hear the sound of his own voice, so he decided to take a chance on logic.

"Excuse me. I'm his son. I'm Macon Dead's son. Not the one you knew."

She stopped smiling.

"My name is Macon Dead too, but I'm thirty-two years old. You knew my father and his father too." So far, so good. His voice was the same. Now he needed only to know if he had assessed the situation correctly. She did not answer him. "You're Circe, aren't you?"

"Yes; Circe," she said, but she seemed to have lost all interest in him. "My name is Circe."

"I'm just visiting," he said. "I spent a couple of days with Reverend Cooper and his wife. They're the ones brought me out here."

"I thought you were him. I thought you came back to see me. Where is he? *My* Macon?"

"Back home. He's alive. He told me about you. . . ."

"And Pilate. Where is she?"

"There too. She's fine."

"Well, you look like him. You really do." But she didn't sound convinced.

"He's seventy-two years old now," said Milkman. He thought that would clear things up, make her know he couldn't be the Macon she knew, who was sixteen when she last saw him. But all she said was "Uhn," as though seventy-two, thirty-two, any age at all, meant nothing whatsoever to her. Milkman wondered how old she really was.

"Are you hungry?" she asked.

"No. Thank you. I ate breakfast."

"So you've been staying with that little Cooper boy?"

"Yes, ma'am."

"A runt. I told him not to smoke, but children don't listen."

"Do you mind if I do?" Milkman was relaxing a little and he hoped the cigarette would relax him more.

She shrugged. "Do what you like. Everybody does what he likes nowadays anyway."

Milkman lit the cigarette and the dogs hummed at the sound of the match, their eyes glittering toward the flame.

"Ssh!" whispered Circe.

"Beautiful," said Milkman.

"What's beautiful?"

"The dogs."

"They're not beautiful, they're strange, but they keep things away. I'm completely worn out taking care of 'em. They belonged to Miss Butler. She bred them, crossbred them. Tried for years to get them in the AKC. They wouldn't permit it."

"What did you call them?"

"Weimaraners. German."

"What do you do with them?"

"Oh, I keep some. Sell some. Till we all die in here together." She smiled.

She had dainty habits which matched her torn and filthy clothes in precisely the way her strong young cultivated voice matched her wizened face. Her white hair—braided, perhaps; perhaps not—she touched as though replacing a wayward strand from an elegant coiffure. And her smile—an opening of flesh like celluloid dissolving under a drop of acid—was accompanied by a press of fingers on her chin. It was this combination of daintiness and cultivated speech that misled Macon and invited him to regard her as merely foolish.

"You should get out once in a while."

She looked at him.

"Is this your house now? Did they will you this? Is that why you have to stay here?"

She pressed her lips over her gums. "The only reason I'm here alone is because she died. She killed herself. All the money was gone, so she killed herself. Stood right there on the landing where you were a minute ago and threw herself off the banister. She didn't die right away, though; she lay in the bed a week or two and there was nobody here but us. The dogs were in the kennel then. I brought her in the world, just like I did her mother and her grandmother before that. Birthed just about everybody in the county, I did. Never lost one either. Never lost nobody but your mother. Well, grandmother, I guess she was. Now I birth dogs."

"Some friend of Reverend Cooper said she looked white. My grandmother. Was she?"

"No. Mixed. Indian mostly. A good-looking woman, but fierce, for the young woman I knew her as. Crazy about her husband too, overcrazy. You know what I mean? Some women love too hard. She watched over him like a pheasant hen. Nervous. Nervous love."

Milkman thought about this mixed woman's great-granddaughter, Hagar, and said, "Yes. I know what you mean."

"But a good woman. I cried like a baby when I lost her. Like a baby. Poor Sing."

"What?" He wondered if she lisped.

"I cried like a baby when I–"

"No. I mean what did you call her?"

"Sing. Her name was Sing."

"Sing? Sing Dead. Where'd she get a name like that?"

"Where'd you get a name like yours? White people name Negroes like race horses."

"I suppose so. Daddy told me how they got their name."

"What'd he tell you?"

Milkman told her the story about the drunken Yankee.

"Well, he didn't have to keep the name. She made him. She made him keep that name," Circe said when he was through.

"She?"

"Sing. His wife. They met on a wagon going North. Ate pecans all the way, she told me. It was a wagonful of ex-slaves going to the promised land."

"Was she a slave too?"

"No. No indeed. She always bragged how she was never a slave. Her people neither."

"Then what was she doing on that wagon?"

"I can't answer you because I don't know. Never crossed my mind to ask her."

"Where were they coming from? Georgia?"

"No. Virginia. Both of them lived in Virginia, her people and his. Down around Culpeper somewhere. Charlemagne or something like that."

"I think that's where Pilate was for a while. She lived all over the country before she came to us."

"Did she ever marry that boy?"

"What boy?"

"The boy she had the baby by."

"No. She didn't marry him."

"Didn't think she would. She was too ashamed."

"Ashamed of what?"

"Her stomach."

"Oh, that."

"Borned herself. I had very little to do with it. I thought they were both dead, the mother and the child. When she popped out you could have knocked me over. I hadn't heard a heartbeat anywhere. She just came on out. Your daddy loved her. Hurt me to hear they broke away from one another. So it does me good to hear they're back together again." She had warmed up talking about the past and Milkman decided not to tell her that Macon and Pilate just lived in the same city. He wondered how she knew about their split, and if she knew what they broke apart about.

"You knew about their quarrel?" he asked quietly, nonchalantly.

"Not the substance. Just the fact. Pilate came back here just after her baby was born. One winter. She told me they split up when they left here and she hadn't seen him since."

"Pilate told me they lived in a cave for a few days after they left this house."

"Is that right? Must have been Hunters Cave. Hunters used it to rest up in there sometimes. Eat. Smoke. Sleep. That's where they dumped Old Macon's body."

"They who? I thought . . . My father said he buried him. Down by a creek or a river someplace where they used to fish."

"He did. But it was too shallow and too close to the water. The body floated up at the first heavy rain. Those children hadn't been gone a month when it floated up. Some men were fishing down there and saw this body, a Negro. So they knew who it was. Dumped it in the cave, and it was summer too. You'd think they would have buried a body in the summer. I told Mrs. Butler I thought it was a disgrace."

"Daddy doesn't know that."

"Well, don't tell him. Let him have his peace. It's hard enough with a murdered father; he don't need to know what happened to the body."

"Did Pilate tell you why she came back here?"

"Yes. She said her father told her to. She had visits from him, she said."

"I'd like to see that cave. Where he's . . . where they put him."

"Won't be anything left to see now. That's been a long time ago."

"I know, but maybe there's something I can bury properly."

"Now, that's a thought worth having. The dead don't like it if they're not buried. They don't like it at all. You won't have trouble finding it. You go back out the road you came in on. Go north until you come to a stile. It's falling down, but you'll see it's a stile. Right in there the woods are open. Walk a little way in and you'll come to a creek. Cross it. There'll be some more woods, but ahead you'll see a short range of hills. The cave is right on the face of those hills. You can't miss it. It's the only one there. Tell your daddy you buried him properly, in a graveyard. Maybe with a headstone. A nice headstone. I hope they find me soon enough and somebody'll take pity on me." She looked at the dogs. "Hope they find me soon and don't let me lay in here too long."

Milkman swallowed as her thought touched his mind. "People come to see you, don't they?"

"Dog buyers. They come every now and then. They'll find me, I guess."

"Reverend Cooper . . . They think you're dead."

"Splendid. I don't like those Negroes in town. Dog people come and the man that delivers the dog food once a week. They come. They'll find me. I just hope it's soon."

He loosened his collar and lit another cigarette. Here in this dim room he sat with the woman who had helped deliver his father and Pilate; who had risked her job, her life, maybe, to hide them both after their father was killed, emptied their slop jars, brought them food at night and pans of water to wash. Had even sneaked off to the village to have the girl Pilate's name and snuffbox made into an earring. Then healed the ear when it got infected. And after all these years was thrilled to see what she believed was one of them. Healer, deliverer, in another world she would have been the head nurse at Mercy. Instead she tended Weimaraners and had just one selfish wish: that when she died somebody would find her before the dogs ate her.

"You should leave this place. Sell the damn dogs. I'll help you. You need money? How much?" Milkman felt a flood of pity and thought gratitude made her smile at him. But her voice was cold.

"You think I don't know how to walk when I want to walk? Put your money back in your pocket."

Rebuffed from his fine feelings, Milkman matched her cold tone: "You loved those white folks that much?"

"Love?" she asked. "Love?"

"Well, what are you taking care of their dogs for?"

"Do you know why she killed herself? She couldn't stand to see the place go to ruin. She couldn't live without servants and money and what it could buy. Every cent was gone and the taxes took whatever came in. She had to let the upstairs maids go, then the cook, then the dog trainer, then the yardman, then the chauffeur, then the car, then the woman who washed once a week. Then she started selling bits and pieces—land, jewels, furniture. The last few years we ate out of the garden. Finally she couldn't take it anymore. The thought of having no help, no money—well, she couldn't take that. She had to let everything go."

"But she didn't let you go." Milkman had no trouble letting his words snarl.

"No, she didn't let me go. She killed herself."

"And you still loyal."

"You don't listen to people. Your ear is on your head, but it's not connected to your brain. I said she killed herself rather than do the work I'd been doing all my life!" Circe stood up, and the dogs too. "Do you hear me? She saw the work I did all her days and *died*, you hear me, *died* rather than live like me. Now, what do you suppose she thought I was! If the way I lived and the work I did was so hateful to her she killed herself to keep from having to do it, and you think I stay on here because I loved her, then you have about as much sense as a fart!"

The dogs were humming and she touched their heads. One stood on either side of her. "They loved this place. Loved it. Brought pink veined marble from across the sea for it and hired men in Italy to do the chandelier that I had to climb a ladder and clean with white muslin once every two months. They loved it. Stole for it, lied for it, killed for it. But I'm the one left. Me and the dogs. And I will never clean it again. Never. Nothing. Not a speck of dust, not a grain of dirt, will I move. Everything in this world they lived for will crumble and rot. The chandelier already fell down and smashed itself to pieces. It's down there in the ballroom now. All in pieces. Something gnawed through the cords. Ha! And I want to see it all go, make sure it does go, and that nobody fixes it up. I brought the dogs in to make sure. They keep strangers out too. Folks tried to get in here to steal things after she died. I set the dogs on them. Then I just brought them all right in here with me. You ought to see what they did to her bedroom. Her walls didn't have wallpaper. No. Silk brocade that took some Belgian women six years to make. She loved it—oh, how much she loved it. Took thirty Weimaraners one day to rip it off the walls. If I thought the stink wouldn't strangle you, I'd show it to you." She looked at the walls around her. "This is the last room."

"I wish you'd let me help you," he said after a while.

"You have. You came in here and pretended it didn't stink and told me about Macon and my sweet little Pilate."

"Are you sure?"

"Never surer."

They both stood and walked down the hall. "Mind how you step. There's no light." Dogs came from everywhere, humming. "Time for their feeding," she said. Milkman started down the stairs. Halfway down, he turned and looked up at her.

"You said his wife made him keep the name. Did you ever know his real name?"

"Jake, I believe."

"Jake what?"

She shrugged, a Shirley Temple, little-girl-helpless shrug. "Jake was all she told me."

"Thanks," he called back, louder than he needed to, but he wanted his gratitude to cut through the stink that was flooding back over the humming of the dogs.

But the humming and the smell followed him all the way back down the tunnel to the macadam road. When he got there it was ten-thirty. Another hour and a half before Nephew would be back. Milkman paced the shoulder of the road, making plans. When should he return? Should he try to rent a car or borrow the preacher's? Had Nephew got his suitcase? What equipment would he need? Flashlight and what else? What story should be in his mind in case he was discovered? Of course: looking for his grandfather's remains—to collect them and take them for a proper burial. He paced further, and then began to stroll in the direction Nephew would be coming from. After a few minutes, he wondered if he was going the right way. He started back, but just then saw the ends of two or three wooden planks sticking out of the brush. Maybe this was the stile Circe had described to him. Not exactly a stile, but the remains of one. Circe had not left that house in years, he thought. Any stile she knew of would have to be in disrepair now. And if her directions were accurate, he might make it there and back before twelve. At least he would be able to check it out in the daylight.

Gingerly, he parted the brush and walked a little way into the woods. He didn't see even a trace of a track. But as he kept on a bit, he heard water and followed the sound, which seemed to be just ahead of the next line of trees. He was deceived. He walked for fifteen minutes before he came to it. "Cross it," she'd said, and he thought there would be a bridge of some sort. There was none. He looked across and saw hills. It must be there. Right there. He calculated that he could just make it in the hour or so left before he should be back on the road. He sat down, took off his shoes and socks, stuffed the socks in his pocket, and rolled up his pants. Holding his shoes in his hand, he waded in. Unprepared for the coldness of the water and the slimy stones at the bottom, he slipped to one knee and soaked his shoes trying to break his fall. He righted himself with difficulty and poured the water out of his shoes. Since he was already wet, there was no point in turning back; he waded on out. After half a minute, the creek bed dropped six inches and he fell again, only now he went completely under and got a glimpse of small silvery translucent fish as his head went down. Snorting water, he cursed the creek, which was too shallow to swim and too rocky to walk. He should have pulled a stick to check depth before he put his foot down, but his excitement had been too great. He went on, feeling with his toes for firm footing before he put his weight down. It was slow moving—the water was about two or three feet deep and some twelve yards wide. If he hadn't been so eager, maybe he could have found a narrower part to cross. Thoughts of what he should have done instead of just plunging in, fruitless as they were, irritated him so that they kept him moving until he made it to the other side. He threw his shoes on the dry ground and hoisted himself up and out on the bank. Breathless, he reached for his cigarettes and found them soaked. He lay back on the grass and let the high sunshine warm him. He opened his mouth so the clear air could bathe his tongue.

After a while he sat up and put on the wet socks and shoes. He looked at his watch to check the time. It ticked, but the face was splintered and the minute hand was bent. Better move, he thought, and struck out for the hills, which, deceptive as the sound of the creek, were much farther away than they seemed. He had no idea that simply walking through trees, bushes, on untrammeled ground could be so hard. Woods always brought to his mind City Park, the tended woods on Honoré Island where he went for outings as a child and where tiny convenient paths led you through. "He leased ten acres of virgin woods and cleared it all," said the men describing the beginning of Old Macon Dead's farm. Cleared this? Chopped down this? This stuff he could barely walk through?

He was sweating into his wet shirt and just beginning to feel the result of sharp stones on his feet. Occasionally he came to a clear space and he'd alter his direction as soon as the low hills came back into view.

Finally flat ground gave way to a gentle upward slope of bushes, saplings, and rock. He walked along its edge, looking for an opening. As he moved southward, the skirts of the hills were rockier and the saplings fewer. Then he saw, some fifteen to twenty feet above him, a black hole in the rock which he could get to by a difficult, but not dangerous, climb, made more difficult by the thin smooth soles of his shoes. He wiped sweat from his forehead on his coat sleeve, slipped off the narrow black tie that hung open around his collar and put it in his pocket.

The salt taste was back in his mouth and he was so agitated by what he believed, hoped, he would find there, he had to put his hands on warm stone to dry them. He thought of the pitiful hungry eyes of the old men, their eagerness for some word of defiant success accomplished by the son of Macon Dead; and of the white men who strutted through the orchards and ate the Georgia peaches after they shot his grandfather's head off. Milkman took a deep breath and began to negotiate the rocks.

As soon as he put his foot on the first stone, he smelled money, although it was not a smell at all. It was like candy and sex and soft twinkling lights. Like piano music with a few strings in the background. He'd noticed it before when he waited under the pines near Pilate's house; more when the moon lit up the green sack that hung like a kept promise from her ceiling; and most when he tumbled lightly to the floor, sack in hand. Las Vegas and buried treasure; numbers dealers and Wells Fargo wagons; race track pay windows and spewing oil wells; craps, flushes, and sweepstakes tickets. Auctions, bank vaults, and heroin deals. It caused paralysis, trembling, dry throats, and sweaty palms. Urgency, and the feeling that "they" had been mastered or were on your side. Quiet men stood up and threw a queen down on the table hard enough to break her neck. Women sucked their bottom lips and put little red disks down in numbered squares. Lifeguards, A-students, eyed cash registers and speculated on how far away the door was. To win. There was nothing like it in the world.

Milkman became agile, pulling himself up the rock face, digging his knees into crevices, searching with his fingers for solid earth patches or ledges of stone. He left off thinking and let his body do the work. He stood up, finally, on level ground twenty feet to the right of the mouth of the cave. There he saw a crude footpath he might have found earlier if he had not been so hasty. That was the path the hunters used and that Pilate and his father had also used. None of them tore their clothes as he had, climbing twenty feet of steep rock.

He entered the cave and was blinded by the absence of light. He stepped back out and reentered, cupping his eyes. After a while, he could distinguish the ground from the wall of the cave. There was the ledge of rock where they'd slept, much larger than he had pictured. And worn places on the floor where fires had once burned, and several boulders standing around the entrance—one with a kind of V-shaped crown. But where were the bones? Circe said they dumped him in here. Farther back, probably, back where the shallow pit was. Milkman had no flashlight and his matches were certainly wet, but he tried to find a dry one anyway. Only one or two even sputtered. The rest were dead. Still, his eyes were getting used to the dark. He pulled a branch from a bush that grew near the entrance and bending forward, let it graze the ground before him as he walked. He had gone thirty or forty feet when he noticed the cave's walls were closer together. He could not see the roof at all. He stopped and began to move slowly sideways, the branch tip scratching a yard or so ahead. The side of his hand grazed rock and he flung the dry bat shit off it and moved to the left. The branch struck air. He stopped again, and lowered the tip until it touched ground again. Raising it up and down, and pressing it back and around, he could tell that he had found the pit. It was about two feet deep and maybe eight feet wide. Frantically he scraped the branch around the bottom. It hit something hard, again something else hard. Milkman swallowed and dropped to his knees. He squinted his eyes as hard as he could, but he couldn't see a thing. Suddenly he remembered a lighter in his vest pocket. He dropped the branch and fumbled for it, almost faint from the money smell—the twinkling lights, the piano music. He pulled it out, praying it would light. On the second try, it burst into flame and he peered down. The lighter went out. He snapped it back and held his hand over its fragile flame. At the bottom of the hole he saw rocks, boards, leaves, even a tin cup, but no gold. Stretched out on his stomach, holding the lighter in one hand, he swept the bottom with the other, clawing, pulling, fingering, poking. There were no fat little pigeon-breasted bags of gold. There was nothing. Nothing at all. And before he knew it, he was hollering a long, *awwww* sound into the pit. It triggered the bats, which swooped suddenly and dived in the darkness over his head. They startled him and he leaped to his feet, whereupon the sole of his right shoe split away from the soft cordovan leather. The bats drove him out in a lopsided run, lifting his foot high to accommodate the flopping sole.

In the sunlight once more, he stopped for breath. Dust, tears, and too bright light were in his eyes, but he was too angry and disgusted to rub them. He merely threw the lighter in a wide high arc into the trees at the foot of the hills and limped down the footpath, paying no attention to the direction he was going. He put his feet down wherever was most convenient. Quite suddenly, it seemed to him, he was at the creek again, but upstream where the crossing—about twelve feet here and so shallow he could see the stony bottom—was laid across with boards. He sat down and lashed the sole of his shoe to its top with his black string tie, then walked across the homemade bridge. The woods on the other side had a pathway.

Milkman began to shake with hunger. Real hunger, not the less than top-full feeling he was accustomed to, the nervous desire to taste something good. Real hunger. He believed if he didn't get something to eat that instant he would pass out. He examined the bushes, the branches, the ground for a berry, a nut, anything. But he didn't know what to look for, nor how they grew. Trembling, his stomach in a spasm, he tore off a few leaves and put them in his mouth. They were as bitter as gall, but he chewed them anyway, spit them out, and got others. He thought of the breakfast food Mrs. Cooper had put before him, which had disgusted him then. Fried eggs covered with grease, fresh-squeezed orange juice with seed and pulp floating in it, thick hand-cut bacon, a white-hot mound of grits and biscuits. It was her best effort, he knew, but perhaps because of the whiskey he'd drunk the night before, he could only bring himself to drink two cups of black coffee and eat two biscuits. The rest had nauseated him, and what he did eat he had left at Circe's door.

Some brush closed in on him and when he swept it angrily aside, he saw a stile and the road in front of him. Macadam, automobiles, fence posts, civilization. He looked at the sky to gauge the hour. The sun was a quarter of the way down from what even he knew was high noon. About one o'clock, he guessed. Nephew would have come and gone. He felt in his back pocket for his wallet. It was discolored at the edges from the water, but the contents were dry. Five hundred dollars, his driver's license, phone numbers on slips of paper, social security card, airline ticket stub, cleaners receipts. He looked up and down the road. He had to get food, and started walking south, where he believed Danville lay, hoping to hitch as soon as a car came by. He was not only ravenous; his feet hurt. The third car to pass stopped—a 1954 Chevrolet—and the driver, a black man, showed the same interest in Milkman's clothes that Nephew had shown. He seemed not to notice or care about the rip at the knee or under the arm, the tie-tied shoe, the leaves in Milkman's hair, or the dirt all over the suit.

"Where you headed, partner?"

"Danville. As close as I can get."

"Hop on in, then. Little out my way. I cut over to Buford, but I'll get you closer than you was."

" 'Preciate it," answered Milkman. He loved the car seat, loved it. And sank his weary back into its nylon and sighed.

"Good cut of suit," the man said. "I guess you ain't from here'bouts."

"No. Michigan."

"Sure 'nough? Had a aunt move out there. Flint. You know Flint?"

"Yeah. I know Flint." Milkman's feet were singing, the tender skin of the ball louder than the heels. He dared not spread his toes, lest the singing never stop.

"What kinda place is it, Flint?"

"Jive. No place you'd want to go to."

"Thought so. Name sounds good, but I thought it'd be like that."

Milkman had noticed a six-bottle carton of Coca-Cola on the back seat when he got in the car. It was on his mind.

"Could I buy one of those Coca-Colas from you? I'm kinda thirsty."

"It's warm," said the man.

"Long as it's wet."

"Help yourself."

Milkman reached around and pulled a bottle out of its case.

"Got a bottle opener?"

The man took the bottle from him and put its head in his mouth and slowly pried the top off. Foam shot all over his chin and his lap before Milkman could take it from him.

"Hot." The man laughed and wiped himself with a navy-and-white handkerchief.

Milkman gulped the Coke, foam and all, in three or four seconds.

"Like another?"

He did but he said no. Just a cigarette.

"Don't smoke," said the man.

"Oh," said Milkman, and struggled against and lost to a long belch.

"Bus station's right around the bend there." They were just outside Danville. "You can make it easy."

"I really do thank you." Milkman opened the door. "What do I owe you? For the Coke and all?"

The man was smiling, but his face changed now. "My name's Garnett, Fred Garnett. I ain't got much, but I can afford a Coke and a lift now and then."

"I didn't mean . . . I . . ."

But Mr. Garnett had reached over and closed the door. Milkman could see him shaking his head as he drove off.

Milkman's feet hurt him so, he could have cried, but he made it to the diner/bus station and looked for the man behind the counter. He wasn't there, but a woman offered to help. There followed a long discussion in which he discovered that the bag was not there, the man was not there, she didn't know if a colored boy had picked it up or not, they didn't have a checkroom and she was mighty sorry but he could look at the stationmaster's if the boy didn't have it, and was there anything else she could do?

"Hamburgers," he said. "Give me some hamburgers and a cup of coffee."

"Yes, sir. How many?"

"Six," he said, but his stomach cramped on the fourth and bent him double with a pain that lasted off and on all the way to Roanoke. But before he left, he telephoned Reverend Cooper. His wife answered and told him that her husband was still at the freightyard and he could catch him there if he hurried. Milkman thanked her and hung up. Walking like a pimp in delicate shoes, he managed to get to the yard, which was fairly close to the bus station. He entered the gate and asked the first man he saw if Reverend Cooper was still there.

"Coop?" the man said. "I think he went on over to the station house. See it? Right over there."

Milkman followed his finger, and hobbled over the gravel and ties to the station house.

It was empty save for an old man dragging a crate.

"Excuse me," Milkman said. "Is Rev–is Coop still here?"

"Just left. If you run you can catch him," the man said. He wiped the sweat of exertion from his forehead.

Milkman thought about running anywhere on his tender feet and said, "Oh, well. I'll try to catch him another time." He turned to go.

"Say," said the man. "If you ain't gonna try to catch him, could you give me a hand with this?" He pointed down to the huge crate at his feet. Too tired to say no or explain, Milkman nodded. The two of them grunted and groaned over the box, and finally got it up on a dolly, where they could push it to the weighing platform. Milkman slumped over the crate and caught his breath, barely able to nod to the old man's thank yous. Then he went out of the station into the street.

He was tired now. Really tired. He didn't want to see Reverend Cooper and his success-starved friends again. And he certainly didn't want to explain anything to his father or Guitar just yet. So he hobbled back to the bus station and asked for the next bus leaving that was going south. It had to be south. And it had to be Virginia. Because now he thought he knew how to find out what had happened to the gold.

Full of hamburgers, sore of foot, sick to his stomach, but at least sitting down, he couldn't even feel the disappointment that lay in the pit in the cave. He slept heavily for several hours on the bus, woke and daydreamed, napped a little more, woke again at a rest stop and ate a bowl of pea soup. He went into a drugstore and replaced the shaving equipment and toilet articles he'd left at Reverend Cooper's, and decided to wait and get his shoe fixed (it was sealed with chewing gum now), his suit mended, and a new shirt in Virginia.

The Greyhound bus made a sound like the hum of the Weimaraners as it sped down the road, and Milkman shivered a little, the way he had when Circe glanced at them, sitting in the "last room," wondering if she would outlive them. But there were over thirty of them and reproducing all the time.

The low hills in the distance were no longer scenery to him. They were real places that could split your thirty-dollar shoes. More than anything in the world he'd wanted it to be there, for row upon row of those little bags to turn their fat pigeon chests up to his hands. He thought he wanted it in the name of Macon Dead's Georgia peaches, in the name of Circe and her golden-eyed dogs, and especially in the name of Reverend Cooper and his old-timey friends who began to die before their facial hair was out when they saw what happened to a black man like them—"ignorant as a hammer and broke as a convict"—who had made it anyway. He also thought he wanted it in the name of Guitar, to erase what looked like doubt in his face when Milkman left, the "I-know-you-gonna-fuck-up" look. There wasn't any gold, but now he knew that all the fine reasons for wanting it didn't mean a thing. The fact was he wanted the gold because it was gold and he wanted to own it. Free. As he had sat chomping the hamburgers in the bus station, imagining what going home would be like now—not only to have to say there was no gold, but also to know he was trapped there—his mind had begun to function clearly.

Circe said that Macon and Sing had boarded that wagon in Virginia, where they both came from. She also said Macon's body rose up from the ground at the first heavy rain, and that the Butlers, or somebody, dumped it in the hunters' cave one summer night. One summer night. And it was a body, a corpse, when they hauled it away, because they recognized him as a Negro. Yet Pilate said it was winter when she was there, and there were only bones. She said she went to see Circe and visited the cave four years later, in the snow, and took the white man's bones. Why didn't she see her father's bones? There should have been two skeletons. Did she step over one and collect the other? Surely Circe had told her the same thing she told him—that her father's body was in the cave. Did Pilate tell Circe that they had killed a man in there? Probably not, since Circe didn't mention it. Pilate said she took the white man's bones and didn't even look for the gold. But she lied. She had not mentioned the second skeleton because it wasn't there when she got to the cave. She didn't come back four years later—or if she did, it was her *second* trip. She came back *before* they dumped the Negro they found in the cave. She took the bones, all right; Milkman had seen them on the table in the jailhouse. But that's not all she took. She took the gold. To Virginia. And maybe somebody in Virginia would know.

Milkman followed in her tracks.

Chapter 11

The women's hands were empty. No pocketbook, no change purse, no wallet, no keys, no small paper bag, no comb, no handkerchief. They carried nothing. Milkman had never in his life seen a woman on the street without a purse slung over her shoulder, pressed under her arm, or dangling from her clenched fingers. These women walked as if they were going somewhere, but they carried nothing in their hands. It was enough to let him know he was really in the backwoods of Virginia, an area the signs kept telling him was the Blue Ridge Mountains. Danville, with its diner/bus station and its post office on the main street was a thriving metropolis compared to this no-name hamlet, a place so small nothing financed by state funds or private enterprise reared a brick there. In Roanoke, Petersburg, Culpeper he'd asked for a town named Charlemagne. Nobody knew. The coast, some said. Tidewater. A valley town, said others. He ended up at an AAA office, and after a while they discovered it and its correct name: Shalimar. How do I get there? Well, you can't walk it, that's for sure. Buses go there? Trains? No. Well, not very near. There is one bus, but it just goes to . . . He ended up buying a fifty-dollar car for seventy-five dollars out of a young man's yard. It broke down before he could get to the gas station and fill the tank. And when he got pushed to the station, he spent $132 on a fan belt, brake lining, oil filter, gas line filter, two retreads, and a brand-new oil pan, which he didn't need but bought before the mechanic told him the gasket was broken. It was a hard and bitter price to pay. Not because it wasn't worth it, and not because it had to be in cash since the garage owner looked at his Standard Oil credit card like it was a three-dollar bill, but because he had got used to prices in the South: socks two pairs for a quarter, resoled shoes thirty cents, shirt $1.98, and the two Tommys needed to know that he got a shave *and* a haircut for fifty cents.

By the time he bought the car, his morale had soared and he was beginning to enjoy the trip: his ability to get information and help from strangers, their attraction to him, their generosity (Need a place to stay? Want a good place to eat?). All that business about southern hospitality was for real. He wondered why black people ever left the South. Where he went, there wasn't a white face around, and the Negroes were as pleasant, wide-spirited, and self-contained as could be. He earned the rewards he got here. None of the pleasantness was directed at him because of his father, as it was back home, or his grandfather's memory, as it was in Danville. And now, sitting behind a steering wheel, he felt even better. He was his own director—relieving himself when he wanted to, stopping for cold beer when he was thirsty, and even in a seventy-five-dollar car the sense of power was strong.

He'd had to pay close attention to signs and landmarks, because Shalimar was not on the Texaco map he had, and the AAA office couldn't give a nonmember a charted course—just the map and some general information. Even at that, watching as carefully as he could, he wouldn't have known he had arrived if the fan belt hadn't broken again right in front of Solomon's General Store, which turned out to be the heart and soul of Shalimar, Virginia.

He headed for the store, nodding at the four men sitting outside on the porch, and side-stepping the white hens that were strolling about. Three more men were inside, in addition to the man behind the counter, who he assumed was Mr. Solomon himself. Milkman asked him for a cold bottle of Red Cap, please.

"No beer for sale on Sunday," the man said. He was a light-skinned Negro with red hair turning white.

"Oh. I forgot what day it was." Milkman smiled. "Pop, then. I mean soda. Got any on ice?"

"Cherry smash. That suit you?"

"Fine. Suit me fine."

The man walked over to the side of the store and slid open the door of an ancient cooler. The floor was worn and wavy with years of footsteps. Cans of goods on the shelf were sparse, but the sacks, trays, and cartons of perishables and semiperishables were plentiful. The man pulled a bottle of red liquid from the cooler and wiped it dry on his apron before handing it to Milkman.

"A nickel if you drink it here. Seven cents if you don't."

"I'll drink it here."

"Just get in?"

"Yeah. Car broke down. Is there a garage nearby?"

"Naw. Five miles yonder is one, though."

"Five miles?"

"Yep. What's the trouble? Mebbe one a us can fix it. Where you headed?"

"Shalimar."

"You standin in it."

"Right here? This is Shalimar?"

"Yes, suh. Shalimar." The man pronounced it *Shalleemone*.

"Good thing I broke down. I would have missed it for sure." Milkman laughed.

"Your friend almost missed it too."

"My friend? What friend?"

"The one lookin for you. Drove in here early this mornin and axed for ya."

"Asked for me by name?"

"No. He never mentioned your name."

"Then how do you know he was looking for me?"

"Said he was lookin for his friend in a three-piece beige suit. Like that." He pointed to Milkman's chest.

"What'd he look like?"

"Dark-skinned man. 'Bout your complexion. Tall. Thin. What's a matter? Y'all get your wires crossed?"

"Yeah. No. I mean . . . what was his name?"

"Didn't say. Just asked for you. He come a long way to meet you, though. I know that. Drove a Ford with Michigan tags."

"Michigan? You sure Michigan?"

"Sure I'm sure. Was he supposed to meet you in Roanoke?"

When Milkman looked wild-eyed, the man said, "I seen your tags."

Milkman sighed with relief. And then said, "I wasn't sure where we were going to meet up. And he didn't say his name?"

"Naw. Just said to give you some good-luck message if I was to see you. Lemme see . . ."

"Good luck?"

"Yeah. Said to tell you your day was sure coming or your day . . . something like that . . . your day is here. But I know it had a day in it. But I ain't sure if he said it was comin or was already here." He chuckled. "Wish mine was here. Been waitin fifty-seven years and it ain't come yet."

The other men in the store laughed congenially, while Milkman stood frozen, everything in him quiet but his heart. There was no mistaking the message. Or the messenger. Guitar was looking for him, was following him, and for professional reasons. Unless . . . Would Guitar joke about that phrase? That special secret word the Seven Days whispered to their victims?

"The drink abuse you?" Mr. Solomon was looking at him. "Sweet soda water don't agree with me."

Milkman shook his head and swallowed the rest hurriedly. "No," he said. "I'm just . . . car weary. I think I'll sit outside awhile." He started toward the door.

"You want me to see 'bout your car for you?" Mr. Solomon sounded slightly offended.

"In a minute. I'll be right back."

Milkman pushed the screen door and stepped outside on the porch. The sun was blazing. He took off his jacket and held it on his forefinger over his shoulder. He gazed up and down the dusty road. Shotgun houses with wide spaces between them, a few dogs, chickens, children, and the women with nothing in their hands. They sat on porches, and walked in the road swaying their hips under cotton dresses, bare-legged, their unstraightened hair braided or pulled straight back into a ball. He wanted one of them bad. To curl up in a cot in that one's arms, or that one, or that. That's the way Pilate must have looked as a girl, looked even now, but out of place in the big northern city she had come to. Wide sleepy eyes that tilted up at the corners, high cheekbones, full lips blacker than their skin, berry-stained, and long long necks. There must be a lot of intermarriage in this place, he thought. All the women looked alike, and except for some light-skinned red-headed men (like Mr. Solomon), the men looked very much like the women. Visitors to Shalimar must be rare, and new blood that settled here nonexistent.

Milkman stepped off the porch, scattering the hens, and walked down the road toward a clump of trees near a building that looked like a church or clubhouse of some sort. Children were playing behind the trees. Spreading his jacket on the burnt grass, he sat down and lit a cigarette.

Guitar was here. Had asked for him. But why was he afraid? They were friends, close friends. So close he had told him all about the Seven Days. There was no trust heavier than that. Milkman was a confidant, almost an accomplice. So why was he afraid? It was senseless. Guitar must have left that particular message so Milkman could know who was looking for him without his giving his name. Something must have happened back home. Guitar must be running, from the police, maybe, and decided to run toward his friend—the only one other than the Days who would know what it was all about and whom he could trust. Guitar needed to find Milkman and he needed help. That was it. But if Guitar knew Milkman was headed for Shalimar, he must have found that out in Roanoke, or Culpeper—or maybe even in Danville. And if he knew that, why didn't he wait? Where was he now? Trouble. Guitar was in trouble.

Behind him the children were singing a kind of ring-around-the-rosy or Little Sally Walker game. Milkman turned to watch. About eight or nine boys and girls were standing in a circle. A boy in the middle, his arms outstretched, turned around like an airplane, while the others sang some meaningless rhyme:

Jay the only son of Solomon
Come booba yalle, come booba tambee
Whirl about and touch the sun
Come booba yalle, come booba tambee . . .

They went on with several verses, the boy in the middle doing his imitation of an airplane. The climax of the game was a rapid shouting of nonsense words accompanied by more rapid twirling: "Solomon rye balaly *shoo*; yaraba medina hamlet *too*"—until the last line. "Twenty-one children the last one *Jay!*" At which point the boy crashed to earth and the others screamed.

Milkman watched the children. He'd never played like that as a child. As soon as he got up off his knees at the window sill, grieving because he could not fly, and went off to school, his velvet suit separated him from the other children. White and black thought he was a riot and went out of their way to laugh at him and see to it that he had no lunch to eat, nor any crayons, nor ever got through the line to the toilet or the water fountain. His mother finally surrendered to his begging for corduroy knickers or straights, which helped a little, but he was never asked to play those circle games, those singing games, to join in anything, until Guitar pulled those four boys off him. Milkman smiled, remembering how Guitar grinned and whooped as the four boys turned on him. It was the first time Milkman saw anybody really enjoy a fight. Afterward Guitar had taken off his baseball cap and handed it to Milkman, telling him to wipe the blood from his nose. Milkman bloodied the cap, returned it, and Guitar slapped it back on his head.

Remembering those days now, Milkman was ashamed of having been frightened or suspicious of Guitar's message. When he turned up, he would explain everything and Milkman would do what he could to help. He stood up and brushed his jacket. A black rooster strutted by, its blood-red comb draped forward like a wicked brow.

Milkman walked back toward Solomon's store. He needed a place to stay, some information, and a woman, not necessarily in that order. He would begin wherever the beginning was. In a way it was good Guitar had asked for him. Along with waiting for him and waiting for some way to get a new fan belt, he had a legitimate reason to dawdle. Hens and cats gave up their places on the steps as he approached them.

"Feelin better, are ya?" asked Mr. Solomon.

"Much better. Just needed a stretch, I guess." He jutted his chin toward the window. "Nice around here. Peaceful. Pretty women too."

A young man sitting on a chair tilted to the wall pushed his hat back from his forehead and let the front legs of the chair hit the floor. His lips were open, exposing the absence of four front teeth. The other men moved their feet. Mr. Solomon smiled but didn't say anything. Milkman sensed that he'd struck a wrong note. About the women, he guessed. What kind of place was this where a man couldn't even ask for a woman?

He changed the subject. "If my friend, the one who stopped by this morning, was going to wait for me here, where would he be likely to find a place to stay? Any rooming houses around here?"

"Rooming houses?"

"Yeah. Where a man can spend the night."

Mr. Solomon shook his head. "Nothin like that here."

Milkman was getting annoyed. What was all the hostility for? He looked at the men sitting around the store. "You think maybe one of them could help with the car?" he asked Mr. Solomon. "Maybe get another belt somewhere?"

Mr. Solomon kept his eyes on the counter. "Guess I could ask them." His voice was soft; he spoke as if he was embarrassed about something. There was none of the earlier chattiness he'd been full of when Milkman arrived.

"If they can't find one, let me know right away. I may have to buy another car to get back home."

Every one of the faces of the men turned to look at him, and Milkman knew he had said something else wrong, although he didn't know what. He only knew that they behaved as if they'd been insulted.

In fact they had been. They looked with hatred at the city Negro who could buy a car as if it were a bottle of whiskey because the one he had was broken. And what's more, who had said so in front of them. He hadn't bothered to say his name, nor ask theirs, had called them "them," and would certainly despise their days, which should have been spent harvesting their own crops, instead of waiting around the general store hoping a truck would come looking for mill hands or tobacco pickers in the flatlands that belonged to somebody else. His manner, his clothes were reminders that they had no crops of their own and no land to speak of either. Just vegetable gardens, which the women took care of, and chickens and pigs that the children took care of. He was telling them that they weren't men, that they relied on women and children for their food. And that the lint and tobacco in their pants pockets where dollar bills should have been was the measure. That thin shoes and suits with vests and smooth smooth hands were the measure. That eyes that had seen big cities and the inside of airplanes were the measure. They had seen him watching their women and rubbing his fly as he stood on the steps. They had also seen him lock his car as soon as he got out of it in a place where there couldn't be more than two keys twenty-five miles around. He hadn't found them fit enough or good enough to want to know their names, and believed himself too good to tell them his. They looked at his skin and saw it was as black as theirs, but they knew he had the heart of the white men who came to pick them up in the trucks when they needed anonymous, faceless laborers.

Now one of them spoke to the Negro with the Virginia license and the northern accent.

"Big money up North, eh?"

"Some," Milkman answered.

"Some? I hear tell everybody up North got big money."

"Lotta people up North got nothing." Milkman made his voice pleasant, but he knew something was developing.

"That's hard to believe. Why would anybody want to stay there if they ain't no big money?"

"The sights, I guess." Another man answered the first. "The sights and the women."

"You kiddin," said the first man in mock dismay. "You mean to tell me pussy different up North?"

"Naw," said the second. "Pussy the same everywhere. Smell like the ocean; taste like the sea."

"Can't be," said a third. "Got to be different."

"Maybe the pricks is different." The first man spoke again.

"Reckon?" asked the second man.

"So I hear tell," said the first man.

"How different?" asked the second man.

"Wee little," said the first man. "Wee, wee little."

"Naw!" said the second man.

"So they tell me. That's why they pants so tight. That true?" The first man looked at Milkman for an answer.

"I wouldn't know," said Milkman. "I never spent much time smacking my lips over another man's dick." Everybody smiled, including Milkman. It was about to begin.

"What about his ass hole? Ever smack your lips over that?"

"Once," said Milkman. "When a little young nigger made me mad and I had to jam a Coke bottle up his ass."

"What'd you use a bottle for? Your cock wouldn't fill it?"

"It did. After I took the Coke bottle out. Filled his mouth too."

"Prefer mouth, do you?"

"If it's big enough, and ugly enough, and belongs to a ignorant motherfucker who is about to get the livin shit whipped out of him."

The knife glittered.

Milkman laughed. "I ain't seen one of those since I was fourteen. Where I come from *boys* play with knives—if they scared they gonna lose, that is."

The first man smiled. "That's me, motherfucker. Scared to death I'm gonna lose."

Milkman did the best he could with a broken bottle, but his face got slit, so did his left hand, and so did his pretty beige suit, and he probably would have had his throat cut if two women hadn't come running in screaming, "Saul! Saul!"

The store was full of people by then and the women couldn't get through. The men tried to shush them, but they kept on screaming and provided enough lull for Mr. Solomon to interrupt the fight.

"All right. All right. That's enough of that."

"Shut your mouth, Solomon."

"Get them women outta here."

"Stick him, Saul, stick that cocksucker."

But Saul had a jagged cut over his eye and the blood pouring from it made it hard to see. It was difficult but not impossible for Mr. Solomon to pull him away. He left cursing Milkman, but his fervor was gone.

Milkman backed up against the counter, waiting to see if anybody else was going to jump him. When it looked as if no one was, and when the people were drifting outside to watch Saul scuffling and cursing at the men pulling him away, he slumped a little and wiped his face. When the entire store save for the owner was empty, Milkman hurled the broken bottle into a corner. It careened by the cooler and bounced off the wall before splintering on the floor. He walked outside, still panting, and looked around. Four older men still sat on the porch, as though nothing had happened. Blood was streaming down Milkman's face, but it had dried on his hand. He kicked at a white hen and sat down on the top step, wiping the blood with his handkerchief. Three young women with nothing in their hands stood in the road looking at him. Their eyes were wide but noncommittal. Children joined them, circling the women like birds. Nobody said anything. Even the four men on the porch were quiet. Nobody came toward him, offered him a cigarette or a glass of water. Only the children and the hens walked around. Under the hot sun, Milkman was frozen with anger. If he'd had a weapon, he would have slaughtered everybody in sight.

"You pretty good with a bottle. How you with a shotgun?" One of the older men had sidled up to him. The smile on his face was faint. It was as though now that the young men had had their chance, with unsatisfactory results, the older men would take over. Their style, of course, would be different. No name-calling toilet contest for them. No knives either, or hot breath and knotted neck muscles. They would test him, match and beat him, probably, on some other ground.

"Best shot there is," Milkman lied.

"That so?"

"Yeah, it's so."

"Some of us is going huntin later on. Care to join us?"

"That toothless motherfucker going too?"

"Saul? No."

"Cause I might have to knock the rest of them out."

The man laughed. "Sheriff took the others—with the butt of a gun."

"Yeah? Good."

"Well, you comin?"

"Sure I'm coming. Just get me the gun."

He laughed again. "Name's Omar."

"Macon Dead."

Omar blinked at the name, but didn't comment on it. He merely told him to come by King Walker's, a gas station about two miles up the road, right around sundown. "It's straight up yonder. Ain't no way in the world you can miss it."

"I won't miss it." Milkman stood up and walked to his car. He fumbled for the car keys, opened the door, and slid into the seat. He rolled down all four windows, found a towel in the back seat, and stretched out, using his jacket for a pillow and the towel as a bandage for his face. His feet stuck out the open door. Fuck 'em. Who were all these people roaming the world trying to kill him? His own father had tried while he was still in his mother's stomach. But he'd lived. And he had lived the last year dodging a woman who came every month to kill him, and he had lain just like this, with his arm over his eyes, wide open to whatever she had in her hand. He'd lived through that too. Then a witch had stepped out of his childhood nightmares to grab him, and he'd lived through that. Some bats had driven him out of a cave—and he'd lived through that. And at no time did he have a weapon. Now he walked into a store and asked if somebody could fix his car and a nigger pulled a knife on him. And he still wasn't dead. Now what did these black Neanderthals think they were going to do? Fuck 'em. My name's Macon; I'm already dead. He had thought this place, this Shalimar, was going to be home. His original home. His people came from here, his grandfather and his grandmother. All the way down South people had been nice to him, generous, helpful. In Danville they had made him the object of hero worship. In his own home town his name spelled dread and grudging respect. But here, in his "home," he was unknown, unloved, and damn near killed. These were some of the meanest unhung niggers in the world.

He slept, unmolested by everything and everybody except a dream in which he thought he saw Guitar looking down on him. When he woke he bought two cans of pineapple and a box of crackers from Mr. Solomon. He ate on the porch with the hens. The men were gone, and the sun was leaving. Only the children stayed to watch him eat. When he poured the last of the pineapple juice down his throat, one of the children stepped forward to ask, "Can we have your can, mister?" He held it out and they snatched the can and ran off to fashion some game out of it.

He started out for King Walker's. Even if he could have come up with a way to get out of the hunt, he wouldn't have taken it, in spite of the fact that he had never handled a firearm in his life. He had stopped evading things, sliding through, over, and around difficulties. Before he had taken risks only with Guitar. Now he took them alone. Not only had he let Hagar stab him; he had let the nightmare witch catch him and kiss him. To a man surviving that, anything else was a joke.

King Walker was nothing like his name suggested. He was a small man, bald, with a left cheek bulging with tobacco. Years ago he'd been a star pitcher in one of the black baseball leagues and the history of his career was nailed and pasted all over his shop. They had not lied when they said no garage or mechanic on duty was nearer than five miles. King Walker's station had obviously gone broke a long time ago. The pumps were dry; there wasn't even a can of oil in the place. Now it seemed to be used as a kind of clubhouse for the men and Walker lived in the back of the station. In addition to King Walker, who wasn't going, there was Omar and another man who had also been on the porch and who introduced himself as Luther Solomon—no relation to the grocery store Solomon. They were waiting for some others, who came soon after Milkman got there, driving an old Chevy. Omar introduced them as Calvin Breakstone and Small Boy.

Calvin seemed to be the most congenial of them, and followed the introductions with a command to King Walker to "get this city boy some shoes for his feet." King rummaged around, spitting tobacco, and came up with some mud-caked brogans. They outfitted Milkman completely, laughing all the while at his underwear, fingering his vest—Small Boy tried to get his wrestler's arms into Milkman's jacket—and wondering what had happened to his feet. Bits of skin still peeled from his toes because of the two days he had spent in wet shoes and socks. King Walker made him sprinkle Arm & Hammer soda on them before he put on the thick socks they gave him. When Milkman was dressed in World War II army fatigues with a knit cap on his head, they opened some Falstaff beer and began to talk about guns. At which point the revelry mixed with meanness abated and King Walker handed Milkman his Winchester .22.

"Ever use a twenty-two?"

"Not in a good while," Milkman said.

The five men piled into the Chevy and drove off into the lessening light. From what Milkman could tell, after fifteen minutes or so they were going up to high ground. As the car swerved through narrow roads, the conversation picked up again and they talked about other trips, game, kills, misses. Soon the only light came from the moon and it was getting cool enough for Milkman to be grateful for his knit cap. The car pulled ahead and around some sharp bends. In the rear-view mirror Milkman thought he glimpsed the headlights of another car and wondered briefly if they were being met by others. The sky was dark enough now for stars.

"Better make time, Calvin. Coon be done ate and gone on home."

Calvin pulled over and stopped the car.

"Let 'em rip," he said, and handed the car keys to Small Boy, who walked around to the back and unlocked the trunk. Three hounds leaped out, sniffing and wagging their tails. But they didn't make a sound.

"You brought Becky?" asked Luther. "Oh, man! We gonna get some coon tonight!"

The dogs' nervousness, their eagerness to hear the signal that would allow them to race off into the trees, made Milkman jittery. What was he supposed to do? Two feet in any direction from the headlights was black night.

Omar and Small Boy hauled equipment from the trunk: four lamps, one flashlight, rope, shells, and a pint bottle of liquor. When all four lamps were ablaze, they asked Milkman if he wanted to use a lamp or a flashlight. He hesitated, and Calvin said, "He can run with me. Give him the torch."

Milkman put it in his back pocket.

"Take that change out your pocket," said Calvin. "Makes too much noise."

Milkman did as he was told and took King's shotgun, a piece of rope, and a deep swig from the bottle they were passing around.

The dogs padded about, silent, panting, almost faint with excitement. But still they made no sound. Calvin and Omar both loaded their double-gauge shotguns with .22 shells in one barrel and buckshot in the other. Small Boy clapped his hands once, and the three hounds sped screaming into the night. The men didn't take off after them at once, as Milkman had supposed they would. Instead they stood quietly and listened for a while. Small Boy laughed lightly, shaking his head. "Becky's leadin. Let's go. Calvin, you and Macon go off to the right. We'll head this a way, and circle over by the gulch. Don't shoot no bears, now."

"Shoot him if I see him," said Calvin as he and Milkman moved away.

As they left the Chevy, the car that Milkman had noticed sped past them. Obviously, there were no others in the hunting party. Calvin was ahead, the burning lamp swinging low from his hand. Milkman flicked on his flashlight.

"Better save it," said Calvin. "You don't need it now."

They plodded on in a direction that may have been toward the screaming dogs, but Milkman couldn't tell.

"Any bears out here?" he asked in what he hoped was an interested but not anxious voice.

"Just us, and we got the guns." Calvin laughed and was suddenly swallowed up by the dark, only the low swinging lamp marking his path. Milkman watched the lamp until he realized that focusing on it kept him from seeing anything else. If he was to grow accustomed to the dark, he would have to look at what it was possible to see. A long moan sailed up through the trees somewhere to the left of where they were. It sounded like a woman's voice, sobbing, and mingling with the dogs' yelps and the men's shouts. A few minutes later, the distant screaming of the dogs and the calls of the three men stopped. There was only the soughing wind and his and Calvin's footsteps. It took Milkman a while to figure out how to pick up his feet and miss the roots and stones; to distinguish a tree from a shadow; to keep his head down and away from the branches that swept back from Calvin's hand into his face. They were walking upland. Every now and then Calvin stopped, threw his lamplight on a tree, and examined it closely from about three feet off the ground to up as far as his arm could go. Other times he lowered the lamp over the ground, and squatting down on his haunches, peered into the dirt. Each time he seemed to be whispering. Whatever he discovered he kept to himself and Milkman didn't ask him. All he wanted to do was keep up, be ready to shoot whatever the game was when it appeared, and look out for an attempt any of them might make on his life. Within an hour after arriving in Shalimar, a young man had tried to kill him in public. What these older men, under cover of night, were capable of he could only guess.

He heard the sound of the sobbing woman again and asked Calvin, "What the hell is that?"

"Echo," he said. "Ryna's Gulch is up ahead. It makes that sound when the wind hits a certain way."

"Sounds like a woman crying," said Milkman.

"Ryna. Folks say a woman name Ryna is cryin in there. That's how it got the name."

Calvin stopped, but so suddenly that Milkman, deep in thought about Ryna, bumped into him. "Hush!" Calvin closed his eyes and tilted his head into the wind. All Milkman could hear was the dogs again, yelping, but more rapidly, he thought, than before. Calvin whistled. A faint whistle came back to them.

"Son of a fuckin bitch!" Calvin's voice broke with agitation. "Bobcat! Come on, man!" He literally sprang away and Milkman did the same. Now they moved at double time, still on land that sloped upward. It was the longest trek Milkman had ever made in his life. Miles, he thought; we must be covering miles. And hours; it must be two hours now since he whistled. On they walked, and Calvin never broke his stride for anything except an occasional shout and an occasional pause to listen to the sound that came back.

The light was changing and Milkman was getting very tired. The distance between himself and Calvin's lamp was getting wider and wider. He was twenty years younger than Calvin, but found himself unable to keep up the pace. And he was getting clumsy—stepping over big stones rather than around them, dragging his feet and catching them in humped roots, and now that Calvin was not directly in front, he had to push the branches away from his face himself. The doubling down and under branches and pushing things out of his way were as exhausting as the walk. His breath was coming in shorter and shorter gasps and he wanted to sit down more than anything in the world. He believed they were circling now, for it seemed to him that this was the third time he had seen that double-humped rock in the distance. Should they be circling? he wondered. Then he thought he remembered hearing that certain prey circled when it was being stalked. Did bobcat? He didn't even know what a bobcat looked like.

At last he surrendered to his fatigue and made the mistake of sitting down instead of slowing down, for when he got up again, the rest had given his feet an opportunity to hurt him and the pain in his short leg was so great he began to limp and hobble. Soon it wasn't possible for him to walk longer than five minutes at a time without pausing to lean against a sweet gum tree. Calvin was a pinpoint of light bobbing ahead in and out of the trees. Finally Milkman could take no more; he had to rest. At the next tree he sank down to the ground and put his head back on its bark. Let them laugh if they wanted to; he would not move until his heart left from under his chin and went back down into his chest where it belonged. He spread his legs, pulled the flashlight out of his hip pocket, and put his Winchester down near his right leg. At rest now, he could feel the blood pulsing in his temple and the cut on his face stinging in the night wind from the leaf juice and tree sap the branches had smeared on it.

When he was breathing almost normally, he began to wonder what he was doing sitting in the middle of a woods in Blue Ridge country. He had come here to find traces of Pilate's journey, to find relatives she might have visited, to find anything he could that would either lead him to the gold or convince him that it no longer existed. How had he got himself involved in a hunt, involved in a knife-and-broken-bottle fight in the first place? Ignorance, he thought, and vanity. He hadn't been alert early enough, hadn't seen the signs jutting out everywhere around him. Maybe this was a mean bunch of black folk, but he should have guessed it, sensed it, and part of the reason he hadn't was the easy, good treatment he had received elsewhere. Or had he? Maybe the glow of hero worship (twice removed) that had bathed him in Danville had also blinded him. Perhaps the eyes of the men in Roanoke, Petersburg, Newport News, had not been bright with welcome and admiration. Maybe they were just curious or amused. He hadn't stayed in any place long enough to find out. A meal here, gas there—the one real contact was the buying of the car, and the seller needing a buyer would naturally be friendly under those circumstances. The same thing held when he'd had to have those elaborate repairs. What kind of savages were these people? Suspicious. Hot-tempered. Eager to find fault and despise any outsider. Touchy. Devious, jealous, traitorous, and evil. He had done nothing to deserve their contempt. Nothing to deserve the explosive hostility that engulfed him when he said he might have to buy a car. Why didn't they respond the way the man in Roanoke did when he bought the car? Because in Roanoke he did not have a car. Here he had one and wanted another, and perhaps it was that that upset them. Furthermore, he hadn't even suggested that he would trade the old one in. He had hinted that he would abandon the "broken" one and just get another. But so what? What business was it of theirs what he did with his money? He didn't deserve . . .

It sounded old. *Deserve*. Old and tired and beaten to death. Deserve. Now it seemed to him that he was always saying or thinking that he didn't deserve some bad luck, or some bad treatment from others. He'd told Guitar that he didn't "deserve" his family's dependence, hatred, or whatever. That he didn't even "deserve" to hear all the misery and mutual accusations his parents unloaded on him. Nor did he "deserve" Hagar's vengeance. But why shouldn't his parents tell him their personal problems? If not him, then who? And if a stranger could try to kill him, surely Hagar, who knew him and whom he'd thrown away like a wad of chewing gum after the flavor was gone—she had a right to try to kill him too.

Apparently he thought he deserved only to be loved—from a distance, though—and given what he wanted. And in return he would be . . . what? Pleasant? Generous? Maybe all he was really saying was: I am not responsible for your pain; share your happiness with me but not your unhappiness.

They were troublesome thoughts, but they wouldn't go away. Under the moon, on the ground, alone, with not even the sound of baying dogs to remind him that he was with other people, his self—the cocoon that was "personality"—gave way. He could barely see his own hand, and couldn't see his feet. He was only his breath, coming slower now, and his thoughts. The rest of him had disappeared. So the thoughts came, unobstructed by other people, by things, even by the sight of himself. There was nothing here to help him—not his money, his car, his father's reputation, his suit, or his shoes. In fact they hampered him. Except for his broken watch, and his wallet with about two hundred dollars, all he had started out with on his journey was gone: his suitcase with the Scotch, the shirts, and the space for bags of gold; his snap-brim hat, his tie, his shirt, his three-piece suit, his socks, and his shoes. His watch and his two hundred dollars would be of no help out here, where all a man had was what he was born with, or had learned to use. And endurance. Eyes, ears, nose, taste, touch—and some other sense that he knew he did not have: an ability to separate out, of all the things there were to sense, the one that life itself might depend on. What did Calvin see on the bark? On the ground? What was he saying? What did he hear that made him know something unexpected had happened some two miles—perhaps more—away, and that that something was a different kind of prey, a bobcat? He could still hear them—the way they had sounded the last few hours. Signaling one another. What were they saying? "Wait up?" "Over here?" Little by little it fell into place. The dogs, the men—none was just hollering, just signaling location or pace. The men and the dogs were talking to each other. In distinctive voices they were saying distinctive, complicated things. That long *yah* sound was followed by a specific kind of howl from one of the dogs. The low *howm howm* that sounded like a string bass imitating a bassoon meant something the dogs understood and executed. And the dogs spoke to the men: single-shot barks—evenly spaced and widely spaced—one every three or four minutes, that might go on for twenty minutes. A sort of radar that indicated to the men where they were and what they saw and what they wanted to do about it. And the men agreed or told them to change direction or to come back. All those shrieks, those rapid tumbling barks, the long sustained yells, the tuba sounds, the drumbeat sounds, the low liquid *howm howm*, the reedy whistles, the thin *eeeee*'s of a cornet, the *unh unh unh* bass chords. It was all language. An extension of the click people made in their cheeks back home when they wanted a dog to follow them. No, it was not language; it was what there was before language. Before things were written down. Language in the time when men and animals did talk to one another, when a man could sit down with an ape and the two converse; when a tiger and a man could share the same tree, and each understood the other; when men ran *with* wolves, not from or after them. And he was hearing it in the Blue Ridge Mountains under a sweet gum tree. And if they could talk to animals, and the animals could talk to them, what didn't they know about human beings? Or the earth itself, for that matter. It was more than tracks Calvin was looking for—he whispered to the trees, whispered to the ground, touched them, as a blind man caresses a page of Braille, pulling meaning through his fingers.

Milkman rubbed the back of his head against the bark. This was what Guitar had missed about the South—the woods, hunters, killing. But something had maimed him, scarred him like Reverend Cooper's knot, like Saul's missing teeth, and like his own father. He felt a sudden rush of affection for them all, and out there under the sweet gum tree, within the sound of men tracking a bobcat, he thought he understood Guitar now. Really understood him.

Down either side of his thighs he felt the sweet gum's surface roots cradling him like the rough but maternal hands of a grandfather. Feeling both tense and relaxed, he sank his fingers into the grass. He tried to listen with his fingertips, to hear what, if anything, the earth had to say, and it told him quickly that someone was standing behind him and he had just enough time to raise one hand to his neck and catch the wire that fastened around his throat. It cut like a razor into his fingers, tore into the skin so deeply he had to let go. The wire pressed into his neck then and took his breath. He thought he heard himself gurgling and saw a burst of many-colored lights dancing before his eyes. When the music followed the colored lights, he knew he had just drawn the last sweet air left for him in the world. Exactly the way he'd heard it would be, his life flashed before him, but it consisted of only one image: Hagar bending over him in perfect love, in the most intimate sexual gesture imaginable. In the midst of that picture he heard the voice of the someone holding the wire say, "Your Day has come," and it filled him with such sadness to be dying, leaving this world at the fingertips of his friend, that he relaxed and in the instant it took to surrender to the overwhelming melancholy he felt the cords of his struggling neck muscles relax too and there was a piece of a second in which the wire left him room enough to gasp, to take another breath. But it was a living breath this time, not a dying one. Hagar, the lights, the music, disappeared, and Milkman grabbed the Winchester at his side, cocked it, and pulled the trigger, shooting into the trees in front of him. The blast startled Guitar, and the wire slipped again. Guitar pulled it back, but Milkman knew his friend would need both hands to keep it that way. He turned the shotgun backward as far as he could and managed awkwardly, to pull the trigger again, hitting only branches and dirt. He was wondering if there was another blast in the gun when he heard right up close the wild, wonderful sound of three baying dogs who he knew had treed a bobcat. The wire dropped and he heard Guitar breaking into a fast run through the trees. Milkman stood up and grabbed his flashlight, pointing it in the direction of the sound of running feet. He saw nothing but branches resettling themselves. Rubbing his neck, he moved toward the sound of the dogs. Guitar did not have a gun, otherwise he would have used it, so Milkman felt secure heading for the dogs with the gun in his hand even though it had no more shot. He didn't miss; his sense of direction was accurate and he came upon Calvin, Small Boy, Luther, and Omar crouching on the ground a few feet away from the dogs and the glistening night eyes of a bobcat in a tree.

The dogs were trying their best to get up into the tree, and the men were considering whether to shoot the bobcat down, shoot a limb and make him jump down and fight the dogs, or what. They decided to try and kill the cat where he lay. Omar stood up and took his lamp over to the left. The cat crept a little ways out, following the light. Then Small Boy took aim and put a bullet just under the left foreleg and the bobcat dropped through the branches into the jaws of Becky and her companions.

There was a lot of life in the cat; he fought well until Calvin hollered the dogs away and shot it again, and once more, and then it was still.

They held the lamps over the carcass and groaned with pleasure at the size, the ferocity, the stillness of it. All four got down on their knees, pulling rope and knives, cutting a branch the width of a wrist, tying it and binding it for the long walk back.

They were so pleased with themselves it was some time before anybody remembered to ask Milkman what he was shooting at back there. Milkman hoisted the stake he was carrying a little higher and said, "I dropped the gun. I tripped and it went off. Then when I picked it up it went off again."

They burst into laughter. "Tripped? What'd you have the safety off for? Was you scared?"

"Scared to death," said Milkman. "Scared to death."

They hooted and laughed all the way back to the car, teasing Milkman, egging him on to tell more about how scared he was. And he told them. Laughing too, hard, loud, and long. Really laughing, and he found himself exhilarated by simply walking the earth. Walking it like he belonged on it; like his legs were stalks, tree trunks, a part of his body that extended down down down into the rock and soil, and were comfortable there—on the earth and on the place where he walked. And he did not limp.

They met dawn in King Walker's gas station for a rehash of the night they had spent. Milkman was the butt of their humor, but it was good-humored humor, quite unlike the laughter the trip had begun with. "Lucky to be alive. Cat wasn't the problem; this here nigger was the problem. Blastin away at us while we got a mean cat gettin ready to chew us and the dogs up both. Shootin all through the woods. Could have blown his own head off. Don't you city boys know how to handle yourself?"

"You country niggers got it all over us," Milkman answered.

Omar and Small Boy slapped him on the shoulders. Calvin hollered to Luther, "Go get Vernell. Tell her to get breakfast ready. Soon's we skin this cat, we comin in there with a appetite and she better be ready to meet it!"

Milkman went with them to the back of the station, where, on a small cemented area covered by a corrugated tin roof, the dead bobcat lay. Milkman's neck had swollen so it was difficult for him to lower his chin without pain.

Omar sliced through the rope that bound the bobcat's feet. He and Calvin turned it over on its back. The legs fell open. Such thin delicate ankles.

"*Everybody wants a black man's life.*"

Calvin held the forefeet open and up while Omar pierced the curling hair at the point where the sternum lay. Then he sliced all the way down to the genitals. His knife pointed upward for a cleaner, neater incision.

"*Not his dead life; I mean his living life.*"

When he reached the genitals he cut them off, but left the scrotum intact.

"It's the condition our condition is in."

Omar cut around the legs and the neck. Then he pulled the hide off.

"What good is a man's life if he can't even choose what to die for?"

The transparent underskin tore like gossamer under his fingers.

"Everybody wants the life of a black man."

Now Small Boy knelt down and slit the flesh from the scrotum to the jaw.

"Fair is one more thing I've given up."

Luther came back and, while the others rested, carved out the rectal tube with the deft motions of a man coring an apple.

"I hope I never have to ask myself that question."

Luther reached into the paunch and lifted the entrails. He dug under the rib cage to the diaphragm and carefully cut around it until it was free.

"*It* is *about love. What else but love? Can't I love what I criticize?*"

Then he grabbed the windpipe and the gullet, eased them back, and severed them with one stroke of his little knife.

"*It* is *about love. What else?*"

They turned to Milkman. "You want the heart?" they asked him. Quickly, before any thought could paralyze him, Milkman plunged both hands into the rib cage. "Don't get the lungs, now. Get the heart."

"What else?"

He found it and pulled. The heart fell away from the chest as easily as yolk slips out of its shell.

"What else? What else? What else?"

Now Luther went back into the stomach cavity and yanked the entrails out altogether. They sucked up like a vacuum through the hole that was made at the rectum. He slipped the entrails into a paper bag while the others began cleaning up, hosing down, salting, packing, straightening, and then they turned the cat over to let the blood drain down on its own hide.

"What are you going to do with it?" asked Milkman.

"Eat him!"

A peacock soared away and lit on the hood of a blue Buick.

Milkman looked at the bobcat's head. The tongue lay in its mouth as harmless as a sandwich. Only the eyes held the menace of the night.

Hungry as he was, he couldn't eat much of Vernell's breakfast, so he pushed the scrambled eggs, hominy, fried apples around in the plate, gulped coffee and talked a lot. And, somehow, he had to get around to the purpose of his visit to Shalimar.

"You know, my grandfather came from somewhere near here. My grandmother too."

"Did? From around here? What's their name?"

"I don't know her maiden name, but her first name was Sing. Any of you ever know anybody with a name like that?"

They shook their heads. "Sing? No. Never heard of nobody name that."

"I had an aunt live down this way too. Name of Pilate. Pilate Dead. Ever hear of her?"

"Ha! Sound like a newspaper headline: Pilot Dead. She do any flying?"

"No. *P-i-l-a-t-e*, Pilate."

"*P-i-l-a-t-e*. That spell *Pie-late*," Small Boy said.

"Naw, nigger. Not no *Pie-late*. Pilate like in the Bible, dummy."

"He don't read the Bible."

"He don't read nothin."

"He can't read nothin."

They teased Small Boy until Vernell interrupted them. "You all hush. You say Sing?" she asked Milkman.

"Yeah. Sing."

"I believe that was the name of a girl my gran used to play with. I remember the name cause it sounded so pretty. Gran used to talk about her all the time. Seem like her folks didn't like her to play with the colored children from over this way, so her and my gran used to sneak off and go fishin and berry-pickin. You know what I mean? She'd have to meet her in secret." Vernell eyed Milkman carefully. "This Sing girl was light-skinned, with straight black hair."

"That's her!" Milkman said. "She was mixed or Indian, one."

Vernell nodded. "Indian. One of old Heddy's children. Heddy was all right, but she didn't like her girl playin with coloreds. She was a Byrd."

"A what?"

"A Byrd. Belonged to the Byrd family over by the ridge. Near Solomon's Leap."

"Oh, yeah?" said one of the men. "One of Susan Byrd's people?"

"That's right. One of them. They never was too crazy 'bout colored folks. Susan either."

"Do they still live there?" asked Milkman.

"Susan do. Right behind the ridge. Only house back in there with a brick front. She by herself now. All the others moved out so they could pass."

"Can I walk it?" he asked.

"Most folks could, I reckon," said Omar. "But after last night I don't recommend it for you." He laughed.

"Can you drive a car through?"

"Part of the way you can. But the road is narrow and messy back up in there," said Vernell. "Horse, maybe, but not no car."

"I'll make it. Might take me a week, but I'll make it," said Milkman.

"Just don't carry no guns"—Calvin cooled his coffee in his saucer—"and you'll be all right." They all laughed again.

Milkman thought about that. Guitar was out there someplace, and since he seemed to know everything Milkman was doing or getting ready to do, he'd also know he was going out to some ridge. He touched his swollen neck. He didn't want to go anywhere alone without a gun.

"You ought to have a rest before you go trottin off anywhere," Omar said, looking at him. "There's a nice lady up the road a ways. She'd be proud to take you in." The look in his eyes was unmistakable. "Pretty woman too. Real pretty." Vernell grunted and Milkman smiled. Hope she's got a gun, he thought.

She didn't, but she had indoor plumbing and her smile was just like her name, Sweet, as she nodded her head to Milkman's query about whether he could take a bath. The tub was the newest feature in the tiny shotgun house and Milkman sank gratefully into the steaming water. Sweet brought him soap and a boar's-bristle brush and knelt to bathe him. What she did for his sore feet, his cut face, his back, his neck, his thighs, and the palms of his hands was so delicious he couldn't imagine that the lovemaking to follow would be anything but anticlimactic. If this bath and this woman, he thought, are all that come out of this trip, I will rest easy and do my duty to God, country, and the Brotherhood of Elks for the rest of my life. I will walk hot coals with a quart of kerosene in my hand for this. I will walk every railroad tie from here to Cheyenne and back for this. But when the lovemaking came, he decided he would crawl.

Afterward he offered to bathe her. She said he couldn't because the tank was small and there wasn't enough water for another hot bath.

"Then let me give you a cool one," he said. He soaped and rubbed her until her skin squeaked and glistened like onyx. She put salve on his face. He washed her hair. She sprinkled talcum on his feet. He straddled her behind and massaged her back. She put witch hazel on his swollen neck. He made up the bed. She gave him gumbo to eat. He washed the dishes. She washed his clothes and hung them out to dry. He scoured her tub. She ironed his shirt and pants. He gave her fifty dollars. She kissed his mouth. He touched her face. She said please come back. He said I'll see you tonight.

Chapter 12

At four o'clock he knocked on the door of the only house back of the ridge with a brick front. Fresh and shining in the army fatigues Sweet had washed and pressed, he had tramped along feeling ready for anything. But he didn't think Guitar would jump him in the daytime on a winding path (which they called a road) that cut through hilly land that was nevertheless tilled and had a smattering of houses and people. If he did confront him (with anything other than a gun) Milkman was sure he could take him, but it would be best to get back before nightfall. He didn't know what was on Guitar's mind, but he knew it had something to do with the gold. If he knows I'm here and where I have been and what I did in each place, then he must know that I'm trying to get it, doing just what I said I would do. Why would he try to kill me before I got it or even found out what happened to it? Most of it was a total mystery to him, but the part that was clear was enough to keep him alert and jittery all the way.

The Byrd house sat on a neat lawn separated by a white picket fence from the field grass on either side of the property. A child's swing dangled from a cedar tree; four little steps painted blue led up to the porch, and from the window, between fluttering curtains, came the smell of gingerbread baking.

A woman who looked to be about his mother's age answered the door.

"Miss Byrd?" Milkman asked her.

"Yes?"

"How are you? My name is, uh, Macon, and I'm visiting here for a few days. I'm from Michigan and I think some of my people lived here a long time ago. I was hoping you'd be able to help me."

"Help you what?" She sounded arch and Milkman had the distinct impression that this lady did not like the color of his skin.

"Find them. I mean find out about them. We're all split up, my family, and some folks in town thought you might know some of them."

"Who's that, Susan?" Another woman's voice came from behind her.

"Somebody to see *me*, Grace."

"Well, why don't you ask him in? Don't make him state his business on the steps."

Miss Byrd sighed. "Please come in, Mr. Macon."

Milkman followed her into a pleasant living room full up with sunshine. "Excuse me," she said. "I didn't mean to be rude. Please have a seat." She motioned to a gray velvet wing-back chair. A woman in a two-piece print dress came into the room, clutching a paper napkin in her hand and chewing on something.

"Who'd you say?" She addressed her question to Miss Byrd, but ran inquisitive eyes over Milkman.

Miss Byrd held out a hand. "This is a friend of mine—Miss Long. Grace Long—Mr. . . ."

"How do you do?" Grace held out her hand to him.

"Fine, thank you."

"Mr. Macon, is it?"

"Yes."

"Susan, perhaps Mr. Macon would like some refreshment." Miss Long smiled and sat on the sofa facing the gray chair.

"Well, he just stepped foot in the door, Grace. Give me time." Miss Byrd turned to Milkman. "Would you like a cup of coffee or some tea?"

"Sure. Thanks."

"Which one?"

"Coffee's all right."

"You've got butter cookies, Susan. Give him some of those butter cookies."

Miss Byrd gave her friend a tired frown. "I'll just be a minute," she said to Milkman, and left the room.

"Yes, well. Did I hear you say you were visiting in these parts? We don't see too many visitors." Grace crossed her ankles. Like Susan Byrd, she wore black laced shoes and cotton stockings. As she made herself comfortable, she inched her dress up a little.

"Yes, visiting."

"You in the service?"

"Ma'am? Oh, no. I was hunting last night. Some friends lent me these." He smoothed the seam Sweet had made in the fatigues.

"Hunting? Oh, Lord, don't tell me you're one of them. I can't stand those hunting people. They make me sick, always prowling round other people's property. Day and night they're shooting up the world. I tell my students—I'm a schoolteacher, you know, I teach over at the normal school. Have you seen it yet?"

"No, not yet."

"Well, there's nothing to see, really. Just a school, like any other. But you're welcome to stop by. We'd be pleased to have you. Where you from again?"

"Michigan."

"I thought so. Susan!" She turned around. "He's from up North." Then back to Milkman: "Where are you staying?"

"Well, nowhere yet. I just met a few people in town and . . ."

Susan Byrd came in with a tray of coffee cups and a plate of wide pale cookies.

"He's from Michigan," said Grace.

"I heard him. How do you take your coffee?"

"Black."

"Black? No cream or sugar at all?" asked Grace. "Wish I could do that; maybe I could get back into a twelve. But it's never going to happen now." She pressed one hand on her hip and smiled at Milkman.

"What did you want to see me about?" Susan Byrd placed a mild but clear stress on the word "me."

"I'm trying to locate anybody who might have known my grandmother. Her name was Sing."

Grace clapped her hands to her mouth and gave a little squeal. "Relatives! You all are relatives!" Milkman put his cup down. "Well, I'll be!" Grace's eyes were lit and dancing.

"You've come to the right place," said Susan, "but I doubt if I can help you any."

"What are you talking about, Susan? Your mother was named Sing, wasn't she?"

"No, she wasn't, Grace, and if you let me finish a sentence you might learn something you don't know too."

"I thought you said—"

"My mother's name was Mary. *M-a-r-y*, Mary."

"Well, excuse *me*."

Susan turned to Milkman. "My father, Crowell Byrd, had a sister named Sing."

"That must be her! My grandmother! Sing. Did she marry a man named—"

"I knew there was somebody in your family named Sing!"

"She didn't marry anybody that I know of." Susan interrupted them both.

"Oh, this is really something. A stranger walks right into your house and he's your own . . . what? Cousin? I hate to say it, but this is a small world. Isn't it? You have got to visit my class, Mr. Macon."

Milkman joined Susan Byrd in ignoring Grace Long. "Where did she live?" he asked her.

"The last time my father saw her, she was on a wagon headed for Massachusetts to a private school up there. A Quaker school."

"Your people Quakers? You never told me that. See, Mr. Macon, what your friends hide from you? I bet she'd hide you too."

"And she never married?" Milkman couldn't take the time to acknowledge Grace's attentions.

"Not anybody we heard of. After she went to that Quaker school they lost track of her. I believe they tried to locate her, mostly because my grandmother–her name was Heddy–she was so torn up about it. I always believed the same thing my father believed: that she didn't want to be found after she left that school."

"You know darn well she didn't," said Grace. "She probably started passing like the rest of 'em, that's what." She leaned toward Milkman. "There used to be a lot of that. A lot of it. Not so much nowadays, but there used to be a lot of 'em did it–if they could." She shot a glance at Susan. "Like your cousins, Susan. They're passing now. Lilah, John. I know John is, and he knows I know he is."

"Everybody knows that, Grace."

"Mr. Macon doesn't know it. I saw John on the street in Mayville–"

"Mr. Macon doesn't need to know it. He's not even interested."

"How do you know he's not?"

"Because he said the woman he's looking for was his grandmother, and if she's his grandmother she'd be too dark to . . ." Susan Byrd hesitated. "Well, too dark to pass. Wouldn't she?" She flushed a little.

Milkman ignored the question. "And you say she lived in Massachusetts, right?"

"Yes. Boston."

"I see." It looked like a dead end, so he decided to follow another line. "Did you ever know or hear of a woman around here named Pilate?"

"Pilate. No. Never. Have you, Grace?"

Grace shook her head. "No, and I've been here most of my life."

"I've been here *all* of mine," said Susan. "Both my parents were born here and so was I. Never been farther away than St. Phillips County. I have people in South Carolina, but I've never even been to visit them."

"That's because they're passing too. Just like John. You couldn't visit them if you wanted to." Grace leaned over the plate of cookies and selected one.

"They're not the only family I have left." Susan was indignant.

"I hope not. It's a sad thing, Mr. Macon, when you're left without any people to claim you. I keep up with my family. I'm not married, you know, not yet anyway, but my family is *very* close." She gave him a meaningful look. Milkman turned his wrist and looked down to see what time it was.

"Oh, look at that." Grace pointed to his hand. "What a good-looking watch. May I see it?" Milkman stood up to hand it to her and remained standing. "Look, Susan, it doesn't have a single number on it. Just dots. Now, how can anybody figure out what time it is from those dots?"

Susan rose too. "You ever been down here before, Mr. Macon?"

"No. This is my first visit."

"Well, I hope it won't be your last. How long will you be here?"

"Oh, I think I'll get on back tonight or tomorrow at the latest." He looked out the window. The sun was dropping.

"That soon?" asked Grace. "Why don't you give him something to take with him, Susan? Would you like to take some butter cookies with you, Mr. Macon?"

"No, thank you."

"You'll be happy to have them later." The woman was wearing him down. He smiled, though, and said, "If you like."

"I'll fix a little package for you. Okay, Susan?" She fled from the room.

Susan managed a small smile. "Wish you could stay and visit with us awhile." Her words were as mechanical as her smile.

"So do I," he said, "but, well, maybe I'll be back."

"That'd be nice. Sorry I couldn't be of any help to you."

"You have been."

"Have I?"

"Oh, sure. You have to know what's wrong before you can find what's right."

She smiled a genuine smile then. "It's important to you, is it, to find your people?"

Milkman thought about it. "No. Not really. I was just passing through, and it was just—just an idea. It's not important."

Grace returned with a little parcel wrapped in white paper napkins. "Here you are," she said. "You'll appreciate this later on."

"Thank you. Thank you both."

"Nice meeting you."

"And you."

He left the house feeling tired and off center. I'll spend one more night here and then leave, he thought. The car should be fixed by now. There's nothing here to know, no gold or any traces of it. Pilate lived in Virginia, but not in this part of the state. Nobody at all has heard of her. And the Sing that lived here went to Boston, not Danville, Pennsylvania, and passed for white. His grandmother would have been "too dark to pass." She had actually blushed. As though she'd discovered something shameful about him. He was both angry and amused and wondered what Omar and Sweet and Vernell thought of Miss Susan Byrd.

He was curious about these people. He didn't feel close to

them, but he did feel connected, as though there was some cord or pulse or information they shared. Back home he had never felt that way, as though he belonged to anyplace or anybody. He'd always considered himself the outsider in his family, only vaguely involved with his friends, and except for Guitar, there was no one whose opinion of himself he cared about. Once, long ago, he had cared what Pilate and Hagar thought of him, but having conquered Hagar and having disregarded Pilate enough to steal from her, all that was gone. But there was something he felt now—here in Shalimar, and earlier in Danville—that reminded him of how he used to feel in Pilate's house. Sitting in Susan Byrd's living room, lying with Sweet, eating with those men at Vernell's table, he didn't have to get over, to turn on, or up, or even out.

And there was something more. It wasn't true what he'd said to Susan Byrd: that it wasn't important to find his people. Ever since Danville, his interest in his own people, not just the ones he met, had been growing. Macon Dead, also known as Jake somebody. Sing. Who were they, and what were they like? The man who sat for five nights on a fence with a gun, waiting. Who named his baby girl Pilate, who tore a farm out of a wilderness. The man who ate pecans on a wagon going North. Did he have brothers or sisters whom he left behind? Who was his mother, his father? And his wife. Was she the Boston Sing? If so, what was she doing on a wagon? Why would she go off to a northern private school on a wagon? Not a carriage or a train, but a wagon—full of ex-slaves. Maybe she never got to Boston. Maybe she didn't pass. She could have changed her mind about school and run off with the boy she ate pecans with. And whoever she was, why did she want her husband to keep that awful name? To wipe out the past? What past? Slavery? She was never a slave. *His* slave past? And why didn't his own father, and Pilate, know any of their own relatives? Wasn't there any family to notify when the father died? Macon didn't ever try to get to Virginia. Pilate headed straight for it.

Milkman opened the parcel Grace had fixed for him and took

out a cookie. A little piece of paper fluttered to the ground. He picked it up and read: "Grace Long 40 Route 2 three houses down from the Normal School." He smiled. That's why it took her so long to wrap up four cookies. He bit into one of them and sauntered along, crumpling the napkins and Grace's invitation into a wad. The questions about his family still knocked around in his head like billiard balls. If his grandfather, this Jake, was born in the same place his wife was, in Shalimar, why did he tell the Yankee he was born in Macon, thereby providing him with the raw material for the misnaming? And if he and his wife were born in the same place, why did Pilate and his father and Circe all say they "met" on that wagon? And why did the ghost tell Pilate to sing? Milkman chuckled to himself. That wasn't what he was telling her at all; maybe the ghost was just repeating his wife's name, Sing, and Pilate didn't know it because she never knew her mother's name. After she died Macon Dead wouldn't let anybody say it aloud. That was funny. He wouldn't speak it after she died, and after he died that's all he ever said—her name.

Jesus! Here he was walking around in the middle of the twentieth century trying to explain what a ghost had done. But why not? he thought. One fact was certain: Pilate did not have a navel. Since that was true, anything could be, and why not ghosts as well?

He was near the road leading to the town now, and it was getting dark. He lifted his wrist to look at his watch and remembered that Grace had not given it back to him. "Damn," he murmured aloud. "I'm losing everything." He stood still, trying to make up his mind whether to go back for it now or later. If he went now, he'd be forced to return in deep darkness. Totally defenseless before a hit from Guitar. But it would be a real bother to have to come all the way back here—where no car could make it—tomorrow when he was going to leave. But Guitar might be—

"I can't let him direct and determine what I do, where I go or when. If I do that now I'll do it all my life and he'll run me off the earth."

He didn't know what to do, but decided finally that a watch was not worth worrying about. All it could do was tell him the time of day and he really wasn't interested. Wiping cookie crumbs from his mustache, he turned into the main road, and there, outlined in cobalt blue, stood Guitar. Leaned, rather, against a persimmon tree. Milkman stopped, surprised at the calm, steady beat of his heart—the complete absence of fear. But then, Guitar was cleaning his fingernails with a harmless match stick. Any weapon he had would have to be hidden in his denim jacket or pants.

They looked at each other for a minute. No, less. Just long enough for the heart of each man to adjust its throb to the downbeat of the other. Guitar spoke first.

"My man."

Milkman ignored the greeting. "Why, Guitar? Just tell me why."

"You took the gold."

"What gold? There wasn't any gold."

"You took the gold."

"The cave was empty, man. I got down on my stomach and looked in that pit. I put my hands—"

"You took the gold."

"You're crazy, Guitar."

"Angry. Never crazy."

"There wasn't any gold!" Milkman tried hard not to shout.

"I saw you, motherfucker."

"Saw me what?"

"Take the gold."

"Where?"

"In Danville."

"You saw me with gold in Danville?"

"I saw you with gold in Danville."

"You've got to be kidding. What was I doing with it?"

"Shipping it."

"Shipping it?"

"Yeah. Why the game, man? You just greedy, like your old

man? Or what?" Guitar's eyes rested on the last butter cookie in Milkman's hand. He frowned and began to breathe through his lips.

"Guitar, I didn't ship no gold. There wasn't any gold to ship. You couldn't have seen me."

"I saw you, baby. I was in the station."

"What fuckin station?"

"The freight station in Danville."

Milkman remembered then, going to look for Reverend Cooper, looking all over for him. Then going into the station house to see if he'd gone, and there helping a man lift a huge crate onto the weighing platform. He started to laugh. "Oh, shit. Guitar, that wasn't no gold. I was just helping that man lift a crate. He asked me to help him. Help him lift a big old crate. I did and then I split."

Guitar looked at the cookie again, then back into Milkman's eyes. Nothing changed in his face. Milkman knew it sounded lame. It was the truth, but it sounded like a lie. A weak lie too. He also knew that in all his life, Guitar had never seen Milkman give anybody a hand, especially a stranger; he also knew that they'd even discussed it, starting with Milkman's not coming to his mother's rescue in a dream he had. Guitar had accused him of selfishness and indifference; told him he wasn't serious, and didn't have any fellow feeling—none whatsoever. Now he was standing there saying that he willingly, spontaneously, had helped an old white man lift a huge, heavy crate. But it was true. It was true. And he'd prove it.

"Guitar, why am I here? If I was shipping gold back home, why am I here dressed like this? Would I be roaming around in the country like a fool with a crate of gold off somewhere? Would I? What the fuck would I do that for and then come here?"

"Maybe you shipped the gold *here*, you jive-ass."

"What the fuck are you talking about?"

"I looked! I saw it! You hear me? I drove down there, followed you there, because I had a funny feeling that you were pulling a fast one. I wasn't sure, but I felt it. If I was wrong, I'd help you get it. But I wasn't wrong. I got into Danville that afternoon. I drove right past the freight depot and there you were in your little beige suit. I parked and followed you into the station. When I got there I saw you shipping it. Giving it to the man. I waited until you left, and I went back in and asked the cracker if my friend"–he slurred the word–"had shipped a crate to Michigan. The man said no. Just one crate on the load, he said. Just one crate. And when I asked him where it was going, all he could remember was Virginia." Guitar smiled. "The bus you caught wasn't headed for Michigan. It was headed for Virginia. And here you are."

Milkman felt whipped. There was nothing to do but let it play.

"Was my name on the crate?"

"I didn't look."

"Would I send a crate of gold to Virginia–*gold*, man."

"You might. You did."

"Is that why you tried to kill me?"

"Yes."

"Because I ripped you off?"

"Because you ripped *us* off! You are fuckin with our work!"

"You're wrong. Dead wrong."

"The 'dead' part is you."

Milkman looked down at the cookie in his hand. It looked foolish and he started to throw it away, but changed his mind. "So my Day has come?"

"Your Day has come, but on *my* schedule. And believe it: I will run you as long as there is ground. Your name is Macon, but you ain't dead yet."

"Tell me something. When you saw me in the station, with the crate, why did you back off and hide? Why didn't you just walk up to me? It could have been settled there."

"I told you. I had this funny funny feeling."

"That I was going to cut you out?"

"Cut *us* out. Yes."

"And you believe I did?"

"Yes."

"Back there in the woods you were angry."

"Yes."

"Now you're going to wait till the gold comes."

"Yes."

"And I pick it up."

"You won't be able to pick it up."

"Do me a favor. When it gets here. Check it first to see if there's gold in it."

"First?"

"Or last. But before you haul it all the way back home."

"Don't worry yourself about it."

"One more thing. Why the message? Why'd you warn me with a message at the store?"

"You're my friend. It's the least I could do for a friend."

"My man. I want to thank you."

"You're welcome, baby."

Milkman slipped into Sweet's bed and slept the night in her perfect arms. It was a warm dreamy sleep all about flying, about sailing high over the earth. But not with arms stretched out like airplane wings, nor shot forward like Superman in a horizontal dive, but floating, cruising, in the relaxed position of a man lying on a couch reading a newspaper. Part of his flight was over the dark sea, but it didn't frighten him because he knew he could not fall. He was alone in the sky, but somebody was applauding him, watching him and applauding. He couldn't see who it was.

When he awoke the next morning and set about seeing to the repair of his car, he couldn't shake the dream, and didn't really want to. In Solomon's store he found Omar and Solomon shaking sacks of okra into peck baskets and he still felt the sense of lightness and power that flying had given him.

"Got a belt for your car," said Omar. "Ain't new, but it ought to fit."

"Hey, that's good. Thanks, Omar."

"You leavin us right away?"

"Yeah, I have to get on back."

"You see that Byrd woman all right?"

"Yeah, I saw her."

"She help you any?" Omar wiped the okra fuzz from his hands onto his trousers.

"No. Not much."

"Well, King Walker say he be down this morning and put the belt on. You probably ought to get a good checkup on that car once you get on the road."

"I plan to."

"Sweet give you any breakfast?" asked Solomon.

"She tried, but I wanted to get over here early to see about the car."

"What about a cup a coffee; there's a full pot in back."

"No, thanks. I think I'll walk around a little till he comes."

It was six-thirty in the morning and the town was bustling as though it were high noon. Life and business began early in the South so the coolest part of the day could be taken advantage of. People had already eaten, women had already washed clothes and were spreading them on bushes, and in a few days, when the school in the next town opened, children at this hour would already be walking, running over the roads and fields to class. Now they were sauntering about, doing chores, teasing cats, throwing bread to stray chickens, and some of them were playing their endless round games. Milkman could hear them singing and wandered off toward them and the huge cedar that reared up over their heads. Again their sweet voices reminded him of the gap in his own childhood, as he leaned against the cedar to watch them. The boy in the middle of the circle (it seemed always to be a boy) spun around with his eyes closed and his arm stretched out, pointing. Round and round he went until the song ended with a shout and he stopped, his finger pointing at a child Milkman could not see. Then they all dropped to their knees and he was surprised to hear them begin another song at this point, one he had heard off and on all his life. That old blues song Pilate sang all the time: "O Sugarman don't leave me here," except the children sang, "Solomon don't leave me here."

Milkman smiled, remembering Pilate. Hundreds of miles away, he was homesick for her, for her house, for the very people he had been hell-bent to leave. His mother's quiet, crooked, apologetic smile. Her hopeless helplessness in the kitchen. The best years of her life, from age twenty to forty, had been celibate, and aside from the consummation that began his own life, the rest of her life had been the same. He hadn't thought much of it when she'd told him, but now it seemed to him that such sexual deprivation would affect her, hurt her in precisely the way it would affect and hurt him. If it were possible for somebody to force him to live that way, to tell him, "You may walk and live among women, you may even lust after them, but you will not make love for the next twenty years," how would he feel? What would he do? Would he continue as he was? And suppose he were married and his wife refused him for fifteen years. His mother had been able to live through that by a long nursing of her son, some occasional visits to a graveyard. What might she have been like had her husband loved her?

And his father. An old man now, who acquired things and used people to acquire more things. As the son of Macon Dead the first, he paid homage to his own father's life and death by loving what that father had loved: property, good solid property, the bountifulness of life. He loved these things to excess because he loved his father to excess. Owning, building, acquiring—that was his life, his future, his present, and all the history he knew. That he distorted life, bent it, for the sake of gain, was a measure of his loss at his father's death.

As Milkman watched the children, he began to feel uncomfortable. Hating his parents, his sisters, seemed silly now. And the skim of shame that he had rinsed away in the bathwater after having stolen from Pilate returned. But now it was as thick and as tight as a caul. How could he have broken into that house—

the only one he knew that achieved comfort without one article of comfort in it. No soft worn-down chair, not a cushion or a pillow. No light switch, no water running free and clear after a turn of a tap handle. No napkins, no tablecloth. No fluted plates or flowered cups, no circle of blue flame burning in a stove eye. But peace was there, energy, singing, and now his own remembrances.

His mind turned to Hagar and how he had treated her at the end. Why did he never sit her down and talk to her? Honestly. And what ugly thing was it he said to her the last time she tried to kill him? And God, how hollow her eyes had looked. He was never frightened of her; he never actually believed that she would succeed in killing him, or that she really wanted to. Her weapons, the complete lack of cunning or intelligence even of conviction, in her attacks were enough to drain away any fear. Oh, she could have accidentally hurt him, but he could have stopped her in any number of ways. But he hadn't wanted to. He had used her—her love, her craziness—and most of all he had used her skulking, bitter vengeance. It made him a star, a celebrity in the Blood Bank; it told men and other women that he was one bad dude, that he had the power to drive a woman out of her mind, to destroy her, and not because she hated him, or because he had done some unforgivable thing to her, but because he had fucked her and she was driven wild by the absence of his magnificent joint. His hog's gut, Lena had called it. Even the last time, he used her. Used her imminent arrival and feeble attempt at murder as an exercise of his will against hers—an ultimatum to the universe. "Die, Hagar, die." Either this bitch dies or I do. And she stood there like a puppet strung up by a puppet master who had gone off to some other hobby.

O Solomon don't leave me here.

The children were starting the round again. Milkman rubbed the back of his neck. Suddenly he was tired, although the morning was still new. He pushed himself away from the cedar and sank to his haunches.

Jay the only son of Solomon
Come booba yalle, come . . .

Everybody in this town is named Solomon, he thought wearily. Solomon's General Store, Luther Solomon (no relation), Solomon's Leap, and now the children were singing "*Solomon* don't leave me" instead of "*Sugarman.*" Even the name of the town sounded like Solomon: Shalimar, which Mr. Solomon and everybody else pronounced *Shalleemone*.

Milkman's scalp began to tingle. Jay the only son of Solomon? Was that *Jake* the only son of Solomon? Jake. He strained to hear the children. That was one of the people he was looking for. A man named Jake who lived in Shalimar, as did his wife, Sing.

He sat up and waited for the children to begin the verse again. "Come booba yalle, come booba tambee," it sounded like, and didn't make sense. But another line—"Black lady fell down on the ground"—was clear enough. There was another string of nonsense words, then "Threw her body all around." Now the child in the center began whirling, spinning to lyrics sung in a different, faster tempo: "Solomon 'n' Reiner Belali Shalut . . ."

Solomon again, and Reiner? Ryna? Why did the second name sound so familiar? Solomon and Ryna. The woods. The hunt. Solomon's Leap and Ryna's Gulch, places they went to or passed by that night they shot the bobcat. The gulch was where he heard that noise that sounded like a woman crying, which Calvin said came from Ryna's Gulch, that there was an echo there that folks said was "a woman name Ryna" crying. You could hear her when the wind was right.

But what was the rest: Belali . . . Shalut . . . Yaruba? If Solomon and Ryna were names of people, the others might be also. The verse ended in another clear line. "Twenty-one children, the last one *Jake!*" And it was at the shout of *Jake* (who was also, apparently, "the only son of Solomon") that the twirling boy stopped. Now Milkman understood that if the child's finger pointed at nobody, missed, they started up again. But if it pointed directly to another child, that was when they fell to their knees and sang Pilate's song.

Milkman took out his wallet and pulled from it his airplane ticket stub, but he had no pencil to write with, and his pen was in his suit. He would just have to listen and memorize it. He closed his eyes and concentrated while the children, inexhaustible in their willingness to repeat a rhythmic, rhyming action game, performed the round over and over again. And Milkman memorized all of what they sang.

Jake the only son of Solomon
Come booba yalle, come booba tambee
Whirled about and touched the sun
Come konka yalle, come konka tambee

Left that baby in a white man's house
Come booba yalle, come booba tambee
Heddy took him to a red man's house
Come konka yalle, come konka tambee

Black lady fell down on the ground
Come booba yalle, come booba tambee
Threw her body all around
Come konka yalle, come konka tambee

Solomon and Ryna Belali Shalut
Yaruba Medina Muhammet too.
Nestor Kalina Saraka cake.
Twenty-one children, the last one Jake!

O Solomon don't leave me here
Cotton balls to choke me
O Solomon don't leave me here
Buckra's arms to yoke me

Solomon done fly, Solomon done gone
Solomon cut across the sky, Solomon gone home.

He almost shouted when he heard "Heddy took him to a red man's house." Heddy was Susan Byrd's grandmother on her father's side, and therefore Sing's mother too. And "red man's house" must be a reference to the Byrds as Indians. Of course! Sing was an Indian or part Indian and her name was Sing Byrd or, more likely, Sing Bird. No—Singing Bird! That must have been her name originally—Singing Bird. And her brother, Crowell Byrd, was probably Crow Bird, or just Crow. They had mixed their Indian names with American-sounding names. Milkman had four people now that he could recognize in the song: Solomon, Jake, Ryna and Heddy, and a veiled reference to Heddy's Indianness. All of which seemed to put Jake and Sing together in Shalimar, just as Circe had said they were. He couldn't be mistaken. These children were singing a story about his own people! He hummed and chuckled as he did his best to put it all together.

Jake's father was Solomon. Did Jake whirl about and touch the sun? Did Jake leave a baby in a white man's house? No. If the "Solomon don't leave me" line was right, Solomon was the one who left, who "flew away"—meaning died or ran off—not Jake. Maybe it was the baby, or Jake himself, who was begging him to stay. But who was the "black lady" who fell down on the ground? Why did she throw her body all around? It sounded like she was having a fit. Was it because somebody took her baby first to a white man's house, then to an Indian's house? Ryna? Was Ryna the black lady still crying in the gulch? Was Ryna Solomon's daughter? Maybe she had an illegitimate child, and her father— No. It's Solomon she is crying for, not a baby. "Solomon don't leave me." He must have been her lover.

Milkman was getting confused, but he was as excited as a child confronted with boxes and boxes of presents under the skirt of a Christmas tree. Somewhere in the pile was a gift for him.

Yet there were many many missing pieces. Susan Byrd, he thought—she would have to know more than she had told him. Besides, he had to get his watch back.

He ran back to Solomon's store and caught a glimpse of himself in the plate-glass window. He was grinning. His eyes were shining. He was as eager and happy as he had ever been in his life.

Chapter 13

It was a long time after he left, that warm September morning, that she was able to relax enough to drop the knife. When it clattered to the linoleum, she brought her arms down, oh, so slowly, and cradled her breasts as though they were two mangoes thumbed over in the marketplace and pushed aside. She stood that way in the little rented room with the sunshine pouring in until Guitar came home. He could not get her to speak or move, so he picked her up in his arms and carried her downstairs. He sat her on the bottom step while he went to borrow a car to drive her home.

Terrible as he thought the whole business was, and repelled as he was by mindlessness in love, he could not keep the deep wave of sorrow from engulfing him as he looked at this really rather pretty woman sitting straight as a pole, holding her breasts, and staring in front of her out of hollow eyes.

The engine of the old car he'd borrowed roared, but Guitar spoke softly to her. "You think because he doesn't love you that you are worthless. You think because he doesn't want you anymore that he is right—that his judgment and opinion of you are correct. If he throws you out, then you are garbage. You think he belongs to you because you want to belong to him. Hagar, don't. It's a bad word, 'belong.' Especially when you put it with somebody you love. Love shouldn't be like that. Did you ever see the way the clouds love a mountain? They circle all around it; sometimes you can't even see the mountain for the clouds. But you know what? You go up top and what do you see? His head. The clouds never cover the head. His head pokes through, because the clouds let him; they don't wrap him up. They let him keep his head up high, free, with nothing to hide him or bind him. Hear me, Hagar?" He spoke to her as he would to a very young child. "You can't own a human being. You can't lose what you don't own. Suppose you did own him. Could you really love somebody who was absolutely nobody without you? You really want somebody like that? Somebody who falls apart when you walk out the door? You don't, do you? And neither does he. You're turning over your whole life to him. Your whole life, girl. And if it means so little to you that you can just give it away, hand it to him, then why should it mean any more to him? He can't value you more than you value yourself." He stopped. She did not move or give any sign that she had heard him.

Pretty woman, he thought. Pretty little black-skinned woman. Who wanted to kill for love, die for love. The pride, the conceit of these doormat women amazed him. They were always women who had been spoiled children. Whose whims had been taken seriously by adults and who grew up to be the stingiest, greediest people on earth and out of their stinginess grew their stingy little love that ate everything in sight. They could not believe or accept the fact that they were unloved; they believed that the world itself was off balance when it appeared as though they were not loved. Why did they think they were so lovable? Why did they think their brand of love was better than, or even as good as, anybody else's? But they did. And they loved their love so much they would kill anybody who got in its way.

He looked at her again. Pretty. Pretty little black girl. Pretty little black-skinned girl. What had Pilate done to her? Hadn't anybody told her the things she ought to know? He thought of his two sisters, grown women now who could deal, and the litany of their growing up. Where's your daddy? Your mama know you out here in the street? Put something on your head. You gonna catch your death a cold. Ain't you hot? Ain't you cold? Ain't you scared you gonna get wet? Uncross your legs. Pull up your socks. I thought you was goin to the Junior Choir. Your slip is showin. Your hem is out. Come back in here and iron that collar. Hush your mouth. Comb your head. Get up from there and make that bed. Put on the meat. Take out the trash. Vaseline get rid of that ash.

Neither Pilate nor Reba knew that Hagar was not like them. Not strong enough, like Pilate, nor simple enough, like Reba, to make up her life as they had. She needed what most colored girls needed: a chorus of mamas, grandmamas, aunts, cousins, sisters, neighbors, Sunday school teachers, best girl friends, and what all to give her the strength life demanded of her—and the humor with which to live it.

Still, he thought, to have the object of your love, worthy or not, despise you, or leave you . . .

"You know what, Hagar? Everything I ever loved in my life left me. My father died when I was four. That was the first leaving I knew and the hardest. Then my mother. There were four of us and she just couldn't cut it when my father died. She ran away. Just ran away. My aunt took care of us until my grandmother could get there. Then my grandmother took care of us. Then Uncle Billy came. They're both close to dead now. So it was hard for me to latch on to a woman. Because I thought if I loved anything it would die. But I did latch on. Once. But I guess once is all you can manage." Guitar thought about it and said, "But I never wanted to kill her. *Him*, yeah. But not her." He smiled, but Hagar wasn't looking, wasn't even listening, and when he led her out of the car into Reba's arms her eyes were still empty.

All they knew to do was love her and since she would not speak, they brought things to please her. For the first time in life Reba *tried* to win things. And, also for the first time, couldn't. Except for a portable television set, which they couldn't connect because they had no electricity, Reba won nothing. No raffle ticket, no Bingo, no policy slip, no clearing-house number, no magazine sweepstakes, no, nor any unpierced carnival balloon succumbed to her magic. It wore her down. Puzzled and luckless, she dragged herself home clutching stalks of anything that blossomed along the edges of lots and other people's gardens. These she presented to her daughter, who sat in a chair by the window or lay in bed fingering, fingering her hair.

They cooked special things for her; searched for gifts that they hoped would break the spell. Nothing helped. Pilate's lips were still and Reba's eyes full of panic. They brought her lipstick and chocolate milk, a pink nylon sweater and a fuchsia bed jacket. Reba even investigated the mysteries of making jello, both red and green. Hagar didn't even look at it.

One day Pilate sat down on Hagar's bed and held a compact before her granddaughter's face. It was trimmed in a goldlike metal and had a pink plastic lid.

"Look, baby. See here?" Pilate turned it all around to show it off and pressed in the catch. The lid sprang open and Hagar saw a tiny part of her face reflected in the mirror. She took the compact then and stared into the mirror for a long while.

"No wonder," she said at last. "Look at that. No wonder. No wonder."

Pilate was thrilled at the sound of Hagar's voice. "It's yours, baby," she said. "Ain't it pretty?"

"No wonder," said Hagar. "No wonder."

"No wonder what?" asked Pilate.

"Look at how I look. I look awful. No wonder he didn't want me. I look terrible." Her voice was calm and reasonable, as though the last few days hadn't been lived through at all. "I need to get up from here and fix myself up. No *wonder!*" Hagar threw back the bedcover and stood up. "Ohhh. I smell too. Mama, heat me some water. I need a bath. A long one. We got any bath salts left? Oh, Lord, my head. Look at that." She peered into the compact mirror again. "I look like a ground hog. Where's the comb?"

Pilate called Reba and together they flew through the house to find the comb, but when they found it Hagar couldn't get the teeth through her roped and matted hair.

"Wash it," said Reba. "Wash it and we'll comb it while it's wet."

"I need shampoo, then. Real shampoo. I can't use Mama's soap."

"I'll go get some." Reba was trembling a little. "What kind?"

"Oh, any kind. And get some hair oil, Reba. Posner's, and some . . . Oh, never mind. Just that. Mama? Have you seen my . . . Oh, my God. No wonder. No wonder."

Pilate pulled a piece of string from Hagar's bedspread and put it in her mouth. "I'll heat up the water," she said.

When Reba got back she washed Hagar's hair, brushed it, and combed it gently.

"Just make me two braids, Reba. I'm going to have to go to the beauty shop. Today. Oh, and I need something to wear." Hagar stood at the door of the little cardboard closet, running her hands over the shoulders of dresses. "Everything's a mess in here. A mess. All wrinkled . . ."

"Water's hot. Where you want the tub?"

"Bring it in here."

"You think you should be taking a bath so soon?" Reba asked. "You just got up."

"Hush, Reba," said Pilate. "Let the child take care of herself."

"But she's been in the bed three days."

"All the more reason."

"I can't put these things on. Everything's a mess." Hagar was almost in tears.

Reba looked at Pilate. "I hope you right. I don't approve of getting up too fast and jumping right in some water."

"Help me with this tub and stop grumbling."

"All wrinkled. What am I going to wear?"

"That ain't enough water to cover her feet."

"It'll grow when she sits down."

"Where's my yellow dress? The one that buttons all the way down?"

"Somewhere in there, I reckon."

"Find it for me and press it, would you? I know it's a mess. Everything's a mess."

Reba found and pressed the yellow dress. Pilate helped Hagar bathe. Finally a clean and clothed Hagar stood before the two women and said, "I have to buy some clothes. New clothes. Everything I have is a mess."

They looked at each other. "What you need?" asked Pilate.

"I need everything," she said, and everything is what she got. She shopped for everything a woman could wear from the skin out, with the money from Reba's diamond. They had seventy-five cents between them when Hagar declared her needs, and six dollars owed to them from customers. So the two-thousand-dollar two-carat diamond went to a pawnshop, where Reba traded it for thirty dollars at first and then, accompanied by a storming Pilate, she went back and got one hundred and seventy more for it. Hagar stuffed two hundred dollars and seventy-five cents into her purse and headed downtown, still whispering to herself every now and then, "No wonder."

She bought a Playtex garter belt, I. Miller No Color hose, Fruit of the Loom panties, and two nylon slips—one white, one pink—one pair of Joyce Fancy Free and one of Con Brio ("Thank heaven for little Joyce heels"). She carried an armful of skirts and an Evan-Picone two-piece number into the fitting room. Her little yellow dress that buttoned all the way down lay on the floor as she slipped a skirt over her head and shoulders, down to her waist. But the placket would not close. She sucked in her stomach and pulled the fabric as far as possible, but the teeth of the zipper would not join. A light sheen broke out on her forehead as she huffed and puffed. She was convinced that her whole life depended on whether or not those aluminum teeth would meet. The nail of her forefinger split and the balls of her thumbs ached as she struggled with the placket. Dampness became sweat and her breath came in gasps. She was about to weep when the saleswoman poked her head through the curtain and said brightly, "How are you doing?" But when she saw Hagar's gnarled and frightened face, the smile froze.

"Oh, my," she said, and reached for the tag hanging from the skirt's waist. "This is a five. Don't force it. You need, oh, a nine or eleven, I should think. Please. Don't force it. Let me see if I have that size."

She waited until Hagar let the plaid skirt fall down to her ankles before disappearing. Hagar easily drew on the skirt the woman brought back, and without further search, said she would take it and the little two-piece Evan-Picone.

She bought a white blouse next and a nightgown—fawn trimmed in sea foam. Now all she needed was make-up.

The cosmetics department enfolded her in perfume, and she read hungrily the labels and the promise. Myrurgia for primeval woman who creates for him a world of tender privacy where the only occupant is you, mixed with Nina Ricci's L'Air du Temps. Yardley's Flair with Tuvaché's Nectaroma and D'Orsay's Intoxication. Robert Piguet's Fracas, and Calypso and Visa and Bandit. Houbigant's Chantilly. Caron's Fleurs de Rocaille and Bellodgia. Hagar breathed deeply the sweet air that hung over the glass counters. Like a smiling sleepwalker she circled. Round and round the diamond-clear counters covered with bottles, wafer-thin disks, round boxes, tubes, and phials. Lipsticks in soft white hands darted out of their sheaths like the shiny red penises of puppies. Peachy powders and milky lotions were grouped in front of poster after cardboard poster of gorgeous grinning faces. Faces in ecstasy. Faces somber with achieved seduction. Hagar believed she could spend her life there among the cut glass, shimmering in peaches and cream, in satin. In opulence. In luxe. In love.

It was five-thirty when Hagar left the store with two shopping bags full of smaller bags gripped in her hands. And she didn't put them down until she reached Lilly's Beauty Parlor.

"No more heads, honey." Lilly looked up from the sink as Hagar came in.

Hagar stared. "I have to get my hair done. I have to hurry," she said.

Lilly looked over at Marcelline. It was Marcelline who kept the shop prosperous. She was younger, more recently trained, and could do a light press that lasted. Lilly was still using red-hot irons and an ounce of oil on every head. Her customers were loyal but dissatisfied. Now she spoke to Marcelline. "Can you take her? I can't, I know."

Marcelline peered deeply into her customer's scalp. "Hadn't planned on any late work. I got two more coming. This is my eighth today."

No one spoke. Hagar stared.

"Well," said Marcelline. "Since it's you, come on back at eight-thirty. Is it washed already?"

Hagar nodded.

"Okay," said Marcelline. "Eight-thirty. But don't expect nothing fancy."

"I'm surprised at you," Lilly chuckled when Hagar left. "You just sent two people away."

"Yeah, well, I don't feel like it, but I don't want no trouble with that girl Hagar. No telling what she might do. She jump that cousin of hers, no telling what she might do to me."

"That the one going with Macon Dead's boy?" Lilly's customer lifted her head away from the sink.

"That's her. Ought to be shamed, the two of them. *Cousins*."

"Must not be working out if she's trying to kill him."

"I thought he left town."

"Wouldn't you?"

"Well, I know I don't want to truck with her. Not me."

"She don't bother nobody but him."

"Well, Pilate, then. Pilate know I turned her down, she wouldn't like it. They spoil that child something awful."

"Didn't you order fish from next door?"

"All that hair. I hope she don't expect nothing fancy."

"Call him up again. I'm getting hungry."

"Be just like her. No appointment. No nothing. Come in here all late and wrong and want something fancy."

She probably meant to wait somewhere. Or go home and return to Lilly's at eight-thirty. Yet the momentum of the thing held her—it was all of a piece. From the moment she looked into the mirror in the little pink compact she could not stop. It was as though she held her breath and could not let it go until the energy and busyness culminated in a beauty that would dazzle him. That was why, when she left Lilly's, she looked neither right nor left but walked on and on, oblivious of other people, street lights, automobiles, and a thunderous sky. She was thoroughly soaked before she realized it was raining and then only because one of the shopping bags split. When she looked down, her Evan-Picone white-with-a-band-of-color skirt was lying in a neat half fold on the shoulder of the road, and she was far far from home. She put down both bags, picked the skirt up and brushed away the crumbs of gravel that stuck to it. Quickly she refolded it, but when she tried to tuck it back into the shopping bag, the bag collapsed altogether. Rain soaked her hair and poured down her neck as she stooped to repair the damage. She pulled out the box of Con Brios, a smaller package of Van Raalte gloves, and another containing her fawn-trimmed-in-sea-foam shortie nightgown. These she stuffed into the other bag. Retracing her steps, she found herself unable to carry the heavier bag in one hand, so she hoisted it up to her stomach and hugged it with both arms. She had gone hardly ten yards when the bottom fell out of it. Hagar tripped on Jungle Red (Sculptura) and Youth Blend, and to her great dismay, saw her box of Sunny Glow toppling into a puddle. She collected Jungle Red and Youth Blend safely, but Sunny Glow, which had tipped completely over and lost its protective disk, exploded in light peach puffs under the weight of the raindrops. Hagar scraped up as much of it as she could and pressed the wilted cellophane disk back into the box.

Twice before she got to Darling Street she had to stop to retrieve her purchases from the ground. Finally she stood in Pilate's doorway, limp, wet, and confused, clutching her bundles in whatever way she could. Reba was so relieved to see her that she grabbed her, knocking Chantilly and Bandit to the floor. Hagar stiffened and pulled away from her mother.

"I have to hurry," she whispered. "I have to hurry."

Loafers sluicing, hair dripping, holding her purchases in her arms, she made it into the bedroom and shut the door. Pilate and Reba made no move to follow her.

Hagar stripped herself naked there, and without taking time to dry her face or hair or feet, she dressed herself up in the white-with-a-band-of-color skirt and matching bolero, the Maidenform brassiere, the Fruit of the Loom panties, the no color hose, the Playtex garter belt and the Joyce con brios. Then she sat down to attend to her face. She drew charcoal gray for the young round eye through her brows, after which she rubbed mango tango on her cheeks. Then she patted sunny glow all over her face. Mango tango disappeared under it and she had to put it on again. She pushed out her lips and spread jungle red over them. She put baby clear sky light to outwit the day light on her eyelids and touched bandit to her throat, earlobes, and wrists. Finally she poured a little youth blend into her palm and smoothed it over her face.

At last she opened the door and presented herself to Pilate and Reba. And it was in their eyes that she saw what she had not seen before in the mirror: the wet ripped hose, the soiled white dress, the sticky, lumpy face powder, the streaked rouge, and the wild wet shoals of hair. All this she saw in their eyes, and the sight filled her own with water warmer and much older than the rain. Water that lasted for hours, until the fever came, and then it stopped. The fever dried her eyes up as well as her mouth.

She lay in her little Goldilocks'-choice bed, her eyes sand dry and as quiet as glass. Pilate and Reba, seated beside the bed, bent over her like two divi-divi trees beaten forward by a wind always blowing from the same direction. Like the trees, they offered her all they had: love murmurs and a protective shade.

"Mama." Hagar floated up into an even higher fever.

"Hmmm?"

"Why don't he like my hair?"

"Who, baby? Who don't like your hair?"

"Milkman."

"Milkman does too like your hair," said Reba.

"No. He don't. But I can't figure out why. Why he never liked my hair."

"Of course he likes it. How can he not like it?" asked Pilate.

"He likes silky hair." Hagar was murmuring so low they had to bend down to hear her.

"Silky hair? Milkman?"

"He don't like hair like mine."

"Hush, Hagar."

"Silky hair the color of a penny."

"Don't talk, baby."

"Curly, wavy, silky hair. He don't like mine."

Pilate put her hand on Hagar's head and trailed her fingers through her granddaughter's soft damp wool. "How can he not love your hair? It's the same hair that grows out of his own armpits. The same hair that crawls up out his crotch on up his stomach. All over his chest. The very same. It grows out of his nose, over his lips, and if he ever lost his razor it would grow all over his face. It's all over his head, Hagar. It's his hair too. He got to love it."

"He don't love it at all. He hates it."

"No he don't. He don't know what he loves, but he'll come around, honey, one of these days. How can he love himself and hate your hair?"

"He loves silky hair."

"Hush, Hagar."

"Penny-colored hair."

"Please, honey."
"And lemon-colored skin."
"Shhh."
"And gray-blue eyes."
"Hush now, hush."
"And thin nose."
"Hush, girl, hush."
"He's never going to like my hair."
"Hush. Hush. Hush, girl, hush."

The neighbors took up a collection because Pilate and Reba had spent everything getting Hagar the things needed to fix herself up. It didn't amount to much, though, and it was touch and go whether she'd have a decent funeral until Ruth walked down to Sonny's Shop and stared at Macon without blinking. He reached into his cash drawer and pulled out two twenty-dollar bills and put them down on the desk. Ruth didn't stretch out her hand to pick them up, or even shift her feet. Macon hesitated, then wheeled around in his chair and began fiddling with the combination to his safe. Ruth waited. Macon dipped into the safe three separate times before Ruth unclasped her hands and reached for the money. "Thank you," she said, and marched off to Linden Chapel Funeral Home to make the fastest arrangements possible.

Two days later, halfway through the service, it seemed as though Ruth was going to be the lone member of the bereaved family there. A female quartet from Linden Baptist Church had already sung "Abide with Me"; the wife of the mortician had read the condolence cards and the minister had launched into his "Naked came ye into this life and naked shall ye depart" sermon, which he had always believed suitable for the death of a young woman; and the winos in the vestibule who came to pay their respects to "Pilate's girl," but who dared not enter, had begun to sob, when the door swung open and Pilate burst in, shouting, "Mercy!" as though it were a command. A young man stood up and moved toward her. She flung out her right arm and almost knocked him down. "I want mercy!" she shouted, and began walking toward the coffin, shaking her head from side to side as though somebody had asked her a question and her answer was no.

Halfway up the aisle she stopped, lifted a finger, and pointed. Then slowly, although her breathing was fast and shallow, she lowered her hand to her side. It was strange, the languorous, limp hand coming to rest at her side while her breathing was coming so quick and fast. "Mercy," she said again, but she whispered it now. The mortician scurried toward her and touched her elbow. She moved away from him and went right up to the bier. She tilted her head and looked down. Her earring grazed her shoulder. Out of the total blackness of her clothes it blazed like a star. The mortician tried to approach her again, and moved closer, but when he saw her inky, berry-black lips, her cloudy, rainy eyes, the wonderful brass box hanging from her ear, he stepped back and looked at the floor.

"Mercy?" Now she was asking a question. "Mercy?"

It was not enough. The word needed a bottom, a frame. She straightened up, held her head high, and transformed the plea into a note. In a clear bluebell voice she sang it out—the one word held so long it became a sentence—and before the last syllable had died in the corners of the room, she was answered in a sweet soprano: "I hear you."

The people turned around. Reba had entered and was singing too. Pilate neither acknowledged her entrance nor missed a beat. She simply repeated the word "Mercy," and Reba replied. The daughter standing at the back of the chapel, the mother up front, they sang.

In the nighttime.
Mercy.
In the darkness.
Mercy.
In the morning.
Mercy.

At my bedside.
Mercy.
On my knees now.
Mercy. Mercy. Mercy. Mercy.

They stopped at the same time in a high silence. Pilate reached out her hand and placed three fingers on the edge of the coffin. Now she addressed her words to the woman bordered in gray satin who lay before her. Softly, privately, she sang to Hagar the very same reassurance she had promised her when she was a little girl.

Who's been botherin my sweet sugar lumpkin?
Who's been botherin my baby?
Who's been botherin my sweet sugar lumpkin?
Who's been botherin my baby girl?

Somebody's been botherin my sweet sugar lumpkin.
Somebody's been botherin my baby.
Somebody's been botherin my sweet sugar lumpkin.
Some*body's been botherin my baby girl.*

I'll find who's botherin my sweet sugar lumpkin.
I'll find who's botherin my baby.
I'll find who's botherin my sweet sugar lumpkin.
I'll find who's botherin my baby girl.

"My baby girl." The three words were still pumping in her throat as she turned away from the coffin. Looking about at the faces of the people seated in the pews, she fastened on the first pair of eyes that were directed toward her. She nodded at the face and said, "My baby girl." She looked for another pair of eyes and told him also, "My baby girl." Moving back down the aisle, she told each face turned toward her the same piece of news. "My baby girl. That's my baby girl. My baby girl. My baby girl. My baby girl."

Conversationally she spoke, identifying Hagar, selecting her away from everybody else in the world who had died. First she spoke to the ones who had the courage to look at her, shake their heads, and say, "Amen." Then she spoke to those whose nerve failed them, whose glance would climb no higher than the long black fingers at her side. Toward them especially she leaned a little, telling in three words the full story of the stumped life in the coffin behind her. "My baby girl." Words tossed like stones into a silent canyon.

Suddenly, like an elephant who has just found his anger and lifts his trunk over the heads of the little men who want his teeth or his hide or his flesh or his amazing strength, Pilate trumpeted for the sky itself to hear, "And she was *loved!*"

It startled one of the sympathetic winos in the vestibule and he dropped his bottle, spurting emerald glass and jungle-red wine everywhere.

Chapter 14

Perhaps it was because the sun had hit the rim of the horizon, but Susan Byrd's house looked different. The cedar tree was a silvery gray and its bark crinkled all the way up. It looked to Milkman like the leg of an ancient elephant. And now he noticed that the ropes that held the swing were frayed and the picket fence that had looked so bright and perky before was really flaked, peeling, even leaning to the left. The blue steps leading to the porch were faded into a watery gray. In fact the whole house looked seedy.

He lifted his hand to knock on the door and noticed the doorbell. He rang it and Susan Byrd opened the door.

"Hello again," he said.

"Well," she said, "you're as good as your word."

"I'd like to talk to you some more, if you don't mind. About Sing. May I come in?"

"Of course." She stood back from the door and the odor of another batch of gingerbread wafted out. Again they sat in the living room—he in the gray wing-back chair, she on the sofa this time. Miss Long was nowhere in sight.

"I know you don't know who Sing married or if she married, but I was wondering—"

"Of course I know who she married. That is if they *did* marry. She married Jake, that black boy her mother took care of."

Milkman felt dizzy. Everybody kept changing right in front of him. "But yesterday you said nobody heard from her after she left."

"Nobody did. But they knew who she left with!"

"Jake?"

"Jake. Black Jake. Black as coal."

"Where—where did they live? Boston?"

"I don't know where they ended up. North, I guess. We never heard."

"I thought you said she went to a private school in Boston."

She dismissed the whole notion with a wave of her hand. "I just said that in front of *her*, Grace. She talks so much, you know. Carries tales all over the county. It's true she was supposed to go to some school, but she didn't. She left on that double-team wagon with that black boy, Jake. A whole lot of slaves got together. Jake was driving. Can you imagine it? Riding off with a wagonload of slaves?"

"What was Jake's last name? Can you tell me?"

She shrugged. "I don't think he had one. He was one of those flying African children. They must all be dead a long time now."

"Flying African children?"

"Um hm, one of Solomon's children. Or Shalimar. Papa said Heddy always called him Shalimar."

"And Heddy was . . ."

"My grandmother. Sing's mother and Papa's too. An Indian woman. She was the one who took care of Jake when his father left them all. She found him and took him home and raised him. She didn't have any boy children then. My father, Crowell, came later." She leaned forward and whispered, "She didn't have a husband, Heddy. I didn't want to go into all of that with Grace. You can imagine what she'd do with that information.

You're a stranger, so it doesn't matter. But Grace . . ." Susan Byrd looked pleadingly at the ceiling. "This Jake was a baby she found, and he and Sing grew up together, and I guess rather than be packed off to some Quaker school, she ran away with him. You know colored people and Indians mixed a lot, but sometimes, well, some Indians didn't like it—the marrying, I mean. But neither one of them knew their own father, Jake nor Sing. And my own father didn't know his. Heddy never said. I don't know to this day if he was white, red, or—well—*what*. Sing's name was Singing Bird. And my father's name was Crow at first. Later he changed it to Crowell Byrd. After he took off his buckskin." She smiled.

"Why did you call Solomon a flying African?"

"Oh, that's just some old folks' lie they tell around here. Some of those Africans they brought over here as slaves could fly. A lot of them flew back to Africa. The one around here who did was this same Solomon, or Shalimar—I never knew which was right. He had a slew of children, all over the place. You may have noticed that everybody around here claims kin to him. Must be over forty families spread in these hills calling themselves Solomon something or other. I guess he must have been hot stuff." She laughed. "But anyway, hot stuff or not, he disappeared and left everybody. Wife, everybody, including some twenty-one children. And they say they all saw him go. The wife saw him and the children saw him. They were all working in the fields. They used to try to grow cotton here. Can you imagine? In these hills? But cotton was king then. Everybody grew it until the land went bad. It was cotton even when I was a girl. Well, back to this Jake boy. He was supposed to be one of Solomon's original twenty-one—all boys and all of them with the same mother. Jake was the baby. The baby and the wife were right next to him when he flew off."

"When you say 'flew off' you mean he ran away, don't you? Escaped?"

"No, I mean flew. Oh, it's just foolishness, you know, but according to the story he wasn't running away. He was flying.

He flew. You know, like a bird. Just stood up in the fields one day, ran up some hill, spun around a couple of times, and was lifted up in the air. Went right on back to wherever it was he came from. There's a big double-headed rock over the valley named for him. It like to killed the woman, the wife. I guess you could say 'wife.' Anyway she's supposed to have screamed out loud for days. And there's a ravine near here they call Ryna's Gulch, and sometimes you can hear this funny sound by it that the wind makes. People say it's the wife, Solomon's wife, crying. Her name was Ryna. They say she screamed and screamed, lost her mind completely. You don't hear about women like that anymore, but there used to be more—the kind of woman who couldn't live without a particular man. And when the man left, they lost their minds, or died or something. Love, I guess. But I always thought it was trying to take care of children by themselves, you know what I mean?"

She talked on and on while Milkman sat back and listened to gossip, stories, legends, speculations. His mind was ahead of hers, behind hers, with hers, and bit by bit, with what she said, what he knew, and what he guessed, he put it all together.

Sing had said she was going to a Quaker school, but she joined Jake on his wagonful of ex-slaves heading for Boston or somewhere. They must have dropped their passengers all along the way. And then Jake, at the reins, took a wrong turn, because he couldn't read, and they ended up in Pennsylvania.

"But there's a children's game they play around here. And in the game they sing, 'Jake the *only* son of Solomon.' *Only*." He looked at her, hoping she wouldn't mind the interruption.

"Well, they're wrong. He wasn't the only son. There were twenty others. But he was the only one Solomon tried to take with him. Maybe that's what it means. He lifted him up, but dropped him near the porch of the big house. That's where Heddy found him. She used to come over there and help with the soapmaking and the candlemaking. She wasn't a slave, but she worked over at the big house certain times of year. She was melting tallow when she looked up and saw this man holding a baby and flying toward the ridge. He brushed too close to a tree and the baby slipped out of his arms and fell through the branches to the ground. He was unconscious, but the trees saved him from dying. Heddy ran over and picked him up. She didn't have any male children, like I said, just a little bitty girl, and this one just dropped out of the sky almost in her lap. She never named him anything different; she was afraid to do that. She found out the baby was Ryna's, but Ryna was out of her mind. Heddy lived a good ways off from the place Solomon and them others worked on. She tried to keep the girl away from that place too. And you can imagine how she felt when both of them ran off. Just my father was left."

"Did Jake have to register at the Freedmen's Bureau before he left the state?"

"Everybody did. Everybody who had been slaves, that is. Whether they left the state or not. But we were never slaves, so—"

"You told me that. Weren't any of Jake's brothers registering too?"

"I couldn't say. Those must have been some times, back then. Some bad times. It's a wonder anybody knows who anybody is."

"You've helped me a lot, Miss Byrd. I'm grateful." He thought then about asking her if she had a photo album. He wanted to see Sing, Crowell, even Heddy. But he decided against it. She might start asking him questions, and he didn't want to trouble her with a new-found relative who was as black as Jake.

"Now, that's not the woman you're looking for, is it? Pilate?"

"No," he said. "Couldn't be." He made motions of departure and then remembered his watch.

"By the way, did I leave my watch here? I'd like it back."

"Watch?"

"Yes. Your friend wanted to see it. Miss Long. I handed it to her but I forgot—" Milkman stopped. Susan Byrd was laughing out loud.

"Well, you can say goodbye to it, Mr. Macon. Grace will go to dinner all over the county telling people about the watch you gave her."

"What?"

"Well, you know. She doesn't mean any real harm, but it's a quiet place. We don't have many visitors, especially young men who wear gold watches and have northern accents. I'll get it back for you."

"Never mind. Never mind."

"You'll just have to forgive her otherwise. This is a dull place, Mr. Macon. There's absolutely nothing in the world going on here. Not a thing."

Chapter 15

The fan belt didn't last long enough for him to get to the next gasoline station. It broke on the edge of a little town called Jistann, the needle trembling at H. Milkman sold it to the tow-truck man for twenty dollars and caught the first bus out. It was probably best that way, for over the humming wheels, his legs folded in the little space in front of his seat, he had time to come down from the incredible high that had begun as soon as he slammed the Byrd woman's door.

He couldn't get back to Shalimar fast enough, and when he did get there, dusty and dirty from the run, he leaped into the car and drove to Sweet's house. He almost broke her door down. "I want to swim!" he shouted. "Come on, let's go swimming. I'm dirty and I want waaaaater!"

Sweet smiled and said she'd give him a bath.

"Bath! You think I'd put myself in that tight little porcelain box? I need the sea! The whole goddam sea!" Laughing, hollering, he ran over to her and picked her up at the knees and ran around the room with her over his shoulder. "The sea! I have to swim in the sea. Don't give me no itty bitty teeny tiny tub, girl. I need the whole entire complete deep blue sea!"

He stood her on her feet. "Don't you all swim around here?"

"Over at the quarry is where the kids go sometimes."

"Quarry? You all don't have no sea? No ocean?"

"Naw; this hill country."

"Hill country. Mountain country. Flying country."

"A man was here to see you."

"Oh, yeah? That would be Mr. Guitar Bains."

"He didn't give his name."

"He don't have to! He's Guitar Bains. *Gi*tar, *Gi*tar, Gitar Bains!" Milkman did a little dance and Sweet covered her mouth, laughing.

"Come on, Sweet, tell me where the sea is."

"They some water comin down below the ridge on the other side. Real deep; wide too."

"Then let's go! Come on!" He grabbed her arm and pulled her out to the car. He sang all the way: " 'Solomon 'n Ryna Belali Shalut . . .' "

"Where you learn that?" she asked him. "That's a game we used to play when we was little."

"Of course you did. Everybody did. Everybody but me. But I can play it now. It's my game now."

The river in the valley was wide and green. Milkman took off his clothes, climbed a tree and dived into the water. He surfaced like a bullet, iridescent, grinning, splashing water. "Come on. Take them clothes off and come on in here."

"Naw. I don't wanna swim."

"Come in here, girl!"

"Water moccasins in there."

"Fuck 'em. Get in here. Hurry up!"

She stepped out of her shoes, pulled her dress over her head and was ready. Milkman reached up for her as she came timidly down the bank, slipping, stumbling, laughing at her own awkwardness, then squealing as the cold river water danced up her legs, her hips, her waist. Milkman pulled her close and kissed her mouth, ending the kiss with a determined effort to pull her under the water. She fought him. "Oh, my hair! My hair's gonna get wet."

"No it ain't," he said, and poured a handful right in the middle of her scalp. Wiping her eyes, spluttering water, she turned to wade out, shrieking all the way. "Okay, okay," he bellowed. "Leave me. Leave me in here by myself. I don't care. I'll play with the water moccasins." And he began to whoop and dive and splash and turn. "He could fly! You hear me? My great-granddaddy could fly! Goddam!" He whipped the water with his fists, then jumped straight up as though he too could take off, and landed on his back and sank down, his mouth and eyes full of water. Up again. Still pounding, leaping, diving. "The son of a bitch could fly! You hear me, Sweet? That motherfucker could fly! Could fly! He didn't need no airplane. Didn't need no fuckin tee double you ay. He could fly his own self!"

"Who you talkin 'bout?" Sweet was lying on her side, her cheek cupped in her hand.

"Solomon, that's who."

"Oh, him." She laughed. "You belong to that tribe of niggers?" She thought he was drunk.

"Yeah. That tribe. That flyin motherfuckin tribe. Oh, man! He didn't need no airplane. He just took off; got fed up. *All the way up!* No more cotton! No more bales! No more orders! No more shit! He flew, baby. Lifted his beautiful black ass up in the sky and flew on home. Can you dig it? Jesus God, that must have been something to see. And you know what else? He tried to take his baby boy with him. My grandfather. Wow! Woooee! Guitar! You hear that? Guitar, my great-granddaddy could flyyyyyy and the whole damn town is named after him. Tell him, Sweet. Tell him my great-granddaddy could fly."

"Where'd he go, Macon?"

"Back to Africa. Tell Guitar he went back to Africa."

"Who'd he leave behind?"

"Everybody! He left everybody down on the ground and he sailed on off like a black eagle. 'O-o-o-o-o-o Solomon done fly,

Solomon done gone /Solomon cut across the sky, Solomon gone home!' "

He could hardly wait to get home. To tell his father, Pilate; and he would love to see Reverend Cooper and his friends. "You think Macon Dead was something? Huh. Let me tell you about *his* daddy. You ain't heard nothin yet."

Milkman turned in his seat and tried to stretch his legs. It was morning. He'd changed buses three times and was now speeding home on the last leg of his trip. He looked out the window. Far away from Virginia, fall had already come. Ohio, Indiana, Michigan were dressed up like the Indian warriors from whom their names came. Blood red and yellow, ocher and ice blue.

He read the road signs with interest now, wondering what lay beneath the names. The Algonquins had named the territory he lived in Great Water, *michi gami*. How many dead lives and fading memories were buried in and beneath the names of the places in this country. Under the recorded names were other names, just as "Macon Dead," recorded for all time in some dusty file, hid from view the real names of people, places, and things. Names that had meaning. No wonder Pilate put hers in her ear. When you know your name, you should hang on to it, for unless it is noted down and remembered, it will die when you do. Like the street he lived on, recorded as Mains Avenue, but called Not Doctor Street by the Negroes in memory of his grandfather, who was the first colored man of consequence in that city. Never mind that he probably didn't deserve their honor—they knew what kind of man he was: arrogant, color-struck, snobbish. They didn't care about that. They were paying their respect to whatever it was that made him *be* a doctor in the first place, when the odds were that he'd be a yardman all of his life. So they named a street after him. Pilate had taken a rock from every state she had lived in—because she *had* lived there. And having lived there, it was hers—and his, and his father's, his grandfather's, his grandmother's. Not Doctor Street, Solomon's Leap, Ryna's Gulch, Shalimar, Virginia.

He closed his eyes and thought of the black men in Shalimar, Roanoke, Petersburg, Newport News, Danville, in the Blood Bank, on Darling Street, in the pool halls, the barbershops. Their names. Names they got from yearnings, gestures, flaws, events, mistakes, weaknesses. Names that bore witness. Macon Dead, Sing Byrd, Crowell Byrd, Pilate, Reba, Hagar, Magdalene, First Corinthians, Milkman, Guitar, Railroad Tommy, Hospital Tommy, Empire State (he just stood around and swayed), Small Boy, Sweet, Circe, Moon, Nero, Humpty-Dumpty, Blue Boy, Scandinavia, Quack-Quack, Jericho, Spoonbread, Ice Man, Dough Belly, Rocky River, Gray Eye, Cock-a-Doodle-Doo, Cool Breeze, Muddy Waters, Pinetop, Jelly Roll, Fats, Leadbelly, Bo Diddley, Cat-Iron, Peg-Leg, Son, Shortstuff, Smoky Babe, Funny Papa, Bukka, Pink, Bull Moose, B.B., T-Bone, Black Ace, Lemon, Washboard, Gatemouth, Cleanhead, Tampa Red, Juke Boy, Shine, Staggerlee, Jim the Devil, Fuck-Up, and *Dat* Nigger.

Angling out from these thoughts of names was one more—the one that whispered in the spinning wheels of the bus: "Guitar is biding his time. Guitar is biding his time. Your day has come. Your day has come. Guitar is biding his time. Guitar is a very good Day. Guitar is a very good Day. A very good Day, a very good Day, and biding, biding his time."

In the seventy-five-dollar car, and here on the big Greyhound, Milkman felt safe. But there were days and days ahead. Maybe if Guitar was back in the city now, among familiar surroundings, Milkman could defuse him. And certainly, in time, he would discover his foolishness. There was no gold. And although things would never be the same between them, at least the man-hunt would be over.

Even as he phrased the thought in his mind, Milkman knew it was not so. Either Guitar's disappointment with the gold that was not there was so deep it had deranged him, or his "work" had done it. Or maybe he simply allowed himself to feel about

Milkman what he had always felt about Macon Dead and the Honoré crowd. In any case, he had snatched the first straw, limp and wet as it was, to prove to himself the need to kill Milkman. The Sunday-school girls deserved better than to be avenged by that hawk-headed raven-skinned Sunday man who included in his blood sweep four innocent white girls and one innocent black man.

Perhaps that's what all human relationships boiled down to: Would you save my life? or would you take it?

"Everybody wants a black man's life."

Yeah. And black men were not excluded. With two exceptions, everybody he was close to seemed to prefer him out of this life. And the two exceptions were both women, both black, both old. From the beginning, his mother and Pilate had fought for his life, and he had never so much as made either of them a cup of tea.

Would you save my life or would you take it? Guitar was exceptional. To both questions he could answer yes.

"Should I go home first, or go to Pilate's first?" Out in the street, late at night with autumn air blowing cold off the lake, he tried to make up his mind. He was so eager for the sight of Pilate's face when he told her what he knew, he decided to see her first. He'd have a long time at his own house. He took a taxi to Darling Street, paid the driver, and bounded up the stairs. He pushed the door open and saw her standing over a tub of water, rinsing out the green bottles she used for her wine.

"Pilate!" he shouted. "Have I got stuff to tell you!"

She turned around. Milkman opened his arms wide so he could hold all of her in a warm embrace. "Come here, sweetheart," he said, grinning. She came and broke a wet green bottle over his head.

When he came to, he was lying on his side in the cellar. He opened one eye and considered the option of not coming to for a little while more. For a long time now he knew that anything could appear to be something else, and probably was. Nothing could be taken for granted. Women who loved you tried to cut your throat, while women who didn't even know your name scrubbed your back. Witches could sound like Katharine Hepburn and your best friend could try to strangle you. Smack in the middle of an orchid there might be a blob of jello and inside a Mickey Mouse doll, a fixed and radiant star.

So he lay on the cool damp floor of the cellar and tried to figure out what he was doing there. What did Pilate knock him out for? About the theft of her sack of bones? No. She'd come to his rescue immediately. What could it be, what else could he have done that would turn her against him? Then he knew. Hagar. Something had happened to Hagar. Where was she? Had she run off? Was she sick or . . . Hagar was dead. The cords of his neck tightened. How? In Guitar's room, did she . . . ?

What difference did it make? He had hurt her, left her, and now she was dead—he was certain of it. He had left her. While he dreamt of flying, Hagar was dying. Sweet's silvery voice came back to him: "Who'd he leave behind?" He left Ryna behind and twenty children. Twenty-one, since he dropped the one he tried to take with him. And Ryna had thrown herself all over the ground, lost her mind, and was still crying in a ditch. Who looked after those twenty children? Jesus Christ, he left twenty-one children! Guitar and the Days chose never to have children. Shalimar left his, but it was the children who sang about it and kept the story of his leaving alive.

Milkman rolled his head back and forth on the cellar floor. It was his fault, and Pilate knew it. She had thrown him in the cellar. What, he wondered, did she plan to do with him? Then he knew that too. Knew what Pilate's version of punishment was when somebody took another person's life. Hagar. Something of Hagar's must be nearby. Pilate would put him someplace near something that remained of the life he had taken, so he could *have* it. She would abide by this commandment from her father herself, and make him do it too. "You just can't fly on off and leave a body."

Suddenly Milkman began to laugh. Curled up like a Polish sausage, a rope cutting his wrists, he laughed.

"Pilate!" he called. "Pilate! That's not what he meant. Pilate! He didn't mean that. He wasn't talking about the man in the cave. Pilate! He was talking about himself. His own father flew away. He was the 'body.' The body you shouldn't fly off and leave. Pilate! Pilate! Come here. Let me tell you what your father said. Pilate, he didn't even tell you to sing, Pilate. He was calling for his wife—your mother. Pilate! Get me out of here!"

Light exploded in his face. The cellar door opened over his head. Pilate's feet appeared on the stone steps, and paused.

"Pilate," said Milkman, softly now, "that's not what he meant. I know what he meant. Come, let me tell you. And Pilate, those bones. They're not that white man's bones. He probably didn't even die. I went there. I saw. He wasn't there and the gold wasn't there either. Somebody found it and found him too. They must have, Pilate. Long before you got there. But, Pilate . . ."

She descended a few steps.

"Pilate?"

She came all the way down and he looked in her eyes and at her still mouth. "Pilate, your father's body floated up out of the grave you all dug for him. One month later it floated up. The Butlers, somebody, put his body in the cave. Wolves didn't drag the white man to the front of the cave and prop him on a rock. That was your father you found. You've been carrying your father's bones—all this time."

"Papa?" she whispered.

"Yes. And, Pilate, you have to bury him. He wants you to bury him. Back where he belongs. On Solomon's Leap."

"Papa?" she asked again.

Milkman did not speak; he watched her long fingers travel up her dress, to rest like the wing of a starling on her face. "I've been carryin Papa?" Pilate moved toward Milkman, stopped and looked at him for a while. Then her eyes turned to a rickety wooden table that stood against the stone wall of the cellar. It was in a part of the room so dark he had not even seen it. She walked over to the table and lifted from it a green-and-white shoe box, its cover held down with a rubber band. "Joyce," it said on the box. "Thank heaven for little Joyce heels."

"If I bury Papa, I guess I ought to bury this too—somewhere." She looked back at Milkman.

"No," he said. "No. Give it here."

When he went home that evening, he walked into the house on Not Doctor Street with almost none of the things he'd taken with him. But he returned with a box of Hagar's hair.

She wouldn't set foot on an airplane, so he drove. She seemed happy now. Her lips mobile again, she sat next to him in Macon's Buick, a mink stole Reba had won wrapped around her shoulders over her old black dress. The knit cap was pulled down on her forehead and her shoes still had no laces. Every now and then she glanced at the back seat to check on the sack. Peace circled her.

Milkman felt it too. His return to Not Doctor Street was not the triumph he'd hoped it would be, but there was relief in his mother's crooked smile. And Lena, though unforgiving as ever, was civil to him, since Corinthians had moved to a small house in Southside, which she shared with Porter. The Seven Days, Milkman guessed, would be looking for a new recruit, as they had to when Robert Smith jumped off the roof of Mercy. But there were long rambling talks with his father, who could not hear it enough—the "boys" who remembered him in Danville; his mother's running off with his father; the story about his father and his grandfather. He wasn't a bit interested in the flying part, but he liked the story and the fact that places were named for his people. Milkman softened his description of Circe, saying simply that she was alive, and taking care of the dogs.

"I ought maybe to take me a trip down there," said Macon.

"Virginia?" Milkman asked him.

"Danville. I ought to go by and see some of those boys before these legs stop moving. Let Freddie pick up the rents, maybe."

It was nice. No reconciliation took place between Pilate and Macon (although he seemed pleased to know that they were going to bury their father in Virginia), and relations between Ruth and Macon were the same and would always be. Just as the consequences of Milkman's own stupidity would remain, and regret would always outweigh the things he was proud of having done. Hagar was dead and he had not loved her one bit. And Guitar was . . . somewhere.

In Shalimar there was general merriment at his quick return, and Pilate blended into the population like a stick of butter in a churn. They stayed with Omar's family, and on the second and last evening, Milkman and Pilate walked up the road to the path that led to Solomon's Leap. It was the higher of two outcroppings of rock. Both flat-headed, both looking over a deep valley. Pilate carried the sack, Milkman a small shovel. It was a long way to the top, but neither stopped for breath. At the very top, on the plateau, the trees that could stand the wind at that height were few. They looked a long time for an area of earth among the rock faces large enough for the interment. When they found one, Pilate squatted down and opened the sack while Milkman dug. A deep sigh escaped from the sack and the wind turned chill. Ginger, a spicy sugared ginger smell, enveloped them. Pilate laid the bones carefully into the small grave. Milkman heaped dirt over them and packed it down with the back of his shovel.

"Should we put a rock or a cross on it?" Milkman asked.

Pilate shook her head. She reached up and yanked her earring from her ear, splitting the lobe. Then she made a little hole with her fingers and placed in it Sing's snuffbox with the single word Jake ever wrote. She stood up then, and it seemed to Milkman that he heard the shot after she fell. He dropped to his knees and cradled her lolling head in the crook of his arm, barking at her, "You hurt? You hurt, Pilate?"

She laughed softly and he knew right away that she was reminded of the day he first met her and said the most stupid thing there was to say.

The twilight had thickened and all around them it was getting dark. Milkman moved his hand over her chest and stomach, trying to find the place where she might be hit. "Pilate? You okay?" He couldn't make out her eyes. His hand under her head was sweating like a fountain. "Pilate?"

She sighed. "Watch Reba for me." And then, "I wish I'd a knowed more people. I would of loved 'em all. If I'd a knowed more, I would a loved more."

Milkman bent low to see her face and saw darkness staining his hand. Not sweat, but blood oozing from her neck down into his cupped hand. He pressed his fingers against the skin as if to force the life back in her, back into the place it was escaping from. But that only made it flow faster. Frantically he thought of tourniquets and could even hear the rip of cloth he should have been tearing. He shifted his weight and was about to lay her down, the better to wrap her wound, when she spoke again.

"Sing," she said. "Sing a little somethin for me."

Milkman knew no songs, and had no singing voice that anybody would want to hear, but he couldn't ignore the urgency in her voice. Speaking the words without the least bit of a tune, he sang for the lady. "Sugargirl don't leave me here/ Cotton balls to choke me/Sugargirl don't leave me here/ Buckra's arms to yoke me." The blood was not pulsing out any longer and there was something black and bubbly in her mouth. Yet when she moved her head a little to gaze at something behind his shoulder, it took a while for him to realize that she was dead. And when he did, he could not stop the worn old words from coming, louder and louder as though sheer volume would wake her. He woke only the birds, who shuddered off into the air. Milkman laid her head down on the rock. Two of the birds circled round them. One dived into the new grave and scooped something shiny in its beak before it flew away.

Now he knew why he loved her so. Without ever leaving the ground, she could fly. "There must be another one like you," he whispered to her. "There's got to be at least one more woman like you."

Even as he knelt over her, he knew there wouldn't be another mistake; that the minute he stood up Guitar would try to blow his head off. He stood up.

"Guitar!" he shouted.

Tar tar tar, said the hills.

"Over here, brother man! Can you see me?" Milkman cupped his mouth with one hand and waved the other over his head. "Here I am!"

Am am am am, said the rocks.

"You want me? Huh? You want my life?"

Life life life life.

Squatting on the edge of the other flat-headed rock with only the night to cover him, Guitar smiled over the barrel of his rifle. "My man," he murmured to himself. "My main man." He put the rifle on the ground and stood up.

Milkman stopped waving and narrowed his eyes. He could just make out Guitar's head and shoulders in the dark. "You want my life?" Milkman was not shouting now. "You need it? Here." Without wiping away the tears, taking a deep breath, or even bending his knees—he leaped. As fleet and bright as a lodestar he wheeled toward Guitar and it did not matter which one of them would give up his ghost in the killing arms of his brother. For now he knew what Shalimar knew: If you surrendered to the air, you could *ride* it.

ALSO BY

TONI MORRISON

THE SOURCE OF SELF-REGARD

Selected Essays, Speeches, and Meditations

Here is Toni Morrison in her own words: a rich gathering of her most important essays and speeches, spanning four decades. These pages give us her searing prayer for the dead of 9/11, her Nobel lecture on the power of language, her searching meditation on Martin Luther King Jr., her heart-wrenching eulogy for James Baldwin. She looks deeply into the fault lines of culture and freedom: the foreigner, female empowerment, the press, money, "black matter(s)," human rights, the artist in society, the Afro-American presence in American literature. And she turns her incisive critical eye to her own work (*The Bluest Eye* *Sula*, *Tar Baby*, *Jazz*, *Beloved*, *Paradise*) and that of others. An essential collection from an essential writer, *The Source of Self-Regard* shines with the literary elegance, intellectual prowess, spiritual depth, and moral compass that have made Toni Morrison our most cherished and enduring voice.

Essays

ALSO AVAILABLE

Beloved

The Bluest Eye

God Help the Child

Home

Love

Sula

Tar Baby

AND OTHER TITLES

VINTAGE INTERNATIONAL
Available wherever books are sold.
www.vintagebooks.com

ACCLAIM FOR

Toni Morrison

"[Toni Morrison] may be the last classic American writer, squarely in the tradition of Poe, Melville, Twain and Faulkner."

—*Newsweek*

"In the first ranks of our living novelists."

—*St. Louis Post-Dispatch*

"Toni Morrison is not just an important contemporary novelist but a major figure in our national literature."

—*The New York Review of Books*

"She is the best writer in America."

—John Leonard, National Public Radio

"[Toni Morrison] has moved from strength to strength until she has reached the distinction of being beyond comparison."

—*Entertainment Weekly*

"Morrison is one of the most exciting living American writers."

—*The Kansas City Star*

"Toni Morrison has made herself into the D. H. Lawrence of the black psyche, transforming individuals into forces, idiosyncrasy into inevitability." —*New York*

"Morrison is perhaps the finest novelist of our time." —*Vogue*

"Toni Morrison is one of the finest writers in America today."
—*Louisville Courier-Journal*

Toni Morrison

The Bluest Eye

Toni Morrison is the author of eleven novels, from *The Bluest Eye* (1970) to *God Help the Child* (2015). She received the National Book Critics Circle Award, the Pulitzer Prize, and in 1993 she was awarded the Nobel Prize in Literature. She died in 2019.

VINTAGE INTERNATIONAL

ALSO BY TONI MORRISON

FICTION

God Help the Child

Home

A Mercy

Love

Paradise

Jazz

Beloved

Tar Baby

Song of Solomon

Sula

NONFICTION

The Source of Self-Regard

The Dancing Mind

Playing in the Dark:
Whiteness and the Literary Imagination

The Origin of Others

THE BLUEST EYE

A NOVEL

Toni Morrison

VINTAGE INTERNATIONAL
Vintage Books
A Division of Penguin Random House LLC
New York

FIRST VINTAGE INTERNATIONAL EDITION, MAY 2007

Portions of the foreword were previously published as the afterword to the 1993 Knopf edition.

The Library of Congress has cataloged the Knopf edition as follows:
Morrison, Toni.
The bluest eye / by Toni Morrison. —1st ed.
p. cm.
1. Afro-Americans—Ohio—Fiction. 2. Girls—Ohio—Fiction. I. Title
PS3563.08749855 1993
813.54—DC20
93-43124

Vintage International Trade Paperback ISBN: 978-0-307-27844-9
eBook ISBN: 978-0-307-38658-8

Book design by Dorothy S. Baker

www.vintagebooks.com

Printed in the United States of America
50 51 49

To the two who gave me life
and the one who made me free

Foreword

There can't be anyone, I am sure, who doesn't know what it feels like to be disliked, even rejected, momentarily or for sustained periods of time. Perhaps the feeling is merely indifference, mild annoyance, but it may also be hurt. It may even be that some of us know what it is like to be actually hated—hated for things we have no control over and cannot change. When this happens, it is some consolation to know that the dislike or hatred is unjustified—that you don't deserve it. And if you have the emotional strength and/or support from family and friends, the damage is reduced or erased. We think of it as the stress (minor or disabling) that is part of life as a human.

When I began writing *The Bluest Eye*, I was interested in something else. Not resistance to the contempt of others, ways to deflect it, but the far more tragic and disabling consequences of accepting rejection as legitimate, as self-evident. I knew that some victims of powerful self-loathing turn out to be dangerous, violent, reproducing the enemy who has humiliated them over and over. Others surrender their identity; melt into a structure that delivers the strong persona they lack. Most others, however, grow beyond it. But there are some who collapse, silently, anonymously, with no voice to express or acknowledge it. They are invisible. The death of self-esteem can occur quickly, easily in children, before their ego has "legs," so to speak. Couple the vulnerability of youth with indifferent parents, dismissive adults, and a world, which, in its language, laws, and images, re-enforces despair, and the journey to destruction is sealed.

The project, then, for this, my first book, was to enter the life of the one least likely to withstand such damaging forces because of youth, gender, and race. Begun as a bleak narrative of psychological murder, the main character could not stand alone since her passivity made her a narrative void. So I invented friends, classmates, who understood, even sympathized, with her plight, but had the benefit of supportive parents and a feistiness all their own. Yet they were helpless as well. They could not save their friend from the world. She broke.

The origin of the novel lay in a conversation I had with a childhood friend. We had just started elementary school. She said she wanted blue eyes. I looked around to picture her with them and was violently repelled by what I imagined she would look like if she had her wish. The sorrow in her voice seemed to call for sympathy, and I faked it for her, but, astonished by the desecration she proposed, I "got mad" at her instead.

Until that moment I had seen the pretty, the lovely, the nice, the ugly, and although I had certainly used the word "beautiful," I had never experienced its shock—the force of which was equaled by the knowledge that no one recognized it, not even, or especially, the one who possessed it.

It must have been more than the face I was examining: the silence of the street in the early afternoon, the light, the atmosphere of confession. In any case it was the first time I knew beautiful. Had imagined it for myself. Beauty was not simply something to behold; it was something one could *do*.

The Bluest Eye was my effort to say something about that; to say something about why she had not, or possibly ever would have, the experience of what she possessed and also why she prayed for so radical an alteration. Implicit in her desire was racial self-loathing. And twenty years later, I was still wondering about how one learns that. Who told her? Who made her feel that it was better to be a freak than what she was? Who had looked at her and found her so wanting, so small a weight on the beauty scale? The novel pecks away at the gaze that condemned her.

The reclamation of racial beauty in the sixties stirred these thoughts, made me think about the necessity for the claim. Why, although reviled by others, could this beauty not be taken for granted within the community? Why did it need wide public articulation to exist? These are not clever questions. But in 1962 when I began this story, and in 1965 when it began to be a book, the answers were not as obvious to me as they quickly became and are now. The assertion of racial beauty was not a reaction to the self-mocking, humorous critique of cultural/racial foibles common in all groups, but against the damaging internalization of assumptions of immutable inferiority originating in an outside gaze. I focused, therefore, on how something as grotesque as the demonization of an entire race could take root inside the most delicate member of society: a child; the most vulnerable member: a female. In trying to dramatize the devastation that even casual racial contempt can cause, I chose a unique situation, not a representative one. The extremity of Pecola's case stemmed largely from a crippled and crippling family—unlike the average black family and unlike the narrator's. But singular as Pecola's life was, I believed some aspects of her woundability were lodged in all young girls. In exploring the social and domestic aggression that could cause a child to literally fall apart, I mounted a series of rejections, some routine, some exceptional, some monstrous, all the while trying hard to avoid complicity in the demonization process Pecola was subjected to. That is, I did not want to dehumanize the characters who trashed Pecola and contributed to her collapse.

One problem was centering the weight of the novel's inquiry on so delicate and vulnerable a character could smash her and lead readers into the comfort of pitying her rather than into an interrogation of themselves for the smashing. My solution—break the narrative into parts that had to be reassembled by the reader—seemed to me a good idea, the execution of which does not satisfy me now. Besides, it didn't work: many readers remain touched but not moved.

The other problem, of course, was language. Holding the despising glance while sabotaging it was difficult. The novel tried to hit the raw nerve of racial self-contempt, expose it, then soothe it not with narcotics but with language that replicated the agency I discovered in my first experience of beauty. Because that moment was so racially infused (my revulsion at what my school friend wanted: very blue eyes in a very black skin; the harm she was doing to *my* concept of the beautiful), the struggle was for writing that was indisputably black. I don't yet know quite what that is, but neither that nor the attempts to disqualify an effort to find out keeps me from trying to pursue it.

My choices of language (speakerly, aural, colloquial), my reliance for full comprehension on codes embedded in black culture, my effort to effect immediate coconspiracy and intimacy (without any distancing, explanatory fabric), as well as my attempt to shape a silence while breaking it are attempts to transfigure the complexity and wealth of Black American culture into a language worthy of the culture.

Thinking back now on the problems expressive language presented to me, I am amazed by their currency, their tenacity. Hearing "civilized" languages debase humans, watching cultural exorcisms debase literature, seeing oneself preserved in the amber of disqualifying metaphors—I can say that my narrative project is as difficult today as it was then.

The Bluest Eye

Here is the house. It is green and white. It has a red door. It is very pretty. Here is the family. Mother, Father, Dick, and Jane live in the green-and-white house. They are very happy. See Jane. She has a red dress. She wants to play. Who will play with Jane? See the cat. It goes meow-meow. Come and play. Come play with Jane. The kitten will not play. See Mother. Mother is very nice. Mother, will you play with Jane? Mother laughs. Laugh, Mother, laugh. See Father. He is big and strong. Father, will you play with Jane? Father is smiling. Smile, Father, smile. See the dog. Bowwow goes the dog. Do you want to play with Jane? See the dog run. Run, dog, run. Look, look. Here comes a friend. The friend will play with Jane. They will play a good game. Play, Jane, play.

Here is the house it is green and white it has a red door it is very pretty here is the family mother father dick and jane live in the green-and-white house they are very happy see jane she has a red dress she wants to play who will play with jane see the cat it goes meow-meow come and play come play with jane the kitten will not play see mother mother is very nice mother will you play with jane mother laughs laugh mother laugh see father he is big and strong father will you play with jane father is smiling smile father smile see the dog bowwow goes the dog do you want to play do you want to play with jane see the dog run run dog run look look here comes a friend the friend will play with jane they will play a good game play jane play

Hereisthehouseitisgreenandwhiteithasareddooritisverypretty hereisthefamilymotherfatherdickandjaneliveinthegreenandw hitehousetheyareveryhappyseejaneshehasareddressshewants toplaywhowillplaywithjaneseethecatitgoesmeowmeowcomea ndplaycomeplaywithjanethekittenwillnotplayseemothermoth erisverynicemotherwillyouplaywithjanemotherlaughslaughm otherlaughseefatherheisbigandstrongfatherwillyouplaywithja nefatherissmilingsmilefathersmileseethedogbowwowgoesthe dogdoyouwanttoplaydoyouwanttoplaywithjaneseethedogrun rundogrunlooklookherecomesafriendthefriendwillplaywithja netheywillplayagoodgameplayjaneplay

Quiet as it's kept, there were no marigolds in the fall of 1941. We thought, at the time, that it was because Pecola was having her father's baby that the marigolds did not grow. A little examination and much less melancholy would have proved to us that our seeds were not the only ones that did not sprout; nobody's did. Not even the gardens fronting the lake showed marigolds that year. But so deeply concerned were we with the health and safe delivery of Pecola's baby we could think of nothing but our own magic: if we planted the seeds, and said the right words over them, they would blossom, and everything would be all right.

It was a long time before my sister and I admitted to ourselves that no green was going to spring from our seeds. Once we knew, our guilt was relieved only by fights and mutual accusations about who was to blame. For years I thought my sister was right: it was my fault. I had planted them too far down in the earth. It never occurred to either of us that the earth itself might have been unyielding. We had dropped our seeds in our own little plot of black dirt just as Pecola's father had dropped his seeds in his own plot of black dirt. Our innocence and faith were no more productive than his lust or despair. What is clear now is that of all of that hope, fear, lust, love, and grief, nothing remains but Pecola and the unyielding earth. Cholly Breedlove is dead; our innocence too. The seeds shriveled and died; her baby too.

There is really nothing more to say—except why. But since why *is difficult to handle, one must take refuge in* how.

Autumn

Nuns go by as quiet as lust, and drunken men and sober eyes sing in the lobby of the Greek hotel. Rosemary Villanucci, our next-door friend who lives above her father's café, sits in a 1939 Buick eating bread and butter. She rolls down the window to tell my sister Frieda and me that we can't come in. We stare at her, wanting her bread, but more than that wanting to poke the arrogance out of her eyes and smash the pride of ownership that curls her chewing mouth. When she comes out of the car we will beat her up, make red marks on her white skin, and she will cry and ask us do we want her to pull her pants down. We will say no. We don't know what we should feel or do if she does, but whenever she asks us, we know she is offering us something precious and that our own pride must be asserted by refusing to accept.

School has started, and Frieda and I get new brown stockings and cod-liver oil. Grown-ups talk in tired, edgy voices about Zick's Coal Company and take us along in the evening to the railroad tracks where we fill burlap sacks with the tiny pieces of coal lying about. Later we walk home, glancing back to see the great carloads of slag being dumped, red hot and smoking, into the ravine that skirts the steel mill. The dying fire lights the sky with a dull orange glow. Frieda and I lag behind, staring at the patch of color surrounded by black. It is impossible not to feel a shiver when our feet leave the gravel path and sink into the dead grass in the field.

Our house is old, cold, and green. At night a kerosene lamp lights one large room. The others are braced in darkness, peopled by roaches and mice. Adults do not talk to us—they give us directions. They issue orders without providing information. When we trip and fall down they glance at us; if we cut or bruise ourselves, they ask us are we crazy. When we catch colds, they shake their heads in disgust at our lack of consideration. How, they ask us, do you expect anybody to get anything done if you all are sick? We cannot answer them. Our illness is treated with contempt, foul Black Draught, and castor oil that blunts our minds.

When, on a day after a trip to collect coal, I cough once, loudly, through bronchial tubes already packed tight with phlegm, my mother frowns. "Great Jesus. Get on in that bed. How many times do I have to tell you to wear something on your head? You must be the biggest fool in this town. Frieda? Get some rags and stuff that window."

Frieda restuffs the window. I trudge off to bed, full of guilt and self-pity. I lie down in my underwear, the metal in my black garters hurts my legs, but I do not take them off, for it is too cold to lie stockingless. It takes a long time for my body to heat its place in the bed. Once I have generated a silhouette of warmth, I dare not move, for there is a cold place one-half inch in any direction. No one speaks to me or asks how I feel. In an hour or two my mother comes. Her hands are large and rough, and when she rubs the Vicks salve on my chest, I am rigid with pain. She takes two fingers' full of it at a time, and massages my chest until I am faint. Just when I think I will tip over into a scream, she scoops out a little of the salve on her forefinger and puts it in my mouth, telling me to swallow. A hot flannel is wrapped about my neck and chest. I am covered up with heavy quilts and ordered to sweat, which I do—promptly.

Later I throw up, and my mother says, "What did you puke on the bed clothes for? Don't you have sense enough to hold your head out the bed? Now, look what you did. You think I got time for nothing but washing up your puke?"

The puke swaddles down the pillow onto the sheet—green-gray, with flecks of orange. It moves like the insides of an uncooked egg. Stubbornly clinging to its own mass, refusing to break up and be removed. How, I wonder, can it be so neat and nasty at the same time?

My mother's voice drones on. She is not talking to me. She is talking to the puke, but she is calling it my name: Claudia. She wipes it up as best she can and puts a scratchy towel over the large wet place. I lie down again. The rags have fallen from the window crack, and the air is cold. I dare not call her back and am reluctant to leave my warmth. My mother's anger humiliates me; her words chafe my cheeks, and I am crying. I do not know that she is not angry at me, but at my sickness. I believe she despises my weakness for letting the sickness "take holt." By and by I will not get sick; I will refuse to. But for now I am crying. I know I am making more snot, but I can't stop.

My sister comes in. Her eyes are full of sorrow. She sings to me: "When the deep purple falls over sleepy garden walls, someone thinks of me. . . ." I doze, thinking of plums, walls, and "someone."

But was it really like that? As painful as I remember? Only mildly. Or rather, it was a productive and fructifying pain. Love, thick and dark as Alaga syrup, eased up into that cracked window. I could smell it—taste it—sweet, musty, with an edge of wintergreen in its base—everywhere in that house. It stuck, along with my tongue, to the frosted windowpanes. It coated my chest, along with the salve, and when the flannel came undone in my sleep, the clear, sharp curves of air outlined its presence on my throat. And in the night, when my coughing was dry and tough, feet padded into the room, hands repinned the flannel, readjusted the quilt, and rested a moment on my forehead. So when I think of autumn, I think of somebody with hands who does not want me to die.

It was autumn too when Mr. Henry came. Our roomer. Our roomer. The words ballooned from the lips and hovered about our heads—silent, separate, and pleasantly mysterious. My mother was all ease and satisfaction in discussing his coming.

"You know him," she said to her friends. "Henry Washington. He's been living over there with Miss Della

Jones on Thirteenth Street. But she's too addled now to keep up. So he's looking for another place."

"Oh, yes." Her friends do not hide their curiosity. "I been wondering how long he was going to stay up there with her. They say she's real bad off. Don't know who he is half the time, and nobody else."

"Well, that old crazy nigger she married up with didn't help her head none."

"Did you hear what he told folks when he left her?"

"Uh-uh. What?"

"Well, he run off with that trifling Peggy—from Elyria. You know."

"One of Old Slack Bessie's girls?"

"That's the one. Well, somebody asked him why he left a nice good church woman like Della for that heifer. You know Della always did keep a good house. And he said the honest-to-God real reason was he couldn't take no more of that violet water Della Jones used. Said he wanted a woman to smell like a woman. Said Della was just too clean for him."

"Old dog. Ain't that nasty!"

"You telling me. What kind of reasoning is that?"

"No kind. Some men just dogs."

"Is that what give her them strokes?"

"Must have helped. But you know, none of them girls wasn't too bright. Remember that grinning Hattie? She wasn't never right. And their Auntie Julia is still trotting up and down Sixteenth Street talking to herself."

"Didn't she get put away?"

"Naw. County wouldn't take her. Said she wasn't harming anybody."

"Well, she's harming me. You want something to scare

the living shit out of you, you get up at five-thirty in the morning like I do and see that old hag floating by in that bonnet. Have mercy!"

They laugh.

Frieda and I are washing Mason jars. We do not hear their words, but with grown-ups we listen to and watch out for their voices.

"Well, I hope don't nobody let me roam around like that when I get senile. It's a shame."

"What they going to do about Della? Don't she have no people?"

"A sister's coming up from North Carolina to look after her. I expect she wants to get aholt of Della's house."

"Oh, come on. That's a evil thought, if ever I heard one."

"What you want to bet? Henry Washington said that sister ain't seen Della in fifteen years."

"I kind of thought Henry would marry her one of these days."

"That old woman?"

"Well, Henry ain't no chicken."

"No, but he ain't no buzzard, either."

"He ever been married to anybody?"

"No."

"How come? Somebody cut it off?"

"He's just picky."

"He ain't picky. You see anything around here you'd marry?"

"Well . . . no."

"He's just sensible. A steady worker with quiet ways. I hope it works out all right."

"It will. How much you charging?"
"Five dollars every two weeks."
"That'll be a big help to you."
"I'll say."

Their conversation is like a gently wicked dance: sound meets sound, curtsies, shimmies, and retires. Another sound enters but is upstaged by still another: the two circle each other and stop. Sometimes their words move in lofty spirals; other times they take strident leaps, and all of it is punctuated with warm-pulsed laughter—like the throb of a heart made of jelly. The edge, the curl, the thrust of their emotions is always clear to Frieda and me. We do not, cannot, know the meanings of all their words, for we are nine and ten years old. So we watch their faces, their hands, their feet, and listen for truth in timbre.

So when Mr. Henry arrived on a Saturday night, we smelled him. He smelled wonderful. Like trees and lemon vanishing cream, and Nu Nile Hair Oil and flecks of Sen-Sen.

He smiled a lot, showing small even teeth with a friendly gap in the middle. Frieda and I were not introduced to him—merely pointed out. Like, here is the bathroom; the clothes closet is here; and these are my kids, Frieda and Claudia; watch out for this window; it don't open all the way.

We looked sideways at him, saying nothing and expecting him to say nothing. Just to nod, as he had done at the clothes closet, acknowledging our existence. To our surprise, he spoke to us.

"Hello there. You must be Greta Garbo, and you must be Ginger Rogers."

We giggled. Even my father was startled into a smile.

"Want a penny?" He held out a shiny coin to us. Frieda lowered her head, too pleased to answer. I reached for it. He snapped his thumb and forefinger, and the penny disappeared. Our shock was laced with delight. We searched all over him, poking our fingers into his socks, looking up the inside back of his coat. If happiness is anticipation with certainty, we were happy. And while we waited for the coin to reappear, we knew we were amusing Mama and Daddy. Daddy was smiling, and Mama's eyes went soft as they followed our hands wandering over Mr. Henry's body.

We loved him. Even after what came later, there was no bitterness in our memory of him.

She slept in the bed with us. Frieda on the outside because she is brave—it never occurs to her that if in her sleep her hand hangs over the edge of the bed "something" will crawl out from under it and bite her fingers off. I sleep near the wall because that thought *has* occurred to me. Pecola, therefore, had to sleep in the middle.

Mama had told us two days earlier that a "case" was coming—a girl who had no place to go. The county had placed her in our house for a few days until they could decide what to do, or, more precisely, until the family was reunited. We were to be nice to her and not fight. Mama didn't know "what got into people," but that old

Dog Breedlove had burned up his house, gone upside his wife's head, and everybody, as a result, was outdoors.

Outdoors, we knew, was the real terror of life. The threat of being outdoors surfaced frequently in those days. Every possibility of excess was curtailed with it. If somebody ate too much, he could end up outdoors. If somebody used too much coal, he could end up outdoors. People could gamble themselves outdoors, drink themselves outdoors. Sometimes mothers put their sons outdoors, and when that happened, regardless of what the son had done, all sympathy was with him. He was outdoors, and his own flesh had done it. To be put outdoors by a landlord was one thing—unfortunate, but an aspect of life over which you had no control, since you could not control your income. But to be slack enough to put oneself outdoors, or heartless enough to put one's own kin outdoors—that was criminal.

There is a difference between being put *out* and being put out*doors*. If you are put out, you go somewhere else; if you are outdoors, there is no place to go. The distinction was subtle but final. Outdoors was the end of something, an irrevocable, physical fact, defining and complementing our metaphysical condition. Being a minority in both caste and class, we moved about anyway on the hem of life, struggling to consolidate our weaknesses and hang on, or to creep singly up into the major folds of the garment. Our peripheral existence, however, was something we had learned to deal with—probably because it was abstract. But the concreteness of being outdoors was another matter—like the difference between the concept of death and being, in fact, dead. Dead doesn't change, and outdoors is here to stay.

Knowing that there was such a thing as outdoors bred in us a hunger for property, for ownership. The firm possession of a yard, a porch, a grape arbor. Propertied black people spent all their energies, all their love, on their nests. Like frenzied, desperate birds, they overdecorated everything; fussed and fidgeted over their hard-won homes; canned, jellied, and preserved all summer to fill the cupboards and shelves; they painted, picked, and poked at every corner of their houses. And these houses loomed like hothouse sunflowers among the rows of weeds that were the rented houses. Renting blacks cast furtive glances at these owned yards and porches, and made firmer commitments to buy themselves "some nice little old place." In the meantime, they saved, and scratched, and piled away what they could in the rented hovels, looking forward to the day of property.

Cholly Breedlove, then, a renting black, having put his family outdoors, had catapulted himself beyond the reaches of human consideration. He had joined the animals; was, indeed, an old dog, a snake, a ratty nigger. Mrs. Breedlove was staying with the woman she worked for; the boy, Sammy, was with some other family; and Pecola was to stay with us. Cholly was in jail.

She came with nothing. No little paper bag with the other dress, or a nightgown, or two pair of whitish cotton bloomers. She just appeared with a white woman and sat down.

We had fun in those few days Pecola was with us. Frieda and I stopped fighting each other and concentrated on our guest, trying hard to keep her from feeling outdoors.

When we discovered that she clearly did not want to dominate us, we liked her. She laughed when I clowned for her, and smiled and accepted gracefully the food gifts my sister gave her.

"Would you like some graham crackers?"

"I don't care."

Frieda brought her four graham crackers on a saucer and some milk in a blue-and-white Shirley Temple cup. She was a long time with the milk, and gazed fondly at the silhouette of Shirley Temple's dimpled face. Frieda and she had a loving conversation about how cu-ute Shirley Temple was. I couldn't join them in their adoration because I hated Shirley. Not because she was cute, but because she danced with Bojangles, who was *my* friend, *my* uncle, *my* daddy, and who ought to have been soft-shoeing it and chuckling with me. Instead he was enjoying, sharing, giving a lovely dance thing with one of those little white girls whose socks never slid down under their heels. So I said, "I like Jane Withers."

They gave me a puzzled look, decided I was incomprehensible, and continued their reminiscing about old squint-eyed Shirley.

Younger than both Frieda and Pecola, I had not yet arrived at the turning point in the development of my psyche which would allow me to love her. What I felt at that time was unsullied hatred. But before that I had felt a stranger, more frightening thing than hatred for all the Shirley Temples of the world.

It had begun with Christmas and the gift of dolls. The

big, the special, the loving gift was always a big, blue-eyed Baby Doll. From the clucking sounds of adults I knew that the doll represented what they thought was my fondest wish. I was bemused with the thing itself, and the way it looked. What was I supposed to do with it? Pretend I was its mother? I had no interest in babies or the concept of motherhood. I was interested only in humans my own age and size, and could not generate any enthusiasm at the prospect of being a mother. Motherhood was old age, and other remote possibilities. I learned quickly, however, what I was expected to do with the doll: rock it, fabricate storied situations around it, even sleep with it. Picture books were full of little girls sleeping with their dolls. Raggedy Ann dolls usually, but they were out of the question. I was physically revolted by and secretly frightened of those round moronic eyes, the pancake face, and orangeworms hair.

The other dolls, which were supposed to bring me great pleasure, succeeded in doing quite the opposite. When I took it to bed, its hard unyielding limbs resisted my flesh—the tapered fingertips on those dimpled hands scratched. If, in sleep, I turned, the bone-cold head collided with my own. It was a most uncomfortable, patently aggressive sleeping companion. To hold it was no more rewarding. The starched gauze or lace on the cotton dress irritated any embrace. I had only one desire: to dismember it. To see of what it was made, to discover the dearness, to find the beauty, the desirability that had escaped me, but apparently only me. Adults, older girls, shops, magazines, newspapers, window signs—all the world had agreed that a blue-eyed, yellow-haired, pink-skinned doll was what every girl child treasured.

"Here," they said, "this is beautiful, and if you are on this day 'worthy' you may have it." I fingered the face, wondering at the single-stroke eyebrows; picked at the pearly teeth stuck like two piano keys between red bowline lips. Traced the turned-up nose, poked the glassy blue eyeballs, twisted the yellow hair. I could not love it. But I could examine it to see what it was that all the world said was lovable. Break off the tiny fingers, bend the flat feet, loosen the hair, twist the head around, and the thing made one sound—a sound they said was the sweet and plaintive cry "Mama," but which sounded to me like the bleat of a dying lamb, or, more precisely, our icebox door opening on rusty hinges in July. Remove the cold and stupid eyeball, it would bleat still, "Ahhhhhh," take off the head, shake out the sawdust, crack the back against the brass bed rail, it would bleat still. The gauze back would split, and I could see the disk with six holes, the secret of the sound. A mere metal roundness.

Grown people frowned and fussed: "You-don't-know-how-to-take-care-of-nothing. I-never-had-a-baby-doll-in-my-whole-life-and-used-to-cry-my-eyes-out-for-them. Now-you-got-one-a-beautiful-one-and-you-tear-it-up-what's-the-matter-with-you?"

How strong was their outrage. Tears threatened to erase the aloofness of their authority. The emotion of years of unfulfilled longing preened in their voices. I did not know why I destroyed those dolls. But I did know that nobody ever asked me what I wanted for Christmas. Had any adult with the power to fulfill my desires taken me seriously and asked me what I wanted, they would have known that I did not want to have anything to own, or to possess any object. I wanted rather to feel something on Christmas day. The real question would have been, "Dear Claudia, what experience would you like on Christmas?" I could have spoken up, "I want to sit on the low stool in Big Mama's kitchen with my lap full of lilacs and listen to Big Papa play his violin for me alone." The lowness of the stool made for my body, the security and warmth of Big Mama's kitchen, the smell of the lilacs, the sound of the music, and, since it would be good to have all of my senses engaged, the taste of a peach, perhaps, afterward.

Instead I tasted and smelled the acridness of tin plates and cups designed for tea parties that bored me. Instead I looked with loathing on new dresses that required a hateful bath in a galvanized zinc tub before wearing. Slipping around on the zinc, no time to play or soak, for the water chilled too fast, no time to enjoy one's nakedness, only time to make curtains of soapy water careen down between the legs. Then the scratchy towels and the dreadful and humiliating absence of dirt. The irritable, unimaginative cleanliness. Gone the ink marks from legs and face, all my creations and accumulations of the day gone, and replaced by goose pimples.

I destroyed white baby dolls.

But the dismembering of dolls was not the true horror. The truly horrifying thing was the transference of the same impulses to little white girls. The indifference with which I could have axed them was shaken only by my desire to do so. To discover what eluded me: the secret of the magic they weaved on others. What made people look at them and say, "Awwwww," but not for me? The eye slide of black women as they approached them on the street, and the possessive gentleness of their touch as they handled them.

If I pinched them, their eyes—unlike the crazed glint of the baby doll's eyes—would fold in pain, and their cry would not be the sound of an icebox door, but a fascinating cry of pain. When I learned how repulsive this disinterested violence was, that it was repulsive because it was disinterested, my shame floundered about for refuge. The best hiding place was love. Thus the conversion from pristine sadism to fabricated hatred, to fraudulent love. It was a small step to Shirley Temple. I learned much later to worship her, just as I learned to delight in cleanliness, knowing, even as I learned, that the change was adjustment without improvement.

"Three quarts of milk. That's what was *in* that icebox yesterday. Three whole quarts. Now they ain't none. Not a drop. I don't mind folks coming in and getting what they want, but three quarts of milk! What the devil does *any*body need with *three* quarts of milk?"

The "folks" my mother was referring to was Pecola. The three of us, Pecola, Frieda, and I, listened to her downstairs in the kitchen fussing about the amount of milk Pecola had drunk. We knew she was fond of the Shirley Temple cup and took every opportunity to drink milk out of it just to handle and see sweet Shirley's face. My mother knew that Frieda and I hated milk and assumed Pecola drank it out of greediness. It was certainly not for us to "dispute" her. We didn't initiate talk with grown-ups; we answered their questions.

Ashamed of the insults that were being heaped on our friend, we just sat there: I picked toe jam, Frieda cleaned her fingernails with her teeth, and Pecola finger-traced some scars on her knee—her head cocked to one side. My mother's fussing soliloquies always irritated and depressed us. They were interminable, insulting, and although indirect (Mama never named anybody—just talked about folks and *some* people), extremely painful in their thrust. She would go on like that for hours, connecting one offense to another until all of the things that chagrined her were spewed out. Then, having told everybody and everything off, she would burst into song and sing the rest of the day. But it was such a long time before the singing part came. In the meantime, our stomachs jellying and our necks burning, we listened, avoided each other's eyes, and picked toe jam or whatever.

". . . I don't know what I'm suppose to be running here, a charity ward, I guess. Time for me to get out of the *giving* line and get in the *getting* line. I guess I ain't sup*posed* to have nothing. I'm sup*posed* to end up in the poorhouse. Look like nothing I do is going to keep me out of there. Folks just spend all their time trying to figure out ways to send *me* to the poorhouse. I got about as much business with another mouth to feed as a cat has with side pockets. As if I don't have trouble enough trying to feed my own and keep out the poorhouse, now I got something else in here that's just going to *drink* me on in there. Well, naw, she ain't. Not long as I got strength in my body and a tongue in my head. There's a limit to everything. I ain't got nothing to just throw *away*. Don't *no*body need *three* quarts of milk. Henry

Ford don't need three quarts of milk. That's just downright *sin*ful. I'm willing to do what I can for folks. Can't nobody say I ain't. But this has got to stop, and I'm just the one to stop it. Bible say watch as *well* as pray. Folks just dump they children off on you and go on 'bout they business. Ain't nobody even *peeped* in here to see whether that child has a loaf of bread. Look like they would just *peep* in to see whether I had a loaf of bread to give her. But naw. That thought don't cross they mind. That old trifling Cholly been out of jail *two* whole days and ain't been here *yet* to see if his own child was 'live or dead. She could be *dead* for all he know. And that *mama* neither. What kind of something is that?"

When Mama got around to Henry Ford and all those people who didn't care whether she had a loaf of bread, it was time to go. We wanted to miss the part about Roosevelt and the CCC camps.

Frieda got up and started down the stairs. Pecola and I followed, making a wide arc to avoid the kitchen doorway. We sat on the steps of the porch, where my mother's words could reach us only in spurts.

It was a lonesome Saturday. The house smelled of Fels Naphtha and the sharp odor of mustard greens cooking. Saturdays were lonesome, fussy, soapy days. Second in misery only to those tight, starchy, cough-drop Sundays, so full of "don'ts" and "set'cha self downs."

If my mother was in a singing mood, it wasn't so bad. She would sing about hard times, bad times, and somebody-done-gone-and-left-me times. But her voice was so sweet and her singing-eyes so melty I found myself longing for those hard times, yearning to be grown without "a thin di-i-ime to my name." I looked forward to the delicious time when "my man" would leave me, when I would "hate to see that evening sun go down . . ." 'cause then I would know "my man has left this town." Misery colored by the greens and blues in my mother's voice took all of the grief out of the words and left me with a conviction that pain was not only endurable, it was sweet.

But without song, those Saturdays sat on my head like a coal scuttle, and if Mama was fussing, as she was now, it was like somebody throwing stones at it.

". . . and here I am poor as a bowl of yak-me. What do they think I am? Some kind of Sandy Claus? Well, they can just take they stocking down 'cause it *ain't* Christmas. . . ."

We fidgeted.

"Let's do something," Frieda said.

"What do you want to do?" I asked.

"I don't know. Nothing." Frieda stared at the tops of the trees. Pecola looked at her feet.

"You want to go up to Mr. Henry's room and look at his girlie magazines?"

Frieda made an ugly face. She didn't like to look at dirty pictures. "Well," I continued, "we could look at his Bible. *That's* pretty." Frieda sucked her teeth and made a *phttt* sound with her lips. "O.K., then. We could go thread needles for the half-blind lady. She'll give us a penny."

Frieda snorted. "Her eyes look like snot. I don't feel like looking at them. What *you* want to do, Pecola?"

"I don't care," she said. "Anything you want."

I had another idea. "We could go up the alley and see what's in the trash cans."

"Too cold," said Frieda. She was bored and irritable.

"I know. We could make some fudge."

"You kidding? With Mama in there fussing? When she starts fussing at the walls, you know she's gonna be at it all day. She wouldn't even let us."

"Well, let's go over to the Greek hotel and listen to them cuss."

"Oh, who wants to do *that?* Besides, they say the same old words all the time."

My supply of ideas exhausted, I began to concentrate on the white spots on my fingernails. The total signified the number of boyfriends I would have. Seven.

Mama's soliloquy slid into the silence ". . . Bible say feed the hungry. That's fine. That's all right. But I ain't feeding no elephants. . . . Anybody need three quarts of milk to *live* need to get out of here. They in the wrong place. What is this? Some kind of *dairy* farm?"

Suddenly Pecola bolted straight up, her eyes wide with terror. A whinnying sound came from her mouth.

"What's the matter with *you?*" Frieda stood up too.

Then we both looked where Pecola was staring. Blood was running down her legs. Some drops were on the steps. I leaped up. "Hey. You cut yourself? Look. It's all over your dress."

A brownish-red stain discolored the back of her dress. She kept whinnying, standing with her legs far apart.

Frieda said, "Oh. Lordy! I know. I know what that is!"

"What?" Pecola's fingers went to her mouth.

"That's ministratin'."

"What's that?"

"You know."

"Am I going to die?" she asked.

"Noooo. You won't die. It just means you can have a baby!"

"What?"

"How do *you* know?" I was sick and tired of Frieda knowing everything.

"Mildred told me, and Mama too."

"I don't believe it."

"You don't have to, dummy. Look. Wait here. Sit down, Pecola. Right here." Frieda was all authority and zest. "And you," she said to me, "you go get some water."

"Water?"

"Yes, stupid. Water. And be quiet, or Mama will hear you."

Pecola sat down again, a little less fear in her eyes. I went into the kitchen.

"What you want, girl?" Mama was rinsing curtains in the sink.

"Some water, ma'am."

"Right where I'm working, naturally. Well, get a glass. Not no clean one neither. Use that jar."

I got a Mason jar and filled it with water from the faucet. It seemed a long time filling.

"Don't nobody never want nothing till they see me at the sink. Then everybody got to drink water. . . ."

When the jar was full, I moved to leave the room.

"Where you going?"

"Outside."

"Drink that water right here!"

"I ain't gonna break nothing."

"You don't know what you gonna do."

"Yes, ma'am. I do. Lemme take it out. I won't spill none."

"You bed' not."

I got to the porch and stood there with the Mason jar of water. Pecola was crying.

"What you crying for? Does it hurt?"

She shook her head.

"Then stop slinging snot."

Frieda opened the back door. She had something tucked in her blouse. She looked at me in amazement and pointed to the jar. "What's that supposed to do?"

"You told me. You *said* get some water."

"Not a little old jar full. Lots of water. To scrub the steps with, dumbbell!"

"How was I supposed to know?"

"Yeah. How was you. Come on." She pulled Pecola up by the arm. "Let's go back here." They headed for the side of the house where the bushes were thick.

"Hey. What about me? I want to go."

"Shut uuuup," Frieda stage-whispered. "Mama will hear you. You wash the steps."

They disappeared around the corner of the house.

I was going to miss something. Again. Here was something important, and I had to stay behind and not see any of it. I poured the water on the steps, sloshed it with my shoe, and ran to join them.

Frieda was on her knees; a white rectangle of cotton was near her on the ground. She was pulling Pecola's pants off. "Come on. Step out of them." She managed to get the soiled pants down and flung them at me. "Here."

"What am I supposed to do with these?"

"Bury them, moron."

Frieda told Pecola to hold the cotton thing between her legs.

"How she gonna walk like that?" I asked.

Frieda didn't answer. Instead she took two safety pins from the hem of her skirt and began to pin the ends of the napkin to Pecola's dress.

I picked up the pants with two fingers and looked about for something to dig a hole with. A rustling noise in the bushes startled me, and turning toward it, I saw a pair of fascinated eyes in a dough-white face. Rosemary was watching us. I grabbed for her face and succeeded in scratching her nose. She screamed and jumped back.

"Mrs. MacTeer! Mrs. MacTeer!" Rosemary hollered. "Frieda and Claudia are out here playing nasty! Mrs. MacTeer!"

Mama opened the window and looked down at us.

"What?"

"They're playing nasty, Mrs. MacTeer. Look. And Claudia hit me 'cause I seen them!"

Mama slammed the window shut and came running out the back door.

"What you all doing? Oh. Uh-huh. Uh-huh. Playing nasty, huh?" She reached into the bushes and pulled off a switch. "I'd rather raise pigs than some nasty girls. Least I can slaughter *them!*"

We began to shriek. "No, Mama. No, ma'am. We wasn't! She's a liar! No, ma'am, Mama! No, ma'am, Mama!"

Mama grabbed Frieda by the shoulder, turned her around, and gave her three or four stinging cuts on her legs. "Gonna be nasty, huh? Naw you ain't!"

Frieda was destroyed. Whippings wounded and insulted her.

Mama looked at Pecola. "You too!" she said. "Child of mine or not!" She grabbed Pecola and spun her around. The safety pin snapped open on one end of the napkin, and Mama saw it fall from under her dress. The switch hovered in the air while Mama blinked. "What the devil is going on here?"

Frieda was sobbing. I, next in line, began to explain. "She was bleeding. We was just trying to stop the blood!"

Mama looked at Frieda for verification. Frieda nodded. "She's ministratin'. We was just helping."

Mama released Pecola and stood looking at her. Then she pulled both of them toward her, their heads against her stomach. Her eyes were sorry. "All right, all right. Now, stop crying. I didn't know. Come on, now. Get on in the house. Go on home, Rosemary. The show is over."

We trooped in, Frieda sobbing quietly, Pecola carrying a white tail, me carrying the little-girl-gone-to-woman pants.

Mama led us to the bathroom. She prodded Pecola inside, and taking the underwear from me, told us to stay out.

We could hear water running into the bathtub.

"You think she's going to drown her?"

"Oh, Claudia. You so dumb. She's just going to wash her clothes and all."

"Should we beat up Rosemary?"

"No. Leave her alone."

The water gushed, and over its gushing we could hear the music of my mother's laughter.

That night, in bed, the three of us lay still. We were full of awe and respect for Pecola. Lying next to a real person who was really ministratin' was somehow sacred. She was different from us now—grown-up-like. She, herself, felt the distance, but refused to lord it over us.

After a long while she spoke very softly. "Is it true that I can have a baby now?"

"Sure," said Frieda drowsily. "Sure you can."

"But . . . how?" Her voice was hollow with wonder.

"Oh," said Frieda, "somebody has to love you."

"Oh."

There was a long pause in which Pecola and I thought this over. It would involve, I supposed, "my man," who, before leaving me, would love me. But there weren't any babies in the songs my mother sang. Maybe that's why the women were sad: the men left before they could make a baby.

Then Pecola asked a question that had never entered my mind. "How do you do that? I mean, how do you get somebody to love you?" But Frieda was asleep. And I didn't know.

HEREISTHEHOUSEITISGREENANDWH ITEITHASAREDDOORITISVERYPRETT YITISVERYPRETTYPRETTYPRETTYP

There is an abandoned store on the southeast corner of Broadway and Thirty-fifth Street in Lorain, Ohio. It does not recede into its background of leaden sky, nor harmonize with the gray frame houses and black telephone poles around it. Rather, it foists itself on the eye of the passerby in a manner that is both irritating and melancholy. Visitors who drive to this tiny town wonder why it has not been torn down, while pedestrians, who are residents of the neighborhood, simply look away when they pass it.

At one time, when the building housed a pizza parlor, people saw only slow-footed teen-aged boys huddled about the corner. These young boys met there to feel their groins, smoke cigarettes, and plan mild outrages. The smoke from their cigarettes they inhaled deeply, forcing it to fill their lungs, their hearts, their thighs, and keep at bay the shiveriness, the energy of their youth. They moved slowly, laughed slowly, but flicked the ashes from their cigarettes too quickly too often, and exposed themselves, to those who were interested, as novices to the habit. But long before the sound of their lowing and the sight of their preening, the building was leased to a Hungarian baker, modestly famous for his brioche and poppy-seed rolls. Earlier than that, there was a real-estate office there, and even before that, some gypsies used it as a base of operations. The gypsy family gave the large plate-glass window as much distinction and character as it ever had. The girls of the family took turns sitting between yards of velvet draperies and Oriental rugs hanging at the windows. They looked out and occasionally smiled, or winked, or beckoned—only occasionally. Mostly they looked, their elaborate dresses, long-sleeved and long-skirted, hiding the nakedness that stood in their eyes.

So fluid has the population in that area been, that probably no one remembers longer, longer ago, before the time of the gypsies and the time of the teen-agers when the Breedloves lived there, nestled together in the storefront. Festering together in the debris of a realtor's whim. They slipped in and out of the box of peeling gray, making no stir in the neighborhood, no sound in the labor force, and no wave in the mayor's office. Each member of the family in his own cell of consciousness, each making his own patchwork quilt of reality—collecting fragments of experience here, pieces of information there. From the tiny impressions gleaned from one another, they created a sense of belonging and tried to make do with the way they found each other.

The plan of the living quarters was as unimaginative as a first-generation Greek landlord could contrive it to be. The large "store" area was partitioned into two rooms by beaverboard planks that did not reach to the ceiling. There was a living room, which the family called the front room, and the bedroom, where all the living was done. In the front room were two sofas, an upright piano, and a tiny artificial Christmas tree which had been there, decorated and dust-laden, for two years. The bedroom had three beds: a narrow iron bed for Sammy, fourteen years old, another for Pecola, eleven years old, and a double bed for Cholly and Mrs. Breedlove. In the center of the bedroom, for the even distribution of heat, stood a coal stove. Trunks, chairs, a small end table, and a cardboard "wardrobe" closet were placed around the walls. The kitchen was in the back of this apartment, a separate room. There were no bath facilities. Only a toilet bowl, inaccessible to the eye, if not the ear, of the tenants.

There is nothing more to say about the furnishings. They were anything but describable, having been conceived, manufactured, shipped, and sold in various states of thoughtlessness, greed, and indifference. The furniture had aged without ever having become familiar. People had owned it, but never known it. No one had lost a penny or a brooch under the cushions of either sofa and remembered the place and time of the loss or the finding. No one had clucked and said, "But I *had* it just a minute ago. I was sitting right there talking to . . ." or "Here it is. It must have slipped down while I was feeding the baby!" No one had given birth in one of the beds—or remembered with fondness the peeled paint places, because that's what the baby, when he learned to pull himself up, used to pick loose. No thrifty child had tucked a wad of gum under the table. No happy drunk—a friend of the family, with a fat neck, unmarried, you know, but God how he eats!—had sat at the piano and played "You Are My Sunshine." No young girl had stared at the tiny Christmas tree and remembered when she had decorated it, or wondered if that blue ball was going to hold, or if HE would ever come back to see it.

There were no memories among those pieces. Certainly no memories to be cherished. Occasionally an item provoked a physical reaction: an increase of acid irritation in the upper intestinal tract, a light flush of perspiration at the back of the neck as circumstances surrounding the piece of furniture were recalled. The sofa, for example. It had been purchased new, but the fabric had split straight across the back by the time it was delivered. The store would not take the responsibility. . . .

"Looka here, buddy. It was O.K. when I put it on the truck. The store can't do anything about it once it's on the truck. . . ." Listerine and Lucky Strike breath.

"But I don't want no tore couch if'n it's bought new." Pleading eyes and tightened testicles.

"Tough shit, buddy. *Your* tough shit. . . ."

You could hate a sofa, of course—that is, if you could hate a sofa. But it didn't matter. You still had to get together $4.80 a month. If you had to pay $4.80 a month for a sofa that started off split, no good, and humiliating—you couldn't take any joy in owning it. And the joylessness stank, pervading everything. The stink of it kept you from painting the beaverboard walls; from getting a matching piece of material for the chair; even from sewing up the split, which became a gash, which became a gaping chasm that exposed the cheap frame and cheaper upholstery. It withheld the refreshment in a sleep slept on it. It imposed a furtiveness on the loving done on it. Like a sore tooth that is not content to throb in isolation, but must diffuse its own pain to other parts of the body—making breathing difficult, vision limited, nerves unsettled, so a hated piece of furniture produces a fretful malaise that asserts itself throughout the house and limits the delight of things not related to it.

The only living thing in the Breedloves' house was the coal stove, which lived independently of everything and everyone, its fire being "out," "banked," or "up" at its own discretion, in spite of the fact that the family fed it and knew all the details of its regimen: sprinkle, do not dump, not too much. . . . The fire seemed to live, go down, or die according to its own schemata. In the morning, however, it always saw fit to die.

*HEREISTHEFAMILYMOTHERFATHER
DICKANDJANETHEYLIVEINTHEGREE
NANDWHITEHOUSETHEYAREVERYH*

The Breedloves did not live in a storefront because they were having temporary difficulty adjusting to the cutbacks at the plant. They lived there because they were poor and black, and they stayed there because they believed they were ugly. Although their poverty was traditional and stultifying, it was not unique. But their ugliness was unique. No one could have convinced them that they were not relentlessly and aggressively ugly. Except for the father, Cholly, whose ugliness (the result of despair, dissipation, and violence directed toward petty things and weak people) was behavior, the rest of the family—Mrs. Breedlove, Sammy Breedlove, and Pecola Breedlove—wore their ugliness, put it on, so to speak, although it did not belong to them. The eyes, the small eyes set closely together under narrow foreheads. The low, irregular hairlines, which seemed even more irregular in contrast to the straight, heavy eyebrows which nearly met. Keen but crooked noses, with insolent nostrils. They had high cheekbones, and their ears turned forward.

Shapely lips which called attention not to themselves but to the rest of the face. You looked at them and wondered why they were so ugly; you looked closely and could not find the source. Then you realized that it came from conviction, their conviction. It was as though some mysterious all-knowing master had given each one a cloak of ugliness to wear, and they had each accepted it without question. The master had said, "You are ugly people." They had looked about themselves and saw nothing to contradict the statement; saw, in fact, support for it leaning at them from every billboard, every movie, every glance. "Yes," they had said. "You are right." And they took the ugliness in their hands, threw it as a mantle over them, and went about the world with it. Dealing with it each according to his way. Mrs. Breedlove handled hers as an actor does a prop: for the articulation of character, for support of a role she frequently imagined was hers—martyrdom. Sammy used his as a weapon to cause others pain. He adjusted his behavior to it, chose his companions on the basis of it: people who could be fascinated, even intimidated by it. And Pecola. She hid behind hers. Concealed, veiled, eclipsed—peeping out from behind the shroud very seldom, and then only to yearn for the return of her mask.

This family, on a Saturday morning in October, began, one by one, to stir out of their dreams of affluence and vengeance into the anonymous misery of their storefront.

Mrs. Breedlove slipped noiselessly out of bed, put a sweater on over her nightgown (which was an old day dress), and walked toward the kitchen. Her one good foot made hard, bony sounds; the twisted one whispered on the linoleum. In the kitchen she made noises with doors, faucets, and pans. The noises were hollow, but the threats they implied were not. Pecola opened her eyes and lay staring at the dead coal stove. Cholly mumbled, thrashed about in the bed for a minute, and then was quiet.

Even from where Pecola lay, she could smell Cholly's whiskey. The noises in the kitchen became louder and less hollow. There was direction and purpose in Mrs. Breedlove's movements that had nothing to do with the preparation of breakfast. This awareness, supported by ample evidence from the past, made Pecola tighten her stomach muscles and ration her breath.

Cholly had come home drunk. Unfortunately he had been too drunk to quarrel, so the whole business would have to erupt this morning. Because it had not taken place immediately, the oncoming fight would lack spontaneity; it would be calculated, uninspired, and deadly.

Mrs. Breedlove came swiftly into the room and stood at the foot of the bed where Cholly lay.

"I need some coal in this house."

Cholly did not move.

"Hear me?" Mrs. Breedlove jabbed Cholly's foot.

Cholly opened his eyes slowly. They were red and menacing. With no exception, Cholly had the meanest eyes in town.

"Awwwwww, woman!"

"I said I need some coal. It's as cold as a witch's tit in this house. Your whiskey ass wouldn't feel hellfire, but I'm cold. I got to do a lot of things, but I ain't got to freeze."

"Leave me 'lone."

"Not until you get me some coal. If working like a mule don't give me the right to be warm, what am I doing it for?

You sure ain't bringing in nothing. If it was left up to you, we'd all be dead. . . ." Her voice was like an earache in the brain. ". . . If you think I'm going to wade out in the cold and get it myself, you'd better think again."

"I don't give a shit how you get it." A bubble of violence burst in his throat.

"You going to get your drunk self out of that bed and get me some coal or not?"

Silence.

"Cholly!"

Silence.

"Don't try me this morning, man. You say one more word, and I'll split you open!"

Silence.

"All right. All right. But if I sneeze once, just once, God help your butt!"

Sammy was awake now too, but pretending to be asleep. Pecola still held her stomach muscles taut and conserved her breath. They all knew that Mrs. Breedlove could have, would have, and had, gotten coal from the shed, or that Sammy or Pecola could be directed to get it. But the unquarreled evening hung like the first note of a dirge in sullenly expectant air. An escapade of drunkenness, no matter how routine, had its own ceremonial close. The tiny, undistinguished days that Mrs. Breedlove lived were identified, grouped, and classed by these quarrels. They gave substance to the minutes and hours otherwise dim and unrecalled. They relieved the tiresomeness of poverty, gave grandeur to the dead rooms. In these violent breaks in routine that were themselves routine, she could display the style and imagination of what she believed to be her own true self. To deprive her of these fights was to deprive her of all the zest and reasonableness of life. Cholly, by his habitual drunkenness and orneriness, provided them both with the material they needed to make their lives tolerable. Mrs. Breedlove considered herself an upright and Christian woman, burdened with a no-count man, whom God wanted her to punish. (Cholly was beyond redemption, of course, and redemption was hardly the point—Mrs. Breedlove was not interested in Christ the Redeemer, but rather Christ the Judge.) Often she could be heard discoursing with Jesus about Cholly, pleading with Him to help her "strike the bastard down from his pea-knuckle of pride." And once when a drunken gesture catapulted Cholly into the red-hot stove, she screamed, "Get him, Jesus! Get him!" If Cholly had stopped drinking, she would never have forgiven Jesus. She needed Cholly's sins desperately. The lower he sank, the wilder and more irresponsible he became, the more splendid she and her task became. In the name of Jesus.

No less did Cholly need her. She was one of the few things abhorrent to him that he could touch and therefore hurt. He poured out on her the sum of all his inarticulate fury and aborted desires. Hating her, he could leave himself intact. When he was still very young, Cholly had been surprised in some bushes by two white men while he was newly but earnestly engaged in eliciting sexual pleasure from a little country girl. The men had shone a flashlight right on his behind. He had stopped, terrified. They chuckled. The beam of the flashlight did not move. "Go on," they said. "Go on and finish. And, nigger, make it good." The flashlight did not move. For some reason Cholly had not hated the white men; he hated, despised, the girl. Even a half-remembrance of this episode, along with myriad other humiliations, defeats, and emasculations, could stir him into flights of depravity that surprised himself—but only himself. Somehow he could not astound. He could only be astounded. So he gave that up, too.

Cholly and Mrs. Breedlove fought each other with a darkly brutal formalism that was paralleled only by their lovemaking. Tacitly they had agreed not to kill each other. He fought her the way a coward fights a man—with feet, the palms of his hands, and teeth. She, in turn, fought back in a purely feminine way—with frying pans and pokers, and occasionally a flatiron would sail toward his head. They did not talk, groan, or curse during these beatings. There was only the muted sound of falling things, and flesh on unsurprised flesh.

There was a difference in the reaction of the children to these battles. Sammy cursed for a while, or left the house, or threw himself into the fray. He was known, by the time he was fourteen, to have run away from home no less than twenty-seven times. Once he got to Buffalo and stayed three months. His returns, whether by force or circumstance, were sullen. Pecola, on the other hand, restricted by youth and sex, experimented with methods of endurance. Though the methods varied, the pain was as consistent as it was deep. She struggled between an overwhelming desire that one would kill the other, and a profound wish that she herself could die. Now she was whispering, "Don't, Mrs. Breedlove. Don't." Pecola, like Sammy and Cholly, always called her mother Mrs. Breedlove.

"Don't, Mrs. Breedlove. Don't."

But Mrs. Breedlove did.

By the grace, no doubt, of God, Mrs. Breedlove sneezed. Just once.

She ran into the bedroom with a dishpan full of cold

water and threw it in Cholly's face. He sat up, choking and spitting. Naked and ashen, he leaped from the bed, and with a flying tackle, grabbed his wife around the waist, and they hit the floor. Cholly picked her up and knocked her down with the back of his hand. She fell in a sitting position, her back supported by Sammy's bed frame. She had not let go of the dishpan, and began to hit at Cholly's thighs and groin with it. He put his foot in her chest, and she dropped the pan. Dropping to his knee, he struck her several times in the face, and she might have succumbed early had he not hit his hand against the metal bed frame when his wife ducked. Mrs. Breedlove took advantage of this momentary suspension of blows and slipped out of his reach. Sammy, who had watched in silence their struggling at his bedside, suddenly began to hit his father about the head with both fists, shouting "You naked fuck!" over and over and over. Mrs. Breedlove, having snatched up the round, flat stove lid, ran tippy-toe to Cholly as he was pulling himself up from his knees, and struck him two blows, knocking him right back into the senselessness out of which she had provoked him. Panting, she threw a quilt over him and let him lie.

Sammy screamed, "Kill him! Kill him!"

Mrs. Breedlove looked at Sammy with surprise. "Cut out that noise, boy." She put the stove lid back in place, and walked toward the kitchen. At the doorway she paused long enough to say to her son, "Get up from there anyhow. I need some coal."

Letting herself breathe easy now, Pecola covered her head with the quilt. The sick feeling, which she had tried to prevent by holding in her stomach, came quickly in spite of her precaution. There surged in her the desire to heave, but as always, she knew she would not.

"Please, God," she whispered into the palm of her hand. "Please make me disappear." She squeezed her eyes shut. Little parts of her body faded away. Now slowly, now with a rush. Slowly again. Her fingers went, one by one; then her arms disappeared all the way to the elbow. Her feet now. Yes, that was good. The legs all at once. It was hardest above the thighs. She had to be real still and pull. Her stomach would not go. But finally it, too, went away. Then her chest, her neck. The face was hard, too. Almost done, almost. Only her tight, tight eyes were left. They were always left.

Try as she might, she could never get her eyes to disappear. So what was the point? They were everything. Everything was there, in them. All of those pictures, all of those faces. She had long ago given up the idea of running away to see new pictures, new faces, as Sammy had so often done. He never took her, and he never thought about his going ahead of time, so it was never planned. It wouldn't have worked anyway. As long as she looked the way she did, as long as she was ugly, she would have to stay with these people. Somehow she belonged to them. Long hours she sat looking in the mirror, trying to discover the secret of the ugliness, the ugliness that made her ignored or despised at school, by teachers and classmates alike. She was the only member of her class who sat alone at a double desk. The first letter of her last name forced her to sit in the front of the room always. But what about Marie Appolonaire? Marie was in front of her, but she shared a desk with Luke Angelino. Her teachers had always treated her this way. They tried never to glance at her, and called on her only when everyone was required to respond. She also knew that when one of the girls at school wanted to be particularly insulting to a boy, or wanted to get an immediate response from him, she could say. "Bobby loves Pecola Breedlove! Bobby loves Pecola Breedlove!" and never fail to get peals of laughter from those in earshot, and mock anger from the accused.

It had occurred to Pecola some time ago that if her eyes, those eyes that held the pictures, and knew the sights—if those eyes of hers were different, that is to say, beautiful, she herself would be different. Her teeth were good, and at least her nose was not big and flat like some of those who were thought so cute. If she looked different, beautiful, maybe Cholly would be different, and Mrs. Breedlove too. Maybe they'd say, "Why, look at pretty-eyed Pecola. We mustn't do bad things in front of those pretty eyes."

Pretty eyes. Pretty blue eyes. Big blue pretty eyes. Run, Jip, run. Jip runs, Alice runs. Alice has blue eyes. Jerry has blue eyes. Jerry runs. Alice runs. They run with their blue eyes. Four blue eyes. Four pretty blue eyes. Blue-sky eyes. Blue-like Mrs. Forrest's blue blouse eyes. Morning-glory-blue-eyes. Alice-and-Jerry-blue-storybook-eyes.

Each night, without fail, she prayed for blue eyes. Fervently, for a year she had prayed. Although somewhat discouraged, she was not without hope. To have something as wonderful as that happen would take a long, long time.

Thrown, in this way, into the binding conviction that only a miracle could relieve her, she would never know her beauty. She would see only what there was to see: the eyes of other people.

She walks down Garden Avenue to a small grocery store which sells penny candy. Three pennies are in her shoe—slipping back and forth between the sock and the inner sole. With each step she feels the painful press of the coins against her foot. A sweet, endurable, even cherished irritation, full of promise and delicate security. There is plenty of time to consider what to buy. Now, however, she moves down an avenue gently buffeted by the familiar and therefore loved images. The dandelions at the base of the telephone pole. Why, she wonders, do people call them weeds? She thought they were pretty. But grown-ups say, "Miss Dunion keeps her yard so nice. Not a dandelion anywhere." Hunkie women in black babushkas go into the fields with baskets to pull them up. But they do not want the yellow heads—only the jagged leaves. They make dandelion soup. Dandelion wine. Nobody loves the head of a dandelion. Maybe because they are so many, strong, and soon.

There was the sidewalk crack shaped like a Y, and the other one that lifted the concrete up from the dirt floor. Frequently her sloughing step had made her trip over that one. Skates would go well over this sidewalk—old it was, and smooth; it made the wheels glide evenly, with a mild whirr. The newly paved walks were bumpy and uncomfortable, and the sound of skate wheels on new walks was grating.

These and other inanimate things she saw and experienced. They were real to her. She knew them. They were the codes and touchstones of the world, capable of translation and possession. She owned the crack that made her stumble;

she owned the clumps of dandelions whose white heads, last fall, she had blown away; whose yellow heads, this fall, she peered into. And owning them made her part of the world, and the world a part of her.

She climbs four wooden steps to the door of Yacobowski's Fresh Veg. Meat and Sundries Store. A bell tinkles as she opens it. Standing before the counter, she looks at the array of candies. All Mary Janes, she decides. Three for a penny. The resistant sweetness that breaks open at last to deliver peanut butter—the oil and salt which complement the sweet pull of caramel. A peal of anticipation unsettles her stomach.

She pulls off her shoe and takes out the three pennies. The gray head of Mr. Yacobowski looms up over the counter. He urges his eyes out of his thoughts to encounter her. Blue eyes. Blear-dropped. Slowly, like Indian summer moving imperceptibly toward fall, he looks toward her. Somewhere between retina and object, between vision and view, his eyes draw back, hesitate, and hover. At some fixed point in time and space he senses that he need not waste the effort of a glance. He does not see her, because for him there is nothing to see. How can a fifty-two-year-old white immigrant storekeeper with the taste of potatoes and beer in his mouth, his mind honed on the doe-eyed Virgin Mary, his sensibilities blunted by a permanent awareness of loss, *see* a little black girl? Nothing in his life even suggested that the feat was possible, not to say desirable or necessary.

"Yeah?"

She looks up at him and sees the vacuum where curiosity ought to lodge. And something more. The total absence of human recognition—the glazed separateness. She does not know what keeps his glance suspended. Perhaps because he is grown, or a man, and she a little girl. But she has seen interest, disgust, even anger in grown male eyes. Yet this vacuum is not new to her. It has an edge; somewhere in the bottom lid is the distaste. She has seen it lurking in the eyes of all white people. So. The distaste must be for her, her blackness. All things in her are flux and anticipation. But her blackness is static and dread. And it is the blackness that accounts for, that creates, the vacuum edged with distaste in white eyes.

She points her finger at the Mary Janes—a little black shaft of finger, its tip pressed on the display window. The quietly inoffensive assertion of a black child's attempt to communicate with a white adult.

"Them." The word is more sigh than sense.

"What? These? These?" Phlegm and impatience mingle in his voice.

She shakes her head, her fingertip fixed on the spot which, in her view, at any rate, identifies the Mary Janes. He cannot see her view—the angle of his vision, the slant of her finger, makes it incomprehensible to him. His lumpy red hand plops around in the glass casing like the agitated head of a chicken outraged by the loss of its body.

"Christ. Kantcha talk?"

His fingers brush the Mary Janes.

She nods.

"Well, why'nt you say so? One? How many?"

Pecola unfolds her fist, showing the three pennies. He scoots three Mary Janes toward her—three yellow rectangles in each packet. She holds the money toward him. He hesitates, not wanting to touch her hand. She does not know how to move the finger of her right hand from the display counter or how to get the coins out of her left hand. Finally he reaches over and takes the pennies from her hand. His nails graze her damp palm.

Outside, Pecola feels the inexplicable shame ebb.

Dandelions. A dart of affection leaps out from her to them. But they do not look at her and do not send love back. She thinks, "They *are* ugly. They *are* weeds." Preoccupied with that revelation, she trips on the sidewalk crack. Anger stirs and wakes in her; it opens its mouth, and like a hot-mouthed puppy, laps up the dredges of her shame.

Anger is better. There is a sense of being in anger. A reality and presence. An awareness of worth. It is a lovely surging. Her thoughts fall back to Mr. Yacobowski's eyes, his phlegmy voice. The anger will not hold; the puppy is too easily surfeited. Its thirst too quickly quenched, it sleeps. The shame wells up again, its muddy rivulets seeping into her eyes. What to do before the tears come. She remembers the Mary Janes.

Each pale yellow wrapper has a picture on it. A picture of little Mary Jane, for whom the candy is named. Smiling white face. Blond hair in gentle disarray, blue eyes looking at her out of a world of clean comfort. The eyes are petulant, mischievous. To Pecola they are simply pretty. She eats the candy, and its sweetness is good. To eat the candy is somehow to eat the eyes, eat Mary Jane. Love Mary Jane. Be Mary Jane.

Three pennies had bought her nine lovely orgasms with Mary Jane. Lovely Mary Jane, for whom a candy is named.

Three whores lived in the apartment above the Breedloves' storefront. China, Poland, and Miss Marie. Pecola loved them, visited them, and ran their errands. They, in turn, did not despise her.

On an October morning, the morning of the stove-lid triumph, Pecola climbed the stairs to their apartment.

Even before the door was opened to her tapping, she could hear Poland singing—her voice sweet and hard, like new strawberries:

> I got blues in my mealbarrel
> Blues up on the shelf
> I got blues in my mealbarrel
> Blues up on the shelf
> Blues in my bedroom
> 'Cause I'm sleepin' by myself

"Hi, dumplin'. Where your socks?" Marie seldom called Pecola the same thing twice, but invariably her epithets were fond ones chosen from menus and dishes that were forever uppermost in her mind.

"Hello, Miss Marie. Hello, Miss China. Hello, Miss Poland."

"You heard me. Where your socks? You as barelegged as a yard dog."

"I couldn't find any."

"Couldn't find any? Must be somethin' in your house that loves socks."

China chuckled. Whenever something was missing, Marie attributed its disappearance to "something in the house that loved it." "There is somethin' in this house that loves brassieres," she would say with alarm.

Poland and China were getting ready for the evening.

Poland, forever ironing, forever singing. China, sitting on a pale-green kitchen chair, forever and forever curling her hair. Marie never got ready.

The women were friendly, but slow to begin talk. Pecola always took the initiative with Marie, who, once inspired, was difficult to stop.

"How come you got so many boyfriends, Miss Marie?"

"*Boy*friends? *Boy*friends? Chittlin', I ain't seen a *boy* since nineteen and twenty-seven."

"You didn't see none then." China stuck the hot curlers into a tin of Nu Nile hair dressing. The oil hissed at the touch of the hot metal.

"How come, Miss Marie?" Pecola insisted.

"How come what? How come I ain't seen a boy since nineteen and twenty-seven? Because they ain't *been* no boys since then. That's when they stopped. Folks started gettin' born old."

"You mean that's when *you* got old," China said.

"I ain't never got old. Just fat."

"Same thing."

"You think 'cause you skinny, folks think you young? You'd make a haint buy a girdle."

"And you look like the north side of a southbound mule."

"All I know is, them bandy little legs of yours is every bit as old as mine."

"Don't worry 'bout my bandy legs. That's the first thing they push aside."

All three of the women laughed. Marie threw back her head. From deep inside, her laughter came like the sound of many rivers, freely, deeply, muddily, heading for the room of an open sea. China giggled spastically. Each gasp seemed to be yanked out of her by an unseen hand jerking an unseen string. Poland, who seldom spoke unless she was drunk, laughed without sound. When she was sober she hummed mostly or chanted blues songs, of which she knew many.

Pecola fingered the fringe of a scarf that lay on the back of a sofa. "I never seen nobody with as many boyfriends as you got, Miss Marie. How come they all love you?"

Marie opened a bottle of root beer. "What else they gone do? They know I'm rich and good-lookin'. They wants to put their toes in my curly hair, and get at my money."

"You rich, Miss Marie?"

"Puddin', I got money's mammy."

"Where you get it from? You don't do no work."

"Yeah," said China, "where you get it from?"

"Hoover give it me. I did him a favor once, for the F. B. and I."

"What'd you do?"

"I did him a favor. They wanted to catch this crook, you see. Name of Johnny. He was as low-down as they come. . . ."

"We *know* that." China arranged a curl.

". . . the F. B. and I. wanted him bad. He killed more people than TB. And if you *crossed* him? Whoa, Jesus! He'd run you as long as there was ground. Well, I was little and cute then. No more than ninety pounds, soaking wet."

"You ain't never been soaking wet," China said.

"Well, you ain't never been dry. Shut up. Let me tell you, sweetnin'. To tell it true, I was the only one could handle him. He'd go out and rob a bank or kill some people, and I'd say to him, soft-like, 'Johnny, you shouldn't do that.' And he'd say he just had to bring me pretty things. Lacy drawers and all. And every Saturday we'd get a case of beer and fry up some fish. We'd fry it in meal and egg batter, you know, and when it was all brown and crisp—not hard, though—we'd break open that cold beer. . . ." Marie's eyes went soft as the memory of just such a meal sometime, somewhere transfixed her. All her stories were subject to breaking down at descriptions of food. Pecola saw Marie's teeth settling down into the back of crisp sea bass; saw the fat fingers putting back into her mouth tiny flakes of white, hot meat that had escaped from her lips; she heard the "pop" of the beer-bottle cap; smelled the acridness of the first stream of vapor; felt the cold beeriness hit the tongue. She ended the daydream long before Marie.

"But what about the money?" she asked.

China hooted. "She's makin' like she's the Lady in Red that told on Dillinger. Dillinger wouldn't have come near you lessen he was going hunting in Africa and shoot you for a hippo."

"Well, this hippo had a ball back in Chicago. Whoa Jesus, ninety-nine!"

"How come you always say 'Whoa Jesus' and a number?" Pecola had long wanted to know.

"Because my mama taught me never to cuss."

"Did she teach you not to drop your drawers?" China asked.

"Didn't have none," said Marie. "Never saw a pair of drawers till I was fifteen, when I left Jackson and was doing day work in Cincinnati. My white lady gave me some old ones of hers. I thought they was some kind of stocking cap. I put it on my head when I dusted. When she saw me, she liked to fell out."

"You must have been one dumb somebody." China lit a cigarette and cooled her irons.

"How'd I know?" Marie paused. "And what's the use of

putting on something you got to keep taking off all the time? Dewey never let me keep them on long enough to get used to them."

"Dewey who?" This was a somebody new to Pecola.

"Dewey who? Chicken! You never heard me tell of *Dewey?*" Marie was shocked by her negligence.

"No, ma'am."

"Oh, honey, you've missed half your life. Whoa Jesus, one-nine-five. You talkin' 'bout smooth! I met him when I was fourteen. We ran away and lived together like married for three years. You know all those klinker-tops you see runnin' up here? Fifty of 'em in a bowl wouldn't make a Dewey Prince ankle bone. Oh, Lord. How that man loved me!"

China arranged a fingerful of hair into a bang effect. "Then why he left you to sell tail?"

"Girl, when I found out I could sell it—that somebody would pay cold cash for it, you could have knocked me over with a feather."

Poland began to laugh. Soundlessly. "Me too. My auntie whipped me good that first time when I told her I didn't get no money. I said 'Money? For what? He didn't owe me nothin'.' She said, 'The hell he didn't!' "

They all dissolved in laughter.

Three merry gargoyles. Three merry harridans. Amused by a long-ago time of ignorance. They did not belong to those generations of prostitutes created in novels, with great and generous hearts, dedicated, because of the horror of circumstance, to ameliorating the luckless, barren life of men, taking money incidentally and humbly for their "understanding." Nor were they from that sensitive breed of young girl, gone wrong at the hands of fate, forced to cultivate an outward brittleness in order to protect her springtime from further shock, but knowing full well she was cut out for better things, and could make the right man happy. Neither were they the sloppy, inadequate whores who, unable to make a living at it alone, turn to drug consumption and traffic or pimps to help complete their scheme of self-destruction, avoiding suicide only to punish the memory of some absent father or to sustain the misery of some silent mother. Except for Marie's fabled love for Dewey Prince, these women hated men, all men, without shame, apology, or discrimination. They abused their visitors with a scorn grown mechanical from use. Black men, white men, Puerto Ricans, Mexicans, Jews, Poles, whatever—all were inadequate and weak, all came under their jaundiced eyes and were the recipients of their disinterested wrath. They took delight in cheating them. On one occasion the town well knew, they lured a Jew up the stairs, pounced on him, all three, held him up by the heels, shook everything out of his pants pockets, and threw him out of the window.

Neither did they have respect for women, who, although not their colleagues, so to speak, nevertheless deceived their husbands—regularly or irregularly, it made no difference. "Sugar-coated whores," they called them, and did not yearn to be in their shoes. Their only respect was for what they would have described as "good Christian colored women." The woman whose reputation was spotless, and who tended to her family, who didn't drink or smoke or run around. These women had their undying, if covert, affection. They would sleep with their husbands, and take their money, but always with a vengeance.

Nor were they protective and solicitous of youthful innocence. They looked back on their own youth as a period of ignorance, and regretted that they had not made more of it. They were not young girls in whores' clothing, or whores regretting their loss of innocence. They were whores in whores' clothing, whores who had never been young and had no word for innocence. With Pecola they were as free as they were with each other. Marie concocted stories for her because she was a child, but the stories were breezy and rough. If Pecola had announced her intention to live the life they did, they would not have tried to dissuade her or voiced any alarm.

"You and Dewey Prince have any children, Miss Marie?"

"Yeah. Yeah. We had some." Marie fidgeted. She pulled a bobby pin from her hair and began to pick her teeth. That meant she didn't want to talk anymore.

Pecola went to the window and looked down at the empty street. A tuft of grass had forced its way up through a crack in the sidewalk, only to meet a raw October wind. She thought of Dewey Prince and how he loved Miss Marie. What did love feel like? she wondered. How do grown-ups act when they love each other? Eat fish together? Into her eyes came the picture of Cholly and Mrs. Breedlove in bed. He making sounds as though he were in pain, as though something had him by the throat and wouldn't let go. Terrible as his noises were, they were not nearly as bad as the no noise at all from her mother. It was as though she was not even there. Maybe that was love. Choking sounds and silence.

Turning her eyes from the window, Pecola looked at the women.

China had changed her mind about the bangs and was arranging a small but sturdy pompadour. She was adept in creating any number of hair styles, but each one left her with a pinched and harassed look. Then she applied makeup heavily. Now she gave herself surprised eyebrows and a cupid-bow mouth. Later she would make Oriental eyebrows and an evilly slashed mouth.

Poland, in her sweet strawberry voice, began another song:

I know a boy who is sky-soft brown
I know a boy who is sky-soft brown
The dirt leaps for joy when his feet touch the ground.
His strut is a peacock
His eye is burning brass
His smile is sorghum syrup drippin' slow-sweet to the last
I know a boy who is sky-soft brown

Marie sat shelling peanuts and popping them into her mouth. Pecola looked and looked at the women. Were they real? Marie belched, softly, purringly, lovingly.

Winter

My daddy's face is a study. Winter moves into it and presides there. His eyes become a cliff of snow threatening to avalanche; his eyebrows bend like black limbs of leafless trees. His skin takes on the pale, cheerless yellow of winter sun; for a jaw he has the edges of a snowbound field dotted with stubble; his high forehead is the frozen sweep of the Erie, hiding currents of gelid thoughts that eddy in darkness. Wolf killer turned hawk fighter, he worked night and day to keep one from the door and the other from under the windowsills. A Vulcan guarding the flames, he gives us instructions about which doors to keep closed or opened for proper distribution of heat, lays kindling by, discusses qualities of coal, and teaches us how to rake, feed, and bank the fire. And he will not unrazor his lips until spring.

Winter tightened our heads with a band of cold and melted our eyes. We put pepper in the feet of our stockings, Vaseline on our faces, and stared through dark icebox mornings at four stewed prunes, slippery lumps of oatmeal, and cocoa with a roof of skin.

But mostly we waited for spring, when there could be gardens.

By the time this winter had stiffened itself into a hateful knot that nothing could loosen, something did loosen it, or rather someone. A someone who splintered the knot into silver threads that tangled us, netted us, made us long for the dull chafe of the previous boredom.

This disrupter of seasons was a new girl in school named Maureen Peal. A high-yellow dream child with long brown hair braided into two lynch ropes that hung down her back. She was rich, at least by our standards, as rich as the richest of the white girls, swaddled in comfort and care. The quality of her clothes threatened to derange Frieda and me. Patent-leather shoes with buckles, a cheaper version of which we got only at Easter and which had disintegrated by the end of May. Fluffy sweaters the color of lemon drops tucked into skirts with pleats so orderly they astounded us. Brightly colored knee socks with white borders, a brown velvet coat trimmed in white rabbit fur, and a matching muff. There was a hint of spring in her sloe green eyes, something summery in her complexion, and a rich autumn ripeness in her walk.

She enchanted the entire school. When teachers called on her, they smiled encouragingly. Black boys didn't trip her in the halls; white boys didn't stone her, white girls didn't suck their teeth when she was assigned to be their work partners; black girls stepped aside when she wanted to use the sink in the girls' toilet, and their eyes genuflected under sliding lids. She never had to search for anybody to eat with in the cafeteria—they flocked to the table of her choice, where she opened fastidious lunches, shaming our jelly-stained bread with egg-salad sandwiches cut into four dainty squares, pink-frosted cupcakes, stocks of celery and carrots, proud, dark apples. She even bought and liked white milk.

Frieda and I were bemused, irritated, and fascinated by her. We looked hard for flaws to restore our equilibrium, but had to be content at first with uglying up her name, changing Maureen Peal to Meringue Pie. Later a minor epiphany was ours when we discovered that she had a dog tooth—a charming one to be sure—but a dog tooth nonetheless. And when we found out that she had been born with six fingers on each hand and that there was a little bump where each extra one had been removed, we smiled. They were small triumphs, but we took what we could get—snickering behind her back and calling her Six-finger-dog-tooth-meringue-pie. But we had to do it alone, for none of the other girls would cooperate with our hostility. They adored her.

When she was assigned a locker next to mine, I could indulge my jealousy four times a day. My sister and I both suspected that we were secretly prepared to be her friend, if she would let us, but I knew it would be a dangerous friendship, for when my eye traced the white border patterns of those Kelly-green knee socks, and felt the pull and slack of my brown stockings, I wanted to kick her. And when I thought of the unearned haughtiness in her eyes, I plotted accidental slammings of locker doors on her hand.

As locker friends, however, we got to know each other a little, and I was even able to hold a sensible conversation with her without visualizing her fall off a cliff, or giggling my way into what I thought was a clever insult.

One day, while I waited at the locker for Frieda, she joined me.

"Hi."

"Hi."

"Waiting for your sister?"

"Uh-huh."

"Which way do you go home?"

"Down Twenty-first Street to Broadway."

"Why don't you go down Twenty-second Street?"

" 'Cause I live on Twenty-first Street."

"Oh. I can walk that way, I guess. Partly, anyway."

"Free country."

Frieda came toward us, her brown stockings straining at the knees because she had tucked the toe under to hide a hole in the foot.

"Maureen's gonna walk part way with us."

Frieda and I exchanged glances, her eyes begging my restraint, mine promising nothing.

It was a false spring day, which, like Maureen, had pierced the shell of a deadening winter. There were puddles, mud, and an inviting warmth that deluded us. The kind of day on which we draped our coats over our heads, left our galoshes in school, and came down with croup the following day. We always responded to the slightest change in weather, the most minute shifts in time of day. Long before seeds were stirring, Frieda and I were scruffing and poking at the earth, swallowing air, drinking rain. . . .

As we emerged from the school with Maureen, we

began to moult immediately. We put our head scarves in our coat pockets, and our coats on our heads. I was wondering how to maneuver Maureen's fur muff into a gutter when a commotion in the playground distracted us. A group of boys was circling and holding at bay a victim, Pecola Breedlove.

Bay Boy, Woodrow Cain, Buddy Wilson, Junie Bug—like a necklace of semiprecious stones they surrounded her. Heady with the smell of their own musk, thrilled by the easy power of a majority, they gaily harassed her.

"Black e mo. Black e mo. Yadaddsleepsnekked. Black e mo black e mo ya dadd sleeps nekked. Black e mo . . ."

They had extemporized a verse made up of two insults about matters over which the victim had no control: the color of her skin and speculations on the sleeping habits of an adult, wildly fitting in its incoherence. That they themselves were black, or that their own father had similarly relaxed habits was irrelevant. It was their contempt for their own blackness that gave the first insult its teeth. They seemed to have taken all of their smoothly cultivated ignorance, their exquisitely learned self-hatred, their elaborately designed hopelessness and sucked it all up into a fiery cone of scorn that had burned for ages in the hollows of their minds—cooled—and spilled over lips of outrage, consuming whatever was in its path. They danced a macabre ballet around the victim, whom, for their own sake, they were prepared to sacrifice to the flaming pit.

Black e mo Black e mo Ya daddy sleeps nekked.
Stch ta ta stch ta ta
stach ta ta ta ta ta

Pecola edged around the circle crying. She had dropped her notebook, and covered her eyes with her hands.

We watched, afraid they might notice us and turn their energies our way. Then Frieda, with set lips and Mama's eyes, snatched her coat from her head and threw it on the ground. She ran toward them and brought her books down on Woodrow Cain's head. The circle broke. Woodrow Cain grabbed his head.

"Hey, girl!"

"You cut that out, you hear?" I had never heard Frieda's voice so loud and clear.

Maybe because Frieda was taller than he was, maybe because he saw her eyes, maybe because he had lost interest in the game, or maybe because he had a crush on Frieda, in any case Woodrow looked frightened just long enough to give her more courage.

"Leave her 'lone, or I'm gone tell everybody what you did!"

Woodrow did not answer; he just walled his eyes.

Bay Boy piped up, "Go on, gal! Ain't nobody bothering you."

"You shut up, Bullet Head." I had found my tongue.

"Who you calling Bullet Head?"

"I'm calling you Bullet Head, Bullet Head."

Frieda took Pecola's hand. "Come on."

"You want a fat lip?" Bay Boy drew back his fist at me.

"Yeah. Gimme one of yours."

"You gone get one."

Maureen appeared at my elbow, and the boys seemed reluctant to continue under her springtime eyes so wide with interest. They buckled in confusion, not willing to beat up three girls under her watchful gaze. So they listened to a budding male instinct that told them to pretend we were unworthy of their attention.

"Come on, man."

"Yeah. Come on. We ain't got time to fool with them."

Grumbling a few disinterested epithets, they moved away.

I picked up Pecola's notebook and Frieda's coat, and the four of us left the playground.

"Old Bullet Head, he's always picking on girls."

Frieda agreed with me. "Miss Forrester said he was incorrigival."

"Really?" I didn't know what that meant, but it had enough of a doom sound in it to be true of Bay Boy.

While Frieda and I clucked on about the near fight, Maureen, suddenly animated, put her velvet-sleeved arm through Pecola's and began to behave as though they were the closest of friends.

"I just moved here. My name is Maureen Peal. What's yours?"

"Pecola."

"Pecola? Wasn't that the name of the girl in *Imitation of Life?*"

"I don't know. What is that?"

"The picture show, you know. Where this mulatto girl hates her mother cause she is black and ugly but then cries at the funeral. It was real sad. Everybody cries in it. Claudette Colbert too."

"Oh." Pecola's voice was no more than a sigh.

"Anyway, her name was Pecola too. She was so pretty. When it comes back, I'm going to see it again. My mother has seen it four times."

Frieda and I walked behind them, surprised at Maureen's friendliness to Pecola, but pleased. Maybe she wasn't so bad, after all. Frieda had put her coat back on her head, and the two of us, so draped, trotted along enjoying the warm breeze and Frieda's heroics.

"You're in my gym class, aren't you?" Maureen asked Pecola.

"Yes."

"Miss Erkmeister's legs sure are bow. I bet she thinks they're cute. How come she gets to wear real shorts, and we have to wear those old bloomers? I want to die every time I put them on."

Pecola smiled but did not look at Maureen.

"Hey." Maureen stopped short. "There's an Isaley's. Want some ice cream? I have money."

She unzipped a hidden pocket in her muff and pulled out a multifolded dollar bill. I forgave her those knee socks.

"My uncle sued Isaley's," Maureen said to the three of us. "He sued the Isaley's in Akron. They said he was disorderly and that that was why they wouldn't serve him, but a friend of his, a policeman, came in and beared the witness, so the suit went through."

"What's a suit?"

"It's when you can beat them up if you want to and won't anybody do nothing. Our family does it all the time. We believe in suits."

At the entrance to Isaley's Maureen turned to Frieda and me, asking, "You all going to buy some ice cream?"

We looked at each other. "No," Frieda said.

Maureen disappeared into the store with Pecola.

Frieda looked placidly down the street; I opened my mouth, but quickly closed it. It was extremely important that the world not know that I fully expected Maureen to buy us some ice cream, that for the past 120 seconds I had been selecting the flavor, that I had begun to like Maureen, and that neither of us had a penny.

We supposed Maureen was being nice to Pecola because of the boys, and were embarrassed to be caught—even by each other—thinking that she would treat us, or that we deserved it as much as Pecola did.

The girls came out. Pecola with two dips of orange-pineapple, Maureen with black raspberry.

"You should have got some," she said. "They had all kinds. Don't eat down to the tip of the cone," she advised Pecola.

"Why?"

"Because there's a fly in there."

"How you know?"

"Oh, not really. A girl told me she found one in the bottom of hers once, and ever since then she throws that part away."

"Oh."

We passed the Dreamland Theater, and Betty Grable smiled down at us.

"Don't you just love her?" Maureen asked.

"Uh-huh," said Pecola.

I differed. "Hedy Lamarr is better."

Maureen agreed. "Ooooo yes. My mother told me that a girl named Audrey, she went to the beauty parlor where we lived before, and asked the lady to fix her hair like Hedy Lamarr's, and the lady said, 'Yeah, when you grow some hair like Hedy Lamarr's.' " She laughed long and sweet.

"Sounds crazy," said Frieda.

"She sure is. Do you know she doesn't even menstrate yet, and she's sixteen. Do you, yet?"

"Yes." Pecola glanced at us.

"So do I." Maureen made no attempt to disguise her pride. "Two months ago I started. My girl friend in Toledo, where we lived before, said when she started she was scared to death. Thought she had killed herself."

"Do you know what it's for?" Pecola asked the question as though hoping to provide the answer herself.

"For babies." Maureen raised two pencil-stroke eyebrows at the obviousness of the question. "Babies need blood when they are inside you, and if you are having a baby, then you don't menstrate. But when you're not having a baby, then you don't have to save the blood, so it comes out."

"How do babies get the blood?" asked Pecola.

"Through the like-line. You know. Where your belly button is. That is where the like-line grows from and pumps the blood to the baby."

"Well, if the belly buttons are to grow like-lines to give the baby blood, and only girls have babies, how come boys have belly buttons?"

Maureen hesitated. "I don't know," she admitted. "But boys have all sorts of things they don't need." Her tinkling laughter was somehow stronger than our nervous ones. She curled her tongue around the edge of the cone, scooping up a dollop of purple that made my eyes water. We were waiting for a stop light to change. Maureen kept scooping the ice cream from around the cone's edge with her tongue; she didn't bite the edge as I would have done. Her tongue circled the cone. Pecola had finished hers; Maureen evidently liked her things to last. While I was thinking about her ice cream, she must have been thinking about her last remark, for she said to Pecola, "Did you ever see a naked man?"

Pecola blinked, then looked away. "No. Where would I see a naked man?"

"I don't know. I just asked."

"I wouldn't even look at him, even if I did see him. That's dirty. Who wants to see a naked man?" Pecola was agitated. "Nobody's father would be naked in front of his own daughter. Not unless he was dirty too."

"I didn't say 'father.' I just said 'a naked man.' "

"Well . . ."

"How come you said 'father'?" Maureen wanted to know.

"Who else would she see, dog tooth?" I was glad to have a chance to show anger. Not only because of the ice cream, but because we had seen our own father naked and didn't care to be reminded of it and feel the shame brought on by the absence of shame. He had been walking down the hall from the bathroom into his bedroom and passed the open door of our room. We had lain there wide-eyed. He stopped and looked in, trying to see in the dark room whether we were really asleep—or was it his imagination that opened eyes were looking at him? Apparently he convinced himself that we were sleeping. He moved away, confident that his little girls would not lie open-eyed like that, staring, staring. When he had moved on, the dark took only him away, not his nakedness. That stayed in the room with us. Friendly-like.

"I'm not talking to you," said Maureen. "Besides, I don't care if she sees her father naked. She can look at him all day if she wants to. Who cares?"

"You do," said Frieda. "That's all you talk about."

"It is not."

"It is so. Boys, babies, and somebody's naked daddy. You must be boy-crazy."

"You better be quiet."

"Who's gonna make me?" Frieda put her hand on her hip and jutted her face toward Maureen.

"You all ready made. Mammy made."

"You stop talking about my mama."

"Well, you stop talking about my daddy."

"Who said anything about your old daddy?"

"You did."

"Well, you started it."

"I wasn't even talking to you. I was talking to Pecola."

"Yeah. About seeing her naked daddy."

"So what if she did see him?"

Pecola shouted, "I never saw my daddy naked. Never."

"You did too," Maureen snapped. "Bay Boy said so."

"I did not."

"You did."

"I did not."

"Did. Your own daddy, too!"

Pecola tucked her head in—a funny, sad, helpless movement. A kind of hunching of the shoulders, pulling in of the neck, as though she wanted to cover her ears.

"You stop talking about her daddy," I said.

"What do I care about her old black daddy?" asked Maureen.

"Black? Who you calling black?"

"You!"

"You think you so cute!" I swung at her and missed, hitting Pecola in the face. Furious at my clumsiness, I threw my notebook at her, but it caught her in the small of her velvet back, for she had turned and was flying across the street against traffic.

Safe on the other side, she screamed at us, "I *am* cute! And you ugly! Black and ugly black e mos. I *am* cute!"

She ran down the street, the green knee socks making her legs look like wild dandelion stems that had somehow lost their heads. The weight of her remark stunned us, and it was a second or two before Frieda and I collected ourselves enough to shout, "Six-finger-dog-tooth-meringue-pie!" We chanted this most powerful of our arsenal of insults as long as we could see the green stems and rabbit fur.

Grown people frowned at the three girls on the curbside, two with their coats draped over their heads, the collars framing the eyebrows like nuns' habits, black garters showing where they bit the tops of brown stockings that barely covered the knees, angry faces knotted like dark cauliflowers.

Pecola stood a little apart from us, her eyes hinged in the direction in which Maureen had fled. She seemed to fold into herself, like a pleated wing. Her pain antagonized me. I wanted to open her up, crisp her edges, ram a stick down that hunched and curving spine, force her to stand erect and spit the misery out on the streets. But she held it in where it could lap up into her eyes.

Frieda snatched her coat from her head. "Come on, Claudia. 'Bye, Pecola."

We walked quickly at first, and then slower, pausing every now and then to fasten garters, tie shoelaces, scratch, or examine old scars. We were sinking under the wisdom, accuracy, and relevance of Maureen's last words. If she was cute—and if anything could be believed, she *was*—then we were not. And what did that mean? We were lesser. Nicer, brighter, but still lesser. Dolls we could destroy, but we could not destroy the honey voices of parents and aunts, the obedience in the eyes of our peers, the slippery light in the eyes of our teachers when they encountered the Maureen Peals of the world. What was the secret? What did we lack? Why was it important? And so what? Guileless and without vanity, we were still in love with ourselves then. We felt comfortable in our skins, enjoyed the news that our senses released to us, admired our dirt, cultivated our scars, and could not comprehend this unworthiness. Jealousy we understood and thought natural—a desire to have what somebody else had; but envy was a strange, new feeling for us. And all the time we knew that Maureen Peal was not the Enemy and not worthy of such intense hatred. The *Thing* to fear was the *Thing* that made *her* beautiful, and not us.

The house was quiet when we opened the door. The acrid smell of simmering turnips filled our cheeks with sour saliva.

"Mama!"

There was no answer, but a sound of feet. Mr. Henry shuffled part of the way down the stairs. One thick, hairless leg leaned out of his bathrobe.

"Hello there, Greta Garbo; hello, Ginger Rogers."

We gave him the giggle he was accustomed to. "Hello, Mr. Henry. Where's Mama?"

"She went to your grandmaw's. Left word for you to cut off the turnips and eat some graham crackers till she got back. They in the kitchen."

We sat in silence at the kitchen table, crumbling the crackers into anthills. In a little while Mr. Henry came back down the stairs. Now he had his trousers on under his robe.

"Say. Wouldn't you all like some cream?"

"Oh, yes, sir."

"Here. Here's a quarter. Gone over to Isaley's and get yourself some cream. You been good girls, ain't you?"

His light-green words restored color to the day. "Yes, sir. Thank you, Mr. Henry. Will you tell Mama for us if she comes?"

"Sure. But she ain't due back for a spell."

Coatless, we left the house and had gotten all the way to the corner when Frieda said, "I don't want to go to Isaley's."

"What?"

"I don't want ice cream. I want potato chips."

"They got potato chips at Isaley's."

"I know, but why go all that long way? Miss Bertha got potato chips."

"But I want ice cream."

"No you don't, Claudia."

"I do too."

"Well, you go on to Isaley's. I'm going to Miss Bertha's."

"But you got the quarter, and I don't want to go all the way up there by myself."

"Then let's go to Miss Bertha's. You like her candy, don't you?"

"It's always stale, and she always runs out of stuff."

"Today is Friday. She orders fresh on Friday."

"And then that crazy old Soaphead Church lives there."

"So what? We're together. We'll run if he does anything at us."

"He scares me."

"Well, I don't want to go up by Isaley's. Suppose Meringue Pie is hanging around. You want to run into her, Claudia?"

"Come on, Frieda. I'll get candy."

Miss Bertha had a small candy, snuff, and tobacco store. One brick room sitting in her front yard. You had to peep in the door, and if she wasn't there, you knocked on the door of her house in back. This day she was sitting behind the counter reading a Bible in a tube of sunlight.

Frieda bought potato chips, and we got three Powerhouse bars for ten cents, and had a dime left. We hurried back home to sit under the lilac bushes on the side of the house. We always did our Candy Dance there so Rosemary could see us and get jealous. The Candy Dance was a humming, skipping, foot-tapping, eating, smacking combination that overtook us when we had sweets. Creeping between the bushes and the side of the house, we heard voices and laughter. We looked into the living-room window, expecting to see Mama. Instead we saw Mr. Henry and two women. In a playful manner, the way grandmothers do with babies, he was sucking the fingers of one of the women, whose laughter filled a tiny place over his head. The other woman was buttoning her coat. We knew immediately who they were, and our flesh crawled. One was China, and the other was called the Maginot Line. The back of my neck itched. These were the fancy women of the maroon nail polish that Mama and Big Mama hated. And in our house.

China was not too terrible, at least not in our imaginations. She was thin, aging, absentminded, and unaggressive. But the Maginot Line. That was the one my mother said she "wouldn't let eat out of one of her plates." That was the one church women never allowed their eyes to rest on. That was the one who had killed people, set them on fire, poisoned them, cooked them in lye. Although I thought the Maginot Line's face, hidden under all that fat, was really sweet, I had heard too many black and red words about her, seen too many mouths go triangle at the mention of her name, to dwell on any redeeming features she might have.

Showing brown teeth, China seemed to be genuinely enjoying Mr. Henry. The sight of him licking her fingers brought to mind the girlie magazines in his room. A cold wind blew somewhere in me, lifting little leaves of terror and obscure longing. I thought I saw a mild lonesomeness cross the face of the Maginot Line. But it may have been my own image that I saw in the slow flaring of her nostrils, in her eyes that reminded me of waterfalls in movies about Hawaii.

The Maginot Line yawned and said, "Come on, China. We can't hang in here all day. Them people be home soon." She moved toward the door.

Frieda and I dropped down to the ground, looking wildly into each other's eyes. When the women were some distance away, we went inside. Mr. Henry was in the kitchen opening a bottle of pop.

"Back already?"

"Yes, sir."

"Cream all gone?" His little teeth looked so kindly and helpless. Was that really our Mr. Henry with China's fingers?

"We got candy instead."

"You did huh? Ole sugar-tooth Greta Garbo."

He wiped the bottle sweat and turned it up to his lips—a gesture that made me uncomfortable.

"Who were those women, Mr. Henry?"

He choked on the pop and looked at Frieda. "What you say?"

"Those women," she repeated, "who just left. Who were they?"

"Oh." He laughed the grown-up getting-ready-to-lie laugh. A heh-heh we knew well.

"Those were some members of my Bible class. We read the scriptures together, and so they came today to read with me."

"Oh," said Frieda. I was looking at his house slippers to keep from seeing those kindly teeth frame a lie. He walked toward the stairs and then turned back to us.

"Bed' not mention it to your mother. She don't take to

so much Bible study and don't like me having visitors, even if they good Christians."

"No, sir, Mr. Henry. We won't."

He rapidly mounted the stairs.

"Should we?" I asked. "Tell Mama?"

Frieda sighed. She had not even opened her Powerhouse bar or her potato chips, and now she traced the letters on the candy wrappers with her fingers. Suddenly she lifted her head and began to look all around the kitchen.

"No. I guess not. No plates are out."

"Plates? What you talking about now?"

"No plates are out. The Maginot Line didn't eat out of one of Mama's plates. Besides, Mama would just fuss all day if we told her."

We sat down and looked at the graham-cracker anthills we had made.

"We better cut off the turnips. They'll burn, and Mama will whip us," she said.

"I know."

"But if we let them burn, we won't have to eat them."

"Heyyy, what a lovely idea," I thought.

"Which you want? A whipping and no turnips, or turnips and no whippings?"

"I don't know. Maybe we could burn them just a little so Mama and Daddy can eat them, but we can say we can't."

"O.K."

I made a volcano out of my anthill.

"Frieda?"

"What?"

"What did Woodrow do that you was gonna tell?"

"Wet the bed. Mrs. Cain told Mama he won't quit."

"Old nasty."

The sky was getting dark; I looked out of the window and saw snow falling. I poked my finger down into the mouth of my volcano, and it toppled, dispersing the golden grains into little swirls. The turnip pot crackled.

SEETHECATITGOESMEOWMEOWCOM EANDPLAYCOMEPLAYWITHJANETHE KITTENWILLNOTPLAYPLAYPLAYPLA

They come from Mobile. Aiken. From Newport News. From Marietta. From Meridian. And the sound of these places in their mouths make you think of love. When you ask them where they are from, they tilt their heads and say "Mobile" and you think you've been kissed. They say "Aiken" and you see a white butterfly glance off a fence with a torn wing. They say "Nagadoches" and you want to say "Yes, I will." You don't know what these towns are like, but you love what happens to the air when they open their lips and let the names ease out.

Meridian. The sound of it opens the windows of a room like the first four notes of a hymn. Few people can say the names of their home towns with such sly affection. Perhaps because they don't have home towns, just places where they were born. But these girls soak up the juice of their home towns, and it never leaves them. They are thin brown girls who have looked long at hollyhocks in the backyards of Meridian, Mobile, Aiken, and Baton Rouge. And like hollyhocks they are narrow, tall, and still. Their roots are deep, their stalks are firm, and only the top blossom nods in the wind. They have the eyes of people who can tell what time it is by the color of the sky. Such girls live in quiet black neighborhoods where everybody is gainfully employed. Where there are porch swings hanging from chains. Where the grass is cut with a scythe, where rooster combs and sunflowers grow in the yards, and pots of bleeding heart, ivy, and mother-in-law tongue line the steps and windowsills. Such girls have bought watermelon and snapbeans from the fruit man's wagon. They have put in the window the cardboard sign that has a pound measure printed on each of three edges—10 lbs., 25 lbs., 50 lbs.—and NO ICE on the fourth. These particular brown girls from Mobile and Aiken are not like some of their sisters. They are not fretful, nervous, or shrill; they do not have lovely black necks that stretch as though against an invisible collar; their eyes do not bite. These sugar-brown Mobile girls move through the streets without a stir. They are as sweet and plain as buttercake. Slim ankles; long, narrow feet. They wash themselves with orange-colored Lifebuoy soap, dust themselves with Cashmere Bouquet talc, clean their teeth with salt on a piece of rag, soften their skin with Jergens Lotion. They smell like wood, newspapers, and vanilla. They straighten their hair with Dixie Peach, and part it on the side. At night they curl it in paper from brown bags, tie a print scarf around their heads, and sleep with hands folded across their stomachs. They do not drink, smoke, or swear, and they still call sex "nookey." They sing second soprano in the choir, and although their voices are clear and steady, they are never picked to solo. They are in the second row, white blouses starched, blue skirts almost purple from ironing.

They go to land-grant colleges, normal schools, and learn how to do the white man's work with refinement: home economics to prepare his food; teacher education to instruct black children in obedience; music to soothe the weary master and entertain his blunted soul. Here they learn the rest of the lesson begun in those soft houses with porch swings and pots of bleeding heart: how to behave. The careful development of thrift, patience, high morals, and good manners. In short, how to get rid of the funkiness. The dreadful funkiness of passion, the funkiness of nature, the funkiness of the wide range of human emotions.

Wherever it erupts, this Funk, they wipe it away; where it crusts, they dissolve it; wherever it drips, flowers, or clings, they find it and fight it until it dies. They fight this battle all the way to the grave. The laugh that is a little too loud; the enunciation a little too round; the gesture a little too generous. They hold their behind in for fear of a sway too free; when they wear lipstick, they never cover the entire mouth for fear of lips too thick, and they worry, worry, worry about the edges of their hair.

They never seem to have boyfriends, but they always marry. Certain men watch them, without seeming to, and know that if such a girl is in his house, he will sleep on sheets boiled white, hung out to dry on juniper bushes, and pressed flat with a heavy iron. There will be pretty paper flowers decorating the picture of his mother, a large Bible in the front room. They feel secure. They know their work clothes will be mended, washed, and ironed on Monday, that their Sunday shirts will billow on hangers from the door jamb, stiffly starched and white. They look at her hands and know what she will do with biscuit dough; they smell the coffee and the fried ham; see the white, smoky grits with a dollop of butter on top. Her hips assure them that she will bear children easily and painlessly. And they are right.

What they do not know is that this plain brown girl will build her nest stick by stick, make it her own inviolable world, and stand guard over its every plant, weed, and doily, even against him. In silence will she return the lamp to where she put it in the first place; remove the dishes from the table as soon as the last bite is taken; wipe the doorknob after a greasy hand has touched it. A sidelong look will be enough to tell him to smoke on the back porch. Children will sense instantly that they cannot come into her yard to retrieve a ball. But the men do not know these things. Nor do they know that she will give him her body sparingly and partially. He must enter her surreptitiously, lifting the hem of her nightgown only to her navel. He must rest his weight on his elbows when they make love, ostensibly to avoid hurting her breasts but actually to keep her from having to touch or feel too much of him.

While he moves inside her, she will wonder why they didn't put the necessary but private parts of the body in some more convenient place—like the armpit, for example, or the palm of the hand. Someplace one could get to easily, and quickly, without undressing. She stiffens when she feels one of her paper curlers coming undone from the activity of love; imprints in her mind which one it is that is coming loose so she can quickly secure it once he is through. She hopes he will not sweat—the damp may get into her hair; and that she will remain dry between her legs—she hates the glucking sound they make when she is moist. When she senses some spasm about to grip him, she will make rapid movements with her hips, press her fingernails into his back, suck in her breath, and pretend she is having an orgasm. She might wonder again, for the six hundredth time, what it would be like to have *that* feeling while her husband's penis is inside her. The closest thing to it was the time she was walking down the street and her napkin slipped free of her sanitary belt. It moved gently between her legs as she walked. Gently, ever so gently. And then a slight and distinctly delicious sensation collected in her crotch. As the delight grew, she had to stop in the street, hold her thighs together to contain it. That must be what it is like, she thinks, but it never happens while he is inside her. When he withdraws, she pulls her nightgown down, slips out of the bed and into the bathroom with relief.

Occasionally some living thing will engage her affections. A cat, perhaps, who will love her order, precision, and constancy; who will be as clean and quiet as she is. The cat will settle quietly on the windowsill and caress her with his eyes. She can hold him in her arms, letting his back paws struggle for footing on her breast and his forepaws cling to her shoulder. She can rub the smooth fur and feel the unresisting flesh underneath. At her gentlest touch he will preen, stretch, and open his mouth. And she will accept the strangely pleasant sensation that comes when he writhes beneath her hand and flattens his eyes with a surfeit of sensual delight. When she stands cooking at the table, he will circle about her shanks, and the trill of his fur spirals up her legs to her thighs, to make her fingers tremble a little in the pie dough.

Or, as she sits reading the "Uplifting Thoughts" in *The Liberty Magazine,* the cat will jump into her lap. She will fondle that soft hill of hair and let the warmth of the animal's body seep over and into the deeply private areas of her lap. Sometimes the magazine drops, and she opens her legs just a little, and the two of them will be still together, perhaps shifting a little together, sleeping a little together, until four o'clock, when the intruder comes home from work vaguely anxious about what's for dinner.

The cat will always know that he is first in her affections. Even after she bears a child. For she does bear a child—easily, and painlessly. But only one. A son. Named Junior.

One such girl from Mobile, or Meridian, or Aiken who did not sweat in her armpits nor between her thighs, who smelled of wood and vanilla, who had made soufflés in the Home Economics Department, moved with her husband, Louis, to Lorain, Ohio. Her name was Geraldine. There she built her nest, ironed shirts, potted bleeding hearts, played with her cat, and birthed Louis Junior.

Geraldine did not allow her baby, Junior, to cry. As long as his needs were physical, she could meet them—comfort and satiety. He was always brushed, bathed, oiled, and shod. Geraldine did not talk to him, coo to him, or indulge him in kissing bouts, but she saw that every other desire was fulfilled. It was not long before the child discovered the difference in his mother's behavior to himself and the cat. As he grew older, he learned how to direct his hatred of his mother to the cat, and spent some happy moments watching it suffer. The cat survived, because Geraldine was seldom away from home, and could effectively soothe the animal when Junior abused him.

Geraldine, Louis, Junior, and the cat lived next to the playground of Washington Irving School. Junior considered the playground his own, and the schoolchildren coveted his freedom to sleep late, go home for lunch, and dominate the playground after school. He hated to see the swings, slides, monkey bars, and seesaws empty and tried to get kids to stick around as long as possible. White kids; his mother did not like him to play with niggers. She had explained to him the difference between colored people and niggers. They were easily identifiable. Colored people were neat and quiet; niggers were dirty and loud. He belonged to the former group: he wore white shirts and blue trousers; his hair was cut as close to his scalp as possible to avoid any suggestion of wool, the part was etched into his hair by the barber. In winter his mother put Jergens Lotion on his face to keep the skin from becoming ashen. Even though he was light-skinned, it was possible to ash. The line between colored and nigger was not always clear; subtle and telltale signs threatened to erode it, and the watch had to be constant.

Junior used to long to play with the black boys. More than anything in the world he wanted to play King of the Mountain and have them push him down the mound of dirt and roll over him. He wanted to feel their hardness pressing on him, smell their wild blackness, and say "Fuck you" with that lovely casualness. He wanted to sit with them on curbstones and compare the sharpness of jackknives, the distance and arcs of spitting. In the toilet he wanted to share with them the laurels of being able to pee far and long. Bay Boy and P. L. had at one time been his idols. Gradually he came to agree with his mother that neither Bay Boy nor P. L. was good enough for him. He played only with Ralph Nisensky, who was two years younger, wore glasses, and didn't want to *do* anything. More and more Junior enjoyed bullying girls. It was easy making them scream and run. How he laughed when they fell down and their bloomers showed. When they got up, their faces red and crinkled, it made him feel good. The nigger girls he did not pick on very much. They usually traveled in packs, and once when he threw a stone at some of them, they chased, caught, and beat him witless. He lied to his mother, saying Bay Boy did it. His mother was very upset. His father just kept on reading the Lorain *Journal.*

When the mood struck him, he would call a child passing by to come play on the swings or the seesaw. If the child wouldn't, or did and left too soon, Junior threw gravel at him. He became a very good shot.

Alternately bored and frightened at home, the playground was his joy. On a day when he had been especially idle, he saw a very black girl taking a shortcut through the playground. She kept her head down as she walked. He had seen her many times before, standing alone, always alone, at recess. Nobody ever played with her. Probably, he thought, because she was ugly.

Now Junior called to her. "Hey! What are you doing walking through my yard?"

The girl stopped.

"Nobody can come through this yard 'less I say so."

"This ain't your yard. It's the school's."

"But I'm in charge of it."

The girl started to walk away.

"Wait." Junior walked toward her. "You can play in it if you want to. What's your name?"

"Pecola. I don't want to play."

"Come on. I'm not going to bother you."

"I got to go home."

"Say, you want to see something? I got something to show you."

"No. What is it?"

"Come on in my house. See, I live right there. Come on. I'll show you."

"Show me what?"

"Some kittens. We got some kittens. You can have one if you want."

"Real kittens?"

"Yeah. Come on."

He pulled gently at her dress. Pecola began to move toward his house. When he knew she had agreed, Junior ran ahead excitedly, stopping only to yell back at her to come on. He held the door open for her, smiling his encouragement. Pecola climbed the porch stairs and hesitated there, afraid to follow him. The house looked dark. Junior said, "There's nobody here. My ma's gone out, and my father's at work. Don't you want to see the kittens?"

Junior turned on the lights. Pecola stepped inside the door.

How beautiful, she thought. What a beautiful house. There was a big red-and-gold Bible on the dining-room table. Little lace doilies were everywhere—on arms and backs of chairs, in the center of a large dining table, on little tables. Potted plants were on all the windowsills. A color picture of Jesus Christ hung on a wall with the prettiest paper flowers fastened on the frame. She wanted to see everything slowly, slowly. But Junior kept saying, "Hey, you. Come on. Come on." He pulled her into another room, even more beautiful than the first. More doilies, a big lamp with green-and-gold base and white shade. There was even a rug on the floor, with enormous dark-red flowers. She was deep in admiration of the flowers when Junior said, "Here!" Pecola turned. "Here is your kitten!" he screeched. And he threw a big black cat right in her face. She sucked in her breath in fear and surprise and felt fur in her mouth. The cat clawed her face and chest in an effort to right itself, then leaped nimbly to the floor.

Junior was laughing and running around the room clutching his stomach delightedly. Pecola touched the scratched place on her face and felt tears coming. When she started toward the doorway, Junior leaped in front of her.

"You can't get out. You're my prisoner," he said. His eyes were merry but hard.

"You let me go."

"No!" He pushed her down, ran out the door that separated the rooms, and held it shut with his hands. Pecola's banging on the door increased his gasping, high-pitched laughter.

The tears came fast, and she held her face in her hands. When something soft and furry moved around her ankles, she jumped, and saw it was the cat. He wound himself in and about her legs. Momentarily distracted from her fear, she squatted down to touch him, her hands wet from the tears. The cat rubbed up against her knee. He was black all over, deep silky black, and his eyes, pointing down toward his nose, were bluish green. The light made them shine like blue ice. Pecola rubbed the cat's head; he whined, his tongue flicking with pleasure. The blue eyes in the black face held her.

Junior, curious at not hearing her sobs, opened the door, and saw her squatting down rubbing the cat's back. He saw the cat stretching its head and flattening its eyes. He had seen that expression many times as the animal responded to his mother's touch.

"Gimme my cat!" His voice broke. With a movement both awkward and sure he snatched the cat by one of its hind legs and began to swing it around his head in a circle.

"Stop that!" Pecola was screaming. The cat's free paws were stiffened, ready to grab anything to restore balance, its mouth wide, its eyes blue streaks of horror.

Still screaming, Pecola reached for Junior's hand. She heard her dress rip under her arm. Junior tried to push her away, but she grabbed the arm which was swinging the cat. They both fell, and in falling, Junior let go the cat, which, having been released in mid-motion, was thrown full force against the window. It slithered down and fell on the radiator behind the sofa. Except for a few shudders, it was still. There was only the slightest smell of singed fur.

Geraldine opened the door.

"What is this?" Her voice was mild, as though asking a perfectly reasonable question. "Who is this girl?"

"She killed our cat," said Junior. "Look." He pointed to the radiator, where the cat lay, its blue eyes closed, leaving only an empty, black, and helpless face.

Geraldine went to the radiator and picked up the cat. He was limp in her arms, but she rubbed her face in his fur. She looked at Pecola. Saw the dirty torn dress, the plaits sticking out on her head, hair matted where the plaits had come undone, the muddy shoes with the wad of gum peeping out from between the cheap soles, the soiled socks, one of which had been walked down into the heel of the shoe. She saw the safety pin holding the hem of the dress up. Up over the hump of the cat's back she looked at her. She had seen this little girl all of her life. Hanging out of windows over saloons in Mobile, crawling over the porches of shotgun houses on the edge of town, sitting in bus stations holding paper bags and crying to mothers who kept saying "Shet up!" Hair uncombed, dresses falling apart, shoes untied and caked with dirt. They had stared at her with great uncomprehending eyes. Eyes that questioned nothing and asked everything. Unblinking and unabashed, they stared up at her. The end of the world lay in their eyes, and the beginning, and all the waste in between.

They were everywhere. They slept six in a bed, all their pee mixing together in the night as they wet their beds each in his own candy-and-potato-chip dream. In the long, hot days, they idled away, picking plaster from the walls and digging into the earth with sticks. They sat in little rows on street curbs, crowded into pews at church, taking space from the nice, neat, colored children; they clowned on the playgrounds, broke things in dime stores, ran in front of you on the street, made ice slides on the sloped sidewalks in winter. The girls grew up knowing nothing of girdles, and the boys announced their manhood by turning the bills of their caps backward. Grass wouldn't grow where they lived. Flowers died. Shades fell down. Tin cans and tires blossomed where they lived. They lived on cold black-eyed peas and orange pop. Like flies they hovered; like flies they settled. And this one had settled in her house. Up over the hump of the cat's back she looked.

"Get out," she said, her voice quiet. "You nasty little black bitch. Get out of my house."

The cat shuddered and flicked his tail.

Pecola backed out of the room, staring at the pretty milk-brown lady in the pretty gold-and-green house who was talking to her through the cat's fur. The pretty lady's words made the cat fur move; the breath of each word parted the fur. Pecola turned to find the front door and saw Jesus looking down at her with sad and unsurprised eyes, his long brown hair parted in the middle, the gay paper flowers twisted around his face.

Outside, the March wind blew into the rip in her dress. She held her head down against the cold. But she could not hold it low enough to avoid seeing the snowflakes falling and dying on the pavement.

Spring

The first twigs are thin, green, and supple. They bend into a complete circle, but will not break. Their delicate, showy hopefulness shooting from forsythia and lilac bushes meant only a change in whipping style. They beat us differently in the spring. Instead of the dull pain of a winter strap, there were these new green switches that lost their sting long after the whipping was over. There was a nervous meanness in these long twigs that made us long for the steady stroke of a strap or the firm but honest slap of a hairbrush. Even now spring for me is shot through with the remembered ache of switchings, and forsythia holds no cheer.

Sunk in the grass of an empty lot on a spring Saturday, I split the stems of milkweed and thought about ants and peach pits and death and where the world went when I closed my eyes. I must have lain long in the grass, for the shadow that was in front of me when I left the house had disappeared when I went back. I entered the house, as the house was bursting with an uneasy quiet. Then I heard my mother singing something about trains and Arkansas. She came in the back door with some folded yellow curtains which she piled on the kitchen table. I sat down on the floor to listen to the song's story, and noticed how strangely she was behaving. She still had her hat on, and her shoes were dusty, as though she had been walking in deep dirt. She put on some water to boil and then swept the porch; then she hauled out the curtain stretcher, but instead of putting the damp curtains on it, she swept the porch again. All the time singing about trains and Arkansas.

When she finished, I went to look for Frieda. I found her upstairs lying on our bed, crying the tired, whimpering cry that follows the first wailings—mostly gasps and shudderings. I lay on the bed and looked at the tiny bunches of wild roses sprinkled over her dress. Many washings had faded their color and dimmed their outlines.

"What happened, Frieda?"

She lifted a swollen face from the crook of her arm. Shuddering still, she sat up, letting her thin legs dangle over the bedside. I knelt on the bed and picked up the hem of my dress to wipe her running nose. She never liked wiping noses on clothes, but this time she let me. It was the way Mama did with her apron.

"Did you get a whipping?"

She shook her head no.

"Then why you crying?"

"Because."

"Because what?"

"Mr. Henry."

"What'd he do?"

"Daddy beat him up."

"What for? The Maginot Line? Did he find out about the Maginot Line?"

"No."

"Well, what, then? Come on, Frieda. How come I can't know?"

"He . . . *picked* at me."

"Picked at you? You mean like Soaphead Church?"

"Sort of."

"He showed his privates at you?"

"Noooo. He touched me."

"Where?"

"Here and here." She pointed to the tiny breasts that, like two fallen acorns, scattered a few faded rose leaves on her dress.

"Really? How did it feel?"

"Oh, Claudia." She sounded put-out. I wasn't asking the right questions.

"It didn't feel like anything."

"But wasn't it supposed to? Feel good, I mean?" Frieda sucked her teeth. "What'd he do? Just walk up and pinch them?"

She sighed. "First he said how pretty I was. Then he grabbed my arm and touched me."

"Where was Mama and Daddy?"

"Over at the garden weeding."

"What'd you say when he did it?"

"Nothing. I just ran out the kitchen and went to the garden."

"Mama said we was never to cross the tracks by ourselves."

"Well, what would you do? Set there and let him pinch you?"

I looked at my chest. "I don't have nothing to pinch. I'm never going to have nothing."

"Oh, Claudia, you're jealous of everything. You *want* him to?"

"No, I just get tired of having everything last."

"You do not. What about scarlet fever? You had that first."

"Yes, but it didn't last. Anyway, what happened at the garden?"

"I told Mama, and she told Daddy, and we all come home, and he was gone, so we waited for him, and when Daddy saw him come up on the porch, he threw our old tricycle at his head and knocked him off the porch."

"Did he die?"

"Naw. He got up and started singing 'Nearer My God to Thee.' Then Mama hit him with a broom and told him to keep the Lord's name out of his mouth, but he wouldn't stop, and Daddy was cussing, and everybody was screaming."

"Oh, shoot, I always miss stuff."

"And Mr. Buford came running out with his gun, and Mama told him to go somewhere and sit down, and Daddy said no, give him the gun, and Mr. Buford did, and Mama screamed, and Mr. Henry shut up and started running, and Daddy shot at him and Mr. Henry jumped out of his shoes and kept on running in his socks. Then Rosemary came out and said that Daddy was going to jail, and I hit her."

"Real hard?"

"Real hard."

"Is that when Mama whipped you?"

"She didn't whip me, I told you."

"Then why you crying?"

"Miss Dunion came in after everybody was quiet, and Mama and Daddy was fussing about who let Mr. Henry in anyway, and she said that Mama should take me to the doctor, because I might be ruined, and Mama started screaming all over again."

"At you?"

"No. At Miss Dunion."

"But why were you crying?"

"I don't want to be *ruined!*"

"What's ruined?"

"You know. Like the Maginot Line. She's ruined. Mama said so." The tears came back.

An image of Frieda, big and fat, came to mind. Her thin legs swollen, her face surrounded by layers of rouged skin. I too begin to feel tears.

"But, Frieda, you could exercise and not eat."

She shrugged.

"Besides, what about China and Poland? They're ruined too, aren't they? And they ain't fat."

"That's because they drink whiskey. Mama says whiskey ate them up."

"You could drink whiskey."

"Where would I get whiskey?"

We thought about this. Nobody would sell it to us; we had no money, anyway. There was never any in our house. Who would have some?

"Pecola," I said. "Her father's always drunk. She can get us some."

"You think so?"

"Sure. Cholly's always drunk. Let's go ask her. We don't have to tell her what for."

"Now?"

"Sure, now."

"What'll we tell Mama?"

"Nothing. Let's just go out the back. One at a time. So she won't notice."

"O.K. You go first, Claudia."

We opened the fence gate at the bottom of the backyard and ran down the alley.

Pecola lived on the other side of Broadway. We had never been in her house, but we knew where it was. A two-story gray building that had been a store downstairs and had an apartment upstairs.

Nobody answered our knock on the front door, so we walked around to the side door. As we approached, we heard radio music and looked to see where it came from. Above us was the second-story porch, lined with slanting, rotting rails, and sitting on the porch was the Maginot Line herself. We stared up and automatically reached for the other's hand. A mountain of flesh, she lay rather than sat in a rocking chair. She had no shoes on, and each foot was poked between a railing: tiny baby toes at the tip of puffy feet; swollen ankles smoothed and tightened the skin; massive legs like tree stumps parted wide at the knees, over which spread two roads of soft flabby inner thigh that kissed each other deep in the shade of her dress and closed. A dark-brown root-beer bottle, like a burned limb, grew out of her dimpled hand. She looked at us down through the porch railings and emitted a low, long belch. Her eyes were as clean as rain, and again I remembered the waterfall.

Neither of us could speak. Both of us imagined we were seeing what was to become of Frieda. The Maginot Line smiled at us.

"You all looking for somebody?"

I had to pull my tongue from the roof of my mouth to say, "Pecola—she live here?"

"Uh-huh, but she ain't here now. She gone to her mama's work place to git the wash."

"Yes, ma'am. She coming back?"

"Uh-huh. She got to hang up the clothes before the sun goes down."

"Oh."

"You can wait for her. Wanna come up here and wait?"

We exchanged glances. I looked back up at the broad cinnamon roads that met in the shadow of her dress.

Frieda said, "No, ma'am."

"Well," the Maginot Line seemed interested in our problem. "You can go to her mama's work place, but it's way over by the lake."

"Where by the lake?"

"That big white house with the wheelbarrow full of flowers."

It was a house that we knew, having admired the large white wheelbarrow tilted down on spoked wheels and planted with seasonal flowers.

"Ain't that too far for you all to go walking?"

Frieda scratched her knee.

"Why don't you wait for her? You can come up here. Want some pop?" Those rain-soaked eyes lit up, and her smile was full, not like the pinched and holding-back smile of other grown-ups.

I moved to go up the stairs, but Frieda said, "No, ma'am, we ain't allowed."

I was amazed at her courage, and frightened of her sassiness. The smile of the Maginot Line slipped. "Ain't 'llowed?"

"No'm."

"Ain't 'llowed to what?"

"Go in your house."

"Is that right?" The waterfalls were still. "How come?"

"My mama said so. My mama said you ruined."

The waterfalls began to run again. She put the root-beer bottle to her lips and drank it empty. With a graceful movement of the wrist, a gesture so quick and small we never really saw it, only remembered it afterward, she tossed the bottle over the rail at us. It split at our feet, and shards of brown glass dappled our legs before we could jump back. The Maginot Line put a fat hand on one of the folds of her stomach and laughed. At first just a deep humming with her mouth closed, then a larger, warmer sound. Laughter at once beautiful and frightening. She let her head tilt sideways, closed her eyes, and shook her massive trunk, letting the laughter fall like a wash of red leaves all around us. Scraps and curls of the laughter followed us as we ran. Our breath gave out at the same time our legs did. After we rested against a tree, our heads on crossed forearms, I said, "Let's go home."

Frieda was still angry—fighting, she believed, for her life. "No, we got to get it now."

"We can't go all the way to the lake."

"Yes we can. Come on."

"Mama gone get us."

"No she ain't. Besides, she can't do nothing but whip us."

That was true. She wouldn't kill us, or laugh a terrible laugh at us, or throw a bottle at us.

We walked down tree-lined streets of soft gray houses leaning like tired ladies. . . . The streets changed; houses looked more sturdy, their paint was newer, porch posts straighter, yards deeper. Then came brick houses set well back from the street, fronted by yards edged in shrubbery clipped into smooth cones and balls of velvet green.

The lakefront houses were the loveliest. Garden furniture, ornaments, windows like shiny eyeglasses, and no sign of life. The backyards of these houses fell away in green slopes down to a strip of sand, and then the blue Lake Erie, lapping all the way to Canada. The orange-patched sky of the steel-mill section never reached this part of town. This sky was always blue.

We reached Lake Shore Park, a city park laid out with rosebuds, fountains, bowling greens, picnic tables. It was empty now, but sweetly expectant of clean, white, well-behaved children and parents who would play there above the lake in summer before half-running, half-stumbling down the slope to the welcoming water. Black people were not allowed in the park, and so it filled our dreams.

Right before the entrance to the park was the large white house with the wheelbarrow full of flowers. Short crocus blades sheathed the purple-and-white hearts that so wished to be first they endured the chill and rain of early spring. The walkway was flagged in calculated disorder, hiding the cunning symmetry. Only fear of discovery and the knowledge that we did not belong kept us from loitering. We circled the proud house and went to the back.

There on the tiny railed stoop sat Pecola in a light red sweater and blue cotton dress. A little wagon was parked near her. She seemed glad to see us.

"Hi."

"Hi."

"What you all doing here?" She was smiling, and since it was a rare thing to see on her, I was surprised at the pleasure it gave me.

"We're looking for you."

"Who told you I was here?"

"The Maginot Line."

"Who is that?"

"That big fat lady. She lives over you."

"Oh, you mean Miss Marie. Her name is Miss Marie."

"Well, everybody calls her Miss Maginot Line. Ain't you scared?"

"Scared of what?"

"The Maginot Line."

Pecola looked genuinely puzzled. "What for?"

"Your mama let you go in her house? And eat out of her plates?"

"She don't know I go. Miss Marie is nice. They all nice."

"Oh, yeah," I said, "she tried to kill us."

"Who? Miss Marie? She don't bother nobody."

"Then how come your mama don't let you go in her house if she so nice?"

"I don't know. She say she's bad, but they ain't bad. They give me stuff all the time."

"What stuff?"

"Oh, lots of stuff, pretty dresses, and shoes. I got more shoes than I ever wear. And jewelry and candy and money. They take me to the movies, and once we went to the carnival. China gone take me to Cleveland to see the square, and Poland gone take me to Chicago to see the Loop. We going everywhere together."

"You lying. You don't have no pretty dresses."

"I do, too."

"Oh, come on, Pecola, what you telling us all that junk for?" Frieda asked.

"It ain't junk." Pecola stood up ready to defend her words, when the door opened.

Mrs. Breedlove stuck her head out the door and said, "What's going on out here? Pecola, who are these children?"

"That's Frieda and Claudia, Mrs. Breedlove."

"Whose girls are you?" She came all the way out on the stoop. She looked nicer than I had ever seen her, in her white uniform and her hair in a small pompadour.

"Mrs. MacTeer's girls, ma'am."

"Oh, yes. Live over on Twenty-first Street?"

"Yes, ma'am."

"What are you doing 'way over here?"

"Just walking. We came to see Pecola."

"Well, you better get on back. You can walk with Pecola. Come on in while I get the wash."

We stepped into the kitchen, a large spacious room. Mrs. Breedlove's skin glowed like taffeta in the reflection of white porcelain, white woodwork, polished cabinets, and brilliant copperware. Odors of meat, vegetables, and something freshly baked mixed with a scent of Fels Naphtha.

"I'm gone get the wash. You all stand stock still right there and don't mess up nothing." She disappeared behind a white swinging door, and we could hear the uneven flap of her footsteps as she descended into the basement.

Another door opened, and in walked a little girl, smaller and younger than all of us. She wore a pink sunback dress and pink fluffy bedroom slippers with two bunny ears pointed up from the tips. Her hair was corn yellow and bound in a thick ribbon. When she saw us, fear danced across her face for a second. She looked anxiously around the kitchen.

"Where's Polly?" she asked.

The familiar violence rose in me. Her calling Mrs. Breedlove Polly, when even Pecola called her mother Mrs. Breedlove, seemed reason enough to scratch her.

"She's downstairs," I said.

"Polly!" she called.

"Look," Frieda whispered, "look at that." On the counter near the stove in a silvery pan was a deep-dish berry cobbler. The purple juice bursting here and there through crust. We moved closer.

"It's still hot," Frieda said.

Pecola stretched her hand to touch the pan, lightly, to see if it was hot.

"Polly, come here," the little girl called again.

It may have been nervousness, awkwardness, but the pan tilted under Pecola's fingers and fell to the floor, splattering blackish blueberries everywhere. Most of the juice splashed on Pecola's legs, and the burn must have been painful, for she cried out and began hopping about just as Mrs. Breedlove entered with a tightly packed laundry bag. In one gallop she was on Pecola, and with the back of her hand knocked her to the floor. Pecola slid in the pie juice, one leg folding under her. Mrs. Breedlove yanked her up by the arm, slapped her again, and in a voice thin with anger, abused Pecola directly and Frieda and me by implication.

"Crazy fool . . . my floor, mess . . . look what you . . . work . . . get on out . . . now that . . . crazy . . . my floor, my floor . . . my floor." Her words were hotter and darker than the smoking berries, and we backed away in dread.

The little girl in pink started to cry. Mrs. Breedlove turned to her. "Hush, baby, hush. Come here. Oh, Lord, look at your dress. Don't cry no more. Polly will change it." She went to the sink and turned tap water on a fresh towel. Over her shoulder she spit out words to us like rotten pieces of apple. "Pick up that wash and get on out of here, so I can get this mess cleaned up."

Pecola picked up the laundry bag, heavy with wet clothes, and we stepped hurriedly out the door. As Pecola put the laundry bag in the wagon, we could hear Mrs. Breedlove hushing and soothing the tears of the little pink-and-yellow girl.

"Who were they, Polly?"

"Don't worry none, baby."

"You gonna make another pie?"

" 'Course I will."

"Who were they, Polly?"

"Hush. Don't worry none," she whispered, and the honey in her words complemented the sundown spilling on the lake.

SEEMOTHERMOTHERISVERYNICEMO THERWILLYOUPLAYWITHJANEMOTH ERLAUGHSLAUGHMOTHERLAUGHLA

The easiest thing to do would be to build a case out of her foot. That is what she herself did. But to find out the truth about how dreams die, one should never take the word of the dreamer. The end of her lovely beginning was probably the cavity in one of her front teeth. She preferred, however, to think always of her foot. Although she was the ninth of eleven children and lived on a ridge of red Alabama clay seven miles from the nearest road, the complete indifference with which a rusty nail was met when it punched clear through her foot during her second year of life saved Pauline Williams from total anonymity. The wound left her with a crooked, archless foot that flopped when she walked—not a limp that would have eventually twisted her spine, but a way of lifting the bad foot as though she were extracting it from little whirlpools that threatened to pull it under. Slight as it was, this deformity explained for her many things that would have been otherwise incomprehensible: why she alone of all the children had no nickname; why there were no funny jokes and anecdotes about funny things she had done; why no one ever remarked on her food preferences—no saving of the wing or neck for her—no cooking of the peas in a separate pot without rice because she did not like rice; why nobody teased her; why she never felt at home anywhere, or that she belonged anyplace. Her general feeling of separateness and unworthiness she blamed on her foot. Restricted, as a child, to this cocoon of her family's spinning, she cultivated quiet and private pleasures. She liked, most of all, to arrange things. To line things up in rows—jars on shelves at canning, peach pits on the step, sticks, stones, leaves—and the members of her family let these arrangements be. When by some accident somebody scattered her rows, they always stopped to retrieve them for her, and she was never angry, for it gave her a chance to rearrange them again. Whatever portable plurality she found, she organized into neat lines, according to their size, shape, or gradations of color. Just as she would never align a pine needle with the leaf of a cottonwood tree, she would never put the jars of tomatoes next to the green beans. During all of her four years of going to school, she was enchanted by numbers and depressed by words. She missed—without knowing what she missed—paints and crayons.

Near the beginning of World War I, the Williamses discovered, from returning neighbors and kin, the possibility of living better in another place. In shifts, lots, batches, mixed in with other families, they migrated, in six months and four journeys, to Kentucky, where there were mines and millwork.

"When all us left from down home and was waiting down by the depot for the truck, it was nighttime. June bugs was shooting everywhere. They lighted up a tree leaf, and I seen a streak of green every now and again. That was the last time I seen real june bugs. These things up here ain't june bugs. They's something else. Folks here call them fireflies. Down home they was different. But I recollect that streak of green. I recollect it well."

In Kentucky they lived in a real town, ten to fifteen houses on a single street, with water piped right into the kitchen. Ada and Fowler Williams found a five-room frame house for their family. The yard was bounded by a once-white fence against which Pauline's mother planted flowers and within which they kept a few chickens. Some of her brothers joined the Army, one sister died, and two got married, increasing the living space and giving the entire Kentucky venture a feel of luxury. The relocation was especially comfortable to Pauline, who was old enough to leave school. Mrs. Williams got a job cleaning and cooking for a white minister on the other side of town, and Pauline, now the oldest girl at home, took over the care of the house. She kept the fence in repair, pulling the pointed stakes erect, securing them with bits of wire, collected eggs, swept, cooked, washed, and minded the two younger children—a pair of twins called Chicken and Pie, who were still in school. She was not only good at housekeeping, she enjoyed it. After her parents left for work and the other children were at school or in mines, the house was quiet. The stillness and isolation both calmed and energized her. She could arrange and clean without interruption until two o'clock, when Chicken and Pie came home.

When the war ended and the twins were ten years old, they too left school to work. Pauline was fifteen, still keeping house, but with less enthusiasm. Fantasies about men and love and touching were drawing her mind and hands away from her work. Changes in weather began to affect her, as did certain sights and sounds. These feelings translated themselves to her in extreme melancholy. She thought of the death of newborn things, lonely roads, and strangers who appear out of nowhere simply to hold one's hand, woods in which the sun was always setting. In church especially did these dreams grow. The songs caressed her, and while she tried to hold her mind on the wages of sin, her body trembled for redemption, salvation, a mysterious rebirth that would simply happen, with no effort on her part. In none of her fantasies was she ever aggressive; she was usually idling by the river bank, or gathering berries in a field when a someone appeared, with gentle and penetrating eyes, who—with no exchange of words—understood; and before whose glance her foot straightened and her eyes dropped. The someone had no face, no form, no voice, no odor. He was a simple Presence, an all-embracing tenderness with strength and a promise of rest. It did not matter that she had no idea of what to do or say to the Presence—after the wordless knowing and the soundless touching, her dreams disintegrated. But the Presence would know what to do. She had only to lay her head on his chest and he would lead her away to the sea, to the city, to the woods . . . forever.

There was a woman named Ivy who seemed to hold in her mouth all of the sounds of Pauline's soul. Standing a little apart from the choir, Ivy sang the dark sweetness that Pauline could not name; she sang the death-defying death that Pauline yearned for; she sang of the Stranger who *knew* . . .

Precious Lord take my hand
Lead me on, let me stand
I am tired, I am weak, I am worn.
Through the storms, through the night
Lead me on to the light
Take my hand, precious Lord, lead me on.

When my way grows drear
Precious Lord linger near,
When my life is almost gone
Hear my cry hear my call
Hold my hand lest I fall
Take my hand, precious Lord, lead me on.

Thus it was that when the Stranger, the someone, did appear out of nowhere, Pauline was grateful but not surprised.

He came, strutting right out of a Kentucky sun on the hottest day of the year. He came big, he came strong, he came with yellow eyes, flaring nostrils, and he came with his own music.

Pauline was leaning idly on the fence, her arms resting on the crossrail between the pickets. She had just put down some biscuit dough and was cleaning the flour from under her nails. Behind her at some distance she heard whistling. One of these rapid, high-note riffs that black boys make up as they go while sweeping, shoveling, or just walking along. A kind of city-street music where laughter belies anxiety, and joy is as short and straight as the blade of a pocketknife. She listened carefully to the music and let it pull her lips into a smile. The whistling got louder, and still she did not turn around, for she wanted it to last. While smiling to herself and holding fast to the break in somber thoughts, she felt something tickling her foot. She laughed aloud and turned to see. The whistler was bending down tickling her broken foot and kissing her leg. She could not stop her laughter—not until he looked up at her and she saw the Kentucky sun drenching the yellow, heavy-lidded eyes of Cholly Breedlove.

"When I first seed Cholly, I want you to know it was like all the bits of color from that time down home when all us chil'ren went berry picking after a funeral and I put some in the pocket of my Sunday dress, and they mashed up and stained my hips. My whole dress was messed with purple, and it never did wash out. Not the dress nor me. I could feel that purple deep inside me. And that lemonade Mama used to make when Pap came in out the fields. It be cool and yellowish, with seeds floating near the bottom. And that streak of green them june bugs made on the trees the night we left from down home. All of them colors was in me. Just sitting there. So when Cholly come up and tickled my foot, it was like them berries, that lemonade, them streaks of green the june bugs made, all come together. Cholly was thin then, with real light eyes. He used to whistle, and when I heerd him, shivers come on my skin."

Pauline and Cholly loved each other. He seemed to relish her company and even to enjoy her country ways and lack of knowledge about city things. He talked with her about her foot and asked, when they walked through the town or in the fields, if she were tired. Instead of ignoring her infirmity, pretending it was not there, he made it seem like something special and endearing. For the first time Pauline felt that her bad foot was an asset.

And he did touch her, firmly but gently, just as she had dreamed. But minus the gloom of setting suns and lonely river banks. She was secure and grateful; he was kind and lively. She had not known there was so much laughter in the world.

They agreed to marry and go 'way up north, where Cholly said steel mills were begging for workers. Young, loving, and full of energy, they came to Lorain, Ohio. Cholly found work in the steel mills right away, and Pauline started keeping house.

And then she lost her front tooth. But there must have been a speck, a brown speck easily mistaken for food but which did not leave, which sat on the enamel for months, and grew, until it cut into the surface and then to the brown putty underneath, finally eating away to the root, but avoiding the nerves, so its presence was not noticeable or uncomfortable. Then the weakened roots, having grown accustomed to the poison, responded one day to severe pressure, and the tooth fell free, leaving a ragged stump behind. But even before the little brown speck, there must have been the conditions, the setting that would allow it to exist in the first place.

In that young and growing Ohio town whose side streets, even, were paved with concrete, which sat on the edge of a calm blue lake, which boasted an affinity with Oberlin, the underground railroad station, just thirteen miles away, this melting pot on the lip of America facing the cold but receptive Canada—What could go wrong?

"Me and Cholly was getting along good then. We come up north; supposed to be more jobs and all. We moved into two rooms up over a furniture store, and I set about housekeeping. Cholly was working at the steel plant, and everything was looking good. I don't know what all happened. Everything changed. It was hard to get to know folks up here, and I missed my people. I weren't used to so much white folks. The ones I seed before was something hateful, but they didn't come around too much. I mean, we didn't have too much truck with them. Just now and then in the fields, or at the commissary. But they want all over us. Up north they was everywhere—next door, downstairs, all over the streets—and colored folks few and far between. Northern colored folk was different too. Dicty-like. No better than whites for meanness. They could make you feel just as no-count, 'cept I didn't expect it from them. That was the lonesomest time of my life. I 'member looking out them front windows just waiting for Cholly to come home at three o'clock. I didn't even have a cat to talk to."

In her loneliness, she turned to her husband for reassurance, entertainment, for things to fill the vacant places. Housework was not enough; there were only two rooms, and no yard to keep or move about in. The women in the town wore high-heeled shoes, and when Pauline tried to wear them, they aggravated her shuffle into a pronounced limp. Cholly was kindness still, but began to resist her total dependence on him. They were beginning to have less and less to say to each other. He had no problem finding other people and other things to occupy him—men were always climbing the stairs asking for him, and he was happy to accompany them, leaving her alone.

Pauline felt uncomfortable with the few black women she met. They were amused by her because she did not straighten her hair. When she tried to make up her face as they did, it came off rather badly. Their goading glances and private snickers at her way of talking (saying "chil'ren") and dressing developed in her a desire for new clothes. When Cholly began to quarrel about the money she wanted, she decided to go to work. Taking jobs as a day worker helped with the clothes, and even a few things for the apartment, but it did not help with Cholly. He was not pleased with her purchases and began to tell her so. Their marriage was shredded with quarrels. She was still no more than a girl, and still waiting for that plateau of happiness, that hand of a precious Lord who, when her way grew drear, would always linger near. Only now she had a clearer idea of what drear meant. Money became the focus of all their discussions, hers for clothes, his for drink. The sad thing was that Pauline did not really care for clothes and makeup. She merely wanted other women to cast favorable glances her way.

After several months of doing day work, she took a steady job in the home of a family of slender means and nervous, pretentious ways.

"Cholly commenced to getting meaner and meaner and wanted to fight me all of the time. I give him as good as

I got. Had to. Look like working for that woman and fighting Cholly was all I did. Tiresome. But I holt on to my jobs, even though working for that woman was more than a notion. It wasn't so much her meanness as just simpleminded. Her whole family was. Couldn't get along with one another worth nothing. You'd think with a pretty house like that and all the money they could holt on to, they would enjoy one another. She haul off and cry over the leastest thing. If one of her friends cut her short on the telephone, she'd go to crying. She should of been glad she had a telephone. I ain't got one yet. I recollect oncet how her baby brother who she put through dentistry school didn't invite them to some big party he throwed. They was a big to-do about that. Everybody stayed on the telephone for days. Fussing and carrying on. She asked me, 'Pauline, what would you do if your own brother had a party and didn't invite you?' I said ifn I really wanted to go to that party, I reckoned I'd go anyhow. Never mind what he want. She just sucked her teeth a little and made out like what I said was dumb. All the while I was thinking how dumb she was. Whoever told her that her brother was her friend? Folks can't like folks just 'cause they has the same mama. I tried to like that woman myself. She was good about giving me stuff, but I just couldn't like her. Soon as I worked up a good feeling on her account, she'd do something ignorant and start in to telling me how to clean and do. If I left her on her own, she'd drown in dirt. I didn't have to pick up after Chicken and Pie the way I had to pick up after them. None of them knew so much as how to wipe their behinds. I know, 'cause I did the washing. And couldn't pee proper to save their lives.

Her husband ain't hit the bowl yet. Nasty white folks is about the nastiest things they is. But I would have stayed on 'cepting for Cholly come over by where I was working and cut up so. He come there drunk wanting some money. When that white woman see him, she turned red. She tried to act strong-like, but she was scared bad. Anyway, she told Cholly to get out or she would call the police. He cussed her and started pulling on me. I would of gone upside his head, but I don't want no dealings with the police. So I taken my things and left. I tried to get back, but she didn't want me no more if I was going to stay with Cholly. She said she would let me stay if I left him. I thought about that. But later on it didn't seem none too bright for a black woman to leave a black man for a white woman. She didn't never give me the eleven dollars she owed me, neither. That hurt bad. The gas man had cut the gas off, and I couldn't cook none. I really begged that woman for my money. I went to see her. She was mad as a wet hen. Kept on telling me I owed her for uniforms and some old broken-down bed she give me. I didn't know if I owed her or not, but I needed my money. She wouldn't let up none, neither, even when I give her my word that Cholly wouldn't come back there no more. Then I got so desperate I asked her if she would loan it to me. She was quiet for a spell, and then she told me I shouldn't let a man take advantage over me. That I should have more respect, and it was my husband's duty to pay the bills, and if he couldn't, I should leave and get alimony. All such simple stuff. What was he gone give me alimony on? I seen she didn't understand that all I needed from her was my eleven dollars to pay the gas man so I could cook. She couldn't get that one thing through her thick head. 'Are you going to leave him, Pauline?' she kept on saying. I thought she'd give me my money if I said I would, so I said 'Yes, ma'am.' 'All right,' she said. 'You leave him, and then come back to work, and we'll let bygones be bygones.' 'Can I have my money today?' I said. 'No' she said. 'Only when you leave him. I'm only thinking of you and your future. What good is he, Pauline, what good is he to you?' How you going to answer a woman like that, who don't know what good a man is, and say out of one side of her mouth she's thinking of your future but won't give you your own money so you can buy you something besides baloney to eat? So I said, 'No good, ma'am. He ain't no good to me. But just the same, I think I'd best stay on.' She got up, and I left. When I got outside, I felt pains in my crotch, I had held my legs together so tight trying to make that woman understand. But I reckon now she couldn't understand. She married a man with a slash in his face instead of a mouth. So how could she understand?"

One winter Pauline discovered she was pregnant. When she told Cholly, he surprised her by being pleased. He began to drink less and come home more often. They eased back into a relationship more like the early days of their marriage, when he asked if she were tired or wanted him to bring her something from the store. In this state of ease, Pauline stopped doing day work and returned to her own housekeeping. But the loneliness in those two rooms had not gone away. When the winter sun hit the peeling green paint of the kitchen chairs, when the smoked hocks were boiling in the pot, when all she could hear was the truck delivering furniture downstairs, she thought about back home, about how she had been all alone most of the time then too, but that this lonesomeness was different. Then she stopped staring at the green chairs, at the delivery truck; she went to the movies instead. There in the dark her memory was refreshed, and she succumbed to her earlier dreams. Along with the idea of romantic love, she was introduced to another—physical beauty. Probably the most destructive ideas in the history of human thought. Both originated in envy, thrived in insecurity, and ended in disillusion. In equating physical beauty with virtue, she stripped her mind, bound it, and collected self-contempt by the heap. She forgot lust and simple caring for. She regarded love as possessive mating, and romance as the goal of the spirit. It would be for her a well-spring from which she would draw the most destructive emotions, deceiving the lover and seeking to imprison the beloved, curtailing freedom in every way.

She was never able, after her education in the movies, to look at a face and not assign it some category in the scale of absolute beauty, and the scale was one she absorbed in full from the silver screen. There at last were the darkened woods, the lonely roads, the river banks, the gentle knowing eyes. There the flawed became whole, the blind sighted, and the lame and halt threw away their crutches. There death was dead, and people made every gesture in a cloud of music. There the black-and-white images came together, making a magnificent whole—all projected through the ray of light from above and behind.

It was really a simple pleasure, but she learned all there was to love and all there was to hate.

"The onliest time I be happy seem like was when I was in the picture show. Every time I got, I went. I'd go early, before the show started. They'd cut off the lights, and everything be black. Then the screen would light up, and I'd move right on in them pictures. White men taking such good care of they women, and they all dressed up in big clean houses with the bathtubs right in the same room with the toilet. Them pictures gave me a lot of pleasure, but it made coming home hard, and looking at Cholly hard. I don't know. I 'member one time I went to see Clark Gable and Jean Harlow. I fixed my hair up like I'd seen hers on a magazine. A part on the side, with one little curl on my forehead. It looked just like her. Well, almost just like. Anyway, I sat in that show with my hair done up that way and had a good time. I thought I'd see it through to the end again, and I got up to get me some candy. I was sitting back in my seat, and I taken a big bite of that candy, and it pulled a tooth right out of my mouth. I could of cried. I had good teeth, not a rotten one in my head. I don't believe I ever did get over that. There I was, five months pregnant, trying to look like Jean Harlow, and a front tooth gone. Everything went then. Look like I just didn't care no more after that. I let my hair go back, plaited it up, and settled down to just being ugly. I still went to the pictures, though, but the meanness got worse. I wanted my tooth back. Cholly poked fun at me, and we started fighting again. I tried to kill him. He didn't hit me too hard, 'cause I were pregnant I guess, but the fights, once they got started up again, kept up. He begin to make me madder than anything I knowed, and I couldn't keep my hands off him. Well, I had that baby—a boy—and after

that got pregnant again with another one. But it weren't like I thought it was gone be. I loved them and all, I guess, but maybe it was having no money, or maybe it was Cholly, but they sure worried the life out of me. Sometimes I'd catch myself hollering at them and beating them, and I'd feel sorry for them, but I couldn't seem to stop. When I had the second one, a girl, I 'member I said I'd love it no matter what it looked like. She looked like a black ball of hair. I don't recollect trying to get pregnant that first time. But that second time, I actually tried to get pregnant. Maybe 'cause I'd had one already and wasn't scairt to do it. Anyway, I felt good, and wasn't thinking on the carrying, just the baby itself. I used to talk to it whilst it be still in the womb. Like good friends we was. You know. I be hanging wash and I knowed lifting weren't good for it. I'd say to it holt on now I gone hang up these few rags, don't get froggy; it be over soon. It wouldn't leap or nothing. Or I be mixing something in a bowl for the other chile and I'd talk to it then too. You know, just friendly talk. On up til the end I felted good about that baby. I went to the hospital when my time come. So I could be easeful. I didn't want to have it at home like I done with the boy. They put me in a big room with a whole mess of women. The pains was coming, but not too bad. A little old doctor come to examine me. He had all sorts of stuff. He gloved his hand and put some kind of jelly on it and rammed it up between my legs. When he left off, some more doctors come. One old one and some young ones. The old one was learning the young ones about babies. Showing them how to do. When he got to me he said now these here women you don't have any trouble with. They deliver right away and with no pain. Just like horses. The young ones smiled a little. They looked at my stomach and between my legs. They never said nothing to me. Only one looked at me. Looked at my face, I mean. I looked right back at him. He dropped his eyes and turned red. He knowed, I reckon, that maybe I weren't no horse foaling. But them others. They didn't know. They went on. I seed them talking to them white women: 'How you feel? Gonna have twins?' Just shucking them, of course, but nice talk. Nice friendly talk. I got edgy, and when them pains got harder, I was glad. Glad to have something else to think about. I moaned something awful. The pains wasn't as bad as I let on, but I had to let them people know having a baby was more than a bowel movement. I hurt just like them white women. Just 'cause I wasn't hooping and hollering before didn't mean I wasn't feeling pain. What'd they think? That just 'cause I knowed how to have a baby with no fuss that my behind wasn't pulling and aching like theirs? Besides, that doctor don't know what he talking about. He must never seed no mare foal. Who say they don't have no pain? Just 'cause she don't cry? 'Cause she can't say it, they think it ain't there? If they looks in her eyes and see them eyeballs lolling back, see the sorrowful look, they'd know. Anyways, the baby come. Big old healthy thing. She looked different from what I thought. Reckon I talked to it so much before I conjured up a mind's eye view of it. So when I seed it, it was like looking at a picture of your mama when she was a girl. You knows who she is, but she don't look the same. They give her to me for a nursing, and she liked to pull my nipple off right away. She caught on fast. Not like Sammy, he was the hardest child to feed. But Pecola look like she knowed right off what to do. A right smart baby she was. I used to like to watch her. You know they makes them greedy sounds. Eyes all soft and wet. A cross between a puppy and a dying man. But I knowed she was ugly. Head full of pretty hair, but Lord she was ugly."

When Sammy and Pecola were still young Pauline had to go back to work. She was older now, with no time for dreams and movies. It was time to put all of the pieces together, make coherence where before there had been none. The children gave her this need; she herself was no longer a child. So she became, and her process of becoming was like most of ours: she developed a hatred for things that mystified or obstructed her; acquired virtues that were easy to maintain; assigned herself a role in the scheme of things; and harked back to simpler times for gratification.

She took on the full responsibility and recognition of breadwinner and returned to church. First, however, she moved out of the two rooms into a spacious first floor of a building that had been built as a store. She came into her own with the women who had despised her, by being more moral than they; she avenged herself on Cholly by forcing him to indulge in the weaknesses she despised. She joined a church where shouting was frowned upon, served on Stewardess Board No. 3, and became a member of Ladies Circle No. 1. At prayer meeting she moaned and sighed over Cholly's ways, and hoped God would help her keep the children from the sins of the father. She stopped saying "chil'ren" and said "childring" instead. She let another tooth fall, and was outraged by painted ladies who thought only of clothes and men. Holding Cholly as a model of sin and failure, she bore him like a crown of thorns, and her children like a cross.

It was her good fortune to find a permanent job in the home of a well-to-do family whose members were affectionate, appreciative, and generous. She looked at their houses, smelled their linen, touched their silk draperies, and loved all of it. The child's pink nightie, the stacks of white pillow slips edged with embroidery, the sheets with top hems picked out with blue cornflowers. She became what is known as an ideal servant, for such a role filled practically all of her needs. When she bathed the little Fisher girl, it was in a porcelain tub with silvery taps running infinite quantities of hot, clear water. She dried her in fluffy white towels and put her in cuddly night clothes. Then she brushed the yellow hair, enjoying the roll and slip of it between her fingers. No zinc tub, no buckets of stove-heated water, no flaky, stiff, grayish towels washed in a kitchen sink, dried in a dusty backyard, no tangled black puffs of rough wool to comb. Soon she stopped trying to keep her own house. The things she could afford to buy did not last, had no beauty or style, and were absorbed by the dingy storefront. More and more she neglected her house, her children, her man—they were like the afterthoughts one has just before sleep, the early-morning and late-evening edges of her day, the dark edges that made the daily life with the Fishers lighter, more delicate, more lovely. Here she could arrange things, clean things, line things up in neat rows. Here her foot flopped around on deep pile carpets, and there was no uneven sound. Here she found beauty, order, cleanliness, and praise. Mr. Fisher said, "I would rather sell her blueberry cobblers than real estate." She reigned over cupboards stacked high with food that would not be eaten for weeks, even months; she was queen of canned vegetables bought by the case, special fondants and ribbon candy curled up in tiny silver dishes. The creditors and service people who humiliated her when she went to them on her own behalf respected her, were even intimidated by her, when she spoke for the Fishers. She refused beef slightly dark or with edges not properly trimmed. The slightly reeking fish that she accepted for her own family she would all but throw in the fish man's face if he sent it to the Fisher house. Power, praise, and luxury were hers in this household. They even gave her what she had never had—a nickname—Polly. It was her pleasure to stand in her kitchen at the end of a day and survey her handiwork. Knowing there were soap bars by the dozen, bacon by the rasher, and reveling in her shiny pots and pans and polished floors. Hearing, "We'll never let her go. We could never find anybody like Polly. She will *not* leave the kitchen until everything is in order. Really, she is the ideal servant."

Pauline kept this order, this beauty, for herself, a private world, and never introduced it into her storefront, or to her children. Them she bent toward respectability, and in so doing taught them fear: fear of being clumsy, fear of being like their father, fear of not being loved by God, fear of madness like Cholly's mother's. Into her son she beat a loud desire to run away, and into her daughter she beat a fear of growing up, fear of other people, fear of life.

All the meaningfulness of her life was in her work. For her virtues were intact. She was an active church woman, did not drink, smoke, or carouse, defended herself mightily against Cholly, rose above him in every way, and felt she was fulfilling a mother's role conscientiously when she pointed out their father's faults to keep them from having them, or punished them when they showed any slovenliness, no matter how slight, when she worked twelve to sixteen hours a day to support them. And the world itself agreed with her.

It was only sometimes, sometimes, and then rarely, that she thought about the old days, or what her life had turned to. They were musings, idle thoughts, full sometimes of the old dreaminess, but not the kind of thing she cared to dwell on.

"I started to leave him once, but something came up. Once, after he tried to set the house on fire, I was all set in my mind to go. I can't even 'member now what held me. He sure ain't give me much of a life. But it wasn't all bad. Sometimes things wasn't all bad. He used to come easing into bed sometimes, not too drunk. I make out like I'm asleep, 'cause it's late, and he taken three dollars out of my pocketbook that morning or something. I hear him breathing, but I don't look around. I can see in my mind's eye his black arms thrown back behind his head, the muscles like great big peach stones sanded down, with veins running like little swollen rivers down his arms. Without touching him I be feeling those ridges on the tips of my fingers. I sees the palms of his hands calloused to granite, and the long fingers curled up and still. I think about the thick, knotty hair on his chest, and the two big swells his breast muscles make. I want to rub my face hard in his chest and feel the hair cut my skin. I know just where the hair growth slacks out—just above his navel—and how it picks up again and spreads out. Maybe he'll shift a little, and his leg will touch me, or I feel his flank just graze my behind. I don't move even yet.

Then he lift his head, turn over, and put his hand on my waist. If I don't move, he'll move his hand over to pull and knead my stomach. Soft and slow-like. I still don't move, because I don't want him to stop. I want to pretend sleep and have him keep on rubbing my stomach. Then he will lean his head down and bite my tit. Then I don't want him to rub my stomach anymore. I want him to put his hand between my legs. I pretend to wake up, and turn to him, but not opening my legs. I want him to open them for me. He does, and I be soft and wet where his fingers are strong and hard. I be softer than I ever been before. All my strength in his hand. My brain curls up like wilted leaves. A funny, empty feeling is in my hands. I want to grab holt of something, so I hold his head. His mouth is under my chin. Then I don't want his hand between my legs no more, because I think I am softening away. I stretch my legs open, and he is on top of me. Too heavy to hold, and too light not to. He puts his thing in me. In me. In me. I wrap my feet around his back so he can't get away. His face is next to mine. The bed springs sounds like them crickets used to back home. He puts his fingers in mine, and we stretches our arms outwise like Jesus on the cross. I hold on tight. My fingers and my feet hold on tight, because everything else is going, going. I know he wants me to come first. But I can't. Not until he does. Not until I feel him loving me. Just me. Sinking into me. Not until I know that my flesh is all that be on his mind. That he couldn't stop if he had to. That he would die rather than take his thing out of me. Of me. Not until he has let go of all he has, and give it to me. To me. To me. When he does, I feel a power. I be strong, I be pretty, I be young. And then I wait. He shivers and tosses his head. Now I be strong enough, pretty enough, and young enough to let him make me come. I take my fingers out of his and put my hands on his behind. My legs drop back onto the bed. I don't make no noise, because the chil'ren might hear. I begin to feel those little bits of color floating up into me— deep in me. That streak of green from the june-bug light, the purple from the berries trickling along my thighs, Mama's lemonade yellow runs sweet in me. Then I feel like I'm laughing between my legs, and the laughing gets all mixed up with the colors, and I'm afraid I'll come, and afraid I won't. But I know I will. And I do. And it be rainbow all inside. And it lasts and lasts and lasts. I want to thank him, but don't know how, so I pat him like you do a baby. He asks me if I'm all right. I say yes. He gets off me and lies down to sleep. I want to say something, but I don't. I don't want to take my mind offen the rainbow. I should get up and go to the toilet, but I don't. Besides, Cholly is asleep with his leg throwed over me. I can't move and don't want to.

"But it ain't like that anymore. Most times he's thrashing away inside me before I'm woke, and through when I am. The rest of the time I can't even be next to his stinking drunk self. But I don't care 'bout it no more. My Maker will take care of me. I know He will. I know He will. Besides, it don't make no difference about this old earth. There is sure to be a glory. Only thing I miss sometimes is that rainbow. But like I say, I don't recollect it much anymore."

SEEFATHERHEISBIGANDSTRONGFATH ERWILLYOUPLAYWITHJANEFATHER ISSMILINGSMILEFATHERSMILESMILE

When Cholly was four days old, his mother wrapped him in two blankets and one newspaper and placed him on a junk heap by the railroad. His Great Aunt Jimmy, who had seen her niece carrying a bundle out of the back door, rescued him. She beat his mother with a razor strap and wouldn't let her near the baby after that. Aunt Jimmy raised Cholly herself, but took delight sometimes in telling him of how she had saved him. He gathered from her that his mother wasn't right in the head. But he never had a chance to find out, because she ran away shortly after the razor strap, and no one had heard of her since.

Cholly was grateful for having been saved. Except sometimes. Sometimes when he watched Aunt Jimmy eating collards with her fingers, sucking her four gold teeth, or smelled her when she wore the asafetida bag around her neck, or when she made him sleep with her for warmth in winter and he could see her old, wrinkled breasts sagging in her nightgown—then he wondered whether it would have been just as well to have died there. Down in the rim of a tire under a soft black Georgia sky.

He had four years of school before he got courage enough to ask his aunt who and where his father was.

"That Fuller boy, I believe it was," his aunt said. "He was hanging around then, but he taken off pretty quick before you was born. I think he gone to Macon. Him or his brother. Maybe both. I hear old man Fuller say something 'bout it once."

"What name he have?" asked Cholly.

"Fuller, Foolish."

"I mean what his given name?"

"Oh." She closed her eyes to think, and sighed. "Can't recollect nothing no more. Sam, was it? Yeh. Samuel. No. No, it wasn't. It was Samson. Samson Fuller."

"How come you all didn't name me Samson?" Cholly's voice was low.

"What for? He wasn't nowhere around when you was born. Your mama didn't name you nothing. The nine days wasn't up before she throwed you on the junk heap. When I got you I named you myself on the ninth day. You named after my dead brother. Charles Breedlove. A good man. Ain't no Samson never come to no good end."

Cholly didn't ask anything else.

Two years later he quit school to take a job at Tyson's Feed and Grain Store. He swept up, ran errands, weighed bags, and lifted them onto the drays. Sometimes they let him ride with the drayman. A nice old man called Blue Jack. Blue used to tell him old-timey stories about how it was when the Emancipation Proclamation came. How the black people hollered, cried, and sang. And ghost stories about how a white man cut off his wife's head and buried her in the swamp, and the headless body came out at night and went stumbling around the yard, knocking over stuff because it couldn't see, and crying all the time for a comb. They talked about the women Blue had had, and the fights he'd been in when he was younger, about how he talked his way out of getting lynched once, and how others hadn't.

Cholly loved Blue. Long after he was a man, he remembered the good times they had had. How on a July 4 at a church picnic a family was about to break open a watermelon. Several children were standing around watching. Blue was hovering about on the periphery of the circle—a faint smile of anticipation softening his face. The father of the family lifted the melon high over his head—his big arms looked taller than the trees to Cholly, and the melon blotted out the sun. Tall, head forward, eyes fastened on a rock, his arms higher than the pines, his hands holding a melon bigger than the sun, he paused an instant to get his bearing and secure his aim. Watching the figure etched against the bright blue sky, Cholly felt goose pimples popping along his arms and neck. He wondered if God looked like that. No. God was a nice old white man, with long white hair, flowing white beard, and little blue eyes that looked sad when people died and mean when they were bad. It must be the devil who looks like that—holding the world in his hands, ready to dash it to the ground and spill the red guts so niggers could eat the sweet, warm insides. If the devil did look like that, Cholly preferred him. He never felt anything thinking about God, but just the idea of the devil excited him. And now the strong, black devil was blotting out the sun and getting ready to split open the world.

Far away somebody was playing a mouth organ; the

music slithered over the cane fields and into the pine grove; it spiraled around the tree trunks and mixed itself with the pine scent, so Cholly couldn't tell the difference between the sound and the odor that hung about the heads of the people.

The man swung the melon down to the edge of a rock. A soft cry of disappointment accompanied the sound of smashed rind. The break was a bad one. The melon was jagged, and hunks of rind and red meat scattered on the grass.

Blue jumped. "Aw—awww," he moaned, "dere go da heart." His voice was both sad and pleased. Everybody looked to see the big red chunk from the very center of the melon, free of rind and sparse of seed, which had rolled a little distance from Blue's feet. He stooped to pick it up. Blood red, its planes dull and blunted with sweetness, its edges rigid with juice. Too obvious, almost obscene, in the joy it promised.

"Go 'head, Blue," the father laughed. "You can have it."

Blue smiled and walked away. Little children scrambled for the pieces on the ground. Women picked out the seeds for the smallest ones and broke off little bits of the meat for themselves. Blue's eye caught Cholly's. He motioned to him. "Come on, boy. Le's you and me eat the heart."

Together the old man and the boy sat on the grass and shared the heart of the watermelon. The nasty-sweet guts of the earth.

It was in the spring, a very chilly spring, that Aunt Jimmy died of peach cobbler. She went to a camp meeting that took place after a rainstorm, and the damp wood of the benches was bad for her. For four or five days afterward, she felt poorly. Friends came to see about her. Some made camomile tea; others rubbed her with liniment. Miss Alice, her closest friend, read the Bible to her. Still she was declining. Advice was prolific, if contradictory.

"Don't eat no whites of eggs."

"Drink new milk."

"Chew on this root."

Aunt Jimmy ignored all but Miss Alice's Bible reading. She nodded in drowsy appreciation as the words from First Corinthians droned over her. Sweet amens fell from her lips as she was chastised for all her sins. But her body would not respond.

Finally it was decided to fetch M'Dear. M'Dear was a quiet woman who lived in a shack near the woods. She was a competent midwife and decisive diagnostician. Few could remember when M'Dear was not around. In any illness that could not be handled by ordinary means—known cures, intuition, or endurance—the word was always, "Fetch M'Dear."

When she arrived at Aunt Jimmy's house, Cholly was amazed at the sight of her. He had always pictured her as shriveled and hunched over, for he knew she was very, very old. But M'Dear loomed taller than the preacher who accompanied her. She must have been over six feet tall. Four big white knots of hair gave power and authority to her soft black face. Standing straight as a poker, she seemed to need her hickory stick not for support but for communication. She tapped it lightly on the floor as she looked down at Aunt Jimmy's wrinkled face. She stroked the knob with the thumb of her right hand while she ran her left one over Aunt Jimmy's body. The backs of her long fingers she placed on the patient's cheek, then placed her palm on the forehead. She ran her fingers through the sick woman's hair, lightly scratching the scalp, and then looking at what the fingernails revealed. She lifted Aunt Jimmy's hand and looked closely at it—fingernails, back skin, the flesh of the palm she pressed with three fingertips. Later she put her ear on Aunt Jimmy's chest and stomach to listen. At M'Dear's request, the women pulled the slop jar from under the bed to show the stools. M'Dear tapped her stick while looking at them.

"Bury the slop jar and everything in it," she said to the women. To Aunt Jimmy she said, "You done caught cold in your womb. Drink pot liquor and nothing else."

"Will it pass?" asked Aunt Jimmy. "Is I'm gone be all right?"

"I reckon."

M'Dear turned and left the room. The preacher put her in his buggy to take her home.

That evening the women brought bowls of pot liquor from black-eyed peas, from mustards, from cabbage, from kale, from collards, from turnips, from beets, from green beans. Even the juice from a boiling hog jowl.

Two evenings later Aunt Jimmy had gained much strength. When Miss Alice and Mrs. Gaines stopped in to check on her, they remarked on her improvement. The three women sat talking about various miseries they had had, their cure or abatement, what had helped. Over and over again they returned to Aunt Jimmy's condition. Repeating its cause, what could have been done to prevent the misery from taking hold, and M'Dear's infallibility. Their voices blended into a threnody of nostalgia about pain. Rising and falling, complex in harmony, uncertain in pitch, but constant in the recitative of pain. They hugged the memories of illnesses to their bosoms. They licked their lips and clucked their tongues in fond remembrance of pains they had endured—childbirth, rheumatism, croup, sprains, backaches, piles. All of the bruises they had collected from moving about the earth—harvesting, cleaning, hoisting, pitching, stooping, kneeling, picking—always with young ones underfoot.

But they had been young once. The odor of their armpits and haunches had mingled into a lovely musk; their eyes had been furtive, their lips relaxed, and the delicate turn of their heads on those slim black necks had been like nothing other than a doe's. Their laughter had been more touch than sound.

Then they had grown. Edging into life from the back door. Becoming. Everybody in the world was in a position to give them orders. White women said, "Do this." White children said, "Give me that." White men said, "Come here." Black men said, "Lay down." The only people they need not take orders from were black children and each other. But they took all of that and re-created it in their own image. They ran the houses of white people, and knew it. When white men beat their men, they cleaned up the blood and went home to receive abuse from the victim. They beat their children with one hand and stole for them with the other. The hands that felled trees also cut umbilical cords; the hands that wrung the necks of chickens and butchered hogs also nudged African violets into bloom; the arms that loaded sheaves, bales, and sacks rocked babies into sleep. They patted biscuits into flaky ovals of innocence—and shrouded the dead. They plowed all day and came home to nestle like plums under the limbs of their men. The legs that straddled a mule's back were the same ones that straddled their men's hips. And the difference was all the difference there was.

Then they were old. Their bodies honed, their odor sour. Squatting in a cane field, stooping in a cotton field, kneeling by a river bank, they had carried a world on their heads. They had given over the lives of their own children and tendered their grandchildren. With relief they wrapped their heads in rags, and their breasts in flannel; eased their feet into felt. They were through with lust and lactation, beyond tears and terror. They alone could walk the roads of Mississippi, the lanes of Georgia, the fields of Alabama unmolested. They were old enough to be irritable when and where they chose, tired enough to look forward to death, disinterested enough to accept the idea of pain while ignoring the presence of pain. They were, in fact and at last, free. And the lives of these old black women were synthesized in their eyes—a purée of tragedy and humor, wickedness and serenity, truth and fantasy.

They chattered far into the night. Cholly listened and grew sleepy. The lullaby of grief enveloped him, rocked him, and at last numbed him. In his sleep the foul odor of an old woman's stools turned into the healthy smell of horse shit, and the voices of the three women were muted into the pleasant notes of a mouth organ. He was aware, in his sleep, of being curled up in a chair, his hands tucked between his thighs. In a dream his penis changed into a long hickory stick, and the hands caressing it were the hands of M'Dear.

On a wet Saturday night, before Aunt Jimmy felt strong enough to get out of the bed, Essie Foster brought her a peach cobbler. The old lady ate a piece, and the next morning when Cholly went to empty the slop jar, she was dead. Her mouth was a slackened O, and her hands, those long fingers with a man's hard nails, having done their laying by, could now be dainty on the sheet. One open eye looked at him as if to say, "Mind how you take holt of that jar, boy." Cholly stared back, unable to move, until a fly settled at the corner of her mouth. He fanned it away angrily, looked back at the eye, and did its bidding.

Aunt Jimmy's funeral was the first Cholly had ever attended. As a member of the family, one of the bereaved, he was the object of a great deal of attention. The ladies had cleaned the house, aired everything out, notified everybody, and stitched together what looked like a white wedding dress for Aunt Jimmy, a maiden lady, to wear when she met Jesus. They even produced a dark suit, white shirt, and tie for Cholly. The husband of one of them cut his hair. He was enclosed in fastidious tenderness. Nobody talked to him; that is, they treated him like the child he was, never engaging him in serious conversation; but they anticipated wishes he never had: meals appeared, hot water for the wooden tub, clothes laid out. At the wake he was allowed to fall asleep, and arms carried him to bed. Only on the third day after the death—the day of the funeral—did he have to share the spotlight. Aunt Jimmy's people came from nearby towns and farms. Her brother O. V., his children and wife, and lots of cousins. But Cholly was still the major figure, because he was "Jimmy's boy, the last thing she loved," and "the one who found her." The solicitude of the women, the head pats of the men, pleased Cholly, and the creamy conversations fascinated him.

"What'd she die from?"

"Essie's pie."

"Don't say?"

"Uh-huh. She was doing fine, I saw her the very day before. Said she wanted me to bring her some black thread to patch some things for the boy. I should of known just from her wanting black thread that was a sign."

"Sure was."

"Just like Emma. 'Member? She kept asking for thread. Dropped dead that very evening."

"Yeah. Well, she was determined to have it. Kept on reminding me. I told her I had some to home, but naw, she wanted it new. So I sent Li'l June to get some that very morning when she was laying dead. I was just fixing to bring it over, 'long with a piece of sweet bread. You know how she craved my sweet bread."

"Sure did. Always bragged on it. She was a good friend to you."

"I believe it. Well, I had no more got my clothes on when Sally bust in the door hollering about how Cholly here had been over to Miss Alice saying she was dead. You could have knocked me over, I tell you."

"Guess Essie feels mighty bad."

"Oh, Lord, yes. But I told her the Lord giveth and the Lord taketh away. Wasn't her fault none. She makes good peach pies. But she bound to believe it was the pie did it, and I 'spect she right."

"Well, she shouldn't worry herself none 'bout that. She was just doing what we all would of done."

"Yeah. 'Cause I was sure wrapping up that sweet bread, and that could of done it too."

"I doubts that. Sweet bread is pure. But a pie is the worse thing to give anybody ailing. I'm surprised Jimmy didn't know better."

"If she did, she wouldn't let on. She would have tried to please. You know how she was. So good."

"I'll say. Did she leave anything?"

"Not even a pocket handkerchief. The house belongs to some white folks in Clarksville."

"Oh, yeah? I thought she owned it."

"May have at one time. But not no more. I hear the insurance folks been down talking to her brother."

"How much do it come to?"

"Eighty-five dollars, I hear."

"That all?"

"Can she get in the ground on that?"

"Don't see how. When my daddy died last year this April it costed one hundred and fifty dollars. 'Course, we had to have everything just so. Now Jimmy's people may all have to chip in. That undertaker that lays out black folks ain't none too cheap."

"Seems a shame. She been paying on that insurance all her life."

"Don't I know?"

"Well, what about the boy? What he gone do?"

"Well, caint nobody find that mama, so Jimmy's brother gone take him back to his place. They say he got a nice place. Inside toilet and everything."

"That's nice. He seems like a good Christian man. And the boy need a man's hand."

"What time's the funeral?"

"Two clock. She ought to be in the ground by four."

"Where's the banquet? I heard Essie wanted it at her house."

"Naw, it's at Jimmy's. Her brother wanted it so."

"Well, it will be a big one. Everybody liked old Jimmy. Sure will miss her in the pew."

The funeral banquet was a peal of joy after the thunderous beauty of the funeral. It was like a street tragedy with spontaneity tucked softly into the corners of a highly formal structure. The deceased was the tragic hero, the survivors the innocent victims; there was the omnipresence of the deity, strophe and antistrophe of the chorus of mourners led by the preacher. There was grief over the waste of life, the stunned wonder at the ways of God, and the restoration of order in nature at the graveyard.

Thus the banquet was the exultation, the harmony, the acceptance of physical frailty, joy in the termination of misery. Laughter, relief, a steep hunger for food.

Cholly had not yet fully realized his aunt was dead. Everything was so interesting. Even at the graveyard he felt nothing but curiosity, and when his turn had come to view the body at the church, he had put his hand out to touch the corpse to see if it were really ice cold like everybody said. But he drew his hand back quickly. Aunt Jimmy looked so private, and it seemed wrong somehow to disturb that privacy. He had trudged back to his pew dry-eyed amid tearful shrieks and shouts of others, wondering if he should try to cry.

Back in his house, he was free to join in the gaiety and enjoy what he really felt—a kind of carnival spirit. He ate greedily and felt good enough to try to get to know his cousins. There was some question, according to the adults, as to whether they were his real cousins or not, since Jimmy's brother O. V. was only a half-brother, and Cholly's mother had been the daughter of Jimmy's sister, but that sister was from the second marriage of Jimmy's father, and O. V. was from the first marriage.

One of these cousins interested Cholly in particular. He was about fifteen or sixteen years old. Cholly went outside and found the boy standing with some others near the tub where Aunt Jimmy used to boil her clothes.

He ventured a tentative "Hey." They responded with another. The fifteen-year-old named Jake offered Cholly a rolled-up cigarette. Cholly took it, but when he held the cigarette at arm's length and stuck the tip of it into the match flame, instead of putting it in his mouth and drawing on it, they laughed at him. Shamefaced, he threw the cigarette down. He felt it important to do something to reinstate himself with Jake. So when he asked Cholly if he knew any girls, Cholly said, "Sure."

All the girls Cholly knew were at the banquet, and he pointed to a cluster of them standing, hanging, draping on the back porch. Darlene too. Cholly hoped Jake wouldn't pick her.

"Let's get some and walk around," said Jake.

The two boys sauntered over to the porch. Cholly didn't know how to begin. Jake wrapped his legs around the rickety porch rail and just sat there staring off into space as though he had no interest in them at all. He was letting them look him over, and guardedly evaluating them in return.

The girls pretended they didn't see the boys and kept on chattering. Soon their talk got sharp; the gentle teasing they had been engaged in with each other changed to bitchiness, a serious kind of making fun. That was Jake's clue; the girls were reacting to him. They had gotten a whiff of his manhood and were shivering for a place in his attention.

Jake left the porch rail and walked right up to a girl named Suky, the one who had been most bitter in her making fun.

"Want to show me 'round?" He didn't even smile.

Cholly held his breath, waiting for Suky to shut Jake up.

She was good at that, and well known for her sharp tongue. To his enormous surprise, she readily agreed, and even lowered her lashes. Taking courage, Cholly turned to Darlene and said, "Come on 'long. We just going down to the gully." He waited for her to screw up her face and say no, or what for, or some such thing. His feelings about her were mostly fear—fear that she would not like him, and fear that she would.

His second fear materialized. She smiled and jumped down the three leaning steps to join him. Her eyes were full of compassion, and Cholly remembered that he was the bereaved.

"If you want to," she said, "but not too far. Mama said we got to leave early, and it's getting dark."

The four of them moved away. Some of the other boys had come to the porch and were about to begin that partly hostile, partly indifferent, partly desperate mating dance. Suky, Jake, Darlene, and Cholly walked through several backyards until they came to an open field. They ran across it and came to a dry riverbed lined with green. The object of the walk was a wild vineyard where the muscadine grew. Too new, too tight to have much sugar, they were eaten anyway. None of them wanted—not then—the grape's easy relinquishing of all its dark juice. The restraint, the holding off, the promise of sweetness that had yet to unfold, excited them more than full ripeness would have done. At last their teeth were on edge, and the boys diverted themselves by pelting the girls with the grapes. Their slim black boy wrists made G clefs in the air as they executed the tosses. The chase took Cholly and Darlene away from the lip of the gully, and when they paused for breath, Jake and Suky were nowhere in sight. Darlene's white cotton dress was stained with juice.

Her big blue hair bow had come undone, and the sundown breeze was picking it up and fluttering it about her head. They were out of breath and sank down in the green-and-purple grass on the edge of the pine woods.

Cholly lay on his back panting. His mouth full of the taste of muscadine, listening to the pine needles rustling loudly in their anticipation of rain. The smell of promised rain, pine, and muscadine made him giddy. The sun had gone and pulled away its shreds of light. Turning his head to see where the moon was. Cholly caught sight of Darlene in moonlight behind him. She was huddled into a D—arms encircling drawn-up knees, on which she rested her head. Cholly could see her bloomers and the muscles of her young thighs.

"We bed' get on back," he said.

"Yeah." She stretched her legs flat on the ground and began to retie her hair ribbon. "Mama gone whup me."

"Naw she ain't."

"Uh-huh. She told me she would if I get dirty."

"You ain't dirty."

"I am too. Looka that." She dropped her hands from the ribbon and smoothed out a place on her dress where the grape stains were heaviest.

Cholly felt sorry for her; it was just as much his fault. Suddenly he realized that Aunt Jimmy was dead, for he missed the fear of being whipped. There was nobody to do it except Uncle O. V., and he was the bereaved too.

"Let me," he said. He rose to his knees facing her and tried to tie her ribbon. Darlene put her hands under his open shirt and rubbed the damp tight skin. When he looked at her in surprise, she stopped and laughed. He smiled and continued knotting the bow. She put her hands back under his shirt.

"Hold still," he said. "How I gone get this?"

She tickled his ribs with her fingertips. He giggled and grabbed his rib cage. They were on top of each other in a moment. She corkscrewing her hands into his clothes. He returning the play, digging into the neck of her dress, and then under her dress. When he got his hand in her bloomers, she suddenly stopped laughing and looked serious. Cholly, frightened, was about to take his hand away, but she held his wrist so he couldn't move it. He examined her then with his fingers, and she kissed his face and mouth. Cholly found her muscadine-lipped mouth distracting. Darlene released his head, shifted her body, and pulled down her pants. After some trouble with the buttons, Cholly dropped his pants down to his knees. Their bodies began to make sense to him, and it was not as difficult as he had thought it would be. She moaned a little, but the excitement collecting inside him made him close his eyes and regard her moans as no more than pine sighs over his head. Just as he felt an explosion threaten, Darlene froze and cried out. He thought he had hurt her, but when he looked at her face, she was staring wildly at something over his shoulder. He jerked around.

There stood two white men. One with a spirit lamp, the other with a flashlight. There was no mistake about their being white; he could smell it. Cholly jumped, trying to kneel, stand, and get his pants up all in one motion. The men had long guns.

"Hee hee hee heeeee." The snicker was a long asthmatic cough.

The other raced the flashlight all over Cholly and Darlene.

"Get on wid it, nigger," said the flashlight one.

"Sir?" said Cholly, trying to find a buttonhole.

"I said, get on wid it. An' make it good, nigger, make it good."

There was no place for Cholly's eyes to go. They slid about furtively searching for shelter, while his body remained paralyzed. The flashlight man lifted his gun down from his shoulder, and Cholly heard the clop of metal. He dropped back to his knees. Darlene had her head averted, her eyes staring out of the lamplight into the surrounding darkness and looking almost unconcerned, as though they had no part in the drama taking place around them. With a violence born of total helplessness, he pulled her dress up, lowered his trousers and underwear.

"Hee hee hee hee heeeeee."

Darlene put her hands over her face as Cholly began to simulate what had gone on before. He could do no more than make-believe. The flashlight made a moon on his behind.

"Hee hee hee hee heeee."

"Come on, coon. Faster. You ain't doing nothing for her."

"Hee hee hee hee heeee."

Cholly, moving faster, looked at Darlene. He hated her. He almost wished he could do it—hard, long, and painfully, he hated her so much. The flashlight wormed its way into his guts and turned the sweet taste of muscadine into rotten fetid bile. He stared at Darlene's hands covering her face in the moon and lamplight. They looked like baby claws.

"Hee hee hee hee heee."

Some dogs howled. "Thas them. Thas them. I know thas Old Honcy."

"Yep," said the spirit lamp.

"Come on." The flashlight turned away, and one of them whistled to Honey.

"Wait," said the spirit lamp, "the coon ain't comed yet."

"Well, he have to come on his own time. Good luck, coon baby."

They crushed the pine needles underfoot. Cholly could hear them whistling for a long time, and then the dogs' answer no longer a howl, but warm excited yelps of recognition.

Cholly raised himself and in silence buttoned his trousers. Darlene did not move. Cholly wanted to strangle her, but instead he touched her leg with his foot. "We got to get, girl. Come on!"

She reached for her underwear with her eyes closed, and could not find them. The two of them patted about in the moonlight for the panties. When she found them, she put them on with the movements of an old woman. They walked away from the pine woods toward the road. He in front, she plopping along behind. It started to rain. "That's good," Cholly thought. "It will explain away our clothes."

When they got back to the house, some ten or twelve guests were still there. Jake was gone, Suky too. Some people had gone back for more helpings of food—potato pie, ribs. All were engrossed in early-night reminiscences about dreams, figures, premonitions. Their stuffed comfort was narcotic and had produced recollections and fabrications of hallucinations.

Cholly and Darlene's entrance produced only a mild stir.

"Ya'll soaked, ain't you?"

Darlene's mother was only vaguely fussy. She had eaten and drunk too much. Her shoes were under her chair, and the side snaps of her dress were opened. "Girl. Come on in here. Thought I told you . . ."

Some of the guests thought they would wait for the rain to slacken. Others, who had come in wagons, thought they'd best leave now. Cholly went into the little storeroom which had been made into a bedroom for him. Three infants were sleeping on his cot. He took off his rain- and pine-soaked clothes and put on his coveralls. He didn't know where to go. Aunt Jimmy's room was out of the question, and Uncle O. V. and his wife would be using it later anyway. He took a quilt from a trunk, spread it on the floor, and lay down. Somebody was brewing coffee, and he had a sharp craving for it, just before falling asleep.

The next day was cleaning-out day, settling accounts, distributing Aunt Jimmy's goods. Mouths were set in downward crescents, eyes veiled, feet tentative.

Cholly floated about aimlessly, doing chores as he was told. All the glamour and warmth the adults had given him on the previous day were replaced by a sharpness that agreed with his mood. He could think only of the flashlight, the muscadines, and Darlene's hands. And when he was not thinking of them, the vacancy in his head was like the space left by a newly pulled tooth still conscious of the rottenness that had once filled it. Afraid of running into Darlene, he would not go far from the house, but neither could he endure the atmosphere of his dead Aunt's house. The picking through her things, the comments on the "condition" of her goods. Sullen, irritable, he cultivated his hatred of Darlene. Never did he once consider directing his hatred toward the hunters. Such an emotion would have destroyed him. They were big, white, armed men. He was small, black, helpless. His subconscious knew what his conscious mind did not guess—that hating them would have consumed him, burned him up like a piece of soft coal, leaving only flakes of ash and a question mark of smoke. He was, in time, to discover that hatred of white men—but not now. Not in impotence but later, when the hatred could find sweet expression. For now, he hated the one who had created the situation, the one who bore witness to his failure, his impotence. The one whom he had not been able to protect, to spare, to cover from the round moon glow of the flashlight. The hee-hee-hee's. He recalled Darlene's dripping hair ribbon, flapping against her face as they walked back in silence in the rain. The loathing that galloped through him made him tremble. There was no one to talk to. Old Blue was too drunk too often these days to make sense. Besides, Cholly doubted if he could reveal his shame to Blue. He would have to lie a little to tell Blue, Blue the woman-killer. It seemed to him that lonely was much better than alone.

The day Cholly's uncle was ready to leave, when everything was packed, when the quarrels about who gets what had seethed down to a sticking gravy on everybody's tongue, Cholly sat on the back porch waiting. It had occurred to him that Darlene might be pregnant. It was a wildly irrational, completely uninformed idea, but the fear it produced was complete enough.

He had to get away. Never mind the fact that he was leaving that very day. A town or two away was not far enough, especially since he did not like or trust his uncle, and Darlene's mother could surely find him, and Uncle O. V. would turn him over to her. Cholly knew it was wrong to run out on a pregnant girl, and recalled, with sympathy, that his father had done just that. Now he understood. He knew then what he must do—find his father. His father would understand. Aunt Jimmy said he had gone to Macon.

With no more thought than a chick leaving its shell, he stepped off the porch. He had gotten a little way when he remembered the treasure; Aunt Jimmy had left something, and he had forgotten all about it. In a stove flue no longer used, she had hidden a little meal bag which she called her treasure. He slipped into the house and found the room empty. Digging into the flue, he encountered webs and soot, and then the soft bag. He sorted the money; fourteen one-dollar bills, two two-dollar bills, and lots of silver change . . . twenty-three dollars in all. Surely that would be enough to get to Macon. What a good, strong-sounding word, *Macon.*

Running away from home for a Georgia black boy was not a great problem. You just sneaked away and started walking. When night came you slept in a barn, if there were no dogs, a cane field, or an empty sawmill. You ate from the ground and bought root beer and licorice in little country stores. There was always an easy tale of woe to tell inquiring black adults, and whites didn't care, unless they were looking for sport.

When he was several days away, he could go to the back door of nice houses and tell the black cook or white mistress that he wanted a job weeding, plowing, picking, cleaning, and that he lived nearby. A week or more there, and he could take off. He lived this way through the turn of summer, and only the following October did he reach a town big enough to have a regular bus station. Dry-mouthed with excitement and apprehension, he went to the colored side of the counter to buy his ticket.

"How much to Macon, sir?"

"Eleven dollars. Five-fifty for children under twelve."

Cholly had twelve dollars and four cents.

"How old you be?"

"Just on twelve, sir, but my mama only give me ten dollars."

"You jest about the biggest twelve I ever seed."

"Please, sir, I got to get to Macon. My mama's sick."

"Thought you said you mama give you ten dollars."

"That's my play mama. My real mama is in Macon, sir."

"I reckon I knows a lying nigger when I sees one, but jest in case you ain't, jest in case one of them mammies is really dyin' and wants to see her little old smoke before she meets her maker, I gone do it."

Cholly heard nothing. The insults were part of the nuisances of life, like lice. He was happier than he had ever remembered being, except that time with Blue and the watermelon. The bus wasn't leaving for four hours, and the minutes of those hours struggled like gnats on fly paper—dying slow, exhausted with the fight to stay alive. Cholly was afraid to stir, even to relieve himself. The bus might leave while he was gone. Finally, rigid with constipation, he boarded the bus to Macon.

He found a window seat in the back all to himself, and all of Georgia slid before his eyes, until the sun shrugged out of sight. Even in the dark, he hungered to see, and only after the fiercest fight to keep his eyes open did he fall asleep. When he awoke it was very well into day, and a fat black lady was nudging him with a biscuit gashed with cold bacon. With the taste of bacon still in his teeth, they sidled into Macon.

. . .

At the end of the alley he could see men clustered like grapes. One large whooping voice spiraled over the heads of the bended forms. The kneeling forms, the leaning forms, all intent on one ground spot. As he came closer, he inhaled a rife and stimulating man smell. The men were gathered, just as the man in the pool hall had said, for and about dice and money. Each figure was decorated some way with the slight pieces of green. Some of them had separated their money, folded the bills around their fingers, clenched the fingers into fists, so the neat ends of the money stuck out in a blend of daintiness and violence. Others had stacked their bills, creased them down the middle, and held the wad as though they were about to deal cards. Still others had left their money in loosely crumpled balls. One man had money sticking out from under his cap. Another stroked his bills with a thumb and forefinger. There was more money in those black hands than Cholly had ever seen before. He shared their excitement, and the dry-mouthed apprehension on meeting his father gave way to the saliva flow of excitement. He glanced at the faces, looking for the one who might be his father. How would he know him? Would he look like a larger version of himself? At that moment Cholly could not remember what his own self looked like. He only knew he was fourteen years old, black, and already six feet tall. He searched the faces and saw only eyes, pleading eyes, cold eyes, eyes gone flat with malice, others laced with fear—all focused on the movement of a pair of dice that one man was throwing, snatching up, and throwing again. Chanting a kind of litany to which the others responded, rubbing the dice as though they were two hot coals, he whispered to them. Then with a whoop the cubes flew from his hand to a chorus of amazements and disappointments. Then the thrower scooped up money, and someone shouted, "Take it and crawl, you water dog, you, the best I know." There was some laughter, and a noticeable release of tension, during which some men exchanged money.

Cholly tapped an old white-haired man on the back.

"Can you tell me is Samson Fuller 'round here somewhere?"

"Fuller?" The name was familiar to the man's tongue. "I don't know, he here somewhere. They he is. In the brown jacket." The man pointed.

A man in a light-brown jacket stood at the far end of the group. He was gesturing in a quarrelsome, agitated manner with another man. Both of them had folded their faces in anger. Cholly edged around to where they stood, hardly believing he was at the end of his journey. There was his father, a man like any other man, but there indeed were his eyes, his mouth, his whole head. His shoulders lurked beneath that jacket, his voice, his hands—all real. They existed, really existed, somewhere. Right here. Cholly had always thought of his father as a giant of a man, so when he was very close it was with a shock that he discovered that he was taller than his father. In fact, he was staring at a balding spot on his father's head, which he suddenly wanted to stroke. While thus fascinated by the pitiable clean space hedged around by neglected tufts of wool, the man turned a hard, belligerent face to him.

"What you want, boy?"

"Uh. I mean . . . is you Samson Fuller?"

"Who sent you?"

"Huh?"

"You Melba's boy?"

"No, sir, I'm . . ." Cholly blinked. He could not remember his mother's name. Had he ever known it? What could he say? Whose boy was he? He couldn't say, "I'm your boy." That sounded disrespectful.

The man was impatient. "Something wrong with your head? Who told you to come after me?"

"Nobody." Cholly's hands were sweating. The man's eyes frightened him. "I just thought . . . I mean, I was just wandering around, and, uh, my name is Cholly. . . ."

But Fuller had turned back to the game that was about to begin anew. He bent down to toss a bill on the ground, and waited for a throw. When it was gone, he stood up and in a vexed and whiny voice shouted at Cholly, "Tell that bitch she get her money. Now, get the fuck outta my face!"

Cholly was a long time picking his foot up from the ground. He was trying to back up and walk away. Only with extreme effort could he get the first muscle to cooperate. When it did, he walked back up the alley, out of its shade, toward the blazing light of the street. As he emerged into the sun, he felt something in his legs give way. An orange crate with a picture of clasping hands pasted on its side was upended on the sidewalk. Cholly sat down on it. The sunshine dropped like honey on his head. A horse-drawn fruit wagon went by, its driver singing: "Fresh from the vine, sweet as sugar, red as wine."

Noises seemed to increase in volume. The clic-cloc of the women's heels, the laughter of idling men in doorways. There was a streetcar somewhere. Cholly sat. He knew if he was very still he would be all right. But then the trace of pain edged his eyes, and he had to use everything to send it away. If he was very still, he thought, and kept his eyes on one thing, the tears would not come. So he sat in the dripping honey sun, pulling every nerve and muscle into service to stop the fall of water from his eyes. While straining in this way, focusing every erg of energy on his eyes, his bowels suddenly opened up, and before he could realize what he knew, liquid stools were running down his legs. At the mouth of the alley where his father was, on an orange crate in the sun, on a street full of grown men and women, he had soiled himself like a baby.

In panic he wondered should he wait there, not moving until nighttime? No. His father would surely emerge and see him and laugh. Oh, Lord. He would laugh. Everybody would laugh. There was only one thing to do.

Cholly ran down the street, aware only of silence. People's mouths moved, their feet moved, a car jugged by—but with no sound. A door slammed in perfect soundlessness. His own feet made no sound. The air seemed to strangle him, hold him back. He was pushing through a world of invisible pine sap that threatened to smother him. Still he ran, seeing only silent moving things, until he came to the end of buildings, the beginning of open space, and saw the Ocmulgee River winding ahead. He scooted down a gravelly slope to a pier jutting out over the shallow water. Finding the deepest shadow under the pier, he crouched in it, behind one of the posts. He remained knotted there in fetal position, paralyzed, his fists covering his eyes, for a long time. No sound, no sight, only darkness and heat and the press of his knuckles on his eyelids. He even forgot his messed-up trousers.

Evening came. The dark, the warmth, the quiet, enclosed Cholly like the skin and flesh of an elderberry protecting its own seed.

Cholly stirred. The ache in his head was all he felt. Soon, like bright bits of glass, the events of that afternoon cut into him. At first he saw only money in black fingers, then he thought he was sitting on an uncomfortable chair, but when he looked, it turned out to be the head of a man, a head with a bald spot the size of an orange. When finally these bits merged into full memory, Cholly began to smell himself. He stood up and found himself weak, trembling, and dizzy. He leaned for a moment on the pier post, then took off his pants, underwear, socks, and shoes. He rubbed handfuls of dirt on his shoes; then he crawled to the river edge. He had to find the water's beginning with his hands, for he could not see it clearly. Slowly he swirled his clothes in the water and rubbed them until he thought they were clean. Back near his post, he took off his shirt and wrapped it around his waist, then spread his trousers and underwear on the ground. He squatted down and picked at the rotted wood of the pier. Suddenly he thought of his Aunt Jimmy, her asafetida bag, her four gold teeth, and the purple rag she wore around her head. With a longing that almost split him open, he thought of her handing him a bit of smoked hock out of her dish. He remembered just how she held it—clumsy-like, in three fingers, but with so much affection. No words, just picking up a bit of meat and holding it out to him. And then the tears rushed down his cheeks, to make a bouquet under his chin.

Three women are leaning out of two windows. They see the long clean neck of a new young boy and call to him. He goes to where they are. Inside, it is dark and warm. They give him lemonade in a Mason jar. As he drinks, their eyes float up to him through the bottom of the jar, through the slick sweet water. They give him back his manhood, which he takes aimlessly.

The pieces of Cholly's life could become coherent only in the head of a musician. Only those who talk their talk through the gold of curved metal, or in the touch of black-and-white rectangles and taut skins and strings echoing from wooden corridors, could give true form to his life. Only they would know how to connect the heart of a red watermelon to the asafetida bag to the muscadine to the flashlight on his behind to the fists of money to the lemonade in a Mason jar to a man called Blue and come up with what all of that meant in joy, in pain, in anger, in love, and give it its final and pervading ache of freedom. Only a musician would sense, know, without even knowing that he knew, that Cholly was free. Dangerously free. Free to feel whatever he felt—fear, guilt, shame, love, grief, pity. Free to be tender or violent, to whistle or weep. Free to sleep in doorways or between the white sheets of a singing woman. Free to take a job, free to leave it. He could go to jail and not feel imprisoned, for he had already seen the furtiveness in the eyes of his jailer, free to say, "No, suh," and smile, for he had already killed three white men. Free to take a woman's insults, for his body had already conquered hers. Free even to knock her in the head, for he had already cradled that head in his arms. Free to be gentle when she was sick, or mop her floor, for she knew what and where his maleness was. He was free to drink himself into a silly helplessness, for he had already been a gandy dancer, done thirty days on a chain gang, and picked a woman's bullet out of the calf of his leg. He was free to live his fantasies, and free even to die, the how and the when of which held no interest for him. In those days, Cholly was truly free. Abandoned in a junk heap by his mother, rejected for a crap game by his father, there was nothing more to lose. He was alone with his own perceptions and appetites, and they alone interested him.

It was in this godlike state that he met Pauline Williams. And it was Pauline, or rather marrying her, that did for him what the flashlight did not do. The constantness, varietylessness, the sheer weight of sameness drove him to despair and froze his imagination. To be required to sleep with the same woman forever was a curious and unnatural idea to him; to be expected to dredge up enthusiasms for old acts, and routine ploys; he wondered at the arrogance of the female. When he had met Pauline in Kentucky, she was hanging over a fence scratching herself with a broken foot. The neatness, the charm, the joy he awakened in her made him want to nest with her. He had yet to discover what destroyed that desire. But he did not dwell on it. He thought rather of whatever had happened to the curiosity he used to feel. Nothing, nothing, interested him now. Not himself, not other people. Only in drink was there some break, some floodlight, and when that closed, there was oblivion.

But the aspect of married life that dumbfounded him and rendered him totally disfunctional was the appearance of children. Having no idea of how to raise children, and having never watched any parent raise himself, he could not even comprehend what such a relationship should be. Had he been interested in the accumulation of things, he could have thought of them as his material heirs; had he needed to prove himself to some nameless "others," he could have wanted them to excel in his own image and for his own sake. Had he not been alone in the world since he was thirteen, knowing only a dying old woman who felt responsible for him, but whose age, sex, and interests were so remote from his own, he might have felt a stable connection between himself and the children. As it was, he reacted to them, and his reactions were based on what he felt at the moment.

So it was on a Saturday afternoon, in the thin light of spring, he staggered home reeling drunk and saw his daughter in the kitchen.

She was washing dishes. Her small back hunched over the sink. Cholly saw her dimly and could not tell what he saw or what he felt. Then he became aware that he was uncomfortable; next he felt the discomfort dissolve into pleasure. The sequence of his emotions was revulsion, guilt, pity, then love. His revulsion was a reaction to her young, helpless, hopeless presence. Her back hunched that way; her head to one side as though crouching from a permanent and unrelieved blow. Why did she have to look so whipped? She was a child—unburdened—why wasn't she happy? The clear statement of her misery was an accusation. He wanted to break her neck—but tenderly. Guilt and impotence rose in a bilious duet. What could he do for her—ever? What give her? What say to her? What could a burned-out black man say to the hunched back of his eleven-year-old daughter? If he looked into her face, he would see those haunted, loving eyes. The hauntedness would irritate him—the love would move him to fury. How dare she love him? Hadn't she any sense at all? What was he supposed to do about that? Return it? How? What could his calloused hands produce to make her smile? What of his knowledge of the world and of life could be useful to her? What could his heavy arms and befuddled brain accomplish that would earn him his own respect, that would in turn allow him to accept her love? His hatred of her slimed in his stomach and threatened to become vomit. But just before the puke moved from anticipation to sensation, she shifted her weight and stood on one foot scratching the back of her calf with her toe. It was a quiet and pitiful gesture. Her hands were going around and around a frying pan, scraping flecks of black into cold, greasy dishwater. The timid, tucked-in look of the scratching toe—that was what Pauline was doing the first time he saw her in Kentucky. Leaning over a fence staring at nothing in particular. The creamy toe of her bare foot scratching a velvet leg. It was such a small and simple gesture, but it filled him then with a wondering softness. Not the usual lust to part tight legs with his own, but a tenderness, a protectiveness. A desire to cover her foot with his hand and gently nibble away the itch from the calf with his teeth. He did it then, and started Pauline into laughter. He did it now.

The tenderness welled up in him, and he sank to his knees, his eyes on the foot of his daughter. Crawling on all fours toward her, he raised his hand and caught the foot in an upward stroke. Pecola lost her balance and was about to careen to the floor. Cholly raised his other hand to her hips to save her from falling. He put his head down and nibbled at the back of her leg. His mouth trembled at the firm sweetness of the flesh. He closed his eyes, letting his fingers dig into her waist. The rigidness of her shocked body, the silence of her stunned throat, was better than Pauline's easy laughter had been. The confused mixture of his memories of Pauline and the doing of a wild and forbidden thing excited him, and a bolt of desire ran down his genitals, giving it length, and softening the lips of his anus. Surrounding all of this lust was a border of politeness. He wanted to fuck her—tenderly. But the tenderness would not hold. The tightness of her vagina was more than he could bear. His soul seemed to slip down to his guts and fly out into her, and the gigantic thrust he made into her then provoked the only sound she made—a hollow suck of air in the back of her throat. Like the rapid loss of air from a circus balloon.

Following the disintegration—the falling away—of sexual desire, he was conscious of her wet, soapy hands on his wrists, the fingers clenching, but whether her grip was from a hopeless but stubborn struggle to be free, or from some other emotion, he could not tell.

Removing himself from her was so painful to him he cut it short and snatched his genitals out of the dry harbor of her vagina. She appeared to have fainted. Cholly stood up and could see only her grayish panties, so sad and limp around her ankles. Again the hatred mixed with tenderness. The hatred would not let him pick her up, the tenderness forced him to cover her.

So when the child regained consciousness, she was lying on the kitchen floor under a heavy quilt, trying to connect the pain between her legs with the face of her mother looming over her.

SEETHEDOGBOWWOWGOESTHEDOG
DOYOUWANTTOPLAYDOYOUWANT
TOPLAYWITHJANESEETHEDOGRUNR

Once there was an old man who loved things, for the slightest contact with people produced in him a faint but persistent nausea. He could not remember when this distaste began, nor could he remember ever being free of it. As a young boy he had been greatly disturbed by this revulsion which others did not seem to share, but having got a fine education, he learned, among other things, the word "misanthrope." Knowing his label provided him with both comfort and courage, he believed that to name an evil was to neutralize if not annihilate it. Then, too, he had read several books and made the acquaintance of several great misanthropes of the ages, whose spiritual company soothed him and provided him with yardsticks for measuring his whims, his yearnings, and his antipathies. Moreover, he found misanthropy an excellent means of developing character: when he subdued his revulsion and occasionally touched, helped, counseled, or befriended somebody, he was able to think of his behavior as generous and his intentions as noble. When he was enraged by some human effort or flaw, he was able to regard himself as discriminating, fastidious, and full of nice scruples.

As in the case of many misanthropes, his disdain for people led him into a profession designed to serve them. He was engaged in a line of work that was dependent solely on his ability to win the trust of others, and one in which the most intimate relationships were necessary. Having dallied with the priesthood in the Anglican Church, he abandoned it to become a caseworker. Time and misfortune, however, conspired against him, and he settled finally on a profession that brought him both freedom and satisfaction. He became a "Reader, Adviser, and Interpreter of Dreams." It was a profession that suited him well. His hours were his own, the competition was slight, the clientele was already persuaded and therefore manageable, and he had numerous opportunities to witness human stupidity without sharing it or being compromised by it, and to nurture his fastidiousness by viewing physical decay. Although his income was small, he had no taste for luxury—his experience in the monastery had solidified his natural asceticism while it developed his preference for solitude. Celibacy was a haven, silence a shield.

All his life he had a fondness for things—not the acquisition of wealth or beautiful objects, but a genuine love of worn objects: a coffee pot that had been his mother's, a welcome mat from the door of a rooming house he once lived in, a quilt from a Salvation Army store counter. It was as though his disdain of human contact had converted itself into a craving for things humans had touched. The residue of the human spirit smeared on inanimate objects was all he could withstand of humanity. To contemplate, for example, evidence of human footsteps on the mat—absorb the smell of the quilt and wallow in the sweet certainty that many bodies had sweated, slept, dreamed, made love, been ill, and even died under it. Wherever he went, he took along his things, and was always searching for others. This thirst for worn things led to casual but habitual examinations of trash barrels in alleys and wastebaskets in public places. . . .

All in all, his personality was an arabesque: intricate, symmetrical, balanced, and tightly constructed—except for one flaw. The careful design was marred occasionally by rare but keen sexual cravings.

He could have been an active homosexual but lacked the courage. Bestiality did not occur to him, and sodomy was quite out of the question, for he did not experience sustained erections and could not endure the thought of somebody else's. And besides, the one thing that disgusted him more than entering and caressing a woman was caressing and being caressed by a man. In any case, his cravings, although intense, never relished physical contact. He abhorred flesh on flesh. Body odor, breath odor, overwhelmed him. The sight of dried matter in the corner of the eye, decayed or missing teeth, ear wax, blackheads, moles, blisters, skin crusts—all the natural excretions and protections the body was capable of—disquieted him. His attentions therefore gradually settled on those humans whose bodies were least offensive—children. And since he was too diffident to confront homosexuality, and since little boys were insulting, scary, and stubborn, he further limited his interests to little girls. They were usually manageable and frequently seductive. His sexuality was anything but lewd; his patronage of little girls smacked of innocence and was associated in his mind with cleanliness. He was what one might call a very clean old man.

A cinnamon-eyed West Indian with lightly browned skin.

Although his given name was printed on the sign in his kitchen window, and on the business cards he circulated, he was called by the townspeople Soaphead Church. No one knew where the "Church" part came from—perhaps somebody's recollection of his days as a guest preacher—those reverends who had been called but who had no flock or coop, and were constantly visiting other churches, sitting on the altar with the host preacher. But everybody knew what "Soaphead" meant—the tight, curly hair that took on and held a sheen and wave when pomaded with soap lather. A sort of primitive process.

He had been reared in a family proud of its academic accomplishments and its mixed blood—in fact, they believed the former was based on the latter. A Sir Whitcomb, some decaying British nobleman, who chose to disintegrate under a sun more easeful than England's, had introduced the white strain into the family in the early 1800's. Being a gentleman by order of the King, he had done the civilized thing for his mulatto bastard—provided it with three hundred pounds sterling, to the great satisfaction of the bastard's mother, who felt that fortune had smiled on her. The bastard too was grateful, and regarded as his life's goal the hoarding of this white strain. He bestowed his favors on a fifteen-year-old girl of similar parentage. She, like a good Victorian parody, learned from her husband all that was worth learning—to separate herself in body, mind, and spirit from all that suggested Africa; to cultivate the habits, tastes, preferences that her absent father-in-law and foolish mother-in-law would have approved.

They transferred this Anglophilia to their six children and sixteen grandchildren. Except for an occasional and unaccountable insurgent who chose a restive black, they married "up," lightening the family complexion and thinning out the family features.

With the confidence born of a conviction of superiority, they performed well at schools. They were industrious, orderly, and energetic, hoping to prove beyond a doubt De Gobineau's hypothesis that "all civilizations derive from the white race, that none can exist without its help, and that a society is great and brilliant only so far as it preserves the blood of the noble group that created it." Thus, they were seldom overlooked by schoolmasters who recommended promising students for study abroad. The men studied medicine, law, theology, and emerged repeatedly in the powerless government offices available to the native population. That they were corrupt in public and private practice, both lecherous and lascivious, was considered their noble right, and thoroughly enjoyed by most of the less gifted population.

As the years passed, due to the carelessness of some of the Whitcomb brothers, it became difficult to maintain their whiteness, and some distant and some not so distant relatives married each other. No obviously bad effects were noticed from these ill-advised unions, but one or two old maids or gardener boys marked a weakening of faculties and a disposition toward eccentricity in some of the children. Some flaw outside the usual alcoholism and lechery. They blamed the flaw on intermarriage with the family, however, not on the original genes of the decaying lord. In any case, there were flukes. No more than in any other family, to be sure, but more dangerous because more powerful. One of them was a religious fanatic who founded his own secret sect and fathered four sons, one of whom became a schoolmaster known for the precision of his justice and the control in his violence. This schoolmaster married a sweet, indolent half-Chinese girl for whom the fatigue of bearing a son was too much. She died soon after childbirth. Her son, named Elihue Micah Whitcomb, provided the schoolmaster with ample opportunity to work out his theories of education, discipline, and the good life. Little Elihue learned everything he needed to know well, particularly the fine art of self-deception. He read greedily but understood selectively, choosing the bits and pieces of other men's ideas that supported whatever predilection he had at the moment. Thus he chose to remember Hamlet's abuse of Ophelia, but not Christ's love of Mary Magdalene; Hamlet's frivolous politics, but not Christ's serious anarchy. He noticed Gibbon's acidity, but not his tolerance, Othello's love for the fair Desdemona, but not Iago's perverted love of Othello. The works he admired most were Dante's; those he despised most were Dostoyevsky's. For all his exposure to the best minds of the Western world, he allowed only the narrowest interpretation to touch him. He responded to his father's controlled violence by developing hard habits and a soft imagination. A hatred of, and fascination with, any hint of disorder or decay.

At seventeen, however, he met his Beatrice, who was three years his senior. A lovely, laughing big-legged girl who worked as a clerk in a Chinese department store. Velma. So strong was her affection and zest for life, she did not eliminate the frail, sickly Elihue from it. She found his fastidiousness and complete lack of humor touching and longed to introduce him to the idea of delight. He resisted the introduction, but she married him anyway, only to discover that he was suffering from and enjoying an invincible melancholy. When she learned two months into the marriage how important his melancholy was to him, that he was very interested in altering her joy to a more academic gloom, that he equated lovemaking with communion and the Holy Grail, she simply left. She had not lived by the sea all those years, listened to the wharfman's songs all that time, to spend her life in the soundless cave of Elihue's mind.

He never got over her desertion. She was to have been the answer to his unstated, unacknowledged question—where was the life to counter the encroaching nonlife? Velma was to rescue him from the nonlife he had learned on the flat side of his father's belt. But he resisted her with such skill that she was finally driven out to escape the inevitable boredom produced by such a dainty life.

Young Elihue was saved from visible shattering by the steady hand of his father, who reminded him of the family's reputation and Velma's questionable one. He then pursued his studies with more vigor than before and decided at last to enter the ministry. When he was advised that he had no avocation, he left the island, came to America to study the then budding field of psychiatry. But the subject required too much truth, too many confrontations, and offered too little support to a failing ego. He drifted into sociology, then physical therapy. This diverse education continued for six years, when his father refused to support him any longer, until he "found" himself. Elihue, not knowing where to look, was thrown back on his own devices, and "found" himself quite unable to earn money. He began to sink into a rapidly fraying gentility, punctuated with a few of the white-collar occupations available to black people, regardless of their noble bloodlines, in America: desk clerk at a colored hotel in Chicago, insurance agent, traveling salesman for a cosmetics firm catering to blacks. He finally settled in Lorain, Ohio, in 1931, palming himself off as a minister, and inspiring awe with the way he spoke English. The women of the town early discovered his celibacy, and not being able to comprehend his rejection of them, decided that he was supernatural rather than unnatural.

Once he understood their decision, he quickly followed through, accepting the name (Soaphead Church) and the role they had given him. He rented a kind of back-room apartment from a deeply religious old lady named Bertha Reese. She was clean, quiet, and very close to total deafness. The lodgings were ideal in every way but one. Bertha Reese had an old dog, Bob, who, although as deaf and quiet as she, was not as clean. He slept most of his days away on the back porch, which was Elihue's entrance. The dog was too old to be of any use, and Bertha Reese had not the strength or presence of mind to care for him properly. She fed him, and watered him, left him alone. The dog was mangy; his exhausted eyes ran with a sea-green matter around which gnats and flies clustered. Soaphead was revolted by Bob and wished he would hurry up and die. He regarded this wish for the dog's death as humane, for he could not bear, he told himself, to see anything suffer. It did not occur to him that he was really concerned about his own suffering, since the dog had adjusted himself to frailty and old age. Soaphead finally determined to put an end to the animal's misery, and bought some poison with which to do it. Only the horror of having to go near him had prevented Soaphead from completing his mission. He waited for rage or blinding revulsion to spur him.

Living there among his worn things, rising early every morning from dreamless sleeps, he counseled those who sought his advice.

His business was dread. People came to him in dread, whispered in dread, wept and pleaded in dread. And dread was what he counseled.

Singly they found their way to his door, wrapped each in a shroud stitched with anger, yearning, pride, vengeance, loneliness, misery, defeat, and hunger. They asked for the simplest of things: love, health, and money. Make him love me. Tell me what this dream means. Help me get rid of this woman. Make my mother give me back my clothes. Stop my left hand from shaking. Keep my baby's ghost off the stove. Break so-and-so's fix. To all of these requests he addressed himself. His practice was to do what he was bid—not to suggest to a party that perhaps the request was unfair, mean, or hopeless.

With only occasional, and increasingly rare, encounters with the little girls he could persuade to be entertained by him, he lived rather peaceably among his things, admitting to no regrets. He was aware, of course, that something was awry in his life, and all lives, but put the problem where it belonged, at the foot of the Originator of Life. He believed that since decay, vice, filth, and disorder were pervasive, they must be in the Nature of Things. Evil existed because God had created it. He, God, had made a sloven and unforgivable error in judgment: designing an imperfect universe. Theologians justified the presence of corruption as a means by which men strove, were tested, and triumphed. A triumph of cosmic neatness. But this neatness, the neatness of Dante, was in the orderly sectioning and segregating of all levels of evil and decay. In the world it was not so. The most exquisite-looking ladies sat on toilets, and the most dreadful-looking had pure and holy yearnings. God had done a poor job, and Soaphead suspected that he himself could have done better. It was in fact a pity that the Maker had not sought his counsel.

Soaphead was reflecting once again on these thoughts one late hot afternoon when he heard a tap on his door. Opening it, he saw a little girl, quite unknown to him. She was about twelve or so, he thought, and seemed to him pitifully unattractive. When he asked her what she wanted, she did not answer, but held out to him one of his cards advertising his gifts and services: "If you are overcome with trouble and conditions that are not natural, I can remove them; Overcome Spells, Bad Luck, and Evil Influences. Remember, I am a true Spiritualist and Psychic Reader, born with power, and I will help you. Satisfaction in one visit. During many years of practice I have brought together many in marriage and reunited many who were separated. If you are unhappy, discouraged, or in distress, I can help you. Does bad luck seem to follow you? Has the one you love changed? I can tell you why. I will tell you who your enemies and friends are, and if the one you love is true or false. If you are sick, I can show you the way to health. I locate lost and stolen articles. Satisfaction guaranteed."

Soaphead Church told her to come in.

"What can I do for you, my child?"

She stood there, her hands folded across her stomach, a little protruding pot of tummy. "Maybe. Maybe you can do it for me."

"Do what for you?"

"I can't go to school no more. And I thought maybe you could help me."

"Help you how? Tell me. Don't be frightened."

"My eyes."

"What about your eyes?"

"I want them blue."

Soaphead pursed his lips, and let his tongue stroke a gold inlay. He thought it was at once the most fantastic and the most logical petition he had ever received. Here was an ugly little girl asking for beauty. A surge of love and understanding swept through him, but was quickly replaced by anger. Anger that he was powerless to help her. Of all the wishes people had brought him—money, love, revenge—this seemed to him the most poignant and the one most deserving of fulfillment. A little black girl who wanted to rise up out of the pit of her blackness and see the world with blue eyes. His outrage grew and felt like power. For the first time he honestly wished he could work miracles. Never before had he really wanted the true and holy power—only the power to make others believe he had it. It seemed so sad, so frivolous, that mere mortality, not judgment, kept him from it. Or did it?

With a trembling hand he made the sign of the cross over her. His flesh crawled; in that hot, dim little room of worn things, he was chilled.

"I can do nothing for you, my child. I am not a magician. I work only through the Lord. He sometimes uses me to help people. All I can do is offer myself to Him as the instrument through which he works. If He wants your wish granted, He will do it."

Soaphead walked to the window, his back to the girl. His mind raced, stumbled, and raced again. How to frame the next sentence? How to hang on to the feeling of power. His eye fell on old Bob sleeping on the porch.

"We must make, ah, some offering, that is, some contact with nature. Perhaps some simple creature might be the vehicle through which He will speak. Let us see."

He knelt down at the window, and moved his lips. After what seemed a suitable length of time, he rose and went to the icebox that stood near the other window. From it he removed a small packet wrapped in pinkish butcher paper. From a shelf he took a small brown bottle and sprinkled some of its contents on the substance inside the paper. He put the packet, partly opened, on the table.

"Take this food and give it to the creature sleeping on the porch. Make sure he eats it. And mark well how he behaves. If nothing happens, you will know that God has refused you. If the animal behaves strangely, your wish will be granted on the day following this one."

The girl picked up the packet; the odor of the dark, sticky meat made her want to vomit. She put a hand on her stomach.

"Courage. Courage, my child. These things are not granted to faint hearts."

She nodded and swallowed visibly, holding down the vomit. Soaphead opened the door, and she stepped over the threshold.

"Good-bye, God bless," he said and quickly shut the door. At the window he stood watching her, his eyebrows pulled together into waves of compassion, his tongue fondling the worn gold in his upper jaw. He saw the girl bending down to the sleeping dog, who, at her touch, opened one liquid eye, matted in the corners with what looked like green glue. She reached out and touched the dog's head, stroking him gently. She placed the meat on the floor of the porch, near his nose. The odor roused him; he lifted his head, and got up to smell it better. He ate it in three or four gulps. The girl stroked his head again, and the dog looked up at her with soft triangle eyes. Suddenly he coughed, the cough of a phlegmy old man—and got to his feet. The girl jumped. The dog gagged, his mouth chomping the air, and promptly fell down. He tried to raise himself, could not, tried again and half-fell down the steps. Choking, stumbling, he moved like a broken toy around the yard. The girl's mouth was open, a little petal of tongue showing. She made a wild, pointless gesture with one hand and then covered her mouth with both hands. She was trying not to vomit. The dog fell again, a spasm jerking his body. Then he was quiet. The girl's hands covering her mouth, she backed away a few feet, then turned, ran out of the yard and down the walk.

Soaphead Church went to the table. He sat down, with folded hands balancing his forehead on the balls of his thumbs. Then he rose and went to a tiny night table with a drawer, from which he took paper and a fountain pen. A bottle of ink was on the same shelf that held the poison. With these things he sat again at the table. Slowly, carefully, relishing his penmanship, he wrote the following letter:

Att: TO HE WHO GREATLY ENNOBLED HUMAN NATURE BY CREATING IT

Dear God:

The Purpose of this letter is to familiarize you with facts which either have escaped your notice, or which you have chosen to ignore.

Once upon a time I lived greenly and youngish on one of your islands. An island of the archipelago in the

South Atlantic between North and South America, enclosing the Caribbean Sea and the Gulf of Mexico: divided into the Greater Antilles, the Lesser Antilles, and the Bahama Islands. Not the Windward or Leeward Island colonies, mark you, but within, of course, the Greater of the two Antilles (while the precision of my prose may be, at times, laborious, it is necessary that I identify myself to you clearly).

Now.

We in this colony took as our own the most dramatic, and the most obvious, of our white masters' characteristics, which were, of course, their worst. In retaining the identity of our race, we held fast to those characteristics most gratifying to sustain and least troublesome to maintain. Consequently we were not royal but snobbish, not aristocratic but class-conscious; we believed authority was cruelty to our inferiors, and education was being at school. We mistook violence for passion, indolence for leisure, and thought recklessness was freedom. We raised our children and reared our crops; we let infants grow, and property develop. Our manhood was defined by acquisitions. Our womanhood by acquiescence. And the smell of your fruit and the labor of your days we abhorred.

This morning, before the little black girl came, I cried—for Velma. Oh, not aloud. There is no wind to carry, bear, or even refuse to bear, a sound so heavy with regret. But in my silent own lone way, I cried—for Velma. You need to know about Velma to understand what I did today.

She (Velma) left me the way people leave a hotel room. A hotel room is a place to be when you are doing something else. Of itself it is of no consequence to one's major scheme. A hotel room is convenient. But its convenience is limited to the time you need it while you are in that particular town on that particular business; you hope it is comfortable, but prefer, rather, that it be anonymous. It is not, after all, where you *live*.

When you no longer need it, you pay a little something for its use; say, "Thank you, sir," and when your business in that town is over, you go away from that room. Does anybody regret leaving a hotel room? Does anybody, who has a home, a real home somewhere, want to stay there? Does anybody look back with affection, or even disgust, at a hotel room when they leave it? You can only love or despise whatever *living* was done in that room. But the room itself? But you take a souvenir. Not, oh, not, to remember the room. To remember, rather, the time and the place of your business, your adventure. What can anyone feel for a hotel room? One doesn't any more feel for a hotel room than one expects a hotel room to feel for its occupant.

That, heavenly, heavenly Father, was how she left me; or rather, she never left me, because she was never ever there.

You remember, do you, how and of what we are made? Let me tell you now about the breasts of little girls. I apologize for the inappropriateness (is that it?), the imbalance of loving them at awkward times of day, and in awkward places, and the tastelessness of loving those which belonged to members of my family. Do I have to apologize for loving strangers?

But you too are amiss here, Lord. How, why, did you allow it to happen? How is it I could lift my eyes from the contemplation of Your Body and fall deeply into the contemplation of theirs? The buds. The buds on some of these saplings. They were mean, you know, mean and tender. Mean little buds resisting the touch, springing like rubber. But aggressive. Daring me to touch. Commanding me to touch. Not a bit shy, as you'd suppose. They stuck out at me, oh yes, at me. Slender-chested, finger-chested lassies. Have you ever seen them, Lord? I mean, really seen them? One could not see them and not love them. You who made them must have considered them lovely even as an idea—how much more lovely is the manifestation of that idea. I couldn't, as you must recall, keep my hands, my mouth, off them. Salt-sweet. Like not quite ripe strawberries covered with the light salt sweat of running days and hopping, skipping, jumping hours.

The love of them—the touch, taste, and feel of them—was not just an easy luxurious human vice; they were, for me, A Thing To Do Instead. Instead of Papa, instead of the Cloth, instead of Velma, and I *chose* not to do without them. But I didn't go into the church. At least I didn't do that. As to what I did do? I told people I knew all about You. That I had received Your Powers. It was not a complete *lie;* but it was a *complete* lie. I should never have, I admit, I should never have taken their money in exchange for well-phrased, well-placed, well-faced lies. But, mark you, I hated it. Not for a moment did I love the lies or the money.

But consider: The woman who left the hotel room.

Consider: The greentime, the noontime of the archipelago.

Consider: Their hopeful eyes that were outdone only by their hoping breasts.

Consider: How I needed a comfortable evil to prevent my knowing what I could not bear to know.

Consider: How I hated and despised the money.

And now, consider: Not according to my just deserts, but according to *my* mercy, the little black girl that came a-looning at me today. Tell me, Lord, how could you leave a lass so long so lone that she could find her way to me? How could you? I weep for you, Lord. And it is because I weep for You that I had to do your work for You.

Do you know what she came for? Blue eyes. New, blue eyes, she said. Like she was buying shoes. "I'd like a pair of new blue eyes." She must have asked you for them for a very long time, and you hadn't replied. (A habit, I could have told her, a long-ago habit broken for Job—but no more.) She came to *me* for them. She had one of my cards. (Card enclosed.) By the way, I added the Micah—Elihue Micah Whitcomb. But I am called Soaphead Church. I cannot remember how or why I got the name. What makes one name more a person than another? Is the name the real thing, then? And the person only what his name says? Is that why to the simplest and friendliest of questions: "What is your name?" put to you by Moses, You would not say, and said instead "I am who I am." Like Popeye? I Yam What I Yam? Afraid you were, weren't you, to give out your name? Afraid they would know the name and then know you? Then they wouldn't fear you? It's quite all right. Don't be vexed. I mean no offense. I understand. I have been a bad man too, and an unhappy man too. But someday *I* will die. I was always so kind. Why do I have to die? The little girls. The little girls are the only things I'll miss. Do you know that when I touched their sturdy little tits and bit them—just a little—I felt I was being friendly? I didn't want to kiss their mouths or sleep in the bed with them or take a child bride for my own. Playful, I felt, and friendly. Not like the newspapers said. Not like the people whispered. And they didn't mind at all. Not at all. Remember how so many of them came back? No one would even try to understand that. If I'd been hurting them, would they have come back? Two of them, Doreen and Sugar Babe, they'd come together. I gave them mints, money, and they'd eat ice cream with their legs open while I played with them. It was like a party. And there wasn't nastiness, and there wasn't any filth, and there wasn't any odor, and there wasn't any groaning—just the light white laughter of little girls and me. And there wasn't any look—any long funny look—any long funny Velma look afterward. No look that makes you feel dirty afterward. That makes you want to die. With little girls it is all clean and good and friendly.

You have to understand that, Lord. You said, "Suffer little children to come unto me, and harm them not." Did you forget? Did you forget about the children? Yes. You forgot. You let them go wanting, sit on road shoulders, crying next to their dead mothers. I've seen them charred, lame, halt. You forgot, Lord. You forgot how and when to be God.

That's why I changed the little black girl's eyes for her, and I didn't touch her; not a finger did I lay on her. But I gave her those blue eyes she wanted. Not for pleasure, and not for money. I did what You did not, could not, would not do: I looked at that ugly little black girl, and I loved her. I played You. And it was a very good show!

I, I have caused a miracle. I gave her the eyes. I gave her the blue, blue, two blue eyes. Cobalt blue. A streak of it right out of your own blue heaven. No one else will see her blue eyes. But *she* will. And she will live happily ever after. I, I have found it meet and right so to do.

Now you are jealous. You are jealous of me.

You see? I, too, have created. Not aboriginally, like you, but creation is a heady wine, more for the taster than the brewer.

Having therefore imbibed, as it were, of the nectar, I am not afraid of You, of Death, not even of Life, and it's all right about Velma; and it's all right about Papa; and it's all right about the Greater and the Lesser Antilles. Quite all right. Quite.

With kindest regards, I remain,

Your,
Elihue Micah Whitcomb

Soaphead Church folded the sheets of paper into three equal parts and slipped them into an envelope. Although he had no seal, he longed for sealing wax. He removed a cigar box from under the bed and rummaged about in it. There were some of his most precious things: a sliver of jade that had dislodged from a cuff link at the Chicago hotel; a gold pendant shaped like a Y with a piece of coral attached to it that had belonged to the mother he never knew; four large hairpins that Velma had left on the rim of the bathroom sink; a powder blue grosgrain ribbon from the head of a little girl named Precious Jewel; a blackened faucet head from the sink in a jail cell in Cincinnati; two marbles he had found under a bench in Morningside Park on a very fine spring day; an old Lucky Hart catalog that smelled still of nut-brown and mocha face powder, and lemon vanishing cream. Distracted by his things, he forgot what he had been looking for. The effort to recall was too great; there was a buzzing in his head, and a wash of fatigue overcame him. He closed his box, eased himself out on the bed, and slipped into an ivory sleep from which he could not hear the tiny yelps of an old lady who had come out of her candy store and found the still carcass of an old dog named Bob.

Summer

I have only to break into the tightness of a strawberry, and I see summer—its dust and lowering skies. It remains for me a season of storms. The parched days and sticky nights are undistinguished in my mind, but the storms, the violent sudden storms, both frightened and quenched me. But my memory is uncertain; I recall a summer storm in the town where we lived and imagine a summer my mother knew in 1929. There was a tornado that year, she said, that blew away half of south Lorain. I mix up her summer with my own. Biting the strawberry, thinking of storms, I see her. A slim young girl in a pink crepe dress. One hand is on her hip; the other lolls about her thigh—waiting. The wind swoops her up, high above the houses, but she is still standing, hand on hip. Smiling. The anticipation and promise in her lolling hand are not altered by the holocaust. In the summer tornado of 1929, my mother's hand is unextinguished. She is strong, smiling, and relaxed while the world falls down about her. So much for memory. Public fact becomes private reality, and the seasons of a Midwestern town become the *Moirai* of our small lives.

The summer was already thick when Frieda and I received our seeds. We had waited since April for the magic package containing the packets and packets of seeds we were to sell for five cents each, which would entitle us to a new bicycle. We believed it, and spent a major part of every day trooping about the town selling them. Although Mama had restricted us to the homes of people she knew or the neighborhoods familiar to us, we knocked on all doors, and floated in and out of every house that opened to us: twelve-room houses that sheltered half as many families, smelling of grease and urine; tiny wooden four-room houses tucked into bushes near the railroad tracks; the up-over places—apartments up over fish markets, butcher shops, furniture stores, saloons, restaurants; tidy brick houses with flowered carpets and glass bowls with fluted edges.

During that summer of the seed selling we thought about the money, thought about the seeds, and listened with only half an ear to what people were saying. In the houses of people who knew us we were asked to come in and sit, given cold water or lemonade; and while we sat there being refreshed, the people continued their conversations or went about their chores. Little by little we began to piece a story together, a secret, terrible, awful story. And it was only after two or three such vaguely overheard conversations that we realized that the story was about Pecola. Properly placed, the fragments of talk ran like this:

"Did you hear about that girl?"

"What? Pregnant?"

"Yas. But guess who?"

"Who? I don't know all these little old boys."

"That's just it. Ain't no little old boy. They say it's Cholly."

"Cholly? Her daddy?"

"Uh-huh."

"Lord. Have mercy. That dirty nigger."

"'Member that time he tried to burn them up? I knew he was crazy for sure then."

"What's she gone do? The mama?"

"Keep on like she been, I reckon. He taken off."

"County ain't gone let her keep that baby, is they?"

"Don't know."

"None of them Breedloves seem right anyhow. That boy is off somewhere every minute, and the girl was always foolish."

"Don't nobody know nothing about them anyway. Where they come from or nothing. Don't seem to have no people."

"What you reckon make him do a thing like that?"

"Beats me. Just nasty."

"Well, they ought to take her out of school."

"Ought to. She carry some of the blame."

"Oh, come on. She ain't but twelve or so."

"Yeah. But you never know. How come she didn't fight him?"

"Maybe she did."

"Yeah? You never know."

"Well, it probably won't live. They say the way her mama beat her she lucky to be alive herself."

"She be lucky if it don't live. Bound to be the ugliest thing walking."

"Can't help but be. Ought to be a law: two ugly people doubling up like that to make more ugly. Be better off in the ground."

"Well, I wouldn't worry none. It be a miracle if it live."

Our astonishment was short-lived, for it gave way to a curious kind of defensive shame; we were embarrassed for Pecola, hurt for her, and finally we just felt sorry for her. Our sorrow drove out all thoughts of the new bicycle. And I believe our sorrow was the more intense because nobody else seemed to share it. They were disgusted, amused, shocked, outraged, or even excited by the story. But we listened for the one who would say, "Poor little girl," or, "Poor baby," but there was only head-wagging where those words should have been. We looked for eyes creased with concern, but saw only veils.

I thought about the baby that everybody wanted dead, and saw it very clearly. It was in a dark, wet place, its head covered with great O's of wool, the black face holding, like nickels, two clean black eyes, the flared nose, kissing-thick lips, and the living, breathing silk of black skin. No synthetic yellow bangs suspended over marble-blue eyes, no pinched nose and bowline mouth. More strongly than my fondness for Pecola, I felt a need for someone to want the black baby to live—just to counteract the universal love of white baby dolls, Shirley Temples, and Maureen Peals. And Frieda must have felt the same thing. We did not think of the fact that Pecola was not married; lots of girls had babies who were not married. And we did not dwell on the fact that the baby's father was Pecola's father too; the process of having a baby by any male was incomprehensible to us—at least she knew her father. We thought only of this overwhelming hatred for the unborn baby. We remembered Mrs. Breedlove knocking Pecola down and soothing the pink tears of the frozen doll baby that sounded like the door of our icebox. We remembered the knuckled eyes of schoolchildren under the gaze of Meringue Pie and the eyes of these same children when they looked at Pecola. Or maybe we didn't remember; we just knew. We had defended ourselves since memory against everything and everybody, considered all speech a code to be broken by us, and all gestures subject to careful analysis; we had become headstrong, devious and arrogant. Nobody paid us any attention, so we paid very good attention to ourselves. Our limitations were not known to us—not then. Our only handicap was our size; people gave us orders because they were bigger and stronger. So it was with confidence, strengthened by pity and pride, that we decided to change the course of events and alter a human life.

"What we gone do, Frieda?"

"What can we do? Miss Johnson said it would be a miracle if it lived."

"So let's make it a miracle."

"Yeah, but how?"

"We could pray."

"That's not enough. Remember last time with the bird?"

"That was different; it was half-dead when we found it."

"I don't care, I still think we have to do something really strong this time."

"Let's ask Him to let Pecola's baby live and promise to be good for a whole month."

"O.K. But we better give up something so He'll know we really mean it this time."

"Give up what? We ain't got nothing. Nothing but the seed money, two dollars."

"We could give that. Or, you know what? We could give up the bicycle. Bury the money and . . . plant the seeds."

"All of the money?"

"Claudia, do you want to do it or not?"

"O.K. I just thought . . . O.K."

"We have to do it *right,* now. We'll bury the money over by her house so we can't go back and dig it up, and we'll plant the seeds out back of our house so we can watch over them. And when they come up, we'll know everything is all right. All right?"

"All right. Only let me sing this time. You say the magic words."

LOOKLOOKHERECOMESAFRIENDTHE FRIENDWILLPLAYWITHJANETHEYWI LLPLAYAGOODGAMEPLAYJANEPLAY

How many times a minute are you going to look inside that old thing?

I didn't look in a long time.

You did too—

So what? I can look if I want to.

I didn't say you couldn't. I just don't know why you have to look every minute. They aren't going anywhere.

I know it. I just like to look.

You scared they might go away?

Of course not. How can they go away?

The others went away.

They didn't go away. They changed.

Go away. Change. What's the difference?

A lot. Mr. Soaphead said they would last forever.

Forever and ever Amen?

Yes, if you want to know.

You don't have to be so smarty when you talk to me.

I'm not being smarty. You started it.

I'd just like to do something else besides watch you stare in that mirror.

You're just jealous.

I am not.

You are. You wish you had them.

Ha. What would I look like with blue eyes?

Nothing much.

If you're going to keep this up, I may as well go on off by myself.

No. Don't go. What you want to do?

We could go outside and play, I guess.

But it's too hot.

You can take your old mirror. Put it in your coat pocket, and you can look at yourself up and down the street.

Boy! I never would have thought you'd be so jealous.

Oh, come on!

You are.

Are what?

Jealous.

O.K. So I'm jealous.

See. I told you.

No. I told you.

Are they really nice?

Yes. Very nice.

Just "very nice"?

Really, truly, very nice.

Really, truly, bluely nice?

Oh, God. You are crazy.

I am not!

I didn't mean it that way.

Well, what did you mean?

Come on. It's too hot in here.

Wait a minute. I can't find my shoes.

Here they are.

Oh. Thank you.

Got your mirror?

Yes dearie. . . .

Well, let's go then. . . . Ow!

What's the matter?

The sun is too bright. It hurts my eyes.

Not mine. I don't even blink. Look. I can look right at the sun.

Don't do that.

Why not? It doesn't hurt. I don't even have to blink.

Well, blink anyway. You make me feel funny, staring at the sun like that.

Feel funny how?

I don't know.

Yes, you do. Feel funny how?

I told you, I don't know.

Why don't you look at me when you say that? You're looking drop-eyed like Mrs. Breedlove.

Mrs. Breedlove look drop-eyed at you?

Yes. Now she does. Ever since I got my blue eyes, she look away from me all of the time. Do you suppose she's jealous too?

Could be. They are pretty, you know.

I know. He really did a good job. Everybody's jealous. Every time I look at somebody, they look off.

Is that why nobody has told you how pretty they are?

Sure it is. Can you imagine? Something like that happening to a person, and nobody but nobody saying anything about it? They all try to pretend they don't see them. Isn't that funny? . . . I said, isn't that funny?

Yes.

You are the only one who tells me how pretty they are.

Yes.

You are a real friend. I'm sorry about picking on you before. I mean, saying you were jealous and all.

That's all right.

No. Really. You are my very best friend. Why didn't I know you before?

You didn't need me before.

Didn't need you?

I mean . . . you were so unhappy before. I guess you didn't notice me before.

I guess you're right. And I was so lonely for friends. And you were right here. Right before my eyes.

No, honey. Right after your eyes.

What?

What does Maureen think about your eyes?

She doesn't say anything about them. Has she said anything to you about them?

No. Nothing.

Do you like Maureen?

Oh. She's all right. For a half-white girl, that is.

I know what you mean. But would you like to be her friend? I mean, would you like to go around with her or anything?

No.

Me neither. But she sure is popular.

Who wants to be popular?

Not me.

Me neither.

But you couldn't be popular anyway. You don't even go to school.

You don't either.

I know. But I used to.

What did you stop for?

They made me.

Who made you?

I don't know. After that first day at school when I had my blue eyes. Well, the next day they had Mrs. Breedlove come out. Now I don't go anymore. But I don't care.

You don't?

No, I don't. They're just prejudiced, that's all.

Yes, they sure are prejudiced.

Just because I got blue eyes, bluer than theirs, they're prejudiced.

That's right.

They are bluer, aren't they?

Oh, yes. Much bluer.

Bluer than Joanna's?

Much bluer than Joanna's.

And bluer than Michelena's?

Much bluer than Michelena's.

I thought so. Did Michelena say anything to you about my eyes?

No. Nothing.

Did you say anything to her?

No.

How come?

How come what?

How come you don't talk to anybody?

I talk to you.

Besides me.

I don't like anybody besides you.

Where do you live?

I told you once.

What is your mother's name?

Why are you so busy meddling me?

I just wondered. You don't talk to anybody. You don't go to school. And nobody talks to you.

How do you know nobody talks to me?

They don't. When you're in the house with me, even Mrs. Breedlove doesn't say anything to you. Ever. Sometimes I wonder if she even sees you.

Why wouldn't she see me?

I don't know. She almost walks right over you.

Maybe she doesn't feel too good since Cholly's gone.

Oh, yes. You must be right.

She probably misses him.

I don't know why she would. All he did was get drunk and beat her up.

Well, you know how grown-ups are.

Yes. No. How are they?

Well, she probably loved him anyway.

HIM?

Sure. Why not? Anyway, if she didn't love him, she sure let him do it to her a lot.

That's nothing.

How do you know?

I saw them all the time. She didn't like it.

Then why'd she let him do it to her?

Because he made her.

How could somebody make you do something like that?

Easy.

Oh, yeah? How easy?

They just make you, that's all.

I guess you're right. And Cholly could make anybody do anything.

He could not.

He made you, didn't he?

Shut up!

I was only teasing.

Shut up!

O.K. O.K.

He just tried, see? He didn't do anything. You hear me?

I'm shutting up.

You'd better. I don't like that kind of talk.

I said I'm shutting up.

You always talk so dirty. Who told you about that, anyway?

I forget.

Sammy?

No. You did.

I did not.

You did. You said he tried to do it to you when you were sleeping on the couch.

See there! You don't even know what you're talking about. It was when I was washing dishes.

Oh, yes. Dishes.

By myself. In the kitchen.

Well, I'm glad you didn't let him.

Yes.

Did you?

Did I what?

Let him.

Now who's crazy?

I am, I guess.

You sure are.

Still . . .

Well. Go ahead. Still what?

I wonder what it would be like.

Horrible.

Really?

Yes. Horrible.

Then why didn't you tell Mrs. Breedlove?

I did tell her!

I don't mean about the first time. I mean about the second time, when you were sleeping on the couch.

I wasn't sleeping! I was reading!

You don't have to shout.

You don't understand anything, do you? She didn't even believe me when I told her.

So that's why you didn't tell her about the second time?

She wouldn't have believed me then either.

You're right. No use telling her when she wouldn't believe you.

That's what I'm trying to get through your thick head.

O.K. I understand now. Just about.

What do you mean, just about?

You sure are mean today.

You keep on saying mean and sneaky things. I thought you were my friend.

I am. I am.

Then leave me alone about Cholly.

O.K.

There's nothing more to say about him, anyway. He's gone, anyway.

Yes. Good riddance.

Yes. Good riddance.

And Sammy's gone too.

And Sammy's gone too.

So there's no use talking about it. I mean them.

No. No use at all.

It's all over now.

Yes.

And you don't have to be afraid of Cholly coming at you anymore.

No.

That was horrible, wasn't it?

Yes.

The second time too?

Yes.

Really? The second time too?

Leave me alone! You better leave me alone.

Can't you take a joke? I was only funning.

I don't like to talk about dirty things.

Me neither. Let's talk about something else.

What? What will we talk about?

Why, your eyes.

Oh, yes. My eyes. My blue eyes. Let me look again.

See how pretty they are.

Yes. They get prettier each time I look at them.

They are the prettiest I've ever seen.

Really?

Oh, yes.

Prettier than the sky?

Oh, yes. Much prettier than the sky.

Prettier than Alice-and-Jerry Storybook eyes?

Oh, yes. Much prettier than Alice-and-Jerry Storybook eyes.

And prettier than Joanna's?

Oh, yes. And bluer too.

Bluer than Michelena's?

Yes.

Are you sure?

Of course I'm sure.

You don't sound sure. . . .

Well, I am sure. Unless. . . .

Unless what?

Oh, nothing. I was just thinking about a lady I saw yesterday. Her eyes sure were blue. But no. Not bluer than yours.

Are you sure?

Yes. I remember them now. Yours are bluer.

I'm glad.

Me too. I'd hate to think there was anybody around with bluer eyes than yours. I'm sure there isn't. Not around here, anyway.

But you don't know, do you? You haven't seen everybody, have you?

No. I haven't.

So there could be, couldn't there?

Not hardly.

But maybe. Maybe. You said "around here." Nobody "around here" probably has bluer eyes. What about someplace else? Even if my eyes are bluer than Joanna's and bluer than Michelena's and bluer than that lady's you saw, suppose there is somebody way off somewhere with bluer eyes than mine?

Don't be silly.

There could be. Couldn't there?

Not hardly.

But suppose. Suppose a long way off. In Cincinnati, say, there is somebody whose eyes are bluer than mine? Suppose there are *two* people with bluer eyes?

So what? You asked for blue eyes. You got blue eyes.

He should have made them bluer.

Who?

Mr. Soaphead.

Did you say what color blue you wanted them?

No. I forgot.

Oh. Well.

Look. Look over there. At that girl. Look at her eyes. Are they bluer than mine?

No, I don't think so.

Did you look real good?

Yes.

Here comes someone. Look at his. See if they're bluer.

You're being silly. I'm not going to look at everybody's eyes.

You have to.

No I don't.

Please. If there is somebody with bluer eyes than mine, then maybe there is somebody with the bluest eyes. The bluest eyes in the whole world.

That's just too bad, isn't it?

Please help me look.

No.

But suppose my eyes aren't blue enough?

Blue enough for what?

Blue enough for . . . I don't know. Blue enough for something. Blue enough . . . for you!

I'm not going to play with you anymore.

Oh. Don't leave me.

Yes. I am.

Why? Are you mad at me?

Yes.

Because my eyes aren't blue enough? Because I don't have the bluest eyes?

No. Because you're acting silly.

Don't go. Don't leave me. Will you come back if I get them?

Get what?

The bluest eyes. Will you come back then?

Of course I will. I'm just going away for a little while.

You promise?

Sure. I'll be back. Right before your very eyes.

So it was.

A little black girl yearns for the blue eyes of a little white girl, and the horror at the heart of her yearning is exceeded only by the evil of fulfillment.

We saw her sometimes. Frieda and I—after the baby came too soon and died. After the gossip and the slow wagging of heads. She was so sad to see. Grown people looked away; children, those who were not frightened by her, laughed outright.

The damage done was total. She spent her days, her tendril, sap-green days, walking up and down, up and down, her head jerking to the beat of a drummer so distant only she could hear. Elbows bent, hands on shoulders, she flailed her arms like a bird in an eternal, grotesquely futile effort to fly. Beating the air, a winged but grounded bird, intent on the blue void it could not reach—could not even see—but which filled the valleys of the mind.

We tried to see her without looking at her, and never, never went near. Not because she was absurd, or repulsive, or because we were frightened, but because we had failed her. Our flowers never grew. I was convinced that Frieda was right, that I had planted them too deeply. How could I have been so sloven? So we avoided Pecola Breedlove—forever.

And the years folded up like pocket handkerchiefs. Sammy left town long ago; Cholly died in the workhouse; Mrs. Breedlove still does housework. And Pecola is somewhere in that little brown house she and her mother moved to on the edge of town, where you can see her even now, once in a while. The birdlike gestures are worn away to a mere picking and plucking her way between the tire rims and the sunflowers, between Coke bottles and milkweed, among all the waste and beauty of the world—which is what she herself was. All of our waste which we dumped on her and which she absorbed. And all of our beauty, which was hers first and which she gave to us. All of us—all who knew her—felt so wholesome after we cleaned ourselves on her. We were so beautiful when we stood astride her ugliness. Her simplicity decorated us, her guilt sanctified us, her pain made us glow with health, her awkwardness made us think we had a sense of humor. Her inarticulateness made us believe we were eloquent. Her poverty kept us generous. Even her waking dreams we used—to silence our own nightmares. And she let us, and thereby deserved our contempt. We honed our egos on her, padded our characters with her frailty, and yawned in the fantasy of our strength.

And fantasy it was, for we were not strong, only aggressive; we were not free, merely licensed; we were not compassionate, we were polite; not good, but well behaved. We courted death in order to call ourselves brave, and hid like thieves from life. We substituted good grammar for intellect; we switched habits to simulate maturity; we rearranged lies and called it truth, seeing in the new pattern of an old idea the Revelation and the Word.

She, however, stepped over into madness, a madness which protected her from us simply because it bored us in the end.

Oh, some of us "loved" her. The Maginot Line. And Cholly loved her. I'm sure he did. He, at any rate, was the one who loved her enough to touch her, envelop her, give something of himself to her. But his touch was fatal, and the something he gave her filled the matrix of her agony with death. Love is never any better than the lover. Wicked people love wickedly, violent people love violently, weak people love weakly, stupid people love stupidly, but the love of a free man is never safe. There is no gift for the beloved. The lover alone possesses his gift of love. The loved one is shorn, neutralized, frozen in the glare of the lover's inward eye.

And now when I see her searching the garbage—for what? The thing we assassinated? I talk about how I did *not* plant the seeds too deeply, how it was the fault of the earth, the land, of our town. I even think now that the land of the entire country was hostile to marigolds that year. This soil is bad for certain kinds of flowers. Certain seeds it will not nurture, certain fruit it will not bear, and when the land kills of its own volition, we acquiesce and say the victim had no right to live. We are wrong, of course, but it doesn't matter. It's too late. At least on the edge of my town, among the garbage and the sunflowers of my town, it's much, much, much too late.

ALSO BY

Toni Morrison

GOD HELP THE CHILD

At the center: a young woman who calls herself Bride, whose stunning blue-black skin is only one element of her beauty, her boldness and confidence, her success in life, but which caused her light-skinned mother to deny her even the simplest forms of love. There is Booker, the man Bride loves and loses to anger. Rain, the mysterious white child with whom she crosses paths. And finally, Bride's mother herself, Sweetness, who takes a lifetime to come to understand that "what you do to children matters. And they might never forget." A fiery and provocative novel, *God Help the Child* weaves a tale about the way the sufferings of childhood can shape, and misshape, the life of the adult.

Fiction

PARADISE

"They shoot the white girl first. With the rest they can take their time." So begins *Paradise*, which opens with a horrifying scene of mass violence and chronicles its genesis in an all-black small town in rural Oklahoma. Founded by the descendants of freed slaves and survivors in exodus from a hostile world, the patriarchal community of Ruby is built on righteousness, rigidly enforced moral law, and fear. But seventeen miles away, another group of exiles has gathered in a promised land of their own. And it is upon these women in flight from death and despair that nine male citizens of Ruby will lay their pain, terror, and murderous rage. In prose that soars with the rhythms, grandeur, and tragic arc of an epic poem, Toni Morrison challenges our most fiercely held beliefs as she weaves folklore and history, memory and myth into an unforgettable meditation on race, religion, gender, and a far-off past that is ever present.

Fiction

HOME

When Frank Money joined the army to escape his too-small world, he left behind his cherished little sister, Cee. After the war, his shattered life has no purpose until he hears that Cee is in danger. Frank is a modern Odysseus returning to a 1950s America mined with lethal pitfalls for a black man. As he journeys to his native Georgia in search of Cee, it becomes clear that their troubles began before their wartime separation. Together, they return to their hometown of Lotus, where buried secrets are unearthed and where Frank learns at last what it means to be a man, what it takes to heal, and—above all—what it means to come home.

Fiction